"You are of one breed with Gysmay's thought was like a sharp hiss.

"The spear," Charis answered the Wyvern, "this is of your kind, not mine! And a man died of it."

"Those who dream not—they have broken the ancient law and run to do evil in the service of strangers. Those strangers have given them a protection against our Power so that they may not be brought back into order again. Perhaps this was not of your doing, for among us you have dreamed true and know the power in its proper use. And the man Lantee— he, too, has dreamed—though that was out of all custom. But now come those who do not dream, and our world will fall apart unless we hasten to the mending."

There was no mistaking the warning lying in that. Charis could only guess at the meaning behind the circumlocution of speech. An off-world party had freed some of the males from the control of the Wyvern matriarchs. And these were now fighting for the strangers. In return the Wyverns seemed about to organize some counterblow against all off-worlders. "She breaks our pattern here," Gysmay said to the shadowed Wyvern. "Send her into the Place Without Dreams that she may not continue to disrupt what we do here!"

"No—that is against her rights," the other Wyvern answered. "Time grows short, Dreamer," she said to Charis. "Dream true if you would save the breaking of your pattern. Now—get you hence!"

The tiered chamber, the watching Wyverns, vanished. Night was dark about Charis, but as her eyes adjusted to the very dim light, she was able to see that she stood on a high point of rock; around her on all sides was the wash of waves. She must be marooned on a rocky spear in what might be the middle of the ocean.

Afraid to take a step in any direction, Charis dropped down to her knees, hardly believing this could be true. Her breath caught in a half-sob of incredulous protest. . . .

Baen Books by Andre Norton

Time Traders
Time Traders II
Star Soldiers
Warlock
Janus
Darkness and Dawn

WARLOCK

ANDRE NORTON

WARLOCK

This is a work of fiction. All the characters and events portrayed in this book are fictional, and any resemblance to real people or incidents is purely coincidental.

A Baen Books Original

Baen Publishing Enterprises
P.O. Box 1403
Riverdale, NY 10471
www.baen.com

ISBN: 0-7434-7151-2

Cover art by Larry Elmore

First paperback printing, August 2003

Library of Congress Catalog Number 2001049949

Distributed by Simon & Schuster
1230 Avenue of the Americas
New York, NY 10020

Production by Windhaven Press, Auburn, NH
Typeset by Bell Road Press, Sherwood, OR
Printed in the United States of America

Contents

———∞∞∞———

Storm Over Warlock
-1-

Ordeal in Otherwhere
-185-

Forerunner Foray
-359-

STORM OVER
WARLOCK

1

DISASTER

The Throg task force struck the Terran Survey camp without warning a few minutes after dawn. The alien invaders sent eye-searing lances of energy flashing back and forth across the base with methodical accuracy. And a single cowering witness, flattened on a ledge in the heights above, knew that when the last of those yellow-red bolts fell, nothing human would be left alive down there. His teeth clamped hard upon the thick stuff of the sleeve covering his thin forearm, and a scream of terror and rage was stillborn in his heart.

More than caution kept him pinned on that narrow shelf of rock. Watching that holocaust below, Shann Lantee could not force himself to move. The sheer ruthlessness of the Throg attack left him momentarily weak. To listen to a tale of Throgs in action, and to be an eyewitness to such action, were two vastly different things. He shivered in spite of the warmth of the Survey Corps uniform.

As yet he had sighted none of the aliens, only their plateshaped flyers. They would stay aloft until their long-range weapon cleared out all opposition. But how had they been able to annihilate the Terran force so completely? The last report had placed the nearest Throg nest at least two systems away from Warlock. And a patrol lane had been drawn about the Circe system the minute that Survey had marked its second planet ready for colonization. Somehow the beetles had slipped through that supposedly tight cordon and would now consolidate their gains with their usual speed. Once their energy attack finished the small Terran force, then they would simply take over.

A month later, or maybe two months, and they could not have done it. The grids would have been up, and any Throg ship venturing into Warlock's amber-tinted sky would abruptly cease to be. In the race for survival as a galactic power, Terra had that one small edge over the swarms of the enemy. They need only stake out their new-found world and get the grids assembled on its surface; then that planet would be locked to the beetles. The critical period was between the first discovery of a suitable colony world‾and the completion of grid control. Planets in the past had been lost during that time lag, just as Warlock was being lost now.

Throgs and Terrans . . . For more than a century now, planet time, they had been fighting their bitter war among the stars. Terrans hunted worlds for colonization, the old hunger for land of their own driving men from the overpopulated worlds, out of Sol's system to the far stars. And those worlds barren of intelligent native life, open to settlers, were none too many and widely scattered. Perhaps half a dozen were found in a quarter century, and of that six maybe only one was suitable for human life without any costly and lengthy adaptation of man or world. Warlock was one of the lucky finds which came so seldom.

Throgs were predators, living on the loot they garnered. As yet, mankind had not been able to discover whether they did indeed swarm from any home world. Perhaps they lived eternally on board their plate ships with no permanent base, forced into a wandering life by the destruction of the planet on which they had originally been spawned. But they were raiders now, laying waste to defenseless worlds, picking up the wealth of shattered cities in which no native life remained. Although their hidden temporary bases were looped about the galaxy, their need for worlds with an atmosphere similar to Terra's was as necessary as that of man.

For in spite of their grotesque insectile bodies, their wholly alien minds, the Throgs were warm-blooded, oxygen-breathing creatures.

After the first few clashes the early Terran explorers had endeavored to promote a truce between the species, only to discover that between Throg and man there appeared to be no meeting ground at all—a total difference of mental processes producing insurmountable misunderstanding. There was simply no point of communication. So the Terrans had suffered one smarting defeat after another until they perfected the grid. And now their colonies were safe, at least when time worked in their favor.

It had not on Warlock.

A last vivid lash of red cracked over the huddle of domes in the valley. Shann blinked, half blinded by that glare. His jaws ached as he unclenched his teeth. That was the finish. Breathing raggedly, he raised his head, beginning to realize that he was the only one of his kind left alive on a none-too-hospitable world controlled by enemies—without shelter or supplies.

He edged back into the narrow cleft which was the entrance to the ledge. As a representative of his species he was not impressive, and now, with those shudders he could not master shaking his thin body, he looked even smaller and more vulnerable. Shann drew his knees up close under his chin. The hood of his woodsman's jacket was pushed back in spite of the chill of the morning, and he wiped the back of his hand across his lips and chin in an oddly childish gesture.

None of the men below who had been alive only minutes earlier had been close friends of his. Shann had never known anyone but acquaintances in his short, roving life. Most people had ignored him completely except to give orders, and one or two had been actively malicious—like Garth Thorvald. Shann grimaced at a certain recent memory, and then that grimace faded into wonder. If young Thorvald hadn't purposefully tried to get Shann into trouble by opening the wolverines' cage, Shann wouldn't be here now—alive and safe for a time—he'd have been down there with the others.

The wolverines! For the first time since Shann had heard the crackle of the Throg attack he remembered the reason he had been heading into the hills. Of all the men on the Survey team, Shann Lantee had been the least important. The dirty, tedious clean-up jobs, the dull routines which required no technical training but which had to be performed to keep the camp functioning comfortably, those had been his portion. And he had accepted that status willingly, just to have a chance to be included among Survey personnel. Not that he had the slightest hope of climbing up to even an S-E-Three rating in the service.

Part of those menial activities had been to clean the animal cages. And there Shann Lantee had found something new, something so absorbing that most of the tiring dull labor had ceased to exist except as tasks to finish before he could return to the fascination of the animal runs.

Survey teams had early discovered the advantage of using mutated and highly trained Terran animals as assistants in the exploration of strange worlds. From the biological laboratories and breeding farms on Terra came a trickle of specialized assistants to accompany man into space. Some were fighters, silent, more deadly than weapons a man wore at his belt or carried in his hands. Some were keener eyes, keener noses, keener scouts than the human kind could produce. Bred for intelligence, for size, for adaptability to alien conditions, the animal explorers from Terra were prized.

Wolverines, the ancient "devils" of the northlands on Terra, were being tried for the first time on Warlock. Their caution, a quality highly developed in their breed, made them testers for new territory. Able to tackle in battle an animal three times their size, they should be added protection for the man they accompanied into the wilderness. Their wide ranging, their ability to climb and swim, and above all, their curiosity were significant assets.

Shann had begun contact by cleaning their cages; he ended captivated by these miniature bears with long bushy tails. And to his unbounded delight the attraction was mutual. Alone to Taggi and Togi he was a person, an important person. Those teeth, which could tear flesh into ragged strips, nipped gently at his fingers. They closed without any pressure on arm, even on nose and chin in what was the ultimate caress of their kind. Since they were escape artists of no mean ability, twice he had had to track and lead them back to camp from forays of their own devising.

But the second time he had been caught by Fadakar, the chief of animal control, before he could lock up the delinquents. And the memory of the resulting interview still had the power to make him flush with impotent anger. Shann's explanation had been contemptuously brushed aside, and he had been delivered an ultimatum. If his carelessness occurred again, he would be sent back on the next supply ship, to be dismissed without an official sign-off on his work record, thus locked out of even the lowest level of Survey for the rest of his life.

That was why Garth Thorvald's act of the night before had made Shann brave the unknown darkness of Warlock alone when he had discovered that the test animals were gone. He had to locate and return them before Fadakar made his morning inspection; Garth Thorvald's attempt to get him into bad trouble had saved his life.

Shann cowered back, striving to make his huddled body as small as possible. One of the Throg flyers appeared silently out of the misty amber of the morning sky, hovering over the silent camp. The aliens were coming in to inspect the site of their victory. And the safest place for any Terran now was as far from the vicinity of those silent domes as he could get. Shann's slight body was an asset as he wedged through the narrow mouth of a cleft and so back into the cliff wall. The climb before him he knew in part, for this was the path the wolverines had followed on their two other escapes. A few moments of tricky scrambling and he was out in a cuplike depression choked with the purple-leaved brush of Warlock. On the other side of that was a small cut to a sloping hillside, giving on another valley, not as wide as that in which the camp stood, but one well provided with cover in the way of trees and high-growing bushes.

A light wind pushed among the trees, and twice Shann

heard the harsh, rasping call of a clak-clak—one of the batlike leather-winged flyers that laired in pits along the cliff walls. That present snap of two-tone complaint suggested that the land was empty of strangers. For the clak-claks vociferously and loudly resented encroachment on their chosen hunting territory.

Shann hesitated. He was driven by the urge to put as much distance between him and the landing Throg ship as he could. But to arouse the attention of inquisitive clak-claks was asking for trouble. Perhaps it would be best to keep on along the top of the cliff, rather than risk a descent to take cover in the valley the flyers patrolled.

A patch of dust, sheltered by a tooth-shaped projection of rock, gave the Terran his first proof that Taggi and his mate had preceded him, for printed firmly there was the familiar paw mark of a wolverine. Shann began to hope that both animals had taken to cover in the wilderness ahead.

He licked dry lips. Having left secretly without any emergency pack, he had no canteen, and now Shann inventoried his scant possessions—a field kit, heavy-duty clothing, a short hooded jacket with attached mittens, the breast marked with the Survey insignia. His belt supported a sheathed stunner and bush knife, and seam pockets held three credit tokens, a twist of wire intended to reinforce the latch of the wolverine cage, a packet of bravo tablets, two identity and work cards, and a length of cord. No rations—save the bravos—no extra charge for his stunner. But he did have, weighing down a loop on the jacket, a small power torch.

The path he followed ended abruptly in a cliff drop, and Shann made a face at the odor rising from below, even though that scent meant he could climb down to the valley floor here without fearing any clak-clak attention. Chemical fumes from a mineral spring funneled against the wall, warding off any nesting in this section.

Shann drew up the hood of his jacket and snapped the transparent face mask into place. He must get away—then find food, water, a hiding place. That will to live which had made Shann Lantee fight innumerable battles in the past was in command, bracing him with a stubborn determination.

The fumes swirled up in a smoke haze about his waist, but he strode on, heading for the open valley and cleaner air. That sickly lavender vegetation bordering the spring deepened in color to the normal purple-green, and then he was in a grove of trees, their branches pointed skyward at sharp angles to the rust-red trunks.

A small skitterer burst from moss-spotted ground covering, giving an alarmed squeak, skimming out of sight as suddenly as it had appeared. Shann squeezed between two trees and then paused. The trunk of the larger was deeply scored with scratches dripping viscous gobs of sap, a sap which was a bright froth of scarlet. Taggi had left his mark here, and not too long ago.

The soft carpet of moss showed no paw marks, but he thought he knew the goal of the animals—a lake down-valley. Shann was beginning to plan now. The Throgs had not blasted the Terran camp entirely out of existence; they had only made sure of the death of its occupiers. Which meant they must have some use for the installations. For the general loot of a Survey field camp would be relatively worthless to those who picked over the treasure of entire cities elsewhere. Why? What did the Throgs want? And would the alien invaders continue to occupy the domes for long?

Shann was still reeling from the shock of the Throgs' ruthless attack. But from early childhood, when he had been thrown on his own to scratch a living—a borderline existence of a living—on the Dumps of Tyr, he had had to use his wits to keep life in a scrawny and undersized body. However, since he had been eating regularly from Survey rations, he was not quite so scrawny anymore.

His formal education was close to zero, his informal and off-center schooling vast. And that particular toughening process which had been working on him for years now aided in his speedy adaptation to a new set of facts, formidable ones. He was alone on a strange and perhaps hostile world. Water, food, safe shelter, those were important now. And once again, away from the ordered round of the camp where he had been ruled by the desires and requirements of others, he was thinking, planning in freedom. Later (his hand went to the butt of his stunner) perhaps later he might just find a way of extracting an accounting from the beetle-heads, too.

For the present, he would have to keep away from the Throgs, which meant well away from the camp. A fleck of green showed through the amethyst foliage before him—the lake! Shann wriggled through a last bush barrier and stood to look out over that surface. A sleek brown head bobbed up. Shann put fingers to his mouth and whistled. The head turned, black button eyes regarded him, short legs began to churn water. To his relief the swimmer was obeying his summons.

Taggi came ashore, pausing on the fine gray sand of the verge to shake himself vigorously. Then the wolverine ran upslope at a clumsy gallop to Shann. With an unknown feeling swelling inside him the Terran went down on both knees, burying both hands in the coarse brown fur, warming to the uproarious welcome Taggi gave him.

"Togi?" Shann asked as if the other could answer. He gazed back to the lake, but Taggi's mate was nowhere in sight.

The blunt head under his hand swung around, black button nose pointed north. Shann had never been sure just how intelligent, as mankind measured intelligence, the wolverines were. He had come to suspect that Fadakar and the other experts had underrated them and that both beasts understood more than they were given credit for. Now he followed an experiment of his own, one he had had a chance to try only a few times before and never at length. Pressing his palm flat on Taggi's head, Shann thought of Throgs and of their attack, trying to arouse in the animal a corresponding reaction to his own horror and anger.

And Taggi responded. A mutter became a growl, teeth gleamed—those cruel teeth of a carnivore to whom they were weapons of aggression. Danger . . . Shann thought "danger." Then he raised his hand, and the wolverine shuffled off, heading north. The man followed.

They discovered Togi busy in a small cove where a jagged tangle of drift made a mat dating from the last high-water period. She was finishing a hearty breakfast, the remains of a water rat which she was burying thriftily against future need after the instincts of her kind. When she was done she came to Shann, inquiry plain to read in her eyes.

There was water here, and good hunting. But the site was too close to the Throgs. Let one of their exploring flyers sight them, and the little group was finished. Better cover, that's what the three fugitives must have. Shann scowled, not at Togi, but at the landscape. He was tired and hungry, but he must keep on going.

A stream fed into the cove from the west, a guide of sorts. With very little knowledge of the countryside, Shann was inclined to follow that.

Overhead the sun made its usual golden haze of the sky. A flight of vivid green streaks marked a flock of lake ducks coming for a morning feeding. Lake duck was good eating, but Shann had no time to hunt one now. Togi started down the bank of the stream, Taggi behind her. Either they had caught his choice subtly through some undefined mental contact, or they had already picked that road on their own.

Shann's attention was caught by a piece of the drift. He twisted the length free and had his first weapon of his own manufacture, a club. Using it to hold back a low sweeping branch, he followed the wolverines.

Within the half hour he had breakfast, too. A pair of limp skitterers, their long hind feet lashed together with a thong of grass, hung from his belt. They were not particularly good eating, but at least they were meat.

The three, man and wolverines, made their way up the stream to the valley wall and through a feeder ravine into the larger space beyond. There, where the stream was born at the foot of a falls, they made their first camp. Judging that the morning haze would veil any smoke, Shann built a pocket-size fire. He seared rather than roasted the skitterers after he had made an awkward and messy business of skinning them, and tore the meat from the delicate bones in greedy mouthfuls. The wolverines lay side by side on the gravel, now and again raising a head alertly to test the scent on the air, or gaze into the distance.

Taggi made a warning sound deep in the throat. Shann tossed handfuls of sand over the dying fire. He had only time to fling himself face-down, hoping the drab and weathered cloth of his uniform would fade into the color of the earth on which he lay, every muscle tense.

A shadow swung across the hillside. Shann's shoulders hunched, and he cowered again. That terror he had known on the ledge was back in full force as he waited for the beam to lick at him as it had earlier at his fellows. The Throgs were on the hunt . . .

2

DEATH OF A SHIP

That sigh of displaced air was not as loud as a breeze, but it echoed monstrously in Shann's ears. He could not believe in his luck as that sound grew fainter, drew away into the valley he had just left. With infinite caution he raised his head from his arm, still hardly able to accept the fact that he had not been sighted, that the Throgs and their flyer were gone.

But that black plate was spinning out into the sun haze. One of the beetles might have suspected that there were Terran fugitives and ordered a routine patrol. After all, how could the aliens know that they had caught all but one of the Survey party in camp? Though with all the Terran scout flitters grounded on the field, the men dead in their bunks, the surprise would seem to be complete.

As Shann moved, Taggi and Togi came to life also. They had gone to earth with speed, and the man was sure that both beasts had sensed danger. Not for the first time he knew a burning desire for the formal education he had never had. In camp he had listened, dragging out routine jobs in order to overhear reports and the small talk of specialists keen on their own particular hobbies. But so much of the information Shann had thus picked up to store in a retentive memory he had not understood and could not fit together. It had

13

been as if he were trying to solve some highly important puzzle with at least a quarter of the necessary pieces missing, or with unrelated bits from others intermixed. How much control did a trained animal scout have over his furred or feathered assistants? And was part of that mastery a mental rapport built up between man and animal?

How well would the wolverines obey him now, especially when they would not return to camp where cages stood waiting as symbols of human authority? Wouldn't a trek into the wilderness bring about a revolt for complete freedom? If Shann could depend upon the animals, it would mean a great deal. Not only would their superior hunting ability provide all three with food, but their scouting senses, so much keener than his, might erect a slender wall between life and death.

Few large native beasts had been discovered on Warlock by the Terran explorers. And of those four or five different species, none had proved hostile if unprovoked. But that did not mean that somewhere back in the wild lands into which Shann was heading there were not heretofore unknowns, perhaps slyer and as vicious as the wolverines when they were aroused to rage.

Then there were the "dreams," which had afforded the prime source of camp discussion and dispute. Shann brushed coarse sand from his boots and thought about the dreams. Did they or did they not exist? You could start an argument any time by making a definite statement for or against the peculiar sort of dreaming reported by the first scout to set ship on this world.

The Circe system, of which Warlock was the second of three planets, had first been scouted four years ago by one of those explorers traveling solo in Survey service. Everyone knew that the First-In Scouts were a weird breed, almost a mutation of Terran stock—their reports were rife with strange observations.

So an alarming one concerning Circe, a solar-type yellow sun, and her three planets was no novelty. Witch, the world nearest in orbit to Circe, was too hot for human occupancy without drastic and too costly world-changing. Wizard, the third out from the sun, was mostly bare rock and highly poisonous water. But Warlock, swinging through space between two forbidding neighbors, seemed to be just what the settlement board ordered.

Then the Survey scout, even in the cocoon safety of his well-armed ship, began to dream. And from those dreams a horror of the apparently empty world developed, until he fled the planet to preserve his sanity. There had been a second visit to Warlock to confirm this—worlds so well adapted to human emigration could not be lightly thrown away. But this time the report was negative. There was no trace of dreams, no registration of any outside influence on the delicate and complicated equipment the ship carried. So the Survey team had been dispatched to prepare for the coming of the first pioneers, and none of them had dreamed either—at least, no more than the ordinary dreams all men accepted.

Only there were those who pointed out that the seasons had changed between the first and second visits to Warlock. That first scout had planeted in summer; his successors had come in fall and winter. They argued that the final release of world for settlement should not be given until the full year on Warlock had been sampled.

But pressure from Emigrant Control had forced their hands, that and the fear of just what had eventually happened—an attack from the Throgs. So they had speeded up the process of declaring Warlock open. Only Ragnar Thorvald had protested that decision up to the last and had gone back to headquarters on the supply ship a month ago to make a last appeal for a more careful study.

Shann stopped brushing the sand from the tough fabric above his knee. Ragnar Thorvald . . . He remembered back to the port landing apron on another world, remembered with a sense of loss he could not define. That had been about the second biggest day of his short life; the biggest had come earlier when they had actually allowed him to sign on for Survey duty.

He had tumbled off the cross-continent cargo carrier, his kit—a very meager kit—slung over his thin shoulder, a hot eagerness expanding inside him until he thought that he could not continue to throttle down that wild happiness. There was a waiting starship. And he—Shann Lantee from

the Dumps of Tyr, without any influence or schooling—
was going to blast off in her, wearing the brown-green uniform of Survey!

Then he had hesitated, had not quite dared cross the
few feet of apron lying between him and that compact
group wearing the same uniform—with a slight difference,
that of service bars and completion badges and rank
insignia—with the unconscious self-assurance of men who
had done this many times before.

But after a moment that whole group had become in
his own shy appraisal just a background for one man. Shann
had never before known in his pinched and limited childhood, his lost boyhood, anyone who aroused in him hero
worship. And he could not have put a name to the new
emotion that added so suddenly to his burning desire to
make good, not only to hold the small niche in Survey
which he had already so painfully achieved, but to climb,
until he could stand so in such a group talking easily to
that tall man, his uncovered head bronze-yellow in the sunlight, his cool gray eyes pale in his brown face.

Not that any of those wild dreams born in that minute
or two had been realized in the ensuing months. Probably those dreams had always been as wild as the ones
reported by the first scout on Warlock. Shann grinned
wryly now at the short period of childish hope and half-
confidence that he could do big things. Only one Thorvald
had ever noticed Shann's existence in the Survey camp,
and that had been Garth.

Garth Thorvald, a far less impressive—one could say
"smudged"—copy of his brother. Swaggering with an arrogance Ragnar never showed, Garth was a cadet on his first
mission, intent upon making Shann realize the unbridge-
able gulf between a labor hand and an officer-to-be. He had
appeared to know right from their first meeting just how
to make Shann's life a misery.

Now, in this slit of valley wall away from the domes,
Shann's fists balled. He pounded them against the earth
in a way he had so often hoped to plant them on Garth's
smoothly handsome face, his well-muscled body. One
didn't survive the Dumps of Tyr without learning how
to use fists, and boots, and a list of tricks they didn't

teach in any academy. He had always been sure that he could take Garth if they mixed it up. But if he had loosed the tight rein he had kept on his temper and offered that challenge, he would have lost his chance with Survey. Garth had proved himself able to talk his way out of any scrape, even minor derelictions of duty, and he far outranked Shann. The laborer from Tyr had had to swallow all that the other could dish out and hope that on his next assignment he would not be a member of young Thorvald's team. Though, because of Garth Thorvald, Shann's toll of black record marks had mounted dangerously high and each day the chance for any more duty tours had grown dimmer.

Shann laughed, and the sound was ugly. That was one thing he didn't have to worry about any longer. There would be no other assignments for him, the Throgs had seen to that. And Garth . . . well, there would never be a showdown between them now. He stood up. The Throg ship had disappeared; they could push on.

He found a break in the cliff wall which was climbable, and he coaxed the wolverines after him. When they stood on the heights from which the falls tumbled, Taggi and Togi rubbed against him, cried for his attention. They, too, appeared to need the reassurance they got from contact with him, for they were also fugitives on this alien world, the only representatives of their kind.

Since he did not have any definite goal in view, Shann continued to be guided by the stream, following its wanderings across a plateau. The sun was warm, so he carried his jacket slung across one shoulder. Taggi and Togi ranged ahead, twice catching skitterers, which they devoured eagerly. A shadow on a sun-baked rock sent the Terran skidding for cover until he saw that it was cast by one of the questing falcons from the upper peaks. But that shook his confidence, so he again sought cover, ashamed at his own carelessness.

In the late afternoon he reached the far end of the plateau, faced a climb to peaks which still bore cones of snow, now tinted a soft peach by the sun. Shann studied that possible path and distrusted his own powers to take it without proper equipment or supplies. He must turn either north or south, though he would then have to abandon a sure water supply in the stream. Tonight he would camp where he was. He had not realized how tired he was until he found a likely half-cave in the mountain wall and crawled in. There was too much danger in fire here; he would have to do without that basic comfort of his kind.

Luckily, the wolverines squeezed in beside him to fill the hole. With their warm furred bodies sandwiching him, Shann dozed, awoke, and dozed again, listening to night sounds—the screams, cries, hunting calls, of the Warlock wilds. Now and again one of the wolverines whined and moved uneasily.

Fingers of sun picked at Shann through a shaft among the rocks, striking his eyes. He moved, blinked blearily awake, unable for the first few seconds to understand why the smooth plasta wall of his bunk had become rough red stone. Then he remembered. He was alone and he threw himself frantically out of the cave, afraid the wolverines had wandered off. Only both animals were busy clawing under a boulder with a steady persistence which argued there was a purpose behind that effort.

A sharp sting on the back of one hand made that purpose only too clear to Shann, and he retreated hurriedly from the vicinity of the excavation. They had found an earth-wasp's burrow and were hunting grubs, naturally arousing the rightful inhabitants to bitter resentment.

Shann faced the problem of his own breakfast. He had had the immunity shots given to all members of the team, and he had eaten game brought in by exploring parties and labeled "safe." But how long he could keep to the varieties of native food he knew was uncertain. Sooner or later he must experiment for himself. Already he drank the stream water without the aid of purifiers, and so far there had been no ill results from that necessary recklessness. Now the stream suggested fish. But instead he chanced upon another water inhabitant which had crawled up on land for some obscure purpose of its own. It was a sluggish scaled thing, an easy victim to his club, with thin, weak legs it could project at will from a finned and armor-plated body.

Shann offered the head and guts to Togi, who had abandoned the wasp nest. She sniffed in careful investigation and then gulped. Shann built a small fire and seared the firm greenish flesh. The taste was flat, lacking salt, but the food eased his emptiness. Heartened, he started south, hoping to find water sometime during the morning.

By noon he had his optimism justified with the discovery of a spring, and the wolverines had brought down a slender-legged animal whose coat was close in shade to the dusky purple of the vegetation. Smaller than a Terran deer, its head bore, not horns, but a ridge of stiffened hair rising in a point some twelve inches above the skull dome. Shann haggled off some ragged steaks while the wolverines feasted in earnest, carefully burying the head afterward.

It was when Shann knelt by the spring pool to wash that he caught the clamor of the clak-claks. He had seen or heard nothing of the flyers since he had left the lake valley. But from the noise now rising in an earsplitting volume, he thought there was a sizable colony near-by and that the inhabitants were thoroughly aroused.

He crept on his hands and knees to near-by brush cover, heading toward the source of that outburst. If the claks were announcing a Throg scouting party, he wanted to know it.

Lying flat, with branches forming a screen over him, the Terran gazed out on a stretch of grassland which sloped at a fairly steep angle to the south and which must lead to a portion of countryside well below the level he was now traversing.

The clak-claks were skimming back and forth, shrieking their staccato war cries. Following the erratic dashes of their flight formation, Shann decided that whatever they railed against was on the lower level, out of his sight from that point. Should he simply withdraw, since the disturbance was not near him? Prudence dictated that; yet still he hesitated.

He had no desire to travel north, or to try and scale the mountains. No, south was his best path, and he should be very sure that route was closed before he retreated. Since any additional fuss the clak-claks might make on sighting him would be undistinguished in their now general clamor, the Terran crawled on to where tall grass provided a screen at the top of the slope. There he stopped short, his hands digging into the earth in sudden braking action.

Below, the ground steamed from a rocket flare-back, grasses burned away from the fins of a small scoutship. But even as Shann rose to one knee, his shout of welcome choked in his throat. One of those fins sank, canting the ship crookedly, preventing any new take-off. And over the crown of a low hill to the west swung the ominous black plate of a Throg flyer.

The Throg ship came up in a burst of speed, and Shann waited tensely for some countermove from the scout. Those small speedy Terran ships were prudently provided with weapons triply deadly in proportion to their size. He was sure that the Terran ship could hold its own against the Throg, even eliminate the enemy. But there was no fire from the slanting pencil of the scout. The Throg circled warily, obviously expecting a trap. Twice it darted back in the direction from which it had come. As it returned from its second retreat, another of its kind showed, a black coin dot against the amber of the sky.

Shann felt sick inside. Now the Terran scout had lost any advantage and perhaps all hope. The Throgs could box the other in, cut the downed ship to pieces with their energy beams. He wanted to crawl away and not witness this last disaster for his kind. But some stubborn core of will kept him where he was.

The Throgs began to circle while beneath them the flock of clak-claks screamed and dived at the slanting nose of the Terran ship. Then that same slashing energy he had watched quarter the camp snapped from the far plate across the stricken scout. The man who had piloted her, if not dead already (which might account for the lack of defense), must have fallen victim to that. But the Throg was going to make very sure. The second flyer halted, remaining poised long enough to unleash a second bolt—dazzling any watching eyes and broadcasting a vibration to make Shann's skin crawl when the last faint ripple reached his lookout post.

What happened then caught the overconfident Throg by surprise. Shann cried out, burying his face on his arm, as pinwheels of scarlet light blotted out normal sight. There was an explosion, a deafening blast. He cowered, blind, unable to hear. Then, rubbing at his eyes, he tried to see what had happened.

Through watery blurs he made out the Throg ship, not swinging now in serene indifference to Warlock's gravity, but whirling end over end across the sky as might a leaf tossed in a gust of wind. Its rim caught against a rust-red cliff, it rebounded and crumpled. Then it came down, smashing perhaps half a mile away from the smoking crater in which lay the mangled wreckage of the Terran ship. The disabled scout pilot must have played a last desperate game, making his ship bait for a trap.

The Terran had taken one Throg with him. Shann rubbed again at his eyes, just barely able to catch a glimpse of the second ship flashing away westward. Perhaps it was only his impaired sight, but it appeared to him that the Throg followed an erratic path, either as if the pilot feared to be caught by a second shot, or because that ship had also suffered some injury.

Acid smoke wreathed up from the valley making Shann retch and cough. There could be no survivor from that Terran scout, and he did not believe that any Throg had lived to crawl free of the crumpled plate. But there would be other beetles swarming here soon. They would not dare to leave the scene unsearched. He wondered about that scout. Had the pilot been aiming for the Survey camp, the absence of any rider beam from there warning him off so that he made the detour which brought him here? Or had the Throgs tried to blast the Terran ship in the upper atmosphere, crippling it, making this a forced landing? But at least this battle had cost the Throgs, settling a small portion of the Terran debt for the lost camp.

The length of time between Shann's sighting of the grounded ship and the attack by the Throgs had been so short that he had not really developed any strong hope of rescue to be destroyed by the end of the crippled ship. On the other hand, seeing the Throgs taking a beating had exploded his subconscious acceptance of their superiority. He might not have even the resources of a damaged scout at his command. But he did have Taggi, Togi, and his own brain. Since he was fated to permanent exile on Warlock, there might just be some way to make the beetles pay for that.

He licked his lips. Real action against the aliens would take a lot of planning. Shann would have to know more about what made a Throg a Throg, more than all the wild stories he had heard over the years. There *had* to be some way a Terran could move effectively against a beetle-head. And he had a lot of time, maybe the rest of his life to work out a few answers. That Throg ship lying wrecked at the foot of the cliff . . . perhaps he could do a little investigating before any rescue squad arrived. Shann decided such a move was worth the try and whistled to the wolverines.

3

TO CLOSE RANKS

Shann made his way at an angle to avoid the smoking pit cradling the wreckage of the Terran ship. There were no signs of life about the Throg plate as he approached. A quarter of its bulk was telescoped back into the rest, and surely none of the aliens could have survived such a smash, tough as they were reputed to be within those those horny carapaces.

He sniffed. There was a nauseous odor heavy on the morning air, one which would make a lasting impression on any human nose. The port door in the black ship stood open, perhaps having burst in the impact against the cliff. Shann had almost reached it when a crackle of chain lightning beat across the ground before him, turning the edge of the buckled entrance panel red.

Shann dropped to the ground, drawing his stunner, knowing at the same moment that such a weapon was about as much use in meeting a blaster as a straw wand would be to ward off a blazing coal. A chill numbness held him as he waited for a second blast to char the flesh between his shoulders. So there had been a Throg survivor, after all.

But as moments passed and the Throg did not move in to make an easy kill, Shann collected his wits. Only one shot! Was the beetle injured, unable to make sure of even an almost defenseless prey? The Throgs seldom took prisoners. When they did . . .

The Terran's lips tightened. He worked his hand under his prone body, feeling for the hilt of his knife. With that he could speedily remove himself from the status of Throg prisoner, and he would do it gladly if there was no hope of escape. Had there been only one charge left in that blaster? Shann could make half a dozen guesses as to why the other had made no move, but that shot had come from behind him, and he dared not turn his head or otherwise make an effort to see what the other might be doing.

Was it only his imagination, or had that stench grown stronger during the last few seconds? Could the Throg be creeping up on him? Shann strained his ears, trying to catch some sound he could interpret. The few clak-claks that had survived the blast about the ship were shrieking overhead, and Shann made one attempt at counterattack.

He whistled the wolverines' call. The pair had not been too willing to follow him down into this valley, and they had avoided the crater at a very wide circle. But if they would obey him now, he just might have a chance.

There! That *had* been a sound, and the smell *was* stronger. The Throg must be coming to him. Again Shann whistled, holding in his mind his hatred for the beetle-head, the need for finishing off that alien. If the animals could pick either thoughts or emotions out of their human companion, this was the time for him to get those unspoken half-orders across.

Shann slammed his hand hard against the ground, sent his body rolling, his stunner up and ready.

And now he could see that grotesque thing, swaying weakly back and forth on its thin legs, yet holding a blaster, bringing that weapon up to center it on him. The Throg was hunched over and perhaps to Taggi presented the outline of some four-footed creature to be hunted. For the wolverine male sprang for the hard-shelled shoulders.

Under that impact the Throg sagged forward. But Taggi, outraged at the nature of the creature he had attacked, squalled and retreated. Shann had had his precious seconds of distraction. He fired, the core of the stun beam striking full into the flat dish of the alien's face.

That bolt, which would have shocked a mammal into insensibility, only slowed the Throg. Shann rolled again, gaining a temporary cover behind the wrecked ship. He squirmed under metal hot enough to scorch his jacket and saw the reflection of a second blaster shot which had been fired seconds late.

Now the Throg had him tied down. But to get at the Terran the alien would have to show himself, and Shann had one chance in fifty, which was better than that of three minutes ago—when the odds had been set at one in a hundred. He knew that he could not press the wolverines in again. Taggi's distaste was too manifest; Shann had been lucky that the animal had made one abortive attack.

Perhaps the Terran's escape and Taggi's action had made the alien reckless. Shann had no clue to the thinking processes of the non-human but now the Throg staggered around the end of the plate, his digits, which were closer to claws than fingers, fumbling with his weapon. The Terran snapped another shot from his stunner, hoping to slow the enemy down. But he was trapped. If he turned to climb the cliff at his back, the beetle-head could easily pick him off.

A rock hurtled from the heights above, striking with deadly accuracy on the domed, hairless head of the Throg. His armored body crashed forward, struck against the ship, and rebounded to the ground. Shann darted forward to seize the blaster, kicking loose the claws which still grasped it, before he flattened back to the cliff, the strange weapon over his arm, his heart beating wildly.

That rock had not bounded down the mountainside by chance; it had been hurled with intent and aimed carefully at its target. And no Throg would kill one of his fellows. Or would he? Suppose orders had been issued to take a Terran prisoner and the Throg by the ship had disobeyed? Then, why a rock and not a blaster bolt?

Shann edged along until the upslanted, broken side of the Throg flyer provided him with protection from any overhead attack. Under that shelter he waited for the next move from his unknown rescuer.

The clak-claks wheeled closer to earth. One lit boldly on the carapace of the inert Throg, shuffling ungainly along that horny ridge. Cradling the blaster, the Terran continued to wait. His patience was rewarded when that investigating clak-clak took off uttering an enraged snap or two. He heard what might be the scrape of boots across rock, but that might also have come from horny skin meeting stone.

Then the other must have lost his footing not too far above. Accompanied by a miniature landslide of stones and earth, a figure slid down several yards away. Shann waited in a half-crouch, his looted blaster covering the man now getting to his feet. There was no mistaking the familiar uniform, or even the man. How Ragnar Thorvald had reached that particular spot on Warlock or why, Shann could not know. But that he was there, there was no denying.

Shann hurried forward. It had been when he caught his first sight of Thorvald that he realized just how deep his unacknowledged loneliness had bit. There were two Terrans on Warlock now, and he did not need to know why. But Thorvald was staring back at him with the blankness of non-recognition.

"Who are you?" The demand held something close to suspicion.

That note in the other's voice wiped away a measure of Shann's confidence, threatened something which had flowered in him since he had struck into the wilderness on his own. Three words had reduced him again to Lantee, unskilled laborer.

"Lantee. I'm from the camp . . ."

Thorvald's eagerness was plain in his next question:

"How many of you got away? Where are the rest?" He gazed past Shann up the plateau slope as if he expected to see the personnel of the camp sprout out of the cloak of grass along the verge.

"Just me and the wolverines," Shann answered in a colorless voice. He cradled the blaster on his hip, turned a little away from the officer.

"You . . . and the wolverines?" Thorvald was plainly startled. "But . . . where? How?"

"The Throgs hit very early yesterday morning. They caught the rest in camp. The wolverines had escaped from their cage, and I was out hunting them . . ." He told his story baldly.

"You're sure about the rest?" Thorvald had a thin steel of rage edging his voice. Almost, Shann thought, as if he could turn that blade of rage against one Shann Lantee for being yet alive when more important men had not survived. "I saw the attack from an upper ridge," the younger man said, having been put on the defensive. Yet he had a right to be alive, hadn't he? Or did Thorvald believe that he should have gone running down to meet the beetle-heads with his useless stunner? "They used energy beams . . . didn't land until it was all over."

"I knew there was something wrong when the camp didn't answer our enter-atmosphere signal," Thorvald said absently. "Then one of those platters jumped us on braking orbit, and my pilot was killed. When we set down on the automatics here I had just time to rig a surprise for any trackers before I took to the hills—"

"The blast got one of them," Shann pointed out.

"Yes, they'd nicked the booster rocket; she wouldn't climb again. But they'll be back to pick over the remains."

Shann looked at the dead Throg. "Thanks for taking a hand." His tone was as chill as the other's this time. "I'm heading south . . ."

And, he added silently, I intend to keep on that way. The Throg attack had dissolved the pattern of the Survey team. He didn't owe Thorvald any allegiance. And he had been successfully on his own here since the camp had been overrun.

"South," Thorvald repeated. "Well, that's as good a direction as any right now."

But they were not united. Shann found the wolverines and patiently coaxed and wheedled them into coming with him over a circuitous route which kept them away from both ships. Thorvald went up the cliff, swung down again, a supply bag slung over one shoulder. He stood watching as Shann brought the animals in.

Then Thorvald's arm swept out, his fingers closing possessively about the barrel of the blaster. Shann's own hold on the weapon tightened, and the force of the other's pull dragged him partly around.

"Let's have that—"

"Why?" Shann supposed that because it had been the other's well-aimed rock which had put the Throg out of commission permanently, the officer was going to claim their only spoils of war as personal booty, and a hot resentment flowered in the younger man.

"We don't take that away from here." Thorvald made the weapon his with a quick twist.

To Shann's utter astonishment, the Survey officer walked back to kneel beside the dead Throg. He worked the grip of the blaster under the alien's lax claws and inspected the result with the care of one arranging a special and highly important display. Shann's protest became vocal. "We'll need that!"

"It'll do us far more good right where it is . . ." Thorvald paused and then added, with impatience roughening his voice as if he disliked the need for making any explanations, "There is no reason for us to advertise our being alive. If the Throgs found a blaster missing, they'd start thinking and looking around. I want to have a breathing spell before I have to play quarry in one of their hunts."

Put that way, his action did make sense. But Shann regretted the loss of an arm so superior to their own weapons. Now they could not loot the plateship either. In silence he turned and started to trudge southward, without waiting for Thorvald to catch up with him.

Once away from the blasted area, the wolverines ranged ahead at their clumsy gallop, which covered ground at a surprising rate of speed. Shann knew that their curiosity made them scouts surpassing any human and that the men who followed would have ample warning of any danger to come. Without reference to his silent trail companion, he sent the animals toward another strip of woodland which would give them cover against the coming of any Throg flyer.

As the hours advanced he began to cast about for a

proper night camp. The woods ought to give them a usable site.

"There's water in this wood," Thorvald said, breaking the silence for the first time since they had left the wrecks.

Shann knew that the other had knowledge, not only of the general countryside, but of exploring techniques which he himself did not possess, but to be reminded of that fact was an irritant rather than a reassurance. Without answering, the younger man bored on to locate the water promised.

The wolverines found the small lake first and were splashing along its shore when the Terrans caught up. Thorvald went to work, but to Shann's surprise he did not unstrap the forceblade ax at his belt. Bending over a sapling, he pounded away with a stone at the green wood a few inches above the root line until he was able to break through the slender trunk. Shann drew his own knife and bent to tackle another treelet when Thorvald stopped him with an order: "Use a stone on that, the way I did."

Shann could see no reason for such a laborious process. If Thorvald did not want to use his ax, that was no reason that Shann could not put his heavy belt knife to work. He hesitated, ready to set the blade to the outer bark of the tree.

"Look"—again that impatient edge in the officer's tone, the need for explanation seeming to come very hard to the other—"sooner or later, the Throgs might just trace us here and find this camp. If so, they are *not* going to discover any traces to label us Terran—"

"But who else could we be?" protested Shann. "There is no native race on Warlock."

Thorvald tossed his improvised stone ax from hand to hand.

"But do the Throgs know that?"

The implications, the possibilities, in that idea struck home to Shann. Now he began to understand what Thorvald might be planning.

"Now there *is* going to be a native race." Shann made that a statement instead of a question and saw that the other was watching him with a new intentness, as if he had at last been recognized as a person instead of rank and file and very low rank at that—Survey personnel.

"There is going to be a native race," Thorvald affirmed.

Shann resheathed his knife and went ·to search the pond beach for a suitable stone to use in its place. Even so, he made harder work of the clumsy chopping than Thorvald had. He worried at one sapling after another until his hands were skinned and his breath came in painful gusts from under aching ribs. Thorvald had gone on to another task, ripping the end of a long tough vine from just under the powdery surface of the thick leaf masses fallen in other years.

With this the officer lashed together the tops of the poles, having planted their splintered butts in the ground, so that he achieved a crudely conical structures. Leafy branches were woven back and forth through this framework, with an entrance, through which one might crawl on hands and knees, left facing the lakeside. The shelter they. completed was compact and efficient but totally unlike anything Shann had ever seen before, certainly far removed from the domes of the camp. He said so, nursing his raw hands.

"An old form," Thorvald replied, "native to a primitive race on Terra. Certainly the beetle-heads haven't come across its like before."

"Are we going to stay here? Otherwise it is pretty heavy work for one night's lodging."

Thorvald tested the shelter with a sharp shake. The matted leaves whispered, but the framework held.

"Stage dressing. No, we won't linger here. But it's evidence to support our play. Even a Throg isn't dense enough to believe that natives would make a cross-country trip without leaving evidence of their passing."

Shann sat down with a sigh he made no effort to suppress. He had a vision of Thorvald traveling southward, methodically erecting these huts here and there to confound Throgs who might not ever chance upon them. But already the Survey officer was busy with a new problem.

"We need weapons—"

"We have our stunners, a force ax, and our knives," Shann pointed out. He did not add, as he would have liked that they could have had a blaster.

"Native weapons," Thorvald countered with his usual snap. He went back to the beach and crawled about there, choosing and rejecting stones picked out of the gravel.

Shann scooped out a small pit just before their hut and set about the making of a pocket-sized fire. He was hungry and looked longingly now and again to the supply bag Thorvald had brought with him. Dared he rummage in that for rations? Surely the other would be carrying concentrates.

"Who taught you how to make a fire that way?" Thorvald was back from the pond, a selection of round stones about the size of his fist resting between his chest and forearm.

"It's regulation, isn't it?" Shann countered defensively.

"It's regulation," Thorvald agreed. He set down his stones in a row and then tossed the supply bag over to his companion. "Too late to hunt tonight. But we'll have to go easy on those rations until we can get more."

"Where?" Did Thorvald know of some supply cache they could raid?

"From the Throgs," the other answered matter of factly.

"But they don't eat our kind of food . . ."

"All the more reason for them to leave the camp supplies untouched."

"The camp?"

For the first time Thorvald's lips curved in a shadow smile which was neither joyous nor warming. "A native raid on an invader's camp. What could be more natural? And we'd better make it soon."

"But how can we?" To Shann what the other proposed was sheer madness.

"There was once an ancient service corps on Terra," Thorvald answered, "which had a motto something like this: 'The improbable we do at once; the impossible takes a little longer.' What did you think we were going to do? Sulk around out here in the bush and let the Throgs claim Warlock for one of their pirate bases without opposition?"

Since that was the only future Shann had visualized, he was ready enough to admit the truth, only some shade of tone in the officer's voice kept him from saying so aloud.

4

SORTIE

Five days later they came up from the south so that this time Shann's view of the Terran camp was from a different angle. At first sight there had been little change in the general scene. He wondered if the aliens were using the Terran dome shelters themselves. Even in the twilight it was easy to pick out such landmarks as the com dome with the shaft of a broadcaster spearing from its top and the greater bulk of the supply warehouse.

"Two of their small flyers down on the landing field..." Thorvald materialized from the shadow, his voice a thread of whisper.

By Shann's side the wolverines were moving restlessly. Since Taggi's attack on the Throg neither beast would venture near any site where they could scent the aliens. This was the nearest point to which the men could urge either animal, which was a disappointment, for the wolverines would have been an excellent addition to the surprise sortie they planned for tonight, halving the danger for the men.

Shann ran his fingers across the coarse fur on the animals' shoulders, exerting a light pressure to signal them to wait. But he was not sure of their obedience. The foray was a crazy idea, and Shann wondered again why he had agreed to it. Yet he had gone along with Thorvald, even suggested a few modifications and additions of his own, such as the contents of the crude leaf sack now resting between his knees.

Thorvald flitted away, seeking his own post to the west. Shann was still waiting for the other's signal when there arose from the camp a sound to chill the flesh of any listener, a wail which could not have come from the throat of any normal living thing, intelligent being or animal. Ululating in ear-torturing intensity, the cry sank to a faint, ominous echo of itself, to waver up the scale again.

The wolverines went mad. Shann had witnessed their quick kills in the wilds, but this stark ferocity of spitting, howling rage was new. They answered that challenge from the camp, streaking out from under his hands. Yet both animals skidded to a stop before they passed the first dome and were lost in the gloom. A spark glowed for an instant to his right; Thorvald was ready to go, so Shann had no time to try and recall the animals.

He fumbled for those balls of soaked moss in his leaf bag. The chemical smell from them blotted out that alien mustiness which the wind brought from the campsite. Shann readied the first sopping mess in his sling, snapped his fire sparker at it, and had the ball awhirl for a toss almost in one continuous movement. The moss burst into fire as it curved out and fell.

To a witness it might have seemed that the missile materialized out of the air, the effect being better than Shann had hoped.

A second ball for the sling—spark . . . out . . . down. The first had smashed on the ground near the dome of the com station, the force of impact flattening it into a round splatter of now fiercely burning material. And his second, carefully aimed, lit two feet beyond.

Another wail tearing at the nerves. Shann made a third throw, a fourth. He had an audience now. In the light of those pools of fire the Throgs were scuttling back and forth, their hunched bodies casting weird shadows on the dome walls. They were making efforts to douse the fires, but Shann knew from careful experimentation that once ignited the stuff he had skimmed from the lip of one of the hot springs would go on burning as long as a fraction of its viscous substance remained unconsumed.

Now Thorvald had gone into action. A Throg suddenly halted, struggled frantically, and toppled over into the edge of a fire splotch, legs looped together by the coils of the curious weapon Thorvald had put together on their first night of partnership. Three round stones of comparable weight had each been fastened at the end of a vine cord, and those cords united at a center point. Thorvald had demonstrated the effectiveness of his creation by bringing down one of the small "deer" of the grasslands, an animal normally fleet enough to feel safe from both human and animal pursuit. And those weighted ropes now trapped the Throg with the same efficiency.

Having shot his last fireball, Shann ran swiftly to take up a new position, downgrade and to the east of the domes. Here he put into action another of the primitive weapons Thorvald had devised, a spear hurled with a throwing stick, giving it double range and twice as forceful penetration power. The spears themselves were hardly more than crudely shaped lengths of wood, their points charred in the fire. Perhaps these missiles could neither kill nor seriously wound. But more than one thudded home in a satisfactory fashion against the curving back carapace or the softer front parts of a Throg in a manner which certainly shook up and bruised the target. And one of Shann's victims went to the ground, to lie kicking in a way which suggested he had been more than just bruised.

Fireballs, spears . . . Thorvald had moved too. And now down into the somewhat frantic melee of the aroused camp fell a shower of slim weighted reeds, each provided with a clay-ball head. The majority of those balls broke on landing as the Terrans had intended. So, through the beetle smell of the aliens, spread the acrid, throat-parching fumes of the hot spring water. Whether those fumes had the same effect upon Throg breathing apparatus as they did upon Terran, the attackers could not tell, but they hoped such a bombardment would add to the general confusion.

Shann began to space the hurling of his crude spears with more care, trying to place them with all the precision of aim he could muster. There was a limit to their

amount of varied ammunition, although they had dedicated every waking moment of the past few days to
manufacture and testing. Luckily the enemy had had none
of their energy beams at the domes. And so far they had
made no move to lift their flyers for retaliation blasts.

But the Throgs were pulling themselves into order.
Blaster fire cut the dusk. Most of the aliens were now
flat on the ground, sending a creeping line of fire into
the perimeter of the camp area. A dark form moved
between Shann and the nearest patch of burning moss.
The Terran raised a spear to the ready before he caught
a whiff of the pungent scent emitted by a wolverine hot
with battle rage. He whistled coaxingly. With the Throgs
eager to blast any moving thing, the animals were in
danger if they prowled about the scene.

That blunt head moved. Shann caught the glint of eyes
in a furred mask; it was either Taggi or his mate. Then
a puff of mixed Throg and chemical scent from the camp
must have reached the wolverine. The animal coughed
and fled westward, passing Shann.

Had Thorvald had time and opportunity to make his
planned raid on the supply dome? Time during such an
embroilment was hard to measure, and Shann could not
be sure. He began to count aloud, slowly, as they had
agreed. When he reached one hundred he would begin
his retreat; on two hundred he was to run for it, his goal
the river a half mile from the camp.

The stream would take the fugitives to the sea where
fiords cut the coastline into a ragged fringe offering a
wealth of hiding places. Throgs seldom explored any
territory on foot. For them to venture into that maze
would be putting themselves at the mercy of the Terrans
they hunted. And their flyers could comb the air above
such a rocky wilderness without result.

Shann reached the count of one hundred. Twice a
blaster bolt singed ground within distance close enough
to make him wince, but most of the fire carried well
above his head. All of his spears were gone, save for
one he had kept, hoping for a last good target. One of
the Throgs who appeared to be directing the fire of the
others was facing Shann's position. And on pure chance

that he might knock out that leader, Shann chose him for his victim.

The Terran had no illusions concerning his own marksmanship. The most he could hope for, he thought, was to have the primitive weapon thud home painfully on the other's armored hide. Perhaps, if he were very lucky, he could knock the other from his clawed feet. But that chance which hovers over any battlefield turned in Shann's favor. At just the right moment the Throg stretched his head up from the usual hunched position where the carapace extended over his wide shoulders to protect one of the alien's few vulnerable spots, the soft underside of his throat. And the fire-sharpened point of the spear went deep.

Throgs were mute, or at least none of them had ever uttered a vocal sound to be reported by Terrans. This one did not cry out. But he staggered forward, forelimbs up, clawed digits pulling at the wooden pin transfixing his throat just under the mandible-equipped jaw, holding his head at an unnatural angle. Without seeming to notice the others of his kind, the Throg came on at a shambling run, straight at Shann as if he could actually see through the dark and had marked down the Terran for personal vengeance. There was something so uncanny about that forward dash that Shann retreated. As his hand groped for the knife at his belt his boot heel caught in a tangle of weed and he struggled for balance. The wounded Throg, still pulling at the spear shaft protruding above the swelling barrel of his chest, pounded on.

Shann sprawled backward and was caught in the elastic embrace of a bush, so he did not strike the ground. He fought the grip of prickly branches and kicked to gain solid earth under his feet. Then again he heard that piercing wail from the camp, as chilling as it had been the first time. Spurred by that, he won free. But he could not turn his back on the wounded Throg, keeping instead to a sidewise retreat.

Already the alien had reached the dark beyond the rim of the camp. His progress now was marked by the crashing through low brush. Two of the Throgs back on the firing line started up after their leader. Shann caught a whiff of their odor as the wounded alien advanced with the single-mindedness of a robot.

It would be best to head for the river. Tall grass twisted about the Terran's legs as he began to run. In spite of the gloom, he hesitated to cross that open space. At night Warlock's peculiar vegetation displayed a very alien attribute—ten . . . twenty varieties of grass, plant, and tree emitted wan phosphorescence, varying in degree, but affording each an aura of light. And the path before Shann now was dotted by splotches of that radiance, not as brilliant as the chemical-born flames the attackers had kindled in the camp, but as quick to betray the unwary who passed within their dim circles. And there had never been any reason to believe that Throg powers of sight were less than human; there was perhaps some evidence to the contrary. Shann crouched, charting the clumps ahead for a zigzag course which would take him to at least momentary safety in the river bed.

Perhaps a mile downstream was the transport the Terrans had cobbled together no earlier than this afternoon, a raft Thorvald had professed to believe would support them to the sea which lay some fifty Terran miles to the west. But now he had to cover that mile.

The wolverines? Thorvald? There was one lure which might draw the animals on to the rendezvous. Taggi had brought down a "deer" just before they had left the raft. And instead of allowing both beasts to feast at leisure, Shann had lashed the carcass to the shaky platform of wood and brush, putting it out to swing in the current, though still moored to the bank.

Wolverines always cached that part of the kill which they did not consume at the first eating, usually burying it. He had hoped that to leave the carcass in such a way would draw both animals back to the raft when they were hungry. And they had not fed particularly well that day.

Thorvald? Well, the Survey officer had made it plain during the past five days of what Shann had come to look upon as an uneasy partnership that he considered himself far abler to manage in the field, while he had grave doubts of Shann's efficiency in the direction of survival potential. The Terran started along the pattern of retreat he had laid out to the river bed. His heart pounded as he ran, not because of the physical effort he was expending, but because again from the camp had come that blood-freezing howl. A lighter line marked the lip of the cut in which the stream was set, something he had not foreseen. He threw himself down to crawl the last few feet, hugging the earth.

That very pale luminescence was easily accounted for by what lay below. Shann licked his lips and tasted the sting of sap smeared on his face during his struggle with the bushes. While the strip of meadow behind him now had been spotted with light plants, the cut below showed an almost solid line of them stringing willow-wise along the water's edge. To go down at this point was simply to spotlight his presence for any Throg on his trail. Hs could only continue along the upper bank, hoping to finally find an end to the growth of luminescent vegetation below.

Shann was perhaps five yards from the point where he had come to the river, when a commotion behind made him freeze and turn his head cautiously. The camp was half hidden, and the fires there must be dying. But a twisting, struggling mass was rolling across the meadow in his general direction.

Thorvald fighting off an attack? The wolverines? Shann drew his legs under him, ready to erupt into a counteroffensive. He hesitated between drawing stunner or knife. In his brush with the injured Throg at the wreck the stunner had had little impression on the enemy. And now he wondered if his blade, though it was super-steel at its toughest, could pierce any joint in the armored bodies of the aliens.

There was surely a fight in progress. The whole crazily weaving blot collapsed and rolled down upon three bright light plants. Dull sheen of Throg casing was revealed . . . no sign of fur, flesh, or clothing. Two of the aliens battling? But why?

One of those figures got up stiffly, bent over the huddle still on the ground, and pulled at something. The wooden shaft of Shann's spear was wanly visible. And the form on the ground did not stir as that was jerked loose. The Throg leader dead? Shann hoped so. He slid his knife back into the sheath, tapped the hilt to make sure it was firmly in place, and crawled on. The river, twisting here and there, was a promising pool of dusky shadow ahead. The bank of willow-things was coming to an end, and none too soon. For when he glanced back again he saw another Throg run across the meadow, and he watched them lift their fellow, carrying him back to camp.

The Throgs might seem indestructible, but he had put an end to one, aided by luck and a very rough weapon. With that to bolster his self-confidence to a higher notch, Shann dropped by cautious degrees over the bank and down to the water's edge. When his boots splashed into the oily flood he began to tramp downstream, feeling the pull of the water, first ankle high and then about his calves. This early in the season they did not have to fear floods, and hereabouts the stream was wide and shallow, save in mid-current.

Twice more he had to skirt patches of light plants, and once a young tree stood bathed in radiance with a pinkish tinge instead of the usual ghostly gray. Within the haze which tented the drooping branches, flitted small glittering, flying things; and the scent of its half-open buds was heavy on the air, neither pleasant nor unpleasant in Shann's nostrils, merely different.

He dared to whistle, a soft call he hoped would carry along the cut between the high banks. But, though he paused and listened until it seemed that every cell in his thin body was occupied in that act, he heard no answering call from the wolverines, nor any suggestion that either the animals or Thorvald were headed in the direction of the raft.

What was he going to do if none of the others joined him downstream? Thorvald had said not to linger there past daylight. Yet Shann knew that unless he actually sighted a Throg patrol splashing after him he would wait until he made sure of the others' fate. Both Taggi and Togi were as important to him as the Survey officer. Perhaps more so, he told himself now, because he understood them to a certain degree and found companionship in their unde-manding company which he could not claim from the man.

Why *did* Thorvald insist upon their going on to the

seashore? To Shann's mind his own first plan of holing
up back in the eastern mountains was better. Those
heights had as many hiding places as the fiord country. But Thorvald had suddenly become so set on this
westward trek that he had given in. As much as he
inwardly rebelled when he took them, he found himself obeying the older man's orders. It was only when
he was alone, as now, that he began to question both
Thorvald's motives and his authority.

Three sprigs of a light bush set in a triangle. Shann
paused and then climbed out on the bank, shaking the
water from his boots as Taggi might shake such drops
from a furred limb. This was the sign they had set to mark
their rendezvous point, but . . .

Shann whirled, drawing his stunner. The raft was a dark
blob on the surface of the water some feet farther on.
And now it was bobbing up and down violently. That was
not the result of any normal tug of current. He heard
an indignant squeal and relaxed with a little laugh. He
need not have worried about the wolverines; that bait had
drawn them all right. Both of them were now engaged
in eating, though they had to conduct their feast on the
rather shaky foundation of the makeshift transport.

They paid no attention as he waded out, pulling at the
anchor cord as he went. The wind must have carried his
familiar scent to them. As the water climbed to his shoulders Shann put one hand on the outmost log of the raft.
One of the animals snarled a warning at being disturbed.
Or had that been at him?

Shann stood where he was, listening intently. Yes, there
was a splashing sound from upstream. Whoever followed
his own recent trail was taking no care to keep that pursuit
a secret, and the pace of the newcomer was fast enough
to spell trouble.

Throgs? Tensely the Terran waited for some reaction
from the wolverines. He was sure that if the aliens had
followed him, both animals would give warning. Save when
they had gone wild upon hearing that strange wail from
the camp, they avoided meeting the enemy.

But from all sounds the animals had not stopped feeding. So the other was no beetle-head. On the other hand,

why would Thorvald so advertise his coming, unless the need for speed was greater than caution? Shann drew taut the mooring cord, bringing out his knife to saw through that tough length. A figure passed the three-sprig signal, ran onto the raft.

"Lantee?" The call came in a hoarse, demanding whisper.

"Here."

"Cut loose. We have to get out of here!"

Thorvald flung himself forward, and together the men scrambled up on the raft. The mangled carcass plunged into the water, dislodged by their efforts. But before the wolverines could follow it, the mooring vine snapped, and the river current took them. Feeling the raft sway and begin to spin, the wolverines whined, crouched in the middle of what now seemed a very frail craft.

Behind them, far away but too clear, sounded that eerie howling, topping the sigh of the night wind.

"I saw—" Thorvald gasped, pausing as if to catch full lungfuls of air to back his words, "they have a 'hound'! That's what you hear."

5

PURSUIT

As the raft revolved slowly it also slipped downstream at a steadily increasing pace, for the current had them in hold. The wolverines pressed close to Shann until the musky scent of their fur, their animal warmth, enveloped him. One growled deep in its throat, perhaps in answer to that wind-borne wail.

"Hound?" Shann asked.

Beside him in the dark Thorvald was working loose one of the poles they had readied to help control the raft's voyaging. The current carried them along, but there was a need for the length of sapling to keep them free from rocks and water-buried snags.

"What hound?" the younger man demanded more sharply when there came no immediate answer.

"The Throgs' tracker. But why did they import one?" Thorvald's puzzlement was plain in his tone. He added a moment later, with some of his usual firmness, "We may be in for bad trouble now. Use of a hound means an attempt to take prisoners—"

"Then they do not know that we are here, as Terrans, I mean?"

Thorvald seemed to be sorting out his thoughts when he replied to that. "They could have brought a hound here just on chance that they might miss one of us in the initial

43

mop-up. Or, if they believe we are natives, they could want a specimen for study."

"Wouldn't they just blast down Terrans on sight?"

Shann saw the dark blot which was Thorvald's head shake in negation.

"They might need a live Terran—badly and soon."

"Why?"

"To operate the camp call beam."

Shann's momentary bewilderment vanished. He knew enough of Survey procedure to guess the reason for such a move on the part of the aliens.

"The settler transport?"

"Yes, the ship. She won't planet here without the proper signal. And the Throgs can't give that. If they don't take her, their time's run out before they have even made a start here."

"But how could they know that the transport is nearly due? When we intercept their calls they're pure gibberish to us. Can they read our codes?"

"The supposition is that they can't. Only, concerning Throgs, all we know is supposition. Anyway, they do know the routine for establishing a Terran colony, and we can't alter that procedure except in small nonessentials," Thorvald said grimly. "If that transport doesn't pick up the proper signal to set down here on schedule, her captain will call in the patrol escort . . . then exit one Throg base. But if the beetle-heads can trick the ship in and take her, then they'll have a clear five or six more months here to consolidate their own position. After that it would take more than just one patrol cruiser to clear Warlock; it will require a fleet. So the Throgs will have another world to play with, and an important one. This lies on a direct line between the Odin and Kulkulkah systems. A Throg base on such a trade route could eventually cut us right out of this quarter of the galaxy."

"So you think they want to capture us in order to bring the transport in?"

"By our type of reasoning, that would be a logical move—*if* they know we are here. They haven't too many of those hounds, and they don't risk them on petty jobs. I'd hoped we'd covered our trail well. But we had to risk that attack on the camp . . . I needed the map case!" Again Thorvald might have been talking to himself. "Time . . . and the right maps"—he brought his fist down on the raft, making the platform tremble—"that's what I have to have now."

Another patch of light-willows stretched along the river-banks, and as they sailed through that ribbon of ghostly radiance they could see each other's faces. Thorvald's was bleak, hard, his eyes on the stream behind them as if he expected at any moment to see a Throg emerge from the surface of the water.

"Suppose that thing"—Shann pointed upstream with his chin—"follows us? What is it anyway?" "Hound" suggested Terran dog, but he couldn't stretch his imagination to believe in a working co-operation between Throg and any mammal.

"A rather spectacular combination of toad and lizard, with a few other grisly touches, is about as close as you can get to a general description. And that won't be too accurate, because like the Throgs its remote ancestors must have been of the insect family. If the thing follows us, and I think we can be sure that it will, we'll have to take steps. There is always this advantage—those hounds cannot be controlled from a flyer, and the beetle-heads never take kindly to foot slogging. So we won't have to expect any speedy chase. If it slips its masters in rough country, we can try to ambush it." In the dim light Thorvald was frowning. "I flew over the territory ahead on two sweeps, and it is a crazy mixture. If we can reach the rough country bordering the sea, we'll have won the first round. I don't believe that the Throgs will be in a hurry to track us in there. They'll try two alternatives to chasing us on foot. One, use their energy beams to rake any suspect valley, and since there are hundreds of valleys all pretty much alike, that will take some time. Or they can attempt to shake us out with a dumdum should they have one here, which I doubt."

Shann tensed. The stories of the effects of the Throgs' dumdum weapon were anything but pretty.

"And to get a dumdum," Thorvald continued as if he were discussing a purely theoretical matter and not a threat of something worse than death, "they'll have to

bring in one of their major ships. Which they will hesitate to do with a cruiser near at hand. Our own danger
spot now is the section we should strike soon after dawn
tomorrow if the rate of this current is what I have timed
it. There is a band of desert on this side of the mountains. The river gorge deepens there and the land is bare.
Let them send a ship over and we could be as visible as
if we were sending up flares—"

"How about taking cover now and going on only at
night?" suggested Shann.

"Ordinarily, I'd say yes. But with time pressing us now,
no. If we keep straight on, we could reach the foothills
in about forty hours, maybe less. And we have to stay with
the river. To strike across country there without good supplies and on foot is sheer folly."

Two days. With perhaps the Throgs unleashing their
hound on land, combing from their flyers. With a
desert . . . Shann put out his hands to the wolverines. The
prospect certainly didn't seem anywhere near as simple
as it had the night before when Thorvald had planned
this escape. But then the Survey officer had left out
quite a few points which were not pertinent. Was he
also leaving out other essentials? Shann wanted to ask,
but somehow he could not.

After a while he dozed, his head resting on his knees.
He awoke, roused out of a vivid dream, a dream so detailed
and so deeply impressed in a picture on his mind that he
was confused when he blinked at the riverbank visible in
the half-light of early dawn.

Instead of that stretch of earth and ragged vegetation
now gliding past him as the raft angled along, he should
have been fronting a vast skull stark against the sky—a
skull whose outlines were oddly inhuman. From its eyeholes issued and returned flying things while its sharply
protruding lower jaw was lapped by water. The skull's color
had been a violent clash of blood-red and purple. Shann
blinked again at the riverbank, seeing transposed on it
still that ghostly haze of bone-bare dome, cavernous eyeholes and nose slit, fanged jaws. That skull was a mountain, or a mountain was a skull—and it was important to
him; he must locate it!

He moved stiffly, his legs and arms cramped but not cold. The wolverines stirred on either side of him. Thorvald continued to sleep, curled up beyond, the pole still clasped in his hands. A flat map case was slung by a strap about his neck, its thin envelope between his arm and his body as if for safekeeping. On the smooth flap was the Survey seal, and it was fastened with a finger lock.

Thorvald had lost some of the bright hard surface he had shown at the spaceport where Shann had first sighted him. There were hollows in his cheeks, sending into high relief those bone ridges beneath his eye sockets, giving him a faint resemblance to the skull of Shann's dream. His face was grimed, his field uniform stained and torn. Only his hair was as bright as ever.

Shann smeared the back of his hand across his own face, not doubting that he must present an even more disreputable appearance. He leaned forward cautiously to look into the water, but that surface was not quiet enough to act as a mirror.

Getting to his feet as the raft bobbed under his shift of weight, Shann studied the territory now about them. He could not match Thorvald's inches, just as he must have a third less bulk than the officer, but standing, he could sight something of what now lay beyond the rising banks of the cut. That grass which had been so thick in the meadowlands around the camp had thinned into separate clumps, pale lavender in color. And the scrawniness of stem and blade suggested dehydration and poor soil. The earth showing between those clumps was not of the usual blue, but pallid, too, bleached to gray, while the bushes along the stream's edge were few and smaller. They must have crossed the line into the desert Thorvald had promised.

Shann edged around to face west. There was light enough in the sky to sight tall black pyramids waiting. They had to reach those distant mountains, mountains whose other side rested in sea water. He studied them carefully, surveying each peak he could separate from its fellows.

Did the skull lie among them? The conviction that the place he had seen in his dreams was real, that it was to be found on Warlock, persisted. Not only was it a definite feature of the landscape somewhere in the wild places of this world, but it was also necessary for him to locate it. Why? Shann puzzled over that, with a growing uneasiness which was not quite fear, not yet, anyway.

Thorvald moved. The raft tilted and the wolverines growled. Shann sat down, one hand out to the officer's shoulder in warning. Feeling that touch Thorvald shifted, one hand striking out blindly in a blow which Shann was just able to avoid while with the other he pinned the map case yet tighter to him.

"Take it easy!" Shann urged.

The other's eyelids flickered. He looked up, but not as if he saw Shann at all.

"The Cavern of the Veil—" he muttered. "Utgard . . ." Then his eyes focused and he sat up, gazing around him with a frown.

"We're in the desert," Shann announced.

Thorvald got up, balancing on feet planted a little apart, looking to the faded expanse of the waste spreading from the river cut. He stared at the mountains before he squatted down to fumble with the lock of the map case.

The wolverines were growing restless, though they still did not try to move about too freely on the raft. They greeted Shann with vocal complaint. He and Thorvald could satisfy their hunger with a handful of concentrates from the survival kit. But those dry tablets could not serve the animals. Shann studied the terrain with more knowledge than he had possessed a week earlier. This was not hunting land, but there remained the bounty of the river.

"We'll have to feed Taggi and Togi," he broke the silence abruptly. "If we don't, they'll be into the river and off on their own."

Thorvald glanced up from one of the tough, thin sheets of map skin, again as if he had been drawn back from some distance. His eyes moved from Shann to the unpromising shore.

"How? With what?" he wanted to know. Then the real urgency of the situation must have penetrated his mental isolation. "You have an idea—?"

"There's those fish we found them eating back by the mountain stream," Shann said, recalling an incident of a few days earlier. "Rocks here, too, like those the fish were hiding under. Maybe we can locate some of them here."

He knew that Thorvald would be reluctant to work the raft inshore, to spare time for such hunting. But there would be no arguing with hungry wolverines, and he did not propose to lose the animals for the officer's whim.

However, Thorvald did not protest. They poled the raft out of the main pull of the current, sending it in toward the southern shore in the lee of a clump of light-willows. Shann scrambled ashore, the wolverines after him, sniffing along at his heels while he overturned likely looking rocks to unroof some odd underwater dwellings. The fish with the rudimentary legs were present and not agile enough even in their native element to avoid well-clawed paws which scooped them neatly out of the river shallows. There was also a sleek furred creature with a broad flat head and paddle-equipped forepaws, rather like a miniature seal, which Taggi appropriated before Shann had a chance to examine it closely. In fact, the wolverines wrought havoc along a half-mile section of bank before the Terran could coax them back to the raft.

As they hunted, Shann got a better idea of the land about the river. It was sere, the vegetation dwindling except for some rough spikes of things pushing through the parched ground like flayed fingers, their puffed redness in contrast to the usual amethyst hues of Warlock's growing things. Under the climbing sun that whole stretch of country was revealed in a starkness which at first repelled, and then began to interest him.

He discovered Thorvald standing on the upper bluff, looking out toward the waiting mountains. The officer turned as Shann urged the wolverines to the raft, and when he jumped down the drop to join them, Shann saw he carried a map strip unrolled in his hand.

"The situation is not as good as we hoped," he told the younger man. "We'll have to leave the river to cross the heights."

"Why?"

"There's rapids—ending in a falls." The officer squatted

down, spreading out the strip and making stabs at it with a nervous finger tip. "Here we have to leave. This is all rough ground. But lying to the south there's a gap which may be a pass. This was made from an aerial survey."

Shann knew enough to realize to what extent such a guide could go wrong. Main features of the landscape would be clear enough from aloft, but there might be insurmountable difficulties at ground level which were not distinguishable from the air. Yet Thorvald had planned this journey as if he had already explored their escape route and that it was as open and easy as a stroll down Tyr's main transport way. Why was it so necessary that they try to reach the sea? However, since he had no objection to voice except a dislike for indefinite information, Shann did not question the other's calm assumption of command, not yet, anyway.

As they embarked and worked back into the current, Shann studied his companion. Thorvald had freely listed the difficulties lying before them. Yet he did not seem in the least worried about their being able to win through to the sea—or if he was, his outer shell of unconcern remained uncracked. Before their first day together had ended, the younger Terran had learned that to Thorvald he was only another tool, to be used by the Survey officer in some project which the other believed of primary importance. And his resentment of the valuation was under control so far. He valued Thorvald's knowledge, but the other's attitude chilled and rebuffed his need for something more than a half partnership of work.

Why had Thorvald come back to Warlock in the first place? And why had it been necessary for him to risk his life—perhaps more than his life if their theory was correct concerning the Throgs' wish to capture a Terran—to get that set of maps from the plundered camp? When he had first talked of that raid, his promised loot had been supplies to fill their daily needs; there had been no mention of maps. By all signs Thorvald was engaged on some mission. And what would happen if he, Shann, suddenly stopped being the other's obedient underling and demanded a few explanations here and now?

Only Shann knew enough about men to also know that he would not get any information out of Thorvald that the latter was not ready to give, and that such a showdown, coming prematurely, would only end in his own discomfiture. He smiled wryly now, remembering his emotions when he had first seen Ragnar Thorvald months ago. As if the officer ever considered the likes, dislikes—or dreams—of one Shann Lantee. No, reality and dreams seldom approached each other. Dreams . . .

"On any of those shoreline maps," he asked suddenly, "do they have marked a mountain shaped like a skull?"

Thorvald thrust with his pole. "Skull?" he repeated, a little absently, as he so often did in answer to Shann's questions unless they dealt with some currently important matter.

"A peculiar sort of skull," Shann said. Just as vividly as when he had first awakened, he could picture that skull mountain with the flying things around its eye sockets. And that, too, was odd; dream impressions usually faded with the passing of waking hours. "It has a protruding jaw and the waves wash that . . . red-and-purple rock—"

"What?"

He had Thorvald's complete attention now.

"Where did you hear about it?" That demand followed quickly.

"I didn't hear about it. I dreamed of it last night. I stood there right in front of it. There were birds—or things flying like birds—going in and out of the eyeholes—"

"What else?" Thorvald leaned across his pole, his eyes alive, avid, as if he would pull the reply he wanted out of Shann by force.

"That's all I remember—the skull mountain." He did not add his other impression, that he was meant to find that skull, that he *must* find it.

"Nothing . . ." Thorvald paused, and then spoke slowly, with a visible reluctance. "Nothing else? No cavern with a green veil—a wide green veil—strung across it?"

Shann shook his head. "Just the skull mountain."

Thorvald looked as if he didn't quite believe that, but Shann's expression must have been convincing, for he laughed shortly.

"Well, there goes one nice neat theory up in smoke!" he commented. "No, your skull doesn't appear on any of our maps, and so probably my cavern does not exist either. They may both be smoke screens—"

"What—?" But Shann never finished that query.

A wind was rising in the desert to blow across the slit which held the river, carrying with it a fine shifting of sand which coasted down into the water as a gray haze, coating men, animals, and raft, and sighing as snow sighs when it falls.

Only that did not drown out another cry, a thin cry, diluted by the miles of land stretching behind them, but yet carrying that long ululating howl they had heard in the Throg camp. Thorvald grinned mirthlessly.

"The hound's on trail."

He bent to the pole, using it to aid the pace of the current. Shann, chilled in spite of the sun's heat, followed his example, wondering if time had ceased to fight on their side.

6

THE HOUND

The sun was a harsh ball of heat baking the ground and then, in some odd manner, drawing back that same fieriness. In the coolness of the eastern mountains Shann would not have believed that Warlock could hold such heat. The men discarded their jackets early as they swung to dip the poles. But they dared not strip off the rest of their clothing lest their skin burn. And again gusts of wind now drove sand over the edge of the cut to blanket the water.

Shann wiped his eyes, pausing in his tedious push-push, to look at the rocks which they were passing in risky proximity. For the slash which held the river had narrowed. And the rock of its walls was naked of earth, save for sheltered pockets holding the drift of sand dust, while boulders of all sizes cut into the path of the flowing water.

He had not been mistaken; they were going faster, faster even than their efforts with the poles would account for. With the narrowing of the bed of the stream, the current was taking on a new swiftness. Shann said as much and Thorvald nodded.

"We're approaching the first of the rapids."

"Where we get off and walk around," Shann croaked wearily. The dust gritted between his teeth, irritated his eyes. "Do we stay beside the river?"

"As long as we can," Thorvald replied somberly. "We have no way of transporting water."

Yes, a man could live on very slim rations of food, continue to beat his way over a bad trail if he had the concentrate tablets they carried. But there was no going without water, and in this heat such an effort would finish them quickly. Always they both listened for another cry from behind, a cry to tell them just how near the Throg hunting party had come.

"No Throg flyers yet," Shann observed. He had expected one of those black plates to come cruising the moment the hound had pointed the direction for their pursuers.

"Not in a storm such as this." Thorvald, without releasing his hold on the raft pole, pointed with his chin to the swirling haze cloaking the air above the cut walls. Here the river dug yet deeper into the beginning of a canyon. They could breathe better. The dust still sifted down but not as thickly as a half hour earlier. Though over their heads the sky was now a grayish lid, shutting out the sun, bringing a portion of coolness to the travelers.

The Survey officer glanced from side to side, watching the banks as if hunting for some special mark or sign. At last he used his pole as a pointer to indicate a rough pile of boulders ahead. Some former landslide had quarter dammed the river at that point, and the drift of seasonal floods was caught in and among the rocky pile to form a prickly peninsula.

"In there—"

They brought the raft to shore, fighting the faster current. The wolverines, who had been subdued by the heat and the dust, flung themselves to the rocks with the eagerness of passengers deserting a sinking ship for certain rescue. Thorvald settled the map case more securely between his arm and side before he took the same leap. When they were all ashore he prodded the raft out into the stream again, pushing the platform along until it was sucked by the current past the line of boulders.

"Listen!"

But Shann had already caught that distant rumble of sound. It was steady, beating like some giant drum.

Certainly it did not herald a Throg ship in flight and it came from ahead, not from their back trail.

"Rapids . . . perhaps even the falls," Thorvald interpreted that faint thunder. "Now, let's see what kind of a road we can find here."

The tongue of boulders, spiked with driftwood, was firmly based against the wall of the cut. But it sloped up to within a few feet of the top of that gap, more than one landslide having contributed to its fashioning. The landing stage paralleled the river for perhaps some fifty feet. Beyond it water splashed a straight wall. They would have to climb and follow the stream along the top of the embankment, maybe being forced well away from the source of the water.

By unspoken consent they both knelt and drank deeply from their cupped hands, splashing more of the liquid over their heads, washing the dust from their skins. Then they began to climb the rough ascent up which the wolverines had already vanished. The murk above them was less solid, but again the fine grit streaked their faces, embedding itself in their hair.

Shann paused to scrape a film of mud from his lips and chin. Then he made the last pull, bracing his slight body against the push of the wind he met there. A palm struck hard between his shoulders, nearly sending him sprawling. He had only wits enough left to recognize that as an order to get on, and he staggered ahead until rock arched over him and the sand drift was shut off.

His shoulder met solid stone, and rubbing the sand from his eyes, Shann realized he was in a pocket in the cliff walls. Well overhead he caught a glimpse of natural amber sky through a slit but here was a twilight which thickened into complete darkness.

There was no sign of the wolverines. Thorvald moved along the pocket southward, and Shann followed him. Once more they faced a dead end. For the crevice, with the sheer descent to the river on the right, the cliff wall at its back, came to an abrupt halt in a drop which caught at Shann's stomach when he ventured to look down.

If some battleship of the interstellar fleet had aimed a force beam across the mountains of Warlock, cutting down to what lay under the first layer of planet-skin, perhaps the resulting wound might have resembled that slash. What had caused such a break between the height on which they stood and the much taller peak beyond, Shann could not guess. But it must have been a cataclysm of spectacular dimensions. There was certainly no descending to the bottom of that cut and reclimbing the rock face on the other side. The fugitives would either have to return to the river with all its ominous warnings of trouble to come, or find some other path across that gap which now provided such an effective barrier to the west.

"Down!" Just as Thorvald had pushed him out of the murk of the dust storm into the crevice, so now did that officer jerk Shann from his feet, forcing him to the floor of the half cave from which they had partially emerged.

A shadow moved across the bright band of sunlit sky.

"Back!" Thorvald caught at Shann again, his greater strength prevailing as he literally dragged the younger man into the dusk of the crevice. And he did not pause, nor allow Shann to do so, even when they were well under cover again. At last they reached the dark hole in the southern wall which they had passed earlier. And a push from Thorvald sent his companion into that.

Then a blow greater than any the Survey officer had aimed at him struck Shann. He was hurled against a rough wall with impetus enough to explode the air from his lungs, the ensuing pain so great that he feared his ribs had given under that thrust. Before his eyes fire lashed down the slit, searing him into temporary blindness. That flash was the last thing he remembered as thick darkness closed in, shutting him into the nothingness of unconsciousness.

It hurt to breathe; he was slowly aware first of that pain and then the fact that he *was* breathing, that he had to endure the pain for the sake of breath. His whole body was jarred into a dull torment as a weight pressed upon his twisted legs. Then strong animal breath puffed into his face. Shann lifted one hand by will power, touched thick fur, felt the rasp of a tongue laid wetly across his fingers.

Something close to terror engulfed him for a second

or two when he knew that he could not see! The black about him was colored by jagged flashes of red which he somehow guessed were actually inside his eyes. He groped through that fire-pierced darkness. An animal whimper from the throat of the shaggy body pressed against him; he answered that movement.

"Taggi?"

The shove against him was almost enough to pin him once more to the wall, a painful crush on his aching ribs, as the wolverine responded to his name. That second nudge from the other side must be Togi's bid for attention.

But what had happened? Thorvald had hurled him back just after that shadow had swung over the ledge. That shadow! Shann's wits quickened as he tried to make sense of what he could remember. A Throg ship! Then that fiery lash which had cut after them could only have resulted from one of those energy bolts such as had wiped out the others of his kind at the camp. But he was still alive—!

"Thorvald?" He called through his personal darkness. When there was no answer, Shann called again, more urgently. Then he hunched forward on his hands and knees, pushing Taggi gently aside, running his hands over projecting rocks, uneven flooring.

His fingers touched what could only be cloth, before they met the warmth of flesh. And he half threw himself against the supine body of the Survey officer, groping awkwardly for heartbeat, for some sign that the other was still living.

"What—?" The one word came thickly, but Shann gave something close to a sob of relief as he caught the faint mutter. He squatted back on his heels, pressed his forearm against his aching eyes in a kind of fierce will to see.

Perhaps that pressure did relieve some of the blackout, for when he blinked again, the complete dark and the fiery trails had faded to gray, and he was sure he saw dimly a source of light to his left.

The Throg ship had fired upon them. But the aliens could not have used the full force of their weapon or neither of the Terrans would still be alive. Which meant,

Shann's thoughts began to make sense—sense which brought apprehension—the Throgs probably intended to disable rather than kill. They wanted prisoners, just as Thorvald had warned.

How long did the Terrans have before the aliens would come to collect them? There was no fit landing place hereabouts for their flyer. The beetle-heads would have to set down at the edge of the desert land and climb the mountains on foot. And the Throgs were not good at that. So, the fugitives still had a measure of time.

Time to do what? The country itself held them securely captive. That drop to the southwest was one barrier. To retreat eastward would mean running straight into the hands of the hunters. To descend again to the river, their raft gone, was worse than useless. There was only this side pocket in which they sheltered. And once the Throgs arrived, they could scoop the Terrans out at their leisure, perhaps while stunned by a controlling energy beam.

"Taggi? Togi?" Shann was suddenly aware that he had not heard the wolverines for some time.

He was answered by a weirdly muffled call—from the south! Had the animals found a new exit? Was this niche more than just a niche? A cave of some length, or even a passage running back into the interior of the peaks? With that faint hope spurring him, Shann bent again over Thorvald, not able to make out the other's huddled form. Then he drew the torch from the inner loop of his coat and pressed the lowest stud.

His eyes smarted in answer to that light, watered until tears patterned the grime and dust on his cheeks. But he could make out what lay before them, a hole leading into the cliff face, the hole which might furnish the door to escape.

The Survey officer moved, levering himself up, his eyes screwed tightly shut.

"Lantee?"

"Here. And there's a tunnel—right behind you. The wolverines went that way . . ."

To his surprise there was a thin ghost of a smile on Thorvald's usually straight-lipped mouth. "And we'd better be away before visitors arrive?"

So he, too, must have thought his way through the sequence of past action to the same conclusion concerning the Throg movements.

"Can you see, Lantee?" The question was painfully casual, but a note in it, almost a reaching for reassurance, cut for the first time through the wall which had stood between them from their chance meeting by the wrecked ship.

"Better now. I couldn't when I first came to," Shann answered quickly.

Thorvald opened his eyes, but Shann guessed that he was as blind as he himself had been. He caught at the officer's nearer hand, drawing it to rest on his own belt.

"Grab hold!" Shann was giving the orders now. "By the look of that opening we had better try crawling. I've a torch on at low—"

"Good enough." The other's fingers fumbled on the band about Shann's slim waist until they gripped tight at his back. He started on into the opening, drawing Thorvald by that hold with him.

Luckily, they did not have to crawl far, for shortly past the entrance the fault or vein they were following became a passage high enough for even the tall Thorvald to travel without stooping. And then only a little later he released his hold on Shann, reporting he could now see well enough to manage on his own.

The torch beam caught on a wall and awoke from there a glitter which hurt their eyes—a green-gold cluster of crystals. Several feet on, there was another flash of embedded crystals. Those might promise priceless wealth, but neither Terran paused to examine them more closely or touch their surfaces. From time to time Shann whistled. And always he was answered by the wolverines, their calls coming from ahead. So the men continued to hope that they were not walking into a trap from which the Throgs could extract them.

"Snap off your torch a moment!" Thorvald ordered.

Shann obeyed. The subdued light vanished. Yet there was still light to be seen—ahead and above.

"Front door," Thorvald observed. "How do we get up?"

The torch showed them that, a narrow ladder of ledges

branching off when the passage they followed took a turn to the left and east. Afterward Shann remembered that climb with wonder that they had actually made it, though their advance had been slow, passing the torch from one to another to make sure of their footing.

Shann was top man when a last spurt of effort enabled him to draw himself out into the open, his hands raw, his nails broken and torn. He sat there, stupefied with his own weariness, to stare about.

Thorvald called impatiently, and Shann reached for the torch to hold it for the officer. Then Thorvald crawled out; he, too, looked around in dull surprise.

On either side, peaks cut high into the amber of the sky. But this bowl in which the men had found refuge was rich in growing things. Though the trees were stunted, the grass grew almost as high here as it did on the meadows of the lowlands. Quartering the pocket valley, galloped the wolverines, expressing in that wild activity their delight in this freedom.

"Good campsite."

Thorvald shook his head. "We can't stay here."

And, to underline that gloomy prophecy, there issued from that hole through which they had just come, muffled and broken, but still threatening, the howl of the Throgs' hound.

The Survey officer caught the torch from Shann's hold and knelt to flash it into the interior of the passage. As the beam slowly circled that opening, he held out his other arm, measuring the size of the aperture.

"When that things gets on a hot scent"—he snapped off the beam—"the beetle-heads won't be able to control it. There will be no reason for them to attempt to. Those hounds obey their first orders: kill or capture. And I think this one operates on 'capture.' So they'll loose it to run ahead of their party."

"And we move to knock it out?" Shann relied now on the other's experience.

Thorvald rose. "It would need a blaster on full power to finish off a hound. No, we can't kill it. But we can make it a doorkeeper to our advantage." He trotted down into the valley, Shann beside him without understanding in the least, but aware that Thorvald did have some plan. The officer bent, searched the ground, and began to pull from under the loose surface dirt one of those nets of tough vines which they had used for cords. He thrust a double handful of this hasty harvest into Shann's hold with a single curt order: "Twist these together and make as thick a rope as you can!"

Shann twisted, discovering to his pleased surprise that under pressure the vines exuded a sticky purple sap which not only coated his hands, but also acted as an adhesive for the vines themselves so that his task was not nearly as formidable as it had first seemed. With his force ax Thorvald cut down two of the stunted pine trees and stripped them of branches, wedging the poles into the rocks about the entrance of the hole.

They were working against time, but on Thorvald's part with practiced efficiency. Twice more that cry of the hunter arose from the depths behind them. As the westering sun, almost down now, shone into the valley hollow Thorvald set up the frame of his trap.

"We can't knock it out, any more than we can knock out a Throg. But a beam from a stunner ought to slow it up long enough for this to work."

Taggi burst out of the grass, approaching the hole with purpose. And Togi was right at his heels. Both of them stared into that opening, drooling a little, the same eagerness in their pose as they had displayed when hunting. Shann remembered how that first howl of the Throg hound had drawn both animals to the edge of the occupied camp in spite of their marked distaste for its alien masters.

"They're after it too." He told Thorvald what he had noted on the night of their sortie.

"Maybe they can keep it occupied," the other commented. "But we don't want them to actually mix with it; that might be fatal."

A clamor broke out in the interior passage. Taggi snarled, backing away a few steps before he uttered his own war cry.

"Ready!" Thorvald jumped to the net slung from the poles; Shann raised his stunner.

Togi underlined her mate's challenge with a series of snarls rising in volume. There was a tearing, scrambling sound from within. Then Shann fired at the jack-in-the-box appearance of a monstrous head, and Thorvald released the deadfall.

The thing squalled. Ropes beat, growing taut. The wolverines backed from jaws which snapped fruitlessly. To Shann's relief the Terran animals appeared content to bait the now imprisoned—or collared—horror, without venturing to make any close attack.

But he reckoned that too soon. Perhaps the stunner had slowed up the hound's reflexes, for those jaws stilled with a last shattering snap, the toad-lizard mask—a head which was against all nature as the Terrans knew it—was quiet in the strangle leash of the rope, the rest of the body serving as a cork to fill the exit hole. Taggi had been waiting only for such a chance. He sprang, claws ready. And Togi went in after her mate to share the battle.

7

UNWELCOME GUIDE

There was a small eruption of earth and stone as the
hound came alive, fighting to reach its tormentors. The
resulting din was deafening. Shann, avoiding by a hand's
breadth a snap of jaws with power to crush his leg into
bone shards and mangled flesh, cuffed Togi across her
nose. He buried his hands in the fur about Taggi's throat
as he heaved the male wolverine back from the struggling
monster. He shouted orders, and to his surprise Togi did
obey, leaving him free to yank Taggi away. Perhaps neither wolverine had expected the full fury of the hound.

Though he suffered a slash across the back of one
hand, delivered by the over-excited Taggi, in the end
Shann was able to get both animals away from the hole,
now corked so effectively by the slavering thing. Thorvald
was actually laughing as he watched his younger companion in action.

"This ought to slow up the beetles! If they haul their
little doggie back, it's apt to take out some of its rage
on them, and I'd like to see them dig around it."

Considering that the monstrous head was swinging
from side to side in a collar of what seemed to be
immovable rocks, Shann thought Thorvald right. He went
down on his knees beside the wolverines, soothing them

with hand and voice, trying to get them to obey his orders willingly.

"Ha!" Thorvald brought his mud-stained hands together with a clap, the sharp sound attracting the attention of both animals.

Shann scrambled up, swung out his bleeding hand in the simple motion which meant to hunt, being careful to signal down the valley westward. Taggi gave a last reluctant growl at the hound, to be answered by one of its ear-torturing howls, and then trotted off, Togi tagging behind.

Thorvald caught Shann's slashed hand, inspecting the bleeding cut. From the aid packet at his belt he brought out powder and a strip of protecting plasta-flesh to cleanse and bind the wound.

"You'll do," he commented. "But we'd better get out of here before full dark."

The small paradise of the valley was no safe campsite. It could not be so long as that monstrosity on the hillside behind them roared and howled its rage to the darkening sky. Trailing the wolverines, the men caught up with the animals drinking from a small spring and thankfully shared that water. Then they pushed on, not able to forget that somewhere in the peaks about must lurk the Throg flyer ready to attack on sight.

Only darkness could not be held off by the will of men. Here in the open there was no chance to use the torch. As long as they were within the valley boundaries the phosphorescent bushes marked a path. But by the coming of complete darkness they were once more out in a region of bare rock.

The wolverines had killed a brace of skitterers, consuming hide and soft bones as well as the meager flesh which was not enough to satisfy their hunger. However, to Shann's relief, they did not wander too far ahead. And as the men stopped at last on a ledge where a fall of rock gave them some limited shelter both animals crowded in against the humans, adding the heat of their bodies to the slight comfort of that cramped resting place.

From time to time Shann was startled out of a troubled half sleep by the howl of the hound. Luckily that sound never seemed any louder. If the Throgs had caught up with their hunter, and certainly they must have done so by now, they either could not, or would not free it from the trap. Shann dozed again, untroubled by any dreams, to awake hearing the shrieks of clak-claks. But when he studied the sky he was able to sight none of the cliff-dwelling Warlockian bats.

"More likely they are paying attention to our friend back in the valley," Thorvald said dryly, rightly reading Shann's glance to the clouds overhead. "Ought to keep them busy."

Clak-claks were meat eaters, only they preferred their chosen prey weak and easy to attack. The imprisoned hound would certainly attract their kind. And those shrill cries now belling through the mountain heights ought to draw everyone of their species within miles.

"There it is!" Thorvald, pulling himself to his feet by a rock handhold, gazed westward, his gaunt face eager.

Shann, expecting no less than a cruising Throg ship, searched for cover on their perch. Perhaps if they flattened themselves behind the fall of stones, they might be able to escape attention. Yet Thorvald made no move into hiding. And so Shann followed the line of the other's fixed stare.

Before and below them lay a maze of heights and valleys, sharp drops, and saw-toothed rises. But on the far rim of that section of badlands shone the green of a Warlockian sea rippling on to the only dimly seen horizon. They were now within sight of their goal.

Had they had one of the exploration sky-flitters from the overrun camp, they could have walked its beach sands within the hour. Instead, they fought their way through a devil-designed country for the next two days. Twice they had narrow escapes from the Throg ship—or ships—which continued to sweep across the rugged line of the coast, and only a quick dive to cover, wasting precious time cowering like trapped animals, saved them from discovery. But at least the hound did not bay again on the tangled trail they left, and they hoped that the trap and the clak-claks had put that monster permanently out of service.

On the third day they came down to one of those fiords

which tongued inland, fringing the coast. There had been no lack of hunting in the narrow valleys through which they had threaded, so both men and wolverines were well fed. Though the animals' fur wore better than the now tattered uniforms of the men.

"Now where?" Shann asked.

Would he now learn the purpose driving Thorvald on to this coastland? Certainly such broken country afforded good hiding, but no better concealment than the mountains of the interior.

The Survey officer turned slowly around on the shingle, studying the heights behind them as well as the angle of the inlet where the wavelets lapped almost at their battered boot tips. Opening his treasured map case, he began a patient checking of landmarks against several of the strips he carried. "We'll have to get on down to the true coast."

Shann leaned against the trunk of a conical branched mountain tree, pulling absently at the shreds of wine-colored bark being shed in seasonal change. The chill they had known in the upper valleys was succeeded here by a humid warmth. Spring was becoming a summer such as this northern continent knew. Even the fresh wind, blowing in from the outer sea, had already lost some of the bite they had felt two days before when its salt-laden mistiness had first struck them.

"Then what'll we do there?" Shann persisted.

Thorvald brought over the map, his black-rimmed nail tracing a route down one of the fiords, slanting out to indicate a lace of islands extending in a beaded line across the sea.

"We head for these."

To Shann that made no sense at all. Those islands . . . why, they would offer less chance of establishing a safe base than the broken land in which they now stood. Even the survey scouts had given those spots of sea-encircled earth the most cursory examination from the air.

"Why?" he asked bluntly. So far he had followed orders because they had for the most part made sense. But he was not giving obedience to Thorvald as a matter of rank alone.

"Because there is something out there, something

which may make all the difference now. Warlock isn't an empty world."

Shann jerked free a long thong of loose bark, rolling it between his fingers. Had Thorvald cracked? He knew that the officer had disagreed with the findings of the team. He had been an unconvinced minority of one who had refused to subscribe to the report that Warlock had no native intelligent life and therefore was ready and waiting for human settlement because it was technically an empty world. But to continue to cling to that belief without a single concrete proof was certainly a sign of mental imbalance.

And Thorvald was regarding him now with frowning impatience. You were supposed to humor delusions, weren't you? Only, could you surrender and humor a wild idea which might mean your death? If Thorvald wanted to go island-hopping in chance of discovering what never had existed, Shann need not accompany him. And if the officer tried to use force, well, Shann was armed with a stunner, and had, he believed, more control over the wolverines. Perhaps if he merely gave lip agreement to this project . . . Only he didn't believe, noting the light deep in those gray eyes holding on him, that anybody could talk Thorvald out of this particular obsession.

"You don't believe me, do you?" The impatience arose hotly in that demand.

"Why shouldn't I?" Shann tried to temporize. "You've had a lot of exploration experience; you should know about such things. I don't pretend to be any authority."

Thorvald refolded the map and placed it in the case. Then he pulled at the sealing of his blouse, groping in an inner secret pocket. He uncurled his fingers to display his treasure.

On his palm lay a coin-shaped medallion, bone-white but possessing an odd luster which bone would not normally show. And it was carved. Shann put out a finger, though he had a strange reluctance to touch the object. When he did he experienced a sensation close to the tingle of a mild electric shock. And once he had made that contact, he was also impelled to pick up that disk and examine it more closely.

The intricately carved pattern had been done with great delicacy and skill, though the whorls, oddly shaped knobs, ribbon tracings, made no connected design he could determine. After a moment or two of study, Shann became aware that his eyes, following those twists and twirls, were "fixed," that it required a distinct effort to look away from the thing. Feeling some of that same alarm as he had known when he first heard the wailing of the Throg hound, he let the disk fall back into Thorvald's hold, even more disturbed when he discovered that to relinquish his grasp required some exercise of will.

"What is it?"

Thorvald restored the coin to his hiding place.

"You tell me. I can say this much, there is no listing for anything even remotely akin to this in the Archives."

Shann's eyes widened. He absently rubbed the fingers which had held the bone coin—if it was a coin—back and forth across the torn front of his blouse. That tingle . . . did he still feel it? Or was his imagination at work again? But an object not listed in the exhaustive Survey Archives would mean some totally new civilization, a new stellar race.

"It's definitely a fabricated article," the Survey officer continued. "And it was found on the beach of one of those sea islands."

"Throg?" But Shann already knew the answer to that.

"Throg work—*this*?" Thorvald was openly scornful. "Throgs have no conception of such art. You must have seen their metal plates—those are the beetle-heads' idea of beauty. Have those the slightest resemblance to this?"

"Then who made it?"

"Either Warlock has—or once had—a native race advanced enough in a well-established form of civilization to develop such a sophisticated type of art, or there have been other visitors from space here before us and the Throgs. And the latter possibility I don't believe—"

"Why?"

"Because this was carved of bone or an allied substance. We haven't been quite able to identify it in the labs, but it's an organic material. It was found exposed to the weather and yet it is in perfect condition, could have been carved any time within the past five years. It has been handled, yes, but not roughly. And we have come across evidences of no other star-cruising races or species in this sector save ourselves and the Throgs. No, I say this was made here on Warlock, not too long ago, and by intelligent beings of a very high level of civilization."

"But they would have cities," protested Shann. "We've been here for months, explored all over this continent. We'd have seen them or some traces of them."

"An old race, maybe," Thorvald mused, "a very old race, perhaps in decline, reduced to a remnant in numbers with good reason to retire into hiding. No, we've discovered no cities, no evidence of a native culture past or present. But this"—he touched the front of his blouse—"was found on the shore of an island. We may have been looking in the wrong place for our natives."

"The sea . . ." Shann glanced with new interest at the green water surging in wavelets along the edge of the fiord.

"Just so, the sea!"

"But scouts have been here for more than a year, one team or another. And nobody saw anything or found any traces."

"All four of our base camps were set inland, our explorations along the coast were mainly carried out by flitter, except for one party—the one which found this. And there may be excellent local reasons why no native ever showed himself to us. For that matter, they may not be able to exist on land at all, any more than we could live without artificial aids in the sea."

"Now—?"

"Now we must make a real attempt to find them if they do exist anywhere near here. A friendly native race could make all the difference in the world in any struggle with the Throgs."

"Then you did have more than the dreams to back you when you argued with Fenniston!" Shann cut in.

Thorvald's eyes were on him again. "When did you hear that, Lantee?"

To his great embarrassment, Shann found himself flushing. "I heard you, the day you left for Headquarters," he admitted, and then added in his own defense, "Probably half the camp did, too."

Thorvald's gathering frown flickered away. He gave a snort of laughter. "Yes, I guess we did rather get to the bellowing point that morning. The dreams"—he came back to the subject—"Yes, the dreams were—are—important. We had their warning from the start. Lorry was the First-In Scout who charted Warlock, and he's a good man. I guess I can break secret now to tell you this his ship was equipped with a new experimental device which recorded—well, you might call it an 'emanation'—a radiation so faint its source could not be traced. And it registered whenever Lorry had one of those dreams. Unfortunately, the machine was very new, very much in the untested stage, and its performance when checked later in the lab was erratic enough so the powers-that-be questioned all its readings. They produced a half dozen answers to account for that tape, and Lorry only caught the signal as long as he was on a big bay to the south.

"Then when two check flights came in later, carrying perfected machines and getting no recordings, it was all written off as a mistake in the first experiment. A planet such as Warlock is too big a find to throw away when there was no proof of occupancy. And the settlement boys rushed matters right along."

Shann recalled his own vivid dream of the skull-rock set in the lap of water—this sea? And another small point fell into place to furnish the beginning of a pattern. "I was asleep on the raft when I dreamed about that skull-mountain," he said slowly, wondering if he were making sense.

Thorvald's hand came up with the alert stance of Taggi on a strong game scent.

"Yes, on the raft you dreamed of a skull-rock. And I of a cavern with a green veil. Both of us were on water—water which had an eventual connection with the sea. Could water be a conductor? I wonder . . ." Once again his hand went into his blouse. He crossed the strip of gravel beach and dipped fingers into the water, letting the drops fall on the carved disk he now held in his other hand.

"What are you doing?" Shann could see no purpose in that.

Thorvald did not answer. He had pressed wet hand to dry now, palm to palm, the coin cupped tightly between them. He turned a quarter circle, to face the still distant open sea.

"That way." He spoke with a new odd tonelessness.

Shann stared into the other's face. All the eager alertness of only a moment earlier had been wiped away. Thorvald was no longer the man he had known, but in some frightening way a husk, holding a quite different personality. The younger Terran answered his fear with an attack from the old days of rough in-fighting in the Dumps of Tyr. He brought his right hand down hard in a sharp chop across the officer's wrists. The bone coin spun to the sand and Thorvald stumbled, staggering forward a step or two. Before he could recover balance Shann had stamped on the medallion.

Thorvald whirled, his stunner drawn with a speed for which Shann gave him high marks. But the younger man's own weapon was already out and ready. And he talked— fast.

"That thing's dangerous! What did you do—what did it do to you?"

His demand got through to a Thorvald who was himself again.

"What was *I* doing?" came a counter demand.

"You were acting like you were mind-controlled."

Thorvald stared at him incredulously, then with a growing spark of interest.

"The minute you dripped water on that thing you changed," Shann continued.

Thorvald reholstered his stunner. "Yes," he mused, "why *did* I want to drip water on it? Something prompted me . . ." He ran his still-damp hand up the angle of his jaw, across his forehead as if to relieve some pain there. "What else did I do?"

"Faced to the sea and said 'that way,'" Shann replied promptly.

"And why did you move in to stop me?"

Shann shrugged. "When I first touched that thing I felt

a shock. And I've seen mind-controlled people—" He could have bitten his tongue for betraying that. The world of the mind-controlled was very far from the life Thorvald and his kind knew.

"Very interesting," commented the other. "For one of so few years you seem to have seen a lot, Lantee—and apparently remembered most of it. But I would agree that you're right about this little plaything; it carries a danger with it, being far less innocent than it looks." He tore off one of the fluttering scraps of rag which now made up his sleeve. "If you'll just remove your foot, we'll put it out of business for now."

He proceeded to wrap the disk well in his bit of cloth, taking care not to touch it again with his bare fingers while he stowed it away.

"I don't know what we have in this—a key to unlock a door, a trap to catch the unwary. I can't guess how or why it works. But we can be reasonably sure it's not just some carefree maiden's locket, nor the equivalent of a credit to spend in the nearest bar. So it pointed me to the sea, did it? Well, that much I am willing to allow. Maybe we'll be able to return it to the owner, *after* we learn who—or what—that owner is."

Shann gazed down at the green water, opaque, not to be pierced to the depths by human sight. Anything might lurk there. Suddenly the Throgs became normal when balanced against an unknown living in the murky depths of an aquatic world. Another attack on the Throg-held camp could be well preferred to such exploration as Thorvald had in mind. Yet Shann did not voice any protest as the Survey officer faced again in the same direction as the disk had pointed him moments before.

8

UTGARD

A wind from the west sprang up an hour before sunset, lashing waves inland until their spray was a salt mist in the air, a mist to sodden clothing, plaster hair to the skull, and leave a briny slime across the skin. Yet Thorvald hunted no shelter in spite of the promise in the rough shoreline at their backs. The sand in which their boots slipped and slid was coarse stuff, hardly finer than gravel, studded with nests of drift—bone-white or grayed or pale lavender—smoothed and stored by the seasons of low tides and high, seasonal storms and hurricanes. A wild shore and a forbidding one, that aroused Shann's distrust, perhaps a fitting goal for that disk's guiding.

Shann had tasted loneliness in the mountains, experienced the strange world of the river lit at night by the wan radiance of glowing shrubs and plants, and faced the starkness of the heights. Yet through all that journeying there had been a general resemblance to his own experience on other worlds. A tree was a tree, whether it bore purple foliage or was red-veined. A rock was a rock, a river a river. They were equally hard and wet on Warlock or Tyr.

But now a veil he could not describe, even in his own thoughts, hung between him and the sand over which he walked, between him and the sea which sent spray to wet his torn clothing, between him and that wild wrack of long-ago storms. He could put out his hand and touch sand, drift, spray; yet they were a setting where something lay hidden behind that setting—something watched, calculatingly, with intelligence, and a set of emotions and values he did not, could not share.

" . . . storm coming." Thorvald paused in the buffeting of wind and spray, watching the fury of the tossing sea. The sun was still a pale smear just above the horizon. And it gave light enough to make out that trickle of islands melting out to obscurity.

"Utgard—"

"Utgard?" Shann repeated, the strange word holding no meaning for him.

"Legend of my people." Thorvald smeared spray from his face with one hand. "Utgard, those outermost islands where dwell the giants who are the mortal enemies of the old gods."

Those dark lumps, most of them bare rock, only a few crowned with stunted vegetation, might well harbor *anything*, Shann decided, from giants to the malignant spirits of any race. Perhaps even the Throgs had their tales of evil things in the night, beetle monsters to populate wild, unknown lands. He caught at Thorvald's arm and suggested a practical course of action.

"We'll need shelter before the storm strikes." To Shann's relief the other nodded.

They trailed back across the beach, their backs now to the sea and Utgard. That harsh-sounding name did so well fit the line of islands and islets, Shann repeated it to himself. Here the beach was narrow, a strip of blue sand-gravel walled by wave-worn boulders. And from that barrier of stones piled into a breastwork by chance, interwoven with bone-bare drift, arose the first of the cliffs, Shann studied the terrain with increasing uneasiness. To be caught between a sea, whipped inland by a storm wind, and that cliff would be a risk he did not like to consider, as ignorant of field lore as he was. They must locate some break nearer than the fiord down which they had come. And they must find it soon, before the daylight was gone and the full fury of bad weather struck.

In the end the wolverines discovered an exit, just as they had found the passage through the mountain. Taggi nosed into a darker line down the face of the cliff and disappeared, Togi duplicating that feat. Shann trailed them, finding the opening a tight squeeze.

He squirmed into dimness, his outstretched hands meeting a rough stone surface sloping upward. After gaining a point about eight feet above the beach he was able to look back and down through the seaward slit. Open to the sky the crevice proved a doorway to a narrow valley, not unlike those which housed the fiords, but provided with a thick growth of vegetation well protected by the high walls.

Working as a now well-rehearsed team, the men set up a shelter of saplings and brush, the back to the slit through which wind was still able to tear a way. Walled in by stone and knowing that no Throg flyer would attempt to fly in the face of the coming storm, they dared make a fire. The warmth was a comfort to their bodies, just as the light of the flames, men's age-old hearth companion, was a comfort to the fugitives' spirits. Those dancing spears of red, for Shann at least, burned away that veil of other-worldliness which had enwrapped the beach, providing in the night an illusion of the home he had never really known.

But the wind and the weather did not keep truce very long. A wailing blast around the upper peaks produced a caterwauling to equal the voices of half a dozen Throg hounds. And in their poor shelter the Terrans not only heard the thunderous boom of surf, but felt the vibration of that beat pounding through the very ground on which they lay. The sea must have long since covered the beach over which they had come and was now trying its strength against the rock of the cliff barrier. They could not talk to each other over that din, although shoulder touched shoulder.

The last flush of amber vanished from the sky with the speed of a dropped curtain. Tonight no period of twilight divided night from day, but their portion of Warlock was plunged abruptly into darkness. The wolverines crowded into their small haven, whining deep in their throats.

Shann ran his hands along their furred bodies, trying to give them a reassurance he himself did not feel. Never before when on stable land had he been so aware of the unleashed terrors nature could exert, the forces against which all mankind's powers were as nothing.

Time could no longer be measured by any set of minutes or hours. There was only darkness, the howling winds, and the salty rain which must be in part the breath of the sea driven in upon them. The comforting fire vanished, chill and dankness crept up to cramp their bodies, so that now and again they were forced to their feet, to swing arms, stamp, drive the blood into faster circulation.

Later came a time when the wind died, no longer driving the rain bullet-hard against and through their flimsy shelter. Then they slept in the thick unconsciousness of exhaustion.

A red-purple skull—and from its eye sockets the flying things—kept coming . . . going . . . Shann trod on an unsteady foundation which dipped under his weight as had the raft of the river voyage. He was drawing nearer to that great head, could see now how waves curled about the angle of the lower jaw, slapping inward between gaps of missing teeth—which were really broken fangs of rock—as if the skull now and then sucked reviving moisture from the water. The aperture marking the nose was closer to a snout, and the hole was dark, dark as the empty eye sockets. Yet that darkness was drawing him past any effort to escape he could summon. And then that on which he rode so perilously was carried forward by the waves, grated against the jawbone, while against his own fighting will his hands arose above his head, reaching for a hold to draw his shrinking body up the stark surface to that snout-passage.

"Lantee!" A hand jerked him back, broke that compulsion—and the dream. Shann opened his eyes with difficulty, his lashes seemed glued to his cheeks.

He might have been surveying a submerged world. Thin streamers of fog twined up from the earth as if they grew from seeds planted by the storm. But there was no wind, no sound from the peaks. Only under his stiff body

Shann could still feel that vibration which was the sea battering against the cliff wall.

Thorvald was crouched beside him, his hand still urgent on the younger man's shoulder. The officer's face was drawn so finely that his features, sharp under the tanned skin, were akin to the skull Shann still half saw among the ascending pillars of fog.

"Storm's over."

Shann shivered as he sat up, hugging his arms to his chest, his tattered uniform soggy under that pressure. He felt as if he would never be warm again. When he moved sluggishly to the pit where they had kindled their handful of fire the night before he realized that the wolverines were missing.

"Taggi—?" His voice sounded rusty in his own ears, as if some of the moisture thick in the air about them had affected his vocal cords.

"Hunting." Thorvald's answer was clipped. He was gathering a handful of sticks from the back of their lean-to, where the protection of their own bodies had kept that kindling dry. Shann snapped a length between his hands, dropped it into the pit.

When they did coax a blaze into being they stripped, wringing out their clothing, propping it piece by steaming piece on sticks by the warmth of the flames. The moist air bit at their bodies and they moved briskly, striving to keep warm by exercise. Still the fog curled, undisturbed by any shaft of sun.

"Did you dream?" Thorvald asked abruptly.

"Yes." Shann did not elaborate. Disturbing as his dream had been, the feeling that it was not to be shared was also strong, as strong as some order.

"And so did I," Thorvald said bleakly. "You saw your skull-mountain?"

"I was climbing it when you awoke me," Shann returned unwillingly.

"And I was going through my green veil when Taggi took off and wakened me. You are sure your skull exists?"

"Yes."

"And so am I that the cavern of the veil is somewhere on this world. But why?" Thorvald stood up, the firelight marking plainly the lines between his tanned arms, his brown face and throat, and the paleness of his lean body. "Why do we dream those particular dreams?"

Shann tested the dryness of a shirt. He had no reason to try and explain the wherefore of those dreams, only was he certain that he would sometime, somewhere, find that skull, and that when he did he would climb to the doorway of the snout, pass behind to depths where the flying things might nest—not because he wanted to make such an expedition, but because he must.

He drew his hands across his ribs, where pressure still brought an aching reminder of the crushing force of the energy whip the Throgs had wielded. There was no extra flesh on his body, yet muscles slid easily under the skin, a darker skin than Thorvald's, deepening to a warm brown where it had been weathered. His hair, unclipped now for a month, was beginning to curl about his head in tight dark rings. Since he had always been the youngest or the smallest or the weakest in the world of the Dumps, of the Service, of the Team, Shann had very little personal vanity. He did possess a different type of pride, born of his own stubborn achievement in winning out over a long roster of discouragements, failures, and adverse odds.

"Why do we dream?" he repeated Thorvald's question. "No answer, sir." He gave the traditional reply of the Service recruit. And a little to his surprise Thorvald laughed with a tinge of real amusement.

"Where do you come from, Lantee?" He asked as if he were honestly interested.

"Tyr."

"Caldon mines." The Survey officer automatically matched planet to product. "How did you come into Service?"

Shann drew on his shirt. "Signed on as casual labor," he returned with a spark of defiance. Thorvald had joined the Service the right way as a cadet, then a Team man, finally an officer, climbing that nice even ladder with every rung ready for him when he was prepared to mount it. What did his kind know about the labor barracks where the dull-minded, the failures, the petty criminals on the run, lived hard under a secret social system of their own?

It had taken every bit of physical endurance and energy, every fraction of stubborn will Shann could summon, for him to survive his first three months in those barracks— unbroken and still eager to be Survey. He could still wonder at the unbelievable chance which had rescued him from that merely because Training Center had needed another odd hand to clean cages and feed troughs for the experimental animals.

And from the center he made a Team, because when working in a smaller group his push and attention to duty had been noticed and had paid off. Three years it had taken, but he *had* made Team stature. Not that that meant anything now. Shann pulled his boots on over the legs of rough dried coveralls and glanced up, to find Thorvald watching him with a new, questioning directness the younger man could not understand.

Shann sealed his blouse and stood up, knowing the bite of hunger, dull but persistent. It was a feeling he had had so many times in the past that now he hardly gave it a second thought.

"Supplies?" He brought the subject back to the present and the practical. What did it matter why or how one Shann Lantee had come to Warlock in the first place?

"What we have left of the concentrates we had better keep for emergencies." Thorvald made no move to open the very shrunken bag he had brought from the scoutship.

He walked over to a rocky outcrop and tugged loose a yellowish tuft of plant, neither moss nor fungi but sharing attributes of both. Shann recognized it without enthusiasm as one of the varieties of native produce which could be safely digested by Terran stomachs. The stuff was almost tasteless and possessed a rather unpleasant odor. Consumed in bulk it would satisfy hunger for a time. Shann hoped that with the wolverines to aid they could go back to hunting soon.

However, Thorvald showed no desire to head inland where they might expect to locate game. He disagreed with Shann's suggestion for tracking Taggi and Togi when those two emerged from the underbrush obviously well fed and contented after their early morning activity.

When Shann protested with some heat, the other countered: "Didn't you ever hear of fish, Lantee? After a storm such as last night's, we ought to discover good pickings along the shore."

But Shann was also sure that it was not only the thought of food which drew Thorvald back to the sea.

They crawled back through the bolt hole. The beach of gravel-sand had vanished save for a narrow ribbon of land just at the foot of the cliffs, where the water curled in white lace about the barrier of boulders. There was no change in the dullness of the sky; no sun broke through the thick lid of clouds. And the green of the sea was ashened to gray which matched that overcast until one could strain one's eyes trying to find the horizon, unable to mark the dividing line between air and water.

Utgard was a broken necklace, the outermost island-beads lost, the inner ones more isolated by the rise in water, more forbidding. Shann let out a startled hiss of breath.

The top of a near-by rock detached itself, drew up into a hunched thing of armor-plated scales and heavy wide-jawed head. A tail cracked into the air; a double tail split into equal forks for half-way down its length. A leg lifted as a forefoot, webbed, clawed for a new hold. This sea beast was the most formidable native thing he had sighted on Warlock, approaching in its ugliness the hound of the Throgs.

Breathing in labored gusts, the thing slapped its tail down on the stones with a limpness which suggested that the raising of that appendage had overtaxed its limited supply of strength. The head sank forward, resting across one of the forelimbs. Then Shann sighted the fearsome wound in the side just before one of the larger hind legs, a ragged hole through which pumped with every one of those breaths a dark purplish stream, licked away by the waves as it trickled slickly down the rock.

"What is that?"

Thorvald shook his head. "Not on our records," he replied absently, studying the dying creature with avid attention. "Must have been driven in by the storm. This proves there is more in the sea then we knew!"

Again the forked tail lifted and fell, the head raised from the forelimb, stretching up and back until the white underfolds of the throat were exposed as the snout pointed almost vertically to the sky. The jaws opened and from between them came a moaning whistle, a complaint which was drowned out by the wash of the waves. Then, as if that was the last effort, the webbed, clawed feet relaxed their grip of the rock and the scaled body slid sidewise, out of their sight, into the water. There was a feather of spume to mark the plunge and nothing else.

Shann, watching to see if the reptile would surface again, sighted another object, a rounded shape floating on the sea, bobbing lightly as had their river raft.

"Look!"

Thorvald's gaze followed his pointing finger and then before Shann could protest, the officer leaped outward from their perch on the cliff to the broad rock where the scaled sea dweller had lain moments earlier. He stood there, watching that drifting object with the closest attention, as Shann made the same crossing in his wake.

The drifting thing was oval, perhaps some six feet long and three wide, the mid point rising in a curve from the water's edge. As far as Shann could make out in the half-light the color was a reddish-brown, the surface rough. And he thought by the way that it moved that it must be flotsam of the storm, buoyant enough to ride the waves with close to cork resiliency. To Shann's dismay his companion began to strip.

"What are you going to do?"

"Get that."

Shann surveyed the water about the rock. The forked tail had sunk just there. Was the Survey officer mad enough to think he could swim unmenaced through a sea which might be infested with more such creatures? It seemed that he was, for Thorvald's white body arched out in a dive. Shann waited, half crouched and tense, as though he could in some way attack anything rising from the depths to strike at his companion.

A brown arm flashed above the surface. Thorvald swam strongly toward the floating object. He reached it, his outstretched hand rasping across the surface. And it responded so quickly to that touch that Shann guessed it was even lighter and easier to handle than he had first thought.

Thorvald headed back, herding the thing before him. And when he climbed out on the rock, Shann was pulling up his trophy. They flipped the find over, to discover it hollow. They had, in effect, a ready-made craft not unlike a canoe with blunted bows. But the substance was surely organic. Was it shell? Shann speculated, running his finger tips over the irregular surface.

The Survey officer dressed. "We have our boat," he commented. "Now for Utgard—"

Use this frail thing to dare the trip to the islands? But Shann did not protest. If the officer was determined to try such a voyage, he would do it. And neither did the younger man doubt that he would accompany Thorvald.

9

ONE ALONE

Once again the beach was a wide expanse of shingle, drying fast under a sun hotter than any Shann had yet known on Warlock. Summer had taken a big leap forward. The Terrans worked in partial shade below a cliff overhang, not only for the protection against the sun's rays, but also as a precaution against any roving Throg air patrol.

Under Thorvald's direction the curious shell dragged from the sea—if it were a shell, and the texture as well as the general shape suggested that—was equipped with a framework to act as a stabilizing outrigger. What resulted was certainly an odd-looking craft, but one which obeyed the paddles and rode the waves easily.

In the full sunlight the outline of islands was clear-cut— red-and-gray rock above an aquamarine sea. The Terrans had sighted no more of the sea monsters, and the major evidence of native life along the shore was a new species of clak-claks, roosting in cliff holes and scavenging along the sands, and various curious fish and shelled things stranded in small tide pools—to the delight of the wolverines, who fished eagerly up and down the beach, ready to investigate all debris of the storm.

"That should serve." Thorvald tightened the last lashing, straightening up, his fists resting on his hips, to regard the craft with a measure of pride.

Shann was not quite so content. He had matched the Survey officer in industry, but the need for haste still eluded him. So the ship—such as it was—was ready. Now they would be off to explore Thorvald's Utgard. But a small and nagging doubt inside the younger man restrained his enthusiasm over such a voyage. Fork-tail had come out of the section of ocean which they must navigate in this very crude transport. And Shann had no desire to meet an uninjured and alert fork-tail in the latter's own territory.

"Which island do we head for?" Shann kept private his personal doubts of their success. The outmost tip of that chain was only a distant smudge lying low on the water.

"The largest . . . that one with trees."

Shann whistled. Since the night of the storm the wolverines were again more amenable to the very light discipline he tried to keep. Perhaps the fury of that elemental burst had tightened the bond between men and animals, both alien to this world. Now Taggi and his mate padded toward him in answer to his summons. But would the wolverines trust the boat? Shann dared not risk their swimming, nor would he agree to leaving them behind.

Thorvald had already stored their few provisions on board. And now Shann steadied the craft against a rock which served them as a wharf, while he coaxed Taggi gently. Though the wolverine protested, he at last scrambled in, to hunch at the bottom of the shell, the picture of apprehension. Togi took longer to make up her mind. And at length Shann picked her up bodily, soothing her with quiet speech and stroking hands, to put her beside her mate.

The shell settled under the weight of the passengers, but Thorvald's foresight concerning the use of the outrigger proved right, for the craft was seaworthy. It answered readily to the dip of their paddles as they headed in a curve, keeping the first of the islands between them and the open sea for a breakwater.

From the air, Thorvald's course would have been a crooked one, for he wove back and forth between the scattered islands of the chain, using their lee calm for the protection of the canoe. About two thirds of the group were barren rock, inhabited only by clak-claks and creatures closer to true Terran birds in that they wore a body plumage which resembled feathers, though their heads were naked and leathery. And, Shann noted, the clak-claks and the birds did not roost on the same islands, each choosing their own particular home while the other species did not invade that territory.

The first large-sized island they approached was crowned by trees, but it had no beach, no approach from sea level. Perhaps it might be possible to climb to the top of the cliff walls. But Thorvald did not suggest that they try it, heading on toward the next large outcrop of land and rock.

Here white lace patterned in a ring well out from the shore to mark a circle of reefs. They nosed their way patiently around the outer circumference of that threatening barrier, hunting the entrance to the lagoon. Within, there were at least two beaches with climbable ascents to the upper reaches inland. Though Shann noted that the vegetation showing was certainly not luxuriant, the few trees within their range of vision being pallid growths, rather like those they had sighted on the fringe of the desert. Leather-headed flyers wheeled out over their canoe, coasting on outspread wings to peer down at the Terran invaders in a manner which suggested intelligent curiosity.

A full flock gathered to escort them as they continued along the outer line of the reef. Thorvald impatiently dug his paddle deeper. They had explored more than half of the reef now without chancing on an entrance channel.

"Regular fence," Shann commented. One could begin to believe that the barrier had been deliberately reared to frustrate visitors. Hot sunshine, reflected back from the surface of the waves, burned their exposed skin, so they dared not discard their ragged clothing. And the wolverines were growing increasingly restless. Shann did not know how much longer the animals would consent to their position as passengers without raising active protest.

"How about trying the next one?" he asked, knowing at the same time his companion was not in any mood to accept such a suggestion with good will.

The officer made no reply, but continued to use his steer paddle in a fashion which spelled out his stubborn determination to find a passage. This was a personal thing now, between Ragnar Thorvald of the Terran Survey and a wall of rock, and the man's will was as strongly rooted as those water-washed stones.

On the southwestern tip of the reef they discovered a possible opening. Shann eyed the narrow space between two fanglike rocks dubiously. To him that width of water lane seemed dangerously limited, the sudden slam of a wave could dash them against either of those pillars, with disastrous results, before they could move to save themselves. But Thorvald pointed their blunt bow toward the passage with seeming confidence, and Shann knew that as far as the officer was concerned, this was their door to the lagoon.

Thorvald might be stubborn, but he was not a fool. And his training and skill in such maneuvers was proved when the canoe rode in a rising swell in and by those rocks to gain the safety, in seconds, of the calm lagoon. Shann sighed with relief, but ventured no comment.

Now they must paddle back along the inner side of the reef to locate the beaches, for fronting them on this side of the well-protected island were cliffs as formidable as those which guarded the first of the chain at which they had aimed.

Shann glanced now and then over the side of the boat, hoping in these shallows to sight the sea bed or some of the inhabitants of these waters. But there was no piercing that green murk. Here and there nodules of rock awash in wavelets projected inches or feet above the surface, to be avoided by the voyagers. Shann's shoulders ached and burned, his muscles were unaccustomed to the steady swing of the paddles, and the fire of the sun stabbed easily through only two layers of ragged cloth to his skin. He ran a dry tongue over drier lips and gazed eagerly ahead in search of the first of the beaches.

What was so important about this island that Thorvald *had* to make a landing here? The officer's stories of a native race which they might turn against the Throgs to their own advantage was thin, very thin indeed. Especially now, as Shann weighed an unsupported theory against that ache in his shoulders, the possibility of being marooned on the inhospitable shore ahead, against the fifty probable dangers he could total up with very little expenditure of effort. A small nagging doubt of Thorvald's obsession began to grow in his mind. How could Shann even be sure that that carved disk and Thorvald's hokus-pokus with it had been on the level? On the other hand what motive would the officer have for trying such an act just to impress Shann?

The beach at last! As they headed the canoe in that direction the wolverines nearly brought disaster on them. The animals' restlessness became acute as they sighted and scented the shore and knew that they were close. Taggi reared, plunged over the side of the craft, and Shann had just time to fling his weight in the opposite direction as a counterbalance when Togi followed. They splashed shoreward while Thorvald swore fluently and Shann grabbed to save the precious supply bag. In a shower of gravel the animals made land and humped well up on the strand before pausing to shake themselves and splatter far and wide the burden of moisture transported by their shaggy fur.

Ashore, the canoe became a clumsy burden and, light as the craft was, both of the men sweated to get it up on the beach without snagging the outrigger against stones and brush. With the thought of a Throg patrol in mind they worked swiftly to cover it.

Taggi raised an egg-patterned snout from a hollow and licked at the stippling of greenish yolk matting his fur. The wolverines had wasted no time in sampling the contents of a wealth of nesting places that began just above the high-water mark, each cupping two to four tough-shelled eggs. Treading a path among those clutches, the Terrans climbed a red-earthed slope toward the interior of the island.

They found water, not the clear running of a mountain spring, but a stalish pool in a stone-walled depression on the crest of a rise, filled by the bounty of the rain. The warm liquid was brackish, but satisfied in part their thirst, and they drank eagerly.

The outer cliff wall of the island was just that, a wall, for there was an inner slope to match the outer. And at the bottom of it purple-green foliage showed where plants and stunted trees fought for living space. But there was nothing else, though they quartered that growing section with the care of men trying to locate an enemy outpost.

That night they camped in the hollow, roasted eggs in a fire, and ate the fishy-tasting contents because it was food, not because they relished what they swallowed. Tonight no cloud bank hung overhead. A man, gazing up, could see the stars. The stars and other things, for over the distant shore of the mainland they sighted the cruising lights of a Throg ship and waited tensely for that circle of small sparkling points to swing out toward their own hiding hole.

"They haven't given up," Shann stated what was obvious to them both.

"The settler transport," Thorvald reminded him. "If they do not take a prisoner to talk her in and allay suspicion, then"—he snapped his fingers—"the Patrol will be on their tails, but quick!"

So just by keeping out of Throg range, they were, in a way, still fighting. Shann settled back, his tender shoulders resting against a tree bole. He tried to count the number of days and nights lying behind him now since that early morning when he had watched the Terran camp die under the aliens' weapons. But one day faded into another so that he could remember only action parts clearly—the attack on the grounded scoutship, the sortie they had made in turn on the occupied camp, the dust storm on the river, the escape from the Throg ship in the mountain crevice, and their meeting with the hound. Then that storm which had driven them to seek cover after their curious experience with the disk. And now this day when they had safely reached the island.

"Why this island?" he asked suddenly.

"That carved piece was found here on the edge of this valley," Thorvald returned matter-of-factly.

"But today we found nothing at all—"

"Yet this island supplies us with a starting point."

A starting point for what? A detailed search of all the

islands, great and small, in the chain? And how did they dare continue to paddle openly from one to the next with the Throgs sweeping the skies? They would have provided an excellent target today as they combed that reef for an hour or more. Wearily, Shann spread out his hands in the very faint light of their tiny fire, poked with a finger tip at smarting points which would have been blisters had those hands not known toughening in the past. More paddling tomorrow? But that was tomorrow, and at least they need not worry tonight about any Throg attack once they had doused the fire, an action which was now being methodically attended to by Thorvald. Shann pushed down on the bed of leaves he had heaped together. The night was quiet. He could hear only the murmur of the sea, a lulling croon of sound to make one sleep deep, perhaps dreamlessly.

Sun struck down, making a dazzle about him. Shann turned over drowsily in that welcome heat, stretching a little as might a cat at ease. When he really awoke under the press of memory, the need for alertness rode him once more. Beaten-down grass, the burnt-out embers of last night's fire were beside him. But of Thorvald and the wolverines there were no signs.

Not only did he now lie alone, but he was possessed by the feeling that he had not been deserted only momentarily, that Taggi, Togi, and the Survey officer were indeed gone. Shann sat up, got to his feet, breathing faster, a prickle of uneasiness spreading in him, bringing him to that inner slope, up it to the crest from which he could see that beach where last night they had concealed the canoe.

Those lengths of brush and tufts of grass they had used for a screen were strewn about as if tossed in haste. And not too long before . . .

For the canoe was out in the calm waters within the reef, the paddle blade wielded by its occupant flashing brightly in the sun. On the shingle below, the wolverines prowled back and forth, whining in bewilderment.

"Thorvald—!"

Shann put the full force of his lungs into that hail, hearing the name ring from one of the small peaks at his back. But the man in the boat did not turn his head; there was no change in the speed of that paddle dip.

Shann leaped down the outer slope to the beach, skidding the last few feet, saving himself from going headfirst into the water only by a painful wrench of his body.

"Thorvald!" He tried calling again. But that head, bright under the sun did not turn; there was no answer. Shann tore at his clothes and kicked off his boots.

He did not think of the possibility of lurking sea monsters as he plunged into the water, swam for the canoe edging along the reef, plainly bound for the sea gate to the southwest. Shann was not a powerful swimmer. His first impetus gave him a good start, but after that he had to fight for each foot he gained, and the fear grew in him that the other would reach the reef passage before he could catch up. He wasted no more time trying to hail Thorvald, putting all his breath and energy into the effort of overtaking the craft.

And he almost made it, his hand actually slipping along the log which furnished the balancing outrigger. As his fingers tightened on that slimy wood he looked up, and loosed that hold again in time perhaps to save his life.

For when he ducked to let the water cover his head in an impromptu half dive, Shann carried with him a vivid picture, a picture so astounding that he was a little dazed.

Thorvald had stopped paddling at last, because that paddle had to be put to another use. Had Shann not released his hold on the log and gone under water, that crudely fashioned piece of wood might have broken his skull. He saw only too clearly the paddle raised in both hands as an ugly weapon, and Thorvald's face, convulsed in a spasm of ugly rage which made it as inhuman as a Throg's.

Sputtering and choking, Shann fought up to the air once more. The paddle was back at the task for which it had been carved, the canoe was underway again, its occupant paying no more attention to what lay behind than if he *had* successfully disposed of the man in the water. To follow would be only to invite another attack, and Shann might not be so lucky next time. He was not good enough a swimmer to try any tricks such as oversetting the canoe, not when Thorvald was an expert who could easily finish off a fumbling opponent.

Shann swam wearily to shore where the wolverines waited, unable yet to make sense of that attack in the lagoon. What had happened to Thorvald? What motive had led the other to leave Shann and the animals on this island, the island Thorvald had called a starting point in his search for the natives of Warlock? Or had every bit of that tall tale been invented by the Survey officer for some obscure purpose of his own, certainly no sane purpose? Against that logic Shann could only set the carved disk, and he had only Thorvald's word that that had been discovered here.

He dragged himself out of the water on his hands and knees and lay, winded and gasping. Taggi came to lick his face, nuzzle him, making a small, bewildered whimpering. While above, the leather-headed birds called and swooped, fearful and angry for their disturbed nesting place. The Terran retched, coughed up water, and then sat up to look around.

The spread of lagoon was bare. Thorvald must have rounded the south point of land and be very close to the reef passage, perhaps through it by now. Not stopping for his clothes, Shann started up the slope, crawling part of the way on his hands and knees.

He reached the crest again and got to his feet. The sun made an eye-dazzling glitter of the waves. But under the shade of his hands Shann saw the canoe again, beyond the reef, heading on out along the island chain, not back to shore as he had expected. Thorvald was still on the hunt, but for what? A reality which existed, or a dream in his own disturbed brain?

Shann sat down. He was very hungry, for that adventure in the lagoon had sapped his strength. And he was a prisoner along with the wolverines, a prisoner on an island which was half the size of the valley which held the Survey camp. As far as he knew, his only supply of drinkable water was that tank of evil-smelling rain which would be speedily evaporated by a sun such as the one now beating down on him. And between him and the shore was the sea, a sea which harbored such creatures as the fork-tail he had watched die.

Thorvald was still steadily on course, not to the next island in the chain, a small, bare knob, but to the one beyond that. He could have been hurrying to a meeting. Where and with what?

Shann got to his feet, started down to the beach once more, sure now that the officer had no intention of returning, that he was again on his own with only his wits and strength to keep him alive—alive and somehow free of this waterwashed prison.

10

A TRAP FOR A TRAPPER

Shann took up the piece of soft chalklike stone he had found and drew another short white mark on the rust-red of a boulder well above tide level. That made three such marks, three days since Thorvald had marooned him. And he was no nearer the shore now than he had been on that first morning! He sat where he was by the boulder, aware that he should be up, trying to climb to the less accessible nests of the sea birds. The prisoners, man and wolverines, had cleaned out all those they had discovered on beach and cliffs. But at the thought of more eggs, Shann's stomach knotted in pain and he began to retch.

There had been no sign of Thorvald since Shann had watched him steer between the two westward islands. And the younger Terran's faint hope that the officer would return had died. On the shore a few feet away lay his own pitiful attempt to solve the problem of escape.

The force ax had vanished with Thorvald, along with all the rest of the meager supplies which had been the officer's original contribution to their joint equipment. Shann had used his knife on brush and small trees, trying to put together some kind of a raft. But he had not been able to discover here any of those vines necessary for binding, and his best efforts had all come to grief when he tried them in a lagoon launching. So far he had achieved no form of raft which would keep him afloat longer than five minutes, let alone support three of them as far as the next island.

Shann pulled listlessly at the framework of his latest try, dully disheartened. He tried not to think of the inescapable fact that the water in the rain tank had sunk to only an inch or so of muddy scum. Last night he had dug in the heart of the interior valley where the rankness of the vegetation was a promise of moisture, to uncover damp clay and then a brackish ooze. Far too little to satisfy both him and the animals.

There were surely fish somewhere in the lagoon. Shann wondered if the raw flesh of sea dwellers could supply the water they needed. But lacking net, line, or hooks, how did one fish? Yesterday, using his stunner, he had brought down a bird, to discover the carcass so rank even the wolverines, never dainty eaters, refused to gnaw it.

The animals prowled the two beaches, and Shann guessed they hunted shell dwellers, for at times they dug energetically in the gravel. Togi was busied in this way now, the sand flowing from under her pumping legs, her claws raking in good earnest.

And it was Togi's excavation which brought Shann a first ray of hope. Her excitement was so marked that he believed she was in quest of some worthwhile game and he moved across to inspect the pit. A patch of brown, which had been skimmed bare by one raking paw, made him shout.

Taggi shambled downslope, going to work beside his mate with an eagerness as open as hers. Shann hovered at the edge of the pit they were rapidly enlarging. The brown patch was larger, disclosing itself as a hump doming up from the gravel. The Terran did not need to run his hands over that rough surface to recognize the nature of the find. This was another shell such as had come floating in after the storm to form the raw material of their canoe.

However, as fast as the wolverines dug, they did not appear to make correspondingly swift headway in uncovering their find as might reasonably be expected. In fact, a witness could guess that the shell was sinking at a pace only a fraction slower than the burrowers were using to free it. Intrigued by that, Shann went back to the water-line, secured one of the lengths he had been trying to weave into his failures, and returned to use it as a make-shift shovel.

Now, with three of them at the digging, the brown hump was uncovered, and Shann pried down around its edge, trying to lever it up and over. To his amazement, his tool was caught and held, nearly jerked from his hands. To his retaliating tug the obstruction below-ground gave way, and the Terran sprawled back, the length of wood coming clear, to show the other end smashed and splin-tered as if it had been caught between mashing gears.

For the first time he understood that they were dealing not with an empty shell casing buried by drift under this small beach, but with a shell still inhabited by the Warlockian creature to whom it was a natural covering, and that that inhabitant would fight to con-tinue ownership. A moment's examination of that splin-tered wood also suggested that the shell's present wearer was well able to defend itself.

Shann attempted to call off the wolverines, but they were out of control now, digging frantically to get at this new prey. And he knew that if he pulled them away by force, they were apt to turn those punishing claws and snapping jaws on him.

It was for their protection that he returned to dig-ging, though he no longer tried to pry up the shell. Taggi leaped to the top of that dome, sweeping paws downward to clear its surface, while Togi prowled around its circumference, pausing now and then to send dirt and gravel spattering, but treading warily as might one alert for a sudden attack.

They had the creature almost clear now, though the shell still rested firmly on the ground, and they had no notion of what it might protect. It was smaller, perhaps two thirds the size of the one which Thorvald had fash-ioned into a seagoing craft. But it could provide them with transportation to the mainland if Shann was able to repeat the feat of turning it into an outrigger canoe.

Taggi joined his mate on the ground and both wolver-ines padded about the dome, obviously baffled. Now and then they assaulted the shell with a testing paw. Claws raked and did not leave any marks but shallow scratches. They could continue that forever, as far as Shann could see, without solving the problem in the least.

He sat back on his heels and studied the scene in detail. The excavation holding the shelled creature was some three yards above the high-water mark, with a few more feet separating that from the point where lazy waves now washed the finer sand. Shann watched the slow inward slip of those waves with growing interest. Where their combined efforts had failed to win this odd battle, perhaps the sea itself could now be pressed into service.

Shann began his own excavation, a trough to lead from the waterline to the pit occupied by the obstinate shell. Of course the thing living in or under that covering might be only too familiar with salt water. But it had placed its burrow, or hiding place, above the reach of the waves and so might be disconcerted by the sudden appearance of water in its bed. However, the scheme was worth trying, and he went to work doggedly, wishing he could make the wolverines understand so they would help him.

They still prowled about their captive, scraping at the sand about the shell casing. At least their efforts would keep the half-prisoner occupied and prevent its escape. Shann put another piece of his raft to work as a shovel, throwing up a shower of sand and gravel while sweat dampened his tattered blouse and was salt and sticky on his arms and face.

He finished his trench, one which ran at an angle he hoped would feed water into the pit rapidly once he knocked away the last barrier against the waves. And, splashing out into the green water, he did just that.

His calculations proved correct. Waves lapped, then flowed in a rapidly thickening stream, puddling out about the shell as the wolverines drew back, snarling. Shann lashed his knife fast to a stout length of sapling, so equipping himself with a spear. He stood with it ready in his hand, not knowing just what to expect. And when the answer to his water attack came, the move was so sudden that in spite of his preparation he was caught gaping.

For the shell fairly erupted out of the mess of sand
and water. A complete fringe of jointed, clawed brown
limbs churned in a forward-and-upward dash. But the
water worked to frustrate that charge. For one of the pit
walls crumbled, over-balancing the creature so that the
fore end of the shell lifted from the ground, the legs
clawing wildly at the air.

Shann thrust with the spear, feeling the knife point go
home so deeply that he could not pull his improvised
weapon free. A limb snapped claws only inches away from
his leg as he pushed down on the haft with all his strength.
That attack along with the initial upset of balance did the
job. The shell flopped over, its rounded hump now embedded in the watery sand of the pit while the frantic struggles
of the creature to right itself only buried it the deeper.

The Terran stared down upon a segmented under
belly where legs were paired in riblike formation. Shann
could locate no head, no good target. But he drew his
stunner and beamed at either end of the oval, and then,
for good measure, in the middle, hoping in one of those
three general blasts to contact the thing's central nervous system. He was not to know which of those shots
did the trick, but the frantic wiggling of the legs slowed
and finally ended, as a clockwork toy might run down
for want of winding—and at last projected, at crooked
angles, completely still. The shell creature might not be
dead, but it was tamed for now.

Taggi had only been waiting for a good chance to do
battle. He grabbed one of those legs, worried it, and then
leaped to tear at the under body. Unlike the outer shell,
this portion of the creature had no proper armor and the
wolverine plunged joyfully into the business of the kill,
his mate following suit.

The process of butchery was a bloody, even beastly job,
and Shann was shaken before it was complete. But he
kept at his labors, determined to have that shell, his one
chance of escape from the island. The wolverines feasted
on the greenish-white flesh, but he could not bring himself
to sample it, climbing to the heights in search of eggs,
and making a happy find of a niche filled with the edible
moss-fungi.

By late afternoon he had the shell scooped fairly clean and the wolverines had carried away for burial such portions as they had not been able to consume at their first eating. Meanwhile, the leather-headed birds had grown bold enough to snatch up the fragments he tossed out on the water, struggling for that bounty against feeders arising from the depths of the lagoon.

At the coming of dusk Shann hauled the bloodstained, grisly trophy well up the beach and wedged it among the rocks, determined not to lose his treasure. Then he stripped and washed, first his clothing and then himself, rubbing his hands and arms with sand until his skin was tender. He was still exultant at his luck. The drift would supply him with materials for an outrigger. One more day's work—or maybe two—and he could leave. He wrung out his blouse and gazed toward the distant line of the shore. Once he had his new canoe ready he would try to make the trip back in the early morning while the mists were still on the sea. That should give him cover against any Throg flight.

That night Shann slept in the deep fog of bodily exhaustion. There were no dreams, nothing but an unconsciousness which even a Throg attack could not have pierced. He roused in the morning with an odd feeling of guilt. The water hole he had scooped in the valley yielded him some swallows tasting of earth, but he had almost forgotten the flavor of a purer liquid. Munching on a fistful of moss, he hurried down to the shore, half fearing to find the shell gone, his luck out once again.

Not only was the shell where he had wedged it, but he had done better than he knew when he had left it exposed in the night. Small things scuttled away from it into hiding, and several birds arose—scavengers had been busy lightening his unwelcome task for that morning. And seeing how the clean-up process had gone, Shann had a second inspiration.

Pushing the thing down the beach, he sank it in the shallows with several rocks to anchor it. Within a few seconds the shell was invaded by a whole school of spiny-tailed fish that ate greedily. Leaving his find to their cleansing, Shann went back to prospect the pile of raft material, choosing pieces which could serve for an outrigger frame. He was handicapped as he had been all along by the absence of the vines one could use for lashings. And he had reached the point of considering a drastic sacrifice of his clothing to get the necessary strips when he saw Taggi dragging behind him one of the jointed legs the wolverines had put in storage the day before.

Now and again Taggi laid his prize on the shingle, holding it firmly pinned with his forepaws as he tried to worry loose a section of flesh. But apparently that feat was beyond even his notable teeth, and at length he left it lying there in disgust while he returned to a cache for more palatable fare. Shann went to examine more closely the triple-jointed limb.

The casing was not as hard as horn or shell, he discovered upon testing; it more resembled tough skin laid over bone. With a knife he tried to loosen the skin—a tedious job requiring a great deal of patience, since the tissue tore if pulled away too fast. But with care he acquired a few thongs perhaps a foot long. Using two of these, he made a trial binding of one stick to another, and experimented further, soaking the whole construction in sea water and then exposing it to the direct rays of the sun.

When he examined his test piece an hour later, the skin thongs had set into place with such success that the one piece of wood might have been firmly glued to the other. Shann shuffled his feet in a little dance of triumph as he went on to the lagoon to inspect the water-logged shell. The scavengers had done well. One scraping, two at the most, would have the whole thing clean and ready to use.

But that night Shann dreamed. No climbing of a skull-shaped mountain this time. Instead, he was again on the beach, laboring under an overwhelming compulsion, building something for an alien purpose he could not understand. And he worked as hopelessly as a beaten slave, knowing that what he made was to his own undoing. Yet he could not halt the making, because just beyond the limit of his vision there stood a dominant will which held him in bondage.

And he awoke on the beach in the very early dawn, not knowing how he had come there. His body was bathed in sweat, as it had been during his day's labors under the sun, and his muscles ached with fatigue.

But when he saw what lay at his feet he cringed. The framework of the outrigger, close to completion the night before, was dismantled—smashed. All those strips of hide he had so laboriously culled were cut—into inch-long bits which could be of no service.

Shann whirled, ran to the shell he had the night before pulled from the water and stowed in safety. Its rounded dome was dulled where it had been battered, but there was no break in the surface. He ran his hands anxiously over the curve to make sure. Then, very slowly, he came back to the mess of broken wood and snipped hide. And he was sure, only too sure, of one thing. He, himself, had wrought that destruction. In his dream he had built to satisfy the whim of an enemy; in reality he had destroyed; and that was also, he believed, to satisfy an enemy.

The dream was a part of it. But who or what could set a man dreaming and so take over his body, make him in fact betray himself? But then, what had made Thorvald maroon him here? For the first time, Shann guessed a new, if wild, explanation for the officer's desertion. Dreams—and the disk which had worked so strangely on Thorvald. Suppose everything the other had surmised was the truth! Then that disk *had* been found on this very island, and here somewhere must lie a clue to the riddle.

Shann licked his lips. Suppose that Thorvald had been sent away under just such a strong compulsion as the one which had ruled Shann last night? Why was he left behind if the other had been moved away to protect some secret? Was it that Shann himself was wanted here, wanted so much that when he at last found a means of escape he was set to destroy it? That act might have been forced upon him for two reasons: to keep him here, and to impress upon him how powerless he was.

Powerless! A flicker of stubborn will stirred to respond to that implied challenge. All right, the mysterious *they* had made him do this. But they had underrated him by letting him learn, almost contemptuously, of their presence by that revelation. So warned, he was in a manner armed; he could prepare to fight back.

He squatted by the wreckage as he thought that through, turning over broken pieces. And, Shann realized, he must present at the moment a satisfactory picture of despondency to any spy. A spy, that was it! Someone or something must have him under observation, or his activities of the day before would not have been so summarily countered. And if there was a spy, then there was his answer to the riddle. To trap the trapper. Such action might be a project beyond his resources, but it was his own counterattack.

So now he had to play a role. Not only must he search the island for the trace of his spy, but he must do it in such a fashion that his purpose would not be plain to the enemy he suspected. The wolverines could help. Shann arose, allowed his shoulders to droop, slouching to the slope with all the air of a beaten man which he could assume, whistling for Taggi and Togi.

When they came, his exploration began. Ostensibly he was hunting for lengths of drift or suitable growing saplings to take the place of those he had destroyed under orders. But he kept a careful watch on the animal pair, hoping by their reactions to pick up a clue to any hidden watcher.

The larger of the two beaches marked the point where the Terrans had first landed and where the shell thing had been killed. The smaller was more of a narrow tongue thrust out into the lagoon, much of it choked with sizable boulders. On earlier visits there Taggi and Togi had poked into the hollows among these with their usual curiosity. But now both animals remained upslope, showing no inclination to descend to the water line.

Shann caught hold of Taggi's scruff, pulling him along. The wolverine twisted and whined, but he did not fight for freedom as he would have upon scenting Throg. Not that the Terran had ever believed one of those aliens was responsible for the happenings on the island.

Taggi came down under Shann's urging, but he was plainly ill at ease. And at last he snarled a warning when

the man would have drawn him closer to two rocks
which met overhead in a crude semblance of an arch.
There was a stick of drift protruding from that hollow
affording Shann a legitimate excuse to venture closer.
He dropped his hold on the wolverines, stooped to
gather in the length of wood, and at the same time
glanced into the pocket.

Water lay just beyond, making this a doorway to the
lagoon. The sun had not yet penetrated into the shadow,
if it ever did. Shann reached for the wood, at the same
time drawing his finger across the flat rock which would
furnish a stepping-stone for anything using that door as
an entrance to the island.

Wet! Which might mean his visitor had recently
arrived, or else merely that a splotch of spray had landed
there not too long before. But in his mind Shann was
convinced that he had found the spy's entrance. Could
he turn it into a trap? He added a piece of drift to his
bundle and picked up two more before he returned to
the cliff ahead.

A trap . . . He revolved in his mind all the traps he
knew which could be used here. He already had decided
upon the bait—his own work. And if his plans went
through—and hope does not die easily—then this time
he would not waste his labor either.

So he went back to the same job he had done the
day before, making do with skin strips he had considered second-best before, smoothing, cutting. Only the
trap occupied his mind, and close to sunset he knew just
what he was going to do and how.

Though the Terran did not know the nature of the
unseen opponent, he thought he could guess two weak-
nesses which might deliver the other into his hands.
First, the enemy was entirely confident of success in this
venture. No being who was able to control Shann as
completely and ably as had been done the night before
would credit any prey with the power to strike back in
force.

Second, such a confident enemy would be unable to
resist watching the manipulation of a captive. The Terran
was certain that his opponent would be on the scene

somewhere when he was led, dreaming, to destroy his work once more.

He might be wrong on both of those counts, but inwardly he didn't believe so. However, he had to wait until the dark to set up his own answer, one so simple he was certain the enemy would not suspect it at all.

11

THE WITCH

There were patches of light in the inner valley marking the phosphorescent plants, some creeping at ground level, others tall as saplings. On other nights Shann had welcomed that wan radiance, but now he lay in as relaxed a position as possible, marking each of those potential betrayers as he tried to counterfeit the attitude of sleep and at the same time plan out his route.

He had purposely settled in a pool of shadow, the wolverines beside him. And he thought that the bulk of the animal's bodies would cover his own withdrawal when the time came to move. One arm lying limply across his middle was in reality clutching to him an intricate arrangement of small hide straps which he had made by sacrificing most of the remainder of his painfully acquired thongs. The trap must be set in place soon!

Now that he had charted a path to the crucial point avoiding all light plants, Shann was ready to move. The Terran pressed his hand on Taggi's head in the one imperative command the wolverine was apt to obey—the order to stay where he was.

Shann sat up and gave the same voiceless instruction to Togi. Then he inched out of the hollow, a worm's progress to that narrow way along the cliff top—the path which anyone or anything coming up from that sea gate on the beach would have to pass in order to watch the shoreline occupied by the half-built outrigger.

So much of his plan was based upon luck and guesses, but those were all Shann had. And as he worked at the stretching of his snare, the Terran's heart pounded, and he tensed at every sound out of the night. Having tested all the anchoring of his net, he tugged at a last knot, and then crouched to listen not only with his ears, but with all his strength of mind and body.

Pound of waves, whistle of wind, the sleepy complaint of some bird . . . A regular splashing! One of the fish in the lagoon? Or what he awaited? The Terran retreated as noiselessly as he had come, heading for the hollow where he had bedded down.

He reached there breathless, his heart pumping, his mouth dry as if he had been racing. Taggi stirred and thrust a nose inquiringly against Shann's arm. But the wolverine made no sound, as if he, too, realized that some menace lay beyond the rim of the valley. Would that other come up the path Shann had trapped? Or had he been wrong? Was the enemy already stalking him from the other beach? The grip of his stunner was slippery in his damp hand; he hated this waiting.

The canoe . . . his work on it had been a careless botching. Better to have the job done right. Why, it was perfectly clear now how he had been mistaken! His whole work plan was wrong; he could see the right way of doing things laid out as clear as a blueprint in his mind. A picture in his mind!

Shann stood up and both wolverines moved uneasily, though neither made a sound. A picture in his mind! But this time he wasn't asleep; he wasn't dreaming a dream—to be used for his own defeat. Only (that other could not know this) the pressure which had planted the idea of new work to be done in his mind—an idea one part of him accepted as fact—had not taken warning from his move. He was supposed to be under control; the Terran was sure of that. All right, so he would play that part. He must if he would entice the trapper into his trap.

He holstered his stunner, walked out into the open, paying no heed now to the patches of light through which he must pass on his way to the path his own feet had already worn to the boat beach. As he went, Shann tried to counterfeit what he believed would be the gait of a man under compulsion.

Now he was on the rim fronting the downslope, fighting against his desire to turn and see for himself if anything had climbed behind. The canoe was all wrong, a bad job which he must make better at once so that in the morning he would be free of this island prison.

The pressure of that other's will grew stronger. And the Terran read into that the overconfidence which he believed would be part of the enemy's character. The one who was sending him to destroy his own work had no suspicion that the victim was not entirely malleable, ready to be used as he himself would use a knife or a force ax. Shann strode steadily downslope. With a small spurt of fear he knew that in a way that unseen other was right; the pressure was taking over, even though he was awake this time. The Terran tried to will his hand to his stunner, but his fingers fell instead on the hilt of his knife. He drew the blade as panic seethed in his head, chilling him from within. He had underestimated the other's power . . .

And that panic flared into open fight, making him forget his careful plans. Now he *must* wrench free from this control. The knife was moving to slash a hide lashing, directed by his hand, but not his will.

A soundless gasp, a flash of dismay rocked him, but neither was his gasp nor his dismay. That pressure snapped off; he was free. But the other wasn't! Knife still in fist, Shann turned and ran upslope, his torch in his other hand. He could see a shape now writhing, fighting, outlined against a light bush. And, fearing that the stranger might win free and disappear, the Terran spotlighted the captive in the beam, reckless of Throg or enemy reinforcements.

The other crouched, plainly startled by the sudden burst of light. Shann stopped abruptly. He had not really built up any mental picture of what he had expected to find in his snare, but this prisoner was as weirdly alien to him as a Throg. The light of the torch was reflected off a skin which glittered as if scaled, glittered with the brilliance of jewels in bands and coils of color spreading from the throat down the chest, spiraling about upper arms, around waist and thighs, as if the stranger wore a treasure house of gems as part of a living body. Except for those patterned loops, coils, and bands, the body had no clothing, though a belt about the slender middle supported a pair of pouches and some odd implements held in loops.

The figure was roughly more humanoid than the Throgs. The upper limbs were not too unlike Shann's arms, though the hands had four digits of equal length instead of five. But the features were nonhuman, closer to saurian in contour. It had large eyes, blazing yellow in the dazzle of the flash, with vertical slits of green for pupils. A nose united with the jaw to make a snout, and above the domed forehead a sharp V-point of raised spiky growth extended back and down until behind the shoulder blades it widened and expanded to resemble a pair of wings.

The captive no longer struggled, but sat quietly in the tangle of the snare Shann had set, watching the Terran steadily as if there were no difficulty in seeing through the brilliance of the beam to the man who held it. And, oddly enough, Shann experienced no repulsion toward its reptilian appearance as he had upon first sighting the beetlelike Throg. On impulse he put down his torch on a rock and walked into the light to face squarely the thing out of the sea.

Still eyeing Shann, the captive raised one limb and gave an absent-minded tug to the belt it wore. Shann, noting that gesture, was struck by a wild surmise, leading him to study the prisoner more narrowly. Allowing for the alien structure of bone, the nonhuman skin; this creature was delicate, graceful, in its way beautiful, with a fragility of limb which backed up his suspicions. Moved by no pressure from the other, but by his own will and sense of fitness, Shann stooped to cut the control line of his snare.

The captive continued to watch as Shann sheathed his blade and then held out his hand. Yellow eyes, never blinking since his initial appearance, regarded him, not with any trace of fear or dismay, but with a calm measurement which was curiosity based upon a strong belief in its own superiority. He did not know how he knew, but Shann was certain that the creature out of the sea was still entirely confident, that it made no fight because it did not conceive of any possible danger from him. And again, oddly enough, he was not irritated by this unconscious arrogance; rather he was intrigued and amused.

"Friends?" Shann used the basic galactic speech devised by Survey and the Free Traders, semantics which depended upon the proper inflection of voice and tone to project meaning when the words were foreign.

The other made no sound, and the Terran began to wonder if his captive had any audible form of speech. He withdrew a step or two then pulled at the snare, drawing the cords away from the creature's slender ankles. Rolling the thongs into a ball, he tossed the crude net back over his shoulder.

"Friends?" he repeated again, showing his empty hands, trying to give that one word the proper inflection, hoping the other could read his peaceful intent in his features if not by his speech.

In one lithe, flowing movement the alien arose. Fully erect, the Warlockian had a frail appearance. Shann, for his breed, was not tall. But the native was still smaller, not more than five feet, that stiff V of head crest just topping Shann's shoulder. Whether any of those fittings at its belt could be a weapon the Terran had no way of telling. However, the other made no move to draw any of them.

Instead, one of the four-digit hands came up. Shann felt the feather touch of strange finger tips on his chin, across his lips, up his cheek, to at last press firmly on his forehead at a spot just between the eyebrows. What followed was communication of a sort, not in words or in any describable flow of thoughts. There was no feeling of enmity—at least nothing strong enough to be called that. Curiosity, yes, and then a growing doubt, not of the Terran himself, but of the other's preconceived ideas concerning him. Shann was other than the native had judged him, and the stranger was disturbed, that self-confidence a little ruffled. And also Shann was right in his guess. He smiled, his amusement growing—not aimed at his companion on this cliff top, but at himself. For he was dealing with a female, a very young female, and someone as fully feminine in her way as any human girl could be.

"Friends?" he asked for the third time.

But the other still exuded a wariness, a wariness mixed with surprise. And the tenuous message which passed between them then astounded Shann. To this Warlockian out of the night he was not following the proper pattern of male behavior at all; he should have been in awe of the other merely because of her sex. A diffidence rather than an assumption of equality should have colored his response, judged by her standards. At first, he caught a flash of anger at this preposterous attitude of his; then her curiosity won, but there was still no reply to his question.

The finger tips no longer made contact between them. Stepping back, her hands now reached for one of the pouches at her belt. Shann watched that movement carefully. And because he did not trust her too far, he whistled.

Her head came up. She might be dumb, but plainly she was not deaf. And she gazed down into the hollow as the wolverines answered his summons with growls. Her profile reminded Shann of something for an instant; but it should have been golden-yellow instead of silver with two jeweled patterns ringing the snout. Yes, that small plaque he had seen in the cabin of one of the ship's officers. A very old Terran legend—"Dragon," the officer had named the creature. Only that one had possessed a serpent's body, a lizard's legs and wings.

Shann gave a sudden start, aware his thoughts had made him careless, or had she in some way led him into that bypath of memory for her own purposes? Because now she held some object in the curve of her curled fingers, regarding him with those unblinking yellow eyes. Eyes . . . eyes . . . Shann dimly heard the alarm cry of the wolverines. He tried to snap draw his stunner, but it was too late.

There was a haze about him hiding the rocks, the island valley with its radiant plants, the night sky, the bright beam of the torch. Now he moved through that haze as one walks through a dream approaching nightmare, striding with an effort as if wading through a deterring flood. Sound, sight—one after another those senses were taken from him. Desperately Shann held to one thing, his own sense of identity. He was Shann Lantee, Terran breed, out of Tyr, of the Survey Service. Some part of him repeated those facts with vast urgency against an almost overwhelming force which strove to defeat that awareness of self, making him nothing but a tool—or a weapon—for another's use.

The Terran fought, soundlessly but fiercely, on a battleground which was within him, knowing in a detached way that his body obeyed another's commands.

"I am Shann—" he cried without audible speech. "I am myself. I have two hands, two legs . . . I think for myself! I am a *man*—"

And to that came an answer of sorts, a blow of will striking at his resistance, a will which struggled to drown him before ebbing, leaving behind it a faint suggestion of bewilderment, of a dawn of concern.

"I am a *man!*" he hurled that assertion as he might have thrust deep with one of the crude spears he had used against the Throgs. For against what he faced now his weapons were as crude as spears fronting blasters. "I am Shann Lantee, Terran, man . . ." Those were facts; no haze could sweep them from his mind or take away that heritage.

And again there was the lightening of the pressure, the slight recoil, which could only be a prelude to another assault upon his last stronghold. He clutched his three facts to him as a shield, groping for others which might have afforded a weapon of rebuttal.

Dreams, these Warlockians dealt in and through dreams. And the opposite of dreams are facts! His name, his breed, his sex—these were facts. And Warlock itself was a fact. The earth under his boots was a fact. The water which washed around the island was a fact. The air he breathed was a fact. Flesh, blood, bones—facts, all of them. Now he was a struggling identity imprisoned in a rebel body. But that body was real. He tried to feel it. Blood pumped from his heart, his lungs filled and emptied; he struggled to feel those processes.

With a terrifying shock, the envelope which had held him vanished. Shann was choking, struggling in water. He flailed out with his arms, kicked his legs. One hand grated painfully against stone. Hardly knowing what he did, but fighting for his life, Shann caught at that rock and drew his head out of water. Coughing and gasping, half drowned, he was weak with the panic of his close brush with death.

For a long moment he could only cling to the rock which had saved him, retching and dazed, as the water washed about his body, a current tugging at his trailing legs. There was light of a sort here, patches of green which glowed with the same subdued light as the bushes of the outer world, for he was no longer under the night sky. A rock-roof was but inches over his head; he must be in some cave or tunnel under the surface of the sea. Again a gust of panic shook him as he felt trapped.

The water continued to pull at Shann, and in his weakened condition it was a temptation to yield to that pull; the more he fought it the more he was exhausted. At last the Terran turned on his back, trying to float with the stream, sure he could no longer battle it.

Luckily those few inches of space above the surface of the water continued, and he had air to breathe. But the fear of that ending, of being swept under the surface, chewed at his nerves. And his bodily danger burned away the last of the spell which had held him, brought him into this place, wherever it might be.

Was it only his heightened imagination, or had the current grown swifter? Shann tried to gauge the speed of his passage by the way the patches of green light slipped by. Now he turned and began to swim slowly, feeling as if his arms were leaden weights, his ribs a cage to bind his aching lungs.

Another patch of light . . . larger . . . spreading across the roof over head. Then, he was out! Out of the tunnel into a cavern so vast that its arching roof was like a skydome far above his head. But here the patches of light were brighter, and they were arranged in odd groups which had a familiar look to them.

Only, better than freedom overhead, there was a shore

not too distant. Shann swam for that haven, summoning
up the last rags of his strength, knowing that if he could
not reach it very soon he was finished. Somehow he made
it and lay gasping, his cheek resting on sand finer than
any of the outer world, his fingers digging into it for
purchase to drag his body on. But when he collapsed, his
legs were still awash in water.

No footfall could be heard on that sand. But he knew
that he was no longer alone. He braced his hands and
with painful effort levered up his body. Somehow he
made it to his knees, but he could not stand. Instead
he half tumbled back, so that he faced them from a
sitting position.

Them—there were three of them—the dragon-headed
ones with their slender, jewel-set bodies glittering even
in this subdued light, their yellow eyes fastened on him
with a remoteness which did not approach any human
emotion, save perhaps that of a cold and limited wonder. But behind them came a fourth, one he knew by the
patterns on her body.

Shann clasped his hands about his knees to still the
trembling of his body, and eyed them back with all the
defiance he could muster. Nor did he doubt that he had
been brought here, his body as captive to their will, as
had been that of their spy or messenger in his crude snare
on the island.

"Well, you have me," he said hoarsely. "Now what?"

His words boomed weirdly out over the water, were
echoed from the dim outer reaches of the cavern. There
was no answer. They merely stood watching him. Shann
stiffened, determined to hold to his defiance and to that
identity which he now knew was his weapon against the
powers they used.

The one who had somehow drawn him there moved
at last, circling around the other three with a suggestion
of diffidence in her manner. Shann jerked back his head
as her hand stretched to touch his face. And then, guessing that she sought her peculiar form of communication,
he submitted to her finger tips, though now his skin
crawled under that light but firm pressure and he shrank
from the contact.

There were no sensations this time. To his amazement a concrete inquiry shaped itself in his brain, as clear as if the question had been asked aloud: "Who are you?"

"Shann . . ." he began vocally, and then turned words into thoughts. "Shann Lantee, Terran, man." He made his answer the same which had kept him from succumbing to their complete domination.

"Name—Shann Lantee, man—yes." The other accepted those. "Terran?" That was a question.

Did these people have any notion of space travel? Could they understand the concept of another world holding intelligent beings?

"I come from another world . . ." He tried to make a cleancut picture in his mind—a globe in space, a ship blasting free . . .

"Look!" The fingers still rested between his eyebrows, but with her other hand the Warlockian was pointing up to the dome of the cavern.

Shann followed her order. He studied those patches of light which had seemed so vaguely familiar at his first sighting, studying them closely to know them for what they were. A star map! A map of the heavens as they could be seen from the outer crust of Warlock.

"Yes, I come from the stars," he answered, booming with his voice.

The fingers dropped from his forehead; the scaled head swung around to exchange glances, which were perhaps some unheard communication with the other three. Then the hand was extended again.

"Come!"

Fingers fell from his head to his right wrist, closing there with surprising strength; and some of that strength together with a new energy flowed from them into him, so that he found and kept his feet as the other drew him up.

12

THE VEIL OF ILLUSION

Perhaps his status was that of a prisoner, but Shann was too tired to press for an explanation. He was content to be left alone in the unusual circular, but roofless, room of the structure to which they had brought him. There was a thick matlike pallet in one corner, short for the length of his body, but softer than any bed he had rested on since he had left the Terran camp before the coming of the Throgs. Above him glimmered those patches of light symbolizing the lost stars. He blinked at them until they all ran together in bands like the jeweled coils on Warlockian bodies; then he slept—dreamlessly.

The Terran awoke with all his senses alert; some silent alarm might have triggered that instant awareness of himself and his surroundings. There had been no change in the star pattern still overhead; no one had entered the round chamber. Shann rolled over on his mat bed, conscious that all his aches had vanished. Just as his mind was clearly active, so did his body also respond effortlessly to his demands. He was not aware of any hunger or thirst, though a considerable length of time must have passed since he had made his mysteriously contrived exit from the outer world.

In spite of the humidity of the air, his ragged garments had dried on his body. Shann got to his feet, trying to order the sorry remnants of his uniform, eager to be on the move. Though to where and for what purpose he could not have answered.

The door through which he had entered remained closed, refusing to yield to his push. Shann stepped back, eyeing the distance to the top of the partition between the roofless rooms. The walls were smooth with the gloss of a sea shell's interior, but the exuberant confidence which had been with him since his awakening refused to accept such a minor obstacle.

He made two test leaps, both times his fingers striking the wall well below the top of the partition. Shann gathered himself together as might a cat and tried the third time, putting into that effort every last ounce of strength, determination and will. He made it, though his arms jerked as the weight of his body hung from his hands. Then a scramble, a knee hooked over the top, and he was perched on the wall, able to study the rest of the building.

In shape, the structure was unlike anything he had seen on his home world or reproduced in any of the tri-dee records of Survey accessible to him. The rooms were either circular or oval, each separated from the next by a short passage, so that the overall impression was that of ten strings of beads radiating from a central knot of one large chamber, all with the uniform nacre walls and a limited amount of furnishings.

As he balanced on the narrow perch, Shann could sight no other movement in the nearest line of rooms, those connected by corridors with his own. He got to his feet to walk the tightrope of the upper walls toward that inner chamber which was the heart of the Warlockian—palace? town apartment dwelling? At least it was the only structure on the island, for he could see the outer rim of that smooth soft sand ringing it about. The island itself was curiously symmetrical, a perfect oval, too perfect to be a natural outcrop of sand and rock.

There was no day or night here in the cavern. The light from the roof patches remained constantly the same, and that flow was abetted within the building by a soft radiation from the walls. Shann reached the next room in line, hunkering down to see within it. To all appearances the chamber was exactly the same as the one he had just left; there were the same unadorned walls, a thick mat bed against the far side, and no indication whether it was in use or had not been entered for days.

He was on the next section of corridor wall when he caught that faint taint in the air, the very familiar scent of wolverines. Now it provided Shann with a guide as well as a promise of allies.

The next bead-room gave him what he wanted. Below him Taggi and Togi paced back and forth. They had already torn to bits the sleeping mat which had been the chamber's single furnishing, and their temper was none too certain. As Shann squatted well above their range of vision, Taggi reared against the opposite wall, his claws finding no hold on the smooth coating of its surface. They were as completely imprisoned as if they had been dropped into a huge fishbowl, and they were not taking to it kindly.

How had the animals been brought here? Down that water tunnel by the same unknown method he himself had been transported until that almost disastrous awakening in the center of the flood? The Terran did not doubt that the doors of the room were as securely fastened as those of his own further down the corridor. For the moment the wolverines were safe; he could not free them. And he was growing increasingly certain that if he found any of his native jailers, it would be at the center of that wheel of rooms and corridors.

Shann made no attempt to attract the animals' attention, but kept on along his tightrope path. He passed two more rooms, both empty, both differing in no way from those he had already inspected; and then he came to the central chamber, four times as big as any of the rest and with a much brighter wall light.

The Terran crouched, one hand on the surface of the partition top as an additional balance, the other gripping his stunner. For some reason his captors had not disarmed him. Perhaps they believed they had no necessity to fear his off-world weapon.

"Have you grown wings?"

The words formed in his brain, bringing with them a sense of calm amusement to reduce all his bold exploration to the level of a child's first staggering steps. Shann fought his first answering flare of pure irritation. To lose even a fraction of control was to open a door for them. He remained where he was as if he had never "heard" that question, surveying the room below with all the impassiveness he could summon.

Here the walls were no smooth barrier, but honeycombed with niches in a regular pattern. And in each of the niches rested a polished skull, a nonhuman skull. Only the outlines of those ranked bones were familiar; for just so had looked the great purple-red rock where the wheeling flyers issued from the eye sockets. A rock island had been fashioned into a skull—by design or nature?

And upon closer observation the Terran could see that there was a difference among these ranked skulls, a mutation of coloring from row to row, a softening of outline, perhaps by the wearing of time.

There was also a table of dull black, rising from the flooring on legs which were not more than a very few inches high, so that from his present perch the board appeared to rest on the pavement itself. Behind the table in a row, as shopkeepers might await a customer, three of the Warlockians, sat cross-legged on mats, their hands folded primly before them. And at the side a fourth, the one whom he had trapped on the island.

Not one of those spiked heads rose to view him. But they knew that he was there; perhaps they had known the very instant he had left the room or cell in which they had shut him. And they were so very sure of themselves . . . Once again Shann subdued a spark of anger. That same patience with its core of stubborn determination which had brought him to Warlock backed his moves now. The Terran swung down, landing lightly on his feet, facing the three behind the table, towering well over them as he stood erect, yet gaining no sense of satisfaction from that merely physical fact.

"You have come." The words sounded as if they might be a part of some polite formula. So he replied in kind and aloud.

"I have come." Without waiting for their bidding, he

dropped into the same cross-legged pose, fronting them now on a more equal level across their dead black table.

"And why have you come, star voyager?" That thought seemed to be a concentrated effort from all three rather than any individual questioning.

"And why did you bring me?" He hesitated, trying to think of some polite form of address. Those he knew which were appropriate to their sex on other worlds seemed incongruous when applied to the bizarre figures now facing him. "Wise ones," he finally chose.

Those unblinking yellow eyes conveyed no emotion; certainly his human gaze could detect no change of expression on their nonhuman faces.

"You are a male."

"I am," he agreed, not seeing just what that fact had to do with either diplomatic fencing or his experiences of the immediate past.

"Where then is your thoughtguider?"

Shann puzzled over that conception, guessed at its meaning.

"I am my own thoughtguider," he returned stoutly, with all the conviction he could manage to put into that reply.

Again he met a yellow-green stare, but he sensed a change in them. Some of their complacency had ebbed; his reply had been as a stone dropped into a quiet pool, sending ripples out afar to disturb the customary mirror surface of smooth serenity.

"The star-born one speaks the truth!" That came from the Warlockian who had been his first contact.

"It would appear that he does." The agreement was measured, and Shann knew that he was meant to "overhear" that.

"It would seem, Readers-of-the-rods"—the middle one of the triumvirate at the table spoke now—"that all living things do not follow our pattern of life. But that is possible. A male who thinks for himself . . . unguided, who dreams perhaps! Or who can understand the truth of dreaming! Strange indeed must be his people. Sharers-of-my-visions, let us consult the Old Ones concerning this." For the first time one of those crested heads moved, the gaze shifted from Shann to the ranks of the skulls, pausing at one.

Shann, ready for any wonder, did not betray his amazement when the ivory inhabitant of that particular niche moved, lifted from its small compartment, and drifted buoyantly through the air to settle at the right-hand corner of the table. Only when it had safely grounded did the eyes of the Warlockian move to another niche on the other side of the curving room, this time bringing up from close to floor level a time-darkened skull to occupy the left corner of the table.

There was a third shifting from the weird storehouse, a last skull to place between the other two. And now the youngest native arose from her mat to bring a bowl of green crystal. One of her seniors took it in both hands, making a gesture of offering it to all three skulls, and then gazed over its rim at the Terran.

"We shall cast the rods, man-who-thinks-without-a-guide. Perhaps then we shall see how strong *your* dreams are—to be bent to your using, or to break you for your impudence."

Her hands swayed the bowl from side to side, and there was an answering whisper from its interior as if the contents slid loosely there. Then one of her companions reached forward and gave a quick tap to the bottom of that container, spilling out upon the table a shower of brightly colored slivers each an inch or so long.

Shann, staring at the display in bewilderment, saw that in spite of the seeming carelessness of that toss the small needles had spread out on the blank surface to form a design in arrangement and color. And he wondered how that skillful trick had been accomplished.

All three of the Warlockians bent their heads to study the grouping of the tiny sticks, their young subordinate leaning forward also, her eagerness less well controlled than her elders'. And now it was as if a curtain had fallen between the Terran and the aliens, all sense of communication which had been with him since he had entered the skull-lined chamber was summarily cut off.

A hand moved, making the jeweled pattern—braceleting wrist and extending up the arm—flash subdued fire. Fingers

swept the sticks back into the bowl; four pairs of yellow
eyes raised to regard Shann once more, but the blanket
of their withdrawal still held.

The youngest Warlockian took the bowl from the elder
who held it, stood for a long moment with it resting
between her palms, fixing Shann with an unreadable stare.
Then she came toward him. One of those at the table
put out a restraining hand.

This time Shann did *not* master his start as he heard
the first audible voice which had not been his own. The
skull at the left hand on the table, by its yellowed color
the oldest of those summoned from the niches, was
moving, moving because its jaws gaped and then snapped,
emitting a faint bleat which might have been a word or
two.

She who would have halted the young Warlockian's
advance, withdrew her hand. Then her fingers curled in
an unmistakable beckoning gesture. Shann came to the
table, but he could not quite force himself near that
chattering skull, even though it had stopped its jig of
speech.

The bowl of sticks was offered to him. Still no message
from mind to mind, but he could guess at what they wanted
of him. The crystal substance was not cool to the touch
as he had expected; rather it was warm, as living flesh might
feel. And the colored sticks filled about two thirds of the
interior, lying all mixed together without any order.

Shann concentrated on recalling the ceremony the Warlockian had used before the first toss. She had offered
the bowl to the skulls in turn. The skulls! But he was no
consulter of skulls. Still holding the bowl close to his chest,
Shann looked up over the roofless walls at the star map
on the roof of the cavern. There, that was Rama; and to
its left, just a little above, was Tyr's system where swung
the stark world of his birth, and of which he had only
few good memories, but of which he was a part. The
Terran raised the bowl to that spot of light which marked
Tyr's pale sun.

Smiling with a wry twist, he lowered the bowl, and on
impulse of pure defiance he offered it to the skull that
had chattered. Immediately he realized that the move had

had an electric effect upon the aliens. Slowly at first, and then faster, he began to swing the bowl from side to side, the needles slipping, mixing within. And as he swung it, Shann held it out over the expanse of the table.

The Warlockian who had given him the bowl was the one who struck it on the bottom, causing a rain of splinters. To Shann's astonishment, mixed as they had been in the container, they once more formed a pattern, and not the same pattern the Warlockians had consulted earlier. The dampening curtain between them vanished; he was in touch mind to mind once again.

"So be it." The center Warlockian spread out her four-fingered thumbless hands above the scattered needles. "What is read, is read."

Again a formula. He caught a chorus of answer from the others.

"What is read, is read. To the dreamer the dream. Let the dream be known for what it is, and there is life. Let the dream encompass the dreamer falsely, and all is lost."

"Who can question the wisdom of the Old Ones?" asked their leader. "We are those who read the messages they send, out of their mercy. This is a strange thing they bid us do, man—open for you our own initiates' road to the veil of illusion. That way has never been for males, who dream without set purpose and have not the ability to know true from false, have no the courage to face their dreams to the truth. Do so—if you can!" There was a flash of mockery in that; combined with something else—stronger than distaste, not as strong as hatred, but certainly not friendly.

She held out her hands and Shann saw now, lying on a slowly closing palm, a disk such as the one Thorvald had shown him. The Terran had only one moment of fear and then came blackness, more absolute than the dark of any night he had ever known.

Light once more, green light with an odd shimmering quality to it. The skull-lined walls were gone; there were no walls, no building held him. Shann strode forward, and his boots sank in sand, that smooth, satin sand which had ringed the island in the cavern. But he was certain he was no longer on that island, even within that cavern, though far above him there was still a dome of roof.

The source of the green shimmer lay to his left. Somehow he found himself reluctant to turn and face it. That would commit him to action. But Shann turned.

A veil, a veil of rippling green. Material? No, rather mist or light. A veil depending from some source so far over his head that its origin was hidden in the upper gloom, a veil which was a barrier he must cross.

With every nerve protesting, Shann walked forward, unable to keep back. He flung up his arm to protect his face as he marched into that stuff. It was warm, and the gas—if gas it was—left no slick of moisture on his skin in spite of its foggy consistency. And it was no veil or curtain, for although he was already well into the murk, he saw no end to it. Blindly he trudged on, unable to sight anything but the rolling billows of green, pausing now and again to go down on one knee and pat the sand underfoot, reassured at the reality of that footing.

And when he met nothing menacing, Shann began to relax. His heart no longer labored; he made no move to draw the stunner or knife. Where he was and for what purpose, he had no idea. But there *was* a purpose in this and that the Warlockians were behind it, he did not doubt. The "initiates' road," the leader had said, and the conviction was steady in his mind that he faced some test of alien devising.

A cavern with a green veil—his memory awoke. Thorvald's dream! Shann paused, trying to remember how the other had described this place. So he was enacting Thorvald's dream! And could the Survey officer now be caught in Shann's dream in turn, climbing up somewhere into the nose slit of a skull-shaped mountain?

Green fog without end, and Shann lost in it. How long had he been here? Shann tried to reckon time, the time since his coming into the water-world of the starred cavern. He realized that he had not eaten, nor drank, nor desired to do so either—nor did he now. Yet he was not weak; in fact, he had never felt such tireless energy as possessed his spare body.

Was this *all* a dream? His threatened drowning in the underground stream a nightmare? Yet there was a pattern in this, just as there had been a pattern in the needles he had spilled across the table. One even led to another with discernible logic; because he had tossed that particular pattern he had come here.

According to the ambiguous instructions or warnings of the Warlockian witch, his safety in this place would depend upon his ability to tell true dreams from false. But how . . . why? So far he had done nothing except walk through a green fog and for all he knew, he might well be traveling in circles.

Because there was nothing else to do, Shann walked on, his boots pressing sand, rising from each step with a small sucking sound. Then, as he stooped to search for some indication of a path or road which might guide him, his ears caught the slightest of noises—other small sucking whimpers. He was not the only wayfarer in this place!

13

HE WHO DREAMS...

The mist was not a quiet thing; it billowed and curled until it appeared to half-conceal darker shadows, any one of which could be an enemy. Shann remained hunkered on the sand, every sense abnormally alert, watching the fog. He was still sure he could hear sounds which marked the progress of another. What other? One of the Warlockians tracing him to spy? Or was there some prisoner like himself lost out there in the murk? Could it be Thorvald?

Now the sound had ceased. He was not even sure from what direction it had first come. Perhaps that other was listening now, as intent upon locating him. Shann ran his tongue over dry lips. The impulse to call out, to try and contact any fellow traveler here, was strong. Only hard-learned caution kept him silent. He got to his hands and knees, uncertain as to his previous direction.

Shann crept. Someone expecting a man walking erect might be suitably distracted by the arrival of a half-seen figure on all fours. He halted again to listen.

He had been right! The sound of a very muffled foot-fall or footfalls carried to his ears. He was sure that the sound was louder, that the unknown was approaching. Shann stood, his hand close to his stunner. He was almost tempted to spray that beam blindly before him, hoping to hit the unseen by chance.

A shadow—something more swift than a shadow, more than one of the tricks the curling fog played on eyes— was moving with purpose and straight for him. Still, prudence restrained Shann from calling out.

The figured grew clearer. A Terran! It could be Thorvald! But remembering how they had last parted, Shann did not hurry to meet him.

That shadow-shape stretched out a long arm in a sweep as if to pull aside some of the vapor concealing them from each other. Then Shann shivered as if that fog had suddenly turned into the drive of frigid snow. For the mist did roll back so that the two of them stood in an irregular clearing in its midst.

And he did not front Thorvald.

Shann was caught up in the ice grip of an old fear, frozen by it, but somehow clinging to a hope that he did not see the unbelievable.

Those hands drawing the lash of a whip back into striking readiness . . . a brutal nose broken askew, a blaster burn puckering across cheek to misshapen ear . . . that evil, gloating grin of anticipation. Flick, flick, the slight dance of the lash in a master's hand as those thick fingers tightened about the stock of the whip. In a moment it would whirl up to lay a ribbon of fire about Shann's defenseless shoulders. Then Logally would laugh and laugh, his sadistic mirth echoed by those other men who played jackals to his rogue lion.

Other men . . . Shann shook his head dazedly. But he did not stand again in the Dump-sized bar of the Big Strike. And he was no longer a terrorized youngster, fit meat for Logally's amusement. Only the whip rose, the lash curled out, catching Shann just as it had that time years ago, delivering a red slash of pure agony. But Logally was dead, Shann's mind screamed, fighting frantically against the evidence of his eyes, of that pain in his chest and shoulder. The Dump bully had been spaced by off-world miners, now also dead, whose claims he had tried to jump out in the Ajax system.

Logally drew back the lash, preparing to strike again. Shann faced a man five years dead who walked and fought. Or, Shann bit hard upon his lower lip, holding desperately to sane reasoning—did he indeed face anything? Logally was the ancient devil of his boyhood, produced anew by the witchery of Warlock. Or had Shann himself been led to recreate both the man and the circumstances of their first meeting with fear as a weapon to pull the creator down? Dream true or false. Logally *was* dead; therefore, this dream was false, it had to be.

The Terran began to walk toward that grinning ogre rising out of his old nightmares. His hand was no longer on the butt of his stunner, but swung loosely at his side. He saw the coming lash, the wicked promise in those small narrowed eyes. This was Logally at the acme of his strength, when he was most to be feared, as he had continued to exist over the years in the depths of a boy-child's memory. But Logally was *not* alive; only in a dream could he be.

For the second time the lash bit at Shann, curling about his body, to dissolve. There was no alteration in Logally's grin. His muscular arm drew back as he aimed a third blow. Shann continued to walk forward, bringing up one hand, not to strike at that sweating, bristly jaw, but as if to push the other out of his path. And in his mind he held one thought; this was not Logally, it could not be. Ten years had passed since they had met. And for five of those years Logally had been dead. Here was Warlockian witchery, to be met by sane Terran reasoning.

Shann was alone. The mist, which had formed walls, enclosed him again. But still there was a smarting brand across his shoulder. Shann drew aside the rags of his uniform blouse to discover a welt, raw and red. And seeing that, his unbelief was shaken.

When he had believed in Logally and in Logally's weapon, the other had had reality enough to strike that blow, make the lash cut deep. But when the Terran had faced the phantom with the truth, then neither Logally nor his lash existed. Shann shivered, trying not to think what might lie before him. Visions out of nightmares which could put on substance! He had dreamed of Logally in the past, many times. And he had had other dreams, just as frightening. Must he front those nightmares, all of them—? Why? To amuse his captors, or to prove their contention that he was a fool to challenge the powers of such mistresses of illusion?

How did they know just what dreams to use in order to break him? Or did he himself furnish the actors and the action, projecting old terrors in this mist as a tri-dee tape projected a story in three dimensions for the amusement of the viewer?

Dream true—was this progress through the mist also a dream? Dreams within dreams . . . Shann put his hand to his head, uncertain, badly shaken. But that stubborn core of determination within him was still holding. Next time he would be prepared at once to face down any resurrected memory.

Walking slowly, pausing to listen for the slightest sound which might herald the coming of a new illusion, Shann tried to guess which of his nightmares might come to face him. But he was to learn that there was more than one kind of dream. Steeled against old fears, he was met by another emotion altogether.

There was a fluttering in the air, a little crooning cry which pulled at his heart. Without any conscious thought, Shann held out his hands, whistling on two notes a call which his lips appeared to remember more quickly than his mind. The shape which winged through the fog came straight to his waiting hold, tore at long-walled-away hurt with its once familiar beauty. It flew with a list; one of the delicately tinted wings was injured, had never healed straight. But the seraph nestled into the hollow of Shann's two palms and looked up at him with all the old liquid trust.

"Trav! Trav!" He cradled the tiny creature carefully, regarded with joy its feathered body, the curled plumes on its proudly held head, felt the silken patting of those infinitesimal claws against his protecting fingers.

Shann sat down in the sand, hardly daring to breathe. Trav—again! The wonder of this never-to-be-hoped-for return filled him with a surge of happiness almost too great to bear, which hurt in its way with as great a pain as Logally's lash; it was a pain rooted in love, not fear and hate.

Logally's lash . . .

Shann trembled. Trav raised one of those small claws toward the Terran's face, crooning a soft caressing cry for recognition, for protection, trying to be a part of Shann's life once more.

Trav! How could he bear to will Trav into nothingness, to bear to summon up another harsh memory which would sweep Trav away? Trav was the only thing Shann had ever known which he could love wholeheartedly, that had answered his love with a return gift of affection so much greater than the light body he now held.

"Trav!" he whispered softly. Then he made his great effort against this second and far more subtle attack. With the same agony which he had known years earlier, he resolutely summoned a bitter memory, sat nursing once more a broken thing which died in pain he could not ease, aware himself of every moment of that pain. And what was worse, this time there clung that nagging little doubt. What if he had not forced the memory? Perhaps he could have taken Trav with him unhurt, alive, at least for a while.

Shann covered his face with his now empty hands. To see a nightmare flicker out after facing squarely up to its terror, that was no great task. To give up a dream which was part of a lost heaven, that cut cruelly deep. The Terran dragged himself to his feet, drained and weary, stumbling on.

Was there no end to his aimless circling through a world of green smoke? He shambled ahead, moving his feet leadenly. How long had he been here? There was no division in time, just the unchanging light which was a part of the fog through which he plodded.

Then he heard more than any shuffle of foot across sand, any crooning of a long dead seraph, the rising and falling of a voice: a human voice—not quite singing or reciting, but something between the two. Shann paused, searching his memory, a memory which seemed bruised, for the proper answer to match that sound.

But, though he recalled scene after scene out of the years, that voice did not trigger any return from his past. He turned toward its source, dully determined to get over quickly the meeting which lay behind that signal.

Only, though he walked on and on, Shann did not appear any closer to the man behind the voice, nor was he able to make out separate words composing that chant, a chant broken now and then by pauses, so that the Terran grew aware of the distress of his fellow prisoner. For the impression that he sought another captive came out of nowhere and grew as he cast wider and wider in his quest.

Then he might have turned some invisible corner in the mist, for the chant broke out anew in stronger volume, and now he was able to distinguish words he knew.

" . . . where blow the winds between the worlds,
And hang the suns in dark of space.
For Power is given a man to use.
Let him do so well before the last accounting—"

The voice was hoarse, cracked, the words spaced with uneven catches of breath, as if they had been repeated many, many times to provide an anchor against madness, form a tie to reality. And hearing that note, Shann slowed his pace. This was out of no memory of his; he was sure of that.

" . . . blow the winds between the worlds,
And hang the suns in . . . dark—of—of—"

That harsh croak of voice was running down, as a clock runs down for lack of winding. Shann sped on, reacting to a plea which did not lay in the words themselves.

Once more the mist curled back, provided him with an open space. A man sat on the sand, his fists buried wrist deep in the smooth grains on either side of his body, his eyes set, red-rimmed, glazed, his body rocking back and forth in time to his labored chant.

" . . . the dark of space—"

"Thorvald!" Shann skidded in the sand, went down on his knees. The manner of their last parting was forgotten as he took in the officer's condition.

The other did not stop his swaying, but his head turned with a stiff jerk, the gray eyes making a visible effort to focus on Shann. Then some of the strain smoothed out of the gaunt features and Thorvald laughed softly.

"Garth!"

Shann stiffened but had no chance to protest that mistaken identification as the other continued: "So you made class one status, boy! I always knew you could if you'd work for it. A couple of black marks on your record, sure. But those can be rubbed out, boy, when you're willing to try. Thorvalds always have been Survey. Our father would have been proud."

Thorvald's voice flattened, his smile faded, there was a growing spark of some emotion in those gray eyes. Unexpectedly, he hurled himself forward, his hands clawing for Shann's throat. He bore the younger man down under him to the sand where Lantee found himself fighting desperately for his life against a man who could only be mad.

Shann used a trick learned on the Dumps, and his opponent doubled up with a gasp of agony to let the younger man break free. He planted a knee on the small of Thorvald's back, digging the officer into the sand, pinning down his arms in spite of the other's struggles. Regaining his own breath in gulps, Shann tried to appeal to some spark of reason in the other.

"Thorvald! This is Lantee—Lantee—" His name echoed in the mist-walled void like an unhuman wail.

"Lantee—? No, Throg! Lantee—Throg—killed my brother!"

Sand puffed out with the breath which expelled that indictment. But Thorvald no longer fought, and Shann believed him close to collapse.

Shann relaxed his hold, rolling the other man over. Thorvald obeyed his pull limply, lying face upward, sand in his hair and eyebrows, crusting his slack lips. The younger man brushed the dirt away gently as the other opened his eyes to regard Shann with his old impersonal stare.

"You're alive," Thorvald stated bleakly. "Garth's dead. You ought to be dead too."

Shann drew back, rubbed sand from his hands, his concern dampened by the other's patent hostility. Only that angry accusation vanished in a blink of those gray eyes.

Then there was a warmer recognition in Thorvald's expression.

"Lantee!" The younger man might just have come into sight. "What are you doing here?"

Shann tightened his belt. "Just about what you are." He was still aloof, giving no acknowledgment of difference in rank now. "Running around in this fog hunting the way out."

Thorvald sat up, surveying the billowing walls of the hole which contained them. Then he reached out a hand to draw fingers down Shann's forearm.

"You *are* real," he observed simply, and his voice was warm, welcoming.

"Don't bet on it," Shann snapped. "The unreal can be mighty real—here." His hand went up to the smarting brand on his shoulder.

Thorvald nodded. "Masters of illusion," he murmured.

"Mistresses," Shann corrected. "This place is run by a gang of pretty smart witches."

"Witches? You've seen them? Where? And what—who are they?" Thorvald pounced with a return of his old-time sharpness.

"They're females right enough, and they can make the impossible happen. I'd say that classifies them as witches. One of them tried to take me over back on the island. I set a trap and caught her; then somehow she transported me—" Swiftly he outlined the chain of events leading from his sudden awakening in the river tunnel to his present penetration of this fog-world.

Thorvald listened eagerly. When the story was finished, he rubbed his hands across his drawn face, smearing away the last of the sand. "At least you have some idea of who they are and a suggestion of how you got here. I don't remember that much about my own arrival. As far as I can remember I went to sleep on the island and woke up here!"

Shann studied him and knew that Thorvald was telling the truth. He could remember nothing of his departure in the outrigger, the way he had fought Shann in the lagoon. The Survey officer must have been under the control of the Warlockians then. Quickly he gave the older

man his version of the other's actions in the outer world
and Thorvald was clearly astounded, though he did not
question the facts Shann presented.

"They just took me!" Thorvald said in a husky half
whisper. "But why? And why are we here? Is this a
prison?"

Shann shook his head. "I think all this"—a wave of his
hand encompassed the green wall, what lay beyond it, and
in it—"is a test of some kind. This dream business . . . A
little while ago I got to thinking that I wasn't here at all,
that I might be dreaming it all. Then I met you."

Thorvald understood. "Yes, but this *could* be a dream
meeting. How can we tell?" He hesitated, almost diffi-
dently, before he asked: "Have you met anyone else here?"

"Yes." Shann had no desire to go into that.

"People out of your past life?"

"Yes." Again he did not elaborate.

"So did I." Thorvald's expression was bleak; his encoun-
ters in the fog must have proved no more pleasant than
Shann's. "That suggests that we do trigger the hallucinations ourselves. But maybe we can really lick it now."

"How?"

"Well, if these phantoms are born of our memories
there are about only two or three we could see together—
maybe a Throg on the rampage, or that hound we left
back in the mountains. And if we do sight anything like
that, we'll know what it is. On the other hand, if we stick
together and one of us sees something that the other
can't . . . well, that fact alone will explode the ghost."

There was sense in what he said. Shann aided the officer to his feet.

"I must be a better subject for their experiments than
you," the older man remarked ruefully. "They took me
over completely at the first."

"You were carrying that disk," Shann pointed out.
"Maybe that acted as a focusing lens for whatever power
they use to make us play trained animals."

"Could be!" Thorvald brought out the cloth-wrapped
bone coin. "I still have it." But he made no move to pull
off the bit of rag about it. "Now"—he gazed at the wall
of green—"which way?"

Shann shrugged. Long ago he had lost any idea of keeping a straight course through the murk. He might have turned around any number of times since he first walked blindly into this place. Then he pointed to the packet Thorvald held.

"Why not flip that?" he asked. "Heads, we go that way"—he indicated the direction in which they were facing—"tails we do a rightabout-face."

There was an answering grin on Thorvald's lips. "As good a guide as any we're likely to find here. We'll do it." He pulled away the twist of cloth and with a swift snap, reminiscent of that used by the Warlockian witch to empty the bowl of sticks, he tossed the disk into the air.

It spun, whirled, but—to their open-jawed amazement—it did not fall to the sand. Instead it spun until it looked like a small globe instead of a disk. And it lost its dead white for a glow of green. When that glow became dazzling for Terran eyes the miniature sun swung out, not in orbit but in a straight line of flight, heading to their right.

With a muffled cry, Thorvald started in pursuit, Shann running beside him. They were in a tunnel of the fog now, and the pace set by the spinning coin was swift. The Terrans continued to follow it at the best pace they could summon, having no idea of where they were headed, but each with the hope that they finally did have a guide to lead them through this place of confusion and into a sane world where they could face on more equal terms those who had sent them there.

14

ESCAPE

"Something ahead!" Thorvald did not slacken the pace set by the brilliant spot of green they trailed. Both of the Terrans feared to fall behind, to lose touch with that guide. Their belief that somehow the traveling disk would bring them to the end of the mist and its attendant illusions had grown firmer with every foot of ground they traversed.

A dark, fixed point, now partly veiled by mist, lay beyond, and it was toward that looming half-shadow that the spinning disk hurtled. Now the mist curled away to display its bulk—larger, blacker and four or five times Thorvald's height. Both men stopped short, for the disk no longer played path-finder. It still whirled on its axis in the air, faster and faster, until it appeared to be throwing off sparks, but the sparks faded against a monolith of dark rock unlike the native stone they had seen elsewhere. For it was neither red nor warmly brown, but a dull, dead black. It could have been a huge stone slab, trimmed, smoothed, set up on end as a monument or marker, except that only infinite labor could have accomplished such a task, and there was no valid reason for such toil as far as the Terrans could perceive.

"This is it." Thorvald moved closer.

By the disk's action, they deduced that their guide had

drawn them to this featureless black steel with the precision of a beam-controlled ship. However, the purpose still eluded them. They had hoped for some exit from the territory of the veil, but now they faced a solid slab of dark stone, neither a conventional exit or entrance, as they proved by circling its base. Beneath their boots was the eternal sand, around them the fog.

"Now what?" Shann asked. They had made their trip about the slab and were back again where the disk whirled with unceasing vigor in a shower of emerald sparks.

Thorvald shook his head, scanning the rock face before them glumly. The eagerness had gone out of his expression, a vast weariness replacing it.

"There must have been some purpose in coming here," he replied, but his tone had lost the assurance of moments earlier.

"Well, if we strike away from here, we'll just get right back in again." Shann waved a hand toward the mist, waiting as if with a hunter's watch upon them. "And we certainly can't go down." He dug a boot toe into the sand to demonstrate the folly of that. "So, what about up?"

He ducked under the spinning disk to lay his hands against the surface of the giant slab. And in so doing he made a discovery, revealed to his touch although hidden from sight. For his fingers, running aimlessly across the cold, slightly uneven surface of the stone, slipped into a hollow, quite a deep hollow.

Excited, half fearing that his sudden guess might be wrong, Shann slid his hand higher in line with that hollow, to discover a second. The first had been level with his chest, the second perhaps eighteen inches or so above. He jumped, to draw his fingers down the rock, with damage to his nails but getting his proof. There *was* a third niche, deep enough to hold more than just the toe of a boot, and a fourth above that . . .

"We've a ladder of sorts here," he reported. Without waiting for any answer from Thorvald, Shann began to climb. The holds were so well matched in shape and size that he was sure they could not be natural; they had been bored there for use—the use to which he was now putting

them—a ladder to the top of the slab. Though what he
might find there was beyond his power to imagine.

The disk did not rise. Shann passed that core of light,
climbing above it into the greater gloom. But the holes
did not fail him; each was waiting in a direct line with
its companion. And to an active man the scramble was
not difficult. He reached the summit, glanced around, and
made a quick grab for a secure handhold.

Waiting for him was no level platform such as he had
confidently expected to find. The surface he had just
climbed fly-fashion was the outer wall of a well or chim-
ney. He looked down now into a pit where black nothingness began within a yard of the top, for the radiance
of the mist did not penetrate far into that descent.

Shann fought an attack of giddiness. It would be very
easy to lose control, to tumble over and be swallowed up
in what might well be a bottomless chasm. And what was
the purpose of this well? Was it a trap to entice a prisoner into an unwary climb and then let gravity drag him
over? The whole setup was meaningless. Perhaps meaningless only to him, Shann conceded, with a flash of level
thinking. The situation could be quite different as far as
the natives were concerned. This structure did have a
reason, or it would never have been erected in the first
place.

"What's the matter?" Thorvald's voice was rough with
impatience.

"This thing's a well." Shann edged about a fraction to
call back. "The inside is open and—as far as I can tell—
goes clear to the planet's core."

"Ladder on the inside too?"

Shann squirmed. That was, of course, a very obvious
supposition. He kept a tight hold with his left hand, and
with the other, he did some exploring. Yes, here was a
hollow right enough, twin to those on the outside. But
to swing over that narrow edge of safety and begin a
descent into the black of the well was far harder than
any action he had taken since the morning the Throgs
had raided the camp. The green mist could hold no
terrors greater than those with which his imagination
peopled the depths now waiting to engulf him. But Shann

swung over, fitted his boot into the first hollow, and started down.

The only encouragement he gained during that nightmare ordeal was that those holes were regularly spaced. But somehow his confidence did not feed on that fact. There always remained the nagging fear that when he searched for the next it would not be there and he would cling to his perch lacking the needed strength in aching arms and legs to reclimb the inside ladder.

He was fast losing that sense of well-being which had been his during his travels through the fog; fatigue tugged at his arms and weighed leaden on his shoulders. Mechanically he prospected for the next hold, and then the next. Above, the oblong of half-light grew smaller and smaller, sometimes half blotted out by the movement of Thorvald's body as the other followed him down that interior way.

How far *was* down? Shann giggled lightheadedly at the humor of that, or what seemed to be humor at the moment. He was certain that they were now below the level of the sand floor outside the slab. And yet no end had come to the well hollow.

No break of light down here; he might have been sightless. But just as the blind develop an extra perceptive sense of unseen obstacles, so did Shann now find that he was aware of a change in the nature of the space about him. His weary arms and legs held him against the solidity of a wall, yet the impression that there was no longer another wall at his back grew stronger with every niche which swung him downward. And he was as sure as if he could see it, that he was now in a wide-open space, another cavern, perhaps, but this one totally dark.

Deprived of sight, he relied upon his ears. And there was a sound, faint, distorted perhaps by the acoustics of this place, but keeping up a continuous murmur. Water! Not the wash of waves with their persistent beat, but rather the rippling of a running stream. Water must lie below!

And just as his weariness had grown with his leaving behind the fog, so now did both hunger and thirst gnaw at Shann, all the sharper for the delay. The Terran wanted to reach that water, could picture it in his mind, putting away the possibility—the probability—that it might be sea-borne and salt, and so unfit to drink.

The upper opening to the cavern of the fog was now so far above him that he had to strain to see it. And that warmth which had been there was gone. A dank chill wrapped him here, dampened the holds to which he clung until he was afraid of slipping. While the murmur of the water grew louder, until its *slap-slap* sounded within arm's distance. His boot toe skidded from a niche. Shann fought to hold on with numbed fingers. The other foot went. He swung by his hands, kicking vainly to regain a measure of footing.

Then his arms could no longer support him, and he cried out as he fell. Water closed about him with an icy shock which for a moment paralyzed him. He flailed out, fighting the flood to get his head above the surface where he could gasp in precious gulps of air.

There was a current here, a swiftly running one. Shann remembered the one which had carried him into that cavern in which the Warlockians had their strange dwelling. Although there were no clusters of crystals in this tunnel to supply him with light, the Terran began to nourish a faint hope that he was again in that same stream, that those light crystals would appear, and that he might eventually return to the starting point of this meaningless journey.

So he strove only to keep his head above water. Hearing a splashing behind him, he called out: "Thorvald?"

"Lantee?" The answer came back at once; the splashing grew louder as the other swam to catch up.

Shann swallowed a mouthful of the water lapping against his chin. The taste was brackish, but not entirely salt, and though it stung his lips, the liquid relieved a measure of his thirst.

Only no glowing crystals appeared to stud these walls, and Shann's hope that they were on their way to the cavern of the island faded. The current grew swifter, and he had to fight to keep his head above water, his tired body reacting sluggishly to commands.

The murmur of the racing flood drummed louder in his ears, or was that sound the same? He could no longer be sure. Shann only knew that it was close to impossible to snatch the necessary breath as he was rolled over and over in the hurrying flood.

In the end he was ejected into blazing, blinding light, into a suffocation of wild water as the bullet in an ancient Terran gun might have been fired at no specific target. Gasping, beaten, more than half-drowned, Shann was pummeled by waves, literally driven up on a rocky surface which skinned his body cruelly. He lay there, his arms moving feebly until he contrived to raise himself in time to be wretchedly sick. Somehow he crawled on a few feet farther before he subsided again, blinded by the light, flinching from the heat of the rocks on which he lay, but unable to do more for himself.

His first coherent thought was that his speculation concerning the reality of this experience was at last resolved. This could not possibly be an hallucination; at least this particular sequence of events was not. And he was still hazily considering that when a hand fell on his shoulder, fingers biting into his raw flesh.

Shann snarled, rolled over on his side. Thorvald, water dripping from his rags—or rather streaming from them—his shaggy hair plastered to his skull, sat there.

"You all right?"

Shann sat up in turn, shielding his smarting eyes. He was bruised, battered badly enough, but he could claim no major injuries.

"I think so. Where are we?"

Thorvald's lips stretched across his teeth in what was more a grimace than a smile. "Right off the map, any map I know. Take a look."

They were on a scrap of beach—beach which was more like a reef, for it lacked any covering comparable to sand except for some cupfuls of coarse gravel locked in rock depressions. Rocks, red as the rust of dried blood, rose in fantastic water-sculptured shapes around the small semi-level space they had somehow won.

This space was V-shaped, washed by equal streams on either side of the prong of rock by water which spouted from the face of a sheer cliff not too far away, with force enough to spray several feet beyond its exit point. Shann, seeing that and guessing at its significance, drew a deep breath, and heard the ghost of an answering chuckle from his companion.

"Yes, that's where we came out, boy. Like to make a return trip?"

Shann shook his head, and then wished that he had not so rashly made that move, for the world swung in a dizzy whirl. Things had happened too fast. For the moment it was enough that they were out of the underground ways, back under the amber sky, feeling the bite of Warlock's sun.

Steadying his head with both hands, Shann turned slowly, to survey what might lie at their backs. The water, pouring by on either side, suggested that they were again on an island. Warlock, he thought gloomily, seemed to be for Terrans a succession of islands, all hard to escape.

The tangle of rocks did not encourage any exploration. Just gazing at them added to his weariness. They rose, tier by tier, to a ragged crown against the sky. Shann continued to sit staring at them.

"To climb that . . ." His voice trailed into the silence of complete discouragement.

"You climb—or swim," Thorvald stated. But, Shann noted, the Survey officer was not in a hurry to make either move.

Nowhere in that wilderness of rock was there the least relieving bit of purple foliage. Nor did any clak-claks or leather-headed birds tour the sky over their heads. Shann's thirst might have been partially assuaged, but his hunger remained. And it was that need which forced him at last into action. The barren heights promised nothing in the way of food, but remembering the harvest the wolverines had taken from under the rocks along the river, he got to his feet and lurched out on the reef which had been their salvation, hunting some pool which might hold an edible captive or two.

So it was that Shann made the discovery of a possible path consisting of a ledge running toward the other end of the island, if this were an island where they had taken refuge. The spray of the water drenched that way, feeding small pools in the uneven surface, and strips of yellow weed trailed in slimy ribbons back below the surface of the waves.

He called to Thorvald and gestured to his find. And then, close together, linking hands when the going became hazardous, the men followed the path. Twice they made finds in the pools, finned or clawed grotesque creatures, which they killed and ate, wolfing down the few fragments of odd-tasting flesh. Then, in a small crevice, which could hardly be dignified by the designation of "cave," Thorvald chanced upon quite an exciting discovery—a clutch of four greenish eggs, each as large as his doubled fist.

Their outer covering was more like a tough membrane than a true shell, and the Terrans worried it open with difficulty. Shann shut his eyes, trying not to think of what he mouthed as he sucked his share dry. At least that semi-liquid stayed put in his middle, though he expected disastrous results from the experiment.

More than a little heartened by this piece of luck, they kept on, though the ledge changed from a reasonably level surface to a series of rising, unequal steps, drawing them away from the water. At long last they came to the end of that path. Shann leaned back against a convenient spur of rock.

"Company!" he alerted Thorvald.

The Survey officer joined him to share an outcrop of rock from which they were provided with an excellent view of the scene below. It was a scene to hold their full attention.

That soft sweep of sand which had floored the cavern of the fog lay here also, a gray-blue carpet sloping gently out of the sea. For Shann had no doubt that the wide stretch of water before them was the western ocean. Walling the beach on either side were pillars of stone that extended well out into the water so that the farthest piles were awash except for their crowns. All were shaped with the same finish as that slab which had provided them a ladder of escape. And because of the regularity of their spacing, Shann did not believe them works of nature.

Grouped between them now were the players of the drama. One of the Warlockian witches, her gem body patterns glittering in the sunlight, was walking backward out of the sea, her hands held palms together, breast high, in a Terran attitude of prayer. And following her something swam in the water, clearly not another of her own species. But her actions suggested that by some invisible means she was drawing that water dweller after her. Waiting on shore were two others of her kind, viewing her actions with close attention, the attention of scholars for an instructor.

"Wyverns!"

Shann looked inquiringly at his companion. Thorvald added a whisper of explanation. "A legend of Terra—they were supposed to have a snake's tail instead of hind legs, but the heads . . . They're Wyverns!"

Wyverns. Shann liked the sound of that word; to his mind it well fitted the Warlockian witches. And the one they were watching in action continued her steady backward retreat, rolling her bemused captive out of the water. What emerged into the blaze of sunlight was one of those fork-tailed sea dwellers such as the Terrans had seen die after the storm. The thing crawled out of the shallows, its eyes focused in a blind stare on the praying hands of the Wyvern.

She halted, well up on the sand, when the body of her victim or prisoner—Shann was certain that the fork-tail was one or the other—was completely out of the water. Then, with lightning speed, she dropped her hands.

Instantly fork-tail came to life. Fanged jaws snapped. Aroused, the beast was the incarnation of evil rage, a rage which had a measure of intelligence to direct it into deadly action. And facing it, seemingly unarmed and defenseless, were the slender, fragile Wyverns.

Yet none of the small group of natives made any attempt to escape. Shann thought them suicidal in their indifference as the fork-tail, short legs sending the fine sand flying in a dust cloud, made a rush toward its enemies.

The Wyvern who had led the beast ashore did not move. But one of her companions swung up a hand, as if negligently waving the monster to a stop. Between her first two digits was a disk. Thorvald caught at Shann's arm.

"See that! It's a copy of the one I had; it must be!"

They were too far away to be sure it was a duplicate, but it was coin-shaped and bone-white. And now the Wyvern swung it back and forth in a metronome sweep. The fork-tail skidded to a stop, its head beginning—reluctantly at first, and then, with increasing speed—to echo that left-right sweep. This Wyvern had the sea beast under control, even as her companion had earlier held it.

Chance dictated what happened next. As had her sister charmer, the Wyvern began a backward withdrawal up the length of the beach, drawing the sea thing in her wake. They were very close to the foot of the drop above which the Terrans stood, fascinated, when the sand betrayed the witch. Her foot slipped into a hole and she was thrown backward, her control disk spinning out of her fingers.

At once the monster she had charmed shot forth its head, snapped at that spinning trifle—and swallowed it. Then the fork-tail hunched in a posture Shann had seen the wolverines use when they were about to spring. The weaponless Wyvern was the prey, and both her companions were too far away to interfere.

Why he moved he could not have explained. There was no reason for him to go to the aid of the Warlockian, one of the same breed who had ruled him against his will. But Shann sprang, landing in the sand on his hands and knees.

The sea thing whipped around, undecided between two possible victims. Shann had his knife free, was on his feet, his eyes on the beast's, knowing that he had appointed himself dragon slayer for no good reason.

15

DRAGON SLAYER

"Ayeeee!" Sheer defiance, not only of the beast he fronted, but of the Wyverns as well, brought that old rallying cry to his lips—the call used on the Dumps of Tyr to summon gang aid against outsiders. Fork-tail had crouched again for a spring, but that throat-crackling blast appeared to startle it.

Shann, blade ready, took a dancing step to the right. The thing was scaled, perhaps as well armored against frontal attack as was the shell-creature he had fought with the aid of the wolverines. He wished he had the Terran animals now—with Taggi and his mate to tease and feint about the monster, as they had done with the Throg hound—for he would have a better chance. If only the animals were here!

Those eyes—red-pitted eyes in a gargoyle head following his every movement—perhaps those were the only vulnerable points.

Muscles tensed beneath that scaled hide. The Terran readied himself for a sidewise leap, his knife hand raised to rake at those eyes. A brown shape with a V of lighter fur banding its back crossed the far range of Shann's vision. He could not believe what he saw, not even when a snarling animal, slavering with rage, came at a lumbering gallop to stand beside him, a second animal on its heels.

Uttering his own battle cry, Taggi attacked. The fork-tail's head swung, imitating the movements of the wolverine as it had earlier mimicked the swaying of the disk in the Wyvern's hand. Togi came in from the other side. They might have been hounds keeping a bull in play. And never had they shown such perfect team work, almost as if they could sense what Shann desired of them.

That forked tail lashed viciously, a formidable weapon. Bone, muscles, scaled flesh, half buried in the sand, swept up a cloud of grit into the face of the man and the animals. Shann fell back, pawing with his free hand at his eyes. The wolverines circled warily, trying for the attack they favored—the spring to the shoulders, the usually fatal assault on the spine behind the neck. But the armored head of the fork-tail, slung low, warned them off. Again the tail lashed, and this time Taggi was caught and hurled across the beach.

Togi uttered a challenge, made a reckless dash, and raked down the length of the fork-tail's body, fastening on that tail, weighing it to earth with her own poundage while the sea creature fought to dislodge her. Shann, his eyes watering from the sand, but able to see, watched that battle for a long second, judging that fork-tail was completely engaged in trying to free its best weapon from the grip of the wolverine. The latter clawed and bit with a fury which suggested Togi intended to immobilize that weapon by tearing it to shreds.

Fork-tail wrenched its body, striving to reach its tormentor with fangs or clawed feet. And in that struggle to achieve an impossible position, its head slued far about, uncovering the unprotected area behind the skull base which usually lay under the spiny collar about its shoulders.

Shann went in. With one hand he gripped the edge of that collar—its serrations tearing his flesh—and at the same time he drove his knife blade deep into the soft underfolds, ripping on toward the spinal column. The blade nicked against bone as the fork-tail's head slammed back, catching Shann's hand and knife together in a trap. The Terran was jerked from his feet, and flung to one side with the force of the beast's reaction.

Blood spurted up, his own blood mingled with that of the monster. Only Togi's riding of the tail prevented Shann's being beaten to death. The armored snout pointed skyward as the creature ground the sharp edge of its collar down on the Terran's arm. Shann, frantic with pain, drove his free fist into one of those eyes.

Fork-tail jerked convulsively; its head snapped down again and Shann was free. The Terran threw himself back, keeping his feet with an effort. Fork-tail was writhing, churning up the sand in a cloud. But it could not rid itself of the knife Shann had planted with all his strength, and which the blows of its own armored collar were now driving deeper and deeper into its back.

It howled thinly, with an abnormal shrilling. Shann, nursing his bleeding forearm against his chest, rolled free from the waves of sand it threw about, bringing up against one of the rock pillars. With that to steady him, he somehow found his feet, and stood weaving, trying to see through the rain of dust.

The convulsions which churned up that concealing cloud were growing more feeble. Then Shann heard the triumphant squall from Togi, saw her brown body still on the torn tail just above the forking. The wolverine used her claws to hitch her way up the spine of the sea monster, heading for the fountain of blood spouting from behind the head. Fork-tail fought to raise that head once more; then the massive jaw thudded into the sand, teeth snapping fruitlessly as a flood of grit overrode the tongue, packed into the gaping mouth.

How long had it taken—that frenzy of battle on the bloodstained beach? Shann could have set no limit in clock-ruled time. He pressed his wounded arm tighter to him, lurched past the still-twitching sea thing to that splotch of brown fur on the sand, shaping the wolverine's whistle with dry lips. Togi was still busy with the kill, but Taggi lay where that murderous tail had thrown him.

Shann fell on his knees, as the beach around him developed a curious tendency to sway. He put his good hand to the ruffled back fur of the motionless wolverine.

"Taggi!"

A slight quiver answered. Shann tried awkwardly to

raise the animal's head with his own hand. As far as he could see, there were no open wounds; but there might be broken bones, internal injuries he did not have the skill to heal.

"Taggi?" He called again gently, striving to bring that heavy head up on his knee.

"The furred one is not dead."

For a moment Shann was not aware that those words had formed in his mind, had not been heard by his ears. He looked up, eyes blazing at the Wyvern coming toward him in a graceful glide across the crimsoned sand. And in a space of heartbeats his thrust of anger cooled into a stubborn enmity.

"No thanks to you," he said deliberately aloud. If the Wyvern witch wanted to understand him, let her make the effort; he did not try to touch her thoughts with his.

Taggi stirred again, and Shann glanced down quickly. The wolverine gasped, opened his eyes, shook his miniature bear head, scattering pellets of sand. He sniffed at a dollop of blood, the dark, alien blood, spattered on Shann's breeches, and then his head came up with a reassuring alertness as he looked to where his mate was still worrying the now quiet fork-tail.

With an effort, Taggi got to his feet, Shann aiding him. The man ran his hand down over ribs, seeking any broken bones. Taggi growled a warning once when that examination brought pain in its wake, but Shann could detect no real damage. As might a cat, the wolverine must have met the shock of that whip-tail stroke relaxed enough to escape serious injury. Taggi had been knocked out, but now he was able to navigate again. He pulled free from Shann's grip, lumbering across the sand to the kill.

Someone else was crossing that strip of beach. Passing the Wyverns as if he did not see them, Thorvald came directly to Shann. A few seconds later he had the torn arm stretched across his own bent knee, examining the still bleeding hurt.

"That's a nasty one," he commented.

Shann heard the words and they made sense, but the instability of his surroundings was increasing, while Thorvald's handling sent sharp stabs of pain up his arm and somehow into his head, where they ended in red bursts to cloud his sight.

Out of the reddish mist which had fogged most of the landscape there emerged a single object, a round white disk. And in Shann's clouded mind a well-rooted apprehension stirred. He struck out with his one hand, and through luck connected. The disk flew out of sight. His vision cleared enough so he could sight the Wyvern who had been leaning over Thorvald's shoulder centering her weird weapon on him. Making a great effort, Shann got out the words, words which he also shaped in his mind as he said them aloud: "You're not taking me over—again!"

There was no emotion to be read on that jewel-banded face or in her unblinking eyes. He caught at Thorvald, determined to get across his warning.

"Don't let them use those disks on us!"

"I'll do my best."

Only the haze had taken Thorvald again. Did one of the Wyverns have a disk focused on them? Were they being pulled into one of those blank periods, to awaken as prisoners once more—say, in the cavern of the veil? The Terran fought with every ounce of will power to escape unconsciousness, but he failed.

This time he did not awaken half-drowning in an underground stream or facing a green mist. And there was an ache in his arm which was somehow reassuring with the very insistence of pain. Before opening his eyes, his fingers crossed the smooth slick of a bandage there, went on to investigate by touch a sleep mat such as he had found in the cavern structure. Was he back in that set of rooms and corridors?

Shann delayed opening his eyes until a kind of shame drove him to it. He first saw an oval opening almost the length of his body as it was stretched only a foot or two below the sill of that window. And through its transparent surface came the golden light of the sun—no green mist, no crystals mocking the stars.

The room in which he lay was small with smooth walls, much like that in which he had been imprisoned on the island. And there were no other furnishings save the mat on which he rested. Over him was a light cover netted of fibers resembling yarn, with feathers knotted into it to provide a downy upper surface. His clothing was gone, but the single covering was too warm and he pushed it away from his shoulders and chest as he wriggled up to see the view beyond the window.

His torn arm came into full view. From wrist to elbow it was encased in an opaque skin sheath, unlike any bandage of his own world. Surely that had not come out of any Survey aid pack. Shann gazed toward the window, but beyond lay only a reach of sky. Except for a lemon cloud or two ruffled high above the horizon, nothing broke that soft amber curtain. He might be quartered in a tower well above ground level, which did not match his former experience with Wyvern accommodations.

"Back with us again?" Thorvald, one hand lifting a door panel, came in. His ragged uniform was gone, and he wore only breeches of a sleek green material and his own scuffed-and-battered boots.

Shann settled back on the mat. "Where are we?"

"I think you might term this the capital city," Thorvald answered. "In relation to the mainland, we're on an island well out to sea—westward."

"How did we get here?" That climb in the slab, the stream underground . . . Had it been an interior river running under the bed of the sea? But Shann was not prepared for the other's reply.

"By wishing."

"By *what*?"

Thorvald nodded, his expression serious. "They wished us here. Listen, Lantee, when you jumped down to mix it with that fork-tailed thing, did you wish you had the wolverines with you?"

Shann thought back; his memories of what had occurred before that battle were none too clear. But, yes, he had wished Taggi and Togi present at that moment to distract the enraged beast.

"You mean I wished them?" The whole idea was probably a part of the Wyvern jargon of dreaming and he added, "Or did I just dream everything?" There was the bandage on his arm, the soreness under that bandage. But also there had been Logally's lash brand back in the cavern, which had bitten into his flesh with the pain of a real blow.

"No, you weren't dreaming. You happened to be tuned in on one of those handy little gadgets our lady friends here use. And, so tuned in, your desire for the wolverines being pretty powerful just then, they came."

Shann grimaced. This was unbelievable. Yet there were his meetings with Logally and Trav. How could anyone rationally explain them? And how had he, in the beginning, been jumped from the top of the cliff on the island of his marooning into the midst of an underground flood without any conscious memory of an intermediate journey?

"How does it work?" he asked simply.

Thorvald laughed. "You tell me. They have these disks, one to a Wyvern, and they control forces with them. Back there on the beach we interrupted a class in such control; they were the novices learning their trade. We've stumbled on something here which can't be defined or understood by any of our previous standards of comparison. It's frankly magic, judged by our terms."

"Are we prisoners?" Shann wanted to know.

"Ask me something I'm sure of. I've been free to come and go within limits. No one's exhibited any signs of hostility; most of them simply ignore me. I've had two interviews, via this mind-reading act of theirs, with their rulers, or elders, or chief sorceresses—all three titles seem to apply. They ask questions, I answer as best I can, but sometimes we appear to have no common meeting ground. Then I ask some questions, they evade gracefully, or reply in a kind of unintelligible double-talk, and that's as far as our communication has progressed so far."

"Taggi and Togi?"

"Have a run of their own and as far as I can tell are better satisfied with life than I am. Oddly enough, they respond more quickly and more intelligently to orders. Perhaps this business of being shunted around by the disks has conditioned them in some way."

"What about these Wyverns? Are they all female?"

"No, but their tribal system is strictly matriarchal, which follows a pattern even Terra once knew: the fertile earth mother and her priestesses, who became the witches when the gods overruled the goddesses. The males are few in number and lack the power to activate the disks. In fact," Thorvald laughed ruefully, "one gathers that in this civilization our opposite numbers have, more or less, the status of pets at the best, and necessary evils at the worst. Which put *us* at a disadvantage from the start."

"You think that they won't take us seriously because we are males?"

"Might just work out that way. I've tried to get through to them about danger from the Throgs, telling them what it would mean to them to have the beetle-heads settle in here for good. They just brush aside the whole idea."

"Can't you argue that the Throgs are males, too? Or aren't they?"

The Survey officer shook his head. "That's a point no human can answer. We've been sparring with Throgs for years and there have been libraries of reports written about them and their behavior patterns, all of which add up to about two paragraphs of proven facts and hundreds of surmises beginning with the probable and skimming out into the wild fantastic. You can claim anything about a Throg and find a lot of very intelligent souls ready to believe you. But whether those beetle-heads squatting over on the mainland are able to answer to 'he,' 'she,' or 'it,' your solution is just as good as mine. We've always considered the ones we fight to be males, but they might just as possibly be amazons. Frankly, these Wyverns couldn't care less either; at least that's the impression they give."

"But anyway," Shann observed, "it hasn't come to 'we're all girls together' either."

Thorvald laughed again. "Not so you can notice. We're not the only unwilling visitor in the vicinity."

Shann sat up. "A Throg?"

"A something. Non-Warlockian, or non-Wyvern. And perhaps trouble for us."

"You haven't seen this other?"

Thorvald sat down cross-legged. The amber light from the window made red-gold of his hair, added ruddiness to his less-gaunt features.

"No, I haven't. As far as I can tell, the stranger's not right here. I caught stray thought beams twice—surprise expressed by newly arrived Wyverns who met me and apparently expected to be fronted by something quite physically different."

"Another Terran scout?"

"No. I imagine that to the Wyverns we must look a lot alike. Just as we couldn't tell one of them from her sister if their body patterns didn't differ. Discovered one thing about those patterns—the more intricate they run, the higher the 'power,' not of the immediate wearer, but of her ancestors. They're marked when they qualify for their disk and presented with the rating of the greatest witch in their family line as an inducement to live up to those deeds and surpass them if possible. Quite a bit of logic to that. Given the right conditioning, such a system might even work in our service."

That nugget of information was the stuff from which Survey reports were made. But at the moment the information concerning the other captive was of more value to Shann. He steadied his body against the wall with his good hand and got to his feet. Thorvald watched him.

"I take it you have visions of action. Tell me, Lantee, why *did* you take that header off the cliff to mix it with the fork-tail?"

Shann wondered himself. He had no reason for that impulsive act. "I don't know—"

"Chivalry? Fair Wyvern in distress?" the other prodded. "Or did the back lash from one of those disks draw you in?"

"I don't know—"

"And why did you use your knife instead of your stunner?"

Shann was startled. For the first time he realized that he had fronted the greatest native menace they had discovered on Warlock with the more primitive of his weapons. Why had he not tried the stunner on the beast? He had just never thought of it when he had taken that leap into the role of dragon slayer.

"Not that it would have done you any good to try the ray; it has no effect on fork-tails."

"You tried it?"

"Naturally. But you didn't know that, or did you pick up that information earlier?"

"No," answered Shann slowly. "No, I don't know why I used the knife. The stunner would have been more natural." Suddenly he shivered, and the face he turned to Thorvald was very sober.

"How much do they control us?" he asked, his voice dropping to a half whisper as if the walls about them could pick up those words and relay them to other ears. "What can they do?"

"A good question." Thorvald lost his light tone. "Yes, what can they feed into our minds without our knowledge? Perhaps those disks are only window dressing, and they can work without them. A great deal will depend upon the impression we can make on these witches." He began to smile again, more wryly. "The name we gave this planet is certainly a misnomer. A warlock is a male sorcerer, not a witch."

"And what are the chances of our becoming warlocks ourselves?"

Again Thorvald's smile faded, but he gave a curt little nod to Shann as if approving that thought. "That is something we are going to look into, and now! If we have to convince some stubborn females, as well as fight Throgs, well"—he shrugged—"we'll have a busy, busy time."

16

THIRD PRISONER

"Well, it works as good as new." Shann held his hand and arm out into the full path of the sun. He had just stripped off the skin-case bandage, to show the raw seam of a half-healed scar, but as he flexed muscles, bent and twisted his arm, there was only a small residue of soreness left.

"Now what, or where?" he asked Thorvald with some eagerness. Several days' imprisonment in this room had made him impatient for the outer world again. Like the officer, he now wore breeches of the green fabric, the only material known to the Wyverns, and his own badly worn boots. Oddly enough, the Terrans' weapons, stunner and knife, had been left to them, a point which made them uneasy, since it suggested that the Wyverns believed they had nothing to fear from clumsy alien arms.

"Your guess is as good as mine," Thorvald answered that double question. "But it is you they want to see; they insisted upon it, rather emphatically in fact."

The Wyvern city existed as a series of cell-like hollows in the interior of a rock-walled island. Outside there had been no tampering with the natural rugged features of the escarpment, and within, the silence was almost complete. For all the Terrans could learn, the population of the stone-walled hive might have been several thousand, or just the handful that they had seen with their own eyes along the passages which had been declared open territory for them.

Shann half expected to find again a skull-walled chamber where witches tossed colored sticks to determine his future. But he came with Thorvald into an oval room in which most of the outer wall was a window. And seeing what lay framed in that, Shann halted, again uncertain as to whether he actually saw that, or whether he was willed into visualizing a scene by the choice of his hostesses.

They were lower now than the room in which he had nursed his wound, not far above water level. And this window faced the sea. Across a stretch of green water was his red-purple skull, the waves lapping its lower jaw, spreading their foam in between the gaping rock-fringe which formed its teeth. And from the eye hollows flapped the clak-claks of the sea coast, coming and going as if they carried to some brain imprisoned within that giant bone case messages from the outer world.

"My dream—" Shann said.

"Your dream." Thorvald had not echoed that; the answer had come in his brain.

Shann turned his head and surveyed the Wyvern awaiting them with a concentration which was close to the rudeness of an outright stare, a stare which held no friendship. For by her skin patterns he knew her for the one who had led that trio who had sent him into the cavern of the mist. And with her was the younger witch he had trapped on the night that all this baffling action had begun.

"We meet again," he said slowly. "To what purpose?"

"To our purpose . . . and yours—"

"I do not doubt that it is to yours." The Terran's thoughts fell easily now into a formal pattern he would not have used with one of his own kind. "But I do not expect any good to me . . ."

There was no readable expression on her face; he did not expect to see any. But in their uneven mind touch he caught a fleeting suggestion of bewilderment on her part, as if she found his mental processes as hard to understand as a puzzle with few leading clues.

"We mean you no ill, star voyager. You are far more than we first thought you, for you have dreamed false and have known. Now dream true, and know it also."

"Yet," he challenged, "you would set me a task without my consent."

"We have a task for you, but already it was set in the pattern of your true dreaming. And we do not set such patterns, star man; that is done by the Greatest Power of all. Each lives within her appointed pattern from the First Awakening to the Final Dream. So we do not ask of you any more than that which is already laid for your doing."

She arose with that languid grace which was a part of their delicate jeweled bodies and came to stand beside him, a child in size, making his Terran flesh and bones awkward, clodlike in contrast. She stretched out her four-digit hand, her slender arm ringed with gemmed circles and bands, measuring it beside his own, bearing that livid scar.

"We are different, star man, yet still are we both dreamers. And dreams hold power. Your dreams brought you across the dark which lies between sun and distant sun. Our dreams carry us on even stranger roads. And yonder"—one of her fingers stiffened to a point, indicating the skull—"there is another who dreams with power, a power which will destroy us all unless the pattern is broken speedily."

"And I must go to seek this dreamer?" His vision of climbing through that nose hole was to be realized then.

"You go."

Thorvald stirred and the Wyvern turned her head to him. "Alone," she added. "For this is your dream only, as it has been from the beginning. There is for each his own dream, and another cannot walk through it to alter the pattern, even to save a life."

Shann grinned crookedly, without humor. "It seems that I'm elected," he said as much to himself as to Thorvald. "But what do I do with this other dreamer?"

"What your pattern moves you to do. Save that you do not slay him—"

"Throg!" Thorvald started forward. "You can't just walk

in on a Throg barehanded and be bound by orders such as that!"

The Wyvern must have caught the sense of that vocal protest, for her communication touched them both. "We cannot deal with that one as his mind is closed to us. Yet he is an elder among his kind and his people have been searching land and sea for him since his air rider broke upon the rocks and he entered into hiding over there. Make your peace with him if you can, and also take him hence, for his dreams are not ours, and he brings confusion to the Reachers when they retire to run the Trails of Seeking."

"Must be an important Throg," Shann deduced. "They could have an officer of the beetle-heads under wraps over there. Could we use him to bargain with the rest?"

Thorvald's frown did not lighten. "We've never been able to establish any form of contact in the past, though our best qualified minds, reinforced by training, have tried . . ."

Shann did not take fire at that rather delicate estimate of his own lack of preparation for the carrying out of diplomatic negotiations with the enemy; he knew it was true. But there was one thing he could try—if the Wyvern permitted.

"Will you give a disk of power to this star man?" He pointed to Thorvald. "For he is my Elder One and a Reacher for Knowledge. With such a focus his dream could march with mine when I go to the Throg, and perhaps that can aid in my doing what I could not accomplish alone. For that is the secret of *my* people, Elder One. We link our powers together to make a shield against our enemies, a common tool for the work we must do."

"And so it is with us also, star voyager. We are not so unlike as the foolish might think. We learned much of you while you both wandered in the Place of False Dreams. But our power disks are our own and can not be given to a stranger while their owners live. However . . ." She turned again with an abruptness foreign to the usual Wyvern manner and faced the older Terran.

The officer might have been obeying an unvoiced order as he put out his hands and laid them palm to palm on those she held up to him, bending his head so gray eyes met golden ones. The web of communication which had held all three of them snapped. Thorvald and the Wyvern were linked in a tight circuit which excluded Shann.

Then the latter became conscious of movement beside him. The younger Wyvern had joined him to watch the clak-claks in their circling of the bare dome of the skull island.

"Why do they fly so?" Shann asked her.

"Within they nest, care for their young. Also they hunt the rock creatures that swarm in the lower darkness."

"The rock creatures?" If the skull's interior was infested by some other native fauna, he wanted to know it.

By some method of her own the young Wyvern conveyed a strong impression of revulsion, which was her personal reaction to the "rock creatures."

"Yet you imprison the Throg there—" he remarked.

"Not so!" Her denial was instantaneous and vehement. "The other worlder fled into that place in spite of our calling. There he stays in hiding. Once we drew him out to the sea, but he broke the power and fled inside again."

"Broke free—" Shann pounced upon that. "From disk control?"

"But surely." Her reply held something of wonder. "Why do you ask, star voyager? Did you not also break free from the power of the disk when I led you by the underground ways, awaking in the river? Do you then rate this other one as less than your own breed that you think him incapable of the same action?"

"Of Throgs I know as much as this . . ." He held up his hand, measuring off a fraction of space between thumb and forefinger.

"Yet you knew them before you came to this world."

"My people have known them for long. We have met and fought many times among the stars."

"And never have you talked mind to mind?"

"Never. We have sought for that, but there has been no communication between us, neither of mind nor voice."

"This one you name Throg is truly not as you," she assented. "And we are not as you, being alien and female. Yet, star man, you and I have shared a dream."

Shann stared at her, startled, not so much by what she said as the human shading of those words in his mind. Or had that also been illusion?

"In the veil . . . that creature which came to you on wings when you remembered that. A good dream, though it came out of the past and so was false in the present. But I have gathered it into my own store: such a fine dream, one that you have cherished."

"Trav was to be cherished," he agreed soberly. "I found her in a broken sleep cage at a spaceport when I was a child. We were both cold and hungry, alone and hurt. So I stole and was glad that I stole Trav. For a little space we both were very happy . . ." Forcibly he stifled memory.

"So, though we are unlike in body and in mind, yet we find beauty together if only in a dream. Therefore, between your people and mine there can *be* a common speech. And I may show you my dream store for your enjoyment, star voyager."

A flickering of pictures, some weird, some beautiful, all a little distorted—not only by haste, but also by the haze of alienness which was a part of her memory pattern—crossed Shann's mind.

"Such a sharing would be a rich feast," he agreed.

"All right!" Those crisp words in his own tongue brought Shann away from the window to Thorvald. The Survey officer was no longer locked hand to hand with the Wyvern witch, but his features were alive with a new eagerness.

"We are going to try your idea, Lantee. They'll provide me with a new, unmarked disk, show me how to use it. And I'll do what I can to back you with it. But they insist that you go today."

"What do they really want me to do? Just root out that Throg? Or try to talk him into being a go-between with his people? That *does* come under the heading of dreaming!"

"They want him out of there, back with his own kind if possible. Apparently he's a disruptive influence for them; he causes some kind of a mental foul up which interferes drastically with their 'power.' They haven't been able to get him to make any contact with them. This Elder One is firm about your being the one ordained for the job, and that you'll know what action to take when you get here."

"Must have thrown the sticks for me again," Shann commented.

"Well, they've definitely picked you to smoke out the Throg, and they can't be talked into changing their minds about that."

"I'll be the smoked one if he has a blaster."

"They say he's unarmed—"

"What do they know about our weapons or a Throg's?"

"The other one has no arms." Wyvern words in his mind again. "This fact gives him great fear. That which he has depended upon is broken. And since he has no weapon, he is shut into a prison of his own terrors."

But an adult Throg, even unarmed, was not to be considered easy meat, Shann thought. Armored with horny skin, armed with claws and those crushing mandibles of the beetle mouth . . . a third again as tall as he himself was. No, even unarmed, the Throg had to be considered a menace.

Shann was still thinking along that line as he splashed through the surf which broke about the lower jaw of the skull island, climbed up one of the pointed rocks which masqueraded as a tooth, and reached for a higher hold to lead him to the nose slit, the gateway to the alien's hiding place.

The clak-claks screamed and dived about him, highly resentful of his intrusion. And when they grew so bold as to buffet him with their wings, threaten him with their tearing beaks, he was glad to reach the broken rock edging his chosen door and duck inside. Once there, Shann looked back. There was no sighting the cliff window where Thorvald stood, nor was he aware in any way of mental contact with the Survey officer; their hope of such a linkage might be futile.

Shann was reluctant to venture farther. His eyes had sufficiently adjusted to the limited supply of light, and now the Terran brought out the one aid the Wyverns had granted him, a green crystal such as those which had played the role of stars on the cavern roof. He clipped its simple loop setting to the front of his belt, leaving his hands free. Then, having filled his lungs for the last time with clean, sea-washed air, he started into the dome of the skull.

There was a fetid thickness to this air only a few feet away from the outer world. The odor of clak-clak droppings and refuse from their nests was strong, but there was an added staleness, as if no breeze ever scooped out the old atmosphere to replace it with new. Fragile bones crunched under Shann's boots, but as he drew away from the entrance, the pale glow of the crystal increased its radiance, emitting a light not unlike that of the phosphorescent bushes, so that he was not swallowed up by dark.

The cave behind the nose hole narrowed quickly into a cleft, a narrow cleft which pierced into the bowl of the skull. Shann proceeded with caution, pausing every few steps. There came a murmur rising now and again to a shriek, issuing, he guessed, from the clak-clak rookery above. And the pound of sea waves was also a vibration carrying through the rock. He was listening for something else, at the same time testing the ill-smelling air for that betraying muskiness which spelled Throg.

When a twist in the narrow passage cut off the splotch of daylight, Shann drew his stunner. The strongest bolt from that could not jolt a Throg into complete paralysis, but it would slow up any attack.

Red—pinpoints of red—were edging a break in the rock wall. They were gone in a flash. Eyes? Perhaps of the rock dwellers which the Wyverns hated? More red dots, farther ahead. Shann listened for a sound he could identify.

But smell came before sound. That trace of effluvia which in force could sicken a Terran, was his guide. The cleft ended in a space to which the limited gleam of the crystal could not provide a far wall. But that faint light did show him his quarry.

The Throg was not on his feet, ready for trouble, but hunched close to the wall. And the alien did not move at Shann's coming. Did the beetle-head sight him? Shann wondered. He moved cautiously. And the round head, with its bulbous eyes, turned a fraction; the mandibles about the ugly mouth opening quivered. Yes, the Throg could see him.

But still the alien made no move to rise out of his crouch, to come at the Terran. Then Shann saw the fall of rock, the stone which pinned a double-kneed leg to the floor. And in a circle about the prisoner were the small, crushed, furred things which had come to prey on the helpless to be slain themselves by the well-aimed stones which were the Throg's only weapons of defense.

Shann sheathed his stunner. It was plain the Throg was helpless and could not reach him. He tried to concentrate mentally on a picture of the scene before him, hoping that Thorvald or one of the Wyverns could pick it up. There was no answer, no direction. Choice of action remained solely his.

The Terran made the oldest friendly gesture of his kind; his empty hands held up, palm out. There was no answering move from the Throg. Neither of the other's upper limbs stirred, their claws still gripping the small rocks in readiness for throwing. All Shann's knowledge of the alien's history argued against an unarmed advance. The Throg's marksmanship, as borne out by the circle of small bodies, was excellent. And one of those rocks might well thud against his own head, with fatal results. Yet he had been sent there to get the Throg free and out of Wyvern territory.

So rank was the beetle smell of the other that Shann coughed. What he needed now was the aid of the wolverines, a diversion to keep the alien busy. But this time there was no disk working to produce Taggi and Togi out of thin air. And he could not continue to just stand there staring at the Throg. There remained the stunner. Life on the Dumps tended to make a man a fast draw, a matter of survival for the fastest and most accurate marksman. And now one of Shann's hands swept down with a speed which, learned early, was never really to be forgotten.

He had the rod out and was spraying on tight beam straight at the Throg's head before the first stone struck his shoulder and his weapon fell from a numbed hand. But a second stone tumbled out of the Throg's claw. The alien tried to reach for it, his movements slow, uncertain.

Shann, his arm dangling, went in fast, bracing his good shoulder against the boulder which pinned the Throg. The alien aimed a blow at the Terran's head, but again so slowly Shann had no difficulty in evading it. The boulder gave, rolled, and Shann cleared out of range, back to the opening of the cleft, pausing only to scoop up his stunner.

For a long moment the Throg made no move; his dazed wits must have been working at very slow speed. Then the alien heaved up his body to stand erect, favoring the leg which had been trapped. Shann tensed, waiting for a rush. What now? Would the Throg refuse to move? If so, what could he do about it?

With the impact of a blow, the message Shann had hoped for struck into his mind. But his initial joy at that contact was wiped out with the same speed.

"Throg ship . . . overhead."

The Throg stood away from the wall, limped out, heading for Shann, or perhaps only the cleft in which he stood. Swinging the stunner awkwardly in his left hand, the Terran retreated, mentally trying to contact Thorvald once more. There was no answer. He was well up into the cleft, moving crabwise, unwilling to turn his back on the Throg. The alien was coming as steadily as his injured limb would allow, trying for the exit to the outer world.

A Throg ship overhead . . . Had the castaway somehow managed to call his own kind? And what if he, Shann Lantee, were to be trapped between the alien and a landing party from the flyer? He did not expect any assistance from the Wyverns, and what could Thorvald possibly do? From behind him, at the entrance of the nose slit, he heard a sound—a sound which was neither the scolding of a clak-clak nor the eternal growl of the sea.

17

THROG JUSTICE

The musty stench was so strong that Shann could no longer fight the demands of his outraged stomach. He rolled on his side, retching violently until the sour smell of his vomit battled the foul odor of the ship. His memories of how he had come into this place were vague; his body was a mass of dull pain, as if he had been scorched. Scorched! Had the Throgs used one of their energy whips to subdue him? The last clear thing he could recall was that slow withdrawal down the cleft inside the skull rock, the Throg not too far away—the sound from the entrance.

A Throg prisoner! Through the pain and the sickness the horror of that bit doubly deep. Terrans did not fall alive into Throg hands, not if they had the means of ending their existence within reach. But his hands and arms were caught behind him in an unbreakable lock, some gadget not unlike the Terran force bar used to restrain criminals, he decided groggily.

The cubby in which he lay was black-dark. But the quivering of the deck and the bulkheads about him told Shann that the ship was in flight. And there could be but two destinations, either the camp where the Throg force had taken over the Terran installations or the mother ship of the raiders. If Thorvald's earlier surmise was true and the aliens were hunting a Terran to talk in the transport, then they were heading for the camp.

And because a man who still lives and who is not yet broken can also hope, Shann began to think ahead to the camp—the camp and a faint, thin chance of escape. For on the surface of Warlock there was a thin chance; in the mother ship of the Throgs none at all.

Thorvald—and the Wyverns! Could he hope for any help from them? Shann closed his eyes against the thick darkness and tried to reach out to touch, somewhere, Thorvald with his disk—or perhaps the Wyvern who had talked of Trav and shared dreams. Shann focused his thoughts on the young Wyvern witch, visualizing with all the detail he could summon out of memory the brilliant patterns about her slender arms, her thin, fragile wrists, those other designs overlaying her features. He could see her in his mind, but she was only a puppet, without life, certainly without power.

Thorvald . . . Now Shann fought to build a mental picture of the Survey officer, making his stand at that window, grasping his disk, with the sun bringing gold to his hair and showing the bronze of his skin. Those gray eyes which could be ice, that jaw with the tight set of a trap upon occasion . . .

And Shann made contact! He touched something, a flickering like a badly tuned tri-dee—far more fuzzy than the mind pictures the Wyvern had paraded for him. But he had touched! And Thorvald, too, had been aware of his contact.

Shann fought to find that thread of awareness again. Patiently he once more created his vision of Thorvald, adding every detail he could recall, small things about the other which he had not known that he had noticed—the tiny arrow-shaped scar near the base of the officer's throat, the way his growing hair curled at the ends, the look of one eyebrow slanting abruptly toward his hairline when he was dubious about something. Shann strove to make a figure as vividly as Logally and Trav had been in the mist of the illusion.

" . . . where?"

This time Shann was prepared; he did not let that mind

image dissolve in his excitement at recapturing the link. "Throg ship," he said the words aloud, over and over, but still he held to his picture of Thorvald.

" . . . will . . ."

Only that one word! The thread between them snapped again. Only then did Shann become conscious of a change in the ship's vibration. Were they setting down? And where? Let it be at the camp! It must be the camp!

There was no jar at that landing, just that one second the vibration told him the ship was alive and air-borne, and the next a dead quiet testified that they had landed. Shann, his sore body stiff with tension, waited for the next move on the part of his captors.

He continued to lie in the dark, still queasy from the stench of the cell, too keyed up to try to reach Thorvald. There was a dull grating over his head, and he looked up eagerly—to be blinded by a strong beam of light. Claws hooked painfully under his arms and he was man-handled up and out, dragged along a short passage and pitched free of the ship, falling hard upon trodden earth and rolling over gasping as the seared skin of his body was rasped and abraded.

The Terran lay face up now, and as his eyes adjusted to the light, he saw a ring of Throg heads blotting out the sky as they inspected their catch impassively. The mouth mandibles of one moved with a faint clicking. Again claws fastened in his armpits, brought Shann to his feet, holding him erect.

Then the Throg who had given that order moved closer. His hand-claws clasped a small metal plate surmounted by a hoop of thin wire over which was stretched a web of threads glistening in the sun. Holding that hoop on a level with his mouth, the alien clicked his mandibles, and those sounds became barely distinguishable basic galactic words.

"You Throg meat!"

For a moment Shann wondered if the alien meant that statement literally. Or was it a conventional expression for a prisoner among their kind.

"Do as told!"

That was clear enough, and for the moment the Terran

did not see that he had any choice in the matter. But Shann refused to make any sign of agreement to either of those two limited statements. Perhaps the beetle-heads did not expect any. The alien who had pulled him to his feet continued to hold him erect, but the attention of the Throg with the translator switched elsewhere.

From the alien ship emerged a second party. The Throg in their midst was unarmed and limping. Although to Terran eyes one alien was the exact counterpart of the other, Shann thought that this one was the prisoner in the skull cave. Yet the indications now suggested that he had only changed one captivity for another and was in disgrace among his kind. Why?

The Throg limped up to front the leader with the translator, and his guards fell back. Again mandibles clicked, were answered, though the sense of that exchange eluded Shann. At one point in the report—if report it was—he himself appeared to be under discussion, for the injured Throg waved a hand-claw in the Terran's direction. But the end to the conference came quickly enough and in a manner which Shann found shocking.

Two of the guards stepped forward, caught at the injured Throg's arms and drew him away, leading him out into a space beyond the grounded ship. They dropped their hold on him, returning at a trot. The officer clicked an order. Blasters were unholstered, and the Throg in the field shriveled under a vicious concentration of cross bolts. Shann gasped. He certainly had no liking for Throgs, but this execution carried overtones of a cold-blooded ferocity which transcended anything he had known, even in the callous brutality of the Dumps.

Limp, and more than a little sick again, he watched the Throg officer turn away. And a moment later he was forced along in the other's wake to the domes of the once Terran camp. Not just to the camp in general, he discovered a minute later, but to that structure which had housed the com unit linking them with ships cruising the solar lanes and with the patrol. So Thorvald had been right; they needed a Terran to broadcast—to cover their tracks here and lay a trap for the transport.

Shann had no idea how much time he had passed

among the Wyverns; the transport with its load of unsuspecting settlers might already be in the system of Circe, plotting a landing orbit around Warlock, broadcasting her recognition signal and a demand for a beam to ride her in. Only, this time the Throgs were out of luck. They had picked up one prisoner who could not help them, even if he wanted to do so. The mysteries of the highly technical installations in this dome were just that to Shann Lantee—complete mysteries. He had not the slightest idea of how to activate the machines, let alone broadcast in the proper code.

A cold spot of terror gathered in his middle, spreading outward through his smarting body. For he was certain that the Throgs would not believe that. They would consider his protestations of ignorance as a stubborn refusal to co-operate. And what would happen to him then would be beyond human endurance. Could he bluff—play for time? But what would that time buy him except to delay the inevitable? In the end, that small hope based on his momentary contact with Thorvald made him decide to try that bluff.

There had been changes in the com dome since the capture of the camp. A squat box on the floor sprouted a collection of tubes from its upper surface. Perhaps that was some Throg equivalent of Terran equipment in place on the wide table facing the door.

The Throg leader clicked into his translator: "You call ship!"

Shann was thrust down into the operator's chair, his bound arms still twisted behind him so that he had to lean forward to keep on the seat at all. Then the Throg who had pushed him there, roughly forced a set of com earphones and speech mike onto his head.

"Call ship!" clicked the alien officer.

So time must be running out. Now was the moment to bluff. Shann shook his head, hoping that the gesture of negation was common to both their species.

"I don't know the code," he said aloud.

The Throg's bulbous eyes gazed at his moving lips. Then the translator was held before the Terran's mouth. Shann repeated his words, heard them reissue as a series of clicks, and waited. So much depended now on the reaction of the beetle-head officer. Would he summarily apply pressure to enforce his order, or would he realize that it was possible that all Terrans did not know that code, and so he could not produce in a captive's head any knowledge that had never been there—with or without physical coercion?

Apparently the latter logic prevailed for the present. The Throg drew the translator back to his mandibles.

"When ship call—you answer—make lip talk your words! Say had sickness here—need help. Code man dead—you talk in his place. I listen. You say wrong, you die—you die a long time. Hurt bad all that time—"

Clear enough. So he had been able to buy a little time! But how soon before the incoming ship would call? The Throgs seemed to expect it. Shann licked his blistered lips. He was sure that the Throg officer meant exactly what he said in that last grisly threat. Only, would anyone— Throg or human—live very long in this camp if Shann got his warning through? The transport would have been accompanied on the big jump by a patrol cruiser, especially now with Throgs littering deep space the way they were in this sector. Let Shann alert the ship, and the cruiser would know; swift punitive action would be visited on the camp. Throgs could begin to make their helpless prisoner regret his rashness; then all of them would be blotted out together, prisoner and captors alike, when the cruiser came in.

If that was his last chance, he'd play it that way. The Throgs would kill him anyhow, he hadn't the least doubt of that. They kept no long-term Terran prisoners and never had. And at least he could take this nest of devil beetles along with him. Not that the thought did anything to dampen the fear which made him weak and dizzy. Shann Lantee might be tough enough to fight his way out of the Dumps, but to stand up and defy Throgs face-to-face like a video hero was something else. He knew that he could not do any spectacular act; if he could hold out to the end without cracking he would be satisfied.

Two more Throgs entered the dome. They stalked to the far end of the table which held the com equipment, and frequently pausing to consult a Terran work tape set in a reader, they made adjustments to the spotter beam broadcaster. They worked slowly but competently, testing each circuit. Preparing to draw in the Terran transport, holding the large ship until they had it helpless on the ground. The Terran began to wonder how they proposed to take the ship over once they did have it on planet.

Transports were armed for ground fighting. Although they rode in on a beam broadcast from a camp, they were prepared for unpleasant surprises on a planet's surface; such were certainly not unknown in the history of Survey. Which meant that the Throgs had in turn some assault weapon they believed superior, for they radiated confidence now. But could they handle a patrol cruiser ready to fight?

The Throg technicians made a last check of the beam, reporting in clicks to the officer. The alien gave an order to Shann's guard before following them out. A loop of wire rope dropped over the Terran's head, tightened about his chest, dragging him back against the chair until he grunted with pain. Two more loops made him secure in a most uncomfortable posture, and then he was left alone in the com dome.

An abortive struggle against the wire rope taught him the folly of such an effort. He was in deep freeze as far as any bodily movement was concerned. Shann closed his eyes, settled to that same concentration he had labored to acquire on the Throg ship. If there was any chance of the Wyvern communication working again, here and now was the time for it!

Again he built his mental picture of Thorvald, as detailed as he had made it in the Throg ship. And with that to the forefront of his mind, Shann strove to pick up the thread which could link them. Was the distance between this camp and the seagirt city of the Wyverns too great? Did the Throgs unconsciously dampen out that mental reaching as the Wyverns had said they did when they had sent him to free the captive in the skull?

Drops gathered in the unkempt tight curls on his head, trickled down to sting on his tender skin. He was bathed in the moisture summoned by an effort as prolonged and severe as if he labored physically under a hot sun at the top speed of which his body was capable.

Thorvald—

Thorvald! But not standing by the window in the Wyvern stronghold! Thorvald with the amethyst of heavy Warlockian foliage at his back. So clear was the new picture that Shann might have stood only a few feet away. Thorvald there, with the wolverines at his side. And behind him sun glinted on the gem-patterned skin of more than one Wyvern.

"Where?"

That demand from the Survey officer, curt, clear—so perfect the word might have rung audibly through the dome.

"The camp!" Shann hurled that back, frantic with fear that once again their contact might fail.

"They want me to call in the transport." He added that.

"How soon?"

"Don't know. They have the guide beam set. I'm to say there's illness here; they know I can't code."

All he could see now was Thorvald's face, intent, the officer's eyes cold sparks of steel, bearing the impress of a will as implacable as a Throg's. Shann added his own decision.

"I'll warn the ship off; they'll send in the patrol."

There was no change in Thorvald's expression. "Hold out as long as you can!"

Cold enough, no promise of help, nothing on which to build hope. Yet the fact that Thorvald was on the move, away from the Wyvern city, meant something. And Shann was sure that thick vegetation could be found only on the mainland. Not only was Thorvald ashore, but there were Wyverns with him. Could the officer have persuaded the witches of Warlock to forsake their hands-off policy and join him in an attack on the Throg camp? No promise, not even a suggestion that the party Shann had envisioned was moving in his direction. Yet somehow he believed that they were.

There was a sound from the doorway of the dome. Shann opened his eyes. There were Throgs entering, one to go to the guide beam, two heading for his chair. He closed his eyes again in a last attempt, backed by every remaining ounce of his energy and will.

"Ship's in range. Throgs here."

Thorvald's face, dimmer now, snapped out while a blow on Shann's jaw rocked his head cruelly, made his ears sing, his eyes water. He saw Throgs—Throgs only. And one held the translator.

"You talk!"

A tri-jointed arm reached across his shoulder, triggered a lever, pressed a button. The head set cramping his ear let out a sudden growl of sound—the com was activated. A claw jammed the mike closer to Shann's lips, but also slid in range the webbed loop of the translator.

Shann shook his head at the incoming rattle of code. The Throg with the translator was holding the other head set close to his own ear pit. And the claws of the guard came down on Shann's shoulder in a cruel grip, a threat of future brutality.

The rattle of code continued while Shann thought furiously. This was it! He had to give a warning, and then the aliens would do to him just what the officer had threatened. Shann could not seem to think clearly. It was as if in his efforts to contact Thorvald, he had exhausted some part of his brain, so that now he was dazed just when he needed quick wits the most!

This whole scene had a weird unreality. He had seen its like a thousand times on fiction tapes—the Terran hero menaced by aliens intent on saving . . . saving . . .

Was it out of one of those fiction tapes he had devoured in the past that Shann recalled that scrap of almost forgotten information?

The Terran began to speak into the mike, for there had come a pause in the rattle of code. He used Terran, not basic, and he shaped the words slowly.

"Warlock calling—trouble—sickness here—com officer dead."

He was interrupted by another burst of code. The claws of his guard twisted into the naked flesh of his shoulders in vicious warning.

"Warlock calling—" he repeated. "Need help—"

"Who are you?"

The demand came in basic. On board the transport they would have a list of every member of the Survey team.

"Lantee." Shann drew a deep breath. He was so conscious of those claws on his shoulders, of what would follow.

"This is Mayday!" he said distinctly, hoping desperately that someone in the control cabin of the ship now in orbit would catch the true meaning of that ancient call of complete disaster. "Mayday—beetles—over and out!"

18

STORM'S ENDING

Shann had no answer from the transport, only the continuing hum of a contact still open between the dome and the control cabin miles above Warlock. The Terran breathed slowly, deeply, felt the claws of the Throg bite his flesh as his chest expanded. Then, as if a knife slashed, the hum of that contact was gone. He had time to know a small flash of triumph. He had done it; he had aroused suspicion in the transport.

When the Throg officer clicked to the alien manning the landing beam, Shann's exultation grew. The beetle-head must have accepted that cut in communication as normal; he was still expecting the Terran ship to drop neatly into his claws.

But Shann's respite was to be very short, only timed by a few breaths. The Throg at the riding beam was watching the indicators. Now he reported to his superior, who swung back to face the prisoner. Although Shann could read no expression on the beetle's face, he did not need any clue to the other's probable emotions. Knowing that his captive had somehow tricked him, the alien would now proceed relentlessly to put into effect the measures he had threatened.

How long before the patrol cruiser would planet? That crew was used to alarms, and their speed was three or four times greater than that of the bulkier transports. If the Throgs didn't scatter now, before they could be caught in one attack . . .

The wire rope which held Shann clamped to the chair was loosened, and he set his teeth against the pain of restored circulation. This was nothing compared to what he faced; he knew that. They jerked him to his feet, faced him toward the outer door, and propelled him through it with a speed and roughness indicative of their feelings.

The hour was close to dusk and Shann glanced wistfully at promising shadows, though he had given up hope of rescue by now. If he could just get free of his guards, he could at least give the beetle-heads a good run.

He saw that the camp was deserted. There was no sign about the domes that any Throgs sheltered there. In fact, Shann saw no aliens at all except those who had come from the com dome with him. Of course! The rest must be in ambush, waiting for the transport to planet. What about the Throg ship or ships? Those must have been hidden also. And the only hiding place for them would be aloft. There was a chance that the Throgs had so flung away their chance for any quick retreat.

Yes, the aliens could scatter over the countryside and so escape the first blast from the cruiser. But they would simply maroon themselves to be hunted down by patrol landing parties who would comb the territory. The beetles could so prolong their lives for a few hours, maybe a few days, but they were really ended on that moment when the transport cut communication. Shann was sure that the officer, at least, understood that.

The Terran was dragged away from the domes toward the river down which he and Thorvald had once escaped. Moving through the dusk in parallel lines, he caught sight of other Throg squads, well armed, marching in order to suggest that they were not yet alarmed. However, he had been right about the ships—there were no flyers grounded on the improvised field.

Shann made himself as much of a burden as he could. At the best, he could so delay the guards entrusted with his safekeeping; at the worst, he could earn for himself a quick ending by blaster which would be better than the one they had for him. He went limp, falling forward into the trampled grass. There was an exasperated click from the Throg who had been herding him, and the Terran tried not to flinch from a sharp kick delivered by a clawed foot.

Feigning unconsciousness, the Terran listened to the unintelligible clicks exchanged by Throgs standing over him. His future depended now on how deep lay the alien officer's anger. If the beetle-head wanted to carry out his earlier threats he would have to order Shann's transportation by the fleeing force. Otherwise his life might well end here and now.

Claws hooked once more on Shann. He was boosted up on the horny carapace of a guard, the bonds on his arms taken off and his numbed hands brought forward, to be held by his captor so that he lay helpless, a cloak over the other's hunched shoulders.

The ghost flares of bushes and plants blooming in the gathering twilight gave a limited light to the scene. There was no way of counting the number of Throgs on the move. But Shann was sure that all the enemy ships must have been emptied except for skeleton crews, and perhaps others had been ferried in from their hidden base somewhere in Circe's system.

He could only see a little from his position on the Throg's back, but ahead a ripple of beetle bodies slipped over the bank of the river cut. The aliens were working their way into cover, fitting into the dapple shadows with a skill which argued a long practice in such elusive maneuvers. Did they plan to try to fight off a cruiser attack? That was pure madness. Or, Shann wondered, did they intend to have the Terrans met by one of their own major ships somewhere well above the surface of Warlock?

His bearer turned away from the stream cut, carrying Shann out into that field which had first served the Terrans as a landing strip, then offered the same service to the Throgs. They passed two more parties of aliens on the move, manhandling bulky objects the Terran could not identify. Then he was dumped unceremoniously to the hard earth, only to lie there a few seconds before he was flopped over on a framework which grated unpleasantly against his raw shoulders, his wrists and ankles being made fast so that his body was spread-eagled. There was a click of orders; the frame was raised and dropped with a jarring movement into a base, and he was held erect, once more facing the Throg with the translator. This was it! Shann began to regret every small chance he had had to end more cleanly. If he had attacked one of the guards, even with his hands bound, he might have flustered the Throg into retaliatory blaster fire.

Fear made a thicker fog about him than the green mist of the illusion. Only this was no illusion. Shann stared at the Throg officer with sick eyes, knowing that no one ever quite believes that at last evil will strike at him, that he had clung to a hope which had no existence.

"Lantee!"

The call burst in his head with a painful force. His dazed attention was outwardly on the alien with the translator, but that inner demand had given him a shock.

"Here! Thorvald? Where?

The other struck in again with an urgent demand singing through Shann's brain.

"Give us a fix point—away from camp but not too far. Quick!"

A fix point—what did the Survey officer mean? A fix point . . . For some reason Shann thought of the ledge on which he had lain to watch the first Throg attack. And the picture of it was etched on his mind as clearly as memory could paint it.

"Thorvald—" Again his voice and his mind call were echoes of each other. But this time he had no answer. Had that demand meant Thorvald and the Wyverns were moving in, putting to use the strange distance-erasing power the witches of Warlock could use by desire? But why had they not come sooner? And what could they hope to accomplish against the now scattered but certainly unbroken enemy forces? The Wyverns had not been able to turn their power against one injured Throg—by their own accounting—how could they possibly cope with well-armed and alert aliens in the field?

"You die—slow—" The Throg officer clicked, and the

emotionless, toneless translation was all the more daunting for that lack of color. "Your people come—see—"

So that was the reason they had brought him to the landing field. He was to furnish a grisly warning to the crew of the cruiser. However, there the Throgs were making a bad mistake if they believed that his death by any ingenious method could scare off Terran retaliation.

"I die—you follow—" Shann tried to make that promise emphatic.

Did the Throg officer expect the Terran to beg for his life or a quick death? Again he made his threat—straight into the web, hearing it split into clicks.

"Perhaps," the Throg officer returned. "But you die the first."

"Get to it!" Shann's voice scaled up. He was close to the ragged edge, and the last push toward the breaking point had not been the Throg speech, but that message from Thorvald. If the Survey officer was going to make any move in the mottled dusk, it would have to be soon.

Mottled dusk . . . the Throgs had moved a little away from him. Shann looked beyond them to the perimeter of the cleared field, not really because he expected to see any rescuers break from cover there. And when he did see a change, Shann thought his own sight was at fault.

Those splotches of waxy light which marked certain trees, bushes, and scrubby ground-hugging plants were spreading, running together in pools. And from those center cores of concentrated glow, tendrils of mist lazily curled out, as a many-armed creature of the sea might allow its appendages to float in the water which supported it. Tendrils crossed, met, and thickened. There was a growing river of eerie light which spread, again resembling a sea wave licking out onto the field. And where it touched, unlike the wave, it did not retreat, but lapped on. Was he actually seeing that? Shann could not be sure.

Only the gray light continued to build, faster now, its speed of advance matching its increase in bulk. Shann somehow connected it with the veil of illusion. If it was real, there was a purpose behind it.

There was an aroused clicking from the Throgs. A blaster bolt cracked, its spiteful, sickly yellow slicing into the nearest tongue of gray. But that luminous fog engulfed the blast and was not dispelled. Shann forced his head around against the support which held him. The mist crept across the field from all quarters, walling them in.

Running at the ungainly lope which was their best effort at speed were half a dozen Throgs emerging from the river section. Their attitude suggested panic-stricken flight, and when one tripped on some unseen obstruction and went down—to fall beneath a descending tongue of phosphorescence—he uttered a strange high-pitched squeal, thin and faint, but still a note of complete, mindless terror.

The Throgs surrounding Shann were firing at the fog, first with precision, then raggedly, as their bolts did nothing to cut that opaque curtain drawing in about them. From inside that mist came other sounds—noises, calls, and cries all alien to him, and perhaps also to the Throgs. There were shapes barely to be discerned through the swirls; perhaps some were Throgs in flight. But certainly others were non-Throg in outline. And the Terran was sure that at least three of those shapes, all different, had been in pursuit of one fleeing Throg, heading him off from that small open area still holding about Shann.

For the Throgs were being herded in from all sides— the handful who had come from the river, the others who had brought Shann there. And the action of the mist was pushing them into a tight knot. Would they eventually turn on him, wanting to make sure of their prisoner before they made a last stand against whatever lurked in the fog? To Shann's continued relief the aliens seemed to have forgotten him. Even when one cowered back against the very edge of the frame on which the Terran was bound, the beetle-head did not look at this helpless prey.

They were firing wildly, with desperation in every heavy thrust of bolt. Then one Throg threw down his blaster, raised his arms over his head, and voicing the same high wail uttered by his comrade-in-arms earlier, he ran straight into the mist where a shape materialized, closed in behind him, cutting him off from his fellows.

That break demoralized the others. The Throg commander burned down two of his company with his blaster, but three more broke past him to the fog. One of the remaining party reversed his blaster, swung the stock against the officer's carapace, beating him to his knees, before the attacker raced on into the billows of the mist. Another threw himself on the ground and lay there, pounding his claws against the baked earth. While a remaining two continued with stolid precision to fire at the lurking shapes which could only be half seen; and a third helped the officer to his feet.

The Throg commander reeled back against the frame, his musky body scent filling Shann's nostrils. But he, too, paid no attention to the Terran, though his horny arms scraped across Shann's. Holding both of his claws to his head, he staggered on, to be engulfed by a new arm of the fog.

Then, as if the swallowing of the officer had given the mist a fresh appetite, the wan light waved in a last vast billow over the clear area about the frame. Shann felt its substance cold, slimy, on his skin. This was a deadly breath of un-life.

He was weakened, sapped of strength, so that he hung in his bonds, his head lolling forward on his breast. Warmth pressed against him, a warm wet touch on his cold skin, a sensation of friendly concern in his mind. Shann gasped, found that he was no longer filling his lungs with that chill staleness which was the breath of the fog. He opened his eyes, struggling to raise his head. The gray light had retreated, but though a Throg blaster lay close to his feet, another only a yard beyond, there was no sign of the aliens.

Instead, standing on their hind feet to press against him in a demand for his attention, were the wolverines. And seeing them, Shann dared to believe that the impossible could be true; somehow he was safe.

He spoke. And Taggi and Togi answered with eager whines. The mist was withdrawing more slowly than it had come. Here and there things lay very still on the ground.

"Lantee!"

This time the call came not into his mind but out of the air. Shann made an effort at reply which was close to a croak.

"Over here!"

A new shape in the fog was moving with purpose toward him. Thorvald strode into the open, sighted Shann, and began to run.

"What did they—?" he began.

Shann wanted to laugh, but the sound which issued from his dry throat was very little like mirth. He struggled helplessly until he managed to get out some words which made sense.

" . . . hadn't started in on me yet. You were just in time."

Thorvald loosened the wires which held the younger man to the frame and stood ready to catch him as he slumped forward. And the officer's hold wiped away the last clammy residue of the mist. Though he did not seem able to keep on his feet, Shann's mind was clear.

"What happened?" he demanded.

"The power." Thorvald was examining him hastily but with attention for every cut and bruise. "The beetle-heads didn't really get to work on you—"

"Told you that," Shann said impatiently. "But what brought that fog and got the Throgs?"

Thorvald smiled grimly. The ghostly light was fading as the fog retreated, but Shann could see well enough to note that around the other's neck hung one of the Wyvern disks.

"It was a variation of the veil of illusion. You faced your memories under the influence of that; so did I. But it would seem that the Throgs had ones worse than either of us could produce. You can't play the role of thug all over the galaxy and not store up in the subconscious a fine line of private fears and remembered enemies. We provided the means for releasing those, and they simply raised their own devils to order. Neatest justice ever rendered. It seems that the 'power' has a big kick—in a different way—when a Terran will manages to spark it."

"And you did?"

"I made a small beginning. Also I had the full backing of the Elders, and a general staff of Wyverns in support. In a way I helped to provide a channel for their concentration. Alone they can work 'magic'; with us they can spread out into new fields. Tonight we hunted Throgs as a united team—most successfully."

"But they wouldn't go after the one in the skull."

"No. Direct contact with a Throg mind appears to short-circuit them. I did the contacting; they fed me what I needed. We have the answer to the Throgs now—one answer." Thorvald looked back over the field where those bodies lay so still. "We can kill Throgs. Maybe someday we can learn another trick—how to live with them." He returned abruptly to the present. "You did contact the transport."

Shann explained what had happened in the com dome. "I think when the ship broke contact that way they understood."

"We'll take it that they did, and be on the move." Thorvald helped Shann to his feet. "If a cruiser berths here shortly, I don't propose to be under its tail flames when it sets down."

The cruiser came. And a mop-up squad patrolled outward from the reclaimed camp, picked up two living Throgs, both wandering witlessly. But Shann only heard of that later. He slept, so deep and dreamlessly that when he roused he was momentarily dazed.

A Survey uniform—with a cadet's badges—lay across the wall seat facing his bunk in the barracks he had left . . . how many days or weeks before? The garments fitted well enough, but he removed the insignia to which he was not entitled. When he ventured out he saw half a dozen troopers of the patrol, together with Thorvald, watching the cruiser lift again into the morning sky.

Taggi and Togi, trailing leashes, galloped out of nowhere to hurl themselves at him in uproarious welcome. And Thorvald must have heard their eager whines even through the blast of the ship, for he turned and waved Shann to join him.

"Where is the cruiser going?"

"To punch a Throg base out of this system," Thorvald answered. "They located it—on Witch."

"But we're staying on here?"

Thorvald glanced at him oddly. "There won't be any

settlement now. But we have to establish a conditional embassy post. And the patrol has left a guard."

Embassy post. Shann digested that. Yes, of course, Thorvald, because of his close contact with the Wyverns, would be left here for the present to act as liaison officer-in-charge.

"We don't propose," the other was continuing, "to allow to lapse any contact with the one intelligent alien race we have discovered who can furnish us with full-time partnership to our mutual benefit. And there mustn't be any bungling here!"

Shann nodded. That made sense. As soon as possible Warlock would witness the arrival of another team, one slated this time to the cultivation of an alien friendship and alliance, rather than preparation for Terran colonists. Would they keep him on? He supposed not; the wolverines' usefulness was no longer apparent.

"Don't you know your regulations?" There was a snap in Thorvald's demand which startled Shann. He glanced up, discovered the other surveying him critically. "You're not in uniform—"

"No, sir," he admitted. "I couldn't find my own kit."

"Where are your badges?"

Shann's hand went up to the marks left when he had so carefully ripped off the insignia.

"My badges? I have no rank," he replied, bewildered.

"Every team carries at least one cadet on strength."

Shann flushed. There had been one cadet on this team; why did Thorvald want to remember that?

"Also," the other's voice sounded remote, "there can be appointments made in the field—for cause. Those appointments are left to the discretion of the officer-in-charge, and they are never questioned. I repeat, you are not in uniform, Lantee. You will make the necessary alteration and report to me at headquarters dome. As sole representatives of Terra here we have a matter of protocol to be discussed with our witches, and they have a right to expect punctuality from a pair of warlocks, so get going!"

Shann still stood, staring incredulously at the officer. Then Thorvald's official severity vanished in a smile which was warm and real.

"Get going," he ordered once more, "before I have to log you for inattention to orders."

Shann turned, nearly stumbling over Taggi, and then ran back to the barracks in quest of some very important bits of braid he hoped he could find in a hurry.

ORDEAL IN
OTHERWHERE

I

Charis crouched behind the stump, her thin hands pressed tight to the pain in her side. Her breath came in tearing gasps which jerked her whole body, and her hearing was dimmed by the pounding blood in her ears. It was still too early in the morning to distinguish more than light and dark, shadow and open. Even the blood-red of the spargo stump was gray-black in this predawn. But it was not too dark for her to pick out the markers on the mountain trail.

Though her will and mind were already straining ahead for that climb, her weak body remained here on the edge of the settlement clearing, well within reach—within reach. Charis fought back the panic which she still had wit enough to realize was an enemy. She forced her trembling body to remain in the shadow of the stump, to be governed by her mind and not by the fear which was a fire eating her. Now she could not quite remember when that fear had been born. It had ridden her for days, coming to its full blaze yesterday.

Yesterday! Charis strove to throw off the memory of yesterday, but that, too, she forced herself to face now. Blind panic and running; she dared not give in to either or she was lost. She knew the enemy and she had to fight, but since a trial of physical strength was out of the question, this meant a test of wits.

As she crouched there, striving to rest, she drew upon

memory for any scraps of information which might mean
weapons. The trouble had begun far back; Charis knew a
certain dull wonder at why she had not realized before *how*
far back it had begun. Of course, she and her father had
expected to be greeted by some suspicion—or at least some
wariness when they had joined the colonists just before
takeoff on Varn.

Ander Nordholm had been a government man. He and
his daughter were classed as outsiders and strangers by the
colony group, much as were the other representatives of
law from off-world—the Ranger Franklyn, Post Officer Kaus
and his two guards, the medical officer and his wife. But
every colony had to have an education officer. In the past
too many frontier-world settlements had split away from the
Confederation, following sometimes weird and dangerous
paths of development when fanatics took control, warped
education, and cut off communications with other worlds.

Yes, the Nordholms had expected a period of adjust-
ment, of even semi-ostracization since this was a Believer
colony. But her father had been winning them over—he
had! Charis could not have deceived herself about that.
Why, she had been invited to one of the women's "mend"
parties. Or had it been a blind even then?

But this—this would never have happened if it had not
been for the white death! Charis's breath came now in
a real sob. There were so many shadows of fear on a
newly opened planet. No safeguard could keep them all
from striking at the fragile life of a newly planted colony.
And here had been waiting a death no one could see,
could meet with blaster or hunting knife or even the
medical knowledge her species had been able to amass
during centuries of space travel, experimentation, and
information acquired across the galaxy.

And in its striking, the disease had favored the fanatical
prejudices of the colonists. For it struck first the resented
government men. The ranger, the port captain and his
men, her father—Charis's fist was at her mouth, and she
bit hard upon her knuckles. Then it struck the medic—
always the men. Later the colonists—oddly enough, those
who had been most friendly with the government party—
and only the men and boys in those families.

The ugly things the survivors had said—that the government was behind the plague. They had yelled that when they burned the small hospital. Charis leaned her forehead against the rough stump and tried not to remember that. She had been with Aldith Lasser, the two of them trying to find some meaning in a world which in two weeks had taken husband and father from them and turned their kind into mad people. She would not think of Aldith now; she would not! nor of Visma Unskar screaming horrors when Aldith had saved her baby for her—

Charis's whole body was shaking with spasms she could not control. Demeter had been such a fair world. In the early days after their landing, Charis had gone on two expeditions with the ranger, taking the notes for his reports. That was what they had held against her in the colony—her education, her equality with the government men. So—Charis put her hands against the stump and pulled herself up—so now she had three choices left.

She could return; or she could remain here until the hunt found her—to take her as a slave down to the foul nest they were fast making of the first human settlement on Demeter; or somehow she could reach the mountains and hide out like a wild thing until sooner or later some native peril would finish her. That seemed much the cleaner way to end. Still steadying herself with one hand on the stump, Charis stooped to pick up the small bundle of pitiful remnants she had grubbed out of the ruins of the government domes.

A hunting knife, blackened by fire, was her only weapon. And there were formidable beasts in the mountains. Her tongue moved across dry lips, and there was a dull ache in her middle. She had eaten last when? Last night? A portion of bread, hard and with the mustiness of mold on it, was in the bag. There would be berries in the heights. She could actually see them—yellow, burstingly plump—hanging so heavy on willowy branches that they pulled the boughs groundward. Charis swallowed again, pushed away from the stump, and stumbled on.

Her safety depended upon what the settlers would decide. She had no means of concealing her back trail. In the morning it would be found. But whether their temper would be to follow her, or if they would shruggingly write her off to be finished by the wild, Charis could not guess. She was the one remaining symbol of all Tolskegg preached against—the liberal off-world mind, the "un-female," as he called it. The wild, with every beast Ranger Franklyn had catalogued lined up ready to tear her, was far better than facing again the collection of cabins where Tolskegg now spouted his particular brand of poison, that poison, bred of closed minds, which her father had taught her early to fear. And Visma and her ilk had lapped that poison to grow fat and vigorous on it. Charis weaved on along the trail.

There was no sign of a rising sun, she realized some time later. Instead, clouds were thicker overhead. Charis watched them in dull resignation, awaiting a day of chill, soaking rain. The thickets higher up might give her some protection from the full force of a steady pour, but they would not keep out the cold. Some cave or hole into which she could crawl before full exposure weakened her to the point that she could go no farther—

She tried to remember all the features of this trail. Twice she had been along it—the first time when they had cut the trace, the second time when she had taken the little ones to the spring to show them the wonderful sheaths of red flowers and the small, jeweled, flying lizards that lived among those loops of blossoming vines.

The little ones . . . Charis's cracked lips shaped a grimace. Jonan had thrown the stone which had made the black bruise on her arm. Yet, on that other day, Jonan had stood drinking in the beauty of the flowers.

Little ones and not so little ones. Charis began to reckon how many boys had survived the white death. All the little ones, she realized with some wonder, were still alive—that is, all under twelve years. Of those in their teens, five remained, all representing families who had had least contact with the government group, been the most fanatical in their severance. And of adult men . . . Charis forced herself to recall every distorted face in the mob bent on destruction, every group she had spied upon while hiding out.

Twenty adult men out of a hundred! The women would

go into the fields, but they could not carry on the heavy work of clearing. How long would it take Leader Tolskegg to realize that, in deliberately leading the mob to destroy the off-world equipment, he might also have sentenced all of the remaining colonists to slow death?

Of course, sooner or later, Central Control would investigate. But not for months was any government ship scheduled to set down on Demeter. And by that time the whole colony could be finished. The excuse of an epidemic would cover the activities of any survivors. Tolskegg, if he *were* still alive then, could tell a plausible tale. Charis was sure that the colony leader now believed he and his people were free from the government and that no ship would come, that the Power of their particular belief had planned this so for them.

Charis pushed between branches. The rain began, plastering her hair to her head, streaming in chill trickles down her face, soaking into the torn coat on her shoulders. She stooped under its force, still shivering. If she could only reach the spring. Above that was broken rock where she might find a hole.

But it was harder and harder for her to pull herself up the rising slope. Several times she went down to hands and knees, crawling until she could use a bush or a boulder to pull upright once more. All the world was gray and wet, a sea to swallow one. Charis shook her head with a jerk. It would be so easy to drift into the depths of that sea, to let herself go.

This was real—here and now. She could clutch the bushes, pull herself along. Above was safety; at least, freedom of a sort still undefiled by the settlers. And here was the spring. The curtain of blossoms was gone, seed pods hung in their place. No lizards, but something squat and hairy drank at the pool, a thing with a long muzzle that looked at her from a double set of eyes, coldly, without fear. Charis paused to stare back.

A purple tongue flicked from the snout, lapped at the water in a farewell lick. The creature reared on stumpy hind feet, standing about three feet tall; and Charis recognized it, in this normal pose, as one of the tree-dwelling fruit eaters that depended upon overdeveloped arms and shoulders for a method of progress overhead. She had never seen one on the ground before, but she thought it harmless.

It turned with more speed than its clumsy build suggested and used the vines for a ladder to take it up out of her sight. There was a shrill cry from where it vanished and the sound of more than one body moving away.

Charis squatted by the pool side and drank from her cupped hands. The water was cold enough to numb her palms, and she rubbed them back and forth across the front of her jacket when she was finished, not in any hopes of drying them but to restore circulation. Then Charis struck off to the left where the vegetation gave way to bare rock.

How long it was, that struggle to gain the broken country, Charis could not have told. The effort stripped her of her few remaining rags of energy, and sheer, stubborn will alone kept her crawling to the foot of an outcrop, where a second pillar of stone leaned to touch the larger and so formed a small cup of shelter. She drew her aching body into that and huddled, sobbing with weakness.

The pain which had started under her ribs spread now through her whole body. She drew her knees up to her chest and wrapped her arms about them, resting her chin on one kneecap. For a long moment she was as still as her shaking body would allow her to rest. And it was some time later that she realized chance had provided her with a better hideout than her conscious mind had directed.

From this niche and out of the full drive of the rain, Charis had a relatively unobstructed view of the downslope straight to the field on which their colony ship had first set down. The scars of its braking thrusters were still visible there even after all these months. Beyond, to her right, was the straggle of colony cabins. The dim gray of the storm lessened the range of visibility, but Charis thought she could see a trail or two of smoke rising there.

If Tolskegg was following the usual pattern, he had already herded the majority of the adults into the fields in that race for planting. With the equipment destroyed, it would be a struggle to get the mutated seed in the ground in time for an early harvest. Charis did not move her head. From here the fields were masked by the rounded slope; she could not witness the backbreaking toil in progress there. But if the new ruler of the colony was holding to schedule, she need not fear the trailers would be early on her track—if they came at all.

Her head was heavy on her knee; the need for sleep was almost as great as the ache of hunger. She roused herself to open her bundle and take out the dry bread to gnaw. The taste almost made her choke. If she had only had warning enough to hide some of the trail rations the explorers had used! But by the time she had nursed her father to the end, the main stores had largely been raided or destroyed because of their "evil" sources.

As she chewed the noisome mouthful, Charis watched downtrail. Nothing moved in the portion of the settlement she could see. Whether or not she wanted to, whether or not it was safe, she must rest. And this was the best hole she could find. Perhaps the steady rain would wash away the traces she had left. It was a small hope but all she had left to cling to.

Charis thrust the rest of the bread back into her bundle. Then she strove to wriggle deeper into her half-cave. Spray from the rain striking the rocks reached her in spite of her efforts. But finally she lapsed into quiet, her forehead down on her knees, her only movements the shivers she could not control.

Was it sleep or unconsciousness which held her, and for how long? Charis rose out of a nightmare with a cry, but any sound she made was swallowed up by a roar from outside.

She blinked dazedly at what seemed to be a column of fire reaching from earth to gray, weeping sky. Only for a moment did that last, and then the fire was at ground level, boiling up the very substance of the soil. Charis scrambled forward on hands and knees, shouting but still blanketed by that other sound.

There was a spacer, a slim, scoured shape, pointing nose to sky, the heat of its braking fire making a steam mist about it. But this was no vision—it was real! A spacer had set down by the village!

Charis tottered forward. Tears added to the rain, wet

on her cheeks. There was a ship—help—down there. And it had come too soon for Tolskegg to hide the evidence of what had happened. The burned bubble domes, all the rest—they would be seen; questions would be asked. And she would be there to answer them!

She lost her footing on a patch of sleek clay, and before she could regain her balance, Charis was skidding down, unable to stop her fall. The sick horror lasted for an endless second or two. Then came a sudden shock, bringing pain and blackness.

Rain on her face roused Charis again. She lay with her feet higher than her head, a mass of rubble about her. Panic hit her, the fear that she was trapped or that broken bones would immobilize her, away from the wonderful safety and help of the ship. She must get there—now!

In spite of the pain, she wriggled and struggled out of the debris of the slide, crawled away from it. Somehow she got to her feet. There was no way of telling how long she had lain there and the thought of the ship waiting drove her on to make an effort she could not have faced earlier.

No time to go back to the spring trail—if she could reach it from this point. Better straight down, with the incline of the slope to keep her going in the right direction. She had been almost directly above and behind the landing point when she had sheltered among the rocks. She must have slid in the right direction, so she only had to keep on going that way.

Was it a Patrol ship, Charis wondered as she stumbled on. She tried to remember its outline. It was certainly not a colony transport—it was not rotund enough; nor was it a regulation freighter. So it could only be a Patrol or a government scout landing off-schedule. And its crew would know how to deal with the situation here. Tolskegg might already be under arrest.

Charis forced herself to cut down her first headlong pace. She knew she must not risk another fall, the chance of knocking herself out just when help was so near. No, she wanted to walk in on her own two feet, to be able to tell her story and tell it clearly. Take it slowly: the ship would not lift now.

She could smell the stench of the thruster-burn, see the steam as a murky fog through the trees and brush. Better circle here; it no longer mattered if Tolskegg or his henchmen sighted her. They would be afraid to make any move against her.

Charis wavered out of the brush into the open and started for the village without fear. She would show up on the vistaplates in the ship, and none of the colonists would risk a hostile move under that circumstance.

So—she would stay right here. There was no sign of anyone's coming out of the village. Of course not! They would be trying to work out some plausible story, whining to Tolskegg. Charis faced around toward the ship and waved vigorously, looking for the insignia which would make it Patrol or Scout.

There was none! It took a moment for that fact to make a conscious impression on her mind. Charis had been so sure that the proper markings would be there that she had almost deceived herself into believing that she sighted them. But the spacer bore no device at all. Her arm dropped to her side suddenly as she saw the ship as it really was.

This was not the clean-lined, well-kept spacer of any government service. The sides were space-dust cut, the general proportions somewhere between scout and freighter, with its condition decidedly less than carefully tended. It must be a Free Trader of the second class, maybe even a tramp—one of those plying a none-too-clean trade on the frontier worlds. And the chances were very poor that the commander or crew of such would be lawfully engaged here or would care at all about what happened to the representatives of government they were already aligned against in practice. Charis could hope for no help from such as these.

A port opened and the landing ramp snaked out and down. Somehow Charis pulled herself together, she turned to run. But out of the air spun a rope, jerking tight about her arms and lower chest, pulling her back and off her feet to roll, helplessly entangled, a prisoner. While behind she heard the high-pitched, shrill laughter of Tolskegg's son, one of the five boys who had survived the epidemic.

II

She must keep her wits, she must! Charis sat on the backless bench, her shoulders braced against the log wall, and thought furiously. Tolskegg was there and Bagroof, Sidders, Mazz. She surveyed what now must be the ruling court of the colony. And then, the trader. Her attention kept going back to the man at the end of the table who sat there, nursing a mug of quaffa, eyeing the assembly with a spark of amusement behind the drooping lids of his very bright and wary eyes.

Charis had known some Free Traders. In fact, among that class of explorer-adventurer-merchant her father had had some good friends, men who carried with them a strong desire for knowledge, who had added immeasurably to the information concerning unknown worlds. But those were the aristocrats of their calling. There were others who were scavengers, pirates on occasion, raiders who took instead of bargained when the native traders of an alien race were too weak to stand against superior off-world weapons.

"It is simple, my friend." The trader's insolent tone to Tolskegg must have cut the colonist raw, yet he took it because he must. "You need labor. Your fields are not going to plow, plant, and reap themselves. All right, in freeze I have labor—good hands all of them. I had my pick; not one can't pull his weight, I promise you. There was a flare on Gonwall's sun, they had to evacuate to Sallam, and

Sallam couldn't absorb the excess population. So we were allowed to recruit in the refugee camp. My cargo's prime males—sturdy, young, and all under indefinite contracts. The only trouble is, friend, what do you have to offer in return? Oh—" his hand went up to silence the beginning rumble from Tolskegg. "I beg of you, do not let us have again this talk of furs. Yes, I have seen them, enough to pay for perhaps three of *my* cargo. Your wood does not interest me in the least. I want small things, of less bulk, a money cargo for a fast turnover elsewhere. Your furs for three laborers—unless you have something else to offer."

So that was it! Charis drew a deep breath and knew there was no use in appealing to this captain. If he had shipped desperate men on indefinite labor contracts, he was no better than a slaver, even though there was a small shadow of legality to his business. And his present offer was sheer torment to Tolskegg.

"No native treasures—gems or such?" the captain continued. "Sad that your new world has so few resources to aid you now, friend."

Mazz was pulling at his leader's grimed sleeve, hissing into Tolskegg's ear. The frown on the other's face lightened a little.

"Give us a moment to do some reckoning, captain. We may have something else."

The trader nodded. "All the time you wish, friend. I thought that might move your memories."

Charis tried to think what Mazz had in mind. There was nothing of immediate value to trade, she was sure, save the bundle of pelts the ranger had gathered as specimens. Those had been cured to send off-world as scientific material.

The buzz of whispers among the colonists came to an end and Tolskegg faced about. "You trade in labor. What if we offer you labor in return?"

For the first time, the captain displayed a faint trace of surprise—deliberately, Charis decided. He was too old a hand at any bargaining to show any emotion unless for a purpose.

"Labor? But you are poor in labor. Do you wish to strip yourselves of what few assets you possess?"

"You deal in labor," Tolskegg growled. "And there is more than one kind of labor. Is that not so? We need strong backs, men for our fields. But there are other worlds where they may need women."

Charis stiffened. For the first time she saw more than one reason for her having been dumped here. She had thought it was merely to impress upon her the folly of hoping for any rescue. But this—

"Women?" The captain's surprise grew more open. "You would trade your women?"

Mazz was grinning, a twisted and vicious grin centered on Charis. Mazz still smarted from Ander Nordholm's interference when he had wanted to beat his wife and daughter into the fields.

"Some women," Mazz said. "Her—"

Charis had been aware that the trader had pointedly ignored her from his entrance into the cabin. To interfere in the internal affairs of any colony was against trading policy. To the captain, a girl with her arms tied behind her back, her feet pinioned, was a matter involving the settlement and not his concern. But now he accepted Mazz's statement as an excuse for giving her a measuring stare. Then he laughed.

"And of what possible value is this one? A child, a reed to break if you set her to any useful labor."

"She is older than she looks and has the learning of books," Tolskegg retorted. "She was a teacher of useless knowledge, and speaks more than one tongue. On some worlds such are useful or deemed so by the fools that live there."

"Who are you, then?" The captain spoke to her directly.

Was this a chance? Could she persuade him to take her, hoping to contact authority off-world and so obtain her freedom?

"Charis Nordholm. My father was education officer here."

"So? Oh, daughter of a learned one, what has chanced in this place?" He had slipped from Basic into the sibilant Zacathan tongue. She answered him readily in the same language.

"First, winged one, a sickness, and then the blight of ignorance."

Tolskegg's great fist struck the table with a drum thud. "Speak words we can understand!"

The captain smiled. "You have claimed for this child knowledge. I have the right to decide whether that knowledge makes her worth my buying. In the water of the north there are splinters of ice." Again he used one of the Five Tongues—that of Danther.

"But the winds of the south melt them swiftly." Charis replied to that code address almost mechanically.

"I say—speak what a man can understand. She has learning, this one. She is useless to us here. But to you she is worth at least another laborer!"

"How say you, Gentle Fem?" The trader addressed Charis. "Do you deem yourself worth a man?"

For the first time the girl allowed herself a thrust in return. "I am worth several of some!"

The captain laughed. "Well said. And if I take you, will you sign an indefinite contract?"

For a long moment Charis stared at him, her small spark of hope crushed before it had time to warm her. As her eyes met his, she knew the truth—he was not really an escape at all. This man would not take her from Demeter to someone in authority. Any bargain would be made on his terms, and those terms would bind her on almost every planet he would visit. With a labor cargo he would set down only on those worlds where such a shipment would be welcome and legal. With an indefinite contract to bind her, she could not appeal for freedom.

"That is slavery," she said.

"Not so." But his smile held almost as much malice as Mazz's grin. "To every contract there comes an end in time. Of course, you need not sign, Gentle Fem. You may remain here—if that is your wish."

"We trade her!" Tolskegg had followed this exchange with growing exasperation. "She is not one of us, nor our kind. We trade her!"

The captain's smile grew broader. "It would seem, Gentle Fem, that you have little choice. I do not think that this world will be very kind to you under the circumstances if you remain."

Charis knew he was right. Left to Tolskegg and the rest, their hatred of her the hotter for losing out on what they thought was a bargain, she would be truly lost. She drew a ragged breath; the choice was already made.

"I'll sign," she said dully.

The captain nodded. "I thought you would. You are in full possession of your senses. You—" he pointed to Mazz, "loose the Gentle Fem!"

"Already once she has run to the woods," Tolskegg objected. "Let her remain bound if you wish to control her. She is a demon's daughter and full of sin."

"I do not think she will run. And since she is about to become marketable property, I have a voice in this matter. Loose her now!"

Charis sat rubbing her wrists after the cords were cut. The captain was right—her strength and energy were gone; she could not make a break for freedom now. Since the trader had tested her education to a small degree, it was possible that learning *was* a marketable commodity for which he already foresaw profit. And to be off-world, away from Demeter, would be a small measure of freedom in itself.

"You present a problem." The captain spoke to her again. "There is no processing station here, and we cannot ship you out in freeze—"

Charis shivered. Most labor ships stacked their cargo in the freeze of suspended animation, thus saving room, supplies, all the needs of regular passengers. Space on board a trader ship was strictly limited.

"Since we lift without much cargo," he continued, "you'll bunk in the strong room. And now—what's the matter—are you sick?"

She had striven to rise, only to have the room whirl about her with a sickening lurch of floor and ceiling.

"Hungry." Charis clutched at the nearest hold, the arm the captain had put out involuntarily when she swayed.

"Well, that can be remedied easily enough."

Charis remembered little of how she got to the spacer. She was most aware of a cup pushed into her hands, warm to her cold palms, and the odor which rose from it. Somehow she managed to get the container to her lips and drink. It was a thick soup, savory, though she could not identify any of its contents. When she had finished, she settled back on the bunk and looked about the room.

Each Free Trader had a cabin with extra security devices intended to house particularly rich, small cargo. The series of cupboards and drawers about her were plainly marked with thumbprint locks which only the captain and his most trusted officers could open. And the bunk on which she sat was for a port-side guard when such were needed.

So she, Charis Nordholm, was no longer a person but valuable cargo. But she was tired, too tired to worry, to even think, about the future. She was tired—

The vibration of the walls, the bunk under her, were a part of her body, too. She tried to move and could not; panic caught at her until she saw that the webbing of the take-off belts laced her in. Thankful, Charis touched the release button and sat up. They were off-planet, headed toward what new port of call? She almost did not want to know.

Since there was no recording of time in the treasure cabin, Charis could portion hours, days, only by the clicking of the tray which brought her food through a hatch at intervals—long intervals, for the food was mostly the low-bulk, high-energy tablets of emergency rations. She saw no one and the door did not open. She might have been imprisoned in an empty ship.

At first Charis welcomed the privacy, feeling secure in it. She slept a lot, slowly regaining the strength which had been drained from her during those last weeks on Demeter. Then she became bored and restless. The drawers and cupboards attracted her, but those she could open were empty. At the fifth meal-period there was a small packet beside her rations, and Charis opened it eagerly to find a reader with a tape threaded through it.

Surprisingly enough, the tape proved to be one of the long epic poems of the sea world of Kraken. She read it often enough to commit long passages to heart, but it spurred her imagination to spin fantasies of her own which broke up the dull apathy induced by her surroundings. And always she could speculate about the future and what it might hold.

The captain—odd that she had never heard his name—
had hers now, along with her thumbprint, on his contract.
She was signed and sealed to a future someone else would
direct. But always she could hope that chance would take
her where she could appeal for aid and freedom. And
Charis was very sure now that a future off-world would
be better than any on Demeter.

She was reciting aloud her favorite passage from the
saga when a loud clang, resounding from the walls of the
cabin, sent her flat on the bunk, snapping the webbing
in place. The spacer was setting down. Was this the end
of the trip for her or just a way stop? She endured the
pressure of planeting and lay waiting for the answer.

Though the ship must be in port, no one came to free
her, and as the moments passed she grew impatient, pacing back and forth in the cabin, listening for any sound.
But, save that the vibration had ceased, they could as well
have been in space.

Charis wanted to pound the door, scream her desire
to be out of what was now not a place of security but a
cage. By stern effort she controlled that impulse. Where
were they now? What was happening? How long would
this continue—this being sealed away? Lacing her fingers
tightly together, she went back to the bunk, willed herself to sit there with an outward semblance of patience.
She might be able to communicate through the ration
hatch if this went on.

She was still sitting when the door opened. The captain stood there with a bundle under his arm which he
tossed to the bunk beside her.

"Get into this." He nodded curtly at the bundle. "Then
come!"

Charis pulled at the fastening of the bundle to unroll
a coverall uniform, the kind worn by spacemen off duty.
It was clean and close enough to her size to fit if she rolled
up the sleeves and pants legs. She changed in the pocket-
sized refresher of the cabin, glad to discard her soiled and
torn Demeter clothing. But she had to keep her scuffed
and worn boots. Her hair was shoulder-length now, its light
brown strands fair against her tanned skin, curling up a little
at the ends. Charis drew it back to tie with a strip of cloth,

forming a bobbing tail at the back of her head. There was no need to consult any mirror; she was no beauty by the standards of her race and never had been. Her mouth was too wide, her cheekbones too clearly defined, and her eyes—a pale gray—too colorless. She was of Terran stock, of middle height which made her taller than some of the mutated males, and altogether undistinguished.

But she was feminine enough to devote several seconds making sure the coverall fitted as well as she could manage and that she made the best appearance possible under the circumstances. Then, a little warily, she tried the door, found it open, and stepped out onto the level landing.

The captain was already on the ladder; only his head and shoulders were in sight. He beckoned impatiently to her. She followed him down for three levels until they came to the open hatch from which sprang the door ramp.

Outside was a glare of sunlight which made Charis blink and raise her hands to shield her eyes. The captain caught her elbow and steered her ahead into a harsh warmth, desert-like in its baking heat. And as her eyes adjusted she saw that they had indeed set down in a wasteland.

Sand, which was a uniform red outside the glassy slag left by the thruster blast, lapped out to the foot of a range of small hills, the outline of which shimmered in heat waves. There was no sign of any building, no look of a port, save for the countless slag scars which pecked and pitted the surface of the desert sand, evidence of many landings and take-offs.

There were ships—two, three, a fourth farther away. And all of them, Charis saw, were of the same type as the one she had just left, second- and third-class traders. This seemed to be a rendezvous for fringe merchants.

The captain's hold on her arm left Charis no time to examine her surroundings more closely; he was pulling rather than guiding her to the next ship, a twin to his own. And a man, with an officer's winged cap but no uniform except nondescript coveralls, stood waiting for them at the foot of the ramp.

He stared at Charis intently as she and the captain approached. But the stare was impersonal, as if she were not a woman or even a human being at all, but a new tool of which the stranger was not quite sure.

"Here she is." The captain brought Charis to a stop before the strange officer.

His stare held for a moment and then he nodded and turned to go up the ramp. The other two followed. Once inside the ship, Charis, sandwiched between the two men, climbed the core ladder up to the level of the commander's cabin. There he signaled for her to sit at a swing-down desk, pushed a reader before her.

What followed was, Charis discovered, an examination into her ability to keep accounts, her knowledge of X-tee contact procedures, and the like. In some fields she was very ignorant, but in others she appeared to satisfy her questioner.

"She'll do." The stranger was very sparing of words.

Do for what? The question was on the tip of Charis's tongue when the stranger saw fit to enlighten her.

"I'm Jagan, Free Trader, and I've a temporary permit for a world named Warlock. Heard of it?"

Charis shook her head. There were too many worlds; one could never keep up with their listing.

"Probably not—back of beyond," Jagan had already added. "Well, the natives have an unusual system. Their females rule, make all off-world contacts; and they don't like to deal with males, even strangers like us. So we have to have a woman to palaver with them. You know some X-tee stuff and you've enough education to keep the books. We'll put you at the post, and then they'll trade. I'm buying your contract, and that's that. Got it, girl?"

He did not wait for her to answer, but waved her away from the desk. She backed against the cabin wall and watched him thumbprint the document which transferred her future into his keeping.

Warlock—another world—unsettled by human beings except at a trading post. Charis considered the situation. Such trading posts were visited at intervals by officials. She might have a chance to plead her case before such an inspector.

Warlock— She began to wonder about that planet and what might await her there.

III

"It's simple. You discover what they want and give it to them for as near your price as you can get." Jagan sat at the wall desk, Charis on a second pull-seat by the wall. But the captain was not looking at her; he was staring at the cabin wall as if the answer to some dilemma was scratched there as deeply as a blaster ray could burn it. "They have what we want. Look here—" He pulled out a strip of material as long as Charis's forearm and as wide as her palm.

It was fabric of some type, a pleasant green color with an odd shimmer to its surface. And it slipped through her fingers with a caressing softness. Also, she discovered, it could be creased and folded into an amazingly small compass, yet would shake out completely unwrinkled.

"That's waterproof," Jagan said. "They make it. Of what we don't know."

"For their clothing?" Charis was entranced. This had the soft beauty of the fabulously expensive Askra spider silk.

"No, this fabric is used commonly to package things— bags and such. The Warlockians don't wear clothing. They live in the sea as far as we know. And that's the only thing we've been able to trade out of them so far. We can't get to them—" He scowled, flipping record tapes about the top of the desk. "This is our chance, the big one, the one every trader dreams of having someday—a permit on a

newly opened world. Make this spin right and it means—"
His voice trailed off, but Charis understood him.

Trading empires, fortunes, were made from just such
chances. To get at the first trade of a new world *was* a
dream of good luck. But she was still puzzled as to how
Jagan had achieved the permit for Warlock. Surely one
of the big Companies would have made contact with
Survey and bid in the rights to establish the first post.
Such plums were not for the fringe men. But it was hardly
tactful under the circumstances to ask Jagan how he had
accomplished the nigh to impossible.

She had been spending a certain period of each
ship's day with Jagan, going over the tapes he considered necessary for her briefing. And Charis had, after
her first instruction hour, realized that to Jagan she was
not a person at all, but a key with which he might
unlock the mysteriously shut door of Warlockian trade.
Oddly enough, while the captain supplied her with a
wealth of information about his goods, the need for
certain prices and profits, the mechanics of trading with
aliens, he seemed to have very little to say about the
natives themselves, save that they were strongly matriarchal in their beliefs, holding males in contempt. And
they had been wary of the post after a first curious
interest in it.

Jagan was singularly evasive over why the first contact had failed so thoroughly. And Charis, treading warily,
dared not ask too many questions. This was like forsaking
a well-worn road for a wilderness. She still had a little
knowledge to guide her, but she had to pick a new path,
using all her intuition.

"They have something else." Jagan came out of the
thoughtful silence into which he had retreated. "It's a
tool, a power. They travel by it." He rubbed one hand
across his square chin and looked at Charis oddly as if
daring her to take his words lightly. "They can vanish!"

"Vanish?" She tried to be encouraging. Every bit of
information she could gain she must have.

"I saw it." His voice sank to a mumble. "She was right
there—" one finger stabbed at the corner of the cabin,
"and then—" He shook his head. "Just—just gone! They

work it some way. Get us the secret of how they do that and we won't need anything else."

Charis knew that Jagan believed in the truth of what he had seen. And aliens *had* secrets. She was beginning to look forward to Warlock more than for just a chance of being free of this spacer.

But when they did planet, she was not so certain once again. The sky of mid-afternoon was amber, pure gold in places. The ship had set down among rough cliffs of red and black which shelved or broke abruptly to the green sea. Except for that sea and the sky, Warlock appeared a somber world of dark earth, a world which, to Charis, repelled rather than invited the coming of her species.

On Demeter the foliage had been a light, bright green, with hints of yellow along stem or leaf edge. Here it held a purple overcast, as if it were eternally night-shadowed even in the full sun of day.

Charis had welcomed and fiercely longed for the fresh air of the open, untainted by spacer use. But after her first tasting of that pleasure, she was more aware of a chill, a certain repulsion. Yet the breeze from the sea was no more than fresh; the few odors it bore, while perhaps strange, were not offensive in any way.

There was no settlement, no indication except for slag scars, that any spacer had set down here before. She followed Jagan down the ramp, away from the thruster steam, to the edge of a cliff drop, for they had landed on a plateau well above sea level. Below was an inlet running like a sharp sword thrust of sea into the land. And at its innermost tip bubbled the dome of the post, a gray dome of quickly hardened plasta-skin—the usual temporary structure on a frontier planet.

"There she is." Jagan nodded. But it seemed to Charis that he was in no hurry to approach his gate to fortune. She stood there, the breeze tugging at her hair and the coveralls they had given her. Demeter had been a frontier world, alien, but until after the white death had struck it had seemed open, willing to welcome her kind. Was that because it had had no native race? Or because its very combination of natural features, of sights, sounds, smells, had been more attuned to Terran stock? Charis had only begun to assess what made that difference, trying to explore the emotions this first meeting with Warlock aroused in her, when Jagan moved.

He lifted a hand to summon her on and led the way down a switchback trail cut into the native rock by blaster fire. Behind she could hear the voices of his crew as they formed a line of men to descend.

The foliage had been thinned about the post, leaving a wide space of bare, blue soil and gray sand ringing the bubble, an elementary defense precaution. Charis caught the scent of perfume, looked into a bush where small lavender-pink balls bobbed and swung with the wind's touch. That was the first light and delicate thing she had seen in this rugged landscape.

Now that she was on a level with the post, she saw that the dome was larger than it looked from above. Its surface was unbroken by any windows; visa-screens within would be set to pick up what registered on sensitive patches of the walls. But at the seaward end there was the outline of a door. Jagan fronted that and Charis, alert to any change in the trader's attitude, was sure he was puzzled. But his pause was only momentary. He strode forward and slapped his palm against the door as if in irritation.

The portal split open and they were inside the large foreroom. Charis looked about her. There was a long table, really only a flat surface mounted on easily assembled pipelegs. A set of shelves, put together in a like manner and now occupied by a mass of trade goods, followed the curve of the dome wall along, flanking the door, and added to the portion cutting this first chamber off from the rest.

There was a second door midway of that inner wall; the man who stood there must be Gellir, Jagan's cargomaster and now post keeper. He had the deep tan of a space man, but his narrow face, with its sharp jet of chin and nose, bore signs of fatigue. There were lines bracketing his lips, dark smudges under his eyes. He was a man who was under a strain, Charis thought. And he carried a stunner, not holstered at his belt as all the crew wore them when planetside, but free in his hand, as if he expected not his captain but some danger he was not sure he could meet.

"You made it." His greeting was a flat statement of fact. Then he sighted Charis and his expression tightened into one that she thought, with surprise, was a mingling of fear and repulsion. "Why—" He stopped, perhaps at some signal from Jagan the girl had not seen.

"Through here," the captain spoke to her quickly. She was almost pushed past Gellir into a passage so narrow that the shoulders of her escort brushed the plasta walls. He took her to the end of that way where the dome began to curve down overhead and then opened another door. "In here," he ordered curtly.

Charis went in, but as she turned, the door was already shut. Somehow she knew that if she tried to separate it by palm pressure, it would be locked.

With growing apprehension Charis looked about the room. There was a folding cot against the slope of the wall—she would have to move carefully to fit in under that curve. A stall fresher occupied a considerable space in the room where the roof was higher. For the rest, there was a snap-down table and a pull-out seat to fit beneath it and, at the foot of the cot, a box she guessed was to hold personal possessions.

More like a cell than living quarters in its design to conserve space. But, she thought, probably equal to any within the post. She wondered how big a staff Jagan thought necessary to keep here. Gellir had been in charge while the captain was off-world, and he could have been alone, a situation which would cause him to be jumpy under the circumstances. Normally a spacer of the Free Trader class would carry—Charis reckoned what she did know about such ships—normally a captain, cargomaster, assistant pilot-navigator, engineer and his assistant, a jet man, a medico, a cook—perhaps an assistant cargomaster. But that was a fully staffed ship, not a fringe tramp. She thought there had been four men on board beside Jagan.

Think things out, assemble your information before you act. Ander Nordholm had been a systematic thinker and his training still held in the odd turn her life had taken. Charis pulled out the seat and folded her hands on the table surface as she sat down to follow her father's way of facing a problem.

If she only knew more about Jagan! That he was desperately intent upon this project she could understand.
Success meant a great deal for a fringe tramp; the
establishment of a post on a newly opened planet was a
huge step up. But—how had one on the ragged edge of
respectability gotten the franchise for such a post in the
beginning? Or—Charis considered a new thought—or had
Jagan broken in here without a license? Suppose, just
suppose, he had seen the chance to land well away from
any government base, start trading. Then, when he was
located by a Patrol from whatever headquarters did exist
on Warlock, he could present an established fact. With
the trade going, he could pay his fine and be left alone,
because the situation could be so delicate locally that the
legal representatives would not want the natives to have
any hint of dissension between two off-world groups.

Then a time lapse in establishing proper contact with
the aliens *would* goad Jagan into action. He would have
to take any short cut, make any move he could devise,
to get started. So, he needed her—

But that meeting on the desert of the unknown world
where she had been traded from the labor ship to Jagan—
what was that place and why had Jagan been there? Just
to pick her up—or some other woman? An illegal meeting
place where traders in contraband exchanged cargoes—
of that she was sure. Smugglers operated all over space.
A regular stop for the labor ship and Jagan was there,
waiting on the chance of their carrying a woman for sale?

Which meant she had been taken by an illegal trader.
Charis smiled slowly; she could be lucky because this trade
had gone through. Somewhere on Warlock there was a
government base where all contacts between off-worlders
and natives were supervised. If she could reach that base
and protest an illegal contract, she might be free even
with Jagan holding her signature and thumbprint against
her!

For the time being she would go along with Jagan's
trading plans. Only—if the captain were working against
time—Suddenly Charis felt as cold as she had when
crouched on the Demeter mountainside. She was only a
tool for Jagan; let that tool fail and . . .

She took an iron grip on herself, fought the cold inside her which was a gathering storm to send her beating at the door of what might be a trap. Her hands were palm-down on the table, their flesh wet. Charis strove to master the sickness in her middle and then she heard movements. Not in this cell—no—but beyond its wall.

A pounding—now heavy, now hardly more than a tapping—at irregular intervals. She was straining to hear more when the sound of metallic space-boot plates clicking against the flooring made her tense. Coming here?

She slipped sidewise on the seat to face the door. But that did not open. Instead, she heard another sound from beyond the wall—a thin mewling, animal-like, yet more frightening than any beast's cry. A human voice—low; Charis could not make out any words, just a man's tone close to the level of a whisper.

Now the sound of footsteps just without her own door. Charis sat very still, willing herself into what she hoped was the outer semblance of calm. Not Jagan entered as the door split open, but one of the crew she did not recognize. In one hand he carried a sack-bag such as the crew used for personal belongings, which he tossed in the general direction of her cot. In the other, he balanced a sealed, hot ration tray which he slid on to the table before her. The room was so small he need hardly step inside the door to rid himself of both burdens.

Charis was ready to speak, but the expression on his face was forbidding and his movements were those of a man in a hurry. He was back and gone, the door sealed behind him before she could ask a question.

A finger-tip pressure released the lid of the tray and Charis savored the fragrance of stew, hot quaffa. She made a quick business of eating, and her plate was cleared before she heard more sounds. Not the thumping this time but a low cry which was not quite a moan.

As suddenly as that plaint began, it stopped and there was silence. A prisoner? A member of the crew ill? Charis's imagination could supply several answers, but imagination was not to be relied upon.

As the silence continued, Charis rose to investigate the bag on the cot. Jagan or someone had made a selection of trade goods, for the articles which spilled out were items intended to catch the eye of an alien or primitive. Charis found a comb with the back set in a fanciful pattern of bits of crystal; a mirror adorned to match; a box containing highly scented soap powder, the too strong perfume of which made her sniff in fastidious disgust. There were several lengths of cloth in bright colors; a small hand-sew kit; three pairs of ornamented sandals in different sizes for a fitting choice; a robe, which was too short and too wide, of a violent blue with a flashy pattern of oblak birds painted on it.

Apparently the captain wished her to present a more feminine appearance than she now made wearing the coveralls. Which was logical considering her duties here—that she register as a woman with the natives.

Suddenly Charis yielded to the desire to be just that again—a woman. The colonists of Demeter had been a puritanical sect with strong feelings concerning the wrongness of frivolous feminine clothing. Suiting themselves outwardly as well as they could to the people they must live among, all members of the government party not generally in uniform had adapted to the clumsy, drab clothing the sect believed fitting. Such colors as now spilled across the cot had been denied Charis for almost two years. While they were not the ones she would have chosen for herself, she reached out to stroke their brightness with an odd lightening of spirit.

There were no patterns by which to cut, but she thought she had skill enough to put together a straight robe and skirt, a very modified version of the colony clothing. The yellow went with the green in not too glaring a combination. And one pair of sandals did fit.

Charis set out the toilet articles on the table, piled the material and the robe on the chair. Of course, they must have brought her the least attractive and cheapest of their supplies. But still—she remembered the strip of native material Jagan had shown her. The color of that was far better than any of these garish fabrics. Someone who used that regularly would not be attracted by what she had here. Perhaps that was one of the points which had defeated Jagan so far; his wares were not fitted to the taste of his customers. But surely the captain was no amateur; he would know that for himself.

No—definitely she would not combine the yellow with the green after all. One color alone and, if there was not enough material, Jagan would have to give her the run of his shelves to make a better selection. If she was going to represent her race before alien females, she must appear at her best.

Charis measured the length of green against her body. Another modification of the cut she had planned might do it.

"Pretty—pretty—"

She swung around. That sibilant whisper was so startling that Charis was badly shaken. The figure in the slit of the opened door whipped through and drew the portal tight shut behind her as she stood, facing Charis, her back to the door, her lips stretched in a frightening caricature of a smile.

IV

The newcomer was of a height with Charis so they could match eye to eye as they stood there, Charis gripping the fabric length tightly with both hands, the other woman continuing to laugh in a way which was worse than any scream. She must have been plump once, for her skin was loose in pouches and wrinkles on her face and in flabby flaps on her arms. Her black hair hung in lank, greasy strings about her wrinkled neck to her hunched shoulders.

"Pretty." She reached out crooked fingers and Charis instinctively retreated, but not until those crooked nails caught in the material and jerked at it viciously.

The stranger's own garments were a bundle of stuffs—a gaudy robe much like the one Charis had been given, pulled on crookedly over a tunic of another and clashing shade. And she wore the heavy, metal-plated boots of a space man.

"Who are you?" Charis demanded. Oddly enough, something in her tone appeared to awaken a dim flash of reason in the other.

"Sheeha," she replied as simply as a child. "Pretty." Her attention returned again to the fabric. "Want—" she snatched, ripping the length from Charis's grasp. "Not to the snakes—not give to the snakes!" Her lips drew flat across her teeth in an ugly way and she retreated until her shoulders were once more set against the door panel,

214

the material now wreathed and twisted in her own claw hands.

"The snakes won't get this pretty?" she announced. "Even if they dream. No—not even if they dream . . ."

Charis was afraid to move. Sheeha had crossed the border well into a country for which there was no map of any sane devising.

"They have dreamed," Sheeha's croak of a voice was crooning, "so many times they have dreamed—calling Sheeha. But she did not go, not to the snakes, no!" Her locks of hair bobbed as she shook her head vigorously. "Never did she go. Don't you go—never—not to the snakes."

She was busy thrusting the material she had balled into a wad into a bag in her robe. Now she looked beyond Charis at the blue robe on the cot, reaching out for that, also.

"Pretty—not for the snakes—no!"

Charis snatched the garment up and pushed it into that clawing hand.

"For Sheeha—not the snakes," she agreed, trying to keep her fear from showing.

Again the woman nodded. But this time as she took the robe, she caught at Charis with her other hand, linking fingers tight about the girl's wrist. Charis was afraid to struggle. But the touch of the other's dry, burning skin against her own made her flesh shrink, and a shudder ran through her.

"Come!" Sheeha ordered. "Snakes will get nothing. We shall make sure."

She jerked Charis toward her as she swung around. The door-slit opened and Sheeha pulled the unresisting girl out into the corridor. Dared she call for help? Charis wondered. But the grasp on her wrist, the strength the other displayed, was a warning against centering Sheeha's attention on her.

As far as Charis could see, the trading post was deserted save for the two of them. The doors along the hall were shut, but that to the store was open and the light there beckoned them on. It must be early evening. Was Sheeha going out into the night? Charis, remembering the broken country about the perimeter of the post, had hopes of escape there if she could break the hold the other had on her.

But it appeared that Sheeha was bound no farther than the outer room where the shelves were crowded with the trade wares. As her eyes settled on that wealth of miscellaneous goods, she did drop her hold on Charis.

"Not to the snakes!"

She had moved down the corridor at a rapid shuffle, as if the weight of the space boots had been a handicap. But now she fairly sprang at the nearest shelf on which stood rows of small glass bottles, sweeping her arms along to send them smashing to the floor. A cloud of overpowering and mingled scents arose. Not content with clearing them from the shelves, Sheeha was now stamping on the shards which survived the first crash, her cry of "Not to the snakes!" becoming a chant.

"Sheeha!"

She had finished with the bottles and was now grabbing at rolls of materials, tearing at the stuff with her claws. But her first assault had brought a response from the owner of the post. Charis was brushed aside with a force which sent her back against the long table as Jagan burst in from the corridor and hurled himself at the frantic woman, his arms clamping hers tight to her body though she threshed and fought in his grasp, her teeth snapping as her head turned back and forth trying for a wolfish-fang grip on her captor. She was screaming, high, harsh, and totally without mind.

Two more men came on the run, one from outside, the other—whom Charis recognized as the one who had brought her the food—from the corridor. But it took all three of them to control Sheeha.

She cried as they looped a length of unrolled fabric about her, imprisoning her arms against her body, making her into a package.

"The dreams—not the dreams—not the snakes!" The words broke from her as a plea.

Charis was surprised to see the emotion on Jagan's face. His hands rested gently on Sheeha's shoulders as he turned her around to face, not the interior corridor of the post but the outer door.

"She goes to the ship," he said. "Maybe there . . ." He did not complete that sentence but, steering the woman before him, he went out into the night.

The overwhelming odors of the spilt perfumes were thick enough to make Charis sneeze. Trails of trade fabrics cascaded down from the second shelf Sheeha had striven to clean off. Mechanically Charis went over to loop the material up from the mess on the floor, circling about the glass shards which were still visible in the powder Sheeha's boots had ground.

"You—" She glanced up as the man by the table spoke. "You'd better go back now."

Charis obeyed, glad to be out of the wreckage. She was shivering as she sat down upon her cot once again, trying to understand what had happened. Jagan said he needed a woman to contact the natives. But before Charis's coming there had already been a woman here— Sheeha. And that Sheeha was to the captain something more than a tool Charis was sure, having watched his handling of her frenzy.

The snakes—the dreams? What had moved Sheeha to her wild talk and acts? Charis's own first impression of Warlock, that it was not a world to welcome her kind— was that the truth and not just a semiconscious, emotional reaction to certain landscape coloring? What *was* happening here?

She could go out, demand an explanation. But Charis discovered that her will this time was not strong enough to make her cross that threshold again. And when she did try the door and found she could not open it, she sighed in relief. In this small cell she felt safe; she could see every inch of it and know she was alone.

The light from the glow-track running along the ceiling of the bubble was growing dimmer. Charis deduced they were slacking power for the night. She curled up on the cot. Odd. Why was she so sleepy all at once? There was a flicker of alarm at her realization of that oddness. Then . . .

Light again, all around her. Charis was aware of that light even though her eyes were closed. Light and warmth. Then came the desire to know from whence they reached her. She opened her eyes and looked up into a serene, golden sky. *Golden* sky? She had seen a golden sky— where? When? A part of her pushed away memory. It was good to lie here under the gold of the sky. She had not rested so, uncaring, for a long, long time.

A tickle at her toes, a lapping about her ankles, up around her calves. Charis stirred, used her elbows to prop herself up. She lay in warm, gray sand in which there were small, glittering points of red, blue, yellow, green. Her body was bare, but she felt no need for any clothing; the warmth was covering of a sort. And she lay on the very verge of a green sea with its foremost wavelets lapping gently at her feet and legs. A green sea . . . As with the golden sky, that triggered memory, memory which some-thing within her feared and fought.

She was languorous, relaxed, happy—if this freedom could be called happiness. This was right! Life should always be a clear gold sky, a green sea, jeweled sand, warmth, no memories—just here and now!

Save for the kiss and go of the waves there was no movement. Then Charis wanted more than this flaccid content and sat up. She turned her head to find that she was in a pocket of rock with a steep red cliff behind and about her and, seemingly, no path out. Yet that did not disturb her in the least. With her fingers she idly shifted the sand, blinking at the winks of color. The water was washing higher, up to her knees now, but she had no wish to withdraw from its warm caress.

Then—all the languor, the content, vanished. She was not afraid, but aware. Aware of what? one part of her awakening mind demanded. Of what? Of—of an intelli-gence, another awareness. She scrambled up from the sand which had hollowed about her body and stood, this time giving the rock walls about her a closer examina-tion. But there was nothing there, nothing save herself stood alive in this pocket cup of rock and sand.

Charis looked to the sea. Surely there—right there— was a troubling of the water. Something was emerging, coming to her. And she . . .

Charis gasped, gasped as if the air could not readily fill too empty lungs. She was on her back, and it was no longer gold day but dim pale night about her. To her right was the curve of the bubble wall. She could barely make it out, but her outflung hand proved it solid and real. But—that sand had also been real as it had shifted between her fingers. The soft lap of the sea water, the sun and air on her skin? They, too, had been real.

A dream—more vivid and substantial than any she had ever known before? But dreams were broken bits of things, like the shards Sheeha had left on the floor of the trade room. And this had not been broken, contained nothing which did not fit. That awareness at the end, that belief that there was something rising from the sea to meet her?

Was it that which had broken the dream pattern, brought her awake and into that frightening sense, for a fraction of a second, that she was drowning—not in the sea which had welcomed and caressed her but in something which now lay between the realization of that sea and this room?

Charis wriggled off the cot and padded to the seat by the table. She was excited, experiencing the sensation which she had known when she anticipated some pleasure yet to come. Would a second try at sleep return her to the sea, the sand, the place in space and time where something—or someone—awaited her?

But the sensation of well-being which she had brought with her from the dream, if dream it had been, was seeping away. In its place flowed the same vague discomfort and repugnance which had claimed her from her first leaving the spacer. Charis found herself listening, as it seemed, not only with her ears but with every part of her.

No sound at all. Without knowing exactly why, she went to the door. There was still light from the roof, dimmed to twilight but enough to see her way around. Charis set her hands on either side of the slit and applied pressure. And the portal opened, allowing her to look down the corridor.

This time she faced no string of closed doors; they all gaped open. Again she listened, trying to still her own breathing. What did she expect to hear? A murmur of

voices, the sound of some sleeper's heavy intake and
expulsion of air? But there was nothing at all.

Earlier her room had seemed a haven of safety, the
only security she could hope to find. Now she was not
so sure, just as she could not put name to the intangible
atmosphere which made her translate her growing uneasiness into action she could not have assayed before.

Charis started down the hall. Her bare feet made no
sound on the floor which was too chill as she paused at
the first door. That was open wide enough to show her
another cot—empty, just as the room was empty. The
second room, more sleeping quarters without a sleeper.
A third room with the same deserted bareness. But the
fourth room was different. Even by this dim light she
could make out one promising feature, a com visa-screen
against the far wall. There was a table here, two chairs,
a pile of record tapes. Ugly, distorted—

She was startled into immobility. It was almost as if
she had seen this room and its furnishings through eyes
which measured and disdained it and all it stood for. But
that odd disorientation had been only a flash, the visa-
screen drew her. It was undoubtedly set there to be a
link between a planeting ship and the post. But, too, it
might just furnish her with a key to freedom. Somewhere
on Warlock there was a government base. And this com
could pick up that station, would pick it up if she had
the patience and time to make a sweep-beam search.
Patience she could produce; time was another matter.
Where were the traders? All back to the spacer for some
reason? But why?

Where earlier she had crept, now Charis sped, making the round of the post: the sleeping rooms—all empty;
the cook unit with its smell of recently heated rations and
quaffa still lingering but otherwise closed tight; the larger
outer room, where the smashed glass had been brushed
into a pile and then left, where one strip of tangled and
creased material still fluttered from a hastily wrapped roll;
back to the com room. She was alone in the post. Why
and for how long she could not tell, but for the moment
she *was* alone.

Now it was a matter of time, luck, and distance. She

could operate the sweep, set its probe going to pick up
any other com-beam within a good portion of planet
surface. If this was the middle of a Warlockian night, there
might be no one on duty at the government base com.
Still she could set a message to be picked up on its duty
tape, a message which would bring the authorities here
and give her a chance to tell her story.

Pity she could not increase the glow of lights, but she
had not found the control switch. So Charis had to lean
very close to the keyboard of the unit to pick out the
proper combination to start the sweep.

For a moment or two Charis was bewildered by a
strange and unorthodox arrangement of buttons. Then she
understood. Just as the ship Jagan captained was certainly
not new or first class, this was a com of an older type
than any she had seen before. And a small worry dampened her first elation. What *would* be the range of sweep
on such an antiquated installation? If the government base
was too far away, she might have little hope of a successful
contact.

Charis pressed the button combination slowly, intent
upon making no error in setting up a sweep. But the
crackles of sound which the activated beam fed back into
the room was only the natural atmospheric response of
an empty world. Charis had heard that on Demeter the
times she had practiced the same drill.

Only the beep-beep spark traveling from one side of
a small scan-plate to the other assured her that the sweep
was active. Now she had nothing to do but wait, either
to catch another wave or face the return of the traders.

Having set the com to work, Charis returned to her
other problem. Why had she been left alone in the station at night? From the deeply cleft valley of the inlet
she could not see the landing site of the plateau where
the spacer had planeted. Jagan had taken Sheeha to the
ship, but he had left at least two men here. Had they
believed her safely locked in her room so they could leave
for some other necessary duty? All she knew of the
general routine of the post she had learned from the
captain, and that had been identical to the cramming of
what he had wanted her to know of his business.

The faint beeping of the sweep was a soothing monotone, too soothing. Charis's head jerked as she shook herself fully awake. One third of the circle had registered no pick-up, and at least a fourth of the circumference must be largely sea, from which direction she could expect no positive response.

That came just when Charis was almost convinced there was no hope for her, it came—weak, so weak that the distance must be great. But she had a direct beam on it and so could increase receptive volume. Somewhere to the northeast, another off-world com was beaming.

Charis's fingers flew, centering her sweep, adding to its intensity. The visa-plate before her clouded, began to clear again. She was picking up an answer! Charis reacted more quickly than she had thought possible as some instinct sent her dodging to one side, away from the direct line of the plate and so out of sight—or at least out of focus—for a return cast.

The figure which emerged from the clearing mist was no government man, though he *was* a man or at least humanoid in appearance. He wore the same dingy coveralls as the traders used; belted at his thick waist was not the legal stunner but a highly illegal blaster. Charis's hand shot out and thumbed the lever which broke connection just as the expression of open surprise on his face turned to one of searching inquiry.

Breathing fast, the girl crept back to her place before the screen. Another post—somewhere to the north. But the blaster? Such a weapon was strictly forbidden to anyone except a member of the Patrol or Defense forces. She hesitated. Dare she put the sweep to work again? Try it south? She had not recognized the man pictured on the plate as one of the ship's crew, but still he could be one of Jagan's men. And so the captain's actions here could be more outside the law than she had guessed.

Standing well to one side of the screen, Charis triggered the sweep again. Moments later she had a pick-up to the south. However, what flashed on the screen this time was no armed space man but a very familiar standby pattern—the insignia of Survey surmounted by a small Embassy seal, signifying an alien contact mission manned by Survey personnel. There was no operator on duty; the standby pattern clarified that. But they would have a pick-up tape ready to record. She could send a message and know that it would be read within hours. Charis began to click out the proper code words.

V

A soft swish of sound, a light touch on her body.

Charis looked about her with an acceptance which was in itself part of the strangeness of this experience. She had been huddled in the seat before the com, beating out on its keys her call for attention. Then—she was here, back somehow in the dream.

But, she knew a second or so later after the dawn of that realization, this was not quite the same dream after all. She wore the coverall she had pulled on before she began her night's prowling of the deserted post. Her bare feet sent small messages of pain along nerves and she glanced down at them. They were bruised and there was a scrape along one instep which oozed drops of blood. Instead of that feeling of oneness and satisfaction she had had before, now she was tired and confused.

There, as it had before, rolled the sea under the light of morning. And about her were rocky cliffs, while her sore feet sank into loose and powdery sand. She was on the shore—there was no doubting that, but this could not be a dream.

Charis turned, expecting to see the post on its narrow tongue of water, but behind her was a cliff wall. She could sight a line of depressions in the sand, ending at the point where she now stood, marking her trail, and those led back out of sight. Where she was and how she had come here she did not know.

Her heart picked up the beat of fear, her breath came faster in shallow gasps. She could not remember. No forcing of thought could bring back memory.

Back? Maybe she could trace her way back along her trail. But even as she turned to try that, Charis found she could not. There was a barrier somehow, a sensation almost as keen as physical pain, which kept her from retracing. Literally she could not take the first step back. Shaking, Charis faced around and tried again to move. And the energy she expended nearly sent her sprawling on her face. If she could not return, there was nothing to prevent her going forward.

She tried to equate the points of the compass. Had she strayed north or south from the post? She thought south. South—the government base lay to the south. If she kept on, she had a chance of reaching that.

How small that chance might be Charis dared not consider. Without supplies, without even shoes, how long could she keep going? Some wild thoughts troubled her. Had she brought this upon herself because she had striven to contact the base by com? She cupped her hands over her eyes and stood, trying to understand, trying to trace the compulsion which must have led her to this place. Had her conscious mind blanked out? Her need for escape, for reaching the government base, had that then taken over? It made sense of a sort, but it had also led her into trouble.

Charis limped down to the sea and sat on a rock to inspect her feet. They were bruised, and there was another cut on the tip of a toe. She lowered them into the water and bit her lip against the sting of the liquid in her wounds.

This might be a world without life, Charis thought. The golden-amber sky held floating clouds, but no birds or winged things cut across its serenity. The sand and rocks about her were bare of any hint of growing things, and there was no break on the smooth surface of the beach save the hollows of her own footprints.

Charis pulled open the seal of her coverall and took off her undershirt. It was a struggle to tear that, but at the cost of a broken nail she at last had a series of strips which she bound about her feet. They would be some protection since she could not remain where she was forever.

Some hundred feet or so to the south, the cliff pointed out to meet the sea with no strip of easily traveled beach at its foot. She would have to climb there. But Charis sat where she was for a while, marking the hand- and foot-holds to use, when she had to.

She was hungry—as hungry as she had been back on the mountain on Demeter, and there was not even a hunk of bread for her this time. Hungry and thirsty—although the water washed before her mockingly. To go on into a bare wilderness was sheer folly, yet there was that invisible barrier on the back trail. Now, even to turn her head and retrace by eye the hollow sand prints required growing effort.

Grimly she rose on her bandaged feet and limped to the cliff. She could not stay there, growing weaker with hunger. There could be hope that beyond the cliff there was more than just sand and rock.

The climb taxed her strength, scraped her palms and fingers almost as badly as her feet. She pulled out on the pitted surface of the crest and lay with her hands tight against her breast, sobbing a little. Then she raised her head to look about.

She had reached the lip of another foliage-choked, narrow valley such as the one which held the trading post. But here were no buildings, nothing but trees and brush. However, not too far away a thread of water splashed down to make a stream flowing seaward. Charis licked dry lips and started for that. Within seconds she crouched on blue earth, her hands tingling in the chill of the spring water as she drank from cupped palms, not caring whether her immunization shots, intended for any lurking danger on Demeter, would hold on Warlock.

If the sea beach had been empty of life, the same was not true of this valley. Her thirst assuaged, Charis squatted back on her heels and noticed a gauzy-winged flying thing skim across the water. It rose again, a white thread-like creature writhing in the hold of its two pincer-equipped forelegs, and was gone with its victim between a bush and the cliff wall.

Then, from over her head, burst a clap of sound as if someone had brought two pieces of bone sharply together. Another flyer, a great deal more substantial and a hundred times larger than the insect hunter, shot out of a hole in the cliff and darted back and forth over her. The thing had leathery skin-wings, its body naked of any feathers or fur, the hide wrinkled and seamed. The head was very large in proportion and split halfway down its length most of the time as an enormous fang-set mouth uttered "clak-clak" noises.

A second flyer joined the first, then a third, and the racket of their cries was deafening. They swooped lower and lower and Charis's first curiosity turned to real alarm. One alone would have been no threat, but a flock of the things, plainly set upon her as a target for their dives, could mean real trouble. She looked about for cover and plunged in under the matted branches of the stunted-tree grove.

Apparently her passage was not hidden from the clakers even though they could not reach her, for she could hear their cries following her as she moved toward the sea. Something leaped up from just before her and squealed as it ran for the deeper shadows.

Now she hesitated, unsure of what else might lie in this wood—waiting. The smell of growing things—some pleasant, some disagreeable to her off-world senses—was strong here. Her foot came down on a soft object which burst before she could shift her weight and she saw a mashed fruit. More of these hung from the branches of the tree under which she stood and lay on the ground where the squealing creature had been feeding.

Charis plucked one and held it to her nose, sniffing an unfamiliar odor which she could not decide was pleasant or the reverse. It was food, but whether she could eat it was another question. Still holding the fruit, Charis pushed on seaward.

The clamor of the clakers had not stilled but kept pace with her progress, yet the open water tugged at her with a strange promise of safety. She came to the last screen of brush from which the vegetation straggled on to vanish in a choke of gray sand.

There was a smudge on the horizon which was more, Charis believed, than a low-flying cloud bank. An island? She was so intent upon that that she did not, at first, note the new activity of the clakers.

They were no longer circling about her but had changed course, flying out to sea where they wheeled and wove aerial patterns over the waves. And there was a disturbance in those same waves, marking action below their surface. Something was coming inshore, heading directly toward her.

Charis unconsciously squeezed the fruit until its squashed pulp oozed between her fingers. Judging by the traces, the swimmer—who or what that might be—was large.

But she did not expect nightmare to splash out of the surf and face her across so narrow a strip of beach. Armor plate in the form of scales, greened by clinging seaweed laced over the brown serrations, a head which was also armed with hornlike extensions projecting above each wide eye, a snout to gape in a fang-filled mouth . . .

The creature clawed its way up out of the wash of the waves. Its legs ended in web-jointed talons. Then it whipped up a tail, forked into two spike-tipped equal lengths, spattering water over and ahead. The clakers set up a din and scattered, soaring up, but they did not abandon the field to the sea monster. But the creature paid them no attention in return.

At first Charis was afraid it had seen her, and when it did not advance she was temporarily relieved. A few more wadding steps brought it out of the water, and then it flattened its body on the sand with a plainly audible grunt.

The head swung back and forth and then settled, snout resting outstretched on the scaled forelegs. It had all the appearance of desiring a nap in the warmth of the sun. Charis hesitated. Since the clakers had directed their attention to the fork-tail they might have forgotten her. It was the time to withdraw.

Her inner desire was to run, to crash back into the brush and so win out of the valley, which had taken on the semblance of a trap. But wisdom said she was to creep rather than race. Still facing the beast on the shingle, Charis retreated. For some precious seconds she thought her hope was succeeding. Then . . .

The screech overhead was loud, summoning. A claker spied her. And its fellows screamed in to join it. Then Charis heard that other sound, a whistling, pitched high to hurt her ears. She did not need to hear those big feet pounding on the shingle or the crackle of broken brush to know that the fork-tail thing was aroused and coming.

Her only chance now was the narrow upper end of the valley where the cliff wall might give her handholds to rise. Bushes raked and tore at her clothing and skin as she thrust through any thin spot she could sight. Past the spring and its draining brook she staggered to a glade where lavender grass grew thickly, twisted about her feet, whipped blood from her with sharp leaf edges.

Always above, the clakers screamed, whirled, dived to get at her, never quite touching her head but coming so close that she ducked and turned until she realized that she was losing ground in her efforts to evade their harassing. She threw herself into the cover on the other side of that open space, using her arm as a shield to protect her face as she beat her way in by the weight of her body.

Then she was at her goal, the rock wall which rimmed the valley. But would the clakers let her climb? Charis flattened herself against the stone to look up at the flock of leather-wings from under the protection of her crooked arm. She glanced back where shaking foliage marked the sea beast moving in.

They were *all* coming down at her! Charis screamed, beat out with both arms.

Cries . . .

She flailed out defensively, wildly, before she saw what was happening. The flight of the clakers had brought them to a line which crossed the more leisurely advance of the fork-tail. And so they had run into trouble. For, as storm lightning might strike, the forked tail swept up and lashed at the flyers, hurling bodies on and out to smash against the cliff wall.

Twice that tail struck, catching the avid first wave of attackers, and then some of the second wave who were too intent upon their target or too slow to change course. Perhaps five screeched their way up into the air to circle and clak, but not to venture down again.

Charis spun around and feeling for hand- and foot-holds, began to climb. The fork-tail was now between her and the remaining clakers. Until she had reached a higher point, she might not have to fear a second attack. She centered all her energy upon reaching a ledge where some vines dropped ragged loops not too far from her grop-ing fingers.

She pushed up and into the tangle of vine growth which squashed under her squirming body, rolling over as fast as she could to look back at the enemy. The clakers were in a frenzy, rising as if wishing to skim down at her, while below, Charis cringed back.

The fork-tail was at the foot of the cliff, its webbed talons clawing at the rock. Twice it managed to gain a small hold and was able to pull up a little, only to crash back again. Either the holds were not deep enough to sustain its weight or some clumsiness hindered its climb. For it moved awkwardly, as if on land its bulk were a liability.

But its determination to follow her was plain in those continued efforts to find talon-holds on the stone. Charis sidled along the vine-grown ledge with care lest one of those loops of tough vegetation trip her. She stopped once to tear loose a small length of the stuff, using it to lash out at a claker which had gathered resolution enough to dive at her head. The whip of vine did not touch the flyer, but it did send it soaring away in haste.

She could use that defense as long as she traveled the ledge, but when she turned to climb once more, she could not so arm herself. And she was approaching a point where the shelf was too narrow to afford foot room.

The fork-tail still raised on hind feet below, clawing at the cliff wall with single-minded tenacity. A slip on her part would topple her into its reach. And she dared not climb with the clakers darting at her head and shoulders. Now she could keep them off with the lashing vine, but they were growing bolder, their attacks coming closer together, so that her arm was already tired of wielding the improvised whip.

Charis leaned against the cliff wall. So far it looked as if the reptilian attacker could not reach her. But the clakers' harassment continued unabated, and she was tired, so tired that she was beginning to fear that even if they did withdraw, she would not have the strength left to finish the pull up to the top of the cliff.

She rubbed her hand across her eyes and tried to think, though the continuing din of the attackers made her feel stupid, as if her brain was befuddled and cocooned in the noise. It was the cessation of that clamor which brought her to full consciousness again.

Overhead the ugly creatures had ceased to wheel. Instead they turned almost as one and winged across the valley, to snap into the holes in the rock from which they had earlier emerged. Bewildered, the girl could only stare after them. Then, that sound from below— Steadying her body with one hand on the rock wall, Charis looked down.

The fork-tail had turned and, on four feet once again, was making a ponderous way back through the smashed and crushed growth, heading seaward without a backward glance to the ledge where she stood. It was almost as if the clakers and the sea beast had been ordered away from her . . .

What made her put that interpretation on their movements? Charis absently rubbed the rest of the sticky fruit pulp from her hand on a fibrous vine leaf. Silence— nothing stirring. The whole valley as she could now see it, save for the waving foliage where the fork-tail retreated, could have been empty of life. She must make the most of this oddly granted breathing spell.

Doggedly she set about reaching the top of the rise, expecting any moment to have the clakers burst at her. But the silence held. She stood up on the crest, looked beyond for cover.

This was a plateau much like the one Jagan had used as a landing space. Only this showed no rocket scarring. South, it stretched on as might the surface of a wall well above the sea, open to air and sun with no cover. But Charis doubted if she could descend again. So she turned south, limping on her tender feet, always listening for the clak-clak of the enemy.

A splotch of color, vivid against the dull, black-veined, deep red of the rocks. Odd that she had not seen that earlier when she first surveyed this height. It was so brightly visible now that it drew her as might a promise of food.

Food . . . Her hand came up over her eyes and fell again as she strove to make sure that this was not a hallucination but that it did exist outside of her craving hunger.

But if part of a hallucination, would not the so-pictured foods have been familiar—viands she had known on Demeter or other worlds where she had lived? This was no pile of emergency rations, no setting out of known breads, fruits, meats. On the strip of green were several round balls of a deeper green, a shining white basin filled with a yellow lumpy substance, a pile of flat rounds which were a light blue. A tablecloth spread with a meal! It *had* to be a hallucination! It could not have been there earlier or she would have seen it at once.

Charis shuffled to the cloth and looked at the objects on it. She put out a scratched and grimy hand and touched fingers to the side of the bowl to find it warm. The odor which rose from it was strange—neither pleasant nor unpleasant—just strange. She hunkered down, fighting the wild demand of her body to be fed while she considered the strangeness of this food out of nowhere. Dream? But she could touch it.

She took up one of the blue rounds, found it had the consistency of a kind of tough pancake. Rolling it into a scoop, Charis ladled up a mouthful of the yellow—was it stew? Dream or not, she could chew it, taste it, swallow it down. After that first experimental mouthful, she ate, greedily, without caring in the least about dream or reality.

VI

Charis found the tastes were as difficult to identify as the odors—sweet, sour, bitter. But on the whole, the food was pleasant. She devoured it avidly and then ate with more control. It was not until she had emptied the bowl by the aid of her improvised pancake spoon that she began to wonder once more about the source of that feast.

Hallucination? Surely not that. The bowl about which she cupped a hand was very real to the touch, just as the food had been real in her mouth and now was warm and filling in her stomach. She turned the basin about, studying it. The color was a pure, almost radiant white; and, while the shape was utilitarian and without any ornamentation, it was highly pleasing to the eye and suggested, Charis thought, a sophistication of art which marked a high degree of civilization.

And she did not need to give the cloth a closer inspection to know that it matched the strip Jagan had shown her. So this must have all come from the natives of Warlock. But why left here—on this barren rock as if awaiting her arrival?

On her knees, the bowl still in her hands, Charis slowly surveyed the plateau. By the sun's position she guessed that the hour was well past midday, but there were no shadows here, no hiding place. She was totally alone in the midst of nowhere, with no sign of how this largesse had arrived or why.

Why? That puzzled her almost more than how. She could only believe that it had been left here for her. But that meant that "they" knew she was coming, could gauge the moment of her arrival so well that the yellow stew had been hot when she first tasted it. There was no mark that any aircraft had landed.

Charis moistened her lips.

"Please—" her own voice sounded thin and reedy and, she had to admit, a little frightened as she listened to it "—please, where are you?" She raised that plea to a call. There was no answer.

"Where are you?" Again she made herself call, louder, more beseechingly.

The echoing silence made her shrink a little. It was as if she were exposed here to the view of unseen presences—a specimen of her kind under examination. And she wanted away from here—now.

Carefully she placed the now empty bowl on the rock. There were several of the fruit and two pancakes left. Charis rolled these up in the cloth. She got to her feet, and for some reason she could not quite understand, she faced seaward.

"Thank you." Again she dared raise her voice. "Thank you." Perhaps this had not been meant for her, but she believed that it had.

With the bundle of food in her hand, Charis went on across the plateau. At its southern tip she looked back. The shining white of the bowl was easy to see. It sat just where she had left it, exposed on the rock. Yet she had half expected to find it gone, had kept her back turned and her eyes straight ahead for that very reason.

To the south, the terrain was like a flight of steps, devised for and by giants, descending in a series of ledges. Some of these bedded growths of purple and lavender vegetation, but all of it spindly short bushes and the tough knife-bladed grass. Charis made her way carefully from one drop to the next, watching for another eruption of clakers or others signs of hostile life.

She had to favor her sore feet and that journey took a long time, though she had no way of measuring the passing of planet hours save by the sun's movements. It was necessary that she look forward for shelter against the night. The sense of well-being which had warmed her along with the food was fading as she considered what the coming of Warlockian darkness might mean if she did not discover an adequate hiding place.

At last she determined to stay where she was on the ledge she had just reached. The stubby growth could not mask any large intruder, and she had a wide view against any sudden attack. Though how she might defend herself without weapons, Charis did not know. Carefully she unwrapped the remains of the food and put it aside on some leaves she pulled from a sprawling plant. She began to twist the alien fabric into a cord, finding that its soft length did crush well in the process, so that she ended with a rope of sorts.

With a withered branch she was able to pry a stone about as big as her fist from the earth, and she worked hurriedly to knot it into one end of her improvised rope. Against any real weapon this would be a laughable defense, but it gave her some small protection against native beasts. Charis felt safer when she had it under her hand and ready for use.

The sunlight had already faded from the lower land where she now was. With the going of that brighter light, splotches of a diffused gleam were beginning to show here and there. Bushes and shrubs glowed with phosphorescence as the twilight grew deeper, and from some of them, as the heat of the day chilled away, a fragrance was carried by a rising sea breeze.

Charis settled her back against the wall of the drop down which she had come, facing the open. Her weapon lay under her right hand, but she knew that sooner or later she would sleep, that she could not keep long at bay the fatigue which weighted not only her drooping eyelids but her whole body. And when she slept . . . Things happened while one slept on Warlock! Would she awake once more to find herself in a new and strange part of the wilderness? To be on the safe side, she put the food in its leaf-wrapping into the front of her coverall and tied the loose end of the scarf weapon about her wrist. When she went this time, she would take what small supplies she had with her.

Tired as she was, Charis tried to fight that perhaps betraying sleep. There was no use speculating about what force was in power here. To keep going she must concentrate on the mechanics of living. Something had turned the clakers and the sea beast from attack. Could she ascribe that to the will of the same presence which had left the food? If so, what was "their" game?

Study of an alien under certain conditions? Was she being used as an experimental animal? It was one answer and a logical one to what had happened to her so far. But at least "they" had kept her from real harm—her left hand folded over the lump of food inside her coverall; as yet any active move on "their" part had been to her advantage.

So sleepy . . . Why fight this leaden cloud? But—where would she wake again?

On the ledge, chilled and stiff, and in a dark which was not a true dark because of those splotches of light-diffusing plants and shrubs. Charis blinked. Had she dreamed again? If so, she could not remember doing so this time. But there was some reason why she must move here and now, get down from the ledge, then get over there.

She got up stiffly, looping the scarf about her wrist. Was it night or early morning? Time did not matter, but the urgency to move did. Down—and over there. She did not try to fight that pressure but went.

The light plants were signposts for her, and she saw that either their light or scent had attracted small flying things that flickered with sparkles of their own as they winged in and out of those patches of eerie radiance. The somberness of Warlock in the day became a weird ethe-reality by night.

Darkness which was true shadow beyond—that was her goal. As had happened on the beach when she had struggled to turn north to try and retrace her path to the post, so now she could not fight against the influence which aimed her at that dark blot, which exerted more and more pressure on her will, bringing with it a heightening of that sense of urgency which had been hers at her abrupt awakening.

Unwillingly she came out of the half-light of the vegetation into darkness—a cave or cleft in the rock. Drifts of leaves were under her feet, the sense of enclosing walls about her. Charis's outflung hands brushed rock on either side. She could still see, however, above her the wink of a star in the velvet black of the night sky. This must be a passage then and not a true cave. But again why? *Why?*

A second light moved across the slit of sky, a light with a purpose, direction. The flying light of some aircraft? The traders searching for her? That other she had seen on the com screen? But she thought this had come from the south. A government man alerted to her message? There was no chance of being seen in the darkness and this slit. She had been moved here to hide—from danger or from aid?

And she was being held here. No effort of her struggling will could move her another step or allow her to retreat. It was like being fixed in some stiff and unyielding ground, her feet roots instead of means of locomotion. A day earlier she would have panicked, but she had changed. Now her curiosity was fully aroused and she was willing, for a space, to be governed so. She had always been curious. "Why?" had been her demanding bid for attention when she was so small she remembered having to be carried for most of the exploration journeys Ander Nordholm had made a part of her growing years. "Why were those colors here and not there?" "Why did this animal build a home underground and that one in a tree?" Why?—why?—why?

He had been very wise, her father, using always her thirst for knowledge to suggest paths which had led her to make her own discoveries, each a new triumph and wonder. In fact, he had made her world of learning too perfect and absorbing, so that she was impatient with those who did not find such seeking the main occupation of life. On Demeter she had felt trapped, her "whys" there battered against an unyielding wall of prejudice and things which were and must always be. When she had fought to awaken the desire to reach out for the new among her pupils, she had clashed with a definite will-not-to-know and fear-of-learning which had first rendered her incredulous and then hotly angry and, lastly, stubbornly intent upon battle.

While her father had been alive, he had soothed her, turned her frustrated energy to other pursuits in which she had freedom of action and study. She had been encouraged to explore with the ranger, to record the discoveries of the government party, received as an equal among them. But with the settlers, she had come to an uneasy truce. That had burst into open war at her father's death, her repulsion for their closed minds fanned into hatred by what had happened when Tolskegg took over and turned back the clock of knowledge a thousand years.

Now Charis, free from the frustrations of Demeter, had been presented with a new collection of whys which seemed to have restrictions she could not understand, to be sure, but which she could chew on, fasten her mind to, use as a curtain between past and present.

"I'll find out!" Charis did not realize she had spoken aloud until some trick of the dark cleft in which she stood made a hollow echo of those words. But they were no boast, a promise rather, a promise she had made herself before and always kept.

The star twinkling above was alone in the sky. Charis listened for the sound of a copter engine beat and thought that she caught such a throb, very faint and far in the distance.

"So." Again she spoke aloud, as if who or what she addressed stood within touching distance. "You didn't want them to see me. Why? Danger for me or escape for me? What do you want of me?" There was no reason to expect any reply.

Suddenly the pressure of imprisonment was gone. Charis could move again. She edged back to settle down in the mouth of the cleft, facing the valley with its weird light. A breeze shush-shushed through the foliage, sometimes setting light plants to a shimmer of dance. There was a chirruping, a hum of night creatures, lulling in its monotone. If something larger than the things flying about the light vegetation was present, it made no sound. Once again, since the urgency had left her, Charis was drowsy, unable to fight the sleep which crept up her as a wave might sweep over her body on the shore.

When Charis opened her eyes once again, sunlight fingered down to pattern the earth within reach of her hand. She rose from the dried leaf-drift which had been her bed, pulled by the sound of running water: another cliff-side spring to let her wash and give her drink. Her two attempts to make leaf containers to carry some of the liquid with her were failures and she had to give up that hope.

Prudence dictated a conservation of supplies. She allowed herself only one of the pancakes, now dry and tough, and two of the fruit she had brought from the feast on the plateau. Because such abundance had appeared once, there was no reason to expect it again.

The way was still south but Charis's aching muscles argued against more climbing unless she was forced to it. She returned to the cleft and found that it was indeed a passage to more level territory. The heights continued on the western side, forming a wall between the sea and a stretch of level fertile country. There was a wood to the east with the tallest trees Charis had yet seen on Warlock, their dark foliage a blackened blot which was forbidding. On the edge of that forest was a section of brush, shrub, and smaller growth which thinned in turn to grass—not the tough, sharp-bladed species she had suffered from in the valley of the fork-tail, but a moss-like carpet, broken here and there by clumps of smaller stands bearing flowers, all remarkably pale in contrast to the dark hue of leaf and stem. It was as if they were the ghosts of the more brightly colored blossoms she had known on other worlds.

The mossy sward was tempting, but to cross it would take her into the open in full sight of any hunters. On the other hand, she herself would have unrestricted sight. While in the forest or brush belt, her vision would be limited. Swinging her stone-and-scarf weapon, Charis walked into the open. If she kept by the cliff, it would guide her south.

It was warmer here than it had been by the sea. And the footing proved as soft as she had hoped. Keeping to the moss, she walked on a velvety surface which spared her bruised feet, did not tear the tattered rags of covering she had fashioned for them. Away from the dark of the wood, this stretch of Warlockian earth was the most welcoming she had found.

A flash of wings overhead made her start until she saw that this was not a claker but a truly feathered bird, with plumage as pale as the flowers and a naked head of brilliant coral red. It did not notice Charis but skimmed on, disappearing over the cliff toward the sea.

Charis did not force the pace. Now and again she paused to examine a flower or insect. She might be coming to the end of a journey a little before her appointed time and could now spare attention for the things about her. During one rest she watched, fascinated, as a scaled creature no larger than her middle finger, walking erect on a pair of sturdy hind legs, dug with taloned front "hands" in a patch of earth with the concentration of one employed in a regular business. Its efforts unearthed two round gray globes which it brushed to one side impatiently after it had systematically flattened both. Between those spheres had been packed a curled, many-legged body of what Charis believed was a large insect. The lizard-thing straightened his find out and inspected it with care. Having apparently decided in favor of its usability, it proceeded to dine with obvious relish, then stalked on among the grass clumps, now and again stooping to search the earth with a piercing eye, apparently in search of another such find.

Midday passed while Charis was still in the open. She wondered if food would again appear in her path, and consciously watched for the gleam of a second white bowl and the fruit piled on a green cloth. However, none such was to be seen. But she did come upon a tree growing much to itself, bearing the same blue fruit which had been left for her, and she helped herself liberally.

She had just started on when a sound shattered the almost drowsy content of the countryside. It was a cry—frantic, breathless, carrying with it such an appeal for aid against overwhelming danger that Charis was startled into dropping her load of fruit and running toward the sound, her stone weapon ready. Was it really that small cry which awakened such a response in her or some emotion which she shared in some abnormal way? She only knew that there was danger and she must give aid.

Something small, black, coming in great leaps, broke from the brush wall beyond the rim of the forest. It did not head for Charis but ran for the cliff, and a wave of fear hit the girl as it flashed past. Then the compulsion which had willed against her turning north, which had held her in the cleft last night, struck Charis. But this time it brought the need to run, to keep on running, from some peril. She whirled and followed the bounds of the small black thing, and like it, headed for the sea cliff.

The black creature ran mute now. Charis thought that perhaps those first cries had been of surprise at sudden danger. She believed she could hear something behind— a snarling or a muffled howl.

Her fellow fugitive had reached the cliff face, was making frantic leaps, pawing at a too-smooth surface, unable to climb. It whimpered a little as its most agonizing efforts kept it earthbound. Then, as Charis came up, it turned, crouched, and looked at her.

She had a hurried impression of great eyes, of softness, and the shock of the fear and pleading it broadcast. Hardly aware of her act but conscious she had to do something, she snatched up the warm, furred body which half-leaped to meet her grasp and plastered itself to her, clinging with four clawed feet to the stuff of her coverall, its shivering a vibration against her.

There was a way up that she, with her superior size, could climb. She took it, trying not to scrape her living burden against the rock as she went. Then she was in a fissure, breathless with her effort, and a warm tongue tip made a soft, wet touch against her throat. Charis wriggled back farther into hiding, the rescued creature cradled in her arms. She could see nothing coming out of the wood as yet.

A faint mewing from her companion alerted her as a brown shadow padded out on the lavender-green of the moss—an animal she was sure. But from this distance and height, Charis could not make it out clearly as it slunk on, using bushes for cover. So far it had not headed in their direction.

But the animal was not alone. Charis gasped. For the figure now coming from between two trees was not only humanoid—it wore the green-brown uniform of Survey. She was about to call out, to hail the stranger, when the freezing she had known in the cleft caught and held her as soundless, as motionless, as if she had been plunged into the freeze of a labor ship. Helpless, she had to watch the man walk back and forth as if searching for some trail, and at last disappear back into the wood with his four-footed companion.

They had never approached the cliff, yet the freeze which held Charis did not break until long moments after they had gone.

VII

"Meerrreee?" A soft sound with a definite note of inquiry. For the first time Charis looked closely at her fellow fugitive, meeting as searching a gaze turned up at her.

The fur which covered its whole body was in tight, tiny curls, satin-soft against her hands. It had four limbs ending in clawed paws, but the claws were retractable and no longer caught in her clothing. There was a short tail like a fringed flap, now tucked neatly down against the haunches. The head was round, sloping to a blunt muzzle. Only the ears seemed out of proportion to the rest. They were large and wide, set sideways instead of opening forward toward the front of the skull, and their pointed tips had small tassel-tufts of gray fur of the same color that ringed the large and strikingly blue eyes and ran in narrow lines down the inner sides of the legs and on the belly.

Those eyes— Fascinated, Charis found it difficult to look away from the eyes. She was not trained in beast-empathy, but she could not deny there was an aura of intelligence about this small and appealing creature which made her want to claim a measure of kinship. Yet, for all its charm, it was not to be only cuddled and caressed; Charis was as certain of that as if it had addressed her clearly in Basic. It was more than animal, even if she was not sure how.

"Meerrreee!" No inquiry now but impatience. It

squirmed a little in her hold. Once more a pale yellow tongue made a lightning dab against her skin. Charis released her grip, fearing for an instant that it would leave her. But it jumped from her lap to the rough floor of the crevice and stood looking at the forest from which its enemy had emerged.

Enemy? The Survey man! Charis had almost forgotten him. What had restrained her from hailing him? Perhaps his very being here had been the answer to her call from the post. But why had she not been allowed to meet him? For allowed *was* the proper term. A prohibition she could not explain had been laid upon her. And Charis knew, without trying such an experiment, that if she attempted to go to the wood she would not be able to push past an invisible wall someone or something had used to cut her off.

"Meeerreee?" Again a question from the furred one. It paused, one front paw slightly raised, looking back at her from the entrance to the crevice.

Suddenly Charis wanted to get out of this moss-carpeted land. The frustration of her flight from the very help she wished was sour in her. Up over the cliff wall back to the sea— The longing to be again beside the waves was a pulling pain.

"Back to the sea." She said that aloud as if the furred one could understand. She came out of the crevice and glanced up for a way to climb.

"Meeree . . ."

Charis had expected the animal to vanish into the moss meadow. Instead, it was demanding her attention in its own way before it moved sure-footedly along, angling up the surface of the cliff. Charis followed, warmed by the realization that the animal appeared to have joined forces with her, if only temporarily. Perhaps its fear of the enemy in the forest was so overpowering it wanted the promised protection of her company.

While she was not as agile as the animal, Charis was not far behind when they reached the crest of the cliff. From here one could look down on the expanse of the sea and a line of silver beach. There was a feeling of peace. Peace? For an instant Charis recaptured the feeling

she had known in that first dream—contentment and
peace. The animal trotted ahead, south along the cliff top.
From this point the drop to the sand was too sheer to
descend, so Charis again followed the other's lead.

They came down to the silver strand by a path her
companion found. But when Charis would have gone on
south, the Warlockian creature brushed about her ankles,
uttering now and then an imperative cry, plainly wanting her to remain. At last she dropped down to sit facing the sea, and then, looking about her, she was startled.
This *was* the cove of her first dream exactly.

"Meerree?" That tongue-tip touch, a sense of reassurance, a small warm body pressed against hers, a feeling of
contentment—that all was well . . . coming from her companion or out of some depth within herself? Charis did not
know.

They came out of the sea, though the girl had not seen
them swimming in. But these were not a threat like the
fork-tail. Charis drew a deep breath of wonder and delight
or welcome as the contentment flowered within her. They
came on, walking through the wash of the waves, then
stood to look at her.

Two of them, glittering in the sun, sparkling with light.
They were shorter than she, but they walked and stood
with a delicate grace which Charis knew she would never
equal, as if each movement, conscious or unconscious,
were a part of a very ancient and beautiful dance. Bands
of jewel colors made designs about each throat in gemmed
collars, ran down in spirals over chest, waist, thigh,
braceleting the slender legs and arms. Large eyes with
vertical slits of green pupils were fixed on her. She did
not find the saurian shape of their heads in the least
repulsive—different, yes, but not ugly, truly beautiful in
their own fashion. Above their domed, jewel-marked
foreheads stood a sharp V point of spiky growth, a delicate green perhaps two shades lighter than the sea from
which they had come. This extended down in two bands,
one for each shoulder, wider as if aping wings.

They wore no clothing, save a belt each from which hung
various small implements, and a pair of pouches. Yet their
patterned, scaled skin gave the impression of rich robes.

"Meeerrreeee!" The furred body against hers stirred. Charis could not doubt that was a cry of pleasure. But she did not need that welcome from the animal. She had no fear of these sea ones—the Wyverns surely, the masters—or rather the mistresses—of Warlock.

They advanced and Charis arose, picking up the furred one, waiting.

"You are—" she began in Basic, but a four-digit hand came out, touched her forehead between the eyes. And in that touch was not the feel of cold reptilian flesh but of warmth like her own.

No words. Rather it was a flow of thought, of feeling, which Charis's off-world mind turned into speech: "Welcome, Sister—One."

The claim of kinship did not disturb Charis. Their bodies were unlike, yes—but that flow of mind to mind—it was good. It was what she wanted now and forever.

"Welcome." She found it hard to think, not to speak. "I have come—"

"You have come. It is good. The journey has been weary, but now it will be less so."

The Wyvern's other hand moved up into the line of Charis's vision. Cupped against the scaled palm was a disk of ivory-white. And once seeing it, she found she could not look away. A momentary flash of uneasiness at that sudden control and then . . .

There was no beach, no whispering sea waves. She was in a room with smooth walls that were faintly opalescent as if they were coated with sea-shell lining. A window broke one of those surfaces, giving her a view of open sea and sky. And there was a thick mat spread under that, a covering of fluffy feathers folded neatly upon it.

"For the weary—rest."

Charis was alone except for the furred one she still held. Yet that suggestion or order was as emphatic as if she had heard the words spoken. She stumbled to the mat and lay down, drew the fluffy cover over her bruised and aching body, and then plunged into another time—world—existence . . .

There was no arbitrary measurement of time where she went, nor was memory ever sharp set enough to give her more than bits and pieces of what she experienced, learned, saw in that other place. Afterward, things she had garnered sank past full consciousness in her mind and rose in time of need when she was unaware that she held such secrets. Schooling, training, testing—all three in one.

When she awoke again in her windowed room, she was Charis Nordholm still, but also she was someone else, one who had tasted a kind of knowledge her species had never known. She could touch the fringe of that power, hold a little of it; yet the full mystery of it slipped through her fingers much as if she had tried to hold tightly the waters of the sea.

Sometimes she sensed disappointment in her teachers, a kind of exasperation, as if they found her singularly obtuse just when they hovered on the edge of a crucial revelation, and then her own denseness was a matter of anger and shame for her. She had such limitations. But yet she fought and labored against them.

Which was the dream—existence in that other world or this waking? She knew the room at times and the Citadel in the island kingdom of the Wyverns, of which it was a part, and other rooms in other places she knew were not the Citadel. She knew sea depths: Had she gone there in body or in her dream? She danced and ran along the sands of shores with companions who sported and played joyously with the same bursting sense of happy release that she knew. That, she believed, was real.

She learned to communicate with the furred one, if on a limited plane. Tsstu was her name and she was one of a rare species from the forest lands, not merely animal, not quite equivalent to "human," but a link between such as Charis's own kind had sought for years.

Tsstu and the Wyverns and their half-dream existence in which she was caught up, absorbed, in which memory faded into another and far less real dream. But there was to be an awakening as sudden and as racking as that of a warrior startled from slumber by the onslaught of the enemy.

It came during one of the periods Charis believed real, when she was in the Citadel on an island apart from the land mass where the post stood. She had been teasing her companion Gytha to share dreams with her, a process of communication which swept one wholly adrift in wonder. But the young Wyvern seemed absent-minded and Charis guessed a portion of her attention was elsewhere in rapport with her kind, whom Charis could only reach if they willed it so.

"There is trouble?" She thought her question, her hand going instinctively to the pouch at her belt in which rested her guide, the carved disk they had given her. She could use it, though haltingly, to control dangerous life such as the fork-tails or to travel. Of course, she could not draw upon the full Power; maybe she never would. Even the Wise One, Gysmay, who was a Reader of Rods, could not say yes or no on that though, in a way Charis did not understand, the elder Wyvern could read the future in part.

"Not so, Sharer of my Dreams." But even as the answer came, Gytha vanished with a will-to-Otherwise. The impression she left—Charis frowned—that faint trail of impression was of trouble, and trouble connected with herself.

She brought out her guide, felt it warm comfortingly on her palm. Practice with it—that was important. Each time she bent the Power to her will she was that much more proficient. The day was fair; she would like to be free in it. What harm in her using the disk ashore? And Tsstu had been restless. For both of them to return to the moss meadow might be enjoyable. Memory moved— the Survey man there. Somehow she had forgotten about him, just as the post and the traders had receded so far into the dreamy past that they were far less real than a shared dream.

Cupping the disk, she thought of Tsstu and then heard the answering "Meerreee" from the corridor. Charis pictured the moss meadow, questioned, and was answered with an eager assent. She caught up the small body as it bounded toward her and held it against her as she breathed upon the disk and made a new mind-picture— the meadow as she remembered it most vividly by that solitary fruit tree.

Then Tsstu wriggled out of Charis's hold, pranced on

her hind legs, waving her front paws in the air ecstatically, until the girl laughed. She had not felt as young and free as this for as long as she could remember. To be Ander Nordholm's assistant had once absorbed all her interest and energy, and then there had been nothing but dark shadows until she had seen the Wyverns coming to her through the sea. But now, no Wyverns—nothing but Charis and Tsstu, removed from the need for care, in a wide and welcoming stretch of countryside.

Charis threw out her arms, put up her head, so that the warmth of the sun was directly on her face. Her hair, which always intrigued the Wyverns so, she had caught back with a tie the same green as the clinging tunic she now wore.

This time her feet were shielded from hurt with sandals of shell seemingly impervious to wear, yet as light as if she were barefoot. She felt as if she might emulate Tsstu and dance on the moss. She had taken a few tentative steps when she heard it, a sound which sent her backing swiftly into the cover of the tree branches—the hum of an airborne motor.

A copter was coming from the southeast. In general appearance it was like any other atmosphere flyer imported from off-world. Only this one had service insignia, the Winged Planet of Survey surmounted by a gold key. It was slanting away, out to sea in the general direction of the Citadel.

In all the time she had been with the natives, they had had no contact that she had known of with any off-worlders save herself. Nor had the Wyverns ever mentioned such. For the first time Charis speculated about that. Why had she herself never asked any questions about the government base, made any attempt to get the Wyverns to take or send her there? She had seemed to forget her own species while she was with the Warlockians. And that was so unnatural that she was uneasy when she realized it now.

"Meeerrreee?" A paw patted her ankle. Tsstu had caught Charis's thought or at least her uneasiness. But the animal's concern was only partly comforting.

The Wyverns had not wanted Charis to return to her

own kind. It had been their interference on her first awakening that had kept her from retracing her trail to the post, had made her take cover from the flyer in the night, avoid the Survey man. She had had only kindness—yes—and an emotion which her species could term love, and care and teaching from them. But why had they brought her here, tried to cut her off from her own blood? What use did they have for her?

Use—a cold word, and yet one her mind fastened upon now only too readily. Jagan had brought her here to use as a contact with these same wielders of strange powers. Then she had been skillfully detached from the post, led to the meeting by the sea. And understanding that, Charis broke free of the enchantment which had bound her to the Otherwhere of the Wyverns.

The copter was out of sight. Had it been summoned for her? Charis was sure not. But she could have been there when it arrived. She called Tsstu, caught her up, and concentrated upon the disk to return.

Nothing happened. She was not back in the Citadel room but still under the tree in the meadow. Again Charis set her mind to the task of visualizing the place she wanted to be and it was there, as a vivid picture in her mind, but *only* in her mind.

Tsstu whimpered, butted her head under Charis's chin; the girl's fear had spread to her companion. For the third time, Charis tried the disk. But it was as if whatever power had once been conducted through that was turned off at the source. Turned off and by the Wyverns. Charis was as certain of that as if she had been told so, but there was one way to test the truth of her guess.

She raised the disk for the fourth time, this time painting a mind-picture of the plateau top where the mysterious feast had been spread. Sea wind in her hair, rock about— She was just where she had aimed to go. So—she *could* use the disk here, but she could not return to the native stronghold.

They must have known that she had left the Citadel. They did not want her to return while the visitor was there—or ever?

One of those half messages from Tsstu which came not

as words or pictures but obliquely: something wrong near here . . .

Charis looked from the sea to the slit of valley where she had seen the fork-tail, secure in her knowledge that neither the sea beast nor the clakers could attack a disk carrier. From here she could see nothing amiss below. Two clakers screeched and made for her and then abruptly sheered away and fled for their nesting holes. Charis used the disk to reach the scrap of beach below the cliff. She had forgotten to bring Tsstu but she could see the black blot against the red of the rock where the little creature was making a speedy descent.

Tsstu reached the bottom of the cliff and vanished into the cloak of vegetation. Charis moved inland, the mental call bringing her to the spring.

A broken bush, torn turf. Then, on a stone, a dark sticky smear about which flying things buzzed or crawled sluggishly. In the edge of the pool, something gleamed in a spot of sun.

Charis picked up the stunner—not just any off-world weapon but one she knew well. When Jagan had had her in his cabin on the spacer to give her those instructions in what he intended to be her duties, she had seen such a side arm many times. The inlay of cross-within-a-circle set into the butt with small black vors stones had been a personal mark. It was out of the bounds of possibility that two weapons so marked could be here on Warlock.

She tried to fire it, but the trigger snapped on emptiness; its charge was exhausted. The trampled brush, the torn-up sod, and that smear— Charis forced herself to draw her finger through the congealed mess. Blood! She was sure it was blood. There had been a fight here and, judging by the lost stunner, the fight must have gone against the weapon's owner or his weapon would not be left so. Had he faced a fork-tail? But there was no path of wreckage such as that beast had left on its pursuit of her, traces of which still remained to be seen. Only there had been a fight.

Tsstu made a sound deep in her throat, an "rrrrurrgh" of anger and warning. Moved purely by impulse, Charis caught up Tsstu and used the disk.

VIII

The smell caught at Charis's throat, made her cough, even before she knew the source. This was the post clearing—just as she had aimed for—the bubble of the building rising from bare earth. Or the remains of it, for there were splotched holes in its fabric from which the plasta-cover peeled in scorched and stinking strips. Tsstu spat, growled, communication with Charis firm on the need for immediate withdrawal.

But there was a prone figure by the ragged hole which had once been a door. Charis started for that—

"Hoyyy!"

She whirled, her disk ready. There was someone on the trail which led down the cliff face. He moved faster, waving to her. She could escape at any moment she chose and that knowledge led her to stand her ground. Tsstu spat again, caught a clawed grip of Charis's tunic.

From the brush rim of the clearing came a brown animal, trotting purposefully. It walked with its back slightly arched, showing off the bands of lighter color along each side, the fur thick and long. More of the light fur was visible above its eyes. Its ears were small, its face broad, the tail bushy.

Just out of the bushes it stopped to eye Charis composedly. Tsstu made no more audible protests, but the trembling of her body, her fear of mind, was transmitted to Charis. For the second time the girl readied her disk.

The man who had waved disappeared from the trail; he must have jumped down the last few feet. Now a whistle sounded from the foliage. The brown animal squatted down where it was. Charis watched warily as the newcomer burst into the clearing in a rush.

He wore the green-brown of Survey, with the addition of high boots of a dull copper-colored, supple material. On his tunic collar was the glint of metal—the insignia of his corps again modified with a key as it had been on the copter. He was young, though nowadays with the mixture of races and the number of mutants, planet years were hard to guess. Not as tall as the usual Terran breed though, and slender. His skin was an even brown which might be its natural shade or the result of much weathering, and his hair, rather closely cropped to his round skull was almost as tightly curled and just as black, as Tsstu's fur.

His impetuous break into the open halted and he stood staring at Charis in open disbelief. The brown animal rose and went to him, rubbing against his legs.

"Who are you?" he demanded in Basic.

"Charis Nordholm," she replied mechanically. Then she added, "That beast of yours—he frightens Tsstu—"

"Taggi? You need not fear him." The brown animal reared against the man's thigh and he fondled its head, scratched behind the small ears. "But—a curl-cat!" He was gazing now with almost as great surprise at Tsstu. "Where did you get it? And how did you make friends with it?"

"Meeerrreeee." Some of Tsstu's fear had lessened. She wriggled about in Charis's arms as if settling herself in a more comfortable position, watching both man and animal with wary interest.

"She came to me," Charis fitted the past to the present, "when you were hunting her with that animal!"

"But I never—" he began and then stopped "—oh, back in the woods that day Taggi went off on a new scent! But why—who *are* you?" His tone had a new snap; this was official business now. "And what are you doing here? Why did you hide when I searched here earlier?"

"Who are *you*?" she countered.

"Cadet Shann Lantee, Survey Corps, Embassy-Liaison," he replied almost in one breath. "You sent that message, the one entered on our pick-up tape, didn't you? You were here with the traders, though where you were just a little while ago—"

"I wasn't here. I have just come."

He moved toward her, the animal Taggi remaining where it was. Now his eyes were intent, with a new kind of measurement.

"You've been with *them!*"

And Charis had no doubt as to whom that "them" referred.

"Yes." She was not prepared to add to that, but he seemed to need no other answer.

"And you've just come here. Why?"

"What has happened here? That man there—" She turned toward the body once more but the Survey officer in one swift stride was blocking her view of it.

"Don't look! What's happened?—Well, I'd like to know that myself. There's been a raid. But who or why—Taggi and I have been trying to learn what could have happened here. How long have you been with *them?*"

Charis shook her head. "I don't know." It was the truth, but would this Lantee believe it?

He nodded. "Like that, eh? Some of their dreaming . . ."

It was her turn for surprise. What did this officer know of the Wyverns and their Otherwhere? He was smiling slowly, an expression which modified his usual set of mouth, made him even more youthful.

"I, too, have dreamed," he said softly.

"But I thought—!" She had a small prick of emotion which was not amazement but, oddly, resentment.

His smile remained, warm and somehow eager. "That they do not admit males can dream? Yes, that is what they told us, too, once upon a time."

"Us?"

"Ragnar Thorvald and I. We dreamed to order—and came out under our own command, so they had to give us equal status. Did they do the same to you? Make you visit the Cavern of the Veil?"

Charis shook her head. "I dreamed, yes, but I don't

know about your cavern. They taught me how to use this."
On impulse she held up the disk.

Lantee's smile vanished. "A guide! They gave you a guide. So that's how you got here!"

"You don't have one?"

"No, they never offered us those. And you don't ask—"

Charis nodded. She knew what he meant. With the Wyverns, you waited for their giving; you did not ask. But apparently Lantee and this Thorvald had better contact with the natives than the traders had been able to establish.

The traders—the raid here. She did not realize that she was speaking aloud her thoughts as she said:

"That man with the blaster!"

"*What* man?" Again that official voice from Lantee.

Charis told him of that strange last night in the post when she had awakened to find herself in a deserted building, of her use of the com and the answer the sweep had picked up in the north. Lantee shot questions at her, but the answers she had were so limited she could tell him little more than the fact that the stranger in the visaplate had worn an illegal weapon.

"Jagan had a limited permit," Lantee said when she had done. "He was here on sufferance and against our recommendations, and he had only a specified time in which to prove his trade claim. We heard he had brought in a woman as liaison, but that was when he first set up the post . . ."

"Sheeha!" Charis broke in. Rapidly she added that part of the story to the rest.

"Apparently she couldn't take the dreams," Lantee observed. "They reached for her, just as they did for you. But she wasn't receptive in the right way, so it reacted on her, broke her. Then Jagan made another trip and got you. But this other crowd—the one you picked up that night—that spells trouble. It looks as if they hit here—"

Charis glanced at the body. "Is that Jagan? One of his men?"

"It's a crewman, yes. Why did you come here? You taped a call for help to escape that night."

She showed him the stunner, told him of where and how she had found it. Lantee was far from smiling now.

"The com in the post was smashed along with everything else inside that wasn't blast-burned. But—there *was* something else. Have you ever seen a mate to this before, or was it part of Jagan's stock—a keepsake?"

Lantee moved back to the body he had warned her not to approach and picked an object from the ground beside it. When he came back, he held an unusual weapon, now horribly stained for a third of its length. It had the general appearance of a spear or dart, but the sawlike projections extended farther down its shaft than was natural in a spearhead.

Charis's fingers were a tight fist about her disk as Lantee held it closer to her. The bone-white substance was very like that used in the guide.

"I never saw it before." She told the truth, but in her a fear was growing.

"But you have an idea?" He was too acute!

"Suppose, just suppose," Lantee continued, no longer holding her eye to eye as if demanding her thoughts, but regarding the strange spear with a brooding expression, "that this is native to Warlock!"

"*They* don't need such weapons," Charis flashed. "They can control any living thing through these." She waved her balled fist.

"Because they dream," Lantee noted. "But what of those of their race who do not dream?"

"The—the males?" For the first time Charis wondered about that. Now she remembered that, in all the time she had spent with the Wyverns, she had not seen any male of their species. That they existed she knew, but there appeared to be a wall of reticence surrounding any mention of them.

"But—" she could not believe in Lantee's suggestion "—that is the sign of blaster fire." With her chin she pointed to the post.

"Yes. Blaster fire, systematic wrecking of every installation—and then this—used to kill an off-worlder. It's as complicated as a dream, isn't it? But this is real, too real by far!" He dropped the stained spear to lie

between them. "We have to have answers and have
them quick." He looked up at her. "Can you call them?
Thorvald went out to the Citadel for a conference
before he knew about this."

"I tried to go back before—they'd walled me out."

"We have to know what happened here. A body with
this in it. Up there—" Lantée waved toward the plateau, "—an empty ship just sitting. And out of here, as
far as Taggi can trace, not a single trail. Either they
lifted in by aircraft or—"

"The sea!" Charis finished for him.

"And the sea is *their* domain; there is not much happens out there that they are not aware of."

"You mean—*they* planned this?" Charis demanded
coldly. To her mind violence of this kind was not the
Wyvern way. The natives had their own powers and those
did not consist of blaster fire and serrated spears.

"No," Lantee agreed with her promptly. "This has the
stamp of a Jack job, except for that." He toed the spear.
"And if a Jack crew planeted here, the sooner we combine forces against them, the better!"

To that Charis *could* agree. If Jagan's poor outfit had
been fringe trading, it had still been on the side of the
law. A Jack crew was a thoroughly criminal gang, pirates
swooping on out-world trading posts to glut, kill, and be
off again before help could be summoned. And on such
an open world as Warlock, they might well consider lingering for awhile.

"You have a Patrol squad on world?" she asked.

"No. We're in a peculiar situation here. The Wyverns
won't allow any large off-world settlement. They only
accepted Thorvald and me because we did, by chance,
pass their dream test when we were survivors of a Throg
raid. But they wouldn't agree—or haven't yet—to any
Patrol station. We have a scout that visits from time to
time and that's the limit.

"This post of Jagan's was an experiment, pushed on us
by some of the off-world veeps who wanted to see how
a non-government penetration would be accepted. And
the big Companies didn't want to gamble. That's how a
Free Trader got it. There are just Thorvald, Taggi, his

mate Togi and their cubs, and me, plus a com-tech generally resident at headquarters."

As if the mention of his name summoned him, the brown animal lumbered forward. He sniffed the spear and growled. Tsstu spat, her claws pricking through to Charis's skin.

"What is he?" she asked.

"Wolverine, a Terran-mutated team animal," Lantee answered a little absently. "Could you try to raise them again? I have a hunch that time is getting rather tight."

Gytha—among the Wyverns Charis had been the closest to that young witch who had shared some of her instruction—maybe she could break through by beaming the power directly at Gytha and not at the Citadel as a whole. She did not answer Lantee's question in words but breathed upon the disk, and closed her eyes the better to visualize Gytha.

At her first meeting with the Wyverns, they had had a physical uniformity which made it difficult for an off-worlder to see them as individuals. But Charis had learned that their jeweled skin-patterns varied, that this adornment had meaning. The younger members of their species, when they came to adulthood and the use of the Power, could take certain simplifications of designs worn by the elders of their family lines and then gradually add the symbols of their own achievements, spelled out in no code Charis could yet understand, although by it she could now recognize one from another.

So it was easy to visualize Gytha, to beam her desire for her friend. She expected mind contact but, at an exclamation from Lantee, she opened her eyes to see Gytha herself, the gold and crimson circles about her snout agleam in the sun, the spine ridges along her back moving a little as if she had actually used them to fly here.

"He-Who-Dreams-True." The mental greeting reached out to Lantee.

"She-Who-Shares-Dreams." Charis was startled when the Survey man answered in the same way. So he did have communication with the Wyverns in spite of the fact he possessed no disk.

"You have called!" That was aimed at Charis with a

sharpness which suggested her act had been an error of judgment.

"There is trouble here—"

Gytha's head turned; she surveyed the wreckage of the post, glanced once at the body.

"It does not concern us."

"Nor this either?" Lantee made no move to pick up the spear again, but with boot toe he nudged it a little closer to the Wyvern.

She looked down, and a barrier between her and Charis snapped into place, as a door might slam. But Charis had been long enough among Gytha's kind to read the flash of agitation in the sudden quiver of the Wyvern's forehead crest. Her indifference of moments before was gone.

"Gytha!" Charis tried to break through the barrier of silence. But it was as if the Wyvern was not only deaf but that Charis and Lantee had ceased to exist. Only the bloodstained spear had reality and meaning.

The Wyvern made no gesture of warning. But they were there—two more of her kind. And one—Charis took a quick step back—one of the new arrivals had a head crest which was close to black in shade; the whole surface of her scaled skin was covered with such a multiplicity of gemmed design that she flashed. Gysmay—one of the Readers of Rods!

With her came the impact, first of irritation; then, as the Wyvern looked at Lantee, a cold anger, cold enough to strike as a weapon.

Though the Survey officer swayed, his face greenish under the brown, he stood up to her. Under that momentary burst of anger, Charis caught the suggestion of surprise in the Wyvern.

The second Warlockian who had accompanied Gysmay at Gytha's summons made no move. But from her, too, flowed emotion—if one could name it that—a feeling of warning and restraint. Her head crest was also black, but there was no flashing display of patterned skin bright in the sun. At first glance Charis thought she wore no designs at all, even the "encouragement" ones of her ancestors. Then the girl noted that there was a series of markings, deceptively simple, so close in hue to the natural

silver of her skin as to make a brocade effect detectable
only after concentrated study.

For Lantee or Charis this newcomer had no attention
at all; she was staring unwinkingly at the spear. That rose
from the spot where Lantee had dropped it, moving up
horizontally on a level with the Wyvern's eyes, coming to
her. Then it stopped, balanced in the air for a long
moment.

It whirled end for end and dashed groundward. There
was a sharp snapping as it shattered into bits. It might
have been broken against rock instead of bare earth. Then
the splinters whirled about and rose in turn. Charis
watched unbelievingly as those needle-small remnants of
the spear spun madly about. They fell, stilled, but now
they formed what was surely a pattern.

The girl reeled. Tsstu, in her arms, screeched. The wolverine squalled. Charis watched Lantee collapse limply
under a mental blow of rage, so raw and hot as to be a
fire within one's tormented brain. There was a red cloud
about her, but Charis was most aware of the pain in her
head.

That pain accompanied her into the dark, nibbled at
her will, weakened her struggle to pull away from it. Was
it pain or something behind the pain, compelling her, making her no longer Charis Nordholm but a tool to be used,
a key to turn for another, stronger personality?

The pain pushed at her. She crawled through a red
haze—on and on. Where? for what purpose? There was
only the whip of pain and the need to obey that other will
which wielded such a lash. Red, red, all about her. But the
red was fading slowly as a fire falls into ash. Red to gray,
gray which remained about her, a gray she could see . . .

Charis lay on her back. There was an arch of wall close
to her right hand; it sloped inward over her head. She
had seen that wall before. Half-light so dim—bare walls—
a drop table—a seat by it. The trading post—she was back
in the trading post!

IX

It was oddly still. Charis sat up on the cot, pulled her coverall into place. Coverall? Something buried deep inside her questioned, and a seed of doubt plagued her. Yes, the post was very still. She went to the door, set her hands on either side of the sealed slit. Was she locked in? But when she applied pressure, the portal opened and she was able to look out into the corridor.

The doors along it gaped open as she slipped into freedom. Listening brought no trace of sound, no murmur of voices or the heavy breathing of a sleeper. She went on down the hall, the floor chill to her bare feet.

But this—all of this, whispered that rebellious voice deep within her, she had done before. Yet on the surface, this was the here and now. The rooms were empty; she paused at each to make sure of that. Then the fourth room: a com screen against its wall, chairs and piles of record tapes. The com—she could use its sweep, try to pick up the government base. But first she must make sure she was safely alone.

A hurried search of the post, room by room. Time— it was a matter of time. Then she was back in the com room, leaning over the key board, picking out the proper combination to trigger a sweep ray.

A wait, and then a signal to the northeast. The visa-plate clouded and then cleared. Charis dodged from her position before it. A man was standing out of the mist, a man wearing a dingy uniform of a trader. Charis studied him, but he was unknown to her. Only the illegal blaster holstered at his belt made him different from any other fringe crewman. Charis's hand swept out to break contact.

She activated the sweep once again, tried south, and picked a signal—the insignia of Survey with a seal of Embassy. Slowly then she began to click out a message for the tape.

She was on a hillside. It was cold, dark, and she was running, running until her breath made a sharp stab beneath her ribs. The hunt would be up soon. Or would Tolskegg be willing to let her go, to die alone in the heights of exhaustion, starvation, or at the claws of some beast? He had Demeter and the settlement below now within his hold.

Demeter! The part of her which had been denying that this *was* the here and now struggled. Charis shook with more than cold. She was climbing to the heights above the settlement, yet the belief that this was all false grew stronger and stronger.

A dream. And there were those who used dreams and the stuff of dreams as a potter spun clay on his wheel. If she was caught in a dream, then she must wake—wake soon. Not a dream. Yes—a dream. She felt her own exhaustion, the pinch of hunger which was pain, the rough ground over which she stumbled, the bushes she grasped to steady her.

Not real—a dream! The bushes thinned until they were unsubstantial ghosts of themselves. Through their wavering outlines she saw a wall—yes, wall, solid wall. She was not on Demeter—she was—she was . . .

Warlock! As if the recognition of that name were a key, the now shadowy slope of Demeter vanished, driven away like smoke by a rising wind. She lay on a pad of mats. To her right was a window giving on the dark of night with a frosting of stars in the sky. This was Warlock and the Citadel of the Wyverns.

She did not move but lay quietly trying to separate dream from reality. The post—it had been raided. That Survey officer Shann Lantee— She could see him as

plainly now as if he stood before her, the blood-spattered
alien spear held between them.

The spear. It had splintered under the action of the
Wyvern. The broken bits had moved in that weird dance
until they had fallen in a pattern which had awakened such
rage in the Warlockians. And that rage . . .

Charis sat bolt upright on the mats. Lantee crumbling
under the Power of the Wyverns, herself returned to relive
portions of the past—for what purpose she could not
divine. Why had that rage been turned on Lantee? In a
way, it had been her fault for summoning Gytha. She had
been too impulsive.

Her hands went to the pouch at her belt. It was empty
of the disk. That had been in her hand when the Power
had taken her on the shore. Had she dropped it or had
they taken it from her?

That could mean that the Wyverns no longer considered
her in the guise of friend or ally. What *had* the broken
spear meant to them? Without the disk Charis was a prisoner here in this room. At least there was no reason why
she could not attempt at once to find out what bonds had
been set upon her freedom. Would she discover herself
as unable to move as she had been on her flight along the
shore when it had suited the Wyverns to control her?

"Tsstu?" Charis held that call to hardly above a whisper. She did not know how much of an ally the small curl-
cat could be against the Wyverns, but she had come to
depend upon her for companionship more heavily than
she had guessed.

A drowsy sound came from the shadow directly below
the window near which her head had rested. Tsstu lay
there, curled in a ball, her eyes closed, her ears folded
back tight against her head. Charis stooped and drew her
fingers lightly across that head.

"Tsstu," she whispered coaxingly. Was the curl-cat—
she had adopted Lantee's name for Tsstu's species since
it fitted so well—deep in her own kind of dream, too deep
to be aroused now?

The ears twitched and slits of eyes showed between
lids. Then Tsstu yawned widely, her yellow tongue curled
up and out. She lifted her head to eye Charis.

To communicate more than just vague impressions without the aid of the disk—could she do that? Charis made a sudden swoop to gather up the curl-cat, holding Tsstu aloft so that those narrow felinelike eyes looked straight into hers. Was Tsstu so closely linked to the Wyverns that she would serve them rather than Charis now?

Away, the girl thought, out of here.

"Rrrruuuu." That was agreement.

Tsstu wriggled vigorously in her grasp, wanting her freedom. Charis obeyed her wish. The curl-cat approached the doorway on pad-feet, elongating and flattening her body so that she had the appearance of a hunter on stalk. She stared into the corridor, her head raised a little, her ears spread to their widest. Charis guessed that every sense the curl-cat had was analyzing, scouting, for them. Tsstu glanced back at the girl, summoned—

This way led to the assembly rooms, to other private chambers such as hers, prepared for dreamers. Whether or not the corridor would eventually take them outside Charis did not know; she could only hope and rely upon Tsstu.

Even without the disk she strove to pick up any mind touch, any intimation that the Wyverns were about. Twice Charis was sure she had brushed beamed thoughts, not enough to read, just enough to be certain that they did exist. Otherwise, as in the trading post, she might be walking through a deserted dwelling.

Tsstu seemed confident of her path, trotting noiselessly along, choosing without hesitation whenever the corridor branched or was crossed by another passage. Charis was already out of the small portion of the maze that she knew. And she was conscious of the fact that the curl-cat had guided her into a section where the light from the walls was dimmer, the walls themselves rougher, narrower. She gained a feeling of age. Then the light was gone from the whole wall surface, lingering only in some places. Charis had to study closely before she saw the purpose of those remaining patches. They made out a design not unlike the whorls and circling on the disks. Here on the walls were some of the same symbols of power which the Wyverns had harnessed to their bidding.

But these patterns were not finished nor as crisp and cleanly cut as those on the disks. Larger, cruder, could they still open doorways for the initiated?

Tsstu continued with confidence. The even temperature of the other corridors failed. Charis put fingers to the nearest spiral and jerked them away as her flesh shrank from the heat there. She coughed, her throat dry. Where or what was this place?

In spite of an inner warning, she could not help but follow some of the designs with her eyes, looking ahead to pick them up, keeping them in sight until they were behind her. They blanketed her general field of vision until all she could see were the designs, and she halted with a cry of fear.

"Tsstu!"

Soft fur against her ankles, a reassurance in her mind. The curl-cat must not be affected by the same illusions as now imprisoned the girl. But to walk through this blackness where only the whorls, circles, lines had any existence for her was more than Charis could bring herself to do. Fear—overwhelming, panic-raising fear—

"Meeeerreee!"

Charis could feel Tsstu, she could hear her, but she could not see the curl-cat. She could see nothing but the patterns.

"Back!" Her word was a hoarse whisper. Only now Charis was not sure where back was. To take a step could plunge her into unknown chaos.

There was one design out of that mass of patterns— somehow she was able to fasten on that. Larger, sprawled out in crude length where she was used to it in a compact, clearly defined circle—this was her own disk pattern. She was certain of that.

"Tsstu!" She caught up the curl-cat by touch. Only those lines of dull silver glowed in the darkness. Concentrate on this design as she had on the disk and so— escape?

Charis hesitated. Escape to where? Return to the raided post? To the moss meadow? She must have a strong visual picture of her goal or the transport would not occur. Post? Meadow? Neither was where she wanted to go now. It was not just escape she wanted, it was knowledge of what was happening and why. But one could not gain that so . . .

Then—she was there. Lines of Wyverns, all seated cross-legged on mats, all intent upon two in the center. Lines of Wyverns, circles of them, for the chamber was a bowl-shaped place made up of climbing ledges, circling a space.

In that space Gysmay and her shadow-patterned companion stood alone. They faced each other, those two, and between them on the dark of the floor were splinters, needlelike pieces of all colors of the rainbow. The two were intent upon those splinters as were all others in that chamber.

Charis's hair stirred with electricity, her skin prickled. There was such power here, loosed, flowing, that she reacted to it physically. None of those about her had noted her coming; they stared at the splinters, concentrating their power.

The splinters rose upon their points, whirled, danced, spun into the air to form a small cloud which first encircled Gysmay. Three times about her body, beginning at waist height, then at her throat, lastly about her head. Then they spun away to the open between the two Wyverns, came apart in a tinkling rain to form a design on the floor. And from those that watched there came to Charis a ripple of emotion, some decision or demand or bargaining point, she was not sure which, had been stated.

Again the needles rose in their point-dance, leaped into the air to form a cloud which now wreathed the shadowed Wyvern. And Charis thought that they spun more slowly this time and that the cloud did not glint with bright colors but was more subdued. It broke and tinkled down to deliver the answer, counterargument, disagreement—three in one.

And again there was to be sensed a wave of approbation from some of the watchers, but a weaker one. The company was divided upon some issue and their discussion conducted so Charis watched, supposing that Gysmay was about to answer, for the needles were rising again.

But this time their dance was less prolonged and the cloud they formed swayed neither to one of the Wyverns nor to the other. It was a tight saucer-shape rising higher and higher, straight up until it was level with the fourth and top tier of the ledges.

The company watched in shocked surprise. This they had not expected. Gysmay and her companions held their disks. But if they strove to call the needles, those were now out of their control. The cloud swayed back and forth as if it clung to some unseen pendulum. And each swing brought it closer to where Charis stood.

Suddenly it broke from that measured swing to dart at her. She cried out as it whirled about her head, swiftly, almost menacingly. The two nearest Wyverns were on their feet, while all below focused on the girl.

Twice, three times, the cloud wreathed her and then it was gone, out over the open, descending. But Charis could not move; the restraint of the power held her prisoner. The cloud broke, rained its substance down to the floor, but she could see no design, only a meaningless jumble.

At the same time she moved, not of her own volition, but under the will of those about her, descending from tier to tier until she stood in the open, equidistant from the two witches.

"What is read is read. To each dreamer, a dream as is the will of Those Who Have Dreamed Before. It would seem, Dreamer of Other World Dreams, that you, also, have a word in this matter—"

"In what matter?" Charis asked aloud.

"In the matter of life and death, of your blood and our blood, of past and future," was the evasive answer.

Where she found the words and the courage to say them in an even voice, Charis did not know as she replied: "If that is the answer, I have been granted—" she nodded at the fallen needles "—then you needs must read it for me, O One of All Wisdom."

It was the shadow-laced Wyvern who answered: "But this is beyond our reading, though it *has* meaning since the Power moved its fashioning. We can only believe that its time is not yet. But time itself is an enemy in this matter. When one weaves a dream there must be no breaking of the thread of warp and woof. In our dreams, you and yours are unwelcome—"

"Those of my blood have died on the shore," Charis retorted. "Yet I cannot believe that it was by your hands and will—"

"No—by their own. For they began an ill dream and twisted the pattern. They have done a thing which is beyond straightening now." Gysmay was all anger, though that emotion was controlled and perhaps the more deadly because of that control. "They have given those who cannot dream another kind of power to break the long-laid design. Thus they must be hunted! They would overturn all reason and custom, and to that the end is slaying—and the slaying has already begun. We want no more of you. It shall be so." She clapped her hands and the needles jumped, collecting into a heap.

"Perhaps—" the shadowed Wyvern spoke.

"Perhaps?" echoed Charis. "Speak plainly to me now, Holder of Old Wisdom. I have seen a dead man of my race lying by a broken dwelling, and with him was a weapon which was not his. Yet among you I have seen no arms save the disks of Power. What evil walks this world? It is not of my making nor of the man Lantee's." She did not know why she added that, save that Lantee had had friendly contact with the witches.

"You are of one breed with the makers of this trouble!" Gysmay's thought was like a sharp hiss.

"The spear," Charis persisted, "this is of your kind, not mine! And a man died of it."

"Those who dream not—they hunt, they kill with such. And now they have broken the ancient law and run to do evil in the service of strangers. Those strangers have given them a protection against the Power so that they may not be brought back into order again. Perhaps this was not of your doing, for among us you have dreamed true and know the Power in its proper use. And the man Lantee, together with the one other who was with him from the earlier time, he, too, has dreamed—though that was out of all custom. But now come those who do not dream, to uphold the evil of not-dreaming. And our world will fall apart unless we hasten to the mending."

"But still," the shadowed Wyvern's quieter message came, "there is the pattern we cannot read and which we may not push away unheeded, for it was born of what we evoked here to answer us in our need. Therefore, there is a use for you, though we know not yet what it may be, nor do you. This you must learn for yourself and bring to aid the greater design—"

There was no mistaking the warning lying in that. Charis could only guess at the meaning behind the circumlocution of speech. An off-world party—probably the Jacks who had raided the post—had freed some of the males from the control of the Wyvern matriarchs. And these were now fighting for or with the strangers. In return, the Wyverns seemed about to organize some counterblow against all off-worlders.

"This great design—it is being readied against those of my blood?" Charis asked.

"It must be carefully woven, then aimed and dreamed." Again only half an answer. "But it will break your pattern as you have broken ours."

"And I have a part in this?"

"You have received an answer which we could not read. Discover its meaning and maybe it will be for us also."

"She breaks our pattern here," Gysmay interrupted. "Send her into the Place Without Dreams that she may not continue to disrupt what we do here!"

"Not so! She was answered; she has a right to learn the meaning of that answer. Send her forth from this place, yes—that we shall do. But into the Darkness Which Is Naught? No—that is against her rights. Time grows short, Dreamer. Dream true if you would save the breaking of your pattern. Now—get you hence!"

The tiered chamber, the watching Wyverns, vanished. Night was dark about Charis, but she could hear the murmur of sea waves not too far away. She breathed fresh air and above her were stars. Was she back on shore?

No. As her eyes adjusted to the very dim light, she was able to see that she stood on a high point of rock; around her on all sides was the wash of waves. She must be marooned on a rocky spear in what might be the middle of the ocean.

Afraid to take a step in any direction, Charis dropped down to her knees, hardly believing this could be true. Tsstu stirred, made a small questioning sound, and Charis's breath caught in a half-sob of incredulous protest.

X

"The dream is yours. Dream true."

Rock, an islet of bare rock, high above the sea with no path down its steep walls against which waves thundered. Overhead the cries of birds disturbed from their nesting holes by her coming. In the half-light of early morning Charis surveyed her perch. The first bewilderment of her arrival was gone, but her uneasiness now had a base of fear.

There was a series of sharp, shallow ledges leading down from the point of rock where she crouched to a wider open space sheltered on one side by a ridge. Some vegetation, pallid and sickly looking, straggled in that pocket of earth. She rose to look out over the sea, having no idea where she was now in relation to the Citadel or the main continent.

Some distance away there was another blot which must mark a second rock island, but it was too far to make out clearly. The finality which had been in her dismissal from the Wyvern assemblage clung. They had sent her here, and she could only believe that they would do nothing to get her back. Her escape must be of her own devising.

"Meeerrreee?" Tsstu squatted on the rock, her whole stance expressing her dislike of these surroundings.

"Where do we go?" Charis asked. "You know as much as I."

The curl-cat looked at her through eyes slitted against the force of the rising wind. Charis shivered. There was a promise of rain in the feel of that breeze, she thought. To be caught on this barren rock in a storm . . .

Only that half-pocket below offered any shelter at all; best get into it now. Tsstu was prudently already on the way, though with caution as she clawed along the ledges.

Rain sure enough, great drops slapping down. But rain meant water to drink. Charis welcomed those runnels which spattered into the pockets of rock. With the gift of rain water, this storm could be a blessing for them both.

The birds which had cried overhead were now gone. Tsstu, prowling their scrap of ground, went to work at a matted tangle against the ridge wall. She looked up with a trickle of white coursing over her chin, which she swept away with a swift swipe of tongue.

"—ree—" She pushed her head back into the tangle and then backed out, coming to Charis carrying something in her mouth with delicate care. When the girl put out her hand, Tsstu dropped into it a ball which could only be an egg.

Hunger fought with distaste and won. Charis broke a small hole in the top of that sphere and sucked its contents, trying not to notice the taste. Eggs and rain water— How long would they last? How long would the two of them last perched up here, especially if the wind grew strong enough to lick them off?

"The dream is yours. Dream true." Could this be only one of those very real dreams which the Wyverns were able to evoke? Charis could not remember that in any of those visions she had felt the need to eat or drink. Dream or real? Charis had no evidence either way.

But there had to be some way of escape!

The ridge at her back kept a measure of the rain from them, but the water gathering on the higher level drained down into this slight basin, pooling up about the roots of the few small plants. The earth about them grew slick.

If she only had the disk! But she had not had that back in that passage where the patterns had glowed on the walls. Yet her concentration upon those designs had taken her into the Wyvern assembly.

Suppose she had the same means of leaving here—
where would she go? Not back to the Citadel; that was
enemy territory now. To the raided post? No, unless she
was only seeking a hiding place. But that was not what
she wanted.

Wyvern witches against off-worlders. If the natives
moved only against the Jacks and their own renegade
males, that was none of her battle. But they were seeing *all* off-worlders as enemies now. If this rock exile was
merely a device to keep her out of battle, it was a well-
planned one. But she was of one stock; the Wyverns, no
matter how much they had been in accord, were alien.
And when it came to drawing battle lines, she was on the
other side, whether her original sympathies lay there or
not.

No, Charis did not care what happened to the scum
which had turned Jack here; the quicker they were dealt
with the better. But they should be disciplined by their
own kind.

Lantee and this Ragnar Thorvald who represented off-
world law on Warlock and who now were apparently
lumped with those to be finished off, Wyvern-fashion—
they must have a say. If they could be warned, then
there might still be time to summon the Patrol to handle
the Jacks and prove to the Wyverns that all off-worlders
were *not* alike.

A warning. But even with the disk Charis could not
reach the government base. You had to have a previous
memory of any point, be able to picture it in your mind,
in order to use the Power to reach it. And Lantee—what
had happened to him at the post? Was he even still alive
after that mind blast from the Wyverns?

Could—just possibly—could you use a *person* as a journey goal? Not to summon him to you as she had so disastrously done with Gytha at the post, but to go to him?
It was action she had never tried. But it was a thought.

Only first—the means. With a disk, one focused on the
pattern until one's eyes were set, and one's concentration
reached the necessary pitch to use one's will as a springboard into Otherwhere, or through it into another place.

Back in the passage, she had involuntarily used the

glowing design on the wall to project her into the Wyvern council, though then she had not controlled her place of arrival.

What was important then was not the disk itself but the design it bore. Suppose she could reproduce that pattern here, concentrate upon it. Escape? It might be her one chance. Manifestly she had no means of leaving here otherwise. So why not try the illogical?

Then—go where? The post? The moss meadow? Any point on which she could fix an entrance would bring her no closer to the base of the Survey men. But if she could join Lantee—him she could visualize strongly enough to use. The only other possibility was Jagan and she could not obtain any aid from the trader, even if he were still alive.

To join Lantee who, by his own account, had some experience with Wyvern dreaming and Power—might that not make him more receptive as a focal point? There was so much she had to guess about this, but it was the best chance she could see now. *If* she could set up the liberating pattern at all.

What were her means? The rock was too rough to serve as a surface on which to scratch lines. The slick clay at the edge of the growing pool caught Charis's attention. It was a relatively flat stretch and one could make an impression on it with a sharp stone or a branch from one of the bushes. But she had to do it right.

Charis closed her eyes and tried to build within her mind the all-important memory. There was a wavy line which curled back upon its length—so. Then the break which came—thus. Something else—something missing. Her agitation grew as she strove to fit in the part she could not remember. Maybe if she drew it out she would . . .

But the expanse of the clay was now too well covered by the pool water. And the wind was rising. With Tsstu curled close against her, Charis hugged the protecting ridge rock. There was nothing to do until the storm died.

Within a very short time Charis began to fear that they would not survive the fury of the wind, the choking drive of the rain. Only the fact that the ridge wall was there and they were tight against it gave them anchorage. The downpour continued to raise the pool until the water lapped Charis's cold feet and legs, but then it reached new runnels to feed it to the sea below.

Tsstu was a source of warmth in her arms and the curl-cat's vague communication was a reassurance, too. A confidence flowed from the animal to the girl, not steadily, but when she needed it most. Charis wondered just how much of what had happened to them Tsstu understood. Their band of mind-touch was so narrow the girl could not judge the intelligence of the Warlockian animal by the forms of comparison she knew. Tsstu might be far more than she seemed or be assessed as less because of the lack of full communication.

There came a time when the wind no longer lashed at their refuge or poked in finger-gusts to try to loosen their hold. The sky lightened and the rain, from a blustering wall of driven water, slackened into a drizzle. Still Charis was not sure of the design. But she watched the shore of the pool avidly, wondering whether she could bare the clay by cupping out water with her hands.

The sky was streaked with gold when she edged forward and twisted a length of water-soaked frond from one of the bushes. To strip away leaves and give herself a writing point was no problem. Impatience possessed her now—she *must* try this slender hope.

She cupped out some of the pool water by hand, clearing a stretch of smooth blue clay. Now! Charis found her fingers shaking a little; she set her will and muscle power to control that trembling as she put the point of her writing tool in the sticky surface.

Thus—the wavy line which was the base of the design to her thinking. Yes! Now for the sharp counterstroke to bisect it at just the proper angle. There—correct. But the missing part . . .

Charis shut her eyes tightly. Wave, line— What *was* the other? Useless. She could not remember.

Bleakly she looked down at the almost complete pattern. But "almost" would not serve; it had to be perfect. Tsstu sat beside her, staring with feline intensity at the marks in the clay. Suddenly she shot out a paw, planted it flat before

Charis could interfere. At the girl's cry, the curl-cat's ears folded and she growled softly, but she withdrew her forefoot, leaving the impress of three pads set boldly in the mud.

Three indentations! No—two! Charis laughed. Tsstu's memory was the better. She rubbed the mud clear, began to draw again—this time far more swiftly—with self-confidence. Wavy line, cut, two ovals—not quite where Tsstu had placed them, but here and here.

"Meeerrreee!"

"Yes!" Charis echoed that cry of triumph. "Will it work, little one? Will it work? And where do we go?"

But she knew she had already made up her mind as to that. Not a place but a *man* was her goal—at least at first try. If she could not join Lantee, they would try for the moss meadow and the chance of working their way south to the base from there. But that meant a waste of time they might not have to spend. No—for what might be the safety of all their kind on this world, Lantee was her first goal.

First she began to build her mental picture of the Survey officer, fitting in every small detail that memory supplied, and she found there were more of those to summon than she had believed. His hair, black, crisply curling like Tsstu's; his brown face sober and masked until he smiled but then softening about his mouth and eyes; his spare, wiry body in the green-brown uniform, his companion Taggi. Erase the wolverine, a second living thing might confuse the Power.

Charis found that she could not divide the two in her mind-picture. Man and animal, they clung together despite her efforts to forget Taggi and see only Lantee. Once more she built up the picture of Shann Lantee as she had seen him at the post before she had summoned Gytha. Just so he had stood, looked, been. Now!

Tsstu had come back into her arms, her claws caught in Charis's already slitted tunic. Charis regarded the curl-cat with a smile.

"We had better finish this flitting about soon or you will have me reduced to rags. Shall we try it?"

"—reee—" Agreement by mind-touch, eager anticipation. Tsstu appeared to have no doubts that they would go somewhere.

Charis stared down at the pattern.

Cold—no light at all—a terrible emptiness. Life was not. She wanted to scream under a torture which was not of body but of mind. Lantee—where *was* Lantee? Dead? Was this death into which she had followed him?

Cold again—but another kind of cold. Light—light which carried the promise of life she knew and understood. Charis fought down the churning sickness which had come from that terror of the place where life did not exist.

A rank smell, a growling answered by Tsstu's "rrruuugh" or warning. Charis saw the rocky waste about them and—the brown Taggi. The wolverine lumbered back and forth, pausing now and then to snarl. And Charis caught the feeling of fear and bewilderment which moved him. Always his pacing brought him back to the figure which squatted in a small fissure, huddling there, facing outward.

"Lantee!" Charis's cry of recognition was almost a paean of thanksgiving. Her gamble had paid off; they had reached the Survey man.

But if he heard her, saw her, he made no response. Only Taggi turned and came to her at an awkward run, his round head up, his harsh cry sounding not in warning-off anger but as a petition for aid. Lantee must be hurt. Charis ran.

"Lantee?" she called again as she went to her knees before the crevice into which he had crawled. Then she saw his face clearly.

At their first meeting his expression had been guarded, remote, but it had been—alive. This man breathed; she could see the rise and fall of his chest. His skin—she reached out her hand, rested finger tips briefly on his wrist, then raised them to his cheek—his skin was neither burning with fever nor unduly chill. Only what had made him truly a man and not a living husk was gone, sucked or driven out of him. By that bolt of the Wyvern's wrath?

Charis sat back on her heels and looked about. This was not the clearing before the post, so he had not remained where she had seen him fall. She could hear the sea. They were somewhere in the wilds along the coast. How and why he had come here did not matter now.

"Lantee—Shann—" She made a coaxing sound of his name as one might to attract the attention of a child. There was no flicker of response in his dead eyes, on the husk of a face.

The wolverine pushed against her, his rank odor strong. Taggi's head moved, his jaws opened and closed on her hand, not in anger but as a bid for attention. Seeing that he had that, Taggi released his hold, swung around facing inland, his growl a plain warning of danger in that direction.

Tsstu's ears, which had flattened at first sight of the Terran animal, spread again. She clawed at Charis. Something was coming; her own warning was piercingly sharp— they *must* go.

Charis reached again for Lantee's wrist, her fingers closed firmly as she pulled him forward. Whether she could get him moving she did not know.

"Come—come, we must go." Perhaps her words had no meaning, but he *was* responding to her tug, crawling out of the crevice, rising to his feet as she stood up and drew him with her. He would keep moving as long as she kept hold of his arm, Charis discovered, but if she broke contact, he stopped.

So propelling him, the girl turned south, Tsstu prowling ahead, Taggi forming a rear guard. Who or what could be behind them she did not know; her worst suspicions said Jack. Lantee wore no weapon, not even a stunner. And thrown stones were no protection against blasters. To find a refuge in which to hole up was perhaps their only hope if they were trailed.

Luckily, the terrain before them was not too rough. She could not have hauled Lantee, even docile as he was, up or down climbs. Not too far ahead were signs of broken country, an uneven line of outcrops sharp against the sky. And somewhere among those they might find a temporary sanctuary. Taggi had disappeared. Twice Charis had turned to watch for the wolverine, not daring to call. She remembered the whistle she had heard back in the moss meadow when she had first sighted the Survey officer and his four-footed companion. That summons she could not duplicate.

Now she hurried on. Under her urging, Lantee lengthened his stride, but there was no sign that he was
responding to anything but her pull on his arm. He might
have been a robot. Any warning she had would mean
nothing to him in his present condition, and whether that
had been caused only by temporary shock from the
encounter with the blast of Wyvern power or something
more lasting, she could not tell.

It would not be long until sunset, Charis knew. To
reach the broken land before the failing of the light was
her purpose. And she made it. Tsstu scouted out what
they needed, a ledge forming a good overhang which was
half cave. Charis pushed Lantee ahead of her into the
growing pool of shadow and pulled him down. He sat
there, staring unseeingly out into the twilight.

Emergency rations? His uniform belt had a series of
pockets in its broad length and Charis set about searching them. A message or record tape in the first, then a
packet of small tools for which she could not imagine any
use apart from complicated installation repairs, three
credit tokens, a case for identity and permit cards containing four she did not pause to read, another packet
of simple first-aid materials—perhaps more to the purpose now than the rest. She worked from right to left,
emptying each pocket and then restoring its contents,
while Lantee paid no heed to her search. Now—this was
what she had hoped for. She had seen just such tubes
carried by the ranger on Demeter. Sustain tablets. Not
only would they allay hunger, but they added a booster
which restored and nourished nervous energy.

Four of them. Two Charis dropped back into the tube
which she placed in her own belt pouch. One she
mouthed and chewed with vigor. There was no taste at
all, but she got it down. The other she held uncertainly.
How could she get it into Lantee? She doubted if he
would eat in his present condition. She would have to
see if a certain amount of absorption would come by
the only way left. She gathered two pebbles from the
ground and brushed them back and forth on her ragged
tunic to clean them from dust as well as she could, next,
that identity card case, also dusted for surface dirt. With

the rubbing of the tablet between the two pebbles, Charis obtained a powder, caught on the slick surface of the case.

Then, forcing his mouth open, the girl was able to brush that powder into Lantee's mouth. It was the best she could do. And just maybe the reviving powers of the highly concentrated Sustain might cut down the effects of the shock—or whatever affected him now.

XI

While she still had light, Charis set about making their half-cave into more of a fortress, pushing and carrying loose stones to build up a low wall across its front. If they kept well down behind that, the green of her tunic and the green-brown of Lantee's uniform would not be too noticeable. She bit at a ragged nail as she crawled back under cover.

The pocket of shadow had deepened and Charis put out a questioning hand to guide her. She touched Lantee's shoulder and moved, to huddle down close beside him. Tsstu flitted in, "meeerreeed" once, and then left on a hunt of her own. Of Taggi, there had been no sign since they had come into the broken land. Perhaps the wolverine, too, had gone in quest of food.

Charis let her head fall forward to rest on her knees. In this cramped space it was necessary to ball one's body into the smallest possible compass. She was not really tired; the Sustain tablet was working. But she needed to think. The Wyverns had warned her that time was against her. She had won free from the sea-rock to which they had exiled her, but perhaps she had made the wrong choice of escape. In his present condition, Lantee was no ally but a responsibility. With the coming of light she could redraw the pattern, get as far south as the moss meadow. How much farther beyond that lay the government base she had no idea.

But if she kept on following the shore she would eventually reach it.

But—Lantee? She could not take him with her, she was sure of that. And to leave him here in his condition— Charis shied from that solution every time the brutal necessity for action presented it. He was no friend; they had no acquaintance past that one meeting by the post. He had no claim on her at all and the need for action was urgent.

There were times when one human life was expendable for the whole. But, well as she knew the bitter logic of that reasoning, Charis found a barrier in her against her following it as high and firm as the barriers which the Wyverns had used to control her. Well, she could do nothing during the hours of dark. Maybe before morning Lantee would come out of it, out of this state of nonbeing. It was childish to cling to such hope but she did. Now she tried to will herself to sleep, a sleep past the entry of any dream.

"—ah—ahhhhhhh—"

The plaint was that of pain. Charis strove to deafen herself against it.

"—ah—ahhhhhh!"

The girl's head came up. There was a stirring beside her. She could not see Lantee save as a dim bulk in the gloom, but her hand went out to feel the convulsive shudders which tore him. And always came that small thread of a moan which must mark some unendurable agony.

"Lantee!" She shook his arm and he fell over against her, his head now resting on her knee, so that the shivering which rocked him became partly hers. His moaning had stopped, but his breath came and went in great sucking gasps, as if he could not get oxygen enough to satisfy the needs of his trembling body.

"Shann—what is it?" Charis longed for light enough to see his face. When she had nursed those struck down by the white plague on Demeter, she had known this same sick fear, this same courage sapping frustration. What could she do, what could anyone do? She drew him toward her so that his head rested in her lap, tried to hold him still. But just as he had been apathetic and robot-like before, so now he was restless. His head turned back and forth as that horrible gasping racked him.

"Rrrruuuu." Out of nowhere Tsstu came, a shadow. The curl-cat was on Lantee's chest, crouched low, clinging with claws when Charis tried to push her away. Then a growl and Taggi burst around the stones Charis had set up, came to nuzzle against Lantee's twisted body as if, with Tsstu, he strove to hold the sufferer still. Need—it was a cloud about the four of them—the blind call for help which Lantee did not have to put into words for Charis to feel, the concern of the animals, her own helplessness. This was a crisis point, she realized that. The Survey man was fighting a battle, and if he lost—?

"What can I do?" she cried aloud. This was not an affair of the body—she had delved deeply enough into the Wyvern Power to know that—but of mind, of—of identity.

Will—that was the springboard of Wyvern Power. They willed what they wished, and it *was*! She was willing now—willing Lantee to . . .

Dark and cold and that which was nothing once again, this was the space into which her desire to help was drawing her, a space which was utterly alien to her kind. Dark—cold. But now— Two small lights, flickering, then growing stronger, though the dark and cold fought to extinguish them; two lights which drew closer to her and grew and grew. She did not reach out her hands to take up those lights, but they came as if she had called. And then Charis was aware that there was a third light, and *she* furnished the energy on which it fed.

Three lights joined to speed through that dark in search. No thought, no speech among them; just the compulsion to answer a calling need. For the dark and cold were all-encompassing, a sea of black having no shore, no islands.

Island? Faint, *so* faint, a glimmer showed on the sea. They spun together, those three lights, and struck down to the small spark gleaming in that encroaching and swallowing dark. Now there was a fourth light like an ash-encrusted coal in a near-dead fire. Together the three aimed at that fire, but there was no touching it: They had not the power to strike through, and the fire was near extinction.

Then the light which was fed by Charis's energy and will soared, drawing also that which was the animals'. She reached out, not with a physical arm or hand but with an extension of her inner force, and touched one of her companion lights.

It snapped toward her. She was rent, to writhe in pain as emotions which were alien warred against that which was Charis alone—wild, raw emotions which boiled and frothed, which dashed her in and about. But she fought back, strove to master and won to an uneasy stability. And then she reached out again and drew to her the second spark.

Once again she was in tumult, and even greater was the fight she had to wage for supremacy. But the urgency which had drawn all three, the need to go to the dying fire, laid upon them now the need for acting as one. And when Charis called upon that need, they obeyed.

Down to that glimmer which was now far spent sped a bolt of flaming force raised to the highest possible pitch. That broke through, pierced to the heart of the fire.

Turmoil for a space. Then it was as if Charis raced wildly down a corridor into which emptied many doors. From behind each of these came people and things she did not know, who grasped at her, tried to shout messages in her ears, impress upon her their importance, until Charis was deafened, driven close to the edge of sanity. To that corridor she could see no end.

The voices screamed, but through them came other sounds—a growling, a squalling—equal to the voices, demanding attention in their turn. Charis could not run much farther . . .

Silence, abrupt, complete—and in its way terrifying, too. Then—light. And she had a body again. Aware first of that, Charis ran a hand down that body in wonder and thankfulness. She looked about her. Under her sandaled feet was sand, silver sand. But this was not the shore of the sea. In fact, vision in any direction was not clear, for there was a mist which moved in spirals and billows, a mist of green, the same green as the tunic she wore.

The mist curled, writhed, held a darker core. She saw movement in that core, as if an arm had drawn aside a curtain.

"Lantee!"

He stood there, facing her. But it was no longer the shell of a man she saw. There was life and awareness back in his body and mind. He held out his hand to her.

"Dream . . . ?"

Was it all a dream? She had known such clarity of vision before in the dream Otherwhere of the Wyverns.

"I don't know," she answered his half-question.

"You came—*you!*" There was a kind of wondering recognition in his voice which she understood. They had been together in that place where their kind was not. The four fires, joined together, had now broken the bonds which had held him in a place their species should never know.

"Yes." Lantee nodded even though Charis had put none of that into words. "You and Taggi and Tsstu. Together you came, and together we broke out."

"But this?" Charis gazed about at the green mist. "Where is *this?*"

"The Cavern of the Veil—of illusions. But this I believe *is* a dream. Still they strive to keep us that much in bonds."

"For dreams there are answers." Charis went down on her knees and smoothed the sand. With one finger tip she traced her design. It was not clear in the powdery stuff, but there was enough, she hoped, to serve her purpose. Then she looked at Lantee.

"Come." Charis held out her hand. "Think of a half-cave—" swiftly she described the place they had been in at night "—and keep hold. We must try to return."

She felt his grip tense and harden, his stronger fingers cramping hers until her flesh numbed. And then she centered all of her mind on the picture of the ledge cave and the pattern . . .

Charis was stiff and cold, her arm ached, her hand was numb. Behind her was a rock wall, over her head an extension of it, and from before her a breath of sun heat. There was a sigh and she glanced down.

Lantee lay there, curled up awkwardly, his head in

her lap, his hand clutching hers in that numbing grip.
His face was drawn and haggard, as if he had aged
planet years since she had seen him last. But the slack
blankness which had been so terrifying was gone. He
stirred and opened his eyes, first bewildered, but then
knowing, recognizing her.

He raised his head.

"Dream!"

"Maybe. But we are back—here." Charis freed her hand
from his hold and spread her cramped fingers. With her
other hand she patted the nearest stone in her improvised
wall to assure herself of its reality.

Lantee sat up and rubbed his hand across his eyes. But
Charis remembered.

"Tsstu! Taggi!"

There was no sign of either animal. A small nagging
fear began to nibble at her mind. They—*they* were those
other lights. And she had lost them; they had not been
in the place of green mist. Were they lost forever?

Lantee stirred. "They were with you—there?" It was not
a question but a statement. He crawled out from under the
ledge, whistled a clear rising note or two. Then he stooped
and held out his hand again to draw her up beside him.

"Tsstu!" aloud she called the curl-cat.

Faint—very faint—an answer! Tsstu had not been abandoned in that place. But where was she?

"Taggi is alive!" Lantee's smile was real. "And he
answered me. It was different, that answer, from what
it has ever been before, more as if we spoke."

"To have been *there*—might not that bring a change
in us all?"

For a moment he was silent and then he nodded. "You
mean because we were all one for a space? Yes, perhaps
that cannot be ever put aside."

She had a spinning vision of that race down the endless corridor with its opening doors and the shouting
figures emerging from them. Had those represented
Lantee's memories, Lantee's thoughts? Not again did she
want to face that!

"No," he agreed without need of speech from her, "not
again. But there was then the need—"

"More than one kind of need." Charis shied away from any more mention of that mingling. "There's more trouble than Wyvern dreaming for us to consider now." She told him of what she had learned.

Lantee's mouth thinned into a straight line, his jaw thrust forward a little. "Thorvald was with them or at least at the Citadel when we found that spear. They may have put him away as they did me. Now they can move against all off-worlders without interference. We have a com-tech at the base, and a Patrol scout may have set down since I left—one was almost due. If that ship had not come in, Thorvald would have recalled me when he left. Two, maybe three, men were there and none of them armored against Wyvern control. We've been very cautious about trying to expand the base because we did want to maintain good relations. These Jacks have blown the whole plan! You say they have some Wyvern warriors helping them? I wonder how they worked that. From all we've been able to learn, and that's very little, the witches have a firm control over their males. That has always been one of the problems; makes it almost impossible for them to conceive of cooperation with us."

"The Jacks must have something to nullify the Power," Charis commented.

"That's all we need," he said bitterly. "But if they can nullify the Power, then how can the witches go up against them?"

"The Wyverns seem very sure of themselves." Charis had her own first doubts. With the assembly arrayed against her back at the Citadel, she had accepted their warning; her respect for their Power had not been shaken until this moment. But Lantee was right. If the invaders were able to nullify the Power to the extent of releasing the males who had always been under domination, then could the witches hope to battle the strangers themselves?

"No," Lantee continued, "they're very sure of themselves because they've never before come up against anything which threatened their hold on their people and their way of life. Perhaps they can't even conceive of the Power's being broken. We had hoped to make them understand eventually that there *were* other kinds of power, but we have not had time. To them this is a threat, right enough, but not *the* supreme threat I believe it is."

"Their power *has* been broken," Charis said quietly.

"With a nullifier, yes. How soon do you suppose the truth of that will get through to them?"

"But we did not need this machine or whatever the Jacks have. *We* broke it—the four of us!"

Lantee stared at her. Then he threw back his head and laughed, not loudly but with the ring of real amusement.

"You are right. And what will our witches say to this, I wonder? Or do they already know? Yes, you freed me from whatever prison they consigned me to. And it *was* a prison!" His smile vanished, the drawn lines in his face sharpened. "So—their power *can* be broken or circumvented in more ways than one. But I do not think that even that information will deter them from making the first move. And they must be stopped." He hesitated and then added in a rush of words, "I am not arguing that they should take the interference of the Jacks and not fight back. By their way of thinking their way of life is threatened. But if these witches go ahead as they plan and try to wipe us all off Warlock, supposing they *are* able to fight the Jack weapon or weapons, then they will have written the end to their own story themselves.

"For if this band of Jacks has come up with a nullifier to defeat the Power, others can, too. It will just be a matter of time until the Wyverns are under off-world control. And that mustn't happen!"

"You say that?" Charis asked curiously. "*You?*"

"Does that surprise you? Yes, they have worked on me and this was not the first time. But I, too, have shared their dreaming. And because I did and Thorvald did, we were that much closer to bridging the gap between us. We must be changed in part when we are touched by the Power. But though they may have to bend to weather a new wind—which will be very hard for them—they must not be swept away. Now—" he looked about him as if he could summon a copter out of the air "—we have to be on the move."

"I don't think they will allow us to return to the Citadel," Charis demurred.

"No, if they are working up to some stroke against offworlders, they will have all the screens up about their prime base. Our own headquarters is the only place. From there we can signal for help. And if time is good to us, we can handle the Jacks before they do. But where we are now and how far from the base—" Lantee shook his head.

"Do you have your disk?" he added a moment later.

"No. But I don't need it." Just how true that was, Charis could not be sure. She had won off the rock island and out of the place of green mist without it, however. "But I've never seen your base."

"If I described it, as you did this rock hole for me, would that serve?"

"I don't know. The cavern was a dream, I think."

"And our bodies remained here as anchors to draw us back? That could well be. But there's no harm in trying."

The hour must have been close to midday; the sun was burning hot on the baked section of rock. And, as Lantee had pointed out, they were lost as far as landmarks were concerned. His suggestion was as good as any. Charis looked about for a patch of earth and a stone or stick to scratch with. But there was neither.

"I must have something which will make a mark."

"A mark?" Lantee echoed as he, too, surveyed their general surroundings. Then he gave an exclamation and snapped open a belt pocket to bring out the small aid kit. From its contents he selected a slender pencil which Charis recognized as sterile paint, made to cleanse and heal small wounds. It was of a greasy consistency. She tried it on the rock. The mark was faint but she could see it.

"Now," Lantee sat on his heels beside her, "we'll aim for a place I know about a half mile from the base."

"Why not the base itself?"

"Because there may be a reception waiting there that we wouldn't care to meet. I want to do some scouting before I walk into what might be real trouble."

He was right, of course. Either the Wyverns might

already have made their move—for how could Charis guess how much time had actually passed since she had been wafted from the assembly to the island—or the Jacks, learning the undermanned status of the only legal hold on Warlock, had taken it over to save themselves from off-world interference.

"Right here—there's a lake shaped so." Lantee had taken the sterile stick from her and was drawing. "Then trees, a line of them standing this way. The rest is meadow land. We should be at this end of the lake."

It was hard to translate those marks into a real picture and Charis began to shake her head. Suddenly her companion leaned forward and laid his palms flat against her forehead just above her eyes.

XII

What Charis saw was indistinct and fuzzy, not as clean-cut as a picture she recalled from her own memory, but perhaps enough for concentration. Only, with that fogged picture came other things; that corridor with the doors was beginning to take form behind the wood and lake. Charis struck Lantee's hand away and stared at him, breathing hard, trying to read an answering awareness in his eyes.

"We'll have to remember the dangers of that." Lantee spoke first.

"Not again! *Never* again!" Charis heard her voice grow shrill.

But already he was nodding in reply. "No, not again. But did you see enough of the other?"

"I hope so." She took the stick from him and chose a flat rock surface on which to sketch the Power design. It was when she was putting in the ovals Tsstu had remembered for her that Charis paused.

"Tsstu! I cannot leave her behind. And Taggi—"

She closed her eyes and sent out that silent call. "Tsstu, come! Come now!"

Touch! There came an overlapping of thought waves as fuzzy as the picture Lantee had beamed to her. And—refusal! Decided refusal—an abrupt breaking of contact. Why?

"There is no use," she heard Lantee say as she opened her eyes again.

"You reached Taggi." It was not a question.

"I reached him in a different way than I ever have before. He would not listen. He was occupied—"

"Occupied?" Charis wondered at his word choice. "Hunting?"

"I don't think so. He was exploring, trying something new which interested him so greatly he would not come."

"But they are *here*, back with us, not in Otherwhere?" Her relief was threatened by that recurring fear.

"I don't know where they are. But Taggi has no fear; he is only curious, very curious. And Tsstu?"

"She broke contact. But—yes—I think she had no fear either."

"We shall have to leave now!" Lantee continued.

If they could, Charis amended silently. She took his hand once more. "Think of your lake," she ordered and concentrated on the faint pattern on the rock.

Cool breeze—the murmur of it through leaves. The direct baking of the sun had been modified by a weaving of branches, and just before her was the shimmer of lake surface.

"We made it!" The tight grasp on her hand was gone. Lantee surveyed the site with a wary measuring, his nostrils slightly dilated as if, like Taggi, he could pick up and classify some alien scent.

There was a path along the lake shore, defined well enough to be clearly visible. Otherwise the place was as deserted as if no off-worlder had ever been there before.

"This way!" Lantee motioned her south, away from the thread of path. His voice was close to a whisper, as if he suspected they were scouting enemy-held territory.

"There's a hill in this direction and from it we can get a good look at the base."

"But why—?" Charis began and was favored with an impatient frown from her companion.

"If there's any move being made, either by the Jacks or the witches, the first strike will be at the base. With Thorvald and me out of the way, the witches may be able to put Hantin, or any other off-worlder, right under control. And the Jacks could overrun the whole place easily, make a surprise attack and write off the base just as they wrote off the trading post."

She followed him with no more questions. On Demeter Charis had gone exploring with the ranger; she thought she knew a measure of woodcraft. But Lantee was as much at home in this business as Taggi could be. He slipped soundlessly from one piece of cover to another. However, she noted with some surprise, he did not display any outward signs of impatience when her clumsiness slowed them. And she was even a little resentful of what she came to believe was his forbearance.

Hot and very thirsty, Charis wriggled up a slope Lantee had led them to. She had a swelling bite delivered by the rightful inhabitant of an earthen run she had inadvertently crushed, and her throat ached with desert dryness before they lay side by side behind a screen of brush at the top of that rise.

A cluster of four bubble domes lay below and, farther away, a landing field. There was a light copter standing to one side of that, and on the rocket-blasted middle section stood a small spacer—a Patrol scout, Charis believed.

It was very peaceful there below. No one moved about the buildings, but pale flowers native to Warlock grew in the open space. And some brighter spots in those beds suggested that perhaps some off-world plants had been imported as an experiment.

"It looks all right—" she began.

"It looks all wrong!" His whisper carried something of the hiss of Wyvern anger.

There were no blast holes in the fabric of the domes as there had been at the raided post, nothing in sight which suggested trouble. But Lantee's concern was plain to read, and she returned to a second and more searching survey of the scene.

It must be midafternoon and there was a quality of drowsy peace down there. The inhabitants could all be dozing out the hours at their ease. Charis made up her mind not to ask for enlightenment but wait for her companion to volunteer the cause for his suspicion.

He began to talk softly, perhaps more as a listing of his own causes for suspicion aloud rather than as a sharing of information with Charis.

"Com mast down. Hantin's not out in the garden working on that new crossing bed of his. And Togi—Togi and the cubs—"

"Togi?" Charis dared to ask.

"Taggi's mate. She has two cubs and they spend every afternoon that's sunny down among those rocks. They're very fond of earth-wasp grubs and there's several colonies of them to be found there. Togi's been teaching the cubs how to dig them out."

But how could he be sure that just because a wolverine and her cubs were not at a certain place there was trouble below? Then Charis added that to the two other facts he had noted—the com mast down and that he had not seen one of the base personnel outside. But both of those were such little things—

"Put those three together"—Lantee was either able to read her thoughts in part or was following her own line or reasoning with surprising accuracy—"and you have a wrong answer. On a base you come to follow habit. We have the com mast up always. That's orders and you don't change regulations unless there's an emergency. Hantin is experimenting with the crossing of some of the native plants with off-world varieties. He's hybrid-mad and he spends all his free time in the garden. And Togi is earth-wasp minded; only caging would keep her away from those rocks. And since we've yet to find any cage she can't break out of—" He looked glum.

"So—what do we do now?"

"We wait until dark. If the base is deserted and the com not wrecked—both of which are slim chances—there may be an opportunity to get a call off planet. But there's no use in trying to get down there now. Any approach would have to be made across the open."

He was right in that. The usual clearing about buildings ordered by custom in a frontier world was not as open here as it had been about Jagan's post. But there was no brush or trees or other cover growth left within a good distance of any of the four domes or the landing field. To approach those meant advancing in the open.

Lantee rolled over on his back and lay staring up into the bush they were using as a screen with an intentness which suggested that he hoped to read the answer for their problem somewhere within the maze of its drooping branches.

"Togi—" Charis broke the silence "—is she like Taggi? Could you call her?" What aid the wolverine might be Charis did not know, but to try and reach her was action of some sort, and just now she found inaction more frustrating than she could bear.

Exasperation sharpened Lantee's reply. "What do you think I'm trying to do? But since she has had cubs she is less receptive to orders. We have let her go her own way while they are small. Whether she will ever obey spoken commands again, I am not sure."

He closed his eyes, a frown line sharp between his well-marked brows. Charis propped her chin on her hand. As far as she could determine, the base continued to drowse in the sun. Was it really deserted? Through Wyvern Power sending its inhabitants into that strange darkness? Or left so by a Jack raid?

Unlike the rugged setting Jagan had chosen for his post, this more open country was lighter, gave no feeling of somberness darkening into possible menace. Or was she becoming so accustomed to the general Warlockian scenery that it no longer looked the same to her as it had when Jagan had brought her out of the spacer? How long ago? weeks? months? Charis had never been able to reckon how much time she had spent with the Wyverns.

Yes, here Warlock was fair under the amber sky, the golden sun. The amethyst hues of the foliage were sheer splendor. Purple and gold—the ancient colors of royalty in the days when Terra had hailed kings and queens, emperors and empresses. And now Terran blood had spread from star to star, mutated, adapted, even allegiances had changed from world to world as the tides of migration had continued generation after generation. Ander Nordholm had been born on Scandia, but she herself had never seen that planet. Her mother had been from Bran, and she herself could claim Minos for her native soil. Three widely separated and different worlds. And she could not remember Minos at all. Lantee—where had Shann Lantee been born?

Charis turned her head to study him, trying to select some race or planet to fit his name and his general physical appearance. But to her eyes he was not distinctive enough a type to recognize. Survey drew from almost every settled planet of the Confederation. He could even be a native Terran. That he was Survey meant that he had certain basic traits of character, certain very useful skills. And that he was also wearing the gold key of an embassy above his cadet bar meant even more—that he had extra-special attributes into the bargain.

"It's no use." He raised his hand to shade his now open eyes. "If she is still down there, I can't touch her—not mentally anyway."

"What did you think she might do to help us now?" Charis asked, curious.

"Maybe nothing." But that seemed an evasive answer to the girl.

"Are you a Beast Master?" she asked.

"No, Survey doesn't use animals that way—as fighters or sabotage teams. Taggi and Togi are both fighters when they have to be, but they act more as scouts. In lots of ways their senses are more acute than ours; they can learn more in a shorter time about a new stretch of country than any human. But Taggi and Togi were sent here originally as an experiment. We learned after the Throg attack just how much they could help—"

"Listen!" Charis's hand clamped onto his shoulder. She straightened out, flat to the ground, her head to one side. No, she had not been mistaken. The sound *was* growing louder.

"Atmosphere flyer!" Lantee's identification confirmed her own guess. "Back!" He rolled farther under the drooping branches of the bush and tugged at Charis as she wormed in after him.

The flyer was approaching from the north, not coming in over their present perch. As the plane set down on the landing strip, Charis saw that it was larger than the copter already there—probably a six-passenger ship motored for transcontinental service, not for the shorter flights of the copters.

"That's none of ours!" Lantee whispered.

It came to a halt and two men dropped from it to stride purposefully toward the domes. They went so confidently that the watchers knew they must expect welcome or at least believe that no difficulty awaited them. They were too far from the spy post for their features to be distinguished, but while they wore uniforms of a similar cut to those at the post, Charis had never seen these before. The black and silver of Patrol, the green-brown of Survey, the gray and red of the medical service, the blue of Administration, the plain green of the rangers, the maroon of Education—she could identify those at a glance. But these were a light yellow.

"Who?" she wondered. When she heard a small grunt from Lantee, she added, "Do you know?"

"Something—somewhere—" Then he shook his head. "I've seen something like that color, but I can't remember now."

"Would Jacks wear uniforms? The one I saw with the blaster—he was dressed just like any other Free Trader."

"No." Lantee's frown grew deeper. "It means something—if I only could remember!"

"No government service? Perhaps some planetary organization operating off-world," Charis suggested.

"I don't know how that could be. Look!"

A third man had come out of one of the domes. Like the two from the flyer he wore yellow, but sunlight struck glinting sparks from his collar and belt; that could only mark insignia of some type. A uniformed invasion of a government base— A wild idea suddenly struck Charis.

"Shann—could—could a war have broken out?"

For a moment he did not answer her and, when he did, it was almost as if he were trying to deny that idea to himself as much as to her.

"The only war we've waged in centuries has been against the Throgs—and those aren't Throgs down there! I was here just five days ago, and the messages we were receiving from off-world were all only routine. We had no warning of any trouble."

"*Five* days ago?" she challenged him. "How can we be sure of how much time passed while the Wyverns controlled us? It may have been weeks or longer since you were here."

"I know—I know. But I don't think war is the answer. I just don't believe it. But a Company action— If they thought they could get away with a grab— If the gain was big enough—"

Charis considered that. Yes, the Companies—they were regulated, curbed, investigated, as well as the Confederation and the Patrol could manage. But they had their own police, their extra-legal methods when they dared flaunt control. Only what would bring any one of the Companies to send a private army to Warlock? What treasure could be scooped up here before a routine Patrol visit would reveal such lawless activity?

"What could they find here to make it worth their while?" she asked. "Rare metals? What?"

"One thing—" Lantee continued to watch the men below. The two from the flyer were discussing something with the man from the dome. One of them broke away and headed back for the aircraft. "One thing might just be worth it if they could seize it."

"What?" Charis's guesses roved wildly. Surely Jagan would have known and mentioned any outstanding native product during his instruction on trading.

"The Power itself! Think what that secret would mean to men who could use it on other worlds!"

He was right. The Power was a treasure great enough to tempt even one of the companies into piracy of a kind. If they mastered its use they could defy even the Patrol. And Lantee's idea fitted very neatly into place, especially now that she remembered Jagan's mention of the same quest.

"The nullifier." She thought aloud. "That's their answer to the use of the Power against *them*. But how did they develop something of the sort without knowing more about the Power? Maybe they believe they can use it to control the Wyverns and make them yield their secrets."

"The nullifier, whatever it is, can be an adaptation of something already well known. As to the rest—yes—they could believe they have the witches finished."

"But the Jacks? Why?"

Lantee scowled. "Not the first time a Company has shoved some of its hard-fisted boys into plain clothes and tried a Jack cover-screen for a quick steal. If they're caught, then they're just Jacks and nothing else. If they succeed, the Company comes in behind their screen and they all fade out as soon as the grab is over. If they believe now that they've either wiped out all opposition or have it under wraps, then they're in the open with another force to consolidate their position and protect any experts and techs they send in for a real study of the Power. It all fits. Don't you see how it fits?"

"But—if this is a Company at work—" Charis's voice trailed off as the full force of what might be arrayed against them struck home.

"You're beginning to see? Jacks on their own are one thing; a Company pulling a grab is something else." Lantee's tone was bleak. "They will have resources to draw on to back their every move. Right now I wouldn't wager star against comet that they're not in complete control here."

"Maybe," Charis chose to use his gambling symbols, "they may believe that they have every comet on the board blocked, but there are a few wild stars left."

There was a faint suggestion of a smile about his lips.

"*Two* wild stars, perhaps?"

"Four. Do not underestimate Tsstu and Taggi." And she meant that, strange as it sounded.

"Four—you, me, a wolverine, and a curl-cat—against the might of a Company. You fancy high odds, don't you, Gentle Fem?"

"I fancy any odds we can get while the game is still in play. The counters have not been swept from the board yet."

"No, nor the game called. And we might just run those odds to a more even balance. I do not think that our friends below have yet met the witches of Warlock. Even we do not know their full resources."

"I hope they have some good ones left," was her comment.

Only a short time ago the Wyverns had come out in the open as enemies. Now Charis wished with all her heart for their success. In the lines of battle, if what she and Lantee had come to believe was true, they would be on the side of the witches.

"What can we do?" She was again afire for action.

"We wait and still we wait. When it is dark, I want to see a little more of what is going on down there. Make sure, if we can, just what we are up against."

He was entirely right, but waiting now was so very hard.

XIII

They lay side by side, watching the base. The flyer had taken off, leaving behind one of its passengers; with the officer, he had returned to the domes. Again the site was seemingly deserted.

"That is a Patrol scout ship down there," Charis said. "Would any Company dare move outwardly against the Patrol?"

"With a good cover story they could risk it," Lantee replied. "A scout isn't on a tight report schedule, remember. They could say that they found this base deserted and blame any trouble on the Wyverns if it became necessary to provide an explanation. What I'd like to know is—if this *is* a Company grab—how they came to learn of the Power. Jagan ever say anything about it?"

"Yes, he mentioned it once. But he spoke mostly about things such as this cloth." Charis plucked at the stuff of her tunic which was standing the hard usage better than Lantee's uniform. "He was gambling to make a high stake, but I thought trade material was mostly fishing on his part."

"He got in here over Thorvald's protest," Lantee commented. "We couldn't see how he rated a permit in the first place, he was so close to the fringe."

"Could he have been used as a Company cover? Maybe without his even knowing it?"

Lantee nodded. "Could well be. Send him in as an opening wedge and have his reports to add to their general knowledge since our files are closed—if any files are ever closed when the grab is big enough!" he ended cynically. "Somebody passed over a bag of credits in this deal. I'd swear blood-oath on that."

"Just what *can* you do down there?" Charis asked.

"If the com isn't out and if I can reach it, just one signal set on repeat will bring in such help as'll make these blaster merchants think someone's put a couple of earthwasps under their tunic collars!"

"Several ifs in that."

Lantee smiled his humorless, lip-stretching smile. "Life is full of ifs, Gentle Fem. I've carried a pack of them for years."

"Where are you from, Shann?"

"Tyr." The answer was short, bitten off as if meant to be final.

"Tyr," Charis repeated. The name meant nothing to her, but who could ever catalogue the thousands of worlds where Terran blood had rooted, flowered, branched, and broken free to roam inward.

"Mining world. Right—right about there!" He had lifted his head and now he pointed northward into the sky which was displaying the more brilliant shades of sunset.

"I was born on Minos. But that doesn't mean much since my father was an Education officer. I've lived on— five—six—Demeter was the seventh world."

"Education officer?" Lantee echoed. "Then how did you get with Jagan? You beamed in a tape asking for aid. What was that all about anyway?"

She cut the story of Demeter and the labor contract to its bare bones as she told it.

"I don't know whether Jagan could have held you to that contract here on Warlock. On some worlds it'd be legal, but anyway you could have fought him with Thorvald's backing," he observed when she was done.

"Doesn't matter much now. You know—I didn't like Warlock at first. It—it was almost frightening. But now, even with all this, I want to stay here." Charis was surprised at her own words. She had said them impulsively but she knew they were true.

"By ordinary standards, this will never be a settlement world under the code."

"I know—intelligent native life over the fifth degree—so we stay out. How many Wyverns are there anyway?"

He shrugged. "Who knows? They must have more than one settlement among the off-shore islands, but we do not go except to their prime base and then only on permission. You perhaps know more about them than we do."

"This dreaming," Charis mused. "Who can be sure of anything with them? But can the Power really be used by males? They are so certain that it can't. And if they're right about that, what can the Company do?"

"Follow Jagan's lead and bring in women," he retorted. "But we're not sure that they are right. Maybe *their* males can't 'dream true,' as they express it, but I dreamed, and Thorvald did, when they put us through their test at first contact. Whether I could use a disk or pattern as you have I don't know. Their whole setup is so one-sided that contact with another way of life could push it entirely off base. Maybe if they were willing to try—"

"Listen!" Charis caught at his sleeve. Speculation about the future was interesting, but action was needed now. "What if you can use a pattern? You know the whole base; you could get down there and out again if you have to. It would be the perfect way to scout!"

Lantee stared at her. "If it did work—!" She watched him catch some of her enthusiasm. "If it just *would* work!"

He studied the base. The shadows cast by the domes were far more pronounced, though the sky was still bright over their heads. "I could try for my own quarters. But how would I get out again? There's no disk—"

"We'll have to make one or its equivalent. Let's see." Charis wriggled about under their brush cover. The initial pattern to get in by—she could draw that on the ground as she had before. But the other one—to bring Lantee out again—he'd have to carry that with him. How?

"Could you use this?" The Survey man pulled free a wide, dark leaf. Its purple surface was smooth save for a center rib and it was as big as her two hands.

"Try this to mark with." He had out his case of small tools and handed her a sharply pointed rod.

Carefully Charis traced the design which had unlocked so many strange places since she had first used it. Luckily the marks showed up well. When she had done, she handed the leaf to Lantee.

"It works so. First, you picture in your mind as clearly as you can the place you want to go. Then you concentrate on following this design with your eyes, from right to left—"

He glanced from the leaf to the base. "They can't be everywhere," he muttered.

Charis bit back a warning. Lantee knew the terrain better than she. Perhaps he, too, was chafing at inactivity. And, if the leaf pattern worked, he could be in and out of any danger before those who discovered him could move. It would be, or should be, sufficiently disconcerting to have a man materialize out of thin air before one, to give the materializer some seconds of advantage in any surprise confrontation.

Lantee's expression changed. He had made up his mind. "Now!"

Charis could not bring herself to agree in this final moment. As he had said earlier, there were so many ifs. But neither had she the right to persuade him not to make the try.

He slid down the slope behind them, putting the hill between him and the base before getting to his feet, the leaf in his hands. His jaw set, his whole face became a mask of concentration. Nothing happened. When he looked up at her, his expression was bleak and pinched.

"The witches are right. It won't work for me!"

"Perhaps—" Charis had another thought.

"They must be right! It didn't work."

"Maybe for another reason. That's *my* pattern, the one they gave me in the beginning."

"You mean the patterns are individual—separate codes?"

"It's reasonable to believe that. You know how they wear those decorative skin patterns, made up partially of their ancestors' private designs, in order to increase their own Power. But each of them has her disk with her own design on it. It could be that only that works really."

"Then I do it the hard way," he replied. "Go in after dark."

"Or I could go, if you'd give me a reference point as you did when we came here."

"No!" There was no arguing against that; she read an adamant refusal in his whole stance.

"Together—as we came here?"

He balanced the leaf in his hand. Charis knew that he longed to be as decisive with another "no," but there were advantages in her second suggestion which he had to recognize. She pushed that indecision quickly; not that she had any desire to penetrate into the enemy's camp, but neither did she want to remain here alone and perhaps witness Lantee's capture. To her mind, with the Power the two of them would have a better chance working together than the Survey man had as a lone scout.

"We can get in—and out—in a hurry. You've already agreed that's true."

"I don't like it."

She laughed. "What *can* one like about this? It is something we have agreed must be done. Or shall we just take to the countryside and wait out whatever they are planning to do?" Such prodding was not fair of her, but her impatience was rising to a point where it threatened her control.

"All right!" He was angry. "The room is like this." Down on one knee, he sketched out a plan, explaining curtly. Then, before she could move, those same brown fingers were against her forehead, giving her once more that fuzzy picture. Charis jerked away from that contact.

"I told you—not that! Not again!" The girl had no desire to recall any of the earlier dizzy, frightening time when they joined minds after a fashion, when the strange thoughts strove to storm her own mental passages.

Lantee flushed and drew his hand back. Her uneasiness and faint disgust were at once overlaid by a feeling of guilt. After all, he was doing the best he could to insure the success of their action.

"I have the picture now as clearly as I had this place, and we came here safely," she said hurriedly. "Let's go!" For a moment his hand resisted her grasp as she caught it, then his hold tightened on hers.

First the room—then the pattern. It was becoming a familiar exercise, one she had full confidence in. But now—*nothing happened*.

It was as if she had thrown herself against some immovable and impenetrable wall! The barrier the Wyverns had reared to control her movements earlier? It was not that. She would have known it for what it was. This was different—a new sensation altogether.

She opened her eyes. "Did you feel it?" Lantee might not be able to work the transference on his own; but, linked, they had done it successfully once, so perhaps some part of the present failure had reached him.

"Yes. You know what it means? They do have a nullifier to protect them!"

"And it works!" Charis shivered, her hand creasing the leaf into a pulp.

"We were already sure that it did," he reminded her. "Now—I shall go by myself."

She did not want to admit that he was right, but she had to. Lantee knew every inch of the base; she was a stranger there. The invaders might have other safeguards besides the nullifier.

"You don't even have a stunner . . ."

"If I can get in down there, that little matter can be corrected. More than a stunner is needed now. This you *can* do—work your way around to the landing strip. If I succeed, we'll make use of the copter. You can fly one?"

"Of course! But where will we go?"

"To the Wyverns. They'll have to be made to understand what they are up against here. I ought to find evidence of one kind or another as to whether this is a Company grab. The witches may be able to blanket you out of their own mode of travel, but I'll swear they have no way of preventing the copter from reaching their prime base. Let us just get to them and they can pick the truth out of our minds whether they want to or not."

It sounded simple and as if it might work, Charis had to admit. But there was that tall hedge of ifs in between.

"All right. When do we move?"

Lantee crawled up to their former vantage point and she trailed him. After he surveyed the landscape he spoke, but he did not answer her question.

"You circle around in that direction, giving me a hundred-count start. We haven't spotted any guards about the strip, but that doesn't mean that they haven't plugged it with sniffers, and those may even be paired with anti-persona bombs into the bargain."

Was he deliberately trying to make her regret any part in this?

"We could certainly use the wolverines now. No sniffer could baffle them," he continued.

"We could use a detachment of the Patrol, too," Charis retorted tartly.

Lantee did not rise to that. "I'll come in from that direction." He pointed south. "Let's hope our wild stars have the value we hope they do on this board. Luck!"

Before she could more than blink he had gone, vanished into the brush as if one of the disks had whirled him into Otherwhere. Charis strove to fight down her excitement and began a slow count. For some seconds she heard a subdued rustling which she was sure marked his retreat—then nothing.

No movement about the domes. Lantee was right; they *could* have used the wolverines and Tsstu to advantage now. Animal senses, so much keener than human, could have scouted for them both. She thought of an anti-persona bomb twinned to a sniffer detector, and her own part in the action had less and less appeal. The copter was far too tempting a bait; those below *must* have some watch on it! Unless they believed that they had effectively disposed of all resistance.

"—ninety-five—ninety-six—" Charis counted, hoping she was not speeding up. It was always far easier to be on the move than to lie and wait.

"—ninety-nine—one hundred!" She crept down slope to the east on the first lap of her own journey. The light held enough so that she kept to cover, pausing within each shadowed shelter to study the next few feet or yards of advance. And, to keep in concealment, she pulled her circle arc into a segment of oval. When she knew that she must head in again to meet the landing strip, Charis's mouth was dry in contrast to her damp palms, while her heart thudded in a heavy beat.

She found a tree limb, old and brittle—dry but long enough for her purpose. A sniffer activated to catch a prowler would be set about so high—knee-high for a walking man—or less. Would they expect someone to crawl in? All right, then, to be on the safe side—calf-high Charis set about stripping small branches for handfuls of leaves. Several tough ground-vines gave her cords to lash the mass of vegetation to the stick.

As a device for triggering a trap, it was very crude, but it lessened the odds against her somewhat. Now her wriggling advance was even slower as she worked the bundle before her, testing each foot of the way.

The pole was hard to hold in her sweating hands, her shoulders ached with the effort necessary to keep it at what she believed to be the right height. And her goal could have been half the continent away since she appeared to draw no closer to it in spite of her contin-ued struggles.

But so far—no sniffer. And there had to be an end sometime. Charis paused for a breather. No sound came from the domes, no indication there were any guards, either human or machine. Were the invaders under the impression they had nothing to fear, no reason to post sentries?

Must not let growing confidence make her careless, Charis told herself. She did not have one hand on the copter door yet. And—why!—that might be it! The machine itself could be rigged as a trap. And if that were so, could she discover and disarm it?

One thing at a time—just one thing at a time . . .

She had raised her bundle probe, was on the creep again when the twilight breeze brought her a faint scent. Wolverine! When aroused in fear or anger, Charis knew, the animals emitted a rank odor. Was this a mark of the passing of Togi and her cubs?

Could Charis contact the female wolverine who had no knowledge of her as friendly? Lantee had said that afternoon that Togi was less amenable to human contact or control since she had become a mother; the wolverines were noted hunters, accustomed to living off the land. Was Togi now hunting?

Charis sniffed, hoping for some clue as to direction. But the scent was faint, perhaps only a lingering reminder of some earlier passage of an angry wolverine clinging to grass or bush. And there stood the beacon of the Patrol scout not too far to her left. She was close to the fringe of the landing strip. Charis thrust her bundle detector before her and crept on.

A screech—a snarling—a thrashing in the brush to her left. A second cry cut into a horrible bubbling noise.

Charis bit her tongue, painfully muffling a cry of her own. Wide-eyed she watched that wildly waving bush. Another cry—this time not unlike a thin, pulsating whistle. Then suddenly there were figures out in the open, running toward the commotion. As they neared, Charis could see them better.

Not the off-worlders she and Lantee had watched from the hill. Wyverns? No.

For the second time, Charis choked back a cry. For these running figures carried spears, the same type of spear she and Lantee had found at the post. And they were taller than the Wyverns Charis knew, their spiky head and shoulder growths smaller so that they resembled ragged and ugly spines rather than small wings: the Wyvern males Charis had never seen in all her days among the witches!

They cried out shrilly in a way which rasped Charis's nerves and hurt her ears. Two of them hurled spears into the now quiet bush.

A shout from behind, from the domes; this surely had

issued from a human throat. No words Charis could distinguish but it brought confusion to the Wyverns. The two
at the rear stopped, looked over their shoulders; then, at
a second shout, they turned and ran swiftly in the direction of that call. The foremost attackers had reached the
bushes, spears thrust ahead. One of them cried out. Again
no words, but Charis judged the tone to be one of disappointment and rage.

They milled around out of her sight and then came
back into the open, two of them carrying a limp body
between them. One of their own kind killed by some
means. Togi's doing?

But Charis had little time to wonder about that for
there was more shouting from the domes, and all but the
two Wyverns carrying the body began to run in that
direction.

Lantee—had they found Lantee?

XIV

The Wyvern males had left the landing strip. Charis could follow their path through the brush to the open and the waiting copter. Lantee's plan of heading out to sea in the copter, aiming at the witch Citadel, was practical. Lantee?

Charis rubbed her hands together and tried to think clearly. Something had happened back there at the domes; it was only logical to associate the clamor with Lantee's attempt to scout the enemy. He could now be a prisoner— or worse.

But if she took the copter now when the attention of any sentries was fixed elsewhere, she had her best chance of escape, though she might well be deserting a man who had aroused the invaders but managed to evade them. To go—to get to the Citadel and warn the witches of the possible danger, leaving Lantee, his fate unknown? Or to stay in hopes of his coming?

There was no real choice; there never had been, Charis knew that deep within her. But now, at the final test, she felt as bruised and beaten as if those spear carriers had taken her in an unequal struggle. Somehow she got to her feet and ran for the copter.

As she wrenched open the cockpit door, Charis paused for any trap to explode in her face. Then she scrambled in behind the controls. So far, all right. Now— where?

The Citadel was to the west, that was her only clue.

Only, the sea was wide and she had never made the journey by air, as Lantee had. Maybe her guide could be a negative one, and she tracked her goal by the barrier against the Power or rather her use of it. Such a thin chance—but still a chance.

Charis set the control on full, braced herself for the force of a lift-leap, and pushed the proper button. She was slammed back in the cushioned pilot's chair. Copters were not designed for such violent maneuvering. But a lift-leap would take her off the strip with speed enough to startle any guard she had not seen.

She gulped and fought the effects of the spurt upon her body, forcing her fingers to modify the climb. The domes were now small silvery circles just visible in the growing dark. She set a course northward, and put the flyer temporarily on auto-pilot while she tried to think out just how she could track that barrier with any accuracy.

How did you track nothingness? Just try to pierce here and there until you found the wall between you and your goal? Her vague direction was that island home of the Wyverns which stood northwest of the government base, southwest from Jagan's post, and she had not even a com sweep to give her a more definite position.

Below, just visible in the night, was the shore, an irregular division between land and sea. The pattern—she *must* have the pattern. Charis looked about her a little wildly. There was no leaf to scratch, no earth or rock to draw upon. That wall storage pocket at her left hand? Charis plunged fingers into it and spilled out what it contained.

A packet of Sustain tablets—swiftly she scooped that into her own belt pouch and another first-aid kit, bigger and better fitted than the small one Lantee had carried. Joyfully Charis scrabbled in it for the sterile pencil. It was not here, but there was a large tube of the same substance. Last of all, a flat sheet of plasta-board such as could be used for sketch maps, its surface slighted roughened as if it had been marked and erased many times.

This would serve if she could find something with which to mark. Again Charis pawed into the pocket, and her fingers, scraping the bottom of the holder, closed about a thin cylinder. She brought out a fire tube. No use—or was it?

Frantically she twisted its dial to the smallest ray, and pressed the tip tight to the plasta-board. It was such a chance—the whole thing might go up in a burst of flame. But a map sheet should have been proofed against heat as well as moisture. Only this one had been used in the past, perhaps too often. She drew swiftly, fearful of any mistake. The brown heat-lines bit deeply into the surface and spread a little, but not enough to spoil the design.

Charis clicked off the heat unit and studied what she now held. Blurred, yes, but to her distinctive enough in its familiarity. She had a good substitute for the disk which she had lost.

Now—to put it to use. She closed her eyes. The room in the Citadel—concentrate!—the barrier! But in which direction? All she knew was that the barrier still existed. Her one idea of a direction-finder seemed a failure. No one gave up at a first try, though.

Room—design—barrier. Charis opened her eyes. Her head was turned slightly to the left. Was that a clue? Could she test it? She snapped the copter off auto-pilot and altered course inland away from the shore. When she had ceased to see the sea with only the dark mass of land now under her, she brought the flyer about and cruised back.

Room—design— Her head to the left again, but not so much. She had to take that as her lead, slender as it was. Altering the degree of course to that imagined point, she sent the copter on out to sea.

Design—try— She was looking straight ahead when she met what she could not penetrate. Oh, let this *be* right. *Let it be right.*

Charis had no idea how far offshore the Wyvern-held islands were. Any copter had a good ranging allowance, but her goal might still lie hours ahead. She clicked up the speed to full and sat with her hands on the map sheet, waiting.

The stars were low on the horizon. No! Not stars— they were far too low. Lights! Lights at nearly sea level—

the Citadel! On impulse Charis tried the Power and it
was as if she had thrown her body at full force against
an unyielding slab of tri-steel. She gasped at what was
translated into physical pain upon that encounter.

But the copter had met with no barrier. It continued
on, unerringly bound for the lights ahead.

Charis had no idea what she would do when she
reached the Citadel. Only she had her warning, and with
the Power the Wyverns would know that she spoke the
truth. Even with the warning—what could the witches do
in their turn, except avoid outright and quick disaster by
delaying whatever attack they had already organized.

The lights picked out the windows in the massive
block of the Citadel, some of them almost on a level
with the copter. Charis resumed control and circled the
buildings in search of a level site on which to land. She
had rounded the highest of the blocks when she sighted
ground lights marking an open space, almost as if they
had prepared for her coming.

As the flyer touched the pavement, she saw a second
copter at one side. So—the other Survey man, Thorvald,
had not left. An ally for her? Or was he now a prisoner,
tucked away in such a pocket of non-being as Lantee had
been? Lantee— Charis tried to push out of her mind any
thought of Lantee.

She held the plasta-board. In this well-like space between
walls there were no breaks, no doors, and the windows were
at least a story above her. The lights which had directed
her landing burned in portable standards. So the Wyverns
had expected her. Yet no one waited here; she might be
standing in a trap.

Charis nodded. This was all a part of what the shadow-
patterned Wyvern had promised. She must do it all by
her own efforts; the answer had to be *hers*.

The shadow Wyvern had said it, so to her it must be
proven. Charis held the plasta-board in her two hands where
she could see its design in the flickering half-light of the
lamps. Spike-wing crest, pallid skin with only the faint tracings of faded designs—Charis pulled the Wyvern out of
memory and built with care the picture to center upon, until
she was sure no detail she could recall was missing. Then—

"So you *can* dream to a purpose after all." No amazement, only recognition as a greeting.

The room was dusky. Although two lamps stood on either side of a table, their radiance made only a small pool, and Charis sensed larger space stretching far beyond where she stood. That other—the Wyvern—sat in a chair with a high back, its white substance glowing with runnels of color, which in themselves appeared to crawl with life.

She leaned back at her ease, the alien witch, her hands resting on the arms of her chair as she surveyed Charis appraisingly. Now the off-worlder found words to answer.

"I had dreamed to this much purpose, Wise One, that I stand here now."

"Agreed. And to what future purpose do you stand here, Dreamer?"

"That a warning may be delivered."

The vertical pupils in those large yellow eyes narrowed, the snouted head raised a fraction of an inch, and the sense of affront reached Charis clearly.

"You have that which will arm you against us, Dreamer? Then you *have* made a gain since last we were thus, face to face. What great new power have you discovered to be able to say 'I warn you' to us?"

"You mistake my words, Wise One. I do not warn you against myself, but against others."

"And again you take upon yourself more than you have the right to do, Dreamer. Have you then read your answer from Those Gone Before?"

Charis shook her head. "Not so. But still you mistake me, Reader of Patterns. In what is to come, we dream one dream, not dream against dream."

Those eyes searched into her, seemed to pick at her mind.

"It is true that you have done more than we believed you could, Dreamer. Yet you are not one with us in any power save that which we have granted you. Why do you presume to say that we are now to dream the same dream?"

"Because if we do not, then may all dreams be broken."

"And that you truly believe." Not a question but a statement. However, Charis made a quick answer.

"That I truly believe."

"Then you have learned more than how to break a restraint dream since last we have stood together. What have you learned?"

"That those from off-world are more powerful than we thought, that they have with them that which renders all dreams as nothing and protects them, that *their* desire here may be to gather to them the Power that they may use it for their own purposes in other places."

Again that faint pick, pick to uncover the truth behind her words. Then, "But of these facts you are not wholly sure."

"Not wholly," Charis agreed. "Every pattern is made of lines. So, when you have long known a design and see only a portion of it, you can still envision the whole."

"And this is a pattern you have known before?"

"It is one I have heard of, one Lantee has heard of."

Had she made a mistake in mentioning the Survey man's name? That chill which reached from mind to mind suggested that she had.

"What has any man-thing to do with this?" A hissing question hot with rising ire.

Charis's anger woke in turn. "This much, Wise One. He may be dead now, striving to carry war to the enemy— *your* enemy!"

"How can that be when he is—" The thought chain between them broke in mid-sentence. Lids dropped above the yellow eyes. The feeling of withdrawal was so sharp that Charis almost expected the Wyvern to vanish from her chair. Yet her body was still there although her mind was elsewhere.

The minutes were endless, then Charis knew the Wyvern had returned. Fingers had clenched about the chair arms, the yellow eyes were open, fixed upon the girl, though there was no touch of mind.

Charis took a chance. "You did not find him, Wise One, where you had sent him?"

No answer, but Charis was sure the Wyvern understood.

"He is not there," the girl continued, "nor has he been for some time. As I told you in truth, he has been about *your* business elsewhere. And perhaps to his hurt."

"He did not free himself." The frantic grip of the

Wyvern's hands relaxed. Charis thought that the witch was annoyed because she had betrayed her agitation so much. "He could not. He is a man-thing—"

"But also a dreamer after his own fashion," Charis struck in. "And though you strove to remove him from this struggle, yet he returned—not to war against you but against those who threaten all dreaming."

"What dream have you that you can do this thing?"

"Not my dream alone," Charis retorted. "But his dream also, and other dreams together, as a key to unlock this prison."

"I must believe that this is so. Yet such an act is beyond all reason."

"All reason known to you and your sharers of dreams. Look, you." Charis moved to the table, stretched out hand and arm into the full path of the light. "Am I like unto you in the sight of all? Do I wear any dream patterns set upon my skin? Yet I dream. However, need my dreams be any more like unto yours than my body covering resembles that you wear? Perhaps even the Power when I bend it to my will is not the same."

"Words—"

"Words with proving action behind them. You sent me hence and bade me dream myself out of your net if I could, and so I did. Then with Shann Lantee I dreamed a way free from a deeper prison. Did you believe I could do these things?"

"Believe? No," the Wyvern replied. "But there is always a chance of difference, a variable within the Power. And the Talking Rods had an answer for you when we called upon Those Who Once Were. Very well, these are truths accepted. Now say again what you believe to be a truth that had no full proving."

Charis retold her discoveries at the base, Lantee's deductions.

"A machine which nullifies the Power." The Wyvern led her back to that. "Such you believe *can* exist?"

"Yes. Also—what if such a thing be brought to use against you even in this very stronghold? With your dreams broken, how may you fight against slaying weapons in the hands of those who come?"

"We knew—" the Wyvern was musing "—that we could not send dreams to trouble these strangers. Or bring back—" she spoke in anger "—to their proper places those who have broken the law. But that all this is being done so that they may take the Power from us—that we had not thought upon."

Charis knew a small spark of relief. That last admission had changed her own status. It was as if she were now admitted in a small way into the Wyvern ranks.

"However, they must be ignorant to believe that man-things can use the Power."

"Lantee does," Charis reminded her. "And what of the other you have known as a friend here—Thorvald?"

Hesitation, then an unwilling answer. "He, too, in a small way. An ability, you believe, that these others may share because they are not blood, bone, and skin with us?"

"Is that so hard to understand?"

"And what have you to suggest, Dreamer? You speak of battles and warfare. Our only weapons have been our dreams, and now you say they will avail nothing. So—what is your answer?" Hostility again.

And Charis had little with which to meet that. "What these invaders do here is against the law of our kind as much as it is a threat against your people. There are those who will speedily come to our aid."

"From where? Winging down from other stars? And how will you call them? How long will it take them to arrive?"

"I do not know. But you have the man Thorvald, and he would have answers to these questions."

"It would seem, Dreamer, that you believe I, Gidaya, can give all orders here, do as I wish. But that is not so. We sit in council. And there are those among us who would not listen to any truth if you spoke it. We have been divided upon this matter from the first, and to talk against attacking now will require much persuasion. Should you stand openly with me, that persuasion would fail."

"I understand. But also, as you have said to me, Wise One, there is such a thing as a threat by time. Let me speak to Thorvald if you have him here, and learn from him what may be done to gain help from off-world." Had she gone too far with that plea?

Gidaya did not answer at once. "Thorvald is in safe keeping—" she paused and then added "—though I wonder now about the safety of any keeping. Very well, you may go to him. It may be that I shall say to those who will object that you are joining him in custody."

"If you wish." Charis suspected that Gidaya would offer that as a sop to the anti-off-world party. But she greatly doubted that the Wyvern believed any longer Charis herself could be controlled by the Power.

"Go!"

At least Thorvald had not been consigned to that place of nothingness which had been Lantee's prison. Charis stood in a very ordinary sleeping room of the Citadel, its only difference from the one she had called her own being that it had no window. On the pile of sleep-mats lay a man, breathing heavily. His head turned and he muttered, but she could not make out his words.

"Thorvald! Ragnar Thorvald!"

The bronze-yellow head did not lift from the mats nor his eyes open. Charis crossed to kneel beside him.

"Thorvald!"

He was muttering again. And his hand balled into a fist and shot out to thud home painfully on her forearm. Dreaming! Naturally? Or in some fantasy induced by the Wyverns? But she must wake him now.

"Thorvald!" Charis called louder and took hold of his shoulder, shaking him vigorously.

He struck out again, sending her rolling back against the wall, then sat up, his eyes open at last, looking about wildly. But as he sighted her he te₁sed.

"You're real—I think!" His emphatic assertion slid into a less confident conclusion.

"I'm Charis Nordholm." She crouched against the wall, rubbing her arm. "And I'm real all right. This is no dream."

No, no dream but the worst of trouble. And did Thorvald have any of the answers after all? She only hoped that he did.

XV

He was very tall, this officer of Survey, towering over Charis where she sat cross-legged on his mat bed as he strode impatiently back and forth across the chamber, now and then shooting a question at her or making her retell some part of the story again.

"It does look very much like a Company grab." He gave judgment at last. "Which means they must be very sure of themselves, that they think they have all angles covered." Now he might be talking to himself rather than to her. "A deal—somehow they've made a deal!"

Charis guessed at the meaning of that. "You think they've arranged for closed eyes somewhere?"

Thorvald glanced at her sharply, almost in dislike, Charis decided. But he nodded curtly. "Not in our service!" he rapped out.

"But they wouldn't be able to square the Patrol, would they? Not if you were able to get a message through."

He smiled grimly. "Hardly. But the only off-world com is at the base, and from your account they hold that now."

"There's the Patrol ship down on the field. That should have its own com," she pointed out.

Thorvald rubbed one hand along the angle of his jaw, his eyes now fixed unseeingly on the blank wall of the chamber.

"Yes, that Patrol ship—"

"They didn't have any guard on the copter."

"They weren't expecting trouble then. They probably thought they had all the base staff accounted for. That wouldn't be true now."

She could see the reason in that argument. Yes, when they had taken Lantee, as she was now sure they had, and she had flown the copter out, they had been put on the alert. If the Patrol ship had not been guarded before, Charis did not doubt now that it was under strict surveillance.

"What can we do?"

"We'll have to count on it that they do have Lantee."

Or, Charis made herself add silently to Thorvald's statement, he is dead.

"And they know that he had at least one other with him, since the copter was taken. They may scan him, and he's not been brain-locked."

Charis found her hands shaking. There was a cold sickness in her middle, seeping into the rest of her body. Thorvald was only being objective, but she found she could not be the same on this point, not when the man he was discussing was more than a name—a living person who, in a way Charis could hardly describe, had been closer to her than any other being she had known. She was unaware that the Survey officer had paused until he dropped down beside her, his hands covering both of hers.

"We must face the truth," he said quietly.

Charis nodded, her spine stiffened, and her head came up. "I know. But I went off—off and left him—"

"Which was the only thing you could have done. He knew that. Also, there is this. Those male Wyverns—they were attacked by something in the bush—you think it was Togi?"

"I smelled wolverine just before. And one of the Wyverns was killed, or badly injured."

"Which may lead them to believe that there were more than two of you out there. And that could force caution on them. The animals work with trainers—that is universally known. And it's also general knowledge that they are fanatically loyal to their trainers. Lantee has been in charge of the wolverines for two planet years. Those at the base may keep him on ice in order to have control over the animals."

Did he really believe that? Charis wondered. Or was it a very thin attempt to placate her feelings of guilt?

"This nullifier," Thorvald was on his feet again, back to that restless pacing. "As long as they have that they might as well be in a land fortress! And how long will they wait before moving out with it? If they had a trace-beam on that copter, they know—"

"Just where to attack!" Charis finished for him, realizing for the first time what might be the folly of her own move.

"You had no choice." Thorvald caught her up on that quickly. "A warning was important. And with the Wyvern barrier up you had no other way of reaching them."

"No, but I have a way of getting back there." Charis had been thinking. It was a crazy, wild plan, but it might work. She had his full attention.

Sheeha! Charis had gone back to her first night on Warlock, to the trader woman who had been shocked into mental unbalance by contact with the witches.

"These invaders know that Jagan brought me here," Charis began. "Also that I wandered out of the post while under Wyvern control; they can check all that. They might even have the tape recording I made to your base when I appealed for help. But it may be that they do not know that *I* took the copter. Or, if they do—well, how much do they know of the Power? They know the Wyverns used it to dominate and control their males. So, perhaps they will think I was under Wyvern control while taking the copter.

"Now, suppose I let them think I have escaped and that I have headed back to the base because I think there is safety there. I can act as Sheeha did."

"And if they put you under a scanner?" Thorvald demanded harshly, "or if they have already learned from Lantee what you can do with the Power?"

"If they have, they won't want me under a scanner, not right away. They'll want demonstrations," Charis countered. "They can't know too much about it, can they? What have you reported? Those reports must have brought them here."

"Reports? What have we had to say in those except

generalities? We had our instructions to go slow with the witches. After they helped us wipe out a Throg base here—it was entirely their efforts that broke that—they were in no hurry to fraternize. The willingness to communicate had to come from their side, contact was on a delicate basis. I don't understand about this nullifier. No off-world Company could have learned enough from our reports to build it because we didn't know enough ourselves. Unless this machine is a modification of something they already had and they brought it with them, simply as an experiment which did pay off—too well!"

"Then," said Charis, bringing him back to her own suggestion, "they could not know about the Power and how it works?"

"I don't see how they could. They may have subverted some of the male Wyverns. But those have never been able to dream or use the Power. Company scouts could have some idea of what it does, but they'd only be guessing at how it works."

"So as an off-worlder who has had some experience with it, I could make statements they would have no way of testing?"

"Unless they use a scanner," he reminded her.

"But when you're dealing with a mental problem, you don't destroy its roots," Charis countered. "I tell you, if I went to them as a fugitive who had escaped the Wyverns and was willing to cooperate, anyone with any intelligence would not put me under force. He would want me to give freely."

Thorvald studied her. "There's more than one kind of force," he said slowly. "And if they suspected that you were playing a double game, they wouldn't hesitate to use all and every means to crack you for what they wanted. A Company on a grab is moving against time, and their agents here would be ruthless."

"All right. Then what's *your* answer? It seems that I have the best chance of getting into the base on my own terms. Do you or the witches have any at all? If you're taken trying to get in—the way Shann was—then you're expendable too."

"Yes."

"Well, I represent something they want—an off-worlder who has had experience with the use of the Power. There is a good chance to get close to the nullifier under those circumstances. And if I could put that out of action, then the witches could do the rest. As it is now, the Wyverns suspect us too, just because we are off-worlders."

"And how can you convince the Wyverns that you will work against our own species?"

"They read my mind under the Power. There's no hiding the truth from them. Short of leading in an armed force, which we don't have, you aren't going to take back your base. And someone has to make a move before the invaders do."

"You don't know how rough a grab force can be—" Thorvald began.

Charis stood up. "I have been hunted by men before. You can tell me very little about cruelty used as a weapon. But as long as I present a chance of profit to those in command, I shall be guarded. And I think that now I am your only key."

The girl closed her eyes for a second. This was fear, this sick chill. Yes, she knew what it meant to face hostility; before, she had to run from it. Now she must walk defenseless straight into the worst her imagination could picture for her. But there *was* a chance. She had known that from the argument she had had with Gidaya. Perhaps the continued use of the Power did implant in one a confidence. Only, once at the base, she would not have the Power to pull on; the nullifier would see to that. She would have only her wits and luck to back her. Or— could she have more? The wolverines, Togi and her cubs, lurked about the base, apparently free of control and able to prey upon the alien guards. Charis had had no contact with Togi, but with Taggi, who had been so strangely one with her in that search for Lantee, and with Tsstu, it might be different. Where were the animals now?

"You have something more in mind?" A change in her expression must have brought that question from him.

"Tsstu and Taggi—" she began and then explained more fully.

"But I don't understand. You say that they weren't with you in the Cavern of the Veil or afterward."

"No, but they answered when we called. I don't think they were captive in any dream place. Perhaps they had to be free to go their own way for a space after that. It—it was a frightening experience." Charis had a flash thought of the corridor, the opening doors in which Lantee's thoughts had attacked her, and again she shivered. "They may have run from what they remembered."

"Then—will they return?"

"I think they will have to," Charis said simply. "We wove a bond then and still it holds us. Maybe we can never loose it. But if I could find them, they would be allies those at the base would not suspect."

"Suppose the nullifier dampened contact between you?" Thorvald persisted.

"If I reached them before I went in, they would know what they could do in aid."

"You seem to have all the answers!" He did not appear to relish that admission. "So you're to walk alone into a trap and spring it—just like that!"

"Maybe I can't. But I believe there's no other solution."

"Again you read the pattern right, Sharer of Dreams!"

They looked around, startled. Gidaya stood there and with her, Gysmay.

Thorvald opened his mouth, then closed it again. There was a set to his jaw that suggested that, while he knew silence was proper, he resented it.

"You are persuaded it must be thus?" Charis asked of the Wyverns.

Gysmay made a movement of the shoulders approximating a human shrug.

"I, who am a Holder of the Upper Disk, will go with the desires of my Sharers of Dreams in this matter. You believe, one who is not quite a stranger, that this is what must be done. And you are willing to take that doing into your own hands. So let it be. Though we cannot give you any aid, since the evil which has been brought to trouble our world holds about its heart a wall we cannot pierce."

"No, you cannot aid me once I am within that place. But there is that you can do for me before I enter—"

"Such being?" Gidaya asked.

"That Tsstu and Taggi be found and summoned from where they have gone."

"Tsstu at least has power of a sort, but whether that may be harnessed to your purpose—" the older Wyvern hesitated. "However, no power, no aid, is to be despised when one walks into a fork-tail's den without a disk between one's fingers. Yes, we shall search out the small one and also the other who serves these men. Perchance we can do more, using like tools—"

Gysmay nodded eagerly. "That is a good thought, Reader of the Rods! One can build on it. Perchance we can provide some action for these invaders to think upon so that their minds will be in two ways occupied and not fastened alone upon you and what you would do among them. We cannot walk through their rooms, but we shall see." She did not elaborate.

Turning to Charis, Thorvald cut in: "I'm going with you—in the copter."

"You can't!" Charis protested. "I won't take the flyer back. I must wander in as if I have been lost—"

"I didn't say land at the base. But I must be back near the base, near enough to be able to move in when we can." He said that defiantly, glaring at the Wyverns as if he would compel them to his will.

When we can, Charis thought, more likely—*if* we can.

"It is well," Gidaya answered, though there was a small movement from Gysmay as if she were protesting. "Take your machine and fly—to this place—"

Into Charis's mind came instantly a clear picture of a flat rock expanse squared off to make a natural landing strip.

"About a mile from the base!" Thorvald burst out; he must also have had that mind picture and recognized it. "We shall come in from the south—at night—without landing lights. I can set us down there without trouble."

"And Tsstu—Taggi?" demanded Charis of the Wyverns.

"They shall join you there for whatever purpose you think they may serve. Now you may go."

Charis was back in the landing well where the two copters were waiting, but this time Thorvald was with her.

As the girl started for the machine which had brought her to the Citadel, the Survey officer caught at her arm.

"Mine—not that one." He drew her with him toward the other copter. "If it's sighted after we land, they'll believe I returned and am hiding out. They won't connect it with you."

Charis agreed to the sense of that and watched him settle behind the controls as she took her place on the second seat. They lifted with a leap which signaled his impatience more than his words had done. Then, under the night sky, they drove on, the ocean below them.

"They may have a search beam on," he said as his fingers played a dot-dash over course buttons. "We'll take the long way around to make sure we have the best cover we can. North—then west—then up from the south—"

It *was* a long way around. Charis watched with eyes over which the lids were growing very heavy. The smooth sheen of the night-darkened sea underneath them spread on and on in spite of their speed. To be flying away from their goal instead of toward it was hard to be reconciled to now.

"Settle back," Thorvald's voice was low and even; he now had his own impatience under iron control. "Sleep if you can."

Sleep? How could anyone sleep with such a task before her. Sleep—that . . . was . . . impossible . . .

Dark—thick, negative dark. Negative? What did that mean? Dark, and then, deep in the heart of that blackness, a small fire struggling to beat back the dark. A fire threatened, a fire she must reach and feed. Bring it back to bright blaze again! But when Charis strove to speed to the fire, she could move only with agonizing slowness, so that the weight which dragged at her limbs was a pain in itself. And the fire flickered, reblazed, and then flickered. Charis knew that when it died wholly it might not be relit. But she needed more than herself to feed that fire, and she sent out a frantic, soundless call for aid. There was no answer.

"Wake up!"

Charis's body swayed in a rough grip, her head jerked back and forth on her shoulders. She looked up, blinking and half-dazed, into eyes which blazed with some of the intensity of the fire of the dark.

"You were dreaming!" It was an accusation. "They have a hold on you. They never meant—"

"No!" Enough understanding had returned to make her shake off Thorvald's hands. "Not one of *their* dreams."

"But you *were* dreaming!"

"Yes." She huddled in the copter seat as the machine flew on under auto-pilot. "Shann—"

"What about him?" Thorvald caught her up quickly.

"He's still alive." Charis had brought that one small crumb of assurance out of the black with her. "But—"

"But what?"

"He's just holding on." That, too, had come to her although it was not so reassuring. What had strained Lantee to the depths she had witnessed? Physical hurt? A scanner attack? He was alive and he was still fighting. That she knew with certainty and now she said so.

"No real contact? He told you nothing?"

"Nothing. But I almost reached him. If I could try again—"

"No!" Thorvald shouted at her. "If he is under a scanner, you don't know how much they could pick up because of such a contact. You—you'll have to put him out of your mind."

Charis only looked at him.

"You'll have to," he repeated doggedly. "If they pick you up in any way, you haven't a chance of going in as you've planned. Can't you see? You are the only chance Lantee has now. But you'll have to reach him in person in order to help; not this way!"

Thorvald was right. Charis had enough sense left to acknowledge that rightness, though that did not make it any easier when she thought of the small fire flickering close to extinction in a deep and all-abiding darkness.

"Hurry!" She moistened her dry lips with her tongue. He was resetting their course. "Yes."

The copter spiraled away to the right, heading toward the shore they could not see and the task she had set herself.

XVI

The stars were no longer sharp points above as the copter set down under Thorvald's practiced control. An hour close to dawn— Dawn of what day? Time had either stretched slowly or fled swiftly since Charis had walked out onto the soil of Warlock. She could no longer be sure that it followed any ordered marking of minutes or hours. She stood now on the rock, shivering a little in the chill predawn wind.

"Meeerrrreee!" At the cry of welcome, Charis went down on her knees, holding out her arms to the shadow which sped toward her. The warmth of that small body pressing tight to hers, the loving dabs of tongue-tip against her throat, her chin, brought a measure of comforting confidence. Tsstu was again in the circle of Charis's arms, avid for contact, excited in her welcome.

Then the rasp of harsher, coarser fur against the girl's legs signaled Taggi's arrival. A small grunting growl was his vocal hail as she put one hand to his upthrust head, scratching behind his small ears.

"Taggi?" Thorvald walked from the copter.

The wolverine slipped from under Charis's hand, went to the Survey officer. He sniffed inquiringly at the other's field boots, and then reared up against the man, his forepaws scraping Thorvald's thigh as he gave voice to a sound between a whine and a growl. There was no mistaking the questioning note, nor the demand for enlightenment which came to Charis mentally. Taggi wanted the one he knew better than Thorvald.

Charis sat where she was, cradling the nuzzling Tsstu close to her, but reaching out mentally to capture Taggi's thought stream, to try and tap that boiling and, to her, alien flow of brain energy. She touched and savored again, forcing herself not to shrink from the raw savagery, the strange stream. Taggi dropped on all fours. He was swaying from foot to foot, his blunt head swinging about so that he could eye her.

Thoughts—impressions like small sparks—whirled through the air above a stirred fire. Charis built up a picture of Shann Lantee within those sparks—Shann as she had seen him last on the hillside above the base.

Taggi came to her. His teeth closed upon the hand she held out in greeting, not with force enough to even pinch the skin but with the same caress of this kind that she had seen him give to Shann. And, too, inquiry—stronger and much more demanding.

Charis thought of the base as she had viewed it from the hill, knew that Taggi caught that. He dropped his hold upon her, turned halfway around to face in a new direction, and with his head up began sniffing the wind audibly.

Charis approached with some trepidation the real message she must pass along to the wolverine. Tsstu was much more in tune with her. How was she to project into that hunter's brain the sense of danger and an understanding of from whence danger came? By pictures of Shann as a prisoner?

First she thought of Lantee as he stood free by the pool. Then she added imagined bonds, cords about his wrists and ankles, to restrain his freedom. There was a loud snarl of rage from Taggi. She had succeeded so far. But caution! The wolverine must not race recklessly in under that prodding.

"—reeeeuuu—" Tsstu gave a cry Charis knew meant warning. The wolverine looked back at them.

Inquiry flashed not at her but at the curl-cat. The animals had their own band of communication. Perhaps that was her best answer.

Charis changed the direction of her warning, no

longer striving to hold contact with the wild, rich stream of Taggi's thought, but to meet Tsstu's. Strike back against the enemy, yes; free Shann, yes. But for now, caution.

The rumbling growl from Taggi grew fainter. He was still shuffling impatiently from foot to foot, his eagerness to be gone plain to read, but Tsstu had impressed him with the need for caution and the old craftiness of his breed was now in command. Wolverines have great curiosity, but they also have a strong instinct for self-preservation; they do not walk easily into what might be a trap, no matter how attractive the bait. And Taggi knew that he faced a trap.

Again Charis centered on Tsstu, thinking out as simply as she could her own plan for entering the base. Suddenly she looked to Thorvald.

"The nullifier—could it stop communication of mind with mind?"

He gave her the truth. "It could well be so."

The animals must remain outside. Tsstu—the curl-cat was small—she could act as liaison between the wolverine and the base.

"Meeerrreee!" Agreement in that and another swift tongue-tip touch on Charis's cheek.

The girl rose to her feet. "There's no sense in delaying any longer. Time to go." Putting down the curl-cat, she pulled the tie from her hair, shaking the loosened strands about her neck and shoulders. By the time she reached the base, her hair would be sufficiently wild-looking, filled with bits of leaf and twig. She could not tear the Wyvern material of her clothing, but earth stains would adhere to it and the crawling she had already done provided dirty blotches. There were raw and healing scratches on her arms and legs. She would well present the appearance of someone who had been lost in a wilderness for a time. Moreover, the nourishment given by the Sustain tablets had worn off so that she did not have to feign hunger or thirst; she felt them both.

"Take care—" Thorvald's hand went out, almost as if he would hold her back on the very edge of action.

The contrast between that simple warning and what

might lie ahead of her suddenly seemed to Charis so funny that a small, strangled sound of choked laughter was her first answer. Then she added, "Remember those words yourself. If you're spotted by some air scout—"

"They might spot the copter, they won't sight me. I'll be ready to move in to you when I can."

That "when I can" rang in Charis's ears as she walked away. Better make that "if I can." Now that she was committed to the venture, every possible fear—the product of a vivid imagination—swirled about her. She concentrated instead on her memory picture of Sheeha. She had to be Sheeha now as far as the invaders at the base were concerned—Sheeha, a woman brought in by the traders to contact the Wyverns, one who had broken at that meeting with the alien power. She had to *be* Sheeha.

Taggi played guide and advance scout, leading her down from the heights where the copter had landed. Here on the lowlands the predawn was still dark and Charis found the going more difficult. Her hair caught in branches; she tore free, adding more scratches to those she already bore. But that was all to the good.

For a while she carried Tsstu, but as they drew near the base, both animals took to cover and Charis kept touch by mind instead of sight or hearing.

Sun made silver droplets of the bubble shelters as Charis lurched into the open ground around the base. There was no need for her to fake her fatigue, for now she moved in a half-fog of exhaustion, her mouth dry, her ribs heaving with every gasping breath she drew. She must indeed look what she claimed to be—a fugitive, half-crazed, struggling out of the wilderness of a hostile world to seek the shelter and comfort of her own kind.

There was an unsealed door in the second of the bubbles. Charis headed for that. Movement there—a man in yellow coming into the open, staring at her. Charis forced a cry which was really a dry croak and slumped forward.

Calls—voices. She did not try to sort them out just yet but concentrated on lying limply where she had fallen, making no answer when she was rolled over, raised, and carried into the dome.

"What's a woman doing here?" That was one voice.

"She's been bush-runnin'. Lookit how she's all scratched up and dirty. And that ain't no service uniform. She ain't from here. You tell the captain what just blew in?"

"She dead?" asked a third voice.

"Naw—just out on her feet. But where'n Dis did she spring from? Ain't no settlement on this planet—"

"In here, captain. She just came runnin' outta the brush. Then she sees Forg, gives a kinda yip, and falls on her face!"

The click-click of magnetic space-boot plates. A fourth man was coming in to where she lay.

"Off-worlder, all right"—the new voice—"What's that rig she's wearing? That's no uniform, she couldn't be from here."

"From the post maybe, captain?"

"From the post? Wait a minute. That's right. They did bring in a woman to try to contact the snake-hags. But no, we found her when we took over their ship."

"No, there was two women, captain. First one blew up on 'em—went clean out of orbit in her head. So they got 'em another one. And she wasn't there when we took over. What about the tape you found here—the one askin' help from the base? She could be the one who sent it. Got outta the post and started runnin'—"

There was a twitch at her tunic as if one of those gathered about her was fingering the material.

"This is the stuff those snake-hags use. She's been with them."

"Prisoner, eh, captain?"

"Maybe—or something else. You, Nonnan, get the medic over here. He'll bring her around and then we'll have some answers. The rest of you, clear out. She might talk better if she doesn't come to with all of you looking her over."

Charis stirred. She did not care for the idea of a Company-squad medic. Such an expert might use the tongue-loosening drugs she had no guard against. It would be well to regain consciousness before his arrival. She opened her eyes.

She did not have to counterfeit her shriek. That came

naturally as she faced—not the Company officer she had expected—but a creature seemingly out of a nightmare. Leaning toward her was one of the male Wyverns, his snout mouth slightly open to display the fang-teeth with which he was only too generously armed, his slit-pupiled eyes measuring her with no friendly intent.

Charis screamed a second time and jerked her legs up under as she sat bolt upright, squirming as far from the Wyvern as she could manage to move on the cot where they had laid her. The creature's taloned paw swept out and down, wicked claws scraping the foam mattress only inches away from her body.

A very human fist connected at the side of that reptilian head, sending the Wyvern off balance, crashing back against the wall, and a human in uniform took his place. Charis screamed again and cowered away from the Wyvern who had righted himself and was now showing a lipless snarl of rage.

"Keep it off! Snake!" she cried, remembering Sheeha's name for the Wyverns. "Don't let it get me!"

The officer caught the native by his scaled shoulder and headed him out the door with a rough shove. Charis found herself crying, a reaction she did not attempt to control as she shrank against the wall of the room, drawing herself into as small a space as possible.

"Don't let it get me!" she begged as she tried to appraise the man who now faced her.

He was very much of a type, a Company officer in the mercenary forces. Charis had seen his like before in space-port cities, and she thought she dared not depend upon his being less shrewd than any space officer. His very employment on a grab action would make him suspicious of her. But he was fairly young and his attack on the Wyvern made her think that he might be a little prejudiced in her favor.

"Who are you?" The demand was rapped out in a tone meant to force a quick and truthful answer. And up to a point she could supply the truth.

"Charis—Charis Nordholm. You—you are the Resident?" He would believe that she was ignorant of his uniform, that she thought him a government man.

"You might say so. I'm in charge at this base. So your name is Charis Nordholm? And how did you come here to Warlock, Charis Nordholm?"

Not too much coherence in her answer, Charis decided. She tried hard to remember Sheeha. "That was a snake," she accused. "You have them here." She eyed him with what she hoped would register the proper amount of suspicion and fear.

"I tell you the native won't harm you—not if you're what you seem," he added the last with some emphasis.

"What I seem—" she said. "What I seem—I am Charis Nordholm." She held her voice to a colorless recitation of facts as if she repeated some hard-learned lesson. "They—they brought me here to—to meet the snakes! I didn't want to come—they made me!" Her voice lengthened into a wail.

"Who brought you?"

"Captain Jagan, the trader. I was at the trading post—"

"So—you *were* at the trading post. Then what happened?"

Again she could give him part truth. Charis shook her head. "I don't know! The snakes—they gave me to the snakes—snakes all around—they got inside my head—in my head." She set her hands above her ears, rocked back and forth. "In my head—they made me go with them—"

The captain was on to that in a flash. "Where?" His demand was purposely sharp to penetrate the haze that he supposed held her.

"To—to their place—in the sea—their place—"

"If you were with them, how did you get away?" Another man had come into the room and started toward her. The captain caught him back as he waited alertly for her answer. "How did you get away from them?" he repeated again with an emphasis designed to rivet her attention.

"I don't know—I was there—then I was all alone— all alone in a woods. I ran—it was dark—very dark—"

The captain spoke to the newcomer, "Can you get her to make better sense?"

"How do I know?" the other retorted. "She needs food—water."

The medic poured from a container and held out the

cup. She had to steady it in both shaking hands to get it to her mouth. She let coolness roll over her dry tongue. Then she detected a taste. Some drug? She might already have lost the game because she had no defense against drugs and she had finished the draft. As a cover she kept the cup to her lips as long as possible.

"More—" she pushed the cup at the medic.

"Not now, later."

"So—" the captain was eager to get her back to her story "—you just found yourself in a woods and then? How did you get here?"

"I walked," Charis replied simply, keeping her eyes on the cup the medic was now holding as if that mattered far more than the officer's questions. She had never tried to play such a role before and now she hoped that the picture she presented was a reasonably convincing one. "Please—more—" she appealed to the medic.

He filled the cup about a third and gave it to her. She gulped it down. Drug or not this *was* her proper action. Her thirst allayed, her hunger was worse.

"I'm hungry," she told them. "Please, I'm hungry—"

"I'll get her something," the medic volunteered and left.

"You walked," the captain persisted. "How did you know which way to walk—to come here?"

"Which way?" Charis returned to her trick of repetition. "I did not know the way—but it was easier—not so many bushes—so I went that way where it was open. Then I saw the building and I ran—"

The medic returned, to put into her hand a soft plasta-skin tube. Charis, sucking at its cone end, tasted the rich, satisfying paste it contained. She recognized it as the revive ration of a well-equipped base.

"What do you think?" the captain asked the medic. "Could she just head in the right direction that way? Sounds thin to me."

The medic was thoughtful. "We don't know how this Power works. They could have directed her, without her being aware of it."

"Then she's meant to be their key in!" The look the captain directed at Charis was now coldly hostile.

"No, any directive such as that would fail once she got within the Alpha-rim. If they gave her some such hypo-order, it won't work now. You've seen how the warriors are freed from control here. If the hags did have some purpose and pointed her at us, it's finished."

"You're sure of that?"

"You've seen it happen with the males. The control does not operate within the rim."

"So—what do we do with her?"

"Maybe we can learn something. She has been with them—that is obvious."

"Might be more your department than mine," the captain observed. "You can take her on with the other one. He still out?"

"I told you, Lazgah, he's not unconscious in the ordinary sense." The medic was clearly irritated. "I don't know *what* he is except still alive. So far he hasn't responded to any restorative. Such a complete withdrawal—I've never seen its like before."

"Well, at least she isn't like him. And maybe you can learn from her. Try to, and the sooner the better."

"Come." The medic spoke softly. He held out his hand to Charis.

She eyed him over the tube from which she was now sucking the last remnants of paste.

"Where?"

"To a good place, a place where you may rest, where there is more food—water—"

"Out there?" She used the tube to point to the door behind him.

"Yes."

"No. There are snakes there!"

"One of the warriors was here when she came to," the captain explained. "Sent her farther off the beam."

"No, no one will hurt you," the medic assured her. "I won't let them."

Charis allowed herself to be persuaded. That scrap of conversation about the "he" who was being treated—It must be Lantee!

XVII

Four rooms made up a small but very well-equipped medical unit for the base. The worst feature, as far as Charis was concerned, was the single door to the outside, a door by which a blaster-armed guard already sat. To be free one must pass him.

Now the medic shepherded her on, his hand under her arm half-steering, half-supporting, and she made her survey of the quarters in a series of seemingly aimless stares. They came into the third room and that touch on her arm brought her to a halt. She swayed, put out a hand against the wall to steady herself, hoping that her start could be attributed to her dazed condition.

Lantee lay on his back on a narrow cot. His eyes were wide open, but his face had that same blankness it had worn when she had found him among the rocks. He had returned to the husk of a living being, his true identity missing.

"Do you know this man?"

"Know this man?" Charis repeated. "Who is he? Know him—why should I—" Her confusion was the best act she could achieve. She knew the medic was studying her closely.

"Come on." He took her arm again, led her into the next chamber. Two more cots. He pushed her down on the nearest one.

"Stay here."

He went out, sealing the door behind him. Charis ran her hands through the wild tangle of her hair. They could be watching her even now via some visa system, so take no chances. Anyway, she was in the base, and so far their suspicions of her were only normal. But just in case there was a spy system, she lay back on the cot and closed her eyes.

Outwardly she was composed for slumber; inwardly her thoughts were busy. Lantee—what *had* happened to Shann? The first time he had been shocked into such a state by a blast of the Wyvern Power. But that was not in effect here, and those few words Charis had heard exchanged between the captain and the medic suggested that their prisoner's present withdrawal had not come as a result of anything they had done. They were baffled by it.

"Withdrawal" the medic had phrased it—a way of escape. Charis almost sat up, startled by what she thought was the answer. Lantee had chosen this as a way of escape! He had purposely retreated thus before they could use a scanner or a truth drug, fleeing back into the same blackness, really retreating into what might prove death. And the motive for such a choice must have been a very strong one.

The Power would not work inside this Alpha-rim, whatever *that* was. Charis's hand moved against her tunic, feeling the slight bulk of the plasta-board which was her key to the place where Lantee had fled, a key which she could not turn. She had found Lantee, or rather the shell which had encased him. She had yet to find the nullifier or work out a plan against it. Her self-confidence was failing fast.

This was always the worst, this striving to cultivate patience with every nerve in her hammering for action. She must first establish her character as a bewildered fugitive. So she forced herself to lie quietly although she longed to be across that small room, trying the door to see if it was lock-sealed.

It had been early morning when she had come here; now the invaders, both off-worlders and Wyvern males, would be astir. Not a good time to go exploring. Exploring!

Charis summoned concentration, sent out a creeping thought—not backed by the Power, but on her own—striving to reach Tsstu. If this avenue of communication was also blocked by their Alpha-rim—

A mind touch lapped against her probe as delicately as if the curl-cat was here in the room to give her a tongue-caress. Charis knew a throb of excitement, that road was not closed! She had contact, faulty and wavering as it was, with the animals outside the base.

The Tsstu link was no longer a touch but a firm uniting, and then came the feral urge she associated with Taggi—and another! Lantee? No. This was not the passageway link, but a heightening of the Taggi strain—his mate, the female wolverine! A piece of luck Charis had not counted on.

Tsstu was trying to send a message, drawing upon the united power of the wolverines to give it added impetus. A warning? No, not quite that; rather a suggestion that any action be delayed. Charis caught a very fuzzy picture of a Wyvern witch mixed in that. The female Wyverns must be taking a hand as they had promised. Then just as Charis tried to learn more, the curl-cat broke contact.

The girl began to think about Lantee. It had taken the Power to reach him before—the Power plus her own will and that of the two animals. But there in the copter she alone had found him, and without consciously drawing on the Power. Now, if he remained too long in that black world, would he ever come forth again? A small fire could die to ashes, never to be rekindled.

Charis willed herself to think of a black which was the entire absence of any light, the swallowing dark from which her species had fled since first they had learned the secret of fire as a weapon against that which prowled in the shadows. Cold crept up her body, the dark gathered in—A spark far in the heart of that dark . . .

A wrenching at her, dragging her back. Charis moaned at the pain of that wrenching. She opened her eyes to look up into the slitted ones set in a reptilian face where a cruel satisfaction gleamed.

"Snake!" she screamed.

The Wyvern male grinned, obviously highly amused by her shock and terror. He caught at her tunic, his claws in the fabric drawing her to the edge of the cot. But as he raised a paw for another grip, his scaled palm spread wide and then contracted quickly as if it had touched fire. A thin cry had burst from the alien; he jumped away from her.

"What's going on here?" a human voice demanded. Hands appeared on the Wyvern's shoulder as a figure loomed behind the native, dragging him back.

Charis watched the medic pull the Wyvern out of her room. Then she stumbled after—to see the guard come into Lantee's room and aid the medic in forcing the struggling native on, the warrior all the while uttering sharp, shrill cries. She paused at the foot of Lantee's cot as they disappeared toward the outer door.

Shann! She did not cry that name aloud, and even as she made a plea of it in her mind, she knew that there would be no answer. But still she longed now for his support.

His eyes were wide open, but behind them was nothingness. She did not have to touch his limp hand to know that it could not grip hers.

The cries of the Wyvern did not grow fainter. Instead they were augmented outside by a growing chorus. There must be more of the natives gathering. Were the Company men in dispute with their allies?

Charis hesitated. She longed to go to the outer door to see what was going on, but that action would not fit her present role. She should be cowering, frightened to death, in some corner. She listened—the clamor was dying— Better get back to her own room. She scuttled back.

"You—" Captain Lazgah stood in the doorway, his shoulders blocking the medic, and the tone of his voice was a warning.

Charis sat up on her cot, her hands were in her hair as if she had been pulling at it. "The snake—" she took the initiative swiftly "—the snake tried to get me!"

"For good reason." Lazgah's quick stride brought him to the cot side. His fingers were steel-tight and punishing about her right wrist as he pulled her about to face him squarely. "You've been using those hags' tricks. Snake— you're a snake yourself! Those bulls out there have good reason to hate such tricks—they'd like to get their claws into you. Gathgar says you've been working with the Power."

"That's impossible!" the medic cut in. "You've had the complete reading from sensatator since she's been here. There's no indication that anything registered. Gathgar knows that she's been with the females and he built up all this on that fact alone."

"What do we know about this Power anyway?" Lazgah asked. "Sure, there's only been negative register since she's been here. But she might have some way of blanketing reception on that. A scanner could give us the truth."

"You put a scanner on her now and you'll get nothing but a complete burn-out. She'll be another like that fellow in there. What good will that do?"

"Turn the bulls loose on her and we could learn something."

"What can you learn from the dead? They're worked up now to a killing rage. Don't hurry and maybe—"

"Don't hurry!" The captain made a noise not far removed from one of Taggi's snarls. "We don't have much time left. This one knows where those hags have their base. I say—get her under questioning and find that out. Then we move and move fast. We have our orders to cut all corners on this deal."

"Destroy what you want and what good will it do? Sure, you can probably blast your way in and burn out the opposition, but you know what we've learned so far. The Power doesn't work unless you have had the training. It may not operate for males at all. You have a woman here who's already been sensitized to it. Why not use her just as Jagan intended—to pick up the information you need? You won't get that by force—either against her or maybe against the Wyvern females."

Lazgah relaxed his grip on Charis. But he still stood over the girl, staring at her as if he could reach inside her skull by his will and bring her under control.

"I don't like it," he stated, but he did not protest further. "All right—but you keep an eye on her."

The captain tramped out. But the medic did not follow. It was his turn to favor Charis with a measuring survey.

"I wish I knew whether you are playing a game," he said, surprising Charis with his frankness. "Those hags can't possibly control you past the Rim. But—" He shook his head, more at his own thoughts than at her, and did not finish his sentence. Going out abruptly, he closed the seal again.

Charis continued to sit on the cot. The Wyvern male Gathgar had accused her of working with the Power, but she had not. At least not with the aid of the patterns, Wyvern-fashion. Could it be, Charis's hand went to the plasta-board under her tunic, that she did not need such an aid anymore? Was what she had been doing here— her contact with Tsstu, the reach-for Lantee—an easier method of using the same force?

But if that were true, there was a way of using the Power which could not be affected by the nullifier. Charis blinked. That surmise opened up a whole new field of speculations. She could reach Tsstu, and Tsstu could link in turn with the wolverines. Suppose that Tsstu, the wolverines, Charis and Lantee could form a chain to break open the Alpha-rim of the enemy?

Lantee— Somehow her thoughts always returned to Lantee, as if the pattern which was not a pattern needed the element for which he stood—just like the time she could not remember the right design until Tsstu supplied the indentations in her drawing. Charis could not have explained why she was certain of this, but she was.

She lay back on the cot and closed her eyes. Lantee must be summoned out of hiding, be one with them again. Charis released a questing thought, spun it out and away from her as a fisherman might cast a line or as a com beam might search for another installation to activate. A Wyvern witch working under the Power would have been accurate in such a hunt. She herself, using the pattern, could have centered on Tsstu and been reasonably certain of a quick contact, but this blind seeking was a fumbling process.

Touch! Charis tensed. Tsstu! Now she must hold that contact, signal along it her need for energy reserves for the job to be done. But Tsstu was unwilling. It was as if she was in Charis's hand and wriggling for her freedom. But Charis kept the line taut, sent her determined demand along it. There—Taggi came in. The girl braced herself against the impact of the far more savage mind of the wolverine. Through to Taggi went her call for strength and a mutual pointing of their combined wills. Lantee—Charis made that call into form—Lantee. Now a fourth will joined—Togi, the female linked with her mate. The thrusting leap of that striking back to Charis was like a blow.

The girl held that linkage intact for a long moment, as a climber might examine knotted ropes to be sure of his support before facing a dangerous mountainside. Now! The wills were a spear which Charis not only aimed for the throwing but followed in flight.

Into the black of the nothing-place, surely the strangest of those Otherwheres into which the Power of the Wyverns led, she was the point of a fiery arrow shooting on and on, seeking the spark of light there. Now it was before her, very low, an ember close to extinction. But the arrow which was Charis, Tsstu, Taggi, and Togi struck into its heart.

Around them whirled a wild dance of figures. From all the doorways they had come into the corridor to crowd about her. She could not flee from them lest the lifeline break. This was worse than the first time she had walked this forbidden way, for the thoughts and memories of Shann Lantee now gathered more substance in their shadows. Charis knew a terror which balanced her on the thin edge of sanity.

However, the chain held true and pulled her back until she lay again on the cot, aware of its support under her. The contacts broke, the wolverines were gone; Tsstu, gone.

"I am here."

Charis opened her eyes, but no one in a green-brown uniform stood beside her. She turned her head to face the wall which was still between them.

"I am—back."

Again that assurance, clear-cut as audible words but, in her mind, coming with the same ease as the Wyvern witches communicated.

"Why—" Her lips shaped that soundlessly to match the inquiry in her mind.

"It was that or face the scanner," he answered swiftly. "And now?"

"Who knows? Did they take you too?"

"No." Charis outlined what had happened.

"Thorvald here?" Lantee's thoughts dropped away and she did not try to follow deeper. Then he was back to communication level. "The installation we're after is in the main dome. They have it guarded by Wyvern males who are sensitive to any telepathic waves. And they will fight to the death to keep it in action and themselves free."

"Can we reach it?" Charis asked.

"Little chance. At least, I've seen none so far," was his disappointing answer.

"You mean it's impossible for us to do anything?" Charis protested.

"No, but we have to know more. They've stopped trying to rouse me. Perhaps that will give me a chance to make some move."

"The Wyvern male told them I am using the Power. But I haven't tried it with the pattern and it didn't register on some machine of theirs, so they didn't quite believe him."

"You did this—without a pattern?"

"With Tsstu and the wolverines, yes. Does it mean we don't really need a pattern? That the Wyverns don't need them? But why wouldn't it show up on their machine?"

"May hit another wave length," Lantee returned. "But if the Wyvern males pick it up, they may be more sensitive on other bands than their mistresses credit. I wonder if they could have some Power of their own but don't know how to use it. If they picked you up before—"

"Then this last call for you—they could—"

"Be really alerted now? Yes. Which shaves our time to act. I don't even know how many there are here at the base."

"The witches have promised their help."

"How can they? Any sending of theirs will fail at the Rim."

"Shann, the Wyverns control their males with the Power. And the male I saw here believes that I can use it here. Suppose we all link again. *Could* we control them inside the Rim?"

There was a moment of pause in the flow of thought and then he answered.

"How do we know what will work and what won't until we put it to the test? But I want to be ready to get out of here on my own two feet. And from here I can see a guard with a blaster at the outer door. We might be able to link against the Wyvern males, but I wouldn't swear we could link to take out an off-worlder who has never been sensitized to mental control."

"What do we do?"

"Link with the others. See if you can reach Thorvald so—" he ordered.

This time the first link was not Charis, but Lantee and his will strengthened hers in her search for the curl-cat. Tsstu replied with a kind of fretfulness, but she picked up the wolverines.

A line cast out, spinning . . . then the catch of response.

"Wait!" That caution came back link by link. "The witches are moving. Wait for their signal." Break off as the animals dropped contact.

"What can they do?" Charis demanded of Lantee.

"Your guess is as good as mine." He was tense. "The medic's just come in."

Silence. How well could he play *his* role, Charis wondered a little fretfully. But if the medic had given up hope of reviving the Survey man, he might not examine him too closely now. She lay listening for any sound which might come through the walls.

The door of her room opened and the medic came in with a tray on which there was food, *real* food, not rations. He put it down on a drop-table and turned around to look at her. Charis tried to look like one awakening from a nap. The man's expression was set and the motion with which he indicated the food was abrupt.

"You'd better eat. You'll need it!"

She sat up, pushing back her hair, striving to present bewilderment.

"If you're smart," he continued, "you'll tell the captain all about it now. He's an expert on grab raids. If you don't know what that means, you'll soon discover the hard way."

Charis was afraid to ask what this warning did mean. To cling to her cloak of being a dazed fugitive was her only defense.

"You can't hide it—not any longer. Not with a complete burn-out of the sensator this time."

Charis tensed. The linkage—twice the linkage—had at last registered on whatever safeguard the invaders had mounted.

"So you do understand that?" The medic nodded. "I thought you would. Now, you had better talk and fast! The captain might just turn you over to the bulls."

"The snakes!" Charis found words at last. "You mean give me to the snakes?" She did not have to counterfeit her repulsion.

"That gets to you, does it? It should; they hate the Power. And they'll willingly destroy anyone who uses it if they can. So—make your deal with the captain. He's willing to offer a good one."

"Simkin!"

There was such urgency in that hail that the medic whirled to the door. There was a growing murmur of sound—some of it sharp, the rest shouting. The medic ran, leaving the door open. Charis was up and into Lantee's room instantly.

The hissing blatt-blatt of a blaster in action came now. And she had heard that claking before when the birds had hunted her along the Warlockian cliff.

Then, like a swifter beat of her heart, a pulse along all the veins and arteries of her body—

"Now!"

The signal was not spoken but to it all of Charis responded. She saw Lantee slide from the cot in one supple, coordinated movement—as ready as she.

XVIII

Lantee waved Charis back and took the lead as they approached the outer door. The Company guard still stood there, his back blocking their passage, intent upon what was happening outside, his blaster drawn and moving as if he were trying to align its sights on some very elusive mark.

The Survey man crossed the anteroom with the caution of a stalking feline as the din outside covered any sound within. But some instinct must have warned the guard. He turned his head, sighted Lantee and, giving a cry, tried to bring his blaster up and around.

Too late! Just what Lantee did Charis was not sure. The blow he struck was certainly not any conventional one. As the guard crumpled, the blaster fell to the floor and skidded. Charis pounced and closed fingers about the ugly weapon. She tossed it, as she straightened, to Lantee and he caught it easily.

They looked out into a scene of wild confusion, though their view of it was limited to a small segment of the base. Men in yellow uniforms crouched under cover and laced the air with blaster rays, apparently trying to strike back at some menace in the sky. Two of the Wyvern males lay either dead or unconscious by the door of a dome to the right, across from the one in which Shann and Charis had been prisoners. And there were burned and blasted clakers littering the ground in all directions.

"There—" Lantee gestured to the dome by which the Wyvern bodies sprawled. "It's in there."

But to try to reach that would set them up as targets for the marksmen now concentrating on the clakers. The din of the attack cries was lessening; fewer bodies struck the ground. Charis saw Lantee's lips thin, his face assume a grim cast, and she knew he was tensing for action.

"Run! I'll cover you."

She measured the distance by eye. Not far, but at his moment that open space stretched as an endless plain. And the Wyvern males? Those in sight were motionless, but more could be inside that open door.

Charis gave a leap which carried her well into the open. She heard a shout and then the crackle of a blaster beam which was close enough to scorch her upper arm. She cried out, but somehow she kept to her feet and stumbled on into the door, tripping there over the body of a Wyvern. She sprawled forward into the interior, thereby saving her life as one of the murderous, saw-toothed spears flew past her. She rolled, coming up against the wall where she pushed up to look at her assailants.

Wyvern males—three of them, two still holding spears, one of whom raised his weapon with sadistic slowness. The Wyvern was enjoying her fear as well as the fact that he was now in command of the situation.

"Rrrrrrrruuggghhh."

The Wyvern, his spear almost ready to throw, snapped around to face the door. A snarling ball of fury burst through it to launch at the natives. They howled, thrusting wildly at the wolverine. But the animal, using the advantage of its surprise attack to break past them, disappeared into the next room.

"Charis! You all right?"

Shann dodged in. The fabric of his tunic smoldered at rib level and he beat at it with his left hand.

"Surprisingly bad shots for Company men," he commented.

"Maybe they've orders not to kill." Charis tried to match his composure. But though she was on her feet now, she kept her back to the wall, facing the Wyverns, amazed that they had not launched a spear as yet. The eruption of the wolverine into their midst had shaken them oddly.

Shann gestured the three aliens back with his ready blaster.

"Move!" he ordered curtly. And the wariness in their yellow eyes told the two off-worlders that the natives were well aware of the potency of that weapon.

They retreated from the small outer room into the main room of the structure. There had been a good-sized com unit in here, but one glance told Charis that it could not serve them, for the installation had been deliberately rayed with blaster fire until it was half-melted in more than one place.

But that was not all that was in the room. On a base improvised from packing boxes was an intricate machine giving off an aura of rippling light. And, standing about that, almost as if they were cold and were warming their chilled bodies, were six male Wyverns. Now spears were leveled—until they sighted the blaster Shann held.

"Kill!" The word was scorching hate in Charis's mind as it flashed from the warriors.

"And be killed!" Shann returned in the same mental speech.

The snouted, spike-combed heads bobbed. Their surprise, their unease close to the border of fear, played about them much as did the light that rippled from the machine they guarded.

Lantee could do just that—wipe out the Wyverns *and* the machine they were striving to shield with their bodies. In Charis's thought, the natives *were* ready to die in that fashion. But was that the only answer?

"There might be a better one." Shann's thought came in reply to hers.

"Kill!" Not from the Wyverns now, but clear and as a feral demand. Taggi emerged from under the wreckage of the com.

"Here!" The small black shadow which had just flitted in sprang at Charis. The girl stooped and gathered up Tsstu. From her arms the curl-cat regarded the Wyverns with an unwinking stare.

"We die—you die!"

Clear-cut that warning. But the Wyvern who had made it did not raise his spear. Instead he placed his four-digited hands on the installation.

"He means it." This time Lantee used audible speech. "There must be some sort of panic button in that that will blow up the whole thing if necessary. Move away!" He changed to mental order and gestured with the blaster.

Not one of the natives stirred, and their determination not to yield to that command beat back at the off-worlders in a counterblast. How long could such a standoff continue? Charis wondered. Sooner or later the Company men would be in on this.

She put down Tsstu and went back to the anteroom, to discover that while she could close the outer door, there was no way to secure that portal. The palm lock which had once fastened it was now only a blackened hole in the fabric.

"Kill the witch one! With *you*, we shall bargain."

The thought was clear speech in her head as she reentered the wrecked com room.

"You are as we. Kill the witch and be free!" The males appealed to Lantee.

Tsstu hissed, her ears flattened against her round skull as she backed to a stand before Charis. Taggi growled from where he accompanied Shann, his small eyes alight with battle anger.

The spokesman for the natives glanced at both animals. Charis caught the quiver of uncertainty in his mind. Shann the Wyvern could understand; Charis he hated since he classed her with his own females who had always held the Power. But this link with animals was new and so to be feared.

"Kill the witch and those who are hers." He made his decision, lumping the unfamiliar with Charis. "Be free again as now we are."

"Are you?" From somewhere Charis found the words. "Away from this room or from the base where this off-world machine cannot reach—are you then free?"

Stark, hot hate glowing at her from yellow eyes, a snarl lifting scaled skin away from fangs.

"Are you?" Shann took up, and Charis readily gave way

to his leadership. To the Wyvern males, she was a symbol of all they hated most. But Lantee was male and so to them not wholly an enemy.

"Not yet." The truth was hard to admit. "But when the witch ones die, then we shall be!"

"But there may not be a need for such killing or dying."

"What are you thinking of?" Charis asked vocally.

Lantee did not look at her. He was studying the Wyvern leader with intensity, as if he would hold the native in check by his will alone.

"A thought," he said aloud, "just a thought which might resolve the whole problem. Otherwise, this is going to end with a real blood bath. Now that they know what this machine can do for them, do you think the males will ever be anything again but potential murderers of their own kind? And we can destroy this machine—and them, but that will be a failure."

"Not killing?" The Wyvern's thoughts cut in. "But if we do not kill them while they may not dream us defenseless, then they will in time break us and once more use the Power against us."

"Upon me they used the Power and I was in the outer dark where nothing is."

The astonishment of the Wyverns was a wave spreading out to engulf the off-worlders.

"And how came you again from that place?" That the Wyvern recognized the site of Lantee's exile was plain.

"She sought me, and these sought me, and they brought me forth."

"Why?" came flatly.

"Because they were my friends; they wished me well."

"Between witch and male there can be no friendship! She is mistress—he obeys her commands in all things— or he is naught!"

"I was naught, yet here I am now." Shann sought Charis. "Link! Prove it to them—link!"

She tossed the mental cord to Tsstu, to Taggi, and then reached for Shann. They were as one and as one, Shann thrust at the Wyvern's consciousness. Charis saw the spokesman for the natives sway as if buffeted by a storm wind. Then the off-worlders broke apart and were four again.

"Thus it is," Shann said.

"But you are not as we are. With you, male and female may be different. True?"

"True. But also know this: as one, we four have broken the bonds of the Power. But can you live always with a machine and those who have brought you the machine? Can they be trusted? Have you looked into their minds?"

"They use us for their purposes. But that we accept for our freedom."

"Turn off the machine," Shann said abruptly.

"If we do, the witches will come."

"Not unless we will it."

Charis was startled. Was Lantee running his claims too high? But she had begun to understand what he was fighting for. As long as the cleft between male and female existed in the Wyvern species, there would be an opening for just such trouble as the Company men had started here. Shann was going to attempt to close that gap. Centuries of tradition, generations of specialized breeding, stood against his will. And all the terrors and fears of inbred prejudice would be fighting against him, but he was going to try it.

He had not even asked for her backing or consent, and she discovered that she did not resent that. It was as if the linkage had erased all desire to counter a decision she realized as right.

"Link!"

A crackling explosion, the stench of burning plasta-fab. The Company soldiers had turned blasters on the dome! What did Lantee propose to do about that? Charis had only time for one fleeting thought before her mind fell into place beside the others.

Again it was Lantee who aimed that shaft of thought, sent it out past the melting wall of the dome, straight at the enemy minds, open and ill-prepared for such attack. Men dropped where they stood. A still-spitting blaster rolled along the ground, spraying its deadly ray in a wave pattern along a wall.

Shann had had the courage to try that first gamble and

he had won. Could he do the same again in the greater gamble he proposed?

The Wyvern spokesman made a slight motion with his hand. Those who walled the machine with their bodies stood away.

"That is not the Power as we know it."

"But it was born of that Power," Shann caught him up. "Just as other ways of life may issue from those now known to you."

"But you are not sure."

"I am not sure. But I know that killing leaves only the dead, and the dead may not be summoned back by any Power ever known to living creatures. You will die and others shall die if you take the vengeance you wish. Then who will profit by your dying—except perhaps off-worlders for whom you do not fight in truth?"

"But you fight for us?"

"Can I hide the truth when we touch minds?"

That curious quiet came down as a curtain between the off-worlders and the Wyverns as the natives conferred among themselves. At last the spokesman returned to contact.

"We know you speak the truth as you see it. No one before has broken the bonds of the Power. That you have done so means that perhaps you can defend us now. We brought our spears for killing. But it is true that the dead remain dead, and if we make the killing we wish, we as a people shall die. So we shall try your path."

"Link!" Again the command from Lantee. He made a motion with his hand and the Wyvern pressed a lever on the installation.

This time they had not fashioned a spear of the mind-force but a barrier wall, and only just in time. As a wave of determined attack struck against it, Charis swayed and felt the firm brace of Shann's arm as he stood, his feet a little apart, his chin up—as he might have faced a physical fight, fist against fist.

Three times that wave battered at them, striving, Charis knew, to reach the Wyvern males. And each time the linkage held without yielding. Then they were there in person—Gysmay, her brilliant body-patterns seeming to flame in her terrible anger, Gidaya—and two others Charis did not know.

"What do you?" The question seared.

"What we must." Shann Lantee made answer.

"Let us have those who are ours!" Gysmay demanded in full cry.

"They are not yours but their own!"

"They are nothing! They do not dream, they have no Power. They are nothing save what we will them to be."

"They are part of a whole. Without them, you die; without you, they die. Can you still say they are nothing?"

"What say you?" The question Gidaya asked was aimed at Charis, not Shann.

"That he speaks the truth."

"After the manner of your people, not ours!"

"Did I not have an answer from Those Who Have Gone Before which you could not read, Wise One? Perhaps this is the reading of that answer. Four have become one at will, and each time we so will it, that one made of four is stronger. Could you break the barrier we raised here while we were one, even though you must have sent against us the full Power? You are an old people, Wise One, and with much learning. Can it not be that some time, far and long ago, you took a turning into a road which limited your Power in truth? Peoples are strong and grow when they search for new roads. When they say, 'There is no road but this one which we know well, and always must we travel in it,' then they weaken themselves and dim their future.

"Four have made one and yet each one of that four is unlike another. You are all of a kind in your Power. Have you never thought that it takes different threads to weave a real pattern—that you use different shapes to make the design of Power?"

"This is folly! Give us what is ours lest we destroy you." Gysmay's head-comb quivered, the very outlines of her body seemed to shimmer with her rage.

"Wait!" Gidaya interrupted. "It is true that this dreamer has had an answer from the Rods, delivered by the will of Those Who Have Dreamed Before. And it was an answer we could not read, but yet it was sent to her and was a true one. Can any of you deny that?"

There was no answer to her demand.

"Also, there have been said here things which have a core of good thought behind them."

Gysmay stirred, none of her anger abating. But she did not render her protest openly.

"Why do you stand against us now, Dreamer?" Gidaya continued. "You, to whom we have opened many gates, to whom we gave the use of the Power—why should you choose to turn that same gift against us who have never chosen to do you ill?"

"Because here I have seen one true thing: that there is a weakness in your Power, that you have been blind to that which makes evil against you. As long as you are a race divided against itself, with a wall of contempt and hatred keeping you apart, then there is a way of bringing disaster upon your race. It is because you opened doors and made straight a road for me that I will to do the same for you now. This evil came from my people. But we are not all thus. We, too, have our divisions and barriers, our outlaws and criminals.

"But do not, I pray you, Wise Ones," Charis hastened on, "keep open this rift in your own nation so that outside ill can enter. You have seen that there are two answers to the Power on which you lean. One comes through a machine which can be turned on and off at the will of outsiders. Another is a growth from the very seeds you have sown, and so it is possible for you to nourish it also.

"Without this man I have only the Power you gave to my summoning. With him and the animals, I am so much the greater that I no longer need this." From her tunic Charis took the map sheet, holding it out so that the Wyverns could see the pattern drawn upon it. She crumpled the sheet and tossed it to the floor.

"This must be thought upon in council." Gidaya had watched that repudiation of the pattern with narrowed eyes.

"So be it," Charis affirmed, and they were gone.

❖   ❖   ❖

"Will it work?" Charis sat in the commander's quarters of the base. A visa-screen on the wall showed a row of Wyvern warriors squatting on their heels, guards for the still dazed Company men who had been herded into the visitors' dome in temporary imprisonment, awaiting the arrival of the Patrol forces.

Lantee lounged in an Eazi-rest, far down on his spine, while across his outstretched legs sprawled two wolverine cubs now snorting a little from the depths of slumber.

"Talk out, won't you?" Thorvald snapped in exasperation as he looked up from the emergency com. "I pick up only a kind of buzzing in the brain when you do that and it's giving me a headache!"

Shann grinned. "A point to remember, sir. Do I think our argument will convince them? I'm not venturing any guesses. But the witches are smart. And we proved them flat failures, tackling them on their own ground. That rocked them harder than they've ever been, I imagine. Warlock's been theirs to control; with their Power and their dreams, they have thought themselves invincible. Now they know they are not. And they have two answers: to stand still and go under, or to try this new road you've talked about. I'll wager we may have a tentative peace offer first, then some questions."

"They have their pride," Charis said softly. "Don't strip that from them."

"Why should we wish to?" Thorvald asked. "Remember, we, too, have dreamed. But this is just why you will handle the negotiations."

She was surprised at the tone of his voice, but he was continuing. "Jagan was right in his approach, a woman must be a liaison. The witches have to admit that Lantee and, to a lesser degree, myself have some small claim on their respect, but they will be happier to have you take the fore now."

"But I'm not—"

"Empowered to act on a diplomatic level? You are. This mission has wide emergency powers, and you are to represent us. You're drafted, all of you—Tsstu and Taggi included—to conduct a treaty with the witches."

"And it will be a real treaty this time!"

Charis did not know how Shann could be so sure of that, but she accepted his confidence.

"Link!"

Automatically now she yielded to that unspoken order. It was a new pattern, flowing, weaving, and she allowed herself to be swept along, sensing there were treasures to be found so: the subtle skill and neat mind that was Tsstu, the controlled savagery and curiosity that was Taggi and sometimes Togi.

Then there was that other—closer in some ways, different in others, and fast becoming an undissolvable part of her—which was strength, companionship. Hand rising to clasp hand, falling away, but always there to reach and hold again when needed. This had she brought with her from the Otherwhere of the Wyverns and this she would need ever hereafter to be complete.

FORERUNNER
FORAY

PREFACE

Parapsychology is now a subject for serious study around the world, storming barriers of long standing based on ignorance and fear. At one time it was dismissed as wild fantasy, except by those who had direct evidence to the contrary. Now it is the source of varied experiments.

Psychometry—a reading of the past history of an object by a sensitive who is sometimes not even aware of its nature—is a very old and well-documented talent. Recently the British archaeologist T.C. Lethbridge experimented in using this gift in his researches into sites and artifacts of Pict and pre-Roman Britain; one may read about the astonishing results in such books as *E.S.P., Ghost and Divining Rod,* and others.

Before beginning this book and while engaged in work upon it, I was witness to four "readings" by a sensitive who is well versed in this paranormal talent. In all four cases I supplied the object to be "read"; the results were amazing. In three cases the information delivered was clear, detailed, and related without hesitation; the fourth was more obscure since the object in question (a piece of antique jewelry) had passed through many hands.

One of the readings I could verify at once with knowledge I already possessed. Another reading, very detailed (in this instance the object was a rare and very old piece of Chinese manufacture), was verified by an expert some weeks after the reading, the true history being unknown to me before that time.

That this talent can be used in archaeology Mr. Lethbridge proved. That it may become a part of regular historical research in the future seems a good possibility.

1

Ziantha stood before the door smoothing a tight-fitting glove with her other hand. Under its clinging material her flesh tingled from the energy controls which had been woven so skillfully into that covering. She had seen the glove used, had practiced—but before this moment had never tried it to its full potential.

For a last time she mind-searched up and down the corridor. All clear, just as Ennia had promised, not that any Guildsperson ever depended on anything save his or her own wits, skills, and defenses. With that prickling hot on her palm, she reached forward and set her hand flat against the persona-lock. Yasa had paid a fabulous price for the loan of that glove; now it would be demonstrated whether that fee was justified.

Tongue tip pushing a little between set teeth, Ziantha waited for seconds frozen in time. Just when she was sure Yasa had lost her gamble, the door slid noiselessly into the wall. So far, so good!

Mind-seek again, to make sure there were no inner guards except those she had been trained to locate and disarm. It would seem that High Lord Jucundus was old-fashioned enough to use only the conventional protectives which were as child's toys to the Thieves' Guild. But still Ziantha made very sure, her bare hand on that girdle (wherein the supposed decorative gems were tiny but very effective detects) before she crossed into the room beyond, snapping down at that moment her dark sight band—which also masqueraded as part of an elaborate, high-fashion headdress, just as the cloak about her, at the pressure of a collar stud, was now a sight distort. The equipment she wore would have cost the yearly revenue of a small planet had it ever come to buying and selling; her own mathematical sense was not enough even to set a sum to its value.

The chamber had every luxury that could be offered on Korwar, the pleasure world. Treasures . . . but she was here for only one thing. Pulling the cloak tightly about her so that it might not brush against any piece of furniture and so discharge energy, traces of which could later be detected, Ziantha threaded a careful path to the far wall. If all went as Yasa wished, if it were a clean foray, Jucundus would never have a clue that his secrets had been penetrated. That is, until their substance had been safely sold.

With the nightsight at her service she might be in a well-lighted room. And not only was her sight an aid. Twice she paused at warnings offered by her belt detects and was able to mind-hold protection devices long enough to slip by, though each check heightened her uneasiness, drew upon her psychic energy.

On the wall was a tri-dee mural portraying an off-world scene. But she had been briefed as to the next step. With her tongue, answered by a blazing shock, she touched the latch of the glove, not daring to lift her other fingers from the detects. The glove responded by splitting down the back so she could hook it to her belt and pull her hand free.

Then the girl drew from beneath her cloak a pendant, raised it to one of the flashing stars on the wall display, pressed it there. An answering sound her ears could barely catch followed; the vibration of it was a pain in her head.

A portion of the wall lifted to display a cupboard. So far the skills and devices of the Guild had been successful. But the rest of her mission depended upon her own talents.

The cupboard safe was filled with neat piles of cubes so small she could have cradled three or four at a time in her palm. There were so many, and in a very limited time she must sort out the few that mattered, psychometrize their contents.

Her breath quickened as she set finger tip to the first in the top row. Not that, nor that—Her finger flickered on down, none in that row was what she wanted, though she guessed all had value. Jucundus's records: if all the rumors about him were true, it did not matter in the least that he had been forced into exile, his planetary holdings confiscated. With these microrecords he could still use men, build again, perhaps even to greater power.

Here! From the middle shelf she brought out the cube, pushing it above the band of her nightsight so it rested against the bare flesh of her forehead. This was the most dangerous part of her foray, for at this moment she must forget everything else—the detects on her belt, her own mind-barrier—and concentrate only on what she could "read" from the cube. Also, it had little meaning for her: no vivid pictures, only code symbols to be memorized. That was it. With a release of breath that was close to a sigh of relief, she put it back, sliding her finger along the rows seeking another. Yasa had thought two—but make very sure.

The second! Once more she had to wait out in danger that transfer of knowledge that left her so defenseless while it was in progress. Now she must make sure there was not a third cube. But her questing finger did not find one. She closed the panel, new relief flooding in. She had only to leave, to relock the door.

Once more drawing her distort cloak tight, Ziantha turned. Touch nothing else, leave no trace to be picked up. This was—

Ziantha froze. She had reached with her now ungloved hand to draw in a corner of the cloak which had threatened to sweep across a small curio table. Now the edge of material fell from between her fingers, her hand stretched out farther, not by conscious will on her part, but as if her wrist had been seized in a powerful grip and jerked forward.

For a second or two the girl believed that she might have been caught in some new protect device that her belt had not been able to pick up. Then she realized that this was a psychic demand for her attention.

Never before had she had such an experience. When she psychometrized it was always by will, by her own volition. This was a demand she did not understand, which brought with it fear and the beginning of panic. On the table lay something that was "charged," just as the Guild devices were charged, with psychic energy so great it could command her attention.

Ziantha's first stab of fear faded. This was new, so the experience caught her even though she knew the danger of lingering. She had to see what demanded recognition from her by provoking such an answering surge of her talent.

Six objects on the table. There was a weird animal form carved from a semiprecious stone. A flat block of veriform rose-crystal with a gauze-winged free-flower from Virgal III imprisoned in it. A box of Styrian stone-wood and next to that one of those inter-ring puzzles made by the natives of Lysander. A trinket basket of tri-fold filigree sapphire held some acid-sweets. But the last— A lump of dusty clay, or so it looked.

Ziantha leaned closer. The lump had odd markings on it—pulling her— She snatched back her hand as if her fingers had neared leaping flames. But she had not touched that ugly lump, and she must not! She knew that if she did she would be totally lost.

Feverishly she wrapped her hand in a fold of her cloak, edged around the table as if it were a trap. For at that moment that was exactly what she felt it to be. A subtle trap, perhaps set not by Jucundus but by some other power to imperil any one with her talent.

Ziantha scuttled across the room as if she were fleeing the clang of an alarm that would bring the whole city patrol. Outside in the corridor, the room again sealed, she stood breathing with the painful, rib-raising force of one who has fled for her life, fighting back the need to return, to take into her hand that lump of baked clay, or earth-encrusted stone, or whatever it was—to *know!*

With shaking hands she made those swift alterations to her clothing which concealed the double purpose of her garments, allowing her to appear a person who had every right to walk here. What was the matter with her?

She had succeeded, could return to Yasa now with exactly the information she had been sent to get. Still she had no feeling of exultation, only the nagging doubt that she had left behind something of infinitely greater value, disastrously spurned.

The branch corridor united with the main one, and Rhin stepped from the shadows where he had concealed himself so well that he startled even Ziantha on his appearance. He wore the weapon belt of a personal guard, the one branch of the Thieves' Guild that had quasi-legality, since they offered protection against assassins. And some of the galactic elite who made Korwar their playground had good reason to fear sudden death.

At his glance she nodded, but they did not speak as he fell into step a pace or so behind her, as was determined by their present roles. Now and then as she moved, but not with undue haste, Ziantha caught sight of them both in a mirror. It gave her a slight shock to see herself in the trappings of a Zhol Maiden, her natural complexion and features concealed by the paint of an entertainer. Her cloak, its distort switched off, was a golden orange, in keeping with the richness of the gems in her headdress, girdle, and necklace. Garnished like this, she had the haughty look that was part of her role, quite unlike her usual self.

They were on the down ramp now and here were others, a motley of clothing, of racial types, of species. Korwar was both a playground and a crossroads for this part of the galaxy. As such, its transient population was most varied. And among them her present guise attracted no attention. The company of a Zhol Maiden for an evening, a week, a month, was a symbol of prestige for many galactic lords. She had had excellent coaching from Ennia, whose semblance she wore tonight—Ennia, who companied with High Lord Jucundus, keeping him well occupied elsewhere.

They reached the main hall, where the flow of guests moving in and out, seeking banqueting halls, gaming rooms, was a steady river into which they dropped. Yet Ziantha did not turn her head even to look at Rhin, though she longed to search faces, probe. Had her venture of the evening, the drain on her talents, brought this odd feeling of being shadowed? Or was it that her meeting with that lump had shaken her into this uneasiness? She sensed—what? The pull of the rock, yes, but that was something she could and would control.

This was something different, a feeling of being watched—a Patrol sensitive? In these garments she was protected by every device the Guild possessed against mind-touch. And all knew that the Guild had techniques that never appeared on the market or were known to the authorities.

Yet she could not throw off the sensation that somewhere there was a questing—a searching. Though as yet she was sure it had not found her. If it had she would have known instantly.

Rhin went ahead, summoned a private flitter with a Zhol registration. Ziantha pulled up the collar of her cloak as she went into the night, sure now that her imagination was overactive, that she need not fear anything at all—not now.

Tikil was all jewels of light, strains of music, exuberant life, and she felt the lifting of a burden, began to enjoy the knowledge that she had repaid tonight the long years of training and guardianship. Sometimes lately she had chafed under that indebtedness, though Yasa had never reminded her of it. Still Ziantha was not free—would she ever be?

But at least she was freer than some. As their flitter climbed to the upper lanes, swung out in a circle to bring them to Yasa's villa, they crossed the edge of the Dipple, where the jeweled lights of the city were cut off by that wedge of gloom as dark and gray as the huddle of barracks below were by day, as depressing to the spirit to see as they were to those who still endured a dreary existence within their drab walls.

Almost her full lifetime the Dipple had been there, a blot that Korwar, and this part of the galaxy, tried to forget but could not destroy.

Ziantha need only look down on that grayness as they swept over to realize that there were degrees of freedom and that what she now had was infinitely preferable to what lay down there. She was one of the lucky ones. How could she ever doubt that?

All because Yasa had seen her on begging detail that time at the spaceport and had witnessed the guessing trick she had taught herself. She had thought it was only a trick, something anyone could do if he wished. But Yasa had known that only a latent sensitive could have done as well as Ziantha. Perhaps that was because Yasa was an alien, a Salarika.

Through Yasa's interest she had been brought out of the Dipple, taken to the villa, which had seemed a miracle of beauty, put to school. Though the Salarika had demanded instant obedience and grueling hours of learning, it was all meat and drink to Ziantha, who had starved and thirsted for such without knowing it before. She was what those months and years of training had made her, an efficient tool of the Guild, a prized possession of Yasa's.

Like all her feline-evolved race, Yasa was highly practical, utterly self-centered, but able to company with other species to a workable degree without ever losing her individuality. Her intelligence was of a very high order, even if she approached matters from a slightly different angle than would one of Ziantha's species. She had great presence and powers of command and was one of the few fems who had risen to the inner ranks of the Guild. Her own past history was a mystery; even her age was unknown. But on more than one planet her slightly hissed word was law to more beings than the conventional and legal rulers could control.

Ziantha was a human of Terran—or past-Terran—descent. But from what race or planet she had come in that dim beginning, when the inhabitants of dozens of worlds (the noncombatants, that is) had been driven by war to land in the "temporary" camp of the Dipple, she could not tell. Her appearance was not in any way remarkable. She had no outstanding features, hue of skin, inches of height, which could easily place her. And because she was unremarkable in her own person, she was of even more value. She could be taught to take on the appearance of many races, even of one or two nonhuman species, when there was need. Like Yasa, her age was an unsolved question. It was apparent she was longer in maturing than some races, though her mind absorbed quickly all the teaching it was given, and her psychic talent tested very high indeed.

Gratitude, and later the Guild oath, bound her to Yasa. She was part of an organization that operated across the galaxy in a loose confederacy of shadows and underworlds. Governments might rise and fall, but the Guild remained, sometimes powerful enough to juggle the governments themselves, sometimes driven undercover to build in the dark. They had their ambassadors, their veeps, and their own laws, which to defy was quick death. Now and then the law itself dealt with the Guild, as was true in the case of Jucundus.

The Dipple was well behind now as they cruised above the gardens and carefully preserved bits of wild which separated villa from villa. Ziantha's hands clenched under the border of her cloak. The thought of tonight's work—not the work, no, rather that lump—filled her mind. An ache as strong as hunger gripped her.

She must see Ogan as soon as she discharged into the waiting tapes the memories she carried—she must see Ogan, discover what was the matter. This obsession which rode her was not natural, certainly. And it upset her thinking, could be a threat to her talent. Ogan, the renegade parapsychologist who had trained her, was the only one who could tell her the meaning of this need.

The flitter set down on a landing roof, where a dim light was sentinel. As a cover Yasa claimed a Salariki headship of a trading firm and so possessed a profitable and legal business in Tikil. That establishment she ran with the same efficiency as she did her Guild concerns. Nor was she the only one within that organization to live a double existence. On Korwar she was the Lady Yasa, and her wealth brought respect and authority.

Ziantha sped across to the grav shaft. Late as it was, the house was alive, as usual, though the sounds were few and muted. But there was never any unawareness under a roof where Yasa ruled. As if only by eternal vigilance could she continue to hold in her long clawed hands the threads of power she must weave together for her purposes.

At the scratch of her fingernails on a plexiglass panel

into which had been set a glory of ferns, that panel rolled back, and Ziantha faced the heavily scented chamber of Yasa's main quarters. On the threshold she paused dutifully while blowers of perfumed spray set up about that portal gave her a quick bath of the scent which was Yasa's preference at the moment.

Quite used to this, Ziantha allowed her cloak to slip to the floor, turned slowly amid the puffing of vapor. To her own sense of smell the odor was oppressively powerful; to the Salarika it made her acceptable as a close companion. It was the one weakness of the species, their extreme susceptibility to alien scents. And they took precautions to render their lives among aliens bearable in this way.

As she endured that anointing, Ziantha lifted off the headdress of Zhol fashion. Her head ached, but that was only to be expected after the strain she had put on her talent and nerves tonight. Once she had delivered what she brought, Ogan might entrance her into a healing sleep, if she asked for it.

The light in the room was subdued, again because of the mistress here. Yasa did not need bright illumination. She was curled among the cushions which formed her favorite seat. By the open window was an eazi-rest, in which Ogan lay at full length. The rumors, which were many, said that he was a Psycho-tech, one of the proscribed group. Like Yasa, he was ageless on the surface, and could well have had several life-prolonging treatments. But on what world he had been born no one knew.

Unlike the Salarikis who served in Yasa's villa, he was a small frail man, seeming a desiccated shadow beside them. He was not only a master of mental talents, but he possessed certain infighting skills which made him legend. Now he lay with his head turned away, facing the open window, as if the strong perfume bothered him. However, as Ziantha came forward, he turned to watch her, his face expressionless as always.

In that single moment the girl knew that she had no intention of telling him about the lump. Ogan might give her peace, but that she did not want at the price of letting him know what had surprised and frightened her. Let

that remain her secret—at least for now. Why should Ogan
be always full master?

"Welcome—" There was a purring in Yasa's voice. She
was slim, and the most graceful creature in movement
Ziantha had ever seen. And, in her way, the most beautiful as well. Black hair, more like plushy fur, was thick
and satiny on her head and shoulders and down the upper
sides of her arms. Her face, not quite as broad and flat
as those of most of her species, narrowed to an almost
sharply pointed chin. But it was the wonder of her very
large eyes which drew away attention from all other features. Slanted a little in her skull, their pupils contract-
ing and expanding in degrees of light, like those of her
far-off feline ancestors, these were a deep red-gold, their
color so vivid against her naturally grayish skin as to make
them resemble those koros stones that were the marvel
and great wealth of her home world.

Two such stones were set now in a wide collar about
her throat, but they seemed dimmed by her eyes, even
though they radiated slightly in the low-lighted room.

She put forth a hand equipped with retractable nails
now sheathed in filigree metal caps, and beckoned
Ziantha. Her short golden robe, caught in by a girdle from
which hung scent bags, shimmered as she moved. From
down in her throat came a tiny murmur of sound the girl
knew of old. Yasa purred, Yasa was well pleased.

"I do not ask, cubling, if all went well. That is apparent
in your presence here. Ogan—"

He did not answer her, but the eazi-rest moved, bringing him upright. It was his turn to beckon Ziantha. She
sat down on a stool near the table and picked up the
waiting headband. Stripping off the long, now far too hot
wig, she slipped the band over her own close-cropped hair.
A few minutes more and she would be free of all the
knowledge she had brought with her. For following her
report, the machine that recorded it would purge her
memory of factors it might be dangerous for her to know.
It was a safeguard her kind had demanded before they
would use their talents, so that they could not be forced
by any enemy to talk after such a mission.

The girl unlocked her memory, knowing that every

symbol she had read from the cubes was being recorded. What if she kept on, allowed the machine to read and then erase her reaction to the lump? But if she did that, those already reading her report on the visa-screen of the machine would know it too. No—her hand moved close to the cut-off key—she would prevent that.

There. Her finger came down and she experienced the familiar moment or two of giddiness, of disorientation. Now she would remember up to the opening of Jucundus's safe and after, but not what she had "read."

"Excellent." Yasa's purr was louder when Ziantha was again aware of the room and those about her. "A first-level foray in every way. Now, cubling, you must be most tired—go to your nest."

She was tired, achingly tired. The lifting of her mental burden drained her, as it always did, though this was her first really big foray. Those in the past had been but token employment compared to this. Ogan was at her side with a cup of that milky-looking restorative. She gulped that avidly and went to gather up her cloak and head-dress.

"Fair dreams." Yasa's lips wrinkled in her equivalent of a smile. "Dream of what you wish most, cubling. For this night's work I shall make it yours."

Ziantha nodded, too tired to answer with words. What she wanted most—that was no idle promise. Yasa would indeed make it come true. Those of the Guild were not niggardly with anyone who brought off a successful foray. What she wanted most now was sleep, though not of Ogan's sending.

Back in her own chamber Ziantha pulled off the rest of the Zhol dress, dropped the trappings in a bundle on the floor. Tired as she was, she would not go to bed with that stiff, cracking mask of paint and overleaf on her face. She went into the fresher, set the dials, stepped into the waves of cleansing vapor. It was good to be her real self again.

As if to assure herself she had returned to Ziantha, she looked into the cruelly bright mirror, cruel because being so often used to check a disguising makeup, it revealed rather than softened every defect of complexion and feature. There was the real outward Ziantha. And with this hour and her great fatigue, that sight was a blow to any vanity.

She was very thin and her skin was pallid. Her hair, from the warm steam of her bath, curled tightly to her head, no lock of it longer than one of her fingers. In color it was silver fair, though in daylight it would show a little darker. Her eyes were gray, so pale as to seem silver too. The mouth below was large, her lips with little curve, but a clear red. As for the rest— She scowled at the true Ziantha and shrugged on her night robe, letting the light of that revelation die behind her as she left the room.

Dream of what she wanted most, Yasa had said. What if she asked for a complete cosmetic-change—to be some-one else all the time, not just at those intervals when she played games for the Guild? Would Yasa agree to that? Perhaps she would, if Ziantha asked, but she only played with the idea.

But of course, what she wanted most—right now—was that lump of clay or carved stone. To have it right here in her two hands that she might learn its secret!

Ziantha gasped. What had put that in her mind? She had not been thinking of it at all, and then—suddenly— there it was as clear as if she could indeed reach out and cup it in her palms. And she did want it. What had happened to her this night?

Shivering, she ran to the bed, threw herself into its soft hollow, and pulled the covers up over her trembling body—even over her head.

2

Ziantha awoke suddenly from a sleep where, if dreams had crowded, she could not remember, as if she had been summoned. She knew what she must do, as surely as if Yasa had given her an order. Fear chilled her small body, but greater than that fear was the need which was a hunger in her.

The girl remembered Ogan's precept: fear, faith, and obsession were akin. All three could drive a person to complete self-abandonment, removing mind blocks, unleashing emotions. She did not fear that much, but she knew she was obsessed.

Korwar's sun was above the horizon. These chambers were all soundproof; she had only her knowledge of the daily routine to guide her. The quickest way to arouse interest in Yasa's domain was to depart from the usual. Ziantha drew herself into a small brooding bundle on the window seat, laced her arms about her knees, and stared down into the garden.

It was going to be a fair day—good. Psychic powers diminish in a storm. Her talent could also be threatened by other factors; energy fields produced by machines, the sun, planets, even human emotions. What she had in mind was a stern test. She might not be able to do it at all, even if she could station herself at the right site, at the proper moment, with the needed backing.

The needed backing—

Psychokinetic power—

There were devices in plenty in Ogan's lab. But to lay a finger on one of those was to attract instant attention. She must depend upon another source entirely.

Ziantha unclasped her hands, raised them to cover her eyes, though she had already closed them, concentrated on forming a mind-picture and with it a summons. It would depend on whether Harath was free.

She delivered her message. But so far she was favored; Harath was not in the lab. Quickly she went to the fresher, bathed, and sat down before the merciless mirror, no longer intent upon her own shortcomings, but upon applying those aids that would take her into Tikil as a person exciting no second glance.

A companion of the second class, from Ioni, she decided. The factors, such as her height, that she could not alter without wasting some of her power in producing a visual hallucination, would fit that identity. The girl worked swiftly, a wig of brassy-colored hair brushed out in full puffing, the proper skin tint, lenses slipped in, changing her own pale eyes to a much darker hue.

She chose skin-hugging trousers of a metallic blue, a side-slitted overrobe of green, and then hesitated over jewelry that was, for the most part, more than jewelry if carefully examined. Best not, she decided regretfully. Some of those devices had side effects that could be picked up by Patrol detects. Stick to a shoulder collar with no secondary use, wrist rings that covered the back of her hands with a wide, flexible mesh of worked gold between the five joined finger rings and the wrist bracelet, forming mitts without palms.

A last check in the mirror assured her the disguise was complete. She dialed the combination code for morning juice and vita meal and ate to the last crumb and drop that sustaining, if unexciting, breakfast.

Her corridor was silent, but she knew the house was astir. Now the last test— Drawing upon all the resolution and ease she could summon, Ziantha stepped to the visa-panel block and punched a code button.

She thus recorded her present appearance and gave her reason for leaving the villa. Without that her absence would arouse suspicion, although the fact that she went into Tikil in disguise was of no moment. It was customary for those of Yasa's household to make sure of cover in the city.

"I go to Master-Gemologist Kafer on the Ruby Lane," she said. Well enough. Yasa would believe that she might be selecting the promised reward for last night. A gem would be such. And Kafer's shop would place her close to her real destination.

For a moment Ziantha waited, tense. There might be a negative flash in answer. It could be her misfortune that Ogan had set up a plan of some experiment this morning. But only the white flicker of a recording came in return.

Though she wanted to run, to be out of reach of either Ogan or Yasa as quickly as she could, Ziantha disciplined herself to keep to the almost strolling pace of one embarking for a morning's shopping in Tikil. She dared not even summon Harath again, not when Ogan's devices might record such a call. But, before her tight rein on impatience was stretched too far, she was on the roof, where a flitter waited.

One of Yasa's liege-fighters turned his head, his eyes slitted against the full light of the sun striking across them. It was Snasker, a taciturn, older warrior, his pointed ears fringed with old battle scars, another of which ridged his jawline. He was holding out one hand while a shape of soft down jumped to catch at his fingers. His glance at Ziantha was indifferent.

"For Tikil?" His voice was a low growl.

"Yes. If it pleases you, Snasker."

He yawned. "It pleases, fem." Snapping two claws at his companion, he climbed into the flitter.

Ziantha stooped to catch the little creature who now threw himself into her arms, chittering a welcome. Though she could not understand his speech, she met mind-talk easily.

"Harath here. Go with Ziantha now, now!"

She beamed back agreement and settled herself beside Snasker. Harath sat on her lap, panting a little, his beaked mouth open a fraction, his round eyes wide to their fullest extent.

Just what Harath was, what species he represented, or whether he could be classed as "human" or merely as a highly evolved and telepathic animal, Ziantha did not know. His small body was covered with a down which could be either feathers or the lightest and fluffiest fur. But he was wingless, having coiled within deep pockets of his body-covering four short tentacles he could use as one might use rather clumsy arms and hands. His legs and feet were down-covered, though the down was shorter in length and fluffed out as if he were wearing leggings and three-toed slippers on his feet. The toes ended in wicked-looking talons which matched the oddly vicious warning of his large, curved beak. In color he was blue-gray; his eyes, black rimmed, were a vivid blue.

He had come to Ogan still encased in his natal egg, so transported during the incubation period, by a Guild collector. And his talent was psychokinetic to a high degree. Not that he apported as well as Ogan had hoped—perhaps that was because he was still so young, and his powers would grow. But he could "step up" the psychic power of another to an amazing degree.

On Korwar, in Tikil, where outré pets were the rule rather than the exception, he excited little attention. He chaffed against wearing the small harness Ziantha now fitted on, enduring it only because he must. Harath had a vast curiosity, and his favorite treat was a trip away from the villa. Since Ogan had decided such trips were a form of training, it was not unusual for Harath to accompany any one of the household into town.

The sun was very brilliant and on her knees Harath's small body vibrated with the soft click-click of beak with which he expressed contentment.

"Where?" Snasker asked.

"I go to Kafer's."

They were winging over the Dipple but Ziantha would not look at that. She was excited by what she planned, deadly afraid she might betray some of that feeling to Harath. This—this must be like chewing gratz—this sensation that one could do anything if one only set one's determination to it.

She must hold control, she must! Fight down that

tingle of energy which came into being at the end of one's spine, rising slowly to the head. Not here—not yet!

The flitter landed on a platform in the center of the gardened square. Through the trees she could see the flashing jewels of light which marked Ruby Lane of the gem merchants—the brilliant signal visible even in the sun. Now she must curb her impatience, visit Kafer in truth before she tried her experiment.

Normally she would have been totally distracted by Kafer's display. It was sheer pleasure to those who loved the beauty of gems cut and polished. Or else the small toys and oddments, both old and new, made of precious things gathered up from perhaps a thousand worlds to show here, where credits flowed a free river.

In spite of the need which drove her, Ziantha stood for a moment entranced before a diadem lined with small tubes set with flexible thread-thin filaments, each supporting a flower, a leaf, a bud, or a filmy insect, to form a halo which would sway like meadow grass under a breeze with every movement of the wearer. Beyond this was a model town made of karem—that iridescent precious metal of a long-lost alloy from Lydis IV—complete in miniature with even its population, each tiny inhabitant no taller than her thumbnail but equipped with microscopic features and apparel.

She could look and look, but this was not what brought her here. Though most of Tikil kept late hours and the press of shoppers would not come until afternoon, there were customers drifting in and out of the shops, from Kafer's at the proud head of Ruby Lane, all down the road.

Harath rode on her shoulders as she moved along, the leash of his harness looped about her forearm; his head sometimes seemed to turn almost completely around as he tried to see everything at once. Ziantha did not mind-talk, saving energy for later. She forced herself to saunter, pausing here and there.

Now she had reached the end of the lane, and she could wait no longer. Ziantha turned to cross into the luxurious foliage of the garden, nearer to the building which held Jucundus's apartment. She must get as close to that as she could.

Unfortunately she was not the only weary shopper to seek out the shade and rest here. Each bench she came to had its occupant. And the closer she came to her goal, the more crowded these ways appeared to be. Her frustration became almost unbearable when added to the strain of keeping control. Somewhere there must be a place! She was not going to surrender her plan so easily.

Her agitation reached Harath. He was chittering unhappily, shifting his feet about on her shoulder with his claws pricking through to her skin. If she got him too upset he would not perform.

They were almost to the end of the last walk when Ziantha came upon something that might have been intended by fortune for the very purpose she had in mind—a small side way between two Stick palms. She turned into that hopefully, finding a moment later a bench sheltered by growth, almost invisible from the main path, and unoccupied.

The reason for that was plain. Dew had condensed on the plants and wet the surface of the seat with droplets which the sun had not dried because of the heavy screen of foliage overhead. She looked at that and, with a sigh, jerked up her slitted skirt, seating herself gingerly on the damp surface, the chill of which penetrated through her single layer of clothing at once. But more than this minor discomfort was she willing to risk for her plan.

She summoned resolution, removed Harath gently from her shoulder, and turned him about on her knee to face her, feeling the flow of communication between them as his eyes locked on hers. Yes, he was willing to aid her, not needing to be coaxed.

Now Ziantha released that brake on her power she had maintained through the morning. The pulse of energy in her lower back built up slowly, perhaps inhibited by the control. But it was rising to her call, climbing up through her shoulders, now at the nape of her neck, coming at last behind her forehead, pulsing faster in a rhythm that was comforting. She felt her whole being at acute attention, as always happened when she called upon this ability, about which even Ogan knew so little.

The time was—now!

Ziantha no longer stared into Harath's eyes. Rather she fastened on the mind picture that had haunted her since last night. It was as if she no longer dwelt within her body, but rather hung suspended above that table, a swimmer in the air, anchored in place by her desire, her need for that crude lump.

Summoning every fragment of memory, the girl built her mental picture into vivid reality. Now—come! All of her talent surged to feed her desperate desire. And there was that stronger pulse of energy bolstering it, the energy Harath released. Come! As if she shouted that to something which could easily obey her cry, Ziantha shaped that demand in her mind, imprisoning the lump as if her order were a tangible net. *Come!*

She held that at peak force as long as she could. But there came a time when, even with Harath's backing, she could keep it so no longer. It swept away, leaving her so spent she swayed dizzily. Pain ran in ripples along her arms and legs as she became aware of her body again. Her hands dropped from their grasp on the alien, twitching in a lack of coordination. Saliva dribbled from her mouth, sticky wet on her chin. She had never unleashed such a will-to-do before and she was frightened at her present weakness, at the dizzy swirl of bush and tree when she looked up. Harath chittered and pressed against her; there was fear in his nuzzling. If this had so affected her, what might it have done to him? For the first time that day, thought of another broke through the obsession which had haunted her since waking. Ziantha tried to raise her hands to soothe him, found they were numbed, deadened, moved slowly and clumsily.

But—

There was something else. In Harath's struggle to get nearer he had almost shoved it to the ground. Dazedly she brought her hand up to catch it—the lump!

She had done it! A successful apport! She did not rate high on the scale of psychokinetic power, yet with Harath's backing she had brought it here!

Only now she was so drained, so weak, she could hardly force one thought to meet another in her head. She had wanted, she had so fiercely wanted— But now that it lay there on her knee, what did she plan to do with it? She could not think, not yet. It was like trying to catch one's breath after a grueling race; the plight of her body was too intrusive; to it she must surrender for now.

Slowly, far too slowly, her strength began to return. In this side nook, shadowy as it was, Ziantha could not even be sure of the passing of time as man normally lived it. For in the realm into which she had forced herself, time had a different measurement entirely. She could have sat there for a few moments—or hours. The chill of the damp seat struck inward and she was shivering. Yet she could not summon strength enough to get to her feet, out into the heat of the sun.

And she could look at that brown-gray lump with indifference. Only, as she continued to stare at it, that indifference changed. The wild excitement that had gripped her at her first contact with it was growing again. It was worth it! She knew that it was worth any effort she had had to put forth. It was—what—? She knew only that she must find out, that such knowledge was as necessary to her as breathing or thinking—

But she dared not tap it now, not while she was so shaken by the effort made to apport it from Jucundus's apartment to this place. No, she must have the backing of all her energy when she tried to break its secret. Which meant she dared not touch it with her bare hand.

Very awkwardly, for still her hands were numb, Ziantha tugged at her girdle, forced open her sling purse, and, using a portion of her skirt wrapped around her fingers to keep from direct contact, wedged and pushed the chunk into the purse for safekeeping. It was a quite visible lump but the best she could do.

Food—drink—Ziantha had remembered seeing a small serving grotto in the other path. With Harath clinging to the bodice of her robe as she managed to stand erect, she paced slowly toward that haven, striving to fight off dizziness.

Back in the full sun the warmth seeped into her body, displacing that chill, banishing the shivers which had wrung her moments before. Harath climbed now to grip her shoulder once again. Though the energy that had flowed to her from him had been great, still it seemed that their ordeal had not affected him as it had her. That so small a body and brain could have generated that powerful backup was a surprise to her, as she, in turn, began to throw off the mind-dulling fatigue.

Ziantha came to the grotto and wavered into the nearest seat. As she sat down, the listing of drinks and food beamed up at her from the top of the table. She punched the proper buttons to bring her the most sustaining of those dishes.

Chewing on a vita-biscuit, the girl did not forget Harath. She broke off bits, dipped them into a conserve high in energy quotients, and passed them to him. The first shock had worn away; even the pains in her legs and arms were easing as she drank the thick, sweet lingrum juice, its warmth adding to the sun's to banish the last of the chill.

Now, with the ebbing of the worst of her fatigue, Ziantha began to feel a new exuberance. She had done it—had apported, a feat she had never tried before, beyond a few tests in the lab. Most of those had rated her ability too low to warrant concentrated training. Of course she had not done it alone; she could not have. But it was her thought, her plan that had accomplished it. Now the girl longed to take the lump out of her purse, to inspect it. However, good sense kept her from doing so.

Harath's long tongue snaked from his bill as he licked some drops of sweet from the fluff on his chest. Then suddenly, he froze, and through the tautness of his body an alert reached Ziantha, though he did not try to communicate with mind-talk. Slowly his head turned in one of those hardly-to-be-believed side sweeps, so that he was looking almost squarely, not only over her shoulder, but also over his own. And Ziantha nearly cried out as his talons tightened, piercing the fabric of her robe. She sat with the cup raised in both hands to her lips, but she no longer sipped at its contents. Rather she readied her powers as best she could and sent forth a mind-seek.

Harath had his own protection, and that did not depend, save in a last extremity, upon his five senses, but rather on the sixth, or seventh, or whatever number made up his "sensitive" reaction to any threat. He was alert to something now, and the fact that he did not relay what he had picked up to her was a greater warning of danger.

Her earlier exultation was wiped away. She had spent herself too much in that burst of kinetic seeking; her mind-search was now limited, picking up nothing of moment. Ogan? Had he trailed them to Tikil? She could believe that. He might just have set up this whole affair, Ziantha thought. He could have suspected last night that she had held back something in her report, used her to uncover that today. Now it seemed, looking back, that it had all been far too easy—her leaving the villa with Harath—all of it!

She wanted desperately to turn her head, sure that if she did so she would see Ogan come into view. And there was no use running; he could mark her down in an instant by any one of four or five devices she understood only too well.

Harath stirred. He was climbing down from her shoulder, clutching at her robe with his claws, using his two upper tentacles to balance. Then he squatted on the table, flicking forth one of those tentacles, inserting it greedily into the pot of sweet spread, whipping it back to draw through his beak, his tongue curled about it to sweep off the last bit.

But he was acting. Just as she had acted out the role of Zhol Maiden last night. Now he was all small-creature-with-but-a-thought-of-food. And Ziantha, not quite sure how she understood (unless Harath could broadcast on some more subtle mental length) concentrated on watching him. Lick, eat, lick, eat. He did not turn his head again. But now and then he bobbed it energetically up and down, licking splashes of his treat from his chest.

Up—down—slow—now twice fast—Ziantha caught her breath. Harath—Harath was coding! She spread out her hand on the side of the cup as she drank, but her fingers tapped that surface with the same beat.

Bob, bob, bob—she read his warning of a sensitive. Not Ogan—Harath would have no reason to warn of him. To the alien Harath, she and Ogan were of a kind, united. No, this was a stranger. And—

He might only be cruising. One of the Patrol sensitives taping mind levels as their companions, who used physical means of controlling crime, made inspections through those districts where the activities of the Guild might be centered.

Ziantha had been proud of her achievement; now her folly struck her like a forceful blow. If there had been a sensitive anywhere within range of her late exploit, the amount of energy she had loosed would have brought instant investigation. That was why Harath was using code. As long as neither of them tried mind-search they were safe, at least from a spot check. Certainly on suspicion alone no patroller could pick up innocent wayfarers for psychic testing.

Her fingers moved on the mug. Harath bobbed his head. They understood each other. Her one fear was the distance now between them and means of escape. She felt far better than she had when she had crawled out into this place. But she would have to stroll, not hurry, to the flitter park, and she must plan a return route to baffle any trail. Could she trust her exhausted body?

Also, any Patrol sensitive might well be able to recognize the signs of energy exhaustion. He had only to note the least wavering on her part and take her in to be psyched. And then— But she would not let herself think about what would come after that. No, she must summon up all her resolution and make it to the flitter landing without displaying any overt signs to any watcher.

It was growing late, and she could not remain here too long. This place might already have been marked down as one of the sites to look, the need for food and drink . . . Ziantha fumbled for a tal-card made out on a legal business of Yasa's, slipped it into the payment slit. Harath climbed once more to her shoulder as she stood up.

Good. She could walk without believing that each new step was going to spill her forward on her face, that much had food done for her. Now, the flitter park—slow and easy, but not too slow.

Harath had closed his eyes. For all intents he might be sleeping, though his sharp hold on her shoulder did not waver. He had closed his mind, just as she had closed hers. But as she went she used her eyes. Her companion had signaled "he" in relation to the hunter. But the pursuer might just as well be a woman. Four, five, six— a dozen people in sight.

Some were obviously visitors, or at least not in a hurry. There were three others—all men—wearing the dress of merchants. If she could have used mind-touch only for an instant she would know the enemy, but that would have revealed her in turn. Now she must mark faces, make very sure none could follow her back to the villa. All at once that seemed to her to be a very safe refuge.

3

She reached the lift to the flitter landing and was borne aloft, wishing she dared to look back and so sight a follower. But her years of training held, and she drew about her as best she could a concealing cloak of unconcern. A few moments later she dialed the call signal for a robo-flitter. Those last seconds of waiting for the empty transport to slide in before her were the worst, so close to escape, yet at any moment subject to challenge.

The flitter dropped, its cabin door opened, and Ziantha scrambled in with perhaps more haste than was cautious, already reaching for the code key to tap out a destination to confuse the trail. Also she risked a quick glance back at the platform from which she was rising. No sign of pursuit.

But that was no proof that she was not under observation.

Minutes later the flitter set down at the wide and crowded general market just beyond the fringe of the landing port. The dealers who traded here bought from space crewmen, who legally could dabble in the private commerce of small objects, and illegally in contraband. Here the Guild had many contacts planted at strategic points, and no sensitive could pierce their protects. Ziantha relaxed—as much as she could with that lump in her purse—as she threaded a way through the narrow runways between one booth and the next. From those

contacts she might claim transportation back to the villa
to baffle any ordinary Patrol exercise.

She had the pricking of the band on her left wrist to
guide her to the stall where she might claim aid, as that
was activated to pick up a Guild signal. Twilight was close,
Harath clicked his beak in a warning, fluffing up his down.
He did not take kindly to the rising chill of night.

A blink sign proclaimed the name of Kackig, and
Ziantha turned there in obedience to her own recognition prick. The man who faced her was as gray-skinned
as any Salariki, but without the feline features of that
species, clearly more humanoid as to ancestry, in spite
of color.

Ziantha raised her hand as if to settle one of the flower-
headed pins in her brush of wig, displaying to the full
her wrist ring.

"Gentle fem." His voice was a thin pipe, seeming not
to issue from his throat but from some place outside his
body. "Look you—here lie the scents of a hundred stars.
Breathe Flame Spice from Andros, Diamond Dust from
Alaban—"

"You have Sickle-lily of the Tenth Day Bloom?"

His expression did not change beyond that of a polite
merchant's attention. "By the favor of Three-horned Math,
it is ready to pour into your hand, gentle fem, rare as it
is. But not here, as you well know. Such a delicate fragrance is easily tainted in the open." He clapped his hands
sharply, and a small boy wearing his livery overalls arose
from the ground behind the stall.

Kackig snapped his fingers. "Take the gentle fem to
Laros—"

Ziantha nodded her thanks and hurried to keep up with
the boy, who slipped far more easily than she among the
narrow and well-crowded ways of the mart. They came
at last to where the delivery flitters parked in a dusty row.

"The fourth." Her guide underlined his information by
pointing with a grubby finger. He surveyed what lay about
them. "Now!" She crossed the short open space to enter
the flitter.

There was a Salariki at the controls who glanced around
as if to assure himself she was not an intruder. From the

interior also came the subtle fragrance of the Sickle-lily, which the dried petals of the Tenth Day Bloom could retain for years. Yasa's favorite scent was about to be delivered to the villa.

For the first time since Harath's warning, the girl dared use mind-touch with her downy companion.

"We are free?"

"Now." If thought could convey a feeling of irritation, then Harath's curt reply was shadowed by that emotion. He did not add to that, which was not usual, but Ziantha did not press. Now that she was reasonably safe, the fact that she carried with her that which she had no business to have taken began to weigh on her spirits.

It all depended upon how important the apport was. If it had no more meaning for Jucundus than any other of the exotic curiosities which had been with it, then it might not even be missed for some time. And, surely if it did have importance, it would not have been left lying in full sight on the table. It would have been sealed in the safe.

She rested her hand over the bulge in her purse, haunted by the same ambivalence of desires that had ridden her ever since this spell had fallen on her. She wanted to use the lump as a focus for exploration, yet she feared it. But she believed now that her desire for knowledge was greater than her fear. It must be, or it would not have pushed her to risk so much in order to get the lump into her possession.

That she intended to keep it a secret—yes. Not that she could for long, because of Harath. He would share information with Ogan. And to suggest that he not do so would be to make sure that he would. One could not credit Harath with human motives. He was programmed to work by an alien set of impulses—which meant—

Harath snapped his beak peevishly, avoiding mind-touch. She set him on the ground as she left the flitter at the villa in-park, and he disappeared with a flash of speed surprising for his small body. Ziantha took warning from that flight and hurried to her own room. If she were to have any use at all from what she had found, it must be here and now.

Dropping among her cushions, she took out the lump, this time without precautions against touching it. Cupping it in her hands she brought it to her forehead, as if at any moment Ogan and Yasa might break in to wrest it away from her.

She swayed, almost crumpled. That thrust of instant reply was as strong as a harsh blow in the face. And yet—she could sort nothing out of the whirl of impressions that rushed so upon her. The worst was a freezing fear, the like of which she had never known before in her life. Perhaps she screamed as it closed about her; she did not know.

But that overpowering force was gone. Ziantha crouched, staring stupidly at her hands, which lay limply on her knees. The lump—the *thing*—where was it? She shrank from it when she saw it among the cushions as she might from a sudden attack by an alien creature.

Nor could she bring herself to touch it again, though that fear had ebbed, and once more she could feel the faint stirrings of the obsession which had made her covet it. Ziantha dragged herself up, tottered into the fresher, needing to feel the cleansing of water, heat, life, the knowledge that she was herself—Ziantha and not—

"Not who?" She cried that aloud this time, her hands to her head. As she ran she shed wig, clothing, to stand in as hot a mist vapor as her body could tolerate. The warmth that enfolded her skin slowly penetrated to reach that part of her which seemed to remain frozen.

Wrapped in a loose robe, she reluctantly returned to her room. Could she bundle the lump up in a covering—perhaps then bury it in the garden? Still she was drawn to it against her will, though at least she could control herself to the point of not touching it.

Ziantha went on her knees by the cushions, studying the artifact with attention she had not given it when she made that first impulsive attempt to unriddle its secret. Though its appearance was very rough, it was, she was sure, not merely some unworked lump of hard-baked clay or stone. It bore the rude semblance of a crouching figure, so rude one could not rightly say that it was meant to resemble either a monster or a man. There appeared to be four limbs of sorts attached to a barrel body. But the head, if it had even been given one, had vanished. Somehow she believed it had been conceived as it now was.

That it was old past her judging she knew. This extreme age could well have caused that nauseating whirl of impressions from her "reading," for the longer any object wrought by intelligence was in existence, the more impressions it could pick up and store, letting those forth as a chaotic mingling of pictures. It would require many sessions, much careful researching, to untangle even a small fraction of what might be packed into this grotesque object.

For a long time it had been a proved fact that any object wrought by intelligence (or even a natural stone or similar object that had been used for a definite purpose by intelligence) could record. From the fumbling beginnings of untrained sensitives, who had largely developed their own powers, much had been learned. It had been "magic" then; yet the talent was too "wild," because all men did not share it, and because it could not be controlled or used at will but came and went for reasons unknown to the possessors. So that at one instance there had been amazing and clear results that could not be questioned by witnesses, and on a second try, nothing at all.

There had been frauds when those who had reputations of wonder workers could not produce the results called for, and in desperation had turned to trickery. But always there had been a percentage that was unexplained. When man learned to study instead of to scoff, when the talented ones were neither scorned nor feared, progress began. Mind-touch was as well accepted as speech now, and with it all those other "unexplainables" which had been denied for generations. Then when mankind of Ziantha's own species—that first mankind which had neither mutated nor altered as a result of living on planets alien to their home world—when her own species headed into space they found others to whom the "wild talents" were a normal way of life.

There were the Wyverns of Warlock, whose females were age-long mistresses of thought over matter. The Thassa of Yiktor—Ziantha did not need to list them all.

Part of her past training had been to study what each newly discovered world could add to the sum total of learning. What she had been able to absorb she had practiced to the height of her powers under Ogan's careful fostering. But this—

Old—old—old!

"How old?" At first Ziantha was so intent upon the problem she did not realize that question had been asked not by her own mind but by— She looked over her shoulder.

Yasa stood in the doorway, her lily scent creeping in to fill the room. At her feet Harath bobbed up and down, hopping on his clawed feet, as if so greatly excited by something that he could not remain still. His beak opened and shut in a harsh clicking.

"Yesss—" Yasa's voice was more of a hiss than usual, and Ziantha recognized that sign of controlled anger. "How old—and what isss thisss thing which isss ssso old?"

"That—" Ziantha pointed to the lump.

The Salarika moved with fluid grace, coming to stand beside where Ziantha crouched. She leaned over, stared round-eyed.

"For thisss you do what issss forbidden? Why, I asssk you now, why?"

Her amber-red eyes caught and held Ziantha mercilessly. Humanoid Yasa might be in general form, but there was no human type of emotion which Ziantha could detect in that long stare.

The girl wet her lower lip with her tongue. She had met so many trials this day, it was as if she were now numb. Ordinarily she would have known fear of Yasa in this mood; now she could only tell the truth, or what seemed the truth.

"I had to—"

"Sssso? What order had been given you to do thissss?"

"I—when I was in Jucundus's apartment this—this pulled me. I could not forget it. It—it made me reach for it—"

"She could be right, you know."

Just as Yasa had entered unbidden and unexpected, now Ogan appeared. "There are strong compulsions sometimes when a sensitive is at top pitch performance. Tell me"—

he, too, came to stand over Ziantha—"when were you aware of this first? Before or after you read the tapes?"

"After, when I was going out of the room. It was so strong—a call I never felt before."

He nodded. "Could be so. You had the vibrations high; a thing attuned to those vibrations could respond with a summons. Where was this—in the safe?"

"No." She explained how she had seen it first, one of a number of curiosities set out on a small table.

"What isss all thisss—?" Yasa began when an imperative wave from Ogan's hand not only halted her question but turned her attention back to the artifact.

Ogan's hand now rested on Ziantha's head. She longed to jerk away, throw off that touch, light and unmenacing though it was, but submitted to it. Ogan had his own ways of detecting truth or falsehood, and she needed him more at this moment as a protection against Yasa's wrath.

"This then obsessed you until you had to apport it?" His voice was encouraging, coaxing.

"I could not get it otherwise," she returned sullenly.

"So you were able, because of this obsession, to develop powers you did not use before?"

"I had Harath to back me."

"Yesss!" Had Yasa still possessed the tail of her ancestors she might have lashed it at that moment; instead she made her voice a whip to lash with words. "Thisss one takes Harath, and with him sssshe makes trouble!" Harath snapped his beak violently as Yasa paused, as if heartily agreeing with her accusation. "Sssomewhere now in Tikil there isss a Patrol ssssensitive at alert. How long you think before Jucundusss beginsss to wonder?"

To Ziantha's surprise, Ogan smiled. She sensed that under his generally expressionless exterior he was excited, even pleased.

"Lady! Bethink you—how many dwell in that apartment where Jucundus chooses to make his headquarters? Two—three—perhaps four hundred! There are endless possibilities. If Jucundus values this thing so little as to leave it in the open, will he miss it for a while? It is true that a sensitive on patrol might well have picked up the surge of Ziantha's power. But to detect and trace it would be impossible unless he had a scan ready for action. She and Harath were right, or rather Harath was right to shut down on communication when he detected the hunter. All the sensitive can say now is that someone within the park put forth an expenditure of energy in an unusual degree. But"—Ogan looked again at Ziantha—"that you escaped was not due to any intelligence on your part, girl."

She was willing to agree. "No, it was Harath."

"Yes, Harath, who will now tell us what we have here."

"But I—" Ziantha half raised her hand in protest.

"You are of no value in the matter, not now. Have you not already tried?" He spoke impatiently as he might to a child who was being tiresome, as he had in the past when she was younger and would not be as pliable as he wished. "Harath," he repeated coldly.

She wanted to cover the artifact with her hands, her body, hide it. It was hers—from the beginning she had known it to be hers. But she was in no condition to read it; her ill-tried experiment proved that. And she wanted to know what it was, from whence it had come, why it should exert such influence over her.

It seemed that Harath had to be coaxed. For he caught at the fluttering ends of Yasa's fringed skirt, turning his head away, only clicking his beak in a staccato of protest when Ogan ordered him to touch the lump.

Yasa folded her slender legs, gracefully joining Ziantha on the floor. She ran her fingers gently over the head of the small alien, purring soothingly, making no mind-send the girl could detect, but in some manner of her own, communicating, coaxing, bringing Harath to a better temper.

At last, with a final ruffle of beak drum, he loosed his hold on her skirt and crossed the cushions with extreme wariness, as if he fully expected an explosion to follow any touch, even through the mind alone. Squatting down, he advanced from his down-covered pocket a single tentacle, brought it over so that the tip alone just touched the artifact.

Eagerly Ziantha opened her own channel of communication, ready to pick up whatever the alien would report.

"Not early"—that was Ogan's caution. "Give us the latest reading."

Ziantha picked up a sensation of distress.

"All ways at once—much—much—" Harath's answer was a protest.

"Give us the latest," Ogan insisted.

"Hidden—deep hidden—oheee—dark—death—" Harath's thought was as sharp as a scream. He snatched away his tentacle as if the figure were searing hot.

"How did Jucundus get it?" It was Yasa this time who asked. "Little one, little brave one, you can see that for us. What is this precious thing?"

"A place, an old place—where death lies. Hidden, old—strange. It is cold from the long time since it was in sun and light. Death and cold. Many things around it once—a great—great lord there. No—not to see!"

He whipped the tentacle away again, into complete hiding. But he did not turn away, rather stood regarding the artifact.

Then: "It is of those you call Forerunners. The very ancient ones. And it is—was—once one of two—"

Ziantha heard a hiss which formed no word. Yasa's lips were a little apart, there was an avid glow in her large eyes.

"Well done, little one." She put out her hand as if to fondle Harath. But he turned, made his way unsteadily across the pillows to stand beside Ziantha.

"I do not know how," he reported on the open mind-send they all now shared, "but this one, she is a part of it. It is Ziantha who can find, if finding comes at all, where this once lay. Dark and cold and death." His round eyes held unblinkingly on Ziantha. She shivered as she had when she had come out of the trance of the apport. But she knew that what he said was the truth. By some curse of temperament or fortune she was linked to this ugly thing beyond all hope of freedom.

"Forerunner tomb!" Yasa held one of her girdle scent bags to her nose, sniffing in refreshment the strong odor of the powdered lily petals. "Ogan, we must discover whence Jucundus had this—"

"If he bought it, Lady, or if he brought it with him—" It was plain that Ogan was equally excited.

"What matter? Whatever a man has discovered can be found. Do we not have more eyes and ears almost than the number of stars over us?"

"If bought, it could well be loot from a tomb already discovered," Ziantha ventured.

Yasa looked at her. "You believe that? That it is some unknown curiosity picked up perhaps at the port mart with no backtracing for its origin? It has no beauty to the eye— age alone and a link with the Forerunners would make it worthy to be displayed and cherished. Also Jucundus has pretensions to hist-test learning. He backed three survey groups on Fennis, striving to place the mound builders there. But old as those were, they were not true Forerunners, nor were there tombs. No, Jucundus kept this with him because of its history, which we must learn. Now we shall put it in safekeeping until—"

She would have taken it up. But, though her fingers scrabbled in the air, she could not touch its surface.

"Ogan! What is the matter?"

He came swiftly around the mound of cushions. After a slow study of the artifact he caught Yasa's wrist.

"Psychokinetic energy. It is charged past a point I have never seen before. Lady, this—this thing must once have been a focus for some parapsychological use. That which gathered in it during the time it was used has now been brought to life by the power bent on it when apported. It is like mind-power itself. Unless it is discharged in some fashion, it is highly dangerous to the touch. Unless—" He turned on Ziantha. "Pick it up! At once, do you hear!"

The snap of his order made her move before she thought. Her hand closed about the lump with no difficulty. It appeared to be warm—or was that only her imagination, primed by what Ogan had just said? But if Yasa had been unable to touch it, that barrier did not hold for her.

"Psychic tie," Ogan pronounced. "Until it is fully discharged, if it ever will be, Lady, this girl is the only one who can handle it."

"Surely you can neutralize it in some manner! You have all your devices—of what good are those?" Yasa was plainly not prepared to accept his decision.

"Of this condition we have theoretical knowledge, Lady. But in a hundred planet years or more no worship object of an alien race has ever been found to be so studied. An artifact which has been the object of worship of a nation or species acquires, with every ceremony of worship, a certain residue of power. So charged, it literally becomes, as the ancient men said, god-like. There were god-kings and –queens of old who were the objects of worship by those who served them, and who were fed by the psychic energies of those who adored them. Thus they achieved the power which made them perform miracles and brought them indeed close to the might they professed to have."

"And you believe this to be such a god-thing?" There was a shadow of disbelief in the Salarika's voice.

"It is clearly a thing of psychic power far past the ordinary. And I tell you I dare not put it to any test I could devise, because I might destroy what it holds. We may have chanced on such a treasure as we could not have hoped to discover in a lifetime."

Perhaps it was the word "treasure" which brought the throat-purr of satisfaction from Yasa.

"But you believe that you can perhaps use it—through our cubling here—" The look she now gave Ziantha was both forgiving and approving.

"I will and can promise nothing, Lady. But with such a key I think old doors can be opened. We must start, of course, to trace its history while it was in Jucundus's possession. Whether its import was known to him in more than a general way, I greatly doubt. He does not like sensitives, as well we know. Men with secrets to hide do not. I can believe that while it was in his hands no one capable of sensing its real value and meaning could have seen it. Though it must have been aroused by apporting. Only Ziantha knew it for what it was, or felt its pull, when she passed by the table on which it lay. A combination of lucky chances, Lady. That she should be in a heightened state when she first found it, so drawn to it, that she should then set it afire by using psychokinetic means to obtain it. Two factors out of the normal, reacting on it and on her in a short time, have set up a rapport we can use very well.

"Now, my girl," he spoke to Ziantha, "you will be advised to try to read this."

"I cannot!" she cried. "I tried, but I cannot! It—it was horrible."

Yasa laughed. "To teach you, cubling, not to take such grave matters on yourself. You will, however, attend to what Ogan is saying or suffer a mind-lock." She spoke lightly enough, but Ziantha had no doubt that she meant exactly what she threatened. Only the girl did not need such a threat; her fascination with the artifact had not been in any way lessened, though she had suffered enough during that one attempt to solve its mystery to know that she could not try that again—not as she felt now.

"In your guardianship then, cubling." Yasa arose. "Or perhaps in its own, if Ogan's reading of its present state continues. Meanwhile we shall take up the matter of where Jucundus first found it."

4

There was no need of any warning. Ziantha realized she had in truth condemned herself to captivity in the villa while that vast underground of spies Yasa maintained went into action. The girl had expected Ogan to show more interest, though, both in her sudden development of psychokinetic powers and in the artifact. She had anticipated, with dread, hours of lab testing. And, when no such summons came, she was first relieved, then a little piqued at being so ignored. Did the parapsychologist think the artifact would continue to be so "charged" that it would defy his powers of research? Or was he only preparing stiffer tests?

Whatever the cause of her semi-imprisonment, Ziantha became more and more uneasy as the hours, and then the days, wore on. There were amusement and information tapes in plenty to draw upon, and the tri-dee casts from Tikil on her screen if she cared to tune them in. But all the various things with which she had filled waiting hours before no longer had the power to hold her attention.

After she made two tangles in the belt she was knotting by a process Yasa's Salarika maid had taught her, and found that she could not concentrate on a tape of Forerunner "history" she had in the reader, she gave up on the morning of the third day. Sitting in the deep window-sill lounge, she looked out into the garden, which was a type of jungle, carefully maintained in that state to ensure Yasa's privacy.

Forerunners—there were many different kinds, civilizations, species— Not even the Zacathans—those reptilian-evolved, very long-lived Hist-techneers and archaeologists of the galaxy—had ever been able to chart them all. Her own species was late come to the stars, springing from a small system on the very edge of this galaxy, that which contained the fabled Terra of Sol. Waves of emigration and settlement had gone forth from that planet—some fleeing wars at home, some questing for adventure and new beginnings. They had found new worlds—some of them—and in turn those worlds altered, changed the settlers through generations. New suns, different trace elements in soil, air, food, had brought about mutations. There was still a legendary Terran "norm," but she had yet to meet a single person who directly matched it. There were "giants" compared to the given height, as well as "dwarfs." Skin color, hair hue or lack of hair, number of digits, ability or limitation of sight, hearing, the rest of the senses, all these characteristics existed in a vast number of gradations and differences. To realize that, one need only visit the Dipple, where the sweepings of the civilizations of half a hundred planets had been dropped, or walk the streets of Tikil with an intent of measuring those differences.

And if the Terrans had been so modified and altered by their spread to the stars, then those earlier races they called the Forerunners must have suffered in their time the same changes. But they had left behind them enigmatic traces of their passing. When that passing had resulted from titanic conflicts, one found "burned-off" worlds reduced to such cinders as to remain horror monuments to deadly fury. However, there were other planets where wondering men found ruins, tombs, even installations which could still work after what, a million years of planet time?

Each find usually added a new question, did not answer many. For those who studied the discoveries could not string together a quarter of such remains into a pattern they could recognize as belonging to any one civilization or people. Here and there a legend collected by the patient netting of the Zacathans from star to star gave a name— of a race? A ruler? Often they were not even sure. And so, for example, the pillar city on Archon IV and two ports on Mochican and Wotan were tentatively linked as "Zaati" because of some similar carvings.

The hopes were always for the discovery of some storehouse of knowledge, of tapes, or of records that could enlighten a little. Two years ago there had come the discovery of a world which was a single huge city, the apex of one of the civilizations of star-traveling races. That was being explored now.

Ziantha brushed her hand across her forehead. She had always been interested in Forerunners. But now— She glanced over her shoulder to that box on the table. When Yasa had left the artifact in her keeping she had emptied her lockbox and had bundled the lump, still wrapped in the scarf she had put about it, into the box and had not looked at it since. But neither had she been able to put it out of mind.

A ring with a strange and deadly gem stone had been the key to the city-world. The story of that quest had been told and retold on tri-dee casts a thousand times. What had she found? Another key—to open what door and where?

Korwar had its own ancient mystery—Ruhkarv. That was a maze of underground ways built by a people, or entities, totally alien. It was a wicked trap, so the Rangers of the Wild had force-walled it against penetration. No one knew who had dug the ways of Ruhkarv, whether it was to be named "city" or "hive," or whether it was a fort, an indwelling, or a way-station for alien off-worlders.

Slowly Ziantha arose, moving against her will, compelled by the force that the artifact could exert. She shrank from what the box held, yet she picked it up and brought it back into the shaft of strong sunlight which beat through the window, as if something in that natural light could disarm what she held, render it her captive rather than allow her to remain in its thrall.

Drawing out the wrapped lump, she set it in the sun, plucked at the folds of scarf covering it until they fell

away. It was dull, ugly; it could have been the result of
a child's attempt at modeling the clay gouged from some
riverbank. There was certainly nothing about it that hinted
at any higher star-reaching, far ranging civilization—very
primitive.

Greatly daring, Ziantha put forth a hand, touched. But
this time there was no answering flare of energy. Ogan's
theory that the act of apporting might have charged it—
was she now proving the truth of that? The girl began
to run her finger back and forth, with more confidence,
across the upper portion, where there should have been
a head.

Though the lump seemed rough to the eye, to the
touch it was smooth. And she picked up only a faint flicker
of something—

Suddenly Ziantha caught it up between her palms,
pressed thumbs on the top, four fingers underneath, and
gave a quick twist of the right wrist, wrenching at the
lump. She did not know why, only this she must do.

The deceptively rough-looking shell moved at her action.
Half of it turned away from her. It did not crumble but
parted evenly in two as if it were a box.

Within was a nest of silver, glittering thread coiled
about and about, plainly designed to protect an inner core.
Ziantha set the half of the artifact which held this on the
window sill. She was cautious enough not to touch the
thread with her bare fingers. Instead she brought from
the table a long-hafted spoon she had used to stir a glass
of fal-berry juice.

Reversing this, she began to probe the puff of thread
warily, pushing in until she cleared a peephole. The sun
reached beyond the brilliant sparks awakened from the
spun filaments and touched what she had uncovered,
bringing a wink of blue-green.

An oval stone lay there—a gem she was sure, though
she did not recognize it by color alone. It was about half
the length of her thumb and cut smoothly cabochon, not
faceted. She turned her head quickly, pushing the covering back over it, knowing in that instant it had almost
entranced her.

Crystallomancy was one of the oldest ways of inducing

clairvoyance. Focusing on a globe wrought of some clear stone or gem brought the sensitive to the point where the power was released. Ogan was right about such objects. When in long use they built up psychic energy within them. This was what she had—a gazing crystal which had been used for a long time to release talent.

As swiftly as she could Ziantha set the two halves of the lump together, closed it with a counter twist. She studied its surface. There was no sign of that seam, not the slightest indication it could be opened. With a sigh of relief she rewrapped it and stowed it in the box. Only when that was locked away did she relax.

If she had taken it, used it as it was meant to be used, what would she have seen? The death and dark that it had broadcast through its outer protection? She had no intention of trying to find out, nor did she intend to let Ogan or Yasa know of this second discovery. That they would set her to using the stone she did not doubt. And she dared not.

She had time to school herself a mind-protection, though she doubted whether she would be able to hold that if Ogan suspected. However, it seemed that events beyond the villa were in her favor. For before midmorning she was summoned to Yasa's chamber, passing through the cloud of perfumed vapor to find the Salarika veep with a man she knew to be one of the traveling coordinators of the Guild.

He scrutinized Ziantha coldly, as if she were not a person but a tool—or weapon—and he were judging her effectiveness. In Yasa, Ziantha detected no sign of unease, though the upper grades of the Guild were perilous to those who aspired to gain them. Advancement went largely by assassination. An "erase" could be ordered for any veep who was either considered "unsafe," or who stood in the path of some ambitious underling.

When a check was run by one of the coordinators, there was always a question of trouble. But if Yasa had any reservations concerning this visit, no human would be able to read that from her, any more than a detect could ensnare her thoughts when she wished to retire behind her own alien "cover." Now she watched Ziantha with a lazy, unblinking stare, but on her knee sat Harath, his eyes closed as if he were asleep. Ziantha, seeing him, was instantly warned. She had been long enough in this household to mark any deviation from the routine as a battle signal and to take up her part of the defense.

Yasa was *not* as easy as she seemed, or Harath would not be playing the pet role. He had been ordered to pick up any leakage from the visitor's mind-lock. Which meant that Yasa would give no information to this coordinator, and Ziantha must be very careful what she herself said. Since the artifact was the main concern at present, that, above all, must be secret.

She had only a moment or two to grasp this, to prepare a defense, when Yasa waved a hand in her direction.

"This is the sensitive who gathered the tape readings, Mackry. You asked to see her; she is here."

He was a large man, once well-muscled and imposing-looking, now a little jowly, a little too paunchy. The spacer's uniform he wore, with a captain's wings, fit a little too tight. Either it had not been tailored for him, or he had put it aside for some time and now found it irksome. On his chin was a small beard, smoothed and stiffened to curl out in an imperious point. But the rest of his face was smooth, dark red in color; his head was shaved bare and then overlaid with a filigree of silver in swirls, as one might wear a very tight cap.

His eyes were deeply sunken, or perhaps it was the puffiness of his cheeks which made them appear so, and his brows had been treated to stand out in points to match his beard. Those eyes, for all their retreat behind flesh and hair, were very hard and bright, reminding Ziantha unwillingly of the glitter of that thread which nested the seeing gem, a memory she hastily buried.

He grunted, perhaps an acknowledgment to Yasa's half introduction. Then he launched into a sharp questioning of Ziantha concerning her visit to Jucundus's apartment, though he, of course, did not inquire what had been on the tapes, since Ogan had erased that. He took her step by step through the whole foray from the moment the palm lock on the door had yielded, to the end of her journey on her return to the villa. Having Yasa's unspoken warning, the girl omitted all reference to the artifact and the subsequent apporting of it.

When she had finished, and there had not been the slightest change in Yasa's expression to signal either that she was correctly following subtle directions, or making perhaps a totally irredeemable mistake, Mackry grunted again. Yasa uncurled from her usual lounging position.

"You see. Ogan checked with every scanner. It is exactly as we reported, gentle homo. There was no possible hint of detection."

"So it would seem. But the city is hot, blazing hot, I tell you! In some way that heat is tied to Jucundus. But that has-been had not made a single move to suggest that he knows his microrecords were scanned. They have a sensitive out, sniffing hard. You have kept this one"—again he regarded Ziantha, to her rising irritation, with a look that relegated her to the status of tool—"under wraps?"

"You can ask." Yasa yawned daintily. "She is here, and has been here. Our detection devices have not traced any mind-scan as a probe. With Ogan's lab here do you think such would go undetected?"

"Ogan!" He made that name into a snort, as if he classed the parapsychologist with Ziantha. "Well, you cannot keep her here—not now. So far our plans concerning Jucundus are going well; we want no interference. Get her off-world at once!"

Yasa yawned again. "It is near time for my leave. And I have an excellent excuse to go and visit the Romstk trading post. She shall go with my household."

"Agreed. You shall be told when to return." With no further word he stalked from the room, his rudeness deliberate, Ziantha knew. Her guess was confirmed when she looked at Yasa.

The feline contoured face of the Salarika was expressionless as far as the human eye could tell, except that the alien's lips were drawn very tight against her teeth, showing the sharp white points of what in her ancestors had been tearing, death-dealing fangs.

"Mackry," Yasa observed in a thoughtful tone, her voice almost as emotionless as she could make her features, "takes his missions with a seriousness that suggests he sees before him a flight of stairs climbing to heights. Oftentimes when one's attention is fixed too far ahead and at the wrong angle, one can trip over a crevice before one's very feet. But in so much does he serve our purpose—we needed a reason to take off from Korwar without question from those using Mackry—though he does not reckon the truth that he is my servant here, rather than master."

"You have learned something?" Ziantha asked.

Yasa purred. "Naturally, cubling. When Yasa tells eyes to see, ears to listen, noses to sniff, they obey. We know the general direction from which came Jucundus's toy. Now we go in search of those who make it their mission in life to learn what is unknown or long forgotten. We go to Waystar."

Waystar! Ziantha had heard of it all her short life. It was considered a legend by most of the star rovers, but it existed, as all the Guild knew well, though perhaps only a handful of a handful among them even guessed in what part of the galaxy it was located. It served the Guild in some respects, but it was not a possession of the veeps of the underworld as were some other secret bases.

Long before the Guild came into power, before the first of the Terrans felt their way along unmapped stellar roads, Waystar had been. It was a port of outlaws, a rendezvous for space pirates when piracy existed. Now it was a meeting place for Jacks, those outlaws who raided sparsely settled planets and installations, and for the Guildmen, who bought the loot from such raids, or hired Jacks at times to carry out some ship plan of their own.

According to the stories, it had once been a space station located in a system now so old its planets were cinders in orbit around an almost dead red dwarf sun. If it were as old as the worlds it companied, or even as old as the life that had once ruled them, it was beyond any reckoning of age by those who now used it. It had, however, in recorded time, such a dark history as to overshadow all speculation. Going to Waystar was like saying one planned to venture into the bowels of Ruhkarv, with perhaps as good a reason to expect the worst thereafter.

"This Mackry—if we go to Waystar—" Ziantha ventured. Though the Guild did not rule there, their influence would weigh deeply enough so Yasa might be found to be playing traitor. What would happen then? When a veep fell, his or her personal following were also swept away, unless they were extraordinarily fortunate or had secret ties with the one or ones who brought about that downfall.

Yasa smoothed Harath's downy head, uttered a sound amazingly like the snapping of the creature's beak.

"Mackry is one who runs hither and thither with messages, is that not so, my soft one?" she asked Harath aloud.

His mind-send was clear. "He tries to find something with which he can cause trouble for you. So far his search has brought nothing. He believes his detect shields him." There was such a strong note of scorn in that beaming that Ziantha was startled into a question of her own.

"It does not?"

Harath turned his head to look directly at her. Though that seemed an impossible angle for flesh and bone to endure, he held so, his huge eyes unblinking. "Harath can read." Again he beak-clicked scornfully.

Ziantha had not realized that the alien could penetrate the mind-seals worn as a matter of course by Guild men. She was so inured to the marvels of their techs that she accepted as a fact that such a shield could not be pierced by normal means. But then, of course, Harath was not "normal" by her species' standards at all.

Then Yasa did have a guard when Harath was with her. Doubtless he could have relayed to the Salarika every thought passing through Mackry's mind. Or Ziantha's mind—! The stone! No, do not think of that! The trouble was when there was something not to be brought to the readable fore of one's mind, that is the very thought which haunted one. Something else—Waystar—think of Waystar—

Again the Salarika purred. "Harath reads well." There was warm approval not comment. "And there are those at Waystar before whom, for all his ambition, Mackry would dwindle until he was smaller than our Harath is in body, as he is already smaller in talent and courage."

"One has to reach Waystar to evoke the backing of such," Ziantha found the courage to point out.

"One need not put obvious truths into words, cubling. However we have not been idle. Plans were made before Mackry arrived to provide us with cover. But this will not be a luxurious voyage. We must travel in voyage-sleep and a sealed cabin."

Ziantha wished she dared refuse, though there could not ever be a chance for her to set her will against that of the Salarika. Voyage-sleep and a sealed cabin was primitive travel indeed in these days, generations after the first ships traveled with their crews and passengers in frozen sleep, not knowing if they would ever awaken again. She thought now that perhaps it was not the ruggedness of the accommodations which might force this now ancient process on them, but perhaps the secrecy of Yasa's plan.

But she was not given much time to worry about possibilities, because by dusk one of Yasa's private flitters had brought them to the airport where they were escorted on board an inner world liner. Only they did not remain there. For they had no more than stepped within the cabin assigned to them before Yasa whipped two hooded cloaks from her top luggage case. So with distort outer garments they made a circuitous way along empty corridors to a lower hatch and, covered by the dusk and the distorts, swung down to ground level again on a luggage lift.

In spite of her cloak, Ziantha felt vulnerable as she scurried after Yasa across the edge of the landing field and into the shadows. Thus they came to that end of the port where few passenger ships ever sat down, which was reserved for Free Traders and lesser transports. Yasa, without hesitation, seeming to know very well what she sought, caught at Ziantha's hand and urged her to a faster pace to reach the space-scoured side of a transport on which the name and emblem was so badly worn that in this limited light the girl could make out neither symbol.

The landing ramp was out, but there was no crewman on guard at either end. Again Yasa did not hesitate, but, drawing the girl with her, hurried up into the ship. They met no one. It might have been totally deserted; Ziantha decided there must have been orders given that they not be observed entering.

Yasa climbed three levels, bringing them not far above the cargo holds. Here was an open door which they entered, Yasa closing it quickly behind them.

"Pleasant voyaging, gentle fems." Ogan leaned against the wall. He looked oddly out of place in a drab uniform of a workman, as he stood guard over two long, narrow chests. Ziantha could not subdue the shiver which ran through her as she threw off the cloak and looked at those, knowing well what ordeal lay before her now. In spite of all that man had learned to make space flight safe, there were always failures, and she had never been off-world that she could remember. Though, of course, like all those in the Dipple, she had originally come to Korwar from some war-swept planet.

"It has gone well so far." Yasa folded their cloaks small, made pillows of them she stowed in the boxes. "Ziantha, you have the artifact—give it here."

Because she had no reason to defy that, the girl handed over the container for the lump, which she had held tightly to her during their flight across the port. Yasa stood for a moment with it in her hands. If she had intended to open it, to assure herself their prize was within, she did not do so. Instead she set it with extra care beside one of those cloak-pillows.

Ogan smiled. "How perceptive of you, Lady. Naturally if there is any relation between voyage-sleep and trance it should help. Now, Ziantha, in with you, and if our small mystery can answer any questions while you sleep, you can report it later."

Ziantha shrank back against the bulkhead. To sleep with that promise of dark and death so close? She could not! Ogan did not know what he suggested. But he probably did, and did not care. Her talent was of value to the Guild, yes, but she was certain that this was not a Guild operation—that Yasa and Ogan were planning a foray of their own. And in such she would only be useful if she could produce results. She had stepped completely out of any safety she might have known, and there was no turning back, no way to run.

"Come, come!" Ogan put out his hand. "Let us have no child's nonsense. You have been hypnoed before—it is nothing. And think what a tale you may have to tell us later!"

In those close quarters she could not even dodge. He caught her wrists in a grip which brought a gasp from her, pulled her arm out and pressed the injector to her flesh below the elbow. Still holding her, he pulled her to the box. She climbed in numbly, lay down with her head pillowed on the folded cloak. The sides and bottom were well padded, could even be called comfortable, if one did not know the future. Beside her head was the box; she would not allow her eyes to stray in that direction.

"Good. Now you see it is all very simple, not at all painful or frightening. Look here, Ziantha—just as you have done before—before—before—" He repeated the word over and over in a dull even-toned voice as she stared, because she had to, at a swinging disk in his fingers. She had no will left, no defense—

"Before—" The word was gone; she slept.

5

Ziantha had to use all her control to keep from cowering flat on the landing stage with her suited body. Overhead (if there could be "over" or "under" in space) was a threatening mass. They had slept, for how long she never knew, and then awakened, to transfer to another ship which had brought them to the outer ring and through the concealing barrier which protected Waystar.

Such a barrier as perhaps a writer of fantasy tri-dees might have conceived—that was Waystar's first defense. For it was a mass of derelicts and parts of derelicts, as if a giant fleet of some great stellar confederacy had been wrecked by deliberate intent, brought here by traction beams, and welded and tied to form a jagged cover about the station.

Beyond that mass of tortured metal was a stretch of free space, which was reached by traversing a "tunnel" through the wreckage. Centering that was a station which had plainly been the result of intelligent planning and construction. At either end was a landing stage and the rest was encased in a crystalline surface pitted and mended many times. But to land on one of those stages and see the massive roofing of twisted metal overhead was to produce in one, Ziantha thought, the sensation of being under a hammer about to descend. That it had not closed upon the fragile-seeming station in all the generations it had been in position did not somehow reassure her in the least.

Even once Yasa had drawn her into the entrance lock, the memory of that weight around the station was daunting. To the girl's surprise there was a weak gravity within, though how that was maintained she never discovered.

The center was hollow, completely surrounded by corridors and balconies. A greenish light, giving the most unhealthy and unpleasant cast to the faces of the inhabitants, diffused from the walls. And those inhabitants were a mixed lot—X-Tee aliens equaling humanoids in number. In the few moments it took them to leave the lock and traverse a portion of one way, Ziantha saw even more outré forms than she had ever viewed on Korwar, which was famous for being the crossroads of many stellar lines.

The gravity was so weak that it was necessary to hold to bars set into the walls, and there were curved rods with handholds to rise and descend to the various levels. However, Yasa apparently knew the way, traveling at a brisk speed toward one of the upper levels.

Here were very faint tracings of patterns which might once have been painted on the walls, perhaps by those who fashioned this station long before the coming of Ziantha's kind into space. But these were so dimmed that one could make little sense of them; a geometric angle, a curve here and there, was all that could be traced.

They came to a door guarded by a human in space leather, one of the forbidden lasers on his hip, its butt near his hand. But at the sight of Yasa he stepped aside and let them enter. The room beyond was such a crowded space that there was too much to sort out in the first glance, or even the fifth.

The furnishings had apparently been gathered with no thought of harmony; there were pieces which could have been ripped from half a hundred plundered ships. Some were intended for the use of humans, others for alien accommodation. What they had in common was a display of ornate riches (or what had once been that, for they were now battered and dingy).

Stretched at length in the midst of this storehouse of stolen goods was the veep Yasa had chosen to consult about the artifact. He snapped his fingers as they entered and a green-skinned Wyvern male scuttled forward to push and pull out two hassocks for their seating. But the veep did not rise in greeting, only lifted his hand in Yasa's direction in a slight salute.

The Salarika, who on Korwar was accorded the full deference for not only her sex but her standing in the Guild, apparently here was not worthy of formality. But if she were piqued by this reception, she showed no sign of it.

This veep, like his quarters, was a mixture of both magnificence and slovenly disorder. Unlike many beings they had passed outside, he showed almost pure Terran descent in his person, though his clothing was barbaric. Like the heads of mercenaries of some centuries earlier, his skull was shaved save for an upstanding roach of black hair, the stiffness of which was reinforced by a band of green-gold metal. And from this circlet a fine koro stone depended, to rest against his forehead.

His skin was the brown of a spaceman, and there were purposely shaped scars running from the corner of each eye to his chin on either side of his mouth, giving his features a cruel frame, as if living flesh had been carved to produce a mask meant to terrify.

Breech-leggings of a very soft and pliable fur—white with a ripple pattern—covered him to the waist. Above that was the full-dress tunic of a Patrol Admiral, black-silver, with all the be-gemmed stars and decorations such an officer was entitled to wear. The sleeves had been cut away. On his bare arms, just below his elbows, were cuff bracelets of iridium, one thickly set with Terran rubies, the other with rows of vivid blue-and-green stones.

There was a tray resting across his thighs, but it held no dishes. Instead there was something there so exquisitely beautiful that it was totally out of place in this barbaric setting. It was a miniature garden, with tiny trees, bushes, and a lake in which a minute boat sailed for an island that was a single mountain of rock. Ziantha's attention followed it as the Wyvern carried it to a table.

The veep spoke Basic in an educated voice that did not match his pirate chieftain's dress.

"My garden, gentle fem. This is the best one can do on Waystar, where nothing will grow. But this is of spice wood, with scented water for its lake. One can hold it, close the eyes, and wander in one's imagination—a substitute for the real, but it must serve."

Yasa was holding one of her scent bags to her nose, no longer able to do without the reviving stimulation her species needed. The veep smiled, the scars rendering that stretch of lips no more attractive than the grimace of a night demon would have been.

"My apologies, gentle fem. Waystar is rich in many things—including odors, but not of the kind your people delight in. So let us return to business before you discover you can no longer get any reviving sniffs from your supply of lily petals. Your message was received. Perhaps I can serve you, perhaps not—there are difficulties, and arrangements." Again he smiled.

Yasa's smile matched his, with some of the same merciless quality in it. "Of a truth, how could it be otherwise? I am prepared, Sreng, to discuss it at length."

For a moment there was silence as their eyes met. Ziantha knew that any bargaining would be a fiercely fought action. But, since they needed each other, terms would eventually be met. The Salarika had not given her much information as to what they sought here at Waystar, save to say that the riddle of where the artifact might have come from would be best answered by those she could meet there.

"We have used the computer to reckon the coordinates which you sent us," he said. Perhaps Yasa's recognition of the need for bargaining satisfied Sreng. "There is a possible mapping. What do you do now?"

Yasa looked to Ziantha. "We shall search—"

Ziantha's hands tightened on the box she held. She knew what Yasa meant, but she mistrusted her own powers for this; she was not trained to it. What if she could not deliver? Did this Sreng have some sensitive of his own who would then take over? But that would mean relinquishing the box's contents to another, and she believed that Yasa would consent to that only on direst necessity.

The technique of such a search was age old, known to every sensitive. But not all had the talent to use it effectively. And, while she knew it had been applied to planet maps, could it be so used on a star map? She hoped that Yasa did not expect too much, and that they might lose advantage to this veep because she, Ziantha, could not search.

"We need rest, a little," Yasa said now with a certain note of authority in her voice which argued that she considered herself, even in Waystar, to be also a veep whose well-being was to be reckoned on.

"Your desire is my wish—" He made a mockery of that formal reply. "SSssfani will show you to quarters, which, though most rough compared to your own holding, gentle fem, are unfortunately the best we can offer. When you are ready, you have only to send word and we shall to work."

The Wyvern led them farther along the same corridor to a chamber furnished with the same looted jumble. When he had departed Yasa turned briskly to the girl.

"Rest you well, cubling. It now lies on you—" As she spoke her hands moved under the edge of her shoulder scarf in a complicated pattern. Ziantha read the signals.

Snooper rays! Of course in such a place as this those were to be suspected. She probably dared not even try mind-touch—they would be surrounded by more than one type of detect.

"I shall do my best, Lady." She settled on an eazi-rest, which adjusted to her comfort more smoothly than she expected from its battered appearance. Yasa had gone to the food server on the wall and was fingering the dial as she read its code. She sniffed.

"Limited, but at least it will keep life in our bodies— all synthetics. Not much better than E-rations." She seemed only too willing to give her opinion, especially if their host was listening.

Ziantha made do with the tube of concentrate which was Yasa's selection. It was highly nourishing, she knew, even if there was a flatness of taste. She lay back in the eazi-rest. One part of her dreaded the coming test; another wanted it to happen as soon as possible, to learn if it would be success or failure. But here she must follow Yasa's lead. She was supposed to be resting, though her anticipation would not allow that.

There was something else. As she lay back and closed her eyes, clearing her mind, building up her psychic energy, she was aware of a—stirring. In no other way could she describe that odd, disquieting feeling that nibbled at the edge of her inner awareness.

A little alarmed, Ziantha concentrated on that area of faint disturbance. The sensation came and went like the lightest of nudges. Now she was sure that it was not born from some layer of her own subconscious. She was being scanned! Though the touch was so faint she could not hope to trace it.

But perhaps Sreng had a sensitive trying her. Only this—Ziantha could not push away the thought that that touch was not trying to gauge her strength of talent— It was—

Confused, she raised her defenses. What *had* she sensed in that moment or two? Mind-touch. However not with the force she expected from a test. Rather as if some questing net had been thrown over Waystar, or this portion of it, merely to see if there was another sensitive within range.

Ziantha tried to be logical. Sreng would have known in advance who and what she was. Yasa would have made no secret of it. This could be some rival of the veep, intent on gaining knowledge—it could be a Guild representative checking on Yasa. Whoever it was, she believed it the enemy.

But she had so little to give Yasa in confirmation of what she had felt. Best keep quiet until she was entirely sure that she had been touched. Only, keep her own defenses up from now on.

The girl was still on the alert when they returned to Sreng's crowded room, where there was now a difference. Some of the furniture had been ruthlessly cleared away to make room for a table on which was spread a star map. To Ziantha it had little meaning, since she was no astrogator. But that would argue in her behalf if she received any message from the artifact. Concentrating on the lump, even as she unboxed and held it between her hands, she moved it out to hold over the map, beginning a slow progress from left corner to right. So far there was nothing in return.

She had covered nearly three quarters of the map when there was a change. It was as if the lump warmed to life. From it came a sharp mental picture, so very clear that she felt as if what she saw existed, that she could reach out and touch a rock, a wind-blown bush!

"Rocks—" she spoke without knowing she did so until she heard her own voice. "There are trees, a road—yes, a road—it leads to— No!" She might have hurled the lump from her at that moment, but it was as if her own flesh were fastened to its surface and she could not free herself from that touch any more than she could free herself from the cloud of terror that entrapped her, until that was all the world and there was nothing else. She thought she screamed—cried for help!

The cloak of fear fell away, leaving her sobbing, so shaken she was weak and would have fallen had Yasa not supported her.

"Death—death! Death in the dark. In the tomb with Turan—death!"

Who was Turan? Now she could not remember. She must not! Sreng leaned over the table to make quick marks on the map. The lump was free now in her hold. She thrust it away from her so that it slid along the map, would have fallen to the floor had not Sreng caught it, keeping his hand upon it as he looked at them.

"A tomb as you guessed, gentle fem," he spoke to Yasa. "Dare we hope unlooted? At least this system is unknown according to our records. Which is a good sign. What else have you learned, girl? This piece has been in your keeping; surely you have picked up more."

Dumbly Ziantha shook her head. She was still shaking from the aftermath of that panic.

"It is death—death waiting—" she said dully.

"Death waits in every tomb," commented Yasa. "But whatever was there to frighten has long since gone. This is true Forerunner."

"Which in no way certifies that all danger has been eradicated by time," was Sreng's answer. "Though the rewards may be beyond price, the danger can be great. Sometimes there are traps. One may find a Scroll of Shlan or be crushed by an ingenious deadfall."

Yasa smiled. "Does not one each day play a game of chance? I did not come here to listen to warn-offs, nor are you one to sit and give them, Sreng—unless time has softened you. You speak of Shlan—that emperor who was buried with the greatest art treasure of his time encasing his body as a shroud. And that is only one of the finds that has been made. What of Var, and Llanfer, and the Gardens of Arzor, the whole planet of Limbo? Do I need to list the others? This is a chance to hunt in a section where no one else has yet searched."

Sreng looked at the chart. "At least not yet," he said. "If Jucundus—"

Yasa interrupted him. "He has made no move, we know that. But it may be a matter of time. He needs only to have a psychometric reading. However"—she smiled again—"if he has not, he cannot now."

"You"—the veep turned to Ziantha—"this Turan you babbled of, who was he?"

She did not hold that memory. "It is a name, no more."

His stare did not change, but she believed he thought she was lying. What would happen now? Would he put her under a scanner? She was so afraid, she could not control the tremor in her hands, waiting for that fate to come. But he said nothing, instead looked again at the lump, rubbing one finger across its back.

Ziantha stiffened. Had he detected the seam? Would he now open it? Instead, he gave the artifact a push in her direction.

"Keep it with you, girl. I am told the power of these things increases if they continue in a sensitive's hold. We shall need your direction again. It is well"—he spoke now to Yasa—"this is worth the use of a ship. Iuban is in orbit. He had only an abortive raid on Fenris and is under obligation to me for supplies. A class D Free Trader convert. Rough travel, gentle fems—"

"Deep sleep will answer that," Yasa returned. "We have no wish to be cabin passengers on such a ship. You will time-lock our sleep boxes."

"How wise of you, gentle fem," his menace-smile showed two teeth almost as fanglike as Yasa's own. "Deep sleep and time locks—set so myself. Iuban is *my* man, however." Those last words were a warning which Yasa accepted with a surface good humor. To Ziantha the Salarika veep seemed uncommonly trusting. But perhaps here she could do no more than accept Sreng's arrangements.

Where was Ogan? Since their transfer to the shuttle which had brought them to Waystar after their first awakening, they had seen nothing of him. But that he was to be ruled out of this venture, Ziantha did not believe.

The rest of their stay on Waystar was short, and they kept to the chamber Sreng had assigned them. Twice more Ziantha was aware of that illusive scan. It had first alarmed her, but later she sought it, her curiosity aroused. It was not mechanically induced, of that she was certain. The touch was that of a living entity—Ogan? But the wave length seemed different. And she thought it was not seeking her so much as pursuing some purpose of its own.

They joined Iuban's ship and were again boxed for the voyage. From what Ziantha had seen of the ship and its crew, to be so sealed from them was an excellent choice. Once more she prepared to sleep away time ·with the lump beside her. If she had dreamed any dreams induced by its proximity before, she had not remembered them, and this second time she did not fear the long sleep.

When they were aroused, Iuban's ship was already in orbit around a planet, and he summoned Yasa and Ziantha to the control cabin to watch through the visa-screen the changing view of the world below.

"Where do we set down, gentle fem?" he asked harshly.

He was young, or young seeming, for his command, and not unhandsome—until one saw the dead chill of his eyes, which made him the semblance of a man without warmth or emotion. Perhaps he was of mutation or crossbreed, for his hands were six-fingered and his ears mere holes. By the way his space tunic fitted Ziantha guessed that he had other body peculiarities.

It was plain that he had tight command of his motley crew. And it was also apparent that he united in his person the ruthlessness of a top-rated Jack captain with an intelligence that might differ in part from the Terran but in its own way was of a high level.

Yasa put her hand on Ziantha's arm. "Where?" she asked the girl. "Have you any guide?"

As Ziantha hesitated, unable to answer, Iuban uttered an impatient sound. Then he added:

"We have neither time, manpower, nor supplies, gentle fem, to search the whole planet. Besides"—he touched a button and the scene on the visa-screen sharpened— "that's no territory to search. By the looks, it's been near to a burn-off down there."

Ziantha had seen in the video-history tapes the records of planets burned off, not only in war, but in some ancient disaster. Some were cinder balls; on others, mutant and ofttimes radioactive vegetation straggled, attempting to keep a few forms of life in the pockets between churned and twisted swaths of soil and recooled molten rock.

From the picture now flitting before her as the ship swung in orbit, she could see that some disaster, either manmade or a vast convulsion of nature, had struck this unknown world. There were great, deep-riven chasms, their rims knife-sharp; stretches of what could be only deserts, with, at great intervals, some touch of color suggesting vegetation. They were over a sea now, one manifestly shrunken to half its former size.

But she had no guide—

Fool! There was Singakok. It was as if a ripple had crossed the screen. She saw a city, rich land around it. Why, she could easily distinguish the Tower of Vut, long avenues, the—

"There!"

But even as she cried that aloud, Singakok was gone. There was only rock and more rock. Ziantha shook her head. Singakok—Vut—the avenues—from whence had come those names? How had she seen a city, known it as if she had walked its pavements all her life? They had asked her and she had seen it, as if it were real! Yet it could not have been.

Iuban no longer gave her any attention. He spoke to the astro-navigator. "Got it?"

"Within measurable error, yes."

She must tell them, not let them land because of that weird double flash of sight. Then prudence argued that she leave well enough alone. It might be that the artifact had given her vision of something which had once existed on that site, and, since they had picked up nothing else of any promise that was as good a place as any to begin looking. Yet she was uneasy at Iuban's quick acceptance, and of what might happen should her suggestion prove to be wrong.

They strapped down for a landing that had to be carefully plotted in that rough country. Nor did they stir from their places until the readings on atmosphere and the like came through. For all its destroyed surface, it registered Arth-type One, and they would be able to explore without helmets and breathing equipment.

But they had landed close to evening and Yasa and Iuban agreed not to explore until morning. He turned his own cabin over to the women, staying in the control section above. When they were alone Ziantha dared to make plain her fear.

"This may not be what you wish—" she said in a half-whisper, not knowing if some listening device could be now turned on them.

"What made you select it then?" Yasa wanted to know.

Ziantha tried to describe those moments when the picture of Singakok had flowed across the screen, a city which seemingly no longer existed.

"Singakok, Vut," Yasa repeated the names.

"That is the closest I can say them," the girl said. "They are from another language—not Basic."

"Describe this city, try to fix it in your mind," Yasa ordered.

Detail by detail Ziantha strove to remember that fleeting picture. And she found that the harder she tried to remember, the more points came clearer in her mind. As if even now she could "see" what she strove to describe.

"I think you have had a true seeing," Yasa commented. "When Ogan arrives, we can—if we have not by then located any trace—entrance you for a far-seeking reading."

"Then Ogan comes?"

"Cubling, did you think that I throw away any advantage blindly? We needed Sreng's computer records. In their way they are more complete than even those of Survey, since they deal with sections of the starways even the Survey Scouts have not fully pioneered. But to then meekly make a pact with Waystar—no, that is not what any but a fool would do! Ogan will have traced us. He brings with him those sworn to me alone. Whatever treachery Sreng contemplates through Iuban and such trash will not avail. Now listen well—if we find traces of your city tomorrow, well and good. We must keep Iuban tail down here until Ogan arrives. But play your guiding well; delay all you can—try not to bring us to this tomb of Turan until we do have reinforcements of our own."

Tomb of Turan—the words rang in Ziantha's mind. There was a stir deep down—not of memory (how could it be memory?) but of intense fear. She was instantly aware.

6

"Ziantha!"

Not a spoken call to bring her so out of sleep. No, this was a stir within her mind, though it awoke her so she lay in the cramped berth looking into the dark—listening—

"Ziantha?"

She had not been dreaming then. Ogan? She sent out a mind-seek before she thought of the danger that Iuban might be equipped with some Guild device to pick up and register such activity.

"Harath!" Her recognition of the mental force meeting hers was instantaneous and left her bewildered. But Harath must be back on Korwar. Ogan surely had not brought the alien on this foray. And there was no possible method by which mind-touch could cross the stellar distance between this unknown planet and Korwar.

"What—?" Questions crowded. But the beaming of the other overrode all her own thoughts with the intensity of the message he would deliver.

"Think—think of me! We must have a reference point."

Allies after all—this was what Yasa had warned of—her following must be guided in. Obediently Ziantha produced a mental picture of Harath, held that with all the strength she could summon, pushing aside her curiosity in the need for providing a beacon guide to those the Salarika expected.

As suddenly as a clap of hands a new message came. "It is well."

She was cut off by the rise of Harath's mind shield. Having what he needed, the alien had severed connections. And Ziantha knew of old that communication could not be renewed without his cooperation.

The girl turned her head. Through the dim night light she could see Yasa curled up opposite her, hear the soft regularity of her breathing. The Salarika was asleep. Should she wake her, tell her Ogan was on the way?

But Harath—how had he come into this? No, she would wait until she was sure. Twice before morning she mind-called. But if the alien was still within beam, he would not answer, and she had to accept that.

They were roused early, and Ziantha, fearful of some snooper, decided to wait until they were away from the ship before she relayed her news. Iuban had suited up too, plainly prepared to go with them. And she must be most careful about awakening any suspicion.

The Jack captain eyed her while she buckled on belt with ration pouch and water carrier as if he would like to have added a leash to keep her to his hand. And she noted at once that he wore a stunner, but neither she nor Yasa had been offered such a weapon.

They came out on the ramp, to stand for a moment just beyond the lock, looking about them at the wild desolation of this broken country. Her vision of a city—how could she have seen it here?

This earth was scored by deep crevices, blasted into a land which had repudiated life before they set foot on it. Ziantha's hands, without conscious willing, went to the bag she had fashioned, the cord of which hung about her neck, so that the lump rested against her breast. If she were to have any guide, that would be it.

Yasa moved up beside her.

"Singakok," the Salarika said softly. "Is *this* your city?"

She had good reason to question. In all that mass of tortured rock that lay about them there was no resemblance to anything wrought by the work of intelligent beings—unless the destruction itself could be taken for such evidence.

"I—I do not know!" Ziantha turned her head from side to side. Where were the tower, the great avenues—all the rest? Or had that vision been hallucination, born from some quirk of her own imagination and fed into her mind as a "seeing"?

"Which way do we cast?" Iuban, two of his men, armed and ready, caught up with them. "I do not see any signs of a city here. Are you playing games then?"

Yasa turned on him. "Know you nothing of the art of a sensitive, sky rover? The talent cannot be forced. It comes and goes, and sometimes not to any bidding. Let the girl alone; in her own time and way she shall pick our path."

There was little expression on his face, nor did his dead eyes show life. But Ziantha was aware of his emotions none the less, impatience and disbelief being well to the fore. And she did not think he would take kindly to any evasion he could detect. Also she was sure she was not clever enough to play the delaying role Yasa wanted. If she found any hint of what they sought she must use it to satisfy him.

It seemed that they were leaving the leadership of this expedition to her. And, with no way of escape, she walked slowly down the ramp, stepped out on the barren rock below. There she fumbled with the bag, unwrapped the lump, held it in her hands.

Ziantha closed her eyes. The answer came with the force of a blow which nearly beat her to the ground. There was the sensation that she stood in a city street amid a press of people, with the passing of strange machines. The force of life feelings, of random thoughts she could not understand, was so great it made her giddy.

"Ziantha!" A hand tightened on her arm. She opened her eyes. Yasa half supported her, the Salarika's eyes intent upon her.

"This—is—was a city," the girl answered.

Iuban had come to face them. "Well enough, but one we cannot search now—unless we can turn back time. Where do we go to look for anything that remains? Can you tell us that, dreamer?" He made a scoffing challenge of his demand.

There had been no selectivity to that impression of the

city. Ziantha's hold on the artifact tightened. Suppose she were to open the crude outer casing, release the jewel inside, would that lead them to what they sought? But she shrank from that act. Let her try as long as she could to use it as it was.

"Let me try—" she said in a low voice, twisting loose from Yasa's hold. There was a ledge of rock nearby, and she reached that, to sit down, hunched over the lump. Wetting her lips, she forced herself to touch it to her forehead.

It was like being whirled through a vast flow of faces, voices. They shouted, they whispered, they grew large, dwindled, they spoke in tongues she had never heard, they laughed, wept, howled, screamed— She made herself try to steady upon one among the many, concentrate on learning what she could.

Singakok—Turan! The second name she held to, using it as an anchor that she might not be carried away in the sea of faces, deafened by the voices, the clamor of the long-vanished city.

"Turan!" she used the name to demand an answer.

The faces withdrew, formed two lines melting into one another, their cries stilled. Between the lines moved a shadow procession. That was Turan, and behind him was her place, her own place. She must follow—for there was no escape—

"What is she doing?" Very faint, that question.

"Be still! She seeks—" came in answer.

But that exchange had nothing to do with Turan. She must follow him. The shadows grew no denser, but they remained, a little ahead. No longer were there faces on either side—only Turan and her tie to him.

Now and then that scene shimmered, tore, as if it were fashioned of the thinnest gauze, shredded by a breeze. Then she saw only distorted rocks and a barren land that was not Singakok. When that happened she had to stop, call upon Turan, rebuild the vision.

Very dimly she heard chanting, sweet and high, like the caroling of birds released from captivity, or the thud of drums which were of the earth, the earth reluctant to lose Turan. Turan—

✧　✧　✧

The shadows were gone, whipped away. Ziantha could not again summon them. She stood with the artifact before a great rise of bare red rock, a wall of cliff. But she knew that what she had sought lay behind it, that the artifact had led her to a place from which it had once come.

The girl looked back over her shoulder. Yasa, Iuban, his men, all were watching her.

"What you seek—" she said, the energy fast draining from her as it always did when she had made such an effort, "lies there." She pointed ahead at the rock, staggering then to an outcrop where she might sit, for she feared her trembling legs would no longer support her.

Yasa came to her quickly. "You are sure, cubling?"

"I am sure." Ziantha's voice was close to a whisper. She was so spent in her struggle to hold the vision that she longed only for rest and quiet, for no more urging to push her talent.

The Salarika held out two revive capsules, and Ziantha took them with a shaking hand, put them in her mouth to dissolve slowly. Iuban had gone to the face of the cliff, was examining it intently, and at a signal his men split to search left and right.

"I can see nothing—" he was beginning when the crewman to his right gave a hail. The Jack captain hurried toward him.

Yasa bent over Ziantha. "I told you—be slow—do not reveal anything before Ogan comes—"

"He is here, or near." Ziantha felt the aid of the revive. "In the early morning I had a message—"

"Ahhhh—" A purr of satisfaction. "It goes well, very well, then. And you play no game with Iuban; this *is* the place?"

Ziantha regarded the wall. "Turan lies there," she said flatly.

But who was Turan—or what? Why should this artifact bind her to him? She looked at the cliff, and now her fatigue was tinged with fear. Behind that—behind that lay— She wanted to scream, to run. But there was no escape, never any escape from Turan; she might have known that.

Only who was Turan? There seemed to be two iden-
tities within her now. One she knew; it was the Ziantha
she had always been. But another was struggling for life—
the one—the *thing* that knew Turan—Singakok—the one
to whom she must never yield!

Iuban had been conferring with his crewmen, and one
now headed back toward the ship while the Jack captain
came to them.

"There are marks of a sealed way there. We shall have
to laser our way in."

"With care," Yasa warned swiftly. "Or do you have a
depth detect for such purposes?"

"With care, and a detect," he replied. Now he glanced
past the Salarika to Ziantha. "What more can she tell us?
Is this a tomb?"

"Turan lies there," the girl answered.

"And who is Turan?" he prodded her. "A king, an
emperor, a stellar lord? Is this a Forerunner of a star
empire, or only an ancient of some earthbound planet?
What can you tell us?"

Yasa swept in between them fiercely. "She is tired—
such reading weakens a sensitive. Get that storehouse
open and let her psychometrize some artifact from within
and she can tell you. But she must rest now."

"At least she brought us here," he conceded. And with
that he tramped back to the walled-in door. But Yasa sat
down beside Ziantha, putting her arm about the girl's shoulders, drawing her close, as she asked in a very low voice:

"Have you contact now with Ogan? It is now he must
come."

Ogan? Summoning up what strength she had Ziantha
formed a mind picture of the parapsychologist, sent forth
mind-search. Harath had cut communication so summarily earlier she did not try him. The alien could be
capricious on occasion, better aim directly for Ogan. Only
she had no—

Answer? A flash of contact, as instantly gone. Ogan?
It was not Harath, because even so light a touch would
have revealed the alien. This had been wholly human.
Ogan, then—but for some reason unwilling to accept a
message. She said as much.

"Do not seek then. There may be a detect he has reason to fear. But as he did make contact, he will know where we are and the urgency of the matter. You have done well in this matter, cubling. Be sure I shall not forget what I owe you."

The crewman returned, another with him. Between them they carried a box and a portable laser—of the type used for asteroid mining. But it was the detect which Iuban first put into action.

Yasa and Ziantha joined him as he crouched over the box, studying the small visa-tape on its top.

"An open space, three cycles within," he reported. "The tomb chamber perhaps. Low frequency setting to bore us a door without any side flare."

He set the laser with care, aiming it twice at nearby rocks to mark the results before he tried it on the wall. Then he moved the finger of the beam up and down within the faint lines of the ancient opening, cutting out a space no wider than a man. The brilliant beam of a belt torch thrust into the space beyond.

"Let us go to Turan!" Iuban laughed.

Ziantha raised one hand to her throat, the other still cradled the artifact against her breast. She was choking, she could not breathe. For a second or two the sensation was so severe she felt that death itself was a single flicker of an eyelid away. Then the sensation faded, and she could not fight as Yasa pushed her along hard on Iuban's heels through the break in the wall.

The Jack captain's lamp flooded the space into which they had come. But it showed dire destruction. This had been a tomb once, yes, and a richly furnished one. But other grave robbers had preceded them. There was a wreckage of plundered chests, now crumbling into dust, objects which had lost their meaning and value when they had been mishandled by those in search of precious and portable loot.

"An abort!" Iuban swung the torch back and forth. "A thrice-damned abort!"

"Be careful!" Yasa cried and caught his arm as he would have moved forward. "We will not know that until after a careful, and I mean a very careful, search is made of what is still here. Tomb robbers often leave what seems of little value to them, but is worth much to others. So do not disturb anything—but widen the passage in that we may shift and hunt—"

"You think anything of value still lies in this muck?" But he did retreat a step or two. "Well, I think it is an abort. But if you can make something out of it—"

Ziantha leaned back against the wall. How could she fight this terrible fear that came upon her in waves, left her weak and sick? Did not the others feel it? They must! It penetrated all through this foul chamber, born not of the wreckage which filled three-quarters of it, but of something else—something beyond—

She turned and pushed through the crack of door, feeling as if that fear were reaching forth great black claws to drag her back. There was a shout behind, words she could not hear, for the beat of her own pounding heart seemed to deafen her. Then there were hands on her, holding her prisoner though she still struggled feebly to flee that place of black horror.

"Tried to run for it—" Iuban's voice over her head. But Yasa touched her, even as the iron grip of the captain held her.

"What is it?" demanded the Salarika. There was a note in her hissing voice which Ziantha had to obey.

"Death—beyond the far wall—death!" And then she screamed for the horror had her in its hold as if that formless evil rather than the captain kept her from flight, screamed and screamed again.

A slap across her face, hard enough to shock her. She whimpered in pain, at the fact that they would not understand, that they held her captive so close to—to— She would close her mind! She must close her mind!

And with the last bit of strength she could summon, Ziantha hurled the artifact from her desperately, as if in that act alone could she find any safety of body or mind.

"Ziantha!" Yasa's voice was a summons to attention, a demand.

The girl whimpered again, wanting to fall on the ground, to dig into the earth and stone as a cover, to hide—from what? She did not know now, only that it was terror incarnate, and it had almost swallowed her up.

"Ziantha—beyond the wall is what?"

"No—and no—and no!" She cried that into Yasa's face. They could not use her to destroy herself; she would not let them.

Perhaps Yasa could read her resolution, for she spoke now to Iuban. "Loose her! She is at the breaking point; any more will snap either her talent or her mind. Loose her to me!"

"What trick is she trying?" Iuban demanded.

"No trick, Captain. But there is something in there— we had better move with caution."

"Captain—look here!" One of the crewmen had knelt beside a rock to the right. He had picked up a shard in which was nested a glitter of spun silver. The artifact had broken open, the focus-gem must now be revealed. Iuban took that half of the figurine, pulled apart the protecting fiber. The gem blazed forth as if there were a fire lighted in it at this exposure to the open air. Ziantha heard the crewman give a low whistle. As Iuban was about to pick out the gem, Yasa spoke:

"Care with that. If it is what I think it may be, then much is now clear—"

"What it may be—" he echoed. "And what is that? An emperor's toy, perhaps?"

"A focus-stone," she replied. And Ziantha wondered at how Yasa had so quickly guessed.

"A stone," The Salarika continued, "used continually by some sensitive as a focus for power. Such things build up vast psychic energy over the years. If this is such a one and Ziantha can use it—why, no secret on this world pertaining to the race of the one who used it can be hidden from her. We may have found the key to more riches than a single plundered tomb!"

"And we may have listened to a likely tale," he countered. "I would see this proved."

"You shall. But not now; she is too spent. Let her rest while we make certain of what lies within here. And if this does prove an abort, we can try elsewhere with the stone."

Yasa would help her, Yasa *must* help her! Once they were alone she could explain, let the Salarika know that deadly peril waited any further dealings with Turan—or this world—or the focus-stone! If Ogan came, he would know the danger. She could make him understand best of all that there were doors one must not open, for behind those lay— Ziantha would not let herself think of that! She must not!

The girl concentrated on holding that barrier within her so much that she was no longer entirely aware of what went on about her. Somehow she had got back to the ship, was lying on a bunk, shivering with reaction while Yasa gave her reassurance.

"Ogan—" Ziantha whispered. "Ogan must know—it is very dangerous."

Yasa nodded. "That I can believe. A stone of power—able to work through such a disguise. Perhaps only a linkage dares use it. Now rest, cubling, rest well. I shall keep these Jacks busy until Ogan comes and we are able to do as we would about the whole matter."

That Yasa had given her a sedating drug she knew and was thankful for. That would push her so deeply into sleep that dreams would not trouble her. And she carried with her that last reassurance. A linkage, yes— she, Ogan and Harath working together might be able to use the focus-stone. But not alone, she must not do it alone!

She was cold—so cold— She was lost in the dark. This was a dream—

"—another shot, Captain?"

"Try it. She's no use to us this way. And when that she-cat comes out of the one we used on her she'll be after us. Give it to this one now."

Pain and cold. Ziantha opened her eyes. There was a bright light showing broken things covered with dust, a wall beyond. She was held upright facing that wall in a grip she could not resist.

Iuban reached out, caught at her hair in a painful hold, for it was so short his nails scraped her scalp as his fingers tightened. So he held her to face him.

"Wake up, you witch!" He shook her head viciously. "Wake up!"

A dream—it must be a dream. This was Turan's place;

they had no right here. The guards would come and then what would happen to them would be very painful, prolonged, while they cried aloud for the death which was not allowed them. To disturb the rest of Turan was to bring full vengeance.

"She's awake," Iuban, still holding her hair with that painful pull, looked straight into her eyes. "You will do this," he spoke slowly, spacing his words as if he feared she might not understand. "You will take this thing, and you will look into it and tell us what is hidden here. Do you understand?"

Ziantha could not find the words to answer him. This was a dream, it must be. If it was not— No, she could not! She could not use the stone where Turan lay! There was the gate to something—

"Ogan," cried her mind in rising terror. "Ogan, Harath!"

She met—Harath—and through him, with him, not Ogan—a new mind, one which greeted her search with a surge of power. Hold for us, it ordered.

"She has to handle the thing, I think," someone behind her said.

"Take it then!" Iuban set the weight of his will against hers.

She would not! But those behind her, those who held her upright here were forcing her arm up though she fought. Her strength was nothing compared to theirs.

"Harath—I cannot—they are making me use the stone! Harath—they make me—"

Iuban had caught one of her hands, was crushing her fingers, straightening them from the fist she tried to keep clenched. In his other hand she could see the blaze of the gem, afire with a life she knew was evil, though she tried to keep from looking at it.

"Harath!" desperately she pleaded.

"Hold—" came the answer. Harath's, together with that other's—the stranger's. "We are almost—"

Iuban ground the gem into the hollow of her palm. With his grip on her hair he pulled her head forward.

"Look!" he ordered.

His compulsion was such that she was forced to his will. The glowing stone was warm against her shrinking flesh. Its color deepened. It had life, power, reaching out, pulling her, drawing her through—

She screamed and heard shouting far off, the crackle of weapon fire. But it was too late. She was falling forward into the heart of the stone, which was now a lake of blazing energy ready to engulf her utterly.

7

The sickly sweetness of bruised camphor-lilies was drugging her; she could not breathe. No, she could not breathe because she was locked in here with Turan! Turan who was dead, as she would be when the air failed and she would enter the last sleep of all.

She was Vintra, war-captive from Turan's last battle, the one in which he had taken his deathblow.

Vintra? Who was Vintra? Where was this dark place? Ziantha tried to move, heard a harsh clink of metal through the oppressive dark. She was—chained! Chained to a wall, and no frantic fight against those bonds left her with more than cut and bruised wrists and the knowledge that she had used up precious air by her struggles.

She was Vintra—no, Ziantha! Crouching against the wall she tried to sort out her whirling thoughts, decide which were true and which hallucinations. She must be caught in some trance nightmare. Ogan had warned her of such a danger. That was why she must never enter the deep trance alone. Nearby there must be one skilled enough to break the trance if she were caught in a killing hallucination.

Ogan—Harath— The thought of them steadied her.

In the tomb of Turan, Iuban had forced her to focus on the gem. This was the result. But it was real! She felt the chains, gasped in the lack of air. She was—

Vintra! It was like the turning of a wheel in her head,

making her first one person and then the other. Vintra
was to die here, part of a funeral gift to Turan, because
she was the only prisoner of note taken during the last
skirmish at the mountain pass. In her a great rage surged
against Turan and his kind. She would die here, gasping
out her life like a korb drawn from its water home, but
she would be avenged! And that avenging—

The pictures in her mind— What, who was she?

Ziantha! Once more the wheel had turned. She was
Ziantha, and she must get back, out of the trance. Ogan—
Harath—! Frantically the girl sent out mind-calls, begging
for help to save her from this dream that was worse than
any she had ever faced before on the out-plane, though
it was true that when one was trained to enter a sensitive's
calling one had to face all one's fears, meannesses of spirit.
Ill acts were given form and substance in trances. Only
when one conquered those did one win to psychic control.
In the past such terrors had been real also, but now, as she
forced herself to employ one familiar safeguard after
another, there was no change. She had known this was different, that she had no defense here. No, she must be
awakened, anchored to her own time and plane by more
strength than she herself could summon.

Harath—Ogan! She made mind pictures, cast for
them.

A faint stirring! Surely she had caught that! By all the
power of That Which Was Beyond Reckoning, she had
felt that answer! Ziantha turned all her talent force into
one plea: draw me forth—draw me forth—or I die!

Yes! A stir—there was an answer. But it did not come
straight, as she expected. It rather flowed, like water finding its way around great rocks half damming a river
course, as if it fought.

"Harath! I am here! Come for me! Do not leave me
to die in the dark, choking out life, imprisoned in what
I cannot understand. Come!"

Not Harath!

There was a personality here. But not Harath—not
Ogan. From the other plane then? She touched thought.

Shock, horror—a horror so great that that other personality was reeling as a man might under a deathblow.

"Help me," it cried. She could not understand. This had come at her call—why then—?

"Dead! Dead!"

An answer out of the dark fraught with terror.

"I am not dead!" Ziantha denied. She would not accept that, for if she did there would never be any escape. She would be caught in Vintra.

"Dead"—the repetition was fainter. Going—the other was going—to leave her here! No!

She might have screamed that aloud. The sound seemed to ring around and around in her head.

"No!"

There was silence through which she could hear the gasping from her laboring lungs. Then—from the other:

"Where is this place?"

Words—not mind-send, but words to her.

"The tomb of Turan," she answered with the truth that Vintra knew.

"And I—I am Turan—" the voice grated. "But I am *not* Turan!" The denial followed the recognition swiftly, as if the same fear she had known when Vintra had taken over gripped him.

Sounds of movement. Then a mind command, quick and urgent: "Light!"

A glow, growing stronger. Why had she not thought of that? Straightway she sent out her own energy to feed his, to strengthen the glow.

"There is no air, we shall die." She added her urgent warning.

"Go to the sunder plane, quickly!"

His command brought her mind back into the protective pattern, which she should also have done for herself. She took the steps of out-of-body, something she had always been reluctant to try. And so, safe for a time, looked about her.

There lay the body from which she had just freed herself, tangled in chains. To her left was a two-step dais on which rested Turan, his High Commander's cloak spread over him, the lilies massed, brown-petaled, dying. Even as she saw him, candles at the head and foot of his resting place flared high.

"The spirit door!" that other's voice in her head. "There!"

She had not remembered, not until he spoke, for that was of Vintra's knowledge not her own. But there was the spirit door set in the rock above Turan.

"Draw back the bar there—"

Their only hope. For if that faintly twitching body she had just left died, then she was also lost. Ziantha made reentry, knew the life force was fast fading. With the last spurt of energy she could summon, she joined her power to the other's, fastened thought to the bar. Together they wrought; fear rose in her—they could not—

She heard a stir, for it was dark again, since all their talent was focused on that one act.

"My arm—my right arm—" wheezed the voice.

She fed him her power. And then she fell into darkness again without learning whether death came with it.

"Vintra!" Her body ached, she cried out in pain as hands pressed her ribs again and again, forcing air in and out.

"I live—let—be!"

There was light again. The candles flamed steadily to show the spirit door hanging open. From it came air, chill but blessedly fresh. Turan knelt beside her, now inspecting the fastenings of the chains.

"A pretty custom," he commented. "Human sacrifice to honor a war hero."

"You—Turan—" She tried to edge away from him. Turan was dead. Even now his body showed those wounds the priests of Vut had repaired that he might go to Nether World intact of person. Yet they looked fully healed, as if they had been ordinary hurts nature mended.

"Not Turan," he shook his head, "though I appear to share some identity with him from time to time. Not any more than you are Vintra. But it would seem we must play parts until we find a way back."

"You, you were the one with Harath!" Ziantha guessed. "The one who was coming when Iuban made me use the focus-stone."

"I was." But he did not identify himself further. "Now what is this about the focus-stone? Apparently some trick of psychometry hurled us back into this and the more I know how and why the better. Tell me!" It was a sharp order, but she was only too willing to obey it.

He had found the trick of the chain fastening, and now they fell from her, and he kicked them away into a corner. Ziantha began her tale with the first sight of the artifact, and all that had happened to her since she had fallen under the peculiar spell that ugly lump with its hidden and perhaps fatal heart had exerted on her.

"A gem such as that now on your forehead?"

Startled, Ziantha raised her hands to her head. There was an elaborate headdress confining hair much longer than her own. And from those bands a drop set with a gem rested just above her eyes. She wrested the band from her so she could see the stone.

It was the focus-stone! Or enough like it to be. Ziantha thought she could tell with a touch, yet she dared not. Who knew what might happen if she tried again?

"Is it?" he who was now Turan demanded a second time.

Ziantha looked miserably at the crown. She had firmly exiled Vintra, but as she stared down at the stone that other identity stirred, gathered strength. Perhaps she might learn the power of the stone, but in doing so she could also lose that other who had been meant to die here in Turan's tomb.

"Vintra—Vintra might know—" she said with vast reluctance, but she could not suppress the truth.

"If the stone had power enough to hurl you into Vintra and me into Turan, then perhaps its results can be reversed. We must know. Look, you are not alone; my will backs yours. And I promise you I shall not let you be imprisoned in Vintra!"

He was Turan, the enemy, who could not be trusted (that was Vintra growing stronger, bolder). No—he was all the help she could have to win back to Ziantha and reality.

"I will try," she said simply, though she shrank from such exposure to whatever lay within the focus of this deadly bit of colored stone.

The ornament of the crown could be detached from

the rest, Ziantha discovered. She unhooked the pendant, raised it to her forehead, and—

Turan's hands were on her shoulders; he was calling her, not in words, but in the powerful waves of mind-send.

"I was not able to learn—" she said in distress.

"Nornoch-Above-the-Waves, Nornoch of the Three Green Walls— The Lurla to be commanded—" He recited the strange names and words slowly, making almost a pattern of song.

"She who is D'Eyree of the Eyes—" Ziantha found herself answering. "Turan—what does that mean? I do not remember—I am saying words I do not understand."

She rubbed her hand wearily across her forehead. Her hair, loosened from the confinement of the crown, fell thickly about her shoulders like a smothering veil.

"You have returned to Vintra." He still kept that hold upon her, and his touch was comforting, for it seemed to anchor her to this body, controlled that feeling that she was about to whirl out and away from all ties with rational life.

"But before Vintra," he was continuing, "there was another—this D'Eyree, who had the talent, was trained in its use."

"Then I just 'saw' again—in a trance!"

"Yes. And this you have learned for us, though you may not presently remember. This focus-stone has its counterpart, which is tied to it by strong bonds, draws it ever, so that she using it is swept farther back in time. The one stone struggles to be united with the other, and that which lies in the past acts as an anchor."

"Vintra—"

"Vintra did not use the talent," Turan said. "To her the stone was only a beautiful gem, a possession of Turan's clan. But it is a thing unique in my knowledge, an insensate thing which had been so worked upon as a focus that it has come to have a kind of half-life. Awakened, that half-life draws it, and those who focus upon it, so that it may be reunited with its twin. And unless that is done I believe that we are held to it."

"But if its origin lies beyond Vintra's time—how far

beyond Vintra?" she interrupted herself to ask that, fearing the answer.

"I do not know—long, I think."

Ziantha clasped her hands tightly to keep them from shaking. The crown clanged to the floor.

"And if we cannot find . . ." She was afraid to complete that question. If his fears were now as great as hers— she did not want to know. What were they going to do? If they could not return—

"At least," he said, "we shall not remain here. The spirit door is open. We'd best make what use of that we can."

He went to stand on the bier, looking up to the dark hole.

"You"—Ziantha moistened her lips and began again— "you—in *his* body—can you control it?"

To her knowledge, and through Ogan that was not too limited, this experience was totally unknown. Of course the legends of necromancy—the raising of the dead to answer the questions and commands of those using the talent in a forbidden way—were known to more than one galactic race. But this type of transfer was new. Would it last? Could he continue to command a body from which life had ebbed before he entered it? She had come into Vintra while the other lived, merged in a way so that her stronger personality was able to push Vintra aside. But in his case—

He looked at her, the wavering candle flames making his face an unreal mask. "I do not know. For the present I can. This has not been done before, to my knowledge. But there is no reason to dwell on what might be; we must concern ourselves with what is, namely, that to linger here is of no use. Now—" He crouched below that opening and made a leap that she watched with horror, fearing that the body he called upon to make that effort would not obey. However, his hands caught the frame of the spirit door and held for a moment, and then he dropped back.

"We need something to climb on—a ladder." He looked around, but the grave offerings were all on the other side of the wall. There was nothing here but—

He was moving the bier end up. Then he caught up

the chains, jerking them loose from the wall ring so he had a length of links.

"You will have to steady this for me," he told her briskly. One end of the bier was within the opening above. He draped the chain about his neck and climbed. Picking up the crown, careful not to touch the dangling gem, Ziantha came to his call, bracing and steadying the bier as best she could.

He was within the frame of the door, his head and shoulders out of her range of sight now. A moment later he was gone. The candles were burning low, but they gave light enough for her to see the chain end swinging through and knew that he must be fully out and prepared to aid her after him.

Moments later she shivered under the buffeting of a strong wind and the beginning of rain out in the open. Some of Vintra's memories helped her.

"The guards—" She caught at his arm. He was winding the chain about him like a belt, as if he might have further use for it.

"On a night like this," he answered, "perhaps we need not fear they are too alert."

It was wild weather. Her festive garment, for they had arrayed Vintra for this sacrifice in a scanty feast robe, was plastered to her body, and the wind whipped her long hair about her. The chill of wind and rain set her shuddering, and now she could see her companion only as a shadow in the night. But his hand, warm, reassuring, closed about her shoulder.

"To Singakok, I think." His voice, hard to hear through the wail of the wind, reached her with difficulty.

"But they will—" Vintra's fear emerged.

"If Turan returns, as a miracle of Vut's doing?" he asked. "The mere fact that I stand before them will give us the advantage for a space. And we need what Turan, or his people, know about that toy you carry. Guard it well, Ziantha, for it is all we have left to bring us back— if we can achieve a return."

Perhaps there was a flaw in his reasoning, but she was too spent by emotion, by what lay immediately behind her, to see it. Vintra shrank from a return to the place of her imprisonment, her condemnation to death. But she was not Vintra—she dared not be. And when he drew her after him, she yielded.

They came through a screen of trees that had kept the storm from beating them down. And now, from this height, they could see Singakok, or the lights of the city, spread before them.

"The guards or their commander will have a land car." Turan's attention was entirely on the road that angled toward the root of the cliff like a thin tongue thrust out to ring them round and pull them in for Singakok's swallowing.

"You can use Turan's memories?" Ziantha was more than a little surprised. Turan's body had been dead, emptied. How then could this other being know the ways of the guards?

"After a fashion. If we win through this foray we shall have some strange data to deliver. Yes, it appears that I can draw upon the memory of the dead to some degree. Now, you try Vintra also—"

"I hold her in check. If I loose her, can I then regain command?"

"That, too, we cannot know," he returned. "But we must not go too blindly. Try a little to see what you can learn of the city—its ways."

Ziantha loosed the control a fraction, was rewarded by memories, but perhaps not useful ones. For these were the memories of a prisoner, one who had been kept in tight security until she was brought forth to give the final touch to Turan's funeral.

"Vintra was not of Singakok—only a prisoner there."

"True. Well, if you learn anything that is useful, let me know quickly. Now, there is no use skulking here. The sooner we reach the city, the better."

They ended their blind descent of the heights with a skidding rush that landed them on their hands and knees in brush. If Turan found that his badly used body took this ill, he gave no sign, pulling her up to her feet and onto the surface of the road.

And they reached that just in time to be caught in the full, blinding glare of light from a vehicle advancing from the city. They froze, knowing that they must already have been sighted. Then Turan turned deliberately to be full face to whoever was behind that light. They must see him, know him, if they would accept the evidence of their eyes.

Ziantha heard a shout, a demand to stand, rasped in the guttural tongue of the city. Men came into the path of the light, one wearing the weather coat of an officer, behind him two armsmen.

"Who are you?" The three halted warily, weapons at alert. They had hand disruptors, the officer an energy ray. Vintra's memory supplied the information.

"You see my face," Turan replied. "Name me."

"You have the seeming—but it must be a trick—" The officer stood his ground, though both the armsmen edged back a little.

Turan raised his hands to his throat, loosened and turned back the high collar of his tunic. The priests of Vut had closed his death wound, but it was still plain to see.

"No trick this. Do you mark it?"

"Whence came you this night?" The officer was shaken but he retained control. Ziantha granted him courage for this.

"Through that door which the Will of Vut leaves for every man to try," Turan answered promptly. "Now—I would go to Singakok where there is that I am called to do."

"To the Tower of Vut?"

"To the House of Turan," he corrected. "Where else would I go at this hour? There are those who await me there. But first, give me your weather coat."

Dazedly the officer loosed the fastenings and handed the garment over, though he made an effort not to touch Turan's hand in that process.

Shaking it out, Turan set it about Ziantha's shoulders. "This must do," he said, "until better serves you."

"That is an error," she thought-flashed to him. "In this world we are enemies to the death! They will not accept such an act from you."

"To the death," he answered in the same fashion, "but

not beyond. All things of this world are weighed now between us. If any ask, that I shall say." Then he spoke aloud:

"Two of us were left in that place, to abide the mercy of Vut; two return after his fair judgment. Of what happened it is not yet the time to speak."

One of the armsmen had put down his weapon, was peeling off his coat.

"Lord Commander, I was at Spetzk when you broke the rebel charge. Honor me by letting that which is mine be of service to you now." He came to Turan holding out the garment.

"This night I have done a greater thing, comrade. For your good will I give thanks. And now, I—we—must go to the House of Turan—by your aid."

Ziantha did not know what game he would play; she could only follow his lead. Within the curve of her arm, pressed tightly against her, was the crown with that pendant gem. To her mind they were pushing out into a swamp where at any moment some debatable footing would give way and plunge them both into disaster. But she allowed him to lead her to the car. And, silent, she took her seat in the passenger section, huddling within the weather coat for a warmth she could not find elsewhere. He settled beside her, and the vehicle turned to Singakok and all that might await them there.

8

"These," the message flashed to her, "do not have the talent, nor, it seems, any knowledge of it."

That her companion had dared to probe those with them made Ziantha anxious. It would seem that care was better than audacity now. Yet what he had learned made them free to use mind-touch.

"Can you then read their minds?" she asked.

"Not to any extent—emotions rather. They have a different wave pattern. These are disturbed as would be entirely natural. The armsmen accept our appearance as a miracle of return, are in awe. The officer—" He checked, and when he did not continue, Ziantha prompted him:

"What of the officer?"

"I see someone, not clearly—someone to whom he feels he must report this as soon as he can. There is a shadow—" Again his thought trailed off.

Ziantha unleashed her own mind-seek, aimed now not at maintaining communication with her companion, but probing the emotions of those about her. Yes, she could understand Turan's bafflement. It was like trying to keep in steady focus a picture that blurred and changed whenever she strove to distinguish it in detail. But she recognized a woman. And that which was of Vintra awoke with a stormy memory.

Zuha M'Turan!

"The one to whom he would report," she relayed, "is the Lady of Turan. I think, Commander, that you—we—go now into a snarl of matters formerly a danger to him whose body you wear. It cannot be clearly read—but there is danger ahead."

"Which we knew from the first," he replied calmly. "So I am to beware, Lady? It would not be the first time that intrigue brought down a man, intrigue from those whose loyalty he had a right to expect was fully his. Now—we must try to delay any report. Can you bend his will, work upon it? I can sense something of his thoughts but not with the clarity I need for such influencing."

"I can try. But it is very difficult to keep in touch—this wavering—"

Ziantha centered her energy fully upon the problem. Though she knew well the theory of such suggestion, had worked it by Ogan's orders, she had done it surrounded by devices to monitor and restrain. To have used it anywhere outside those villa walls on Korwar would have alerted detects instantly. For such interference by a sensitive was so illegal that it would lead to brain-erase if one were caught practicing it. And the force so used was easily traced.

Delicately she probed, caught the picture of Zuha M'Turan. Drawing on Vintra's memory she built it firmly in her mind. And she felt her companion reach and touch that picture.

Bit by bit she achieved the affect she wanted to feed to the alien: that Zuha M'Turan already knew of this night's work, that it was part of a deep-laid plan not to be revealed yet, that chance had brought the officer into it, but that his superiors would be grateful in the future if he did nothing to disrupt it.

"Excellent!" Turan's accolade gave her confidence. "Now—feed it to him, and I shall back you."

As if she repeated a lesson learned by rote, Ziantha focused now on the mind of the man sitting on the other side of Turan, thrusting her image of Zuha and the message with all the vigor she could muster, feeling the backup force of the other. Twice she was certain she made clear contact, shared mind with the alien. Then, spent, after all this night had demanded of her, she could no longer fight.

Weariness swept in, a sea wave washing out all her strength of mind and will. As it ebbed she was left dull, uncaring, aware only of emptiness. Whether she had succeeded in what Turan had wanted of her she had no way of knowing.

They were into the streets of Singakok now. She was aware of lights through the curtain of rain, of people on the move. Vintra was pushing out of confinement within her; the old hates and fears which were a part of her double past surged up. And Ziantha was hard put to retain her own identity. Now she was Vintra, now Ziantha—and she was too tired to hold much longer.

The vehicle turned into a quieter side avenue where the buildings were farther apart, each separated by walls. This was the Way of the Lords—Turan's palace lay not too far ahead.

The ground car stopped at a gate; guards stepped out to flash a light into the shadowed interior. There was a gasp as that beam caught Turan.

"Admit us!" His voice was impatient as if the momentary halt had been an added irritation.

"Lord Commander—" the voice behind that beam of light was that of a badly shaken man.

"Am I to be kept waiting at my own door?" demanded Turan. "Open the gates!"

The guard jumped back, and the gate swung open. They drove between walls of dark vegetation, where rain-heavy foliage cut off any view beyond the borders. Then the car was through that tunnel and out before a sweep of steps leading to the imposing portal of the building.

Ziantha stumbled as she got out; her fatigue was such that those steps before her seemed insurmountable. But Turan was at her side, his hand slipped under her arm, urging and supporting her. One of the armsmen hurried ahead to make a rattle of noise at the door.

That opened slowly just as they came to it. Light swept forth.

"Who comes to disturb the High Consort of the House of Turan? This is the day of third mourning—"

The man who began that indignant demand was now staring open-mouthed at Turan.

"Would you keep us out in this storm, Daxter? In my own door am I to be challenged?" Evidently Ziantha's companion would play his role boldly. Whether or not his boldness was a good defense, who could judge at the present moment?

The doorman retreated, staring. His face was visibly paler as he raised a hand, making a sign as if to ward off some supernatural danger.

"Lord Commander Turan!"

"Yes, Turan." He looked on into the hall. "The third day of mourning is over. Let the household be made aware of that."

"Lord Commander," Daxter retreated yet farther. "You—you are—"

"Dead? But, no, Daxter, I am not. Do dead men walk, talk, seek out their homes, their kin? And where is the High Consort? Let it be made known to her that there is no need for mourning."

"Yes. Lord Commander—"

"And see that this officer, these armsmen, be given the hospitality of the House. They have brought us through a wild night." He slipped off the weather coat and turned to the armsman to whom it belonged.

"Battle comrade, you named yourself; you now have the right to be comrade-in-arms with me. For I have come from a greater trial than any war, a fiercer battle than you can guess."

The man brought his hand up before his face, palm out, in salute. "Lord Commander, the honor of being ready to your service is mine. Be sure that when you call, I shall answer!"

To Ziantha the whole scene was like a tri-dee play, seen when one was half asleep and not too greatly interested in the story. If she could not relax soon, find some energy restorative, she would collapse.

"To my chambers now." Turan was giving more orders. "And you will bring food, wine. We have a long hunger and thirst, Daxter."

Ziantha knew they were climbing stairs, or rather, Turan

was pulling her up step by step. But the rest was a haze until she was lying down and Turan was forcing between her lips a narrow spout from which came a hot, spicy liquid. Half choking, she swallowed again and again. It warmed her chilled body but also added to her lassitude. She could keep her eyes open no longer; her body was one long ache.

She was warm—too warm. Slowly she opened her eyes. Above her was a ceiling riotous in color, and, as her eyes focused, that color fitted itself within outlines of forms. But she had never seen those before. Those strange animals—if animals they were—or were they plants? This could not be her room in the villa. It was—

With effort she turned her head, looked across a wide bed. There were tall posts at each corner, and they provided support for what appeared to be living vines. Cream-colored flowers, touched with rose at petal tip, hung among those vines. And beyond the embowered bed was the wall of a room, its surface covered also with pictures that had the glint of inset metal here and there.

Ziantha pushed herself up with her hands to brace behind her. This strange room was *not* the villa. Where then was she, and how had she come here? Her thoughts were sluggish as she strove to remember the immediate past. Then, as if some barrier in her mind gave way suddenly, it all rushed in. Turan—Vintra—the tomb—their escape. This must be the palace in Singakok to which they had come. And Turan—where was Turan?

She looked about her wildly, needing at that moment the reassurance that she was not trapped here in the past alone. But there was no sign of any other in the chamber. More than a little lightheaded, the girl worked her way to the edge of the bed, slid her feet over to the floor, and tried to stand. The room seemed to dip and sway and she had to hold on to the bed, creeping down to one of those leaf-covered posts and then hang on for support.

On the wall now facing her was a wide mirror and in that was the reflection of—not Ziantha—but Vintra! For a moment or two the shock of being confronted by a stranger was so great that she would not look, study, learn this new self. And then her need for control, for reasserting her will, dominated, and she made herself give that other a searching survey.

She saw a slender body hardly veiled by a transparent robe of pale rose to match the petal tips of the flower so near her cheek. No, it was more than slender, that body, it was gaunt. She was heavily browned on the arms to the shoulder, legs to the thigh, face and throat, the rest being a yellowish tint, as if some portions of her had been long exposed to sun and air. Her thick hair was in stringy wisps reaching well below her shoulders, not light, but a strange pale blue. And she believed that was natural, not some exotic tinting.

The eyes gazing back at her were bordered in lashes of a darker blue, just as the brows above them were, to her Ziantha memory, of that unnatural shade. For the rest, her face as well as her body were humanoid in contour, though both her forearms and lower legs had a very noticeable down or fluff of blue hair, much lighter against the brown skin.

So this was Vintra—Vintra of the rebels, Chieftainess of the Foewomen of Kark, memory supplied that. But she must not allow that alien personality too much freedom. No, she must be Ziantha, or else there was no future for her.

The crown—the focus-stone! She looked about her. Where was that key, the only one which would—or could—open the way back? Her sharp anxiety gave her strength. She was able to loose her hold, move around the room in search. Table backed by another mirror, holding various small pots, a comb ready for service, two chests— She was struggling to lift the lid of the nearest when a sound brought her attention elsewhere.

One section of that painted wall had disappeared and in the opening stood another woman. Vintra's memory supplied a name.

Zuha M'Turan.

She held herself with the arrogant assurance of one who from birth had given orders that had never been questioned. But her face now, under its heavy mask of paint, silvery overlay, was without expression, schooled to remoteness.

Her overrobe was as filmy as Ziantha's present covering and gave only an illusion of cloud over the inner and much shorter tunic. And her dark blue hair was piled into an elaborate coiffure held with pins from which fine wires supported small wide-winged insects of gauzelike filigree constantly in motion. About her waist was a belt from which depended small chiming bells and more encircled the tops of those tight-fitting silver boots showing through the folds of her upper robe.

She did not speak as she crossed the threshold. Behind her the door slipped shut; they were alone.

Ziantha was wary. Though she had not tried mind-seek, she could sense that danger had entered with the High Consort. Where was Turan? Had that body failed her companion? Would he now be returned to the tomb, she with him? But she was not Vintra to be easily handled—she had a defense and weapon in her own mind that she would use to the utmost.

She must learn what had happened to Turan. Delicately, as she might have made the first attempt to pierce the structure of an explosive that could detonate in her face, she used mind-seek.

The alien wave pattern defeated any open reading. But that this woman hated her, and that there was fear with that hatred, yes, that could be read. Turan—Ziantha tried to bring some feeling for him to Zuha's mind.

The thought of Turan brought an explosion—seething hatred! With it, a fear near panic. Zuha had both. What she felt for Vintra was as nothing compared to the emotions which ravaged her now, although her outer façade gave no sign of that storm within.

But Ziantha had gained a little. Turan was alive—and this woman feared that. She had wanted, had believed, her consort dead—and he lived. Not only lived, but she believed him now an ever-present threat whom she must find a way to finish.

"Sorceress!" Zuha flung that single word as she might have used a flamer to char Ziantha. "You will not gain from this shadow-trickery you have wrought! Be sure that I will see to that!"

"I have wrought no trickery. There was the choice of

Vut, the door given every man. If by Vut's will one comes through it, back to life, how can the right or will of that be questioned?" Vintra's knowledge, to draw upon at her time of need. Ancient beliefs these, long given only lip service by the sophisticated nobles.

Vut's priests taught of possible resurrection through the spirit door, which could only be opened from within the sealed tomb. Fabled miracles, legendary accounts of such returns kept Vut as a power. His priests now would sustain Turan in his return for the very reason that his appearance was a bolster to belief.

"Turan is dead. What outland sorcery do you use to make him move and follow your will? You shall tell me and he shall—"

But before the fury which burned her totally overcame all caution, Zuha was silent. It was plain that she refused to accept any thought of a miracle. Perhaps her questions might bring about discovery. Though the alien had no vestige of talent, Ziantha was certain of that—unless it existed on another range of mind-wave entirely.

"Turan is not dead. Have you not the evidence of your own eyes?" She must tread very warily. Zuha, the girl believed, was near to that pitch of mingled fear and rage that might lead to some hasty attack.

"The evidence of my eyes, say you? Yes, and the evidence of the mouthing priests also. Whether they think sorcery or not, they will not say it, lest Vut lose the advantage of this. But Turan was dead, now he lives—or his body walks—" Her hand moved in that same design the armsman had used. "This is not Turan." This last sentence was delivered with an emphasis that made it a declaration of war.

"And if it is not Turan," the girl countered, "who then is he?"

"Rather *what* is he, sorceress? What have you called from the Cold Depths to bring you out of Turan's tomb? Be sure that we shall learn, and in that learning you will have no profit. The death with Turan shall be as nothing compared to the end your dabbling in shadow lore shall bring upon you."

"So it is sorcery, my High One, my First Companion, which brings me back to you?"

Ziantha had been so intent upon their confrontation, as apparently had Zuha, that his entrance had gone unmarked. For it was Turan who stood there, his gaunt face seamed with the wound of his last battle. In this full light he was no pleasant sight, for his skin was a pallid gray, and only his eyes were alive. That this body still served its inmate was a wonder to Ziantha.

"You speak of sorcery," he moved closer when Zuha did not answer, "but you do not speak of the infinite mercy of Vut, not even when your many prayers to him for my well-being have been so mightily answered. Why this change in you, my dear companion, my High Consort? Have you not told me many times that my death would mean your death also—that you would revive the ancient and highest custom of our people and joyfully follow me through the dark way if Vut chose that I should walk first? But who shared my tomb? Not you, for all those loving vows. Rather did you send with me one who was my battle enemy, who would carry with her no love to ease my path, only hate to draw upon me the shadow wraiths and evils. So did your promises come to little in the final hour of farewell. Is that not so, Zuha of the sweet tongue—of the many lies?"

As he advanced, she shrank back from him. And now under that masking of overlay her mouth worked, her features showed emotion at last. A portion of her mask loosened and fell from her skin as her lips twisted and tightened as if to hold within her some shriek of fear. Back she went before his slow steady talk.

"No! Do not come nigh me, dead man! Back! Get you back to the Cold Depths, from which you crawled, from which that sorceress drew you!"

"From the Cold Depths? Was that what you wished upon me, Zuha? Ill wishing, was it not? Perhaps it was your underdealing that brought me back; perhaps Vut would not be mocked by empty words and so gave me life to serve his purpose. That would be fitting—"

Her back was against the wall now. She flung out her other hand, felt along that surface. Then the hidden door opened and she fell rather than moved through it, scrambling back and away as it closed again, leaving Ziantha and him together.

"Guilt gives birth to fear," he commented, as if to himself. "How deep her hatred must lie. I wonder in what it is rooted."

"Turan"—Ziantha demanded his attention—"what have you learned?"

"A little in the time they left me free. It has taken much contriving on my part to keep out of the priests' hands. They would have me among them for examination, since a miracle is so much to their advantage. So far I have held them off. And I have discovered that, in spite of the intrigues within this palace, Turan also has some faithful followers. It was from one of those that I gained what knowledge I have of this." He put his hand within the breast of his tunic and brought out the focusstone.

"Before the outbreak of the rebellion, Turan made a voyage in the southern sea with the fishers of the giant croob-crabs. There a tumult of nature struck without warning, hitting the fleet, no natural storm. From the description I was given it might have been the result of an underseas eruption, followed by a tidal wave. At any rate they found themselves luckily still afloat thereafter—but only just, for the power of their ship was far reduced. The ocean was much roiled, and dead things from the depths floated on the surface.

"Soon after, they sighted land where no land existed on their charts—an outcropping of rock encrusted with marine life, showing it had until lately been long underwater. At Turan's urging the captain sent a small boat ashore on this new-risen coast, and they made two finds. One where there had been a raw break in a ledge disclosing therein a piece of wall not formed by nature.

"Turan would have them labor to uncover more, but there came two aftershocks which shook the island. And the captain feared for the ship and wanted to be out of such dangerous proximity to a land mass they thought might sink again. They were on their way back to their ship's boat in some haste when Turan became separated from the rest.

"He did not join them at once, and the captain at last shouted to him to come or else be left behind.

When he arrived he did not say what had detained him, only his clothing bore marks as if he had been lifting rocks covered with sea slime. And he said he had sighted what appeared to be an inscribed rock. But it was plain he was highly excited, and he tried to bring pressure on the captain to anchor nearby, to send in another party in the morning. However there was the threat of a storm, and the captain would not agree.

"Storm came rightly enough, driving them far off course, exhausting their power unit so that they had to put into one of the small ports as soon as possible. And though Turan talked now and again of returning to this risen land, the rebellion broke shortly after his return."

"What relation has this to the focus-stone?" Ziantha asked.

"These people do not use sensitives as we know them. But they have certain girls kept in the House of Vut who can go into trances and then answer questions the priests set to them. Apparently their talent is very limited and quickly exhausted, rendering each girl incapable after one or two sessions. Thus the power is the monopoly of the priests, well guarded, used only in times of stress.

"Turan exerted his influence with a priest of the Third Rank who had access to these girls. He produced this gem and asked for its history. Whatever the priest told him was unsettling, for he straightway had it set (he had hitherto carried it on his person) into the crown made for the High Consort to wear to her future entombing. There it remained until Zuha ordered it set on your head when she would have you play the role set for her during her many earlier protestations of loyalty and love for her husband."

"And this follower of Turan told you all this? Did he not suspect when you questioned him concerning a matter you should have already known well?"

Turan's set lips moved in a counterfeit of a smile so ghastly Ziantha looked away in a hurry.

"I saw that he recognized the stone and was astounded to see me handling it. The rest I picked from his memory bit by bit, only he did not know that. In this world a sensitive has that advantage. But that this was found on that island, I believe. Only whether that island still exists—that is another matter. And if the twin stone lies anywhere, that island would be the first place to look."

"If you have any charts as a guide we might make sure." Ziantha remembered her success with the star charts.

"Those are what I—we—must locate and speedily. As I say, I cannot much longer spar with the priests and keep out of their Tower of Vut. And even if their sensitives are of the lowest grade they might discover the Turan who returned is not what they believe. Then Zuha could well raise the cry of sorcery against us both and gain her wish to see the last of her Lord Commander forever. We have very little time—"

She looked at him and nodded. Vintra's body served her well, and to look in the mirror reassured her that she was alive. But, Turan, with those deep-closed wounds, that gray face—he was suspect, and she marveled he had managed so well this long.

9

The need for haste was so great it was as if someone trotted on their heels, urging them in whispers to run—run. She had found an undertunic, such as Zuha wore, in one of the chests and bundled over it a longer, semitransparent robe. She now caught that up in both hands to free her feet as they sped along a corridor that Turan said linked the women's quarters with his own.

Though once or twice they heard the sound of conversation or movement in rooms they passed, no one came into the hall. And, as far as mind-touch reported, they passed unseen. She could hardly believe fortune was favoring them so much.

If any record of Turan's voyage existed, that might be found among his private accounts. But to seek blindly was to waste their precious time. It would require both their talents, one to keep sentry, the other to sift out knowledge, as she had in Jucundus's apartment.

It was difficult to remember now that she was not only on an alien world, but in a time so far lost to her own that this city, these people were not even legends. Ziantha felt no wonder, only the driving need to escape, to find again her own place, dangerous though it might be. For those dangers were familiar, and now they seemed, by comparison, not to be perils at all, but a well-settled pattern of life. It is the unknown that always carries with it the darkest fear.

"Here—" Turan was at a door, waved her to him.

"Records?" She looked around her for something familiar. Even if it might be the very ancient scrolls of actual writing she had seen in a museum.

"For secrecy perhaps, or even because of custom they were kept thus."

He had gone to a cabinet and now brought forth bunches of short cords, knotted together at one end, the rest flapping free. Along each of these many lengths were spaced beads of different shapes and colors. Ziantha stared. To her these made no sense. Records—kept by beads knotted at irregular intervals on bits of cord? That was a device she had never heard of. She looked to Turan, unable to believe that he meant what he said.

As he ran his fingers along the cords, he paused to touch a bead here and there.

"A memorization device. In our time this would be used by a very primitive tribe that had not yet mastered the art of writing in symbols. Yet it can be a personal code, locked for all time. Apparently very secret records are kept here in this fashion. Each type of bead, each knotting, whether it be a finger width less or more from the next, has a meaning. The keeper of such can sit in the dark and 'read' these by running them through his fingers."

"If they are Turan's, then you should be able—"

He shook his head wearily. "I have only very fleeting touch with Turan's memories, and those grow less and less. I—I dare not use too much of my power; it is needed to control this body."

So he was admitting that he was having trouble with the Turan shell? Ziantha put out a hand, stirred the mass of cords. If they were in code, a code known only to him who had devised them, it would require intense concentration to gain anything from them.

Compared to this, dealing with the sealed tapes in Korwar was play for a beginner. For the tapes had been clearly inscribed by one of her own species. An alien code, devised by an alien— Well, since this key was the only one offered them she must try.

"You hold watch then?"

At his nod, she took up the nearest assortment of cords. They were silken soft, and the beads glinted blue, white, and vivid orange-scarlet. She slipped the packet back and forth through her fingers.

Emotion—hate—a vicious and deadly hate, as sharp and imperiling in its intent to threaten her reading as if the cords had taken on serpentine life and struck at her. With a little cry, she threw the bunch from her.

"What is it?"

Ziantha did not answer. Instead she held her hand palm down over the whole collection. Not quite touching, but in her mind seeking what source had broadcast that blast that had met her first probe.

"These—these have been recently handled, by some one who was so filled with hate and anger that emotion blankets all. Unless I can break that I can do nothing."

He lowered himself wearily onto a bench, leaned his head back against the wall, his eyes closed. And without the life of his eyes—Ziantha shuddered, would not look at him. It was as if a dead man rested there. How long could he continue to hold Turan in this pseudo-life?

"Who is responsible? Can you learn that?"

She took up again the first collection. Strong emotion could fog any reception of impressions, and she was already handicapped by trying to read alien minds. She wadded the beads and cords into a packet, held that to her forehead, trying to blot out all else but the picture she must have.

Zuha—yes, there was no mistaking the High Consort. But there was another influence. The girl tried for a name, some identification which perhaps Turan could recognize in turn. Zuha's hate, her frustration—those were so strong a wave that they were as blows against her, yet she probed.

"Zuha," she reported. "But there is another, some one behind Zuha. They came here seeking knowledge they did not discover. Zuha was very angry; she needed something she wanted desperately to find here. She— I think that she took some of these with her—the ones she believed important."

"If we can find no chart soon . . ." His thought trailed away.

Time—she could not defeat time. Ziantha tossed the cord bundle back with the others. Had she hours, perhaps days, she could sort through these. There must be another way, for she did not have those hours or days. She need only glance at Turan to know that.

An island risen from the sea, and on it somewhere a twin to the stone, an equal focus piece. Their piece tied to it, and they, apparently, tied to the first. If they could not release those ties, Turan would die again, and so would she—at the hands of Zuha—and no pleasant death.

One could believe that some essence of personality survived the ending of the body. Those with the talent were sure of that. But inbred in their varied species was so firm a barrier against their body's dismissal that they could not face what man called "death" without that safety device of struggle for existence taking over control. She would not accept the fact that she, Ziantha, was going to come to an end in this world which was not hers, any more than she believed that her companion could likewise surrender.

An island from the sea, and a stone found there— The girl strode back and forth, thinking furiously, before the bench on which Turan had half collapsed. There was one way, but she could not do it here. Not in the midst of enemies when at any moment those who had no reason to wish either of them life could come in upon them. But where?

Ziantha paused, looked around, tried to be objective. She had Vintra's memories to call upon and she did that recklessly. These people had aircraft. There was a landing port outside the city where such were kept. If Turan could pilot one—if they could first reach that landing port—commandeer one of the craft— Too many ifs, too many things that might stand between. But it was her—perhaps their—only hope.

She dropped down beside Turan, took his cold hand to hold between her two warmer ones, willing strength back into him. He opened his eyes, turned his head toward her.

Again that ghastly smile came. "I endure," he said, as if he not only meant to reassure her, but himself. "You have thought of something—what? I would think clearer but I must hold on, and at times that takes all my power."

"I know. Yes, I have thought of something. It may be far beyond what can be done, but it is all I have to offer. When I go into deep trance I must be in a safe place—"

His eyes were very intent. "You would try that, knowing what may come of it?"

"I can see no other way." She wanted him with desperate longing to deny that, to say there was another way, that she need not risk again the baleful influence of the stone that had already cost them so much. But he did not. Though he still regarded her closely, his mind-shield was up, and she believed he was testing her plan for feasibility.

"It is a way—" he said slowly. "But you are right, we must have privacy and safety before you try it. I do not believe we shall find either here. Turan's memories are so little open to me that I do not know what intrigues may be in progress. But they threaten from his own household. It is certainly not the first time a noble family came to an end by being torn apart from within. And where shall we find safety? Have you a plan for that also?"

"A weak one." She again wanted him to refuse, to prove her wrong. "These people have air transport. If we could get one—they are not too unlike our own flitters, I think—we might reach the sea. Find some safe place on the shore to give me time for deep trance—"

"It seems—" he was beginning when Ziantha whirled to face one of the mural-concealed doors in the wall.

The noise, a faint scratching, made her look about for something to use as a weapon. She was reaching for a tall vase on a nearby table when Turan pulled himself from the bench, walked with a slow, heavy tread to release the portal.

A man squeezed through a crack hardly wide enough to admit his stocky body and shut that opening at once behind him. The hair on his head was streaked with light patches, and his face was seamed with two noticeable scars.

"Lord Commander, thank Vut you are here!" He looked beyond Turan to Ziantha. "Also the outland witch with you."

"There is trouble, Wamage?"

The man nodded vigorously. "More than trouble, Lord Commander; there may be black disaster. She"—into that single pronoun he put such a hiss that he spat the word in anger and disgust—"she has sent to the priests. They are to take you and"—he pointed with his thumb to Ziantha—"this one to the Tower of Vut, that the miracle may be made manifest to all on the Tenth Feast Day. But they do not intend that you shall ever reach sanctuary. Behind all is Puvult, Lord Commander! Yes, you exiled him half a year gone, but there have been rumors he returned while you hunted the rebels northward. Since—since you were tomb-laid, he is seen openly. And secretly within these very walls!"

"The High Consort then welcomed him?" Turan asked.

"Lord Commander, it has long been said that she favors the younger branch of your House over the elder." Wamage did not quite meet Turan's eyes. It was as if he had news to give, but feared to offend.

"And with me tomb-laid then Puvult comes into headship?" If Turan meant that for a question, it did not alert Wamage, as far as Ziantha could tell, into any suspicion of his lord's memory.

"You spoke that with the truth-tongue, Lord Commander. They thought you gone—then you return—"

"With the added power of a miracle," Turan commented. "I can see how they want now to finish me."

Wamage ran his tongue over his lips. Once more he would not look at Turan but kept his eyes at some point over the other's shoulder.

"Lord Commander," he paused as if seeking courage to continue, and then went on in a rush of words, "*she* says that you are still tomb-laid—that this—this witch Vintra has only made a semblance of a man. Though one may touch you, as I have done, and you are firm and real! But *she* says that if you are taken to Vut the force will depart, and all men will see that this is sorcery and no real return. The priests, they are angry. For they say that in the past, Vut has returned men to life when their purposes here are not fully accomplished. And they do not believe her but want all the people to witness Vut's power. So they will come for you—only *she* has a way to make sure you do not reach Vut."

Turan smiled. "It would seem that she does not really believe in her own argument that I am but a rather solid shadow walking, or she would leave it to Vut to answer the matter."

Wamage made a small gesture. "Lord Commander, I think she believes two ways—she is fearful her own thought may be wrong. If you die again—then Vut's will is manifest."

"But I do not intend to die again." Turan's voice was firm. It was as if his strong will fed the talent which kept him alive. "At least not yet. Therefore I think I shall be safer—"

"We can get you to the Tower, Lord Commander. Vut's priests will then make a defense wall of their own bodies if the need arises!" Wamage interrupted eagerly.

Turan shook his head. "Do my own armsmen of Turan-la"—a shade of confusion crossed his face. "My armsmen of Turan-la," he repeated with a kind of wonder, Ziantha thought, as if he heard those words but did not fully understand them. Ziantha feared his confusion was visible to Wamage. But it would seem that the other was so intent upon his own message of gloom that his thoughts were for that alone. For he burst out then hotly:

"*She* sent them north after—after your entombing, Lord Commander. They were battle comrades of yours; they knew how you felt concerning Puvult. Me you can command under this roof, and Fomi Tarah, and of the younger men, Kar Su Pyt, Jhantan Su Ixto, and we each have armsmen sworn to us, as you know. Enough, Lord Commander, to see you safely to the Tower."

Turan was frowning. "There is another, not of this household, so he might not be suspected or watched. He lent me his weather coat on the night I returned—"

"Yes. I have sought him out. His father is a Vut priest, one Ganthel Su Rwelt. They live on the southern coast— the boy came with the levy from Sxark a year ago."

"From the southern coast!" Turan caught the significance of that at once. "Can you get word to him secretly?"

"I can summon him, but, Lord Commander, as you well know there are eyes and ears awake, watching, listening always amid these walls."

Turan sighed. His gaunt face looked even less fleshy, as if his grayed skin clung tighter and tighter to his skull. "Wamage." He returned slowly to his bench, sat down as if he could no longer trust the effort standing erect caused him. "I would leave this palace, the Lady Vintra with me. But I do not wish to go—as yet—to Vut. There is something to be done, something of which I learned of late, which cannot be left while I tend this ailing body of mine. For time may be fatal. I must be free to move without question or interference. Now I call upon you for your aid in my service, for if battle comrades cannot ask this, then what justice lies in this world?"

"Truth spoken, Lord Commander. Can you depend upon no other for this deed which must be done?" There was a furrow of what Ziantha believed to be honest anxiety between Wamage's bushy brows. If Turan had not managed to gain the loyalty of his High Consort, in this man, at least, he had one faithful follower.

"No other. I have spoken truth to you; now I shall add more. You know of my visit to the land that the sea gave up? Only recently you spoke of this—"

"A place you have often mentioned yourself, Lord Commander. You wished to take a ship of your own and go seeking it again, but the rebels broke out. But—what of it?"

"Just this—there I made a great find, a find which I must now uncover for my own safety."

"Lord Commander, you are in some fever dream, or else—" he swung to Ziantha, his face hard with suspicion— "there is some truth in the High Consort's babble, and this rebel woman has bewitched you. What could lie on a rock in the sea that would aid you now?"

"Something very old and very powerful, and this is no bewitchment. For what lies there I saw long before Vintra came into my life."

"The gem! The gem which you took to Vut's tower and thereafter put from you, having it made into tombwear so that none could lay hand on it."

"In part, yes, but only in part. How think you that the Lady Vintra, wearing it in a tomb crown, was moved to come to my aid, brought me again to this very room? There were ancients of ancients. Do not men declare that they had strange knowledge we do not possess? What of the old tales?"

"But those are for children, or the simple of mind. And we do with the aid of machines made by our own hands what they did in those tales. Who could fly save with a double-wing?"

"They, perhaps. There were things of great power on that island, Wamage, how great I did not even guess then. I thought of such treasure as delights the eye; now I know it was treasure for the mind. With what I once found there and what still awaits to be discovered, I shall be armed against the forces ready to pull me down. Has part not already brought me from the tomb?"

"And how do you reach the island?"

"By your aid and that of this youth from Sxark. You shall arrange for me and this lady—for she has learned part of the secret—"

Wamage moved with a speed Ziantha had not expected. Only the flash of mind-reading alerted her. He would have flamed her down with a small beamer he brought from his sleeve, but she had thrown herself flat.

"Wamage!" Turan was on his feet. "What do you do?"

"She is Vintra, Lord Commander. Every rebel drinks lorca-toast to her at night. If she has such command over any part of your fate she is better dead!"

"And me with her, is that what you would want, Wamage? For I tell you, it is by her I live, and without her further aid I cannot continue to do so."

"Sorcery, Lord Commander. Have in the priests and gain their aid—"

From where she crouched, Ziantha put all her talent into a mighty effort. His voice suddenly faltered, his hand dropped limply to his side, and from his fingers the beamer thudded to the carpeted floor. She retrieved it swiftly. The operation of it she saw was simple. One aimed and pressed a button. What the results would be Vintra's memory supplied; they were both spectacular and fatal.

"You should not have told him," she mind-sent.

"We need him. Otherwise we can make one blunder after another and achieve nothing."

To Ziantha's thinking one blunder had already been made, but she would have to accept Turan's plan. Could it be that he was making such an effort to retain control of his body that he no longer reasoned clearly, and the time would come when she must take command?

Reluctantly she released Wamage from the mind-lock. The man shook his head as if to banish some feeling of dizziness. As full consciousness returned to him Ziantha laid the beamer on the bench at Turan's hand.

"Look you, man of Singakok." She had from Vintra the heavily accented voice of the rebel leader. "I have now no weapon. There lies yours. At whose hand does it lie? Do you think that if I were your enemy in this hour I would disarm myself before you and your lord? I have no love for Singakok. But that which was beyond any struggle of ours faced me in the tomb of Turan, and he and I were bound together in this. Take up your weapon if you do not believe me, use it—"

If he tried that, Ziantha thought—if I have gambled too high—I hope Turan can stop him. But Wamage, though he put out his hand as if to carry out her suggestion, did not complete that move.

"She speaks the truth," Turan said. "She stands unarmed in the midst of her enemies, and she speaks the truth."

Wamage shook his head. "She is one of tricks, Lord Commander, as you know. How else have the rebels held us off this long? It is their tricks—"

"No trick in this. Vintra is no longer of the rebels."

"Do you want an oath on that before the altars of Vut?" Ziantha demanded. "I was bound to another cause by those hours in the dark before the spirit door opened. Do you think any man or woman could pass through such an ordeal as that and not come forth unchanged? For the present I am pledged to the Lord Commander and will be so until his mission is accomplished." She hoped that Wamage believed her—for in this she spoke Ziantha's truth.

Wamage looked from one to the other. "Lord Commander, I have been a battle comrade of yours since the action at Llymur Bay. I am sworn by my own choice to your service. What you wish—that shall it be."

Was this surrender coming too easily? Ziantha tried mental probe. The confusing in and out pattern of the alien mind could deceive her, whereas with her own kind she could easily have assessed friend or enemy.

"What I wish is a double-wing and the armsman from Sxark as a guide. The hour is late, and I must move tonight."

"It will be difficult—"

"I have not said this would move with ease; it is enough that it does move!" Turan's voice took on a deeper note; there was authority in the look he turned upon the other. "For if we do not go at once, we may be too late."

"This is also true," Wamage agreed. "Well enough." He became brisk, producing weather coats from one of the coffers, these with head hoods, and, as he pointed out, no insignia.

Part of the way out of the palace they could follow corridors private to the Lord Commander, where none could intrude without invitation— A fortunate custom, Turan noted to Ziantha as Wamage went ahead to make sure of their clear passage in the public parts of the building.

"Do you trust him?" Ziantha did not. "He may be more loyal to what he considers best for you than to any order from you. Vintra is too long and bitter an enemy for him to accept otherwise."

"We can not lean too heavily on trust, no. But can you see any other way to get us out of this trap? If he is loyal we have won; if he plays a double game, we shall have mind-search to warn us. It is a pity we can not read their patterns better."

But it seemed Wamage would prove loyal. He led them through an inconspicuous side entrance to a waiting car.

"The armsman will meet us at the port, Lord Commander. But we have half the city to cross. And much can happen before we get there."

"So let us be on our way!"

Wamage slipped behind the controls of the vehicle. It was smaller than the one which had brought them there, and Ziantha was cramped tightly in beside Turan. Wamage was immediately in front of her, and she must be instantly alert, she knew, to any sign that he was not carrying out his orders. Half the city to cross—it would be a long time to hold that guard. Turan had raised barriers again, perhaps because he had to retain his talent to aid his own feat of endurance.

10

Under other conditions, Ziantha thought fleetingly, she would have watched about her with wondering eyes. She was doing what no other, not even the Zacathans with all their learning, had been able to accomplish, seeing a Fore-runner civilization. But all that concerned her now was her own escape from it. It was necessary to concentrate on Wamage throughout this journey.

It would seem he was faithful to Turan's trust. At least the car traveled steadily, without hindrance, first along quiet streets and then along those filled with heavier traffic. If their escape had been discovered they were not yet pursued.

Wamage wove a twisted way from broad avenue to cross street and back. Ziantha had never had too keen a sense of direction; for all she knew they could be heading directly away from their goal. And Vintra's memory held little of Singakok.

The lights were bright as they took a last turn coming to a place where many cars were parked. Wamage slowed as he traversed this line of waiting vehicles, heading on past a lighted building.

To one side was a vast expanse lighted in part by rows of set flood lamps. There Ziantha saw one of the aircraft come into the light, turn rather clumsily, and rush forward, lifting after its run into the air. It was unlike the flitters of her own world, having fixed wings and apparently needing the forward run to make it airborne, rather than rising straight up as was normal.

Yet the Vintra part of her cringed at the sight of it, projecting to Ziantha a vivid and horrifying memory of death falling in objects that exploded upon impact. Objects that came from such a machine.

Was Turan a pilot? Vintra had no such knowledge. As Ziantha probed she received the impression that such a skill was difficult to learn and required long tutorage. Or was Wamage to serve them so, accompany them on what might be a vain search? Did Turan plan to take the other fully into his confidence? Or did he propose to put a mind-lock on the alien and so bend him to their aid? That she did not believe could be held for any length of time.

Wamage drove on. The lights were fewer. They now passed a line of flyers. He circled at the end of this and stopped by one much smaller craft.

What might have been a torch flashed in the night. Wamage turned off the lights of the ground car and leaned out of the window to call softly:

"Doramus Su Ganthel?"

"To answer, Commander!" came swift answer.

"You have done well." Turan spoke for the first time since they had left the palace. "My thanks to you, battle comrade."

"It is in my mind that perhaps I have done ill," Wamage replied, a tired, heavy note in his voice. "I do not know why you must do this thing—" He had half hitched about in his seat. "Lord Commander, this woman is your deadliest enemy. She is Vintra who swore before the Host of Bengaril to have your head on the tri-pole of rebel victory. Yet now—"

"Now, by the will of Vut, she serves me as no other can. Think you of where I have just come from, Wamage. If she wanted me dead would I not have remained there?"

"The High Consort speaks of sorcery—"

"For her own ends, and that you also know, Wamage. Was it not you who warned me of her, not once, but twice and more? I tell you that when I return all which puzzles you now will be resolved. But if I do not go— then between the High Consort and the priests I will indeed be returned to whence I came and that with haste."

Wamage sighed so heavily Ziantha could hear him. "That I cannot doubt, Lord Commander, having heard what I have heard. But if there is a third choice—"

"For my safety, Wamage, in this hour there is not! And above all what I must do now must be speedily done. The longer I waste here—the more chances there are for failure—"

He stepped out of the vehicle, and Ziantha made speed to follow him. The waiting armsman came to them.

"At your service, Lord Commander. What is your will?"

"To fly to the south coast where there is a place we may not be seen. This is of high importance, and it must be done with speed. You are a pilot?"

"Of my father's personal craft, Lord Commander. But a scout—I have not flown one—" He was beginning when Turan interrupted him.

"Then you shall gather air time in one tonight. Battle comrade"—he turned now to Wamage—"for what you have done this night I can never give thanks enough. You have indeed saved my life, or at least lengthened it. Let that always be remembered between us."

"Let me go with you—" Wamage put out a hand as if to clutch Turan's arm.

"I leave you for a rear guard, one to cover me. It is a hard thing I ask of you—"

"But nothing that I will not do. Guard your back, Lord Commander!"

Ziantha was aware he watched her as he delivered that warning.

"Be sure I do," Turan answered.

They climbed aboard the strange flyer, and with the armsman for pilot the machine came to vibrating life, swung around, and ran along the field, until Ziantha was sure there was trouble and it would not lift.

With a bounce it did, and she felt queasy as she never had in a flitter. In the cramped cabin she could feel the vibration through her body. And it seemed to her that flying in this Forerunner world was a more rigorous experience than she had been accustomed to.

"It is fortunate, Lord Commander," their pilot said, "that these scouts have instant clearance from the field with no questioning by the control tower. Else—"

"Else we would have had a story for them," Turan said. "Now we can rather plan on landing. Listen well, for much depends upon this. You must set us down in a place as near to the sea as you can take this flyer. And it must be done with as little chance of discovery as possible. We are seeking a source of power, something which lies on an island and to which we have a single pointer. With this—with this—" Turan had hesitated and then began again, "I can promise the future will be changed."

But he did not say whose future. Ziantha smiled in the dark. Turan's—the real Turan's influence must be great— or had been great that he could bind these two men to his purposes. Though Wamage had had his doubts. Perhaps a sensitive in this civilization where the power was apparently so little known could apply pressure without even realizing it. Though she knew that if there was need she could control the armsman for a short time as she had Wamage.

"There is the Plateau of Xuth, Lord Commander. It— it has such an evil reputation that not many seek it out, not since the days of Lord Commander Rolphri, though that is all countryman's talk—"

Countryman's talk, maybe—Ziantha caught a hint or two of what lay in his mind as he spoke—but he believes it holds a threat. I pick up fear which is not of other men but of something strange. If Turan caught that also he would seem to discount it, for he replied promptly:

"Xuth is to our purpose. You can pilot us there?"

"I believe so, Lord Commander."

"Well enough." Turan had edged a little forward in his place. He was intent upon what the armsman was doing, and Ziantha knew that he was striving to pick up from the other the art of flying this ancient machine.

Had the alien mind-patterns been easier to contact he would have had no difficulty. But having to make allowances for constant disruption of mind-touch, his concentration must be forced to a higher level. Without his asking she began to feed him power, give him extra energy. Nor did she cease to marvel at his great endurance.

They did not speak again. Perhaps their pilot thought they slept. Once or twice they saw the riding lights of what must be other aircraft, but none came near, nor did there appear to be any pursuit. However, doubt nibbled at Ziantha's confidence. Surely they could not have got away from Singakok and the High Consort as easily as this!

The night sky grayed; they were coming into day. Dawn and then the full sunrise caught them. For the first time in hours the armsman spoke:

"The sea, Lord Commander. We turn south now to Xuth."

Turan was half collapsed in his seat. Ziantha regarded him with rising concern. His look of fatal illness was heightened by the sunlight. Could he last? And this was so faint a hope they followed— She fought the fear that uncoiled within her, began to seep coldly through her body.

"Xuth, Lord Commander. I can set down, I think, along this line."

In spite of her resolution Ziantha closed her eyes as the nose of the flyer tilted downward and the machine began a descent. It seemed so vulnerable, so dangerous, compared to the flitters that she could only hope the pilot knew what he was doing and they were not about to crash against some unyielding stretch of rock.

The machine touched ground, bounced, touched again with a jar that nearly shook Ziantha from her seat. She heard a gasp from Turan and looked to him. The gray cast on his face was more pronounced; his mouth was open as if he were gasping for breath. Although the flyer ran forward, the pilot's tension suggested he was fearing some further peril.

They stopped and the pilot exhaled so loudly she could hear him. "Fortune has favored us, Lord Commander."

Ziantha looked out. Ahead was only emptiness, as if they were close to the edge of some cliff, a deduction which proved true as they climbed out into a brisk, whipping breeze and the full sun of midmorning.

Beyond, Ziantha could hear the wash of sea surf,

though there was more distance between the shore and the flyer than she had earlier believed. The pilot had landed on what was an amazingly level stretch of rock running like an avenue between tall monoliths and crags of rock.

There was no vegetation to be seen, and those standing stones were of an unrelieved black, though the surface on which they stood was of a red-veined gray rock. A sudden sobbing wail brought an answering cry from her, as she whirled about to face the direction from which that had come.

"Wind—in the rocks," Turan's voice, strained but no longer only a gasp.

But she wondered. Her sensitive's reaction to this place was sharp. As the armsman had hinted—there was evil here. She would not want to touch any of those strange black rocks, read what they held imprisoned in them. For there was such a sense of the past here—an alien past— as one might gather from the walls of a tomb, entirely inimical to all her life force. Those were not just rocks, standing upright because wind and erosion had whittled them so. No, they were alien, had been placed there for a purpose. Ruins—a long vanished city—a temple— Ziantha did not want to know which.

There were birds with brilliant yellow wings flashing in the sunlight out over the sea. But none approached the cliff edge, nor were there any droppings from roosts among the near stones, as if living things shunned Xuth. Ziantha probed Vintra's memory and received a troubled response. Xuth—yes, it had been known to the rebel. But only as a legend, a haunted place wherein some defeat of the past had overturned all rule and order and from which had sprung many of the ills of this world, ills which had festered until this latter-day rebellion had burst in turn.

Now she tested not Vintra's memory but her own talent. So much could influence that. Not only the weather, emotions, the very geography of the site, but also subtle emanations of her surroundings. Would that very ancient evil, which was like a faint, sickening odor in the nostrils, work to combat what she must do?

Keeping well away from any contact with the rocks, Ziantha went on toward the sound of the sea, coming out on a ledge that projected like the beginning of a long-lost bridge over the surf which constantly assaulted the wall below. There was no sign of any beach; the meeting of cliff and water displayed wicked teeth of smaller rocks, around which the sea washed with intimidating force.

But here, on this prong, she was free of the darkness the black monoliths radiated. If there was any place from which she could search the sea it was here where the spray rose high enough in the air to be borne inland, leaving a spattering of moisture along the ledge.

Having won freedom from that other influence, Ziantha felt she dared not return to it. Here and now she must make her attempt to find their guide.

"Here," she mind-sent. "There is too much residue of some old ill among the stones. I can only do this thing free of them."

"I am coming—"

She turned to watch him moving slowly, with such care as if he must plan and then enforce each movement of his body, none of which were instinctive now. He had waved back the pilot who remained by the flyer. And when he reached her his head was up, his eyes steady and clear.

"You are ready?"

"As much as I shall ever be." Now that the final moment before carrying out her decision had come she wanted to flee it. She had used the focus-stone to its full power before, and it had brought her here. When she used it again—where would it take her? And would the change be as entire, as binding, as it now was? She had the gem in her hand, but before she looked into it, surrendered to the talent, Ziantha made a last appeal.

"Anchor me. Do not let me be lost. For if I am—"

"We both are." He nodded. "I shall give you all I have to give, be sure of that."

"Then—" she cupped the stone between her hands, raised it to her forehead—

❖   ❖   ❖

The sea, the pound of the sea—wild, raging—the devouring sea! Around her the tower room trembled, the air was filled with the thunder of the waters. The anger of the sea against Nornoch. Would these walls stand through this storm? And if they did—what of the next and the next—?

Ziantha—no, who was Ziantha? A name—a faint flash of memory to which she tried to cling even as it vanished, as a dream vanishes upon waking. D'Eyree!

"D'Eyree!" her voice rang above the clamor of the storm, as if she summoned herself from sleep to face what must come.

She raised her hands uncertainly before her. Surely she should have been holding something—on the floor—look! The urgency, the fear of loss gripped her, sent her to her knees, her hands groping across the thick carpet.

Her every movement brought a clash, a jangling from the strings of polished shells which formed her skirt, just as they fashioned the tight, scant bodice which barely covered her flat breasts. Her skin—green, pale green, or gold—or blue—no, that color came from the scales which covered her, like small dim jewels laid edge to edge.

She was D'Eyree of the Eyes. The Eyes!

No longer did she run her hands across the floor in vain search. She had had such a foolish thought. Where would the Eyes be but where they had always rested since the Choosing made her what she was? She raised her fingers now to touch that band about her forehead with the two gems she could not see, only feel, one above each temple, just as they should be. How could she have thought them lost?

She was D'Eyree and—

She was—Ziantha! A flooding of memory, like a fire to cleanse the mist in her mind. Her head snapped up and she looked around at strangeness.

The walls of the oval room were opaline, with many soft colors playing across them, and they were very smooth as might be a shell's interior. The carpet on the floor was rusty red, soft and springy with a strange life of its own.

There were two windows, long and narrow slits. She went hastily to the nearest. She was Ziantha—no, D'Eyree!

The Eyes—they fought to make her D'Eyree. She willed her hands to pull at the band that bound them to her head. Her fingers combed coarse hair like thick seaweed but could not move that band.

Ziantha must hold to Ziantha—learn where Nornoch might be.

She looked out, ducking as spray from the storm-driven waves fell salty on her face. But she glimpsed the other towers; this portion of Nornoch was guardian to the land behind, where she was warden.

Only, the sea was winning; after all these centuries it was winning. Her people held this outpost, and when the Three Walls were breached, when the sea came again— they would be swept away, back and down, to become, if any survived, what they had once been; mindless living things of the under-ooze. But that—that would not be! Not while the Eyes had a voice, a mind! Six eyes and their wearers—one for each wall still.

She leaned against the slit, a hand to each side of it, fighting for calm. Bringing all the power which was D'Eyree's by both inheritance and training to subdue this stranger in her mind, she put her—it—away and concentrated on that which was her mission, to will the walls to hold, to be one with the defense.

Think of her wall, of how the creatures, the Lurla, had built it and the two others from secretions of their own bodies over the centuries, of how those creatures had been fed and tended, bred and cherished by the people of Nornoch to create defenses against the sea. *Will* the Lurla to work, now—will!—will! She was no longer even D'Eyree; she was a will, a call to action so that creatures stirred sluggishly began to respond. Ah, so slowly! Yet they could not be prodded to any greater efforts or speed.

Secrete, build, strengthen—that Nornoch not yield! Move, so that the waves do not eat us into nothingness again. The Eyes—let the power that is in the Eyes goad the Lurla to awake and work.

But so few! Was that because, as D'Fani said, her people had dared turn away from the old ways—the sacrifices? Will—she must not let her thoughts, her concentration stray from what was to be done. Lurla—she

could see them in her mind—their sluglike bodies as they
crawled back and forth across the wall which was her own
responsibility, leaving behind them ever those trails of
froth that hardened on contact with the air and steadily
became another layer within the buttress foundations of
the Three Walls, the towers. Stir, Lurla! Awake, move—
do this for the life of Nornoch!

But they were more sluggish than they had ever been.
Two dropped from the walls, lay inert. What was—?
D'Eyree raised her hands from the walls, pressed her
palms to the Eyes, feeling their chill.

Awake, Lurla! This is no time to sleep. The storm is
high; do you not feel the tower shake? Awake, crawl,
build!

Lurla—it was as if she raised her voice to shriek that
aloud.

The sea's pound was in her ears, but fainter, its fury
lessened. Then D'Fani was wrong; this was not one of
the great storms after all. She need not have feared—

"Ziantha!"

There was no window through which she looked. She
was in the open with a bird's screams sounding above the
surf. And before her, hands on her shoulders (as if those
hands had dragged her out of the time and place that had
been), Turan.

She wrested herself from his grip to wheel about on
the rock, face out over the waves, straining as if she could
from this point catch a glimpse of Nornoch, learn whether
its towers, the Three Walls, were still danger-wrapped,
if the Lurla had been kept to their task.

No, that was all finished long ago. How long? Her talent could not answer that. Perhaps as many years stood
now between D'Eyree and Vintra as between Vintra and
Ziantha. And that number her mind reeled from calcu-
lating.

Only now she knew where Nornoch lay, if any of
Nornoch still survived. That much they had gained. She
pointed with an outflung hand.

"Over sea—or under it—but there!" She spoke aloud,
for the burden of weariness which followed upon a trance

lay on her. And she allowed Turan to take her hand, draw her back to the flyer.

As if their coming was a signal, the armsman came out of the cabin. Beneath his close-fitting helmet hood his face was anxious.

"Lord Commander, I have had it on the wave-speak. They are using S-Code—"

Vintra's memory identified that for her and, lest Turan's memory no longer served him, Ziantha supplies what she knew by mind-touch. "A military code of top security."

"The rebels—" Turan began.

But the armsman shook his head. "Lord Commander, I was com officer for my unit. They hunt you and—they have orders to shoot you down!"

There was a look of misery on his young face, as if the first shock had worn off so he could believe, even if he did not understand.

"Zuha must be desperate," Ziantha commented.

"It does not matter. Only time matters," Turan returned. "Battle comrade, here we must part company. You have served me better than you will ever know. However I cannot take you with us farther—"

"Lord Commander, wherever you go, then I shall fly you!" His determination was plain.

"Not to Nornoch—" what made Ziantha say that she did not know.

His head jerked around. "What—what do you know of Nornoch?"

"That it holds what we seek," she answered.

"Lord Commander, do not let her! Nornoch—that is a story—a tale of the sea that sailors have used to frighten their children since the beginning. There is no Nornoch, no fish-people, except in evil dreams!"

"Then in dreams we must seek it."

The armsman moved between them and the cabin of the flyer. "Lord Commander, this—this rebel has indeed bewitched you. Do not let her lead you to your death!"

Tired as she was Ziantha did what must be done, centering her power, thrusting it at him as she might have thrust with a primitive spear or sword. His hands went to his head; he gave a moaning cry and stumbled back, away, until he wilted to the ground well beyond the wing shadow of the flyer.

"Ill done," she said, "but there was naught else—"

"I know," Turan said, his voice as flat, sounding as tired as she felt. "We must go before he revives. Where we go we cannot take him. You are sure of the course?"

"I am sure," she answered steadily as they climbed into the cabin.

11

Ziantha wanted to close her eyes as Turan brought the flyer's engines to life and headed toward the sea. Would the craft lift into the sky, or would they lose altitude and be licked down by the hungry waves below? That he had learned all he could from the pilot, she knew, but his first flight alone might be his last. They were out—over the water—and for a heart-shaking moment, Ziantha thought they had failed. Then the nose of the flyer came up. There was a terrible look of strain on Turan's gaunt face, as if by will alone he lifted them into the sky.

She held the focus-stone cupped in her hands, ever aware of the thread of force which pulled. But where lay the other Eye now? Beneath the ocean where they could not find it?

She concentrated on that guide, being careful, however, not to let the stone draw her into a trance. And to keep that delicate balance of communication between the focus and the retention of her own identity was exhausting. Also her strength of body was beginning to fail. She was aware of hunger, of thirst, of the need for sleep, and she willed these away from her, employing techniques Ogan had long drilled into her to use her body as a tool and not allow its demands to rise paramount.

How far? That was of the greatest importance. The flyer might not be fueled for a long trip. And if they could not land when they reached their goal—what then?

Ziantha kept her mind closed, asked no questions of
Turan, knowing that his failing strength was now centered
on getting them to their goal. And her part was that of
guide.

Time was no longer measured. But the girl became
aware that that thread which had been so slight on their
setting forth from land was growing stronger, easier to
sense. And with that realization her confidence arose. The
stone was growing warmer, and she glanced at it quickly.
Its brilliance had increased and it gave off flashes of light,
as if it were a communication device.

"The stone," she spoke aloud, not using mind-touch
lest she disturb his concentration, "it is coming to life!"

"Then we must be near—" His voice was very low,
hardly above a whisper.

But if the sea covered—

Ziantha moved closer to the vision port, tried to see
ahead. The sun's reflection from the waves was strong
but— A dark shadow, rising from the sea!

"Turan, an island!"

The flyer circled it. What Ziantha could see was forbidding; jagged spires of rock, no vegetation. Where could
they land? Had this been a flitter of their own time and
world they would need only a reasonably open space to
set down. But she had seen the take-off of these ancient
machines and knew they required much more.

As Turan circled he spoke:

"It is larger than I expected. Either the report was
wrong, or more of it has arisen since the first upheaval."

"Look!" Ziantha cried. "To the south—there!"

A stretch of great blocks of masonry locked together,
stretching from the cliffs of the inner portion of the island
out into the waves. Those dashed against it, leaving it wet
with spray. It might have been a pier fashioned to accom-
modate a whole fleet of vessels.

"Can you land on that?"

"There is one way of proving it." And it would seem
Turan was desperate enough to try.

This time Ziantha did shut her eyes as he banked and
turned to make the run along that strange sea-wet roadway, if road it was. She felt the jarring impact of their

first touch, the bumps and bounces as they hurtled along a surface that was plainly not as smooth as it had appeared from the air. Then the vibration of the motor died. They came to a stop without crashing against a rock or diving headlong into the waiting waves.

When she dared to look she saw the vision port wet with spray. The flyer rocked slightly under the pound of water, diffused though that was by the time it reached them. They were safely down.

"Turan!" She glanced around. He had slumped in his seat. She caught his shoulder, shook him. "Turan!"

He turned his head with painful slowness. There was the starkness of death in his eyes.

"I cannot hold—much longer— Listen, open your mind!"

Stiff with fear, she dropped the focus-stone into her lap so that no emanation of that could befog reception for her and leaned forward, set her hands on either side of his head, held it, as if he were some artifact she must read for her life's sake.

Information flooded into her mind—all that he had picked up from the armsman, how to fly them away when what she had come to do was finished, and what she must do afterward if she were successful here.

She accepted this. Then she protested:

"Hold fast! You must hold fast. For if you cannot—then—"

To be entrapped here forever! In a way that was worse than death. Or would death free him when it took back the body it had never fully released to life? Ziantha did not know. All she was sure of was that she could not allow him to die here. That she must, if she could, not only find the key for her return, but also for his.

She leaned closer to him, and instinct moved her to another kind of touch, one that carried in it the seeds of vigorous life as her kind knew it. As her lips met his cold, flaccid ones, she willed her energy into him.

"Hold!"

But there was so little time. Ziantha struggled with the catch on the cabin door, forced it open, stepped out. She cupped the focus-stone to her breast and started back along the causeway. From the air it had looked shorter than it was. The flyer had come to a halt about halfway along it, and there was a wide stretch to traverse before she would reach the sharp rise of the main portion of the island.

It was plain that this roadway was not natural but the work of hands, and also that it had been long under the sea. It was encrusted with shells, and there were patches of decaying water weeds still rooted to it. The stones from which it was fashioned were huge blocks, some fully the size of the flyer in length, and so well set together that even the centuries and the sea had not pulled one from the other.

The draw of the focus-stone was now so strong that she felt as if a real cord were looped about the gem dragging her forward. Somewhere ahead lay the other end of that cord. But where in that maze of rock could it be?

Her road ended in a jumble of huge blocks, as if some structure had been shaken down there, yet the focus still pulled. Ziantha began a painful climb in and among the stones. The clothing she wore had never been intended for such usage. And her knees were scraped and bleeding after two unlucky falls, two of her fingernails torn to the quick, her palm gashed by a sharp shell edge.

But she fought her way on and up that mountain of tumbled stone until she reached a point above. And there—

Although the cord continued to pull there was no further advance. For before her was another of the incredibly ancient structures, only this had no break. It was a smooth wall projecting from the cliff behind it.

Ziantha ran her bleeding hand across its surface, seeking an opening her eyes might not be able to detect; there was nothing to meet her touch. Yet she knew that behind this lay what she sought. With a whimper of despair, the girl sank down at the foot of the wall. Her hands could not tear a way through that. Perhaps there was some weapon or tool in the flyer—but she doubted it. This masonry which had withstood sea burial for centuries could not easily be broached.

There was only one way, and she dreaded it. She could

not depend on any backing. To call upon Turan to support her through a trance might mean his death. Yet she must take this final step, or they would fail, and failure would mean they would end here. That inborn spark of refusal to accept death without a struggle that was the heritage of her own species stiffened her resolution. She set the focus-stone to her forehead.

Once more she was in that nacre-walled room. The Eyes in their band rested heavy on her forehead, just as a weariness which was of the spirit as well as of the body weighed on her heavily. There was fear as dark about her as if shadows drew in from the gleaming walls to smother her.

The storm—she had lasted out the storm, kept the Lurla to their labor of strengthening the walls—but just barely. They had resisted—resisted! With a small hiss of breath she faced what that meant. Her power, her control over the Eyes, must be fading. And it was time for her—

No! It was not time! She was not that old, that weak! The storm had been greater than any they had known before, that was all. And the Lurla had tired. It was not her control slipping. She looked down at her still-rounded body, firm under the veiling of her shell-string clothing. No, she was not ready to put off the Eyes, to take the next remorseless and inevitable step her abdication would lead to.

D'Eyree crossed to the window slit. Now storm-driven waves had subsided for this time. Still the sea looked sullen, angry, and even the tint of the sky was ominous. If the calculations of D'Ongi were right—

Through the sighing of the sea, she heard a slight sound behind her, turned to face a woman standing at a door that had opened in the apparently seamless wall. She was slight, her coarse hair the darkest green of youth. Her body was bare, sleek, and glistening from recent immersion in the sea, her neck gills still a little open.

"Honor to the Eyes," the woman said, but there was mockery in that hail. "There is good gleaning in the storm leavings. Also, D'Huna has spoken—she finds the burden of the Eyes now beyond her power."

And all the time she watched D'Eyree with cruel and greedy eyes.

Ah, yes, D'Atey, how much you wish that I would also resign this power! D'Eyree forced herself not to put hand to the Eye band. D'Atey, you have never rested content since the Eyes came to me and not to you, and you have so carefully provided that you sister-kin will have the next chance to stand for warden. But D'Huna—she is five seasons younger than I! And that will be remembered. I am not loved too greatly in Nornoch. It has been my way to walk a lone path. Yet that I cannot alter, for it is a part of me. Only now—who will stand to my back if clamor grows?

"D'Huna has served well." Carefully she schooled her voice. This one must not suspect she had scored with her news.

"She may serve even better." A pointed tongue showed, caressed D'Atey's lips as if she savored some taste and would prolong that pleasure. "There is a meeting of the warriors' council—"

D'Eyree stiffened and then forced herself to relax, hoping that the other had not seen that momentary betrayal of emotion, though she feared that nothing escaped those vicious, envious eyes of D'Atey's.

"Such is not by custom. The Eyes did not attend—"

"D'Fani holds by the Law of Triple Danger. In such times the warriors are independent of the Eyes. That, too, is custom."

D'Eyree, by great effort, bit back an exclamation. D'Fani was the fanatic, the believer in the old dark ways the people had set aside—D'Fani who talked of the Feeding— If D'Fani gained followers enough what might happen?

"They meet now, the warriors." D'Atey moved a little closer, her eyes still searching D'Eyree's face for some sign of concern. D'Fani speaks to them. Also the Voice of the Peak—"

"The Voice of the Peak," D'Eyree interrupted her, "has not uttered for as many years as you have been hatched, D'Atey. D'Rubin himself could not make it answer when he worked upon its inner parts this past year. The ancients had their secrets and we have lost them."

"Not so many as we thought were lost. And perhaps it was because we sought other paths, less hard ones, weaker ones. But D'Tor has found a way to make the Voice utter. He follows his brother in seeking the wisdom of the old ways. Rumor says now our future will be shortened if we do not find a way to rebreed the Lurla. D'Huna failed with three of them during the storm."

Three? She had failed to spur *three*! But there had been *four* that resisted D'Eyree. And D'Huna had resigned the Eyes. Thus it would follow that she must also— But what had D'Atey earlier hinted at? She must know more.

"You spoke of D'Huna serving better." She hated to ask a question of D'Atey; there was a gloating about the other which fed her own inner fear. "What mean you by that?"

"If the Voice foretells another storm, then D'Fani will have a powerful voice in the council. Are the Eyes not vowed for their lifetime to the service of Nornoch? How better can they serve, once their power over the Lurla has waned, than to provide strength for the Lurla to procreate in greater abundance? Once the Feeding was custom. It is only the weaklings of these latter days who want it set aside—"

This time D'Eyree could not control her slight hiss of breath, though she writhed inwardly a second later when she saw the flash of triumph in D'Atey's eyes.

"The Feeding was of the old days, when the people followed dark customs. There is the Pledge of D'Gan that we be no longer barbarians of the dark. Have we risen from the muck to choose once more to live in it?"

"D'Fani believes that our weakness in listening to D'Gan and his like has doomed us. How find you the Lurla, Eyes Wearer? Are they as strong, as obedient to your orders as they have always been?"

D'Eyree forced a smile. "Ask that of Nornoch, D'Atey. Has a tower tumbled? Have the walls cracked in any storm?"

"Not this time perhaps. But if the Voice says there will be a second storm, a third—" Now D'Atey smiled. "I think after D'Huna's report, D'Fani will have many listening to him. He may even call for a trial of power, D'Eyree. Think you well on that."

She nodded and slipped away. D'Eyree looked once more to the sea. The Voice—had D'Fani's brother really repaired it? Or was it, as more likely, some trick of D'Fani's to influence the council and the people to plunge back into the old ways from which D'Gan had raised them? The Voice was set on the highest peak within the Three Walls. In the old days it had predicted accurately the coming of storms. But custom had been its conqueror. For by custom only one line of the people serviced the Voice, understood its intricate mechanism. And when the Plague of the Red Tide Year had struck, those who had understood the Voice had been, for some reason, the first stricken.

For years it had continued to operate even though those who had once tended it were gone. And the people had been lulled into believing that it was indestructible. Then it slowed, became inaccurate by days with its warnings. Finally it stopped. Though men had labored for two generations now to relearn its workings, they had been uniformly unsuccessful. The belief had been held for a long time that, like the Lurla, the Voice answered to mental control—a control inherited by the one clan that no longer existed. There were no visible focus points of communication to be discovered, nothing like the Eyes.

The Eyes—and D'Huna had surrendered hers! Perhaps she had surrendered even more as D'Atey had suggested. Of course the Lurla no longer bred as they once did. But their number had always been carefully controlled as was needful. However, suppose that a mutant strain had developed, one not so quick to answer to the dominance of the Eyes? The people had changed over the centuries since they had ventured forth step by step from the sea. They were amphibians now. But the fear had always hung over them that if they were forced out of Nornoch, which was their grip upon the land, they would lose their hard-won intelligence and revert again to sea creatures who could not think of themselves as human.

To return to feeding the Lurla on food long forbidden— could that be right? D'Gan had taught that such practices were savage, reducing those who held them to the status of one of the fanged sea raiders.

The band that held the Eyes seemed to press so tightly on D'Eyree's forehead that it was a burden weighting her head; she could not carry it proudly aloft as became her. She returned to the window slit, resting her head against its solid frame, the breeze from the sea cool and moist against her scaled skin. She was so tired. Let those who had never worn the Eyes, carried that burden, think of the powers and privileges of her position. The weight, fear, and responsibility of it was far heavier than any respect could bolster.

Why then not follow D'Huna, admit that the Lurla had been sluggish for her, that four had failed? But if she did that, she was surrendering another kind of wall to D'Fani and those who followed him. The only possible wearers of the Eyes were very young, easily influenced, and one was D'Wasa, whom D'Eyree did not trust.

No, as long as she could, she must not surrender to her weariness, the more so if the Feeding returned. Not only did her whole being shrink from the very thought of that horror for herself; she knew it would also be throwing open the gate to the worst of the people.

Yet if the Voice proclaimed another such storm ahead, and D'Fani called for a trial of power before that came—

She was like one swimming between a fanged raider and a many-arms, with cause to believe that each was alerted to her passing and ready to put an end to her. And she was so tired—

D'Huna—she would go to D'Huna. She must know more of the failure of the Lurla—whether the other believed what she herself suspected, that it was not the fault of the Eyes, but of a mutation in the Lurla themselves. Knowledge was strength and the more knowledge she could garner the better she could build her own defense.

Even if D'Huna had surrendered her Eyes, she would not have left her tower. That by custom she could not do until the new wearer entered into it and took formal possession. So there was yet time.

D'Eyree threaded a way along nacre-walled corridors, climbed down in one section, up in another. The majority of the people never came into these link-ways between the towers. The privacy of the wearers was well guarded, lest they be disturbed at some time when it was necessary to check upon the Lurla or otherwise use their talent. And with a council in progress and the possibility of the Voice making some pronouncement, the attention of most of Nornoch would be centered elsewhere.

She passed no one during her journey; the towers might be deserted. Though there were six wearers on permanent duty, two for each wall. If D'Caquk and D'Lov had heard the news, there was no indication they stirred to hear more. The pale glow of the in-lights shone above their doors as she passed. Then she came to D'Huna's tower.

With her webbed fingers D'Eyree rapped out their private call code. Slowly, almost reluctantly, the slit door opened, and she stepped into a room the duplicate of her own. D'Huna faced her, looking strange without the Eyes. D'Eyree had never seen her without them since they had become wearers on the same day.

"Kin-close," D'Eyree spoke first, a little daunted by the unfocused stare the other turned on her—as if D'Eyree were not there at all. "I have been told a tale I cannot believe." Her voice trailed away.

"What can you not believe?" D'Huna asked in a voice as lacking in animation as her face. "That I have put aside the Eyes, that I am no longer to watch and ward? If it is of that you speak, it is the truth."

"But why have you done this thing? All—all of us know that the Lurla can be sluggish at times, that it is hard to drive them to their task. Of late years this has grown more and more the case."

"With the storm," D'Huna did not answer her directly, "I learned what the Lurla have become. Three would not answer the Eyes, even when I used the full force of my will. Therefore I failed Nornoch by so much. Let another who can bring more force to bear take my place, lest the wall crack at last."

"Are you sure that another can do better?"

At that sharp question life showed in D'Huna's face; there was a flicker in her large eyes. She stared at D'Eyree as if she still wore the Eyes, was attempting to bring their strength to bear on her sister wearer, to read her thoughts.

"What do you mean?" she asked.

"Have you sensed no difference in the Lurla?" D'Eyree might be grasping now for a small scrap of hope, but if she could make D'Huna question her own self-judgment perhaps there was a way out for them all. "As I have said, they have been sluggish of late. Perhaps it is not that our powers fail, but that the Lurla are more armored against us."

"Be that so—then it will be also said that the Feeding once made them obey, that without it they are beyond our holding. Let another who is newly trained, perhaps stronger, stand in my place and try."

The Feeding! So D'Huna was half converted to that belief. But did she not understand the danger in allowing that thought to spread? Perhaps she, D'Eyree, should keep to herself the observations she had made, or she would be giving ammunition to the enemy.

But even as she reflected, D'Huna's expression changed. She threw off that blankness and her interest awakened.

"So—you have found them sluggish. Tell me—how many failed *you* this time!"

"Why should you—"

"Why should I think that?" D'Huna countered. "Because you are afraid, D'Eyree. Yes, I can read it in you, this fear. You sought me out, wishing to learn why I put off the Eyes. That being so, I think that it follows that you have also found your power failing you. There is no place for a wearer whom the Eyes fail. Would you be humbled before all the people by being forced to a trial? Set aside the Eyes by your own will; let them not be torn from you so that all may see a piteous thing worthy of contempt!"

"It is not so easy." D'Eyree longed to deny the other's accusation. But one cannot tell untruths to a wearer. "D'Fani speaks with the council. He urges a return to the Feeding; he promises the Voice will speak—"

"Suppose that it does and it tells of another storm such as that just past? And suppose a wearer who no longer has full power strives to keep the Lurla to their task and fails—shall Nornoch then fall because of her pride?"

"It is not pride, no—nor fear, save a little," D'Eyree protested. "If we revert to the Feeding, then, I believe, it is better we quickly, cleanly, return through wind and wave to that which brought us forth, not sink back by degrees, forgetting all D'Gan taught. For the Feeding is evil, that I believe above all!"

"Which is strange coming from one sworn to nurture the Lurla above even her own life!" It was a man's voice.

D'Eyree spun around to face the speaker.

D'Fani! she shaped his name with her lips but did not utter it aloud.

12

He stood there arrogantly, taller than most other males, if less robust of body. His quick, dominant mind blazed through his eyes. At that moment D'Eyree in a flash of intuition knew what made him a threat to her and all her kind. D'Fani had part of the power, not as the wearers had it, but enough so he resented that he had not the right to the Eyes. Because he lacked them he was her enemy.

D'Fani was no warrior either. He was inept with any weapon save his tongue and his mind. But those he had sharpened to his use so that he had gained ascendancy over others with greater strength. In their world he had carved a place, now he aspired to a greater one.

In this moment of their eyes' meeting, D'Eyree knew this. Now she not only feared for herself, and vaguely for Nornoch; she feared for a way of life that D'Fani would destroy so that he might rule.

"You are sworn to defend the Lurla," he repeated when she made no answer. "Is that not so, Eye Wearer?" There was in him that same strain of cruel maliciousness which D'Atey showed, save that here it was a hundred times the worse.

"I am sworn so," D'Eyree answered steadily. "I am also sworn to the way of D'Gan." Her future might be forfeit now. She had feared such a meeting, yet at this moment she drew upon some inner strength she had not known she possessed.

"If the Lurla die, then where do the precepts of a man already long dead lead us?" He had assumed the mask of someone being reasonable with a child or one of little understanding. But D'Fani classed all females as such.

To argue with him was folly; she could make no impression, that she knew. And that he would force a trial on her was probable. Would any of the other wearers support her? She thought that she dared not count on that, not after this exchange with D'Huna. It would seem she had dragged disaster upon herself by this impulsive visit here. But, that being so, she must waste no time in regrets but turn her whole mind to the struggle D'Fani would make her face. As much time as she had—

Time? Something dim, a wisp of memory stirred deep in her mind—a strange memory she did not understand. Time was important, not only to her but to someone else— Just as in that flash D'Fani's motives had been clear for her to read, so now did she have an instant of otherness—a sensation of being another person. It was frightening, and her hands went to her forehead, to press above the Eyes.

What had she seen, felt, in that moment of disorientation? It was gone, yet it left behind a residue of feeling, or urgency that she must accomplish some necessary act. With the techniques of a wearer she willed that away. Only D'Fani was important now.

"Do those weigh heavily upon you, Wearer?" he demanded. "There is a remedy. Put them off. Or would you have them taken from you for failure, after proof before the people that the Lurla will no longer answer you?"

"There can be no such proof!" She held her head high. That teasing memory-which-was-not-true was gone. "Who are you to presume to judge a wearer's fitness?"

She was reckless, excited, as if she were forced to challenge him so that no more time would be wasted. And her words reacted on him as one of the mind-thrusts did upon a Lurla. He did not visibly twist under it, but the color of his scaled flesh deepened.

"There is one way to judge a wearer—a trial. And since D'Huna has relinquished her Eyes, there is already one arranged. It would seem you will have a part in it also."

Did he expect her to beg off? If so he would be disappointed. Half-consciously she had known this would be the end. Her voice was still even and controlled as she answered:

"So be it, then."

Whatever mission had brought him to D'Huna's quarters seemed forgotten as, with a gloating look at D'Eyree, he left. When he was gone D'Eyree turned to the other woman.

"You gave him an open door when you put aside the Eyes."

"And you gave him another," D'Huna replied. "I was obeying the law when I could no longer control the Lurla. If you do no better, then the longer you hold the Eyes, the more you are at fault."

"And if D'Fani sweeps the council and the people with him back to the old dark ways? Do you not remember the Chronicles of the Wearers—who were the first to be subjected to the Feeding? Are you martyr enough to ask for that? How much better can D'Fani make plain his power than by such a spectacle?"

"We vowed when we put on the Eyes to abide by the law—"

D'Eyree flung out one hang in an impatient gesture. "Do not quote law to me—not when it means the Feeding! Not when it serves D'Fani to climb to the rulership of Nornoch! Though do not fear—if he has his will *I* shall furnish the banquet—not you."

She turned her back on the other; any more words between them would give D'Fani weapons to use against her. And she was not what she had accused D'Huna of being, a willing martyr.

Back she went to her own tower, trying to think, to control those fears D'Fani brought to her mind. But it was when she looked from the sea-window that she was shocked out of her preoccupation. There were the signs she had been trained to read—another storm was on the way.

For one to follow so quickly upon the last was unnatural. And the Lurla were tired; they should have rest and the nourishment of their specially grown food. Also— D'Huna's section of the wall now had no warden.

The Lurla— D'Eyree used the Eyes to look into their burrows. They lay flaccid, thick rolls of boneless flesh, upon the flooring. There was not even a twitching. She tried a thought probe. One—two—raised their fore-ends a little. The rest lay supine, inert. And they did not have that bloated look of afterfeeding.

For the first time D'Eyree did then what it was against all custom to do. She allowed her thought-sight to invade the Lurla pens of the other wearers. In each she noted those which seemed well fed, but there were a far greater number who were not. and some of those in the other pens were moving restlessly, angrily. If this were reported—more fuel for D'Fani!

Her weather-wise eyes told her there was perhaps a day before the storm gathered to full strength. Long enough for D'Fani to strike. There was nothing she could do—or was there?

The Lurla fed on cultures blended by a time-tested formula devised by D'Gan. But before that— She used the Eyes again in a manner she had never tried before, not certain whether they could so serve her, not to watch, to encourage the Lurla—but rather to trace through the walls and the rock of this island certain ancient channels she knew of only by tradition. And to her relief she found she could do this.

Heartened by her first success, D'Eyree explored farther and farther, concentrating on those hidden ways so they also formed pictures in her mind. At last she found the outer gate, and it did give into the sea, well under the surface waves. Now—

D'Eyree gathered her power. There was plenty of life force in the water, though she could not distinguish the separate forms which emitted it, only the impact of the life itself. She began to use thought even as she used it to send the Lurla to labor. But this time she strove to entice, to draw it after her as a fisherman pulls a loaded net.

She played, angled, worked with concentration. In hardly daring to believe that she was succeeding, D'Eyree retraced those long forgotten and unused inner tunnels, bringing the life down them, and so into those pools where the culture for feeding was kept. Three times she made the awesome journey from the sea to the pool by which the Lurla sprawled inertly.

How much life she had so snared she could not tell, save that the vigorous force of it registered. Now D'Eyree turned her attention to one of the unfed Lurla—that nearest to the pool. As she would urge it to work during the storm, she used her talent as a lash to push it toward the pool. It moved weakly, as if so far spent that the least effort exhausted it, but it did move.

Then—

It had reached the pool side. There was a quiver of interest, of awakening. A moment or so later she knew that the first part of her experiment was working. The Lurla was aroused to feed, and it was absorbing the life force.

Not only that but the radiation of its satisfaction was reaching its fellows. They were beginning to crawl toward the pool, to share the feast. Exhausted, she threw herself on the soft carpet, sundering contact with the Lurla in order to strengthen her control. If the Lurla fed well and throve on the bounty of the sea, then D'Fani would be answered and would not dare propose the Feeding. They need only activate the old food tunnels. Of course, in time they would face the same problem which D'Gan's generation had known before them: the inability to continue to feed the Lurla with natural food in quantity enough to build up their strength, especially after great storms had driven the sea dwellers into the depths. But a breathing space in which to defeat D'Fani's immediate plan was all she wanted now.

Time—

Again she was shaken by an uncurling of strange memory. Something far buried in her clamored for expression. D'Eyree sat up, drawing her bent knees close to her breast, her arms about them, huddling in upon herself as she battled with that part of her mind that seemed to be an invader. There was no time— Why did that haunt her so? Yet she would not explore behind that thought; she was afraid to do so with a fear as deadly as her distrust of D'Fani.

A sound—it echoed, vibrated through the walls of the tower—through her body.

The Voice! It had never been heard in her lifetime, but there was no mistaking it for anything else. D'Fani had in so much backed his boasts—the Voice was speaking.

No words, just the rhythm of its beat. But that entered into one's body, one's mind! D'Eyree cried out. For the vibration centered in the Eyes, and they caused such a blaze of pain that she rolled across the floor, now whimpering in gasps of agony, clawing at the band that held the source of torture against her skull.

Somehow she got it loose, dragged it off. Then she lay panting, the relief so great she could only grasp that the pain was gone. Still the beat of the Voice shook her bone and flesh, and somehow its meaning was clear in her mind.

As she had drawn that life force in the sea to feed the Lurla, just so was she being drawn. Yet something within her, some hard core which was herself, D'Eyree, was still firm against that pull. And random thoughts drew together.

In all the tales of the Voice she had never heard of this effect. This was something different—wrong. The Voice was a warning, a defense for the people. It did not beat down the mind, control one. What had D'Fani done to unleash this?

Wrong, all wrong! The realization of that was strong inside her. This was a tampering, an assault— Still, even as she thought that she was crawling against her will on hands and knees toward the door in answer to the summons of that unending sound.

No, she would not answer the Voice—this Voice that was D'Fani's weapon. D'Eyree fought against the compulsion until she lay writhing on the floor. The band of the Eyes was about one arm like a giant's bracelet that did not fit, now she brought it to her. The Eyes were braziers filled with blue-green fire, as she had never seen them before. To loose the compulsion—could she touch them, then focus her power on breaking the call of the Voice?

The pain—could she stand it? With courage she did

not know she had, D'Eyree laid her hands across the Eyes.
Pain, yes, but not so intense, not so concentrated as when
she wore them.

She could stand this, and the very hurt helped to break
the drag of the Voice. If she went, and she believed she
must see what was happening, then she would be armed
by having her own will back.

She took the way from the tower inward to the heart
of Nornoch. People moved along it with her. But none
spoke to the others; rather they stared straight ahead in
such concentration as she herself knew when she worked
with the Lurla.

So they came to the heart of Nornoch, that tallest spur
of rock which had never been leveled, on which was hung
the Voice in its cage. And on the ledge beneath it was
D'Fani. His entire head was encased in a transparent arg
shell of vast size. And below him were D'Atey and others,
similarly shielded against the sound of the Voice.

But the people stood swaying in time to the beat of
that sound from above. And their faces were blank, without expression. Closer and closer they moved to the foot
of that spur, packed tightly now, yet those on the fringe
still pushed as if it were imperative that they reach the
Voice itself.

D'Eyree halted where she saw, keeping her hold on
reality with her grip on the Eyes. But she saw faces she
knew in that throng. Not only D'Huna, who had divested
herself of her eyes, but the other wearers, and none wore
their bands of office.

She looked from them to D'Fani above. There was a
vast exultation on his face as his head turned slowly from
side to side. He might be numbering those gathered
below, taking pleasure in their subordination to the device.

D'Eyree moved back, but she was too late. He saw her
and at the same instant was aware that the spell of the
Voice did not hold her in thrall. Leaning forward, he
caught at the shoulder of one of the helmeted guards
below him, pointing with his other hand to D'Eyree.

As the guard raised a distance harpoon, D'Eyree turned
and ran. Where could she go? Back to her tower? But
they could easily corner her there. She found one of the

sharply set stairs and scrambled up it, knowing she fled from death.

That the Voice controlled Nornoch there was no doubt. What did it matter now that she had learned how easily the Lurla could be fed? She would never have any chance to tell what she had learned, save to ears rendered already deaf to any words of hers.

Gasping, she reached the roof of the wall, ran along it. Now the sky was dark; she saw lightning split the clouds over the island's crown. It was as if the booming of the Voice had drawn the storm faster.

The Lurla—they must be alerted, sent to their posts! But if she were hunted, if the other wearers had laid aside their Eyes—

If she could find a hiding place then she could try to do her duty. The tower ahead was D'Huna's—her own was a turn of the wall away. She looked back once and saw the first guard come into the open.

Around the tower, on the outer edge—resolutely she kept her eyes from the rocks so far below. She had pushed the Eye band to her shoulder for safekeeping so she could use her two hands to steady her. Step, step, do not think of the pursuers, keep her mind on making this perilous advance.

Again a flatter surface, which looked as wide and open as a road after that narrow detour. She flashed along it as the winds from the sea grew stronger. If the gale became worse she dared not try that outer passage at the other towers too often. The gusts could pluck her forth and dash her to her death below.

Even through the murk of the storm she could see her goal, though whether she had the courage and strength to reach it she did not know. A lesser spur of the rock, like that which supported the Voice, yet not so tall, was within leaping distance from the top of the wall at that point. As she well knew, that had a crevice halfway down its surface on the sea side wherein she could hide.

She reached the take-off point, measured the distance. If she faltered now she could never again summon up the needed spurt to make it. Recklessly she leaped for the spur, landing hard with a force that bruised her badly.

But enough need for self preservation was left to make her crawl down into the break, wedging her body in as soon as she could force entrance.

The smell of the sea arose from below, but she was perched in a cramped space. The winds and waves were beginning their assault. She put on the Eye band, concentrated on the Lurla.

They—they were already at work! And at such a pace as her own prodding could never have won from them. Then this must be the effect of the Voice! No wonder D'Fani had felt safe, had allowed the wearers to be without their Eyes.

But—her mental picture steadied. The Lurla were working, yes, but without proper direction. They spun their congealing exudation along the walls, but also on the floors. And they were spinning too fast. Even as she contacted them, one went utterly limp and fell to the floor where another crawled unheedingly over it, encasing it with the hardening substance.

Frantically D'Eyree tried to slow them, give them direction as she had always done. To no avail. Whatever influence the Eyes had once had was gone, wiped out by the Voice. D'Fani was killing the Lurla, and there was nothing she could do—

D'Eyree was startled out of her concentration as something clanged against the rock near her head clattered down past her perch. A harpoon— She looked up, caught a glimpse of a guard taking fresh aim with another weapon. Cringing, she tried to make herself smaller.

But before the shot came, she heard a hoarse cry from above. Then, past the outer edge of the cleft in which she sheltered, a body plunged out and down. The force of the wind, or some misstep, had torn the guard from his post.

Before a second gained the same advantage she must be on the move, though she had to force herself to leave that illusion of safety to descend farther. So going she passed another hole, but it was too small to hold her. Three quarters of the way down she found what she sought, pulling herself into a deeper opening. She was certain now that she could not be sighted from overhead.

That she could retreat any farther was impossible, as the sea was there, washing with vicious slaps among the rocks.

Once more she sought the Lurla. And her visual impression was so frightening that she was shocked. The expenditure of the sealing exudation was unbelievable. It ran in streams on the floor, dripping, before it could solidify, from the walls. In fact it now appeared to have some quality that kept it from that instant hardening which had been their aid.

Through the spur of rock that sheltered her she could still feel the beat of the Voice, though most of the sound was now deadened by the sea. Was it that which worked upon the Lurla? And did D'Fani know—or care?

Duty urged her to climb again, to cry out to the people what was happening. But it would be to deaf ears, and she would doubtless be killed long before she reached any point from which they could hear her. She sat with the Eye band between her hands and tried to think.

The Eyes—the wearers were sensitive to the Eyes. If she could reach the mind of one of them, or more than one, with her warning—even though they had taken off their bands. She could only try. Earlier she had traced the old ways of communication with the sea, an exploit she had never thought to try before. Why not attempt this other thing? If she put all her strength to it—

She slipped the band from her arm, and as she did so it rapped sharply against the rock. To her horror one of the Eyes loosened, dropped. Before she could grab it, it rolled into a crevice and was gone. Only one left. But she could try, even though any power she might call upon was now halved.

D'Eyree concentrated as she never had before in her whole life, closing her eyes to better summon to mind the faces of the wearers. But she could not hold more than three at a time. Very well then—three— And to them, as if she stood before them, she cried aloud her warning, over and over, with no way of knowing either success or failure. At last she tired, tired so that she could not hold those faces in mind. Wearily she opened her eyes—upon darkness!

The storm— The sound of the sea was only a faint

murmur. But she was in the dark! She put forth her hand and felt a wet, slimy surface.

Frantic, D'Eyree beat upon that surface. At first it seemed to her that it gave a little, but that was only illusion. As she ran her fingers across it, she realized the truth; she was walled in. And the smell of the stuff was fetid. It was Lurla slime. That hole past which she had descended must have direct connection with the wall burrows, and some of that overflow had cascaded through it to cover her refuge's entrance. She was eternally trapped!

The horror of it made her sick. With the band at her breast she rocked back and forth, crying aloud. Entombed— alive—no escape— This was death—death—

Not death—not death—that stranger in her mind was awakening, taking over. Out—get out—not death—get out! But it was not D'Eyree who thought so—it was—

The clamor of the sea—she could breathe—she was out! And in her hands—

Ziantha sat up dazedly looking down at what she held. In one hand was the focus-stone, in the other a circle of shining metal with two settings in it—one held the twin to the stone, the other was empty! D'Eyree's Eyes!

But how—she looked along her body, half expecting to see the scaled skin, the alien form. No, she was in Vintra's body. And she—somehow she had not only found the twin stone, but had apported it from the past. But how long had she been in Nornoch? Turan—was he dead?

Lurching to her feet, she started back to the flyer. The sun was no longer high—instead it was nearly setting, sending a brilliant path across the waves. And the island was a dark and awesome blot. Ziantha shuddered away from the memory of those last moments before she had been able to tear away from D'Eyree. Never could she face that again. She must have won her freedom the very moment that the other had died. And if she had not—

Turan!

She tore open the cabin door to look within. He lay in his seat, his eyes closed. He looked dead.

"Turan!" She caught him by the shoulders, exerted her strength to draw him up, to make him open his eyes and see her.

13

Ziantha leaned over him, so filled with fear she could not immediately use mind-search to explore for any spark of life in Turan's body. But slowly those eyes opened; she saw them focus upon her, know her—

"Not dead." His slack lips tightened to shape the words. "You—got—out—"

"You knew that I was dying—back there?"

He did not seem to have even strength left to nod, but she could read his faint assent. Then she knew in turn—

"You helped me!"

"Trapped—needed—" His voice trailed away. Those eyes closed again, and his head rolled limply on his shoulders.

"No! Not now, Turan—we have won! See!" Before his closed eyes she held the two stones, one free, one in its setting. But perhaps it was too late, or was it?

She thought of the way D'Eyree had used the Eyes. Could she do likewise now? Could she give to Turan through them some of her own life force?

She tried to fit the band on her head, but its shape was too different. It had been fashioned for another species. At length she cupped the stones in her hands, held them to her forehead, and thought—thought life, energy, being, into Turan, seeking that spark almost driven out by death. And in that seeking she found it, united

505

with it, fed it with her will, her belief, and confidence. As D'Eyree had driven the Lurla, so did she now in fact drive Turan, feeding him all she had to give.

He stirred. Once more his eyes opened; he pulled himself up in the seat.

"No." His voice was stronger. "I can hold, but do not exhaust what you have to give. The time is not yet when it may be that all you can offer will be needed. We must get back—back to the beginning—Turan's tomb. And you must pilot this flyer."

Ziantha could not protest. In her mind he had earlier set the proper information. But in what direction? Where would she find a guide?

He might have picked that question out of her mind as he answered:

"I have set it—" Once more he lapsed into that state of nonbeing, hoarding his energy, she knew. Now it was her doing, all of it.

Ziantha pushed into the sea, fronted the controls. His instructions were clear in her mind. One did this and this. But could she lift the flyer off this stretch of rock, or would it crash into the sea, taking them both to a swift ending? There was no way to make sure but to try.

Her hands shaking a little, she brought the motor to life; the flyer moved forward. Now one did this and this. Frantically she worked at the controls, nor could she believe that she had succeeded until they were indeed airborne, climbing into the dusk of evening. She circled the rock that was all that was left of Nornoch, her eyes on the direction dial. The needle swung, steadied, and held. If he had been right that would take them back.

As they winged over the sea she tried to plan. That she had brought the second stone out of the past was still difficult for her to believe, unless the drawing power of its twin already in her hands and in use had been the deciding factor. But she was convinced that without careful study, her contemporaries would not be able to understand the psychic power locked in these gems.

The stones had been ancient in Nornoch, put to psychic uses by generations of sensitives. This in turn had built up in them reserves of energy. Reawakened by her use, that power had, in a manner, exploded. Would it now be as quickly dispersed, or could she harness it to return them to their own time?

Night came and still the flyer was airborne; the needle on the guide held steady. Turan moved once or twice, sighed. But she had not tried to reach him either by speech or mind-send. He was not to be disturbed. He needed all the strength he had to hold on. That he had given her of his last reserves in that moment of D'Eyree's death was a debt she must repay.

It was in the first dawn that she saw the coast lights, and, with those, lights moving in the sky as well, marking at least two other flyers. She could not maneuver this machine off course, nor did she know any way of defending it. She could only hope—

Locked on course, the flyer held steady, and she did not have to constantly monitor the controls. Now Ziantha drew from the breast of her robe the band of the Eyes and the loose gem. If she were taken, she must do all she could to keep the focus-stones. She set herself to pry the second of them from the band. A girdle clasp proved to be a useful tool for this, and a few minutes later she had it out.

The other flyers were boxing them in now, one on either side. Ziantha tensed. How soon would they fire upon them? Vintra's memory could not supply her with information. The rebels did not have many flyers, and Vintra had not used one. Would it be better to try to land? One glance at Turan told her of the impossibility of trying to cross country on foot.

Before her on the instrument board a light flashed on and off in a pattern of several colors. Code—but one she could not read, much less answer. They were helpless until the flyer reached the goal Turan had set.

When no attack came, Ziantha breathed a little easier. Zuha had ordered them shot down on sight, but that had not happened. Therefore it might be that other orders had been issued since. How long had they been on the island? She did not know whether it was only part of a day or much longer.

The flyer bored steadily on into the morning. Ziantha

was very hungry, thirsty, and her sensitive's control could no longer banish those needs. She found a compartment in which emergency rations were carried. The contents of the tube were not appetizing but she gulped them down. Turan? She drew forth a second tube, prepared to uncap it.

"No." His word was hardly more than a whisper. He was looking beyond her to the flyer that was their escort—or guard.

"They have not attacked," she told him the obvious. "For a while they tried to communicate by code. Now they do nothing."

"The focus-stones—" He made such a visible effort to get out those words that her anxiety grew.

"Here," she held out her hand so he could see them lying on her palm.

"Must keep—"

"I know." She had not yet thought of a hiding place. If they were taken, she, at least, would be searched. She had no doubt of that. She ran one hand through her hair. Its thick sweep was a temptation, but there was no safe way of anchoring them in those locks. There remained her mouth. Experimentally she fitted the stones, one within each cheek. They were about the same size as the pits of dried umpa fruit, and she believed she could carry them so.

With them so close, she could draw upon their energy. Somehow, as her tongue moved back and forth touching first one and then the other, Ziantha felt a little cheered. They had had such amazing good fortune in their quest so far; they were still free, with both stones. Yet, she knew that there was danger in any building of confidence. And no sane person depended upon fortune to last.

There was a faint beeping sound from the controls. She had set the flyer on maximum speed when they had left the island, recklessly intent only on reaching their goal as quickly as possible. What fueled the machine she did not know, pushing away that worry when she had so much else to concern her. Was this a signal that that energy was failing them?

But it was the guide dial that made that sound. They

must be near to the tomb. Where could she land—and how?

The flyer shook, broke out of its forward sweep. Ziantha caught at the controls. But they were locked against her attempt to free them!

"Turan!"

He turned his head with painful effort.

"They have us—in—a—traction pull—" he whispered.

A pull that was taking them earthward. They would crash! She sat with her hands on those useless controls and sent out mind-seek. The in-and-out reception of alien thought was blighting, but that they were captive she understood. And they were being brought down to their captor's desire almost within sight of their goal.

"They—want—us—secretly—" Turan was rousing, pulling himself higher in the seat. "No one to know what happens—"

Ziantha probed, fought to reach and hold one of those mind waves. Perhaps it was the Eyes that gave her the skill to seize and hold.

Zuha!

The thoughts were blurred. It was like hearing only a few words of a whispered conversation. But the girl learned something. Yes, Turan was right; they were being brought in for a landing at a small private field, away from Singakok. Zuha wanted no interference while she dealt with them. Had they been of her own world and time, Ziantha could have used the power to control, to alter their memories for long enough to escape.

"Ride with them—not—against," Turan said. "Zuha wants us dead."

Ziantha caught his suggestion. Could they use the hate and fear of the alien woman to take them where they must go? Could she feed Zuha's desires?

"I shall be dead," Turan answered her chain of thought. "You must project to the High Consort a great fear of your own—one she will understand."

"The fear of being once more buried with you," Ziantha agreed. But it would be true, painfully true. All the horror she had known as D'Eyree entombed in that sealed crevice flooded back to make her sick. Could she face such an ordeal again? For it might well prove to be the truth, that, returned to Turan's tomb, they would remain there.

"There is no other way. Our door lies there."

Of course she had always known that in the back of her mind, but she had pushed it from her, refusing to face it squarely. This was the pattern they must follow to the end. Once again the tomb and the hope of return through it.

"I am dead," he said. "Your fear must be fed to her. In this I cannot help you."

"I know."

With the same concentration she had used to learn the method for that invasion of Jucundus's apartment which had begun this whole mad foray, Ziantha began to build her one chance. The irregular wave length meant that Zuha would not have clear reception. And so she could not be sure she had succeeded until some action of the other revealed it.

But she summoned fear, which was easy to do, fear of the dark, of imprisonment in that dark, of death, though she dared not allow panic to disrupt the careful marshaling of thought. Not that—not the tomb again! To die entombed beside the dead. Not that! She built up the strength of her broadcast in vivid mind pictures. Ziantha was shivering now, her hands locked about the useless controls.

The flyer was spiraling down. She saw trees rising to meet them, wondered for a moment if they would crash. But no, Zuha wanted more than any quick death, she wanted vengeance on Turan, and more on the woman she believed responsible for Turan's return. Feed her the thought of death in the tomb. Ziantha held to her mind-send as the flyer bounced along the rough ground.

Turan had been shaken against her in that landing. His body was an inert weight. To her eyes he was dead. Dare she test now? No, she must continue to concentrate on that suggestion—the return of the dead—and the living—to the tomb.

She made no move to escape from the flyer. Let them believe she was cowering here in fear. And they would not be far wrong. The dark passion she had touched in Zuha's mind was enough to promise the worst. But, if only the High Consort believed the worst to be what Ziantha tried to suggest to her!

The door was wrenched open with force, and she saw the face of an armsman. He stared at her, at Turan lying limply against her shoulder; then he was ordered aside by an officer.

"Lord Commander!" The man caught at Turan to draw him away from the girl. The body sprawled forward in his grasp. With an exclamation, the officer involuntarily jerked back, Turan falling, to dangle head and shoulders over the edge of the door.

"Dead!" the officer cried out. "The Lord Commander is dead!!

"As he has been!" There was triumph in the High Consort's reply. "There was only the sorcery of this witch to keep him seemingly alive. But he has eluded her at last." She stood wrapped in a heavy cloak against the snow-laden wind. Her eyes hot as she looked beyond the body to Ziantha. Now she leaned forward, her pose almost reptilian as she hissed:

"He is safely dead. But you still live, witch! And now you are under my hand."

The armsman and the officer had drawn Turan's body out of the flyer, laid it upon the ground. Ziantha did not move; only with her last spurt of mind-send she tried to reach, to implant in the High Consort what must be done.

"Your Grace," the officer looked up from where he knelt by Turan, "what are your orders?"

"What should they be—that my lord be returned to his place of rest where we laid him i i honor and respect. And let this be done without further delay before such witnesses as will bear the proper news to the people and put an end to this wild tale of returns and miracles. Let the Priest-Lord of Vut be summoned to reseal the spirit door with Vut's own seal, which no witchery can break."

She spoke swiftly as one who had planned for this moment and intended to see her orders carried out with all dispatch. Turan, dead, must vanish again, and as speedily as possible. But was he dead? Ziantha could only hope that the spark of that other still clung to life so he could win out in the end.

"And the witch, Your Grace?" The officer arose to his feet, came over to the cabin to draw her forth.

"Ah, yes, the witch. Bring her forth!"

The grasp upon her hurt as he pulled her out roughly. She hoped that her concealment of the Eyes would serve. The armsman twisted her arms behind her back, holding her so to face Zuha.

"The priests would have you," the High Consort said slowly, "to tear forth the secret of your witchery. But priests are men before their vows are taken. I would blast you with the flamer where you stand, save that that is too quick a death. You have companied with my lord and brought him back to life—for your purposes. What purposes?"

"Ask of him," Ziantha said. "I moved by his will, not by my own."

Her head rocked from the blow Zuha struck with lightning speed then. Ziantha feared the most that she might have revealed the presence of the Eyes, for the inside of her mouth was cut by the edges of one of the stones.

But as she stood, dazed a little from the force and pain of that blow, the High Consort stepped back a pace.

"It does not matter. Whatever he, or you, attempted has failed. Turan is dead and will go to the tomb. As for you—"

Ziantha braced herself. This was the crucial moment. Would her attempts to influence Zuha succeed?

"Since my lord saw fit, as you tell me, to use you, then it would seem he found you well suited for his tomb service. Thus you shall return with him. Only this time there shall be no escape, through the spirit door or otherwise! There shall be measures taken to make sure of that, above all else do I swear it so!"

She turned to the officer. "You will take charge of my lord's body and bear it to the lodge. I shall send those to prepare him for sleep, which this time will not be disturbed. You will take this witch also, and her you will keep under strict guard until the time comes that she also be returned whence she came. And your life will answer for hers."

"So be it, Your Grace."

Ziantha was so full of relief, for that moment, that she was hardly aware of the rough handling that stowed her into one of the ground cars, brought her forth again at a building among trees. She was bound and dumped on the floor of a room, left under the eyes of two armsmen who watched her with such an intensity of concentration that it was clear they thought she might disappear before their very eyes.

Lying there, her first relief ebbed as she considered the ordeal before her. Even though she had escaped D'Eyree's death, she was not certain she could make the second transfer to her own time. She had drawn so heavily on her powers, that even with the Eyes she could not be sure she had enough energy left. And she would also have the need to draw "Turan" with her.

Rest was what she needed. And in spite of her present discomfort of body, she set herself to relaxing by sensitive techniques, withdrawing into the inner part of herself to renew and store all the force she could generate.

Ziantha submerged herself now in memory, summoning to mind each detail of that plundered outer room of the tomb. If she was to have a point to focus upon it must be that. Her last memory of it had been when she was in the hands of the Jack captain, being forced to gaze into the focus-stone. But she pushed aside her mind-picture of that action, concentrated instead upon the chamber itself—the walls, the crumbling debris of what long ago thieves had smashed. Bit by bit she built up her mental picture of it as she had seen it the moment they had broken their way in.

She rejected any portion that seemed uncertain, but the reality of that chamber must exist, must *be* so she could center her will and power on returning to it. And that her memory was faulty, too broken by the actions of others for accurate anchorage, she was well aware. Again, until the testing, she could never count on success.

Having made her mind-chamber as clear and precise as she could, she allowed it to slip into memory again. Turan—she wished she dared to arouse him. But perhaps the slight effort of receiving a mind-send might shake his hold—if he was not already gone. No, this was her own battle, and she must not count on any help at hand except from her own strength and knowledge.

She had done what she could in preparation. Now let her once more sink into that half-tranced state of mind which would allow her to conserve her strength—wait— Deliberately she forced away all thought of the next hour—the next moment. Her breathing was shallow, even, her eyes closed. She might have been asleep, save that this state was no sleep of body.

Ziantha visualized her own form of peace and content-ment. There was a pool of silent, fragrant water, and on it her body floated free. Above her only the arch of the sky. She was as light as a leaf on the surface of the pool. She was as free as the sky—

The sound of a voice broke the bubble of her peace in a painful shattering. It came so suddenly she did not understand the meaning of the words. But there were hands on her, jerking her upright with unnecessary rough-ness. As she opened her eyes she saw the officer in the doorway. So it was time.

They dumped her without ceremony in the back of a car, where she was bumped and rolled back and forth by the motion of their going. She could not see out, and she made no effort to tap the minds of those with her. Turan was not here. Doubtless they transported him with more dignity.

The drive seemed long, and she was badly bruised— half dazed—but in time the vehicle came to a stop, and she was pulled out. This place she knew. They were at the foot of that rise down which she and Turan had made such an awkward descent on the night of their escape. It was not night now but late afternoon, and the details of earth, rock, and vegetation were clear.

Her two guards kept her upright to one side, away from the cortege climbing the hill to the spirit door. There was a priest of Vut, of the highest rank, Vintra's memory told her. He intoned a chant as he went, supported by two lesser prelates, one carrying a heavy mallet, the other a box, while the Priest-Lord of Vut scattered on the wind handfuls of ashy powder.

Turan, borne on a bier supported by two officers, followed. Except for his face, he had been covered with a long, richly embroidered drapery, over-worked in metallic threads with designs sacred to Vut. Behind came three armsmen and then the High Consort in her robe of yellow mourning, but her veil was thrown well back as if she wished to see every detail of this recommitment of her lord to the earth she determined would hold him safely this time.

Ziantha shivered with more than the lash of the wind, the bite of the snow settling down around them. She watched the Priest-Lord of Vut lean over the bier, sift upon it more of the ashes. They must be standing by the open spirit door. Two of the armsmen lowered themselves through that door, ready to arrange the commander's body.

Then the bier was attached to ropes and slid through the opening to disappear from sight. When the armsmen reappeared, Zuha made a gesture to Ziantha's guards.

They were eager as they pulled and pushed her along. Now she struggled, cried out, for Zuha must not suspect that she greeted this end with other than the height of fear. The wind was harsh, icy as it met them full at the top of the cliff.

"But we should know how she did this thing—" The Priest-Lord of Vut stood before Zuha, authority in his tone. "If the rebels have such powers—"

"If they have such powers, Reverence, will they not be able to use them to bend living men to their will as well? Did not the armsman we found at Xuth tell of how this one controlled him so when he would go to the Lord Commander's aid she rendered him unconscious? She is a danger to us all. Would you take her to the heart of Vut to practice her sorcery?"

The priest turned to look at Ziantha. Was he going to protest more? Here at the very last would he defeat all she had fought for?

"She seems safe enough a prisoner now, High Consort. Would she allow herself to be so taken if she had the great powers you fear?"

"She does not have the Lord Commander. In some way he aided her in this. I do not know how, but it is so; she even admitted it. I tell you such is a danger as we have not seen before. There is only one thing she fears—look well at her now. She fears return to the tomb. Seal it with the seal of Vut and she will trouble us no more!"

For a moment or two he hesitated. The armsmen and the officers had closed ranks behind Zuha, and it was apparent he decided not to stand against them.

Zuha knew that she had won. She swung around to fully face Ziantha and her guards.

"Strip the witch!" she ordered crisply. "If she has aught which seems a thing of power, let it be given to the Priest-Lord. Let her take nothing but her bare skin this time!"

They ripped her clothing from her, and then one of the officers caught her by the shoulders, pushed her forward. She felt them run a rope about her arms. Half frozen in the lash of the wind, she was dropped over, lowered. A moment later all light vanished as they clapped down the spirit door.

14

Ziantha could hear a dull pounding overhead as she lay there in the freezing dark. They were making very sure that the spirit door was sealed, that Turan would not return again. Turan— She used mind-search—meeting nothing!

He was gone. Dead? She was alone in this place of horror, and if she escaped it would only be through her own efforts.

Ziantha spat the gems out in her hands, pressed them against her forehead as D'Eyree had done to achieve the greatest power.

She was not Vintra left to die in the dark—she was Ziantha! Ziantha! Fiercely she poured all her force of will into that identification. Ziantha!

A whirling, a sense of being utterly alone, lost. With it a fear of this nothingness, of being forever caught and held in a place where there was no life at all. Ziantha— she was *Ziantha!* She had identity, this was *so!*

Ziantha! Her name cried out, offering an anchorage.

In this place which was nothingness she tried to use it as a guide.

Ziantha!

She opened her eyes. Her weakness was such that she would have fallen had she not been held on her feet. Iuban.

"She is coming out of it," he spoke over her shoulder

to someone the girl could not see. But the relief of
knowing that she had made the last transfer successfully
was so great she wilted into unconsciousness.

Noise—shouting, a cry broken off by a scream of agony.
Unwillingly she was being drawn back to awareness once
again. She was lying in the dust, as if Iuban had dropped
or thrown her from him. There was no light except that
which came with the crackle of laser beams well over her
head. Dazed, she pressed against the wall wishing she
could burrow into its substance, free herself from this
scene of battle.

Ziantha? Mind call—from Turan? No. Turan was dead,
this was— Her mind was slow, so exhausted that it
fumbled, this was Ogan! She had a flash of reassurance
at being able to fit a name to that seeking.

The firing had stopped and now a bright beam of light
dazzled her eyes as it swept to illumine the looted tomb.
She saw a huddled body, recognized one of the crewmen
who had brought her here.

Someone bent over her. She saw Ogan, put out a hand
weakly.

"Come!" he swept her up, carried her out of that
black and haunted place into the open where the fresh-
ness of the air she drew in was a promise of safety
ahead. But she was so tired, so drained. Her head lay
heavy on Ogan's shoulder as the darkness closed about
her once more.

How long did she sleep? It had been night, now it was
day. For she did not wake in the ship but out in the open,
with a sunlit sky arching above her. And, for the first
moments of that awakening, Ziantha was content to know
she was free, safely returned to her own time. But that
other—he had not returned!

The sense of loss that accompanied that realization was
suddenly a burden to darken the sky, turning all her triumph into defeat. She sat up in a bedroll, though that
movement brought dizziness to follow.

No ship—then— But where—and how? There were
peaks of rock like shattered walls, and, in a cup among
those, bedrolls. Ogan sat cross-legged on one such within
touching distance, watching her in a contemplative way.

Before him on the ground was a piece of clothing and resting on that—the Eyes!

Ziantha shuddered. Those she never wanted to see again.

"But you must!" Ogan's thought ordered.

"Why?" She asked aloud.

"There are reasons. We shall discuss them later." He picked up one end of that cloth, dropped it to cover the gems. "But first—" He arose and went to fetch her an E-ration tube.

There were two other men in the camp, and they were, she noted, plainly, on sentry duty, facing outward on opposite sides of the cup, weapons in hand. Ogan expected attack. But where was Yasa? The Salarika had expected Ogan to join forces with her. Had Iuban made Yasa a prisoner?

"Where is Yasa?" Ziantha finished the ration, felt its renewing energy spread through her.

Ogan reseated himself on the bedroll. In this rugged setting he looked out of place, overshadowed by the grim rocks—almost helpless. But Ziantha did not make the mistake of believing that.

He did not answer her at once, and he had a mind-shield up. Was—was Yasa dead? So much had changed in her life that Ziantha could even believe the formidable veep might have been removed from it. Iuban had tried to use her powers to his own advantage. She struggled now to remember what she had heard before he had forced her to look into the focus-stone. It was plain he had been moving against Yasa, even as the Salarika had earlier schemed to take over the expedition herself.

"Yasa"—Ogan broke through her jumbled thought— "is on the Jack ship. I believe that they intend to use her as a hostage—or bargaining point."

"With you—for them?" Ziantha gestured to the covered stones.

"With me—for you and them," he assented. "Unfortunately for them I have all the necessities, and I do not need Yasa. In fact I much prefer not having to deal with her."

"But Yasa—she expected you to come, to help—"

"Oh, I had every intention of coming, and, as you see, I did. To your service I did. Yasa may be all powerful on Korwar, but here she has stretched her authority far too thin. I am afraid it has just snapped in her face."

"But—" Ogan had always been Yasa's man, a part of her establishment. Ziantha had believed him so thoroughly loyal to the veep that his attachment could not be questioned.

"You find it difficult to believe that I have plunged into a foray on my own? But this is a matter which touches *my* talents. Such a discovery is not to be left to those who do not understand the power of what has been uncovered. They cannot use it properly; therefore, why should they have it to play with in their bungling fashion? I *know* what it is, they only suspect as yet."

He knew what it was, Ziantha digested that. And he knew she had used it. He would take her in turn, use her, wring her dry of all she had learned. Make her—A small spark of rebellion flared deep in Ziantha. She was not going to serve Ogan's purposes so easily.

And with that determined, she began to think more clearly. That other sensitive—it had not been Ogan who had entered Turan and shared her adventures. But the sensitive had worked with Harath and— Was he someone Ogan had brought in? If so, why had the parapsychologist not mentioned him?

Ziantha realized that there was more than a little mystery left and the sooner she learned all she could, the better. At that moment she felt Ogan's testing probe and snapped down a mind-barrier.

Trace of a frown on his face. The probe grew stronger. She stared back at him level-eyed. Then, for the first time in her relationship with him, she made resistance plain.

"Ask your questions if you wish—aloud."

His probe was withdrawn. "You are a foolish child. Do you think because you have managed to use the stones, after some undisciplined fashion, you are now my equal? That is pure nonsense; your own intelligence should tell you so."

"I do not claim to be anything more than I am." From

somewhere came the words and even as she uttered them Ziantha knew wonder at her defiance. Had she indeed changed? She knew well all that Ogan could do to her mentally and physically to gain his own will. Still there was that in her now which defied him to try it—a new confidence. Though until she was more certain of what she had gained she must be wary.

"That is well." He seemed satisfied, though her statement might be considered an ambiguous one. He must be judging her by what she had been and not what she now was.

"Where is Harath?" she asked abruptly, wishing to clear up the mystery of who had been with her, yet not wanting to ask openly.

"Harath?" He looked at her sharply.

She held tight to her barrier. Had she made an error in asking that?

But Harath had been here; she had known his touch, that she could not have mistaken. Why then should Ogan be surprised that she asked for him? Harath was Ogan's tool; it was natural that they be together, just as it had been natural for the unknown sensitive to use the alien to contact her.

"Harath is on Korwar."

Ziantha was startled by so flat a lie. Why did Ogan think she would believe it? He knew that Harath had been used to contact her; there was no reason to conceal it. And if he denied Harath so, then what of the other sensitive? Was this loss of one who had been a tool such that Ogan must cover with lies? But lies which he knew she would not accept? She felt for an instant or two as if she were plunged back into that whirling place which had no sane anchorage. Ogan was not acting in character, unless he had devised some kind of a test she did not understand.

Another thrust of mind-probe, one forceful enough to have penetrated her defenses in other days. But she held against it. Until she knew more she must hold her barrier.

"Why do you expect to find Harath here?" If his defeat at reading her thoughts baffled him, his chagrin was not betrayed by his tone.

"Why should I not?" Ziantha countered. "Have we not always used him for relaying and intensifying the power? Here do we not need him most?"

To Ziantha, her logic sounded good. But would Ogan accept it? And where was Harath? Why had Ogan made such a mystery of his presence?

Ogan arose. "Harath is too unique to risk," he said. His head turned from her; he stood as if listening. Then, in some haste, he crossed the depression to join one of the sentries.

Ziantha watched him. It was plain he expected trouble. It might be that Iuban had grown impatient, or even that Yasa had once more made common cause with the Jack captain when she discovered Ogan a traitor. The Salarika was no fool. Though she had made an independent bid for what the focus-stone might deliver, she would never have shut off all roads of retreat.

The Eyes—Ziantha's attention shifted to the stones under their cloth covering. That they were a prize beyond any one tomb, no matter how rich, she now realized. Ogan suspected that, and perhaps Yasa also. But they did not have her proof. There was also this: were the Eyes unique in answering to one sensitive alone, or could any, including Ogan, bring them into action?

She had worn them twice in those other worlds, as Vintra, who had not known the power of the stone that was forced upon her by her enemies, and as D'Eyree, who had known it very well and had put it to use. She had not been an onlooker, but had entered into Vintra, D'Eyree. Therefore the stones had answered her will. Were they "conditioned" then to her? And if so, did she now have a bargaining point with Ogan?

But that other kept intruding into her half-plans and hopes. Who was the sensitive who had been sacrificed to help her out of the past—and where was Harath, that source of energy? Ziantha tried not to think of Turan, except as a problem she must solve for her own safety in future relations with Ogan. She tried to hold off the dark shadow that came at the very name of Turan. Turan was a dead man—and he who had accompanied her through that wild adventure had been a stranger, some tool of

Ogan's, to whom she owed nothing now. But she did! The fact that Ogan had used him made him no less. Ogan had used her, too, in the past, over and over again, molded and trained her to do just what he—or Yasa—wanted. So why could she feel that this other was any less than she had been? Ogan had used him and he had died. Ogan would try again to use her, and, if the circumstances answered, he would discard her as easily at any moment.

Ziantha snatched up the stones, put them in the front of her planet suit, resealing it. If Ogan thought to treat her so, he might have a surprise. She knew what D'Eyree had been able to do with the Eyes. It might be that she could put them to far more potent use than Ogan guessed. And that she would try it before the end of this venture, Ziantha was now certain.

There remained Harath. If the alien were still on-planet she would reach him. The bond between them was one which Ogan had first brought into being, that was true. However she wanted to hold that much of the past. Of all who were now on the surface of this half-destroyed world, Harath was the only one whom she could trust.

Ogan came back to her. "We are moving on."

"To your ship?" She hoped not, not yet. Oddly enough while she was in the open she at least had the illusion of freedom.

"Not yet." But he did not amplify that, as he knelt to fasten her bedroll.

With those slung as packs, and the men each carrying in addition a sling of supplies, they edged between the fanglike rocks and climbed down into a very deep valley. In the depths of this a thread of water trickled along, and there were some stunted bushes. Here and there a coarse tuft of grass gave more signs of life than she had seen elsewhere.

What had happened to the world of Turan to reduce Singakok and the land around it to this state? Only a disastrous conflict or some unheard-of natural catastrophe would have wrought this. And how many planet centuries ago had it all happened?

The footing was very rough and, though Ogan apparently wanted to set a fast pace, they did not keep to what was any better than perhaps a slow walk on smoother surface. Also the scrambling up and down was most wearying, and Ogan himself began to breathe heavily, rest more often.

As they traveled, the valley opened out, the vegetation grew in greater luxuriance, though all of it was stunted, rising at the highest no farther than one's shoulder. Yet as it thickened it slowed their advance even more. So far Ziantha had seen no other life except that rooted in the soil. And she wondered if all else had been slaughtered in the doom which came to Singakok.

Then one of the men gave a furious exclamation and flashed a laser beam into the bushes. As he called a warning Ziantha saw on his out-thrust boot the scoring of teeth spattered with yellow foam.

"Lizard thing—watch out for it." He set his foot on a rock and leaned over to examine the boot. "Didn't go through." Then he dabbled his foot in the stream, letting the current wash away that foam. Meanwhile his partner methodically lasered the ground ahead, cleaning it down to the bare rock, until Ogan caught at his arm.

"Do not use all your charge on this—"

The man jerked away. "I am not going to get a poison bite," he returned sullenly. But he did not continue with the laser.

Their progress slowed again beyond that clearer section because they had to watch the ground carefully. Ziantha's legs ached. She was not used to such vigorous and continued exercise, and she liked this ground less with every moment they fought their way across it.

Twice Ogan had fallen back a pace or so behind; then they made one of their frequent halts, his attitude still that of one who listened. Ziantha decided he must be using mind-send to check on some possible pursuer. But she did not release her own probe to follow his. It might be a trick of Ogan's to force her barrier down to his own advantage. She must be on constant guard with him, as she well knew.

They came to a barrier formed by the land. The stream spilled here in a long ribbon of falling water over the edge of a drop. And they must now strike east, climbing up one of the valley walls, since the descent before them was too steep to attempt.

This left them in the open on fairly level ground, and the attitude of both Ogan and his men was that of those exposed to possible attack. So they hurried on, Ogan even taking her by the arm and pulling her forward, coming thus to another upstand of rocks into which they crawled.

Here they broke out rations and ate. Ziantha rubbed her aching legs. She was not sure if she could keep going, though she was very certain Ogan would see to it that she did if they had to drag her. It was plain he wanted to avoid some pursuers. Iuban was perhaps not waiting for negotiations over Yasa but again striking out on his own as he had when he took her to the tomb.

"Is it Iuban?" She rolled the empty E-Tube into a tight ball.

Ogan merely grunted. She recognized the signs of ultraconcentration. He was trying mind-search, striving to learn what he could. But there was no confidence in his tension; rather the strain of his effort grew more apparent. And she was troubled by that. In the ordinary way any crewman such as Iuban led would be well open to reading by a master as competent as Ogan. That the mysterious pursuers were not as his concern suggested, meant they were equipped with shields. But why, if he had discovered that fact, as he would have at once, did he still struggle to touch?

And why had he not ordered her to back him in a thrust? It was, Ziantha decided, as if he had a reason to keep her from learning the nature of what he sought to penetrate. Or was she only imagining things? She leaned her back against an upstanding rock and closed her eyes.

If Ogan was not present she could try herself. Not to cast to what might be trailing them, but for Harath. Somehow it was important that she find out where the alien had gone and why Ogan denied he was here.

And for Harath—again her thoughts slid on to the one whose power Harath had guided to her: Ogan's tool—Turan—but he was not Turan. She tried to recall now all those she had seen from time to time visiting Ogan's lab at the villa. He could have been any one of those, for

Ogan had kept her aloof from the others he used in his experiments. The one thing that puzzled her now was that Turan (he must remain Turan for she knew no other name to call him) was indeed a trained sensitive of such power that she could not easily see him subordinated to Ogan.

He was not one to be used as a tool, but rather one who used tools himself. The physical envelope he had worn as Turan continued to mislead her. Now she strove to build up a personality with no association with the dead Lord Commander. It was like fitting together shards of some artifact of whose real shape she was unaware.

But that depression which she had held in abeyance settled down on her full force. In all her life, in the Dipple and after Yasa had taken her from that place of despair, she had had no one of her own. The Salarika veep had given her shelter, education, a livelihood. But Ziantha had always known that this was not because she was herself, but because she represented an investment that was expected to repay Yasa for her attentions many times over.

Ogan had been a figure of awe at first, then one to be feared and resented. She admitted his mastery, and she hated him—yes, she recognized her depth of emotion now—for it. Sooner or later now she would have to face Ogan and fight for her freedom. She had not been a real person when he had taught her, only a thing he could shape. Now she was herself, and she intended to remain so.

Yasa and Ogan—they had been the main factors in her existence. To neither was she bound by any ties of softer emotion. Harath—the closest she had ever come to having what one might deem a "friend"—was the strange alien creature. She trusted Harath.

Then—Turan. It had not been master and pupil between them, or benefactor and servant, but rather what she imagined was the comradeship between two crewmen, or two of the Patrol who faced a common danger and depended upon one another in times of crisis.

As he had depended upon her at the last!

Ziantha felt moisture gather under her closed eyelids. She had never wept except for physical reasons when a child—cold, hunger. These tears now were for a sense of loss transcending all those, a wound so deep within her that she was just beginning to know what damage it had wrought. And Ogan had done this thing—sent the other after her—and had left him to die.

Therefore her reckoning with Ogan, overdue as it was, would be eagerly sought by her. But at her time, not his. For she did not in the least undervalue her opponent.

She was roused from her thoughts by Ogan's hand on her shoulder.

"Up—we have to get under cover. Mauth has been scouting ahead and has found shelter."

The girl glanced around. One of the men was gone, the other held a click com in his hand, was listening to the message it ticked out. She got to her feet with a sigh. If it were much further she was not sure she could make it.

"Hurry!" Ogan pulled at her.

Of course they had to climb again and took a very roundabout way, as if Ogan was determined they remain as much undercover as possible. Twice Ziantha slipped and fell, and the second time she was unable to regain her feet unaided. But Ogan drew her along, cursing under his breath.

So he brought her to a cave, and thrust her back into the shadows well away from the door. When she sprawled there again he made no move to help her up, but let her lay where she had fallen, while he returned to the entrance, giving a low-voiced order to the crewmen that sent one of them away once more.

15

Night shadows were gathering. The sun, so brazen and naked over this riven land, was gone, though its brilliant banners still lingered in part of the sky. Ziantha crouched at the back of the cave. Her body ached from the unaccustomed exercise, but her mind was alert.

The man Ogan had sent out did not return. Twice click signals she could not decode came, and with each Ogan grew more restless. Whatever his plans, they were manifestly being frustrated. At last he came back to where she sat, hunkered down so that their faces were on a level.

"You are safe here—"

"Safe from Iuban?" she dared to interrupt. "Are his men trailing us?

"Iuban!" He gestured as if the Jack captain were a gaming piece of little value to be swept from the board. "No—there is a greater complication than that. There is a Patrol ship down out there!"

"Patrol! But how—" Among all the possible dangers she had not expected this one.

Ogan shrugged. "How indeed? But there are always ears to listen, mouths to be bought. Yasa went through Waystar. And Waystar is not Guild; it can be infiltrated— in fact it has been, at least once. And there is a chance I may have been followed also. But how they came does not matter. That they are here does."

He was silent for a moment, eyeing her narrowly.

"You know the penalty for using sensitive power for the Guild—remember it well, girl."

Her mouth was suddenly dry. Yes, it had been hammered into her from the earliest days of her training what her fate would be if the forces of the law caught her during a Guild foray. Not death, no. In some ways death would be more welcome. But erasure—brain erasure—so that the person who was Ziantha would vanish from life, and some dull-witted creature fit only for a routine task would stand in her place. All memory, personality, wiped permanently away.

There was a glint of satisfaction in Ogan's expression; he must have seen her recoil.

"Yes, remember that and keep remembering it, Ziantha. Erasure—" Ogan drawled that last word. It became an obscenity when one knew its meaning. "You stay undercover exactly as you are bid. Unfortunately the Patrol ship has landed in just that area where it can cause us the greatest inconvenience, and we have to remain hidden until they convince themselves that the Jack ship is the only one here."

"But your ship—they can locate that."

He shook his head. "Not a ship, Ziantha. I landed from space in an L-B. And that is under detect protection. My ship will return, but it is not in orbit now to be picked up by a Patrol detect."

"They have other detects, persona ones, do they not? What if they use those?" She fought for control, determined not to let the fear he sparked in her become panic.

"Naturally. And they are out there now, combing with such. They will pick up the Jacks, unless they are equipped with distorts. We do have those—"

A distort could throw off a persona, she knew. Just as a visual distort could throw off sight. There was one other way—if they had a sensitive—

"They do not!" Ogan might have read her mind. "Though they might have on such a mission, by so much fortune we are favored. I have probed for one and there is no trace. So we are safe as long as we take precautions. But we do not have much time. The L-B is set on a time return, and unless I can get to it and reset it, it will take off without us."

"You are going to try that?"

"I must. Therefore I shall leave you here with Mauth. There is always the hope that the Patrol and the Jacks will keep each other busy. But understand—if they find you"—he again made that sweep-away gesture—"you are finished. There is no one to lift a hand to save you. So— you have the focus-stones—give them to me. I shall put them in the L-B for safety."

"They will be of no value to you." Ziantha began her own game. It all depended on how much she could make Ogan believe. "They are now mind-linked to me. I have learned their full secret, and they will answer only to the one who awakened them."

Would he accept that? He had no way of testing it one way or the other since his lab equipment was worlds away.

"What can you do with them?" he asked.

Ziantha thought frantically. She had to provide some major advantage now for keeping the stones.

"If the Patrol here has no sensitive, I may be able to use these as a mind distort. They were once used for controlling—" For controlling the Lurla, animal things— would they work on men? But she need not explain that to Ogan.

"You have learned much. When there is time you shall tell me all of it."

"All," she echoed as if she were still under his domination.

"But perhaps it is best that you do keep the stones," Ogan continued to her great relief. "And you shall stay with Mauth until my return."

Ziantha knew that he went unwillingly, that above all he was now intrigued by her disclosures and frustrated that he could not put her statements to instant testing. Ogan had never been the most patient of men where his absorption in parapsychology was concerned.

The girl watched him make a wary exit from the cave. Why she had not gladly surrendered the stones to him she did not know, only that she could not. Just as she had brought what had been in D'Eyree's hands from one past, and both of them out of Vintra's time, so were they joined to her now.

She took them out, holding them in her clenched fist. If she ever looked into them again where would she be— Singakok? Nornoch? Neither did she want to see again.

Nor would she use them to serve Ogan. If the need to choose came she would see that they were lost somewhere in this wilderness of broken rocks, beyond his reach.

There remained Harath. Ogan must have left him at the L-B, though she still could not understand his denial that the alien was on-planet. With Ogan gone she could call—from Harath she could certainly learn the truth.

With the stones in her hands, Ziantha let down her mind barrier for the first time since Ogan had found her. She sent out a thought probe, the image of Harath bright and clear in her mind. Greatly daring she advanced the call farther and farther.

"Harath?"

His recognition was as sharp as her call. And then, before she could question him—

Warning, denial, a surge of need—do not try to communicate—use our touch as a guide.

Harath could not then be at the L-B; perhaps he had wandered away, searching for them. Or had he fled Ogan for some reason? But he would not answer. The thread between them was very faint and thin by his will, a guide but not a way of exchanging information. Save the fact that he held it so conveyed a warning.

She leaned her head forward so her chin rested on her knees as she thought of Harath, kept that thread intact. He was coming to her—there was danger—

A sharp clicking interrupted her thoughts. Her head jerked up and around. It was now dark in the cave. The guard at the mouth was only a blot against the slightly lighter sky. That must be his com in action.

"Gentle fem," his voice out of the gloom, using the customary address of everyday life, seemed strange here, "a message from veep Ogan. We are to move out—to the east."

"He said—stay here." Move now when Harath was on the way? She must not.

"The plans are changed, gentle fem. The Jacks or the Patrol are closing in with some type of persona detect that is new."

Perhaps, she thought anxiously, they have picked up my call to Harath.

"Come on!" Mauth did not speak with any courtesy now. He was plainly prepared to carry out his instructions by force if need be.

Ziantha thought furiously. She had the stones with all the power they represented. This man was no sensitive, and this was her chance for escape. She must take it and wait for Harath.

"I am coming." But she did not stir from her place. Instead she broke that cord with Harath and bent all the energy she could summon into a projection aimed at Mauth.

"We go down—" He turned and scrambled out of the cave. Nor did he look back to see that she was not with him. Her attempt was successful, and to his mind she was beside him now.

Ziantha was honestly astounded at her success. Ogan could do this with those who had no talents. But that she could project a believable hallucination was new. Her confidence in the might of the stones grew.

But she could not hold this long. Which meant that with Mauth away from the cave she must leave also. As soon as her projection faded he would be back hunting her.

Searching, she found a single ration tube, a small water container. She burdened herself with nothing more. But at the mouth of the cave she hesitated. The night was dark and the rocks a maze. The best she could do was to find another hiding place and await Harath.

To go higher was best, reach a point from which she could see more. Thrusting the focus-stones back within her suit, Ziantha began to scramble from one hold to the next.

She was some distance from the cave when she heard a sound from below and froze, her body plastered to the cliff wall. Mauth—he was coming back! She must remain where she was lest some sound betray her.

The night was very still with no wind to howl

mournfully among the erosion-sculptured stones. She could hear, sharp and clear, his movements down there, even a muttered curse which must mean he had found the cave empty. Then a second or so later came the click of the com. Was he signaling to Ogan, or receiving a message?

If she could only read that code! Dared she try mind-probe? But, even as she hesitated, Mauth was on the move again, and, by the sounds issuing from the cave, he was coming in her direction!

Then, out of the night shot a beam of dazzling light. Not to pin Ziantha to the rock, but to show Mauth.

"Freeze—right where you are!"

He obeyed and there followed sounds of others on the move—coming up. Patrolmen? They would question Mauth, learn about her. Ziantha swallowed. She was as helpless here as Mauth was, even if they had no light on her. For her slightest move would make a betraying sound.

Someone climbed into the flood of light centered on Mauth. But that was no Patrol uniform, rather a crewman's planet suit—Iuban's men then. If Yasa had made the deal Ogan expected— Should Ziantha hail them? But she could not be sure if Yasa was a free ally or Iuban's prisoner. No—stay free if she could—find Harath and learn some truths.

The crewman disarmed Mauth, was shoving him down-hill. And they made no move to climb higher. They did not suspect her to be here then. But they would learn speedily enough. Ziantha had no illusion that Mauth would not tell them everything they wanted to know once they applied Jack methods to the matter. As soon as she had the chance to move she should get as far away from here as possible.

They were searching the cave now. But that took no length of time. Ziantha willed them to go. She was not using the power, but sometimes even such willing could exert an influence.

Then she drew a deep breath of relief and would have sagged to the ground had there been anything more than a shallow ledge to support her. They were leaving, at last. She strained her ears to follow the sounds of their withdrawal, waiting poised for what seemed very long moments after the last of those finally died away.

Now—up and up—on! The girl began the ascent with the caution dark demanded, feeling ahead with her hands, testing each step with her foot before she put her full weight upon it. Twice she huddled, with a wildly beating heart, as dislodged stones made noises she was sure would bring the hunters straightway back to track her down.

After what seemed hours of strain, Ziantha reached the top of the rise and found it relatively smooth with no rocks to offer shelter. Which meant pushing on, across here and down the other side. Something in the air—she cringed—and then knew it for a flying thing. So this world had night life of its own. The flapping of wings sounded lazy, assured in a way that gave her courage. At least enough to start on again.

The slope on the other side seemed easier, and she was thankful for that, moving slowly, listening always for any sound. One of the stunted bushes caught at her, thorns raking out along the hand she had flung to the side to steady herself as a foot slipped.

But she lost her footing then, skidded down a slope in a loud cascade of stones and earth, bringing up against the thorny embrace of a second growth more stoutly rooted. For a moment she was too alarmed to try to move on again. Surely anyone within a good distance had heard *that!* Without thinking she tried mind-probe.

Harath!

Since she had broken their thread back in the cave she had longed to find a sanctuary from which she could again link with the alien. This was no hiding place, but from the very vigor of that pickup she knew that Harath must be near.

He must be close—very close! Seconds later she heard a faint noise—Harath on this slope?

Something was indeed moving in her direction, making less noise, Ziantha was certain, than a man. And Harath had nightsight; to him this stretch of gravel and small rocks would be much more visible than to her. She held fast to the bush as an anchor, waiting.

Scuttling—then before her—Harath!

He sprung straight for her, both pairs of his tentacles out to find holds on her body. There radiated from him a need for contact, for a meeting of body to body. Ziantha cuddled his small downy shape against her, though it seemed very odd that the usually self-sufficient Harath needed comfort.

"You were lost?"

"Not lost! Come with Harath—come!"

His excitement was wild and now he struggled in her grasp.

"Must come—he dies!"

"Who dies?" Ogan? Had the parapsychologist met with disaster on his attempt to reach the L-B?

"He!" Harath seemed to be utterly unable to understand that Ziantha did not know. As if the person he meant was of such importance in the world that there was no question of his identity.

"Come!"

She had never seen Harath so excited before. The alien would not answer her questions, but fought for release with the same vigor as he had greeted her. That he wanted her attention for only one thing, to obey his command, was plain. And she could not control him.

He had already struggled out of her hold. Ziantha could not restrain him without applying force, and that she was not prepared to do.

"Come!" He scuttled away as swiftly as he had arrived.

Ziantha got carefully to her feet. That she must not let Harath escape her again was plain. But also she had not his sight and could not trust the path ahead.

"Harath!" Had she made that call as emphatic as she must? "Harath—you must wait—I cannot see you!"

"Come!" She caught a glimpse of movement at the foot of the slope, as if Harath lingered there, bobbing about in his impatience and desire to be gone. Recklessly she half slid, half jumped down to that level. Now he reached with an upper tentacle, took hold of her suit, tugged with all his limited strength.

"Come!"

At least Harath offered a guide. As Ziantha obeyed that tug, the girl discovered she did not have to fear such rough footing, that her companion was picking the smoothest way. There was light in the sky now, as a moon rose. A small pale moon whose radiance was greenish, making her own flesh look strange and unhealthy.

Harath turned east. Ziantha thought she recognized one of the oddly shaped peaks in that wan moonlight. Surely they were not far from the Jack ship.

Yasa? But Harath had insisted on "he," and the alien had never displayed any great liking for the Salarika in the past. No—she did not think he led her to the veep. Now he was showing wariness as he angled back and forth among strange outcrops of rock which arose in clusters like the petrified trunks of long dead trees.

"The Jack ship—" Ziantha ventured.

Harath did not reply; only his grasp on her suit tightened, and he gave a sharp pull as if forbidding communication here. They wound a way beyond those rocks and came to a place where pinnacles were joined at the foot to form a wall. Harath loosed his hold on her, scrambled at a speed wherein his feet were aided by all four tentacles, climbing the curve of that wall at a space between two spires.

"Come!"

Where Harath might go she was not sure she could follow. The space between those prongs of stone looked very narrow. But Ziantha had to try it or lose him entirely. Dragging herself up, she wedged between the outcrops, an action which nearly scraped the suit from her back.

Below was a depression like the one in which Ogan had earlier camped. And that pocket was full of shadow. But she could make out dimly that someone lay on the ground here, and Harath was beside the body.

Harath—and a stranger—the sensitive! But if Harath wanted her—then that other was not dead after all! Ziantha's heart beat so fast that it seemed to shake her. She went on her knees beside the body she could not see.

Now she explored with her hands. He wore the bulk of a planet suit, the heavy boots of an explorer. But his head was uncovered and he lay face up. His skin was very cold, but when she held her hand palm down over his lips she could feel a breath puff against her skin. Entranced? It might well be. If so, to bring him out would be a matter requiring more skill than she possessed. Ogan should be here.

"No—Ogan kill!"

Harath's thought was like a blow, sharp enough to make her start back.

"You—Harath—reach—reach—" The alien's communication was in her mind. The emotion of fear which her suggestion of Ogan had raised in him had upset him to the point where he could not mind-send coherently. What lay behind that fear, Ziantha could not guess, but its reality she did not doubt in the least. If Harath said Ogan was a danger, she was willing to accept his verdict.

"Harath—" she sent the thought in as calm a fashion as she could summon. "How do we reach—?"

He appeared able now to control himself.

"Send—with Harath—send—"

Did he mean reverse the process that one generally used with Harath—lend her energy to the alien, rather than draw upon his as she had in the past?

"Yes, yes!" He was eager in affirmation of that.

"I will send," she agreed without further question.

With one hand she unsealed her suit, brought out the focus-stones. Whether those might lend any force to this quest she could not tell, but that they needed all the energy they could call upon now she firmly believed.

Then she leaned forward again over the limp body, touched her fingers to the cold forehead. Around her wrist closed, in a grip as tight as a punishing bond, one of Harath's tentacles. They were now linked physically as they must be linked mentally if this was to succeed.

There was a dizzy sensation of great speed, as if she—or that part of Ziantha that was her innermost self—was being swung out and out and out into a place where all was chaos and there was no stability except that tie with Harath. Farther and farther they quested. The focus-stones grew warm in her hand; she was aware of those and that from them was flowing now a steady push of energy. It passed through her body, down her arms, to those fingers, to the tentacle, where their three bodies met in touch.

Swing, swing, out and out and out—until Ziantha wanted to cry *Enough!* That if they ventured farther their tie with reality would snap and they would be as lost as he whom they sought and could not find.

16

The flaw in the pattern was that she could not build up any mind picture on which to focus the energy. Turan could have been such a goal, but this man she crouched over now she had never seen, could not picture as his head lay in the shadows and she had only touch to guide her. One must have such a focus—

Did Harath see humans as they were? Could he build such a mind picture as it should be built in order to search? Ziantha doubted it. For their swing was failing now, falling back in waning sweeps.

"Hunt!" Harath's urging was sharp.

"We must have a picture." She forced upon him in return her own conclusion for the reason of their failure. "Build a picture, Harath!"

Only what wavered then into her mind was so distorted that she nearly broke contact, so shocked was she by that weird figure Harath projected, a mixture, unbelievable, of his own species and Ziantha's, something which manifestly did not exist.

"We must have a true picture." They were back in the hollow, still united by touch, but warring in mind.

The alien's frustration was fast turning to rage, perhaps aimed at her because of his own inadequacies. Ziantha summoned patience.

"This is a man of my kind," she told Harath. "But if it is he who followed me into that other time, I do not know him as himself. I cannot build the picture that we need. I must see him as he really is—"

Because Harath was so aroused by their failure, which he appeared to blame on her, she feared he would withdraw altogether. Their mind-touch was snapped by his will, and his tentacle dropped from her wrist.

The moon's greenish light was on the lip of the hollow in which they crouched. If she could somehow pull the inert man at her feet up into that—

It seemed to her that there was no other way to learn what she must. Putting the Eyes into safekeeping once more, she caught the man's body, labored to pull it up to the light. But it was a struggle even though he was smaller, lighter than Ogan or one of the crewmen. Finally she brought him to where the moon touched his face.

It was hard to judge in the weird green glow, but she thought his skin as dark as that of a veteran crewman. His hair was cropped close, also, as if to make the wearing of a helmet comfortable, and it was very tightly curled against his skull.

His features were regular; he might be termed pleasantly endowed according to the standards of her kind. But what she was to do now was to learn that face, learn every portion of it as well as if she had seen it each and every day of her existence, fix it so straight in her mind that she could never forget or lose it.

Ziantha stretched out her hand, drawing fingers, with the lightest touch, across his forehead, down the bridge of his nose, tracing the generous curve of his full lips, the firm angle of his chin and jaw. So was he made and she must remember.

Harath crowded in beside her.

"Hurry—he is lost. If he is too long lost—"

She knew that ancient, eating horror of all sensitives when they evoked the trance state—to be lost out of body. But she had to make sure that she would know now whom they sought in those ways which were unlike any world her kind walked.

"I know—" Ziantha only trusted that it was now true that she did indeed know.

Once more she took the Eyes from concealment,

gripped them tightly in her left hand, set the fingers of the right to the forehead of the stranger, felt Harath loop tentacle touch to her wrist.

"Now—" This time she gave the signal. But she was not aware of that swing out into the void as she had been when the alien had guided their searching. Rather she fastened in her mind, behind her closed eyes, only one thing: the stranger's face.

They were not going in search now; they were calling with all the power they possessed, all that could be summoned through the Eyes. Though she did not have a name to call upon, which would have given her efforts greater accuracy, she must use this picture to the full.

He who has this seeming—wherever he now wanders—let him—COME!

Her body, her mind became one summoning cry. That she could long hold it to this pitch she doubted. But as long as she might, that she would.

"Come!"

A stirring—faint—far away—as if something crawled painfully.

"Come!"

There was indeed an answer, weak, but aiming for her with dogged determination. She dared feel no elation, allow any thought of success to trouble the resolute pull of her call.

"Come!"

So painfully slow. And she was weakening even with the energy that flowed into her from the stones, from Harath—

"Come!"

One last effort to put into that drawing all that she had. Then Ziantha broke, unable any longer to sustain the contact.

The girl fell face down, one arm across the body of the stranger. She was conscious, but strength was so drained out of her, she felt so weak and sick, that she could neither move nor utter a sound, even when she felt the other stir.

He pulled free of her, struggling to sit up. Harath was hopping about them both, uttering those clicks of beak that in him signaled unusual emotion. Faintly Ziantha heard the stranger mutter in some tongue that was not Basic. But there was a roaring in her own ears, a need to just lie there, unable to so much as raise a hand as the great weakness that followed her effort held her fast.

She thought the stranger was dazed, that he did not realize at first where he was or what had happened. But if that were so he made a quick recovery. For he suddenly stooped to look at her, exclaiming in his own language.

Then he lifted her up, straightening her body so she could lie in a more comfortable position, as if he well understood the malaise that gripped her. But he did not try mind-touch, for which she was grateful. Perhaps his long ordeal had exhausted his psychic energy for the time as much as the search had hers.

She watched him stand. Much of his body was still in the shadow, and what she could see gave her the impression that he was indeed short in stature and slender. But he was no boy, however much his face had given the impression of youth. That clicking blob, Harath, ran to him, scrambled up the stranger who might be now a tree to be climbed, and settled on his shoulder as if this was a perch he had known many times before.

The burden of the alien, who was no light weight, might be nothing, as the stranger pulled up between two of the rocks guarding this depression, his attitude one of listening. Ziantha watched him. By rights she should have a long rest now—

But at last her eyes were truly focusing on the other as he turned around. He was holding night-vision glasses to his eyes, and his clothing was plain to distinguish even in this baneful moonlight. There was no mistaking the emblem on the breast of his planet suit. Patrol!

What had Harath done to her? Even Ogan—or Iuban—would have been more her friend! What could she do now? If the sensitive was Patrol, as his uniform clearly testified, he was a deadly enemy, and one who already knew from his own participation just what she was doing on this planet. There was no escape, no form of defense she could offer.

But to be erased—

Black horror worse than any fear she had ever known in her life closed about Ziantha. Harath had done this to her! She must escape—she must!

She willed her weak body to obey orders. Though she wavered to a sitting position, the girl realized that she could not escape without some aid. Harath? She could never trust him again.

Ogan? Much as she feared and now hated the parapsychologist, he did not represent the dreaded fate this stranger threatened. But if she tried to contact Ogan, with her power so depleted, either Harath, the stranger, or both, could pick up her mind-send with ease.

With her eyes, wide with fear, on the stranger, she tried to edge away, put as much space between them as possible. If she could reach the other side of this hollow, somehow crawl up—get out among the rocks— But physical efforts were useless; she did not doubt that Harath would easily track her down. The alien knew her mind-pattern and could follow it as some tracking animal might follow footprints or scent.

Yet Harath was in turn physically limited. And if she could somehow dispose of the stranger, then she might be able to out-travel the alien. Inch by inch she won away from the spot where the stranger had left her, working crabwise over the rough ground without rising to her feet. The effort it cost her left her trembling with weakness, but her will and the danger hanging over her drove her on.

She kept her attention fixed upon the other, alert to any change that would suggest he planned to join her. But he seemed intent on watching beyond the hollow, centering on it with his back half toward her. It was apparent, she believed, that he expected no trouble from her. And at that Ziantha longed to hiss as Yasa might have done.

Harath she had to fear as well, but the alien's head was also turned in the same direction as the attention of the watcher. Perhaps he was mind-searching, feeding any information he could pick up to the stranger.

In her progress Ziantha's hand closed upon a rock. With that she could perhaps bring the Patrolman down. But she greatly doubted her accuracy of aim, and to miss would alert him. Now, she could, she would, fight with all her strength if he tried to master her physically, but she must concentrate on escape. She had almost reached the point where she believed she could hope to pull up to the rim.

Only she was not going to have the chance. For the stranger in a swift movement dropped the glasses to hang on their strap and turned to slide down into the hollow. He stopped short when he saw Ziantha, not where he had left her, but with her back against the wall, the stone gripped tight as a pitiful weapon.

"What—?" He spoke Basic now.

She raised the stone. As far as she could see he wore no weapon. And certainly he must be worn from his ordeal in the limbo between Turan's world and this.

"Stand off!" she warned him.

"Why?"

Ziantha could not see him face to face, for he was again in the shadow. But his bulk she could make out. She wondered at the surprise in his voice. Surely he knew that, being what she was, they were deadly enemies?

"Keep off," she repeated.

But he was moving toward her. If she had only left him lost! Fool to trust Harath—the alien was one with Yasa, Ogan and all the others who used her with no thought of her life.

"I mean you no harm." He stood still. "Why do you—"

She laughed then. Only it did not sound like laughter but a crazed, harsh sound that hurt as she uttered it.

"No harm? No, no more harm than a pleasant visit to the Coordinator—then to be erased!"

"No!"

He need not deny that so emphatically. Did he think she was so brain-weakened by what she had been through (and for him!) that she did not remember what happened to sensitives who served the Guild when the Patrol caught them?

"No—you do not understand—"

Weakly, but with all the strength she had, Ziantha threw the stone she held. Let him come any closer and she was lost. This was her one chance. And in the same instant as the stone left her fingers there was a burst of pain in her head, so terrible, so overwhelming, that she did not even have a chance to voice the scream it brought to her lips as she wilted down under that thrust of agony.

The storm was upon them—she must be in the tower. The Lurla—they lay curled, they would not obey, though she sent the commands. They must! If they did not, she would be thrown to the pounding waves below, and the Eyes given to one who could use them. But when she tried the Eyes were dull—they cracked and shivered into splinters, then to dust, sifting through her fingers. And she was left without any weapon.

They were high in the hills, and below them the enemy forces had gathered. But above and behind, coming steadily with fire beams to hunt them out, were flyers. This was a trap from which there was no escape. She must contrive to have death find her quickly when the jaws of the trap closed. For to be captive in the hands of those from Singakok was a worse ending than the clean death in battle. She was Vintra of the Rebels and would not live to be mocked in the streets of the city. Never! The flyers were very close, already their beams fused the hidden guns. This was death, and she must welcome it.

Heat, light, life—she was alive. And they would find her. She would be captive in Singakok—No! Let her but get her hands on her own weapons and she would make sure of that. But she could not move. Had she been wounded? So hurt in the assault that her body would not obey her?

Fearfully she opened her eyes. There was open sky above her. Of course, she lay among the Cliffs of Quait. But the sounds of the flyers were gone. It was very quiet, too quiet. Was she alone in a camp of the dead? Those dead whom she would speedily join if she could?

Sound now—someone was coming—if one of the rebels she would appeal for the mercy thrust, know it would be accorded her as was her right. She was Vintra; all men knew

that she must not fall alive into the hands of the enemy—
Vintra—but there was someone else—D'Eyree! And
then—Ziantha! As if thinking that name steadied a world
that seemed to spin around her, she ordered her thoughts.
Ziantha—that was right! Unless the Eyes had betrayed
her a second time into another return. She was Ziantha
and Ziantha was—

Her memory seemed oddly full of holes as if parts of
it had been extracted to frighten her. Then she looked
up at a down-furred body perched on two legs ending
in clawed feet, a body leaning over her so round eyes
could stare directly into hers.

This was Ziantha's memory. And that was—Harath! At
first she was joyfully surprised. Then memory was whole.
Harath was an enemy. She fought to move, to even raise
her hand—uselessly. But on wriggling hard to gaze along
her body she saw the telltale cords of a tangler. She was
a prisoner, and she could share to the full Vintra's despair
and hatred for those who had taken her.

That Harath had changed sides did not surprise her
now. He was an alien, and as such he was not to be
subjected to erasure or any of the penalties the Patrol
would inflict on her. Undoubtedly he would aid them as
he had Ogan in the past.

Ziantha made no effort to use mind-touch. Why should
she? Harath had seemed so much in accord with the
stranger she did not believe she could win him back. He
had been too frantic when he had begged her aid to
redeem the other's lost personality. What a fool she had
been to answer his call!

She no longer wanted to look at Harath, wedged her
head around so she could see only sunlit rock. This was
not the same hollow in which she had been struck down.
They were in a more open space. And now she could view
the stranger also.

He lay some distance away, belly down, on what might
be the edge of a drop, his head at an angle to watch
below. Then she heard the crackle of weapon fire. Somewhere on a lower level a struggle was in progress.

Ziantha heard the sharp click of Harath's bill, apparently he was trying to gain her attention. Stubbornly she

kept her eyes turned from him, her mind-barrier up. Harath had betrayed her; she wanted no more contact with him. Then came a sharp and painful pull of her hair. By force her head was dragged around, Harath had her in tentacle grip. And, though she closed her eyes instantly against his compelling gaze, Ziantha could feel the force of his mind-probe seeking to reach her. There was no use wasting power she might need later in such a small struggle. She allow mind-touch.

"Why do you fear?"

She could not believe that Harath would ask that. Surely he well knew what they would do to her.

"You—you gave me to the Patrol. They will—kill my talent, that which is me!" she hurled back.

"Not so! This one, he seeks to understand. Without him you might be dead."

She thought of her escape from D'Eyree's tomb. Better she had died there. What would come out of erasure would no longer be Ziantha!

"Better I had died," she replied.

She was looking straight up into Harath's eyes. Suddenly he loosed his hold on her hair, dropped mind-touch. She watched him cross the rock, his beak clicking as if he chewed so on her words, joining the man who still lay watching the battle below.

Harath uncoiled a tentacle, reached out to touch the stranger's hand. Ziantha saw the other's head turn, though she could catch only a very foreshadowed view of his brown face. She was sure that Harath and he were in communication, but she did not try to probe for any passage of thought between them.

Then the stranger rolled over to look at her. When she stared back, hostile and defiant, he shrugged, as if this was of no matter, returning to his view below.

There was a sound. Under them the rock vibrated. Up over the cliff rose the nose of a ship, pointing outward, the flames of her thrusters heating the air. On she climbed and was gone, with a roar, leaving them temporarily deaf.

Surely not Ogan's L-B. Such a craft was far too small to have made such a spectacular take-off. That must have been the Jack ship! The girl lost all hope now; she had been left in Patrol hands. Ziantha could have wailed aloud. But pride was stubborn enough to keep her lips locked on any weakling whimper.

Who had driven the Jack ship off? The Patrol? Ogan? If the latter, he must have been reinforced. If so, feverishly her mind fastened on that, Ogan was still here—she could reach him—

The stranger walked back toward her, standing now as if he feared no danger of detection. She could see him clearly. Turan she had learned to know, even when she realized that his body was only a garment worn by another. But now more than the uniform this one wore was a barrier between them. There was not only the fear of the Patrol but a kind of shyness.

In the past, on Korwar, she had lived a most retired life. Those forays Yasa had sent her on were tasks upon which it was necessary to concentrate deeply, so that during them she observed only those things that applied directly to the failure or success of her mission. Yasa's inner household had been largely female, Ziantha's life therein strictly ordered as if she were some dedicated priestess—which in a way, she had been.

Ogan had never seemed a man, but rather a master of the craft which exercised her talents—impersonal, remote, a source of awe and sometimes of fear. And the various male underlings of the household had been servants, hardly more lifelike to her than a more efficient metal robo.

But this was a man with a talent akin to hers, equal, she believed. And she could not forget the actions on Turan's time level that had endangered them both, that they had shared as comrades, though he was now the enemy. He made her feel self-conscious, wary in a way she had not experienced before.

Yet he was not in any way imposing; only a fraction perhaps over middle height, and so slender it made him seem less. She had been right about the hue of his skin: that was a warm dark brown, which she was sure was natural, and not induced by long exposure to space. And his hair, in the sun, shown in tight black curls. Of Terran descent she was sure, but he could be a mutation, as so many of the First Wave colonists now were, tens and hundreds of generations later.

He settled down beside her, watching her thoughtfully as if she presented some type of equation he must solve. And because she found that silence between them frightening, she asked a question:

"What ship lifted then?"

"The Jacks'. They tangled with some of their own, at least it looked so. Beat the attackers off, then lifted. But there was not much left of the opposition. I think a couple, three at the most, made it out of range when the ship blasted."

"Ogan! He will be after—" she said eagerly and then could have bitten her tongue in anger at that self-betrayal.

"After you? No—he cannot trace us even if he wants to. We have a shield up no one can break."

"So what are you going to do now?" Ziantha came directly to the point, unwillingly conceding that he might be truthful. No one should underrate the Patrol.

"For a time we wait. And while we do so, this is a good time to make you understand that I do not want to hold you like this." He pointed to the tangle cords which restrained her so completely.

"Do you expect me to promise no attempts to escape, with erasure awaiting me?"

"What would you escape to? This is not exactly a welcoming world." There was a reasonableness in his words that awoke irritation in her. "Food, water—and those others"—now he waved to the cliff—"wandering around. You are far safer here. Safer than you might be in Singakok that was." For the first time he gave indication that he remembered their shared past. "At least the High Consort is not setting her hounds to our trail."

He took a packet of smoke sticks from a seal pocket, snapped the end of one alight, and inhaled thoughtfully the sweet scent. By all appearances he was as much at ease as he would be in some pleasure palace on Korwar, and his placidity fed her irritation.

"What are we waiting for?" Ziantha demanded, determined to know the worst as soon as possible.

"For a chance to get back to my ship. I do not intend

to carry you all the way there. In fact, since I may have to fight for the privilege of seeing it again, I could not if I would. There is an alarm broadcast going out; the Patrol ship in this region must already have picked it up. We can expect company, and we can wait for it here. Unless you are reasonable and agree to make no trouble. Then we shall make for the scout and be, I assure you, far more comfortable."

"Comfortable for you—not for me. When I know what is before me!"

He sighed. "I wish you would listen and not believe that you already know all the answers."

"With the Patrol I do—as far as I am concerned!" she flared.

"And who said," he returned calmly, "that I represent the Patrol?"

17

For a moment Ziantha did not understand. When she did she smiled derisively. What a fool he must believe her to think she would accept that. When he sat before her wearing a Patrol uniform. When—

"Clothes," he continued, "do not necessarily denote status. Yes, I have been working with the Patrol. But on my own account, and I do this only for a space because my case seemed to match one of theirs. You see, I have been hunting the Eyes—without knowing just what I sought— for a long time."

The Eyes! Where were they now—in his keeping? Ziantha wriggled her shoulders in an abortive struggle against the cords and desisted at once when they tightened warningly about her with a pressure sharp enough to teach a lesson.

"They are still yours." He might have been reading her thoughts, though she was unaware of any probe.

"If you are not Patrol—then who are you—wearing that insignia?" She made that a challenge, refusing to believe that he was more than trying to lull her for his own purposes.

"I am a sensitive associated with the Hist-Techneer Zorbjac, leader of a Zacathan expedition to X One. And for your information X One is the sister planet of this in the Yaka system." He inhaled from the scented stick again. Harath clawed his way up over the rocks behind, as if he had been on a scouting expedition, and settled down by the stranger's knee.

"Ogan there." The alien's thoughts were open. "One other—hurt. The rest are dead."

He snapped out his tentacles and took to smoothing his body down with the same unconcern the stranger displayed.

"A year ago," the other continued, "finds made on X One were plundered by a Jack force. I was asked to trace down the stolen objects, since my field is archaeological psychometry. I followed the trail to Korwar. We recovered seven pieces there; that is when I joined forces with the Patrol. The eighth was the Eye you apported from Jucundus's place. The backlash of that apport was what set me on your track—that and Harath." He dropped one hand to the alien's head in a caress to which Harath responded with a broadcast of content.

"Then—was it you at Waystar, too?"

"Yes. When the apport was made I was certain that a sensitive would know what it was, try to trace it. We have our people on Waystar; they alert us as to unusual finds that come in as loot. During the past seasons we have built up a loose accord with a couple of the Jack captains, offering them more than they can get from fences to sell us pieces or information."

"How did you get Harath to join you?"

He laughed. "Ask him that. He came to me on Korwar of his own. I gathered that he had not been too happy at the use Ogan made of him. And I knew that he could serve as a link with you when I might need one. I was right, as you were willing to link with him at once— though I did not bargain for that linkage to be so tight as to pull me into Turan." He grimaced. "That was a challenge I would not want to face again."

"You knew about the Eyes all the time!" She had an odd feeling of being cheated, as if she had performed a difficult task to no purpose at all.

"Not so! I knew that that ugly little lump Jucundus bought was something more powerful than it looked to be. One could sense that easily. But the Eyes—no, I had no idea of their existence. What they are seems to be infinitely greater than any discovery the Zacathans have made in centuries."

"But," Ziantha came directly back to the part of his story that shadowed her future, "you joined with the Patrol to run us down. You wear their uniform."

He sighed. "It was necessary for me to take rank for a while. I am *not* Patrol."

"Then who are you?"

Again he laughed. "I see that I have been backward in the ordinary courtesies of life, gentle fem. My name is Ris Lantee, and I am Wyvern trained if that means anything—"

"It means," she flashed, "that you are a liar! Everyone knows that the Wyverns do not deal with males!"

"That is so," he agreed readily. "Most males. But I was born on their world; my parents are mind-linked liaison officers, both of whom the Wyvern council have accepted. When I was born with the power, they bowed to the fact I possessed it, and they gave me training. Can one sensitive lie to another?"

Though he invited her probe with that, Ziantha was reluctant to let her own barrier down. To hold it against him was her defense. He waited, and when she did not try to test his response, he frowned slightly.

"We waste time with your suspicions," he commented. "Though I suppose they are to be expected. But would I open my mind if I were trying to conceal anything from you? You know that is impossible."

"So far I have thought it impossible. But you say you are Wyvern trained, and the Wyverns deal with hallucinations—"

"You are well schooled."

"Ogan gathered information on every variation of the power known—and some only the Guild know," she answered. "I was given every warning."

"That, too, is to be expected."

"If you are not Patrol"—she pushed aside everything now but what was most important to her—"what do you intend to do with me? Turn me over for erasure when their ship planets in? You know the law."

"It all depends—"

"Upon what—or whom?" Ziantha continued to press.

"Mainly upon you. Give me your word you will not try to escape. Let us go back to my scout."

Ziantha tried to weigh her chances without emotion. Ogan was free; she had no reason to doubt Harath's report. He had said he had hidden a detect-safe L-B connected by a timer to a ship. Therefore he had a way of escape. The Jack ship had lifted, she could not depend on any assistance from Yasa. In fact she was sure she had already been discarded as far as the Salarika veep was concerned. Yasa was never one to hesitate cutting losses.

And somehow, between Ogan and this Ris Lantee, she inclined to trust the latter, even though he admitted connection with the Patrol. At least with freedom she might have a better chance for the future.

"As you have said," she spoke sullenly, trying to let him believe she surrendered because there was no other choice, "where could I escape to? For now, I promise."

"Fair enough." He touched the tangler cords in two places with the point of his belt knife, and they withered away.

Ziantha sat up, rubbing her wrists. Hands fell on her shoulders, drawing her to her feet, steadying her as she moved on stiff limbs.

"Do the Zacathans know about Singakok?" she asked as they went.

Harath had climbed up Lantee, was settled on his shoulder. But the man's hand was under her arm, ready with support when she needed, and they made their way down a steep slope.

"About Singakok—no. But there are ruins on X One that are in a fair state of preservation. Perhaps those who peopled this world—the survivors—fled there after whatever catastrophe turned Singakok into this. As Turan, I recognized a kinship between the buildings of the past and those ruins. And with the aid of the Eyes what will we not be able to discover!" There was excitement in his voice.

"You—you would be willing to evoke the past again—after what happened?" Ziantha was surprised at this. Had she been the one lost in that awful limbo that he entered when he could no longer fight off Turan's "death," she would have fled full speed from such a trip again.

"This time one could go prepared." His confidence was firmly assured. "There would be safeguards, as there are for deep trances. Yes, I would be willing to evoke the past again. Would you?"

To admit her fear was difficult. Yet he would learn it at once if she ever relaxed the barrier between them.

"I do not know."

"I think that you could not deny your own desire to learn if you were given free choice—"

He was interrupted by a wild clicking of Harath's beak. Lantee's arm swung up, formed a barrier against her advance.

"Ogan is near."

"You said you have what can safeguard us."

"Against mental invasion, yes. Just as you hold a barrier for me now. But if Ogan has some means of stepping up power it may be that we must unite against him, the three of us. I do not underestimate this man; he cannot be taken lightly even when he is on the run."

This was her chance. But, no, the word she had given was as tangible a bond as the tangler cords had been. Nor was she sure, even if that promise did not exist, that she would have left these two, sought out Ogan.

"What can he bring against us?" Lantee continued.

"I do not know," she was forced to confess. What equipment was small enough to be packed personally Ziantha could not tell. The Guild was notorious for its gathering of unusual devices. Ogan might even have the equivalent of the Eyes.

"I—" she was beginning when the world around her blurred. The rocks, the withered-looking vegetation, rippled as if all were painted on a curtain stirred by the wind. The change was such to frighten, passing from desolation to land alive.

She stood on a street between two lines of buildings. Before her stretched the length of a city, towering against the brilliances of sunlit sky. People moved, afoot, in vehicles—yet about them was something unreal.

Ziantha gasped, tried to leap aside as a landcar bore straight for her. But she was not allowed to escape; a grasp held her firmly in spite of her cries, her struggles. Then, the car was upon her but there was no impact, nothing! Another came the other way, scraped by her. She shut her eyes against those terrors and went on fighting what held her helpless in the Singakok returned—for this was Singakok.

The Eyes—they had done this! Yet she had not focused upon them. And if they were able to do this without her willing—! She raised her free hand to her breast. Unsealing her pocket slit, she snatched forth the Eyes, hurled them from her.

But she was still in Singakok! Locked in Singakok! Ziantha screamed. With a last surge of strength, backed by panic, she beat with her free hand against that thing which held her, fighting with fist, both feet, in any way she could, to break the hold. While around her—*through* her—the people and cars of the long-dead city went their way.

"Ziantha!"

She had closed her eyes to Singakok. Now she realized that, for all the seeming reality of the city, there had been no sound. Her name called in that demand for attention was real. But she dared not open her eyes.

"Ziantha!" Hands held her in spite of her fierce struggles. And the hands were as real as the voice.

"What do you see?" The demand came clearly, to compel her answer.

"I—I stand in Singakok—" And because her fear was so great she released the barrier against mind-probe.

Instantly touch flowed in, that same strong sense of comradeship she had known with Turan. She no longer fought, but rather stood trembling, allowing the confidence he radiated to still her panic, bring stability. And—she had been a fool not to allow this before—he did not mean her ill! As they had fought together in Singakok, as he had given of his last strength to aid her out of Nornoch, so was he prepared to stand with her now.

Ziantha opened her eyes. The city was still there; it made her giddy to see the cars, the pedestrians, and know that this was hallucination. But who induced it? Not the Wyvern-trained Lantee—he could not have done so and responded to her mental contact as he was now doing. Harath? The Eyes? But those she had thrown away.

"The Eyes! I threw them away, but still I see Sing-akok!" She quavered.

"You see a memory someone is replaying for you. Ogan—" Lantee's voice from close beside her, even as she could hold on to him. But she could not *see* him—only Singakok.

"Do not look, use your mind sense," Lantee ordered. "Do you pick up any thoughts?"

She tested. There was Lantee—Harath—nothing of those alien patterns she had known before. Just as the city had no sounds to make it real to one sense, so it had no mind-pattern to make it real to another.

"It is sight—my sight—"

"Well enough." Lantee's voice was as even as if he fully understood what was happening. "The hallucination is only for one sense. It worked in that it made you throw away the Eyes."

Sent to force her to discard the Eyes? Then it had suc-ceeded.

"I did. I threw them—"

"Not very far. Harath has retrieved them. Now listen, this was meant to engulf us all. But because I am Wyvern trained, and because Harath is alien, we were not caught. But if we stay here to fight for your freedom we may be courting another and stronger attack. Therefore we must push on. You must discount what you see, depend upon mind-send and your other senses, so we can reach my scout. Do you understand?"

"Yes." Ziantha kept her eyes tightly closed. Could she walk so blind, even with them leading her?

"We can do it." Lantee was confident. "Keep your eyes closed if you must, but follow our directions. Harath will work directly with you. I am now putting him on your shoulder."

She felt the weight, the painfully strong clutch of Harath's claws.

"Keep your eyes closed. Harath wishes to try some-thing."

She felt the touch of the alien's tentacles about her head; then their tips were lightly touched to her eyelids. It—it was like seeing and yet unlike—the sensation was strange. But through Harath she could visualize the scene as it had been before the illusion entrapped her. And, with her hand in Lantee's, as he drew her on, with Harath's shared sight, Ziantha started ahead. She went with only a shaky belief that this could be done, but her confidence grew.

They were following one of the small stream trickles now, and, remembering the poisonous lizard, she projected a warning. Lantee reassured her.

"We are sending warn-off vibrations. You need not worry about the native life."

"This is the long way round," he added a moment later. "Ogan may have more weapons. We have the shield; but since he has been able to pierce that in your case, we cannot be sure he will not try more direct methods of attack."

More direct methods of attack—laser fire from ambush? No, she must not let herself think of that, she must concentrate on the journey. There were differences in Harath's sight and her own as she speedily discovered, a distortion that was a trial. But it was far better than being led blindly.

They toiled up a rise where Ziantha found the going harder than it had been before. And there was a second descent as both Harath and Lantee cautioned her, taking so long on the passage down, she felt they would never reach bottom.

But before them stood a ship. Far smaller than the Jack craft that had once been a trader, this, she presumed— though through Harath's intermediacy its outlines were odd—was the Patrol scout.

"Wait!" Lantee's hand was now an anchor.

"What is the matter?" Through Harath Ziantha could not see anything that might be amiss. But this perception could be deceptive.

"The ship—it was left on persona-lock—with the ramp in!"

"But the ramp"—with Harath's aid she could see that— "it is out!"

"Just so. Walk into a trap. Does he think he has panicked us into being utter fools? If so he is wrong—but—"

Ziantha stiffened. "It is not the ship. He *wants* you to try for that—"

She could hear his heightened breathing, so still he was. Harath had tensed in turn on her shoulder until his claws cut her flesh. She welcomed that pain as a tie with reality.

"A distort! Can you not feel it?" Surely he was aware of that stomach turning, that inner churning, as if mind and body were swinging about.

It was growing so much stronger that she knew she could force herself no nearer. Now she felt Harath's tentacles slip from their hold about her head, their touch gone from her eyelids. She no longer had his sense as her guide, while that terrible feeling of disorientation grew and grew.

Harath uttered a shrill cry, carrying the force of a human scream. Apparently he was more susceptible to this attack than even the other two. He lost his hold, and Ziantha caught him, felt the shudders in his body. As she cradled him against her he went limp and she lost his mind-touch.

"Back!" Lantee drew her with him. But the distort centered on them, followed their retreat. Whatever defensive barrier her companion trusted in had not held. And if they were caught by the full force of a powerful distort they could lose all coherent thought.

"I am stepping up barrier power." Lantee's voice had not changed; he still seemed confident. "But," he continued, "that cannot hold too long."

"And when it blows—" she added what he had not said, "we can be overcome."

"There is one thing—" He pulled at her hand. "Get down, behind these rocks." Gently he forced her to her knees. The distort broadcast lessened.

"You say there is something we can do?"

"You have the Eyes."

"I threw them away back here. Harath—"

"Harath returned them to me. Here." His hands on hers, opening her fist, dropping on her flattened palm those two pieces of mineral.

"Since you have used them, they will answer best to you. Now, Ogan has plunged you into a visual hallucination. He is hiding near here somewhere. He could not have forced entrance to the ship, although he hallucinates for us that he has. We must reverse on him his own illusion."

"Can this be done?" She had heard of the master illusionists of Warlock, these Wyverns who ruled with dreams and could make anyone falling under their influence live in a world they had created. Lantee was Wyvern trained, but she had never heard of engulfing someone in his own hallucination.

"We cannot tell until we try. Singakok is your illusion. If we can—we shall send him to Singakok!"

Ziantha gasped. She had never heard of such trial of power. But then she *had* heard strange things of what the Wyverns could do with their dream control. And— she was suddenly sure of one thing—that Lantee could be depended upon in a way she had never dared to depend upon anyone in the past. Yasa, Ogan, for them she was a tool. Lantee sought to use her talent now, but as a part of a combined action from which they might both benefit.

"I—I have never tried this." She moistened her lips, unwilling to let him think that she was more able than she was.

"I have—a little. But this is a full test. Now—open your eyes. Look upon Singakok, if we are still within its boundaries. If not, look upon the land about, focus on it through the stones. Make it as real as you can."

She was afraid, afraid of the city, of what might happen when she did focus, afraid of being once more drawn back into the past. Resolutely she made herself face that fear, acknowledge it, and set it aside.

Pressing the Eyes against her forehead as D'Eyree had to release their maximum energy, Ziantha opened her eyes. She was not on a city street this time, rather in a garden, and before her was the rise of a building that was not unlike the palace of the Lord Commander, though she was sure this was not the same. There were guards at the door; men came and went, as if this were a place in which important affairs were conducted. Since she had not Vintra's memories now she could not identify this place. But it was so real except for the silence that she could hardly believe she had not been plunged once more into the past.

"Hold!" At this order she concentrated with all the power she could summon on the scene, trying, where any detail was hazy, to build more solidly.

What Lantee was doing, she could not guess. And Harath was still a limp weight on her arm. But she held the scene with a fierce intensity. Though it was getting harder to keep those details in such clear relief.

There was a sudden fluttering of the whole landscape before her. It became a painted curtain, torn across, and through those rents Ziantha could see rocks and beyond them the ship standing like a finger pointing to the freedom of space.

Then—the illusion was gone!

At the same time that sick feeling, born of the distort, also vanished. She was free! Ziantha scrambled to her feet, Harath stirring against her. Crouched still on his knees, his face in his hands, was Lantee. When he did not move she took a step forward, placed the hand still holding the Eyes on his shoulder.

He quivered under her touch, raised his head. His eyes were shut, his skin beaded with moisture.

"Ris?" She made a question of his name.

He opened his eyes. At first she feared he was caught in just such an illusion as the one which had held her for so long. Then he blinked and knew her. But before she could speak there came a cry from beyond. As one they turned to look.

From between two mounds of earth staggered Ogan, his hands to his head. He uttered sharp, senseless cries as he ran, making curious detours as if he swerved to avoid things which were not there.

"Come." Lantee held out his hand.

She held back. "He'll see us—"

"He sees Singakok. But how long that will continue I do not know. We must go before the illusion breaks."

Ogan, still crying out, was running along beside the rocks behind which they had taken refuge. Hand in hand they sprinted for the ship, passing him, but he did not heed them. Lantee had a com to his lips; he uttered into it the code to open the hatch, really extend the ramp.

Panting, Ziantha drew herself up that boarding way

as fast as she could, Lantee serving as rear guard. She
expected at any moment to be struck again by the distort
wave, yet she reached the hatch and that attack did not
come.

"Up!" The interior was cramped in comparison with
the two ships she had known. She climbed the ladder in
the same breathless haste as she had taken the ramp.
Behind Lantee the hatch clanged shut.

The control cabin at last and Lantee pushed her into
one of the webbing seats, pressed the button to weave
the take-off binding over her and Harath together. He
was in the pilot's place, his fingers busy with the controls.

She felt the shock of lift-off and blacked out.

A trickle of moisture down her chin. Lantee bent over
her, forcing the spout of a revi-tube into her mouth. As
that instant energy flowed into her, Ziantha straightened
within the webbing.

"Where—?"

"Where are we going? To X One."

"And Ogan?"

"Can wait for the Patrol."

"He will talk." She was sure of that. Perhaps Lantee
had given her a breathing space, but he could not stand
against the Patrol. Sooner or later they would be after
her.

She had forgotten her mind-barrier was down; now she
saw him shake his head.

"If they come—that is not going to do them any good.
The Zacathans do not often take a hand in human affairs,
but when they do, it is to some purpose."

"Why would they protect me?"

"Because, Ziantha-Vintra-D'Eyree, you are about the
most important find, as far as they are concerned, of this
age. You opened a new doorway, and they are going to
bend every effort to keep it open. Do you suppose they
would let your gift be erased?"

He seemed so sure; he believed in what he said. She
wished she could, too.

Again he knew her thoughts.

"Just try to—try to believe one impossible thing a day,

and you will find it the truth. What you did down there"—
Lantee waved to the visa-screen, where the world of
Singakok was fast growing smaller—"was impossible, was
it not? You died twice, I died once, but can you deny we
are alive? Knowing that, why can you not think that the
future is brighter than your fear?"

"I guess because it never has been," Ziantha answered
slowly. But he was right. Death was said to be the end,
but twice she had passed that end. So—she drew a deep
breath. Maybe this was all illusion, like the one they had
left Ogan trapped in. If so—let it hold.

Lantee was smiling, and in her arms Harath gave a soft
click of beak.

"You will see—it shall!" Somehow both their thoughts
came at once with bright promise to warm her mind, just
as the Eyes waited warmly in her hand. Waiting for the
next illusion—the next adventure?

Andre Norton ✪

The Honor Harrington series: *(cont.)*

Flag in Exile

Hounded into retirement and disgrace by political enemies, Honor Harrington has retreated to planet Grayson, where powerful men plot to reverse the changes she has brought to their world. And for their plans to succeed, Honor Harrington must die!

Honor Among Enemies

Offered a chance to end her exile and again command a ship, Honor Harrington must use a crew drawn from the dregs of the service to stop pirates who are plundering commerce. Her enemies have chosen the mission carefully, thinking that either she will stop the raiders or they will kill her . . . and either way, her enemies will win. . . .

In Enemy Hands

After being ambushed, Honor finds herself aboard an enemy cruiser, bound for her scheduled execution. But one lesson Honor has never learned is how to give up!

Echoes of Honor

"Brilliant! Brilliant! Brilliant!"—*Anne McCaffrey*

Ashes of Victory

Honor has escaped from the prison planet called Hell and returned to the Manticoran Alliance, to the heart of a furnace of new weapons, new strategies, new tactics, spies, diplomacy, and assassination.

continued ☞